**Tad Williams** has held more jobs than any sane person should admit to – singing in a band, selling shoes, managing a financial institution, throwing newspapers and designing military manuals, to name just a few. He also hosted a syndicated radio show for ten years, worked in theatre and television production, taught, and worked in multimedia for a major computer firm. He is co-founder of an interactive television company, and is currently writing comic books and film and television scripts. Tad and his family live in San Francisco.

Find out more about Tad Williams and other Orbit authors by registering for the free monthly newsletter at www.orbitbooks.co.uk

# THE DRAGONBONE CHAIR

## Memory, Sorrow and Thorn

## Book One

## Tad Williams

www.orbitbooks.co.uk

ORBIT

First published in Great Britain by Century Hutchinson Ltd 1989
Reprinted by Orbit 1997, 1999, 2000, 2001, 2002, 2003, 2005, 2006, 2007

Maps by Tad Williams

A CIP catalogue record for this book
is available from the British Library.

ISBN 978-1-85723-616-3

Papers used by Orbit are natural, recyclable products made from
wood grown in sustainable forests and certified in accordance with
the rules of the Forest Stewardship Council.

Printed and bound in Great Britain by
Mackays of Chatham PLC, Chatham, Kent
Paper supplied by Hellefoss AS, Norway

Orbit
An imprint of
Little, Brown Book Group
Brettenham House
Lancaster Place
London WC2E 7EN

A Member of the Hachette Livre Group of Compnnies

www.orbitbooks.co.uk

# Author's Note

'I have undertaken a labor, a labor out of love for the world and to comfort noble hearts: those that I hold dear, and the world to which my heart goes out. Not the common world do I mean, of those who (as I have heard) cannot bear grief and desire but to bathe in bliss. (May God then let them dwell in bliss!) Their world and manner of life my tale does not regard: its life and mine lie apart. Another world do I hold in mind, which bears together in one heart its bitter sweetness and its dear grief, its heart's delight and its pain of longing, dear life and sorrowful death, dear death and sorrowful life. In this world let me have my world, to be damned with it, or to be saved.'

— GOTTFRIED VON STRASSBURG
(author of *Tristan und Isolt*)

This work would not have been possible without the help of many people. My thanks go out to: Eva Cumming, Nancy Deming-Williams, Arthur Ross Evans, Peter Stampfel, and Michael Whelan, who all read a dreadfully long manuscript, then offered support, useful advice, and clever suggestions; to Andrew Harris, for logistical support above and beyond the call of friendship; and especially to my editors, Betsy Wollheim and Sheila Gilbert, who worked long and hard to help me write the best book I could. They are great souls all.

This book is dedicated to my mother, Barbara Jean Evans, who taught to me a deep affection for Toad Hall, the Hundred Aker Woods, the Shire, and many other hidden places and countries beyond the fields we know. She also induced in me a lifelong desire to make my own discoveries, and to share them with others. I wish to share this book with her.

# Author's Warning

Wanderers in the land of Osten Ard are cautioned not to put blind trust in old rules and forms, and to observe all rituals with a careful eye, for they often mask *being* with *seeming*.

The Qanuc-folk of the snow-mantled Trollfells have a proverb. 'He who is certain he knows the ending of things when he is only beginning them is either extremely wise or extremely foolish; no matter which is true, he is certainly an *unhappy* man, for he has put a knife in the heart of wonder.'

More bluntly, new visitors to this land should take heed:
Avoid Assumptions.

The Qanuc have another saying: 'Welcome stranger. The paths are treacherous today.'

# Foreword

'. . . The book of the mad priest Nisses is large, say those who have held it, and as heavy as a small child. It was discovered at Nisses' side as he lay, dead and smiling, beside the tower window from which his master King Hjeldin had leaped to his own death moments before.

'The rusty brown ink, concocted of lambsfoil, hellebore, and rue — as well as some redder, thicker liquid — is dry, and flakes easily from the thin pages. The unadorned skin of a hairless animal, the species unprovable, forms the binding.

'Those holy men of Nabban who read it after Nisses' passing pronounced it heretical and dangerous, but for some reason did not burn it, as is usually done with such texts. Instead, it lay for many years in Mother Church's near-endless archives, in the deepest, most secret vaults of the Sancellan Aedonitis. It has now apparently disappeared from the onyx casket which housed it; the never-gregarious Order of the Archives is vague as to its present whereabouts.

'Some who have read Nisses' heretical work claim that it contains all the secrets of Osten Ard, from this land's murky past to the shadows of things unborn. The Aedonite priest-examiners will say only that its subject matter was "unholy".

'It may indeed be true that Nisses' writings predict the what-will-be as clearly – and, we may presume, eccentrically – as they chronicle the what-has-been. It is not known, however, whether the great deeds of our age – especially, for our concern, the rise and triumph of Prester John – are included in the priest's foretellings, although there are suggestions that this may be true. Much of Nisses' writing is mysterious, its meaning hidden in strange rhymes and obscure references. I have never read the full work, and most of those who have are now long dead.

'The book is titled, in the cold, harsh runes of Nisses' northern birthplace, Du Svardenvyrd, which means The Weird of the Swords . . .'

– from
The Life and Reign of King John Presbyter,
by Morgenes Ercestres

# PART ONE

---

# SIMON
# MOONCALF

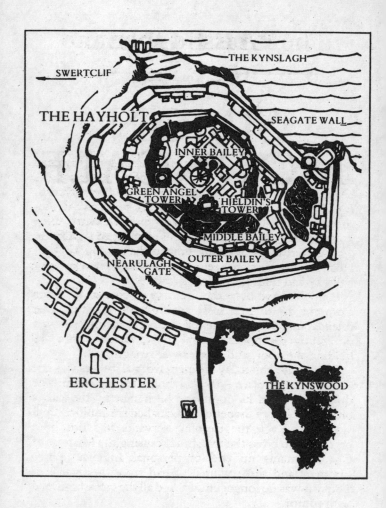

# 1

# The Grasshopper and the King

On this day of days there was an unfamiliar stirring deep inside the dozing heart of the Hayholt, in the castle's bewildering warren of quiet passages and overgrown, ivy-choked courtyards, in the monk's holes and damp, shadowed chambers. Courtiers and servants alike goggled and whispered. Scullions exchanged significant glances across the washing tubs in the steamy kitchen. Hushed conversations seemed to be taking place in every hallway and dooryard of the great keep.

It might have been the first day of spring, to judge from the air of breathless anticipation, but the great calendar in Doctor Morgenes' cluttered chamber showed differently: the month was only Novander. Autumn was holding the door, and Winter was trudging in.

What made this a day different from all others was not a season but a place – the Hayholt's throne room. For three long years its doors had been shut by the king's order, and heavy draperies had cloaked the multicolored windows. Even the cleaning servants had not been permitted to cross the threshold, causing the Mistress of Chambermaids no end of personal anguish. Three summers and three winters it had stood undisturbed. Today it was no longer empty, and all the castle hummed with rumor.

*

3

In truth, there *was* one person in the busy Hayholt whose attention was not fixed on that long-untenanted room, one bee in the murmuring hive whose solitary song was not in key with the greater droning. That one sat in the heart of the Hedge Garden, in an alcove between the dull red stone of the chapel and the leafless side of a skeletal hedge-lion, and thought he was not missed. It had been an irritating day so far – the women all busy, with scant time to answer questions; breakfast late, and cold into the bargain. Confusing orders had been given to him, as usual, and no one had any time to waste with any of *his* problems. . . .

And that was also, he thought grumpily, quite predictable. If it hadn't been for his discovery of this huge, magnificent beetle – which had come strolling across the garden, as self-satisfied as any prosperous villager – then the entire afternoon would have been a waste of time.

With a twig he widened the tiny road he had scraped in the dark, cold earth beside the wall, but still the captive would not walk forward. He tickled gently at its glossy carapace, but the stubborn beetle would not budge. Frowning, he sucked at his upper lip.

'*Simon*! Where in the name of holy Creation have you been!'

The twig dropped from his nerveless fingers, as though an arrow had pierced his heart. Slowly, he turned to look at the looming shape.

'Nowhere . . .' Simon began to say, but even as the words passed his lips a pair of bony fingers caught his ear and brought him sharply to his feet, yelping in pain.

'Don't you dare "nowhere" me, young layabout,' Rachel the Dragon, Mistress of Chambermaids, barked full into his face – a juxtaposition made possible only by Rachel's tiptoed stance and the boy's natural inclination to slouch, for the head chambermaid lacked nearly a foot of Simon's height.

'Sorry, then, mistress, I'm sorry,' Simon muttered, noting with sadness the beetle nosing toward a crack in the chapel wall and freedom.

4

' "Sorry" is not going to get you by forever,' Rachel growled. 'Every single body in the house is at work a–getting things ready but you! And, bad enough that is, but then *I* have to waste my valuable time trying to find you! How can you be such a wicked boy, Simon, when you should be acting like a man? How can you?'

The boy, fourteen gangly years old and furiously embarrassed, said nothing. Rachel stared at him.

*Sad enough*, she thought, *that red hair and those spots, but when he squints his eyes all up that way and scowls – why, the child looks half-witted!*

Simon, staring in turn at his captor, saw Rachel breathing heavily, pluming the Novander air with puffs of vapor. She was shivering, too, although whether from the cold or anger, Simon couldn't tell. It didn't really matter. It just made him feel worse.

*She's still waiting for an answer – how tired and cross she looks!* He curled himself into an even more pronounced slump and glared at his own feet.

'Well, you'll just come with me, then. The good Lord knows I've got things to keep an idle boy busy with. Don't you know *the king* is up out of his sickbed? That he's gone to his throne room today? Are you deaf and blind?' She grabbed his elbow and frog-marched him across the garden.

'The King? King John?' Simon asked, surprised.

'No, you ignorant boy, King Stone-in-the-Road! Of *course* King John!' Rachel halted in her tracks to push a wisp of limp steel-gray hair back under her bonnet. Her hand trembled. 'There, I hope you're happy,' she said. 'You've gotten me so flummoxed and upset that I've gone and been disrespectful to the name of our good old King John. And him so sick and all.' She snuffled loudly and then leaned over to deal Simon a stinging slap on the fat part of his arm. 'Just you come.'

She stumped forward, wicked boy in tow.

Simon had never known any other home but the ageless

5

castle called Hayholt, which meant High Keep. It was well named: Green Angel Tower, its loftiest point, soared far above even the eldest and tallest of trees. If the Angel herself, perched on the tower top, had dropped a stone from her verdigrised hand it would have plummeted nearly two hundred cubits before splashing into the brackish moat and troubling the sleep of the great pikefish bobbing close above the centuried mud.

The Hayholt was older by far than all the generations of Erkynlandish peasants who had been born, labored, and died in the fields and villages surrounding the great keep. The Erkynlanders were only the latest to claim the castle – many others had called it their own, but none had been able to make it wholly so. The outwall around the sprawling keep showed the work of diverse hands and times: the rough-hewn rock and timber of the Rimmersmen, the haphazard patching and strange carvings of the Hernystiri, even the meticulous stonework of Nabbanai craftsmen. But looming over all stood Green Angel Tower, erected by the undying Sithi long before men had come to these lands, when all of Osten Ard had been their dominion. The Sithi had been the first to build here, constructing their primeval stronghold on the headlands overlooking the Kynslagh and the river-road to the sea. They had called their castle *Asu'a*; if it had a true name, this house of many masters, then Asu'a was that name.

The Fair Folk had vanished now from the grassy plains and rolling hill country, fled mostly to the woods and craggy mountains and other dark places inconvenient to men. The bones of their castle – a home to usurpers – remained behind.

Asu'a the paradox; proud yet ramshackle, festive and forbidding, seemingly oblivious to changes of tenantry. Asu'a – the Hayholt. It bulked mountainously above the outlands and town, hunched over its fief like a sleeping, honey-muzzled bear among her cubs.

*

6

It often seemed that Simon was the only dweller in the great castle who had not settled into his place in life. The masons plastered the white-washed facing of the residence and shored up the castle's crumbling walls – although the crumbling did sometimes seem to outpace the restorations – with never a thought toward how the world spun or why. The pantlers and butlers, whistling merrily, rolled huge casks of sack and salted beef here and there. With the castle seneschal beside them, they haggled with farmers over the whiskery onions and soil-moist carrots brought in sacks to the Hayholt's kitchen every morning. And Rachel and her chambermaids were always excruciatingly busy, flourishing their brooms of bound straw, chasing dust balls as if herding skittish sheep, muttering pious imprecations about the way *some people* left a chamber when they departed, and generally terrorizing the slothful and slovenly.

In the midst of such industry, gawky Simon was the fabled grasshopper in the nest of ants. He knew he would never amount to much: many people had told him so, and nearly all of them were older – and presumably wiser – than he. At an age when other boys were clamoring for the responsibilities of manhood, Simon was still a muddler and a meanderer. No matter what task he was given to do, his attention soon wandered, and he would be dreaming of battles, and giants, and sea voyages on tall, shining ships . . . and somehow, things would get broken, or lost, or done wrong.

Other times he could not be found at all. He skulked around the castle like a scrawny shadow, could shinny up a wall as well as the roof-masons and glaziers, and knew so many passageways and hiding holes that the castle folk called him 'ghost boy'. Rachel boxed his ears frequently, and called him a mooncalf.

Rachel had finally let go of his arm, and Simon dragged his feet glumly as he followed the Mistress of Chambermaids like a stick caught in a skirt hem. He had been

7

discovered, his beetle had escaped, and the afternoon was ruined.

'What must I do, Rachel,' he mumbled unpleasantly, 'help in the kitchen?'

Rachel snorted disdainfully and waddled on, a badger in an apron. Simon looked back regretfully on the sheltering trees and hedges of the garden. Their commingled footfalls resounded solemnly down the long stone hallway.

He had been raised by the chambermaids, but since he was certainly never going to be one himself – his boyness aside, Simon was obviously *not* to be trusted with delicate domestic operations – a concerted effort had been made to find suitable labors for him. In a great house, and the Hayholt was doubtless the greatest, there was no place for those who did not work. He found employment of a sort in the castle kitchens, but even at this undemanding job he was not completely successful. The other scullions would laugh and nudge each other to see Simon – elbow-deep in hot water, eyes squinted shut in oblivious reverie – learning the trick of bird flight, or saving dream-maidens from imaginary beasts as his scrubbing stick floated off across the washing vat.

Legend had it that Sir Fluiren – a relative of the famous Sir Camaris of Nabban – had in his youth come to the Hayholt to be a knight, and had worked a year in disguise in this same scullery, due to his ineffable humility. The kitchen workers had teased him – or so the story went – calling him 'Pretty-hands' because the terrible toil did not diminish the fine whiteness of his fingers.

Simon had only to look at his own cracked-nail, pink-boiled paws to know that *he* was no great lord's orphan son. He was a scullion and a corner sweeper, and that was that. At a not much greater age, everyone knew, King John had slain the Red Dragon. Simon wrestled with brooms and pots. Not that it made much difference: it was a different, quieter world than in John's youth,

8

thanks largely to the old king himself. No dragons – living ones, anyway – inhabited the dark, endless halls of the Hayholt. But Rachel – as Simon often cursed to himself – with her sour face and terrible, tweezing fingers, was near enough.

They reached the antechamber before the throne room, the center of the inordinate activity. The chambermaids, moving at a near-run, careened from wall to wall like flies in a bottle. Rachel stood with fists set on hips and surveyed her domain – seeming, from the smile that tightened her thin mouth, to find it good.

Simon lurked against a tapestried wall, forgotten for a moment. Slouching, he stared from the corner of his eyes at the new girl Hepzibah, who was plump and curly-haired and walked with an insolent sway. Passing by with a sloshing bucket of water she caught his glance and smiled widely, amused. Simon felt fire crackling up his neck into his cheeks and turned to pick at the tattered wall hanging.

Rachel had not missed the exchange of looks.

'Lord whip you for a donkey, boy, didn't I tell you to get to work? Have at it, then!'

'At what?! Do what?!' Simon shouted, and was mortified to hear Hepzibah's silvery giggle float out from the hallway. He pinched his own arm in frustration. It hurt.

'Take this broom, and go and sweep out the Doctor's chambers. That man lives like a pack rat, and who knows *where* the king will want to go now that he's up?' It was clear from her tone that Rachel found the general contrariness of men to be undiminished by kingship.

'Doctor Morgenes' chambers?' Simon asked; for the first time since he had been discovered in the garden his spirits rose. 'I'll do it straight away!' He snatched the broom at a dead run and was gone.

Rachel snorted and turned back to examine the spotless perfection of the antechamber. She briefly wondered

9

what could possibly be going on behind the great throne-room door, then dismissed the errant thought as mercilessly as she might swat a hovering gnat. Herding her legions with clapping hands and steely eye, she led them out of the antechamber and off to another pitched battle against her archenemy, disorder.

In that hall beyond the door dusty banners hung, row upon row along the walls, a faded bestiary of fantastic animals: the sun-golden stallion of Clan Mehrdon, Nabban's gleaming kingfisher crest, owl and ox, otter, unicorn, and cockatrice – rank after rank of silent, sleeping creatures. No draft stirred these threadbare hangings; even the spiderwebs sagged empty and un-stitched.

Some small change had come to the throne room, though – something lived once more in the shadowed chamber. Someone was singing a quiet tune in the thin voice of a very young boy or a very old man.

At the farthest end of the hall a massive tapestry hung on the stone wall between the statues of the High Kings of the Hayholt, a tapestry bearing the royal coat of arms, the Firedrake and the Tree. The grim malachite statues, an honor guard of six, flanked a huge, heavy chair that seemed entirely carved from yellowing ivory, the chair arms knobbed and knuckled, the back capped with a huge, many-toothed serpentine skull whose eyes were pools of shadow.

It was on and before this chair that two figures sat. The small one clothed in worn motley was singing; it was his voice that floated up from the foot of the throne, too weak to chip loose even a slight echo. Over him bent a gaunt shape, perched at the end of the chair like an aged raptor – a tired, hobbled bird of prey shackled to the dull bone.

The king, three years sick and enfeebled, had returned to his dusty hall. He listened as the small man at his feet sang; the king's long, mottled hands grasped the arms of his great, yellowing throne.

10

He was a tall man – once very tall, but now hunched like a monk at prayer. He wore a sagging robe of sky blue, and was bearded like a Usirean prophet. A sword lay athwart his lap, shining as though new-polished; on his brow sat an iron crown, studded all about with sea-green emeralds and secretive opals.

The mannekin at the king's feet paused for a long, silent moment, then began another song:

> *'Can tha count th' rain-drops*
> *When th' sun is high?*
> *Can tha swim th' river*
> *When th' bed gang dry?*
> *Can tha catch a cloud?*
> *Nay, canst not, nor I . . .*
> *An' th' wind a cry "Wait".*
> *As a passeth by.*
> *Th' wind a cry "Wait".*
> *As a passeth by . . .'*

When the tune was finished, the tall old man in the blue robe reached down his hand and the jester took it. Neither said a word.

John the Presbyter, Lord of Erkynland and High King of all Osten Ard; scourge of the Sithi and defender of the true faith, wielder of the sword Bright-Nail, bane of the dragon Shurakai . . . Prester John was sitting once more upon his chair made of dragon's bones. He was very, very old, and had been crying.

'Ah, Towser,' he breathed at last, his voice deep but flawed with age, 'it is surely an unmerciful God who could bring me to this sorry pass.'

'Perhaps, my lord.' The little old man in the checkered jerkin smiled a wrinkled smile. 'Perhaps . . . but doubtless many others would not complain of cruelty if brought to your station in life.'

11

'But that is just what I *mean*, old friend!' The king shook his head angrily. 'In this shadow-age of infirmity, all men are leveled. Any thick-witted tailor's apprentice sups more of life than I!'

'Ah, la now my lord, my lord . . .' Towser's grizzled head wagged from side to side, but the bells of his cap – long since clapperless – did not jingle. 'My lord, you complain seasonably, but unreasonably. All men come to this pass, great or small. You have had a fine life.'

Prester John lifted the hilt of Bright-Nail before him, holding it as though it were a Holy Tree. He pulled the back of a long thin hand across his eyes.

'Do you know the story of this blade?' he asked.

Towser looked up sharply: he had heard the story many times.

'Tell me, O King,' he said quietly.

Prester John smiled, but his eyes never left the leather-bound hilt before him. 'A sword, small friend, is the extension of a man's right hand . . . and the end point of his heart.' He lifted the blade up higher, so that it caught a glimmer of light from one of the tiny, high windows. 'Just the same is Man the good right hand of God – Man is the sharp executor of the Heart of God. Do you see?'

Suddenly he was leaning down, eyes bird-bright beneath shaggy brows. 'Do you know what this is?' His shaking finger indicated a bit of crimped, rusty metal bound into the sword haft with golden wire.

'Tell me, Lord.' Towser knew perfectly well.

'This is the only nail of the true Execution Tree still remaining in Osten Ard.' Prester John brought the hilt forward to his lips and kissed it, then held the cool metal against his cheek. 'This nail came from the palm of Usires Aedon, our Savior . . . from His hand . . .' The king's eyes, catching for a moment a strange half-light from above, were fiery mirrors.

'And there is also the relic, of course,' he said after a quiet moment, 'the finger-bone of martyred Saint Eahlstan, the dragon-slain, right here in the hilt. . . .'

There was another interval of silence, and when Towser looked up his master was weeping again.

'Fie, fie on it!' John moaned. 'How can I live up to the honor of God's Sword? With so much sin, such a weight of it, still staining my soul – the arm that once smote the red dragon can now scarce lift a milk-cup. Oh, I am dying, my dear Towser, dying!'

Towser leaned forward, pulling one of the king's bony hands free from the sword-grip and kissing it as the old man sobbed.

'Oh, please, master,' the jester beseeched. 'Weep no more! All men must die – you, I, everyone. If we are not killed by youthful stupidity or ill-luck, then it is our fate to live on like the trees: older and older until at last we totter and fall. It is the way of all things. How can you fight the Lord's will?'

'But I *built* this kingdom!' A quivering rage was on John the Presbyter as he pulled his hand free from the jester's grasp and brought it sharply down on the arm of his throne. 'That *must* weigh against any blot of sin on my soul, however dark! Surely the Good Lord will have that in his Book of Accounts! I dragged these people up from the mud, scourged the cursed, sneaking Sithi out of the countryside, gave the peasantry law and justice . . . the good I have done *must* weigh strongly.' For a moment John's voice became fainter, as though his thoughts wandered elsewhere.

'Ah, my old friend,' he said at last in a bitter voice, 'and now I cannot even walk down to the marketplace on Main Row! I must lie in bed, or shuffle about this cold castle on the arms of younger men. My . . . my *kingdom* lies corrupting on the vine, while servants whisper and tiptoe outside my bedchamber door! All in sin!'

The king's words echoed back from the chamber's stone walls and slowly dissipated up among the swirling dust motes. Towser regained John's hand and squeezed it until the king was composed once more.

'Well,' said Prester John after some time had passed,

13

'my Elias will rule more firmly than I now can, at least. Seeing the decay of all this,' he swept his hand around the throne room, 'today I have decided to call him back from Meremund. He must prepare to take the crown.' The king sighed. 'I suppose I should leave off my womanish weeping, and be grateful I have what many kings have not: a strong son to hold my kingdom together after I am gone.'

'Two strong sons, Lord.'

'Fah.' The king grimaced. 'I should call Josua many things, but I do not believe "strong" is one of them.'

'You are too hard on him, Master.'

'Nonsense. Do you think to instruct me, jester? Do you know the son better than the father does?' John's hand trembled, and for a moment it seemed he would struggle to his feet. Finally, the tension slackened.

'Josua is a cynic,' the king began again in a quieter voice. 'A cynic, a melancholic, cold to his inferiors – and a king's son has nothing *but* inferiors, each one a potential assassin. No, Towse, he is a queer one, my younger – most especially since . . . since he lost his hand. Ah, merciful Aedon, perhaps the fault is mine.'

'What do you mean, Lord?'

'I should have taken another wife after Ebekah died. It has been a cold house without a queen . . . perhaps that caused the boy's odd humors. Elias is not that way, though.'

'There is a certain crude directness to Prince Elias' nature,' Towser muttered, but if the king heard he gave no sign.

'I thank beneficent God that Elias was first-born. He has a brave, martial character, that one – I think that if *he* were the younger, Josua would not be secure upon the throne.' King John shook his head with cold fondness at the thought, then groped down and grasped his jester's ear, tweaking it as if that old worthy were a child of five or six years.

'Promise me one thing, Towse. . . ?'

'What, Lord?'

'When I die – doubtless soon, I do not think I shall last the winter – you must bring Elias to this room . . . do you suppose they will hold the crowning here? Never mind you, if they do then you must wait until it has ended. Bring him here and give him Bright-Nail. Yes, take it now and hold it. I fear that I may die while he is away at Meremund or some other place, and I want it to come straight to his hand with my blessing. Do you understand, Towse?'

With shaking hands Prester John pushed the sword back into its tooled scabbard, and struggled for a moment to unbuckle the baldric on which it hung. The twining was caught, and Towser got up on his knees to work on the knot with his strong old fingers.

'What is the blessing, my Lord?' he asked, tongue between teeth as he picked at the tangle.

'Tell him what I have told you. Tell him that the sword is the point of his heart and hand, just as we are the instruments of the Heart and Hand of God the Father . . . and tell him that *no* prize, however noble, is worth . . . is worth . . .' John hesitated, and drew his trembling fingers to his eyes. 'No, pay that no mind. Speak only what I told you about the sword. Tell him that.'

'I shall, my King,' said Towser. He frowned, although he had solved the knot. 'I will gladly do your wish.'

'Good.' Prester John leaned back once more in his dragonbone chair and closed his gray eyes. 'Sing for me again, Towse.'

Towser did. Above, the dusty banners seemed to sway slightly, as if a whisper passed among the crowd of watchers, among the ancient herons and dull-eyed bears, and others stranger still.

15

# 2
# A Two-Frog Story

*An idle mind is the Devil's seedbed.*

Simon reflected ruefully on this, one of Rachel's favorite expressions, as he stared down at the display of horse-armor which now lay scattered the length of the chaplain's walking-hall. A moment before he had been leaping happily down the long, tiled hallway which ran along the outer length of the chapel, on his way to sweep Doctor Morgenes' chambers. He *had* been waving the broom about a little, of course, pretending it was the Tree and Drake flag of Prester John's Erkynguard, and that he was leading them into battle. Perhaps he should have been paying better heed to where he was waggling it – but what sort of idiot would hang a suit of horse-armor in the chaplain's hallway, anyway? Needless to say, the clatter had been ferocious, and Simon expected skinny, vengeful Father Dreosan to descend at any minute.

Hurrying to gather up the dingy armor plates, some of which had torn loose from the leather straps that bound the suit together, Simon considered another of Rachel's maxims – 'the Devil finds chores for empty hands.' That was silly, of course, and made him angry. It was not the emptiness of his hands, or the idleness of his thoughts that got him into trouble. No, it was the *doing* and the *thinking* that tripped him up time and time again. If only they would leave him alone!

16

Father Dreosan had still not made an entrance by the time he at last worried the armor into a precarious stack, then hastily pushed it beneath the skirt of a table rug. In doing so he nearly upset the golden reliquary seated on the table top, but at last – and with no further mishaps – the sundered armor was gone from view, with nothing but a slightly cleaner-looking patch on the wall to proclaim that the suit had ever existed at all. Simon picked up his broom and scuffed away at the sooty stone, trying to even up the edges so that the bright spot was not so noticeable, then hurried on down the hall and out past the winding choir-loft stairs.

Emerging once more into the Hedge Garden from which he had been so brutally abducted by the Dragon, Simon halted for a moment to inhale the pungent smell of greenery, to drive the last of the tallow-soap stench from his nostrils. His eye was caught by an unusual shape in the upper branches of the Festival Oak, an ancient tree at the far end of the garden, so gnarled and convoluted of branch that it looked as though it had grown for centuries beneath a giant bushel basket. He squinted, hand raised to block the slanting sunlight. A bird's nest! And so late in the year!

It was a very near thing. He had dropped the broom and taken several steps into the garden before he remembered his mission to Morgenes. If it had been any other errand he would have been up the tree in an instant, but getting to see the doctor was a treat, even when it entailed work. He promised himself that the nest would not remain long unexamined, and passed on through the hedges and into the courtyard before the Inner Bailey Gate.

Two figures had just entered the gate and were coming toward him; one slow and stumpy, the other stumpier and slower still. It was Jakob the chandler and his assistant Jeremias. The latter was carrying a large, heavy-looking bag over his shoulder, and walking – if such was possible – more sluggishly than usual. Simon called a greeting as they passed. Jakob smiled and waved.

'Rachel wants new candles for the dining room,' the chandler shouted, 'so candles she gets!' Jeremias made a sour face.

A short trot down the sloping greensward brought Simon to the massive gatehouse. A sliver of afternoon sun still smoldered above the battlements behind him, and the shadows of the pennants of the Western Wall flopped like dark fish on the grass. The red-and-white liveried guard – scarcely older than Simon – smiled and nodded as the master spy pounded past, deadly broom in hand, head held low in case the tyrant Rachel should happen to peep from one of the keep's high windows. Once through the barbican and hidden in the lee of the high gatewall he slowed to a walk. Green Angel Tower's attenuated shadow bridged the moat; the distorted silhouette of the Angel, triumphant on her spire, lay in a pool of fire at the water's farthest edge.

As long as he was here, Simon decided, he might as well catch some frogs. It shouldn't take too long, and the doctor frequently had use for such things. It wouldn't really be putting off the errand so much as expanding the nature of the service. He would have to hurry, though – evening was coming on swiftly. Already he could hear the crickets laboriously tuning up for what would be one of the waning year's last performances and the bullfrogs beginning their muffled, clunking counter-point.

Wading out into the lily-crusted water, Simon paused for a moment to listen, and to watch the eastern sky darkening to a dull violet. Next to Doctor Morgenes' chambers, the moat was his favorite spot in all Creation . . . all of it that he had seen so far, anyway.

With an unconscious sigh he pulled off his shapeless cloth hat and sloshed along toward where the pond grass and hyacinths were thickest.

The sun had completely vanished and the wind was hissing through the cattails ringing the moat by the time

Simon had reached the Middle Bailey to stand, clothes a-drip and a frog in each pocket, before the door of Morgenes' chambers. He knocked on the stout paneling, careful not to touch the unfamiliar symbol chalked on the wood. He had learned by hard experience not to carelessly lay hands on something of the doctor's without asking. Several moments passed before Morgenes' voice was heard.

'Go away,' it said, in a tone of annoyance.

'It's me . . . Simon!' called Simon, and knocked again. There was a longer pause this time, then the sound of rapid footfalls. The door swung open. Morgenes, whose head barely reached Simon's chin, stood framed in bright blue light, the expression on his face obscured. For a moment he seemed to stare.

'What?' he said finally. 'Who?'

Simon laughed. 'Me, of course. Do you want some frogs?' He pulled one of the captives from its prison and held it up by a slippery leg.

'Oh. Oh!' The doctor seemed to be coming awake as from a deep sleep. He shook his head. 'Simon . . . but naturally! Come in, boy! My apologies . . . I am a little distracted.' He opened the door wide enough for Simon to slip past him into the narrow inner hallway, then pulled it closed again.

'Frogs, is it? Hmmmm, frogs . . .' The doctor angled past and led him along the corridor. In the glow of the blue lamps that lined the hall the doctor's spindly form, monkeylike, seemed to bound instead of walk. Simon followed, his shoulders nearly touching the cold stone walls on either side. He could never understand how rooms that seemed as small as the doctor's did from outside – he had looked down on them from the bailey walls, and paced the distance in the courtyard – how they could have such long corridors.

Simon's musings were interrupted by a hideous eruption of noise echoing down the passageway – whistles, bangs, and something that sounded like the hungry baying of a hundred hounds.

Morgenes jumped in surprise and said: 'Oh, Name of a Name, I forgot to snuff the candles. Wait here.' The small man hurried down the hallway, wispy white hair fluttering, pulled the door at the end open just a crack – the howling and whistling doubled its intensity – and slipped quickly inside. Simon heard a muffled shout.

The horrendous noise abruptly ceased – as quickly and completely as . . . as . . .

*As the snuffing of a candle*, he thought.

The doctor poked his head out, smiled, and beckoned him in.

Simon, who had witnessed scenes of this type before, followed Morgenes cautiously into his workshop. A hasty entrance could, at the very least, cause one to step on something strange and unpleasant to contemplate.

There was now not a trace of whatever had set up that fearful yammering. Simon again marveled at the discrepancy between what Morgenes' rooms *seemed* to be – a converted guard-barracks perhaps twenty paces in length, nestled against the ivy-tangled wall of the Middle Bailey's north-eastern corner – and the view inside, which was of a low-ceilinged but spacious chamber almost as long as a tournament field, although not nearly so wide. In the orange light that filtered down from the long row of small windows overlooking the courtyard Simon peered at the farthest end of the room and decided he would be hard-pressed to hit it with a stone from the doorway in which he stood.

This curious stretching effect, however, was quite familiar. In fact, despite the terrifying noises, the whole chamber seemed much as it usually did – as though a horde of crack-brained peddlers had set up shop and then made a hasty retreat during a wild windstorm. The long refectory table that spanned the length of the near wall was littered with fluted glass tubes, boxes, and cloth sacks of powders and pungent salts, as well as intricate structures of wood and metal from which depended retorts and phials and other unrecognizable containers. The centerpiece of the table was a great brazen ball with tiny angled spouts protruding from its shiny skin. It seemed to float in a dish of silvery liquid, the both of them balanced at the apex of a carved ivory tripod. The spouts chuffed steam, and the brass globe slowly revolved.

The floor and shelves were littered with even stranger articles. Polished stone blocks and brooms and leather wings were strewn across the flagstones, vying for space with animal cages – some empty, some not – metal armatures of unknown creatures covered with ragged pelts or mismatched feathers, sheets of seemingly clear crystal stacked haphazardly against the tapestried walls . . . and everywhere books, books, books, dropped half-way open or propped upright here and there about the chamber like huge, clumsy butterflies.

There were also glass balls of colored liquids that bubbled without heat, and a flat box of glittering black sand that rearranged itself endlessly, as if swept by unfelt desert breezes. Wooden cabinets on the wall from time to time disgorged painted wooden birds who cheeped impertinently and disappeared. Beside these hung maps of countries with totally unfamiliar geography – although geography, admittedly, was not something Simon felt too confident about. Taken altogether, the doctor's lair was a paradise for a curious young man . . . without doubt, the most wonderful place in Osten Ard.

Morgenes had been pacing about in the far corner of the room beneath a drooping star-chart that linked the bright celestial points together by painted line to make the shape of an odd, four-winged bird. With a little whistle of triumph the doctor suddenly leaned down and began to dig like a squirrel in spring. A flurry of scrolls, brightly painted flannels, and miniature flatware and goblets from some homunculate supper table rose in the air behind him. At last he straightened up, hefting a large

21

glass-sided box. He waded to the table, set the glass cube down, and picked a pair of flasks out of a rack, apparently at random.

The liquid in one of them was the color of the sunset skies outside; it smoked like a censer. The other was full of something blue and viscous which flowed ever so slowly down into the box as Morgenes upended the two flasks. Mixing, the fluids turned as clear as mountain air. The doctor threw his hand out like a traveling performer, and there was a moment's pause.

'Frogs?' Morgenes asked, waggling his fingers. Simon rushed forward, pulling the two he had caught out of his coat pockets. The doctor took them and dropped them into the tank with a flourish. The pair of surprised amphibians plunked into the transparent liquid, sank slowly to the bottom, then began to swim vigorously about in their new home. Simon laughed with as much surprise as amusement.

'Is it water?'

The old man turned to look at him with bright eyes. 'More or less, more or less . . . So!' Now Morgenes dragged long, bent fingers through his sparse fringe of beard. 'So . . . thank you for the frogs. I think I know what to do with them already. Quite painless. They may even enjoy it, although I doubt they'll like wearing the boots.'

'Boots?' wondered Simon, but the doctor was off and bustling again, this time pushing a stack of maps from a low stool. He beckoned Simon to sit.

'Well then, young man, what will you take as due coin for your day's work! A fithing piece? Or perhaps you would like *Coccindrilis* here for a pet?' Chuckling, the doctor brandished a mummified lizard.

Simon hesitated for a moment over the lizard – it would be a lovely thing to slip into the linen basket for the new girl Hepzibah to discover – but no. The thought of the chambermaids and cleaning stuck in his mind, irritating him. Something wanted to be remembered,

22

but Simon pushed it back. 'No,' he said at last, 'I'd like to hear some stories.'

'Stories?' Morgenes bent forward quizzically. 'Stories? You would be much better off going to old Shem Horsegroom in the stables if you want to hear such things.'

'Not that kind,' Simon said hastily. He hoped he hadn't offended the little man. Old people were so sensitive! 'Stories about real things. How things used to be – battles, dragons – things that happened!'

'Aaahh.' Morgenes sat up, and the smile returned to his pink face. 'I see. You mean *history*.' The doctor rubbed his hands. 'That's better – much better!' He sprang to his feet and began pacing, stepping nimbly over the oddments scattered about the floor. 'Well, what do you want to hear about, lad? The fall of Naarved? The Battle of Ach Samrath?'

'Tell me about the castle,' Simon said. 'The Hayholt. Did the king build it? How old is it?'

'The castle . . .' The doctor stopped pacing, plucked up a corner of his worn-shiny gray robe, and began to rub absently at one of Simon's favorite curiosities: a suit of armor, exotically designed and colored in wildflower-bright blues and yellows, made entirely from polished wood.

'Hmmm . . . the castle . . .' Morgenes repeated. 'Well, that's certainly a two-frog story, at the very least. Actually, if I were to tell you the *whole* story, you would have to drain the moat and bring your warty prisoners in by the cartload to pay for it. But it is the bare bones of the tale that I think you want today, and I can certainly give you that. Hold yourself still for a moment while I find something to wet my throat.'

As Simon tried to sit quietly, Morgenes went to his long table and picked up a beaker of brown, frothy liquid. He sniffed it suspiciously, brought it to his lips, and downed a small gulp. After a moment of consideration he licked his bare upper lip and pulled his beard happily.

23

'Ah, the Stanshire Dark. No doubt on the subject, ale is the stuff! What were we talking about, then? Oh, yes, the castle.' Morgenes cleared a place on the table and then – holding his flask carefully – vaulted up with surprising ease to sit, slippered feet dangling half a cubit above the floor. He sipped again.

'I'm afraid this story starts long before our King John. We shall begin with the first men and women to come to Osten Ard – simple folk, living on the banks of the Gleniwent. They were mostly herdsmen and fisherfolk, perhaps driven out from the lost West over some land-bridge that no longer exists. They caused little trouble for the masters of Osten Ard. . . .'

'But I thought you said they were the first to come here?' Simon interrupted, secretly pleased he had caught Morgenes in a contradiction.

'No. I said they were the first *men*. The Sithi held this land long before any man walked on it.'

'You mean there really *were* Little Folk?' Simon grinned. 'Just like Shem Horsegroom tells of? Pookahs and niskies and all?' This was exciting.

Morgenes shook his head vigorously and took another swallow. 'Not only were, *are* – although that jumps ahead of my narrative – and they are by no means "little folk" . . . wait, lad, let me go on.'

Simon hunched forward and tried to look patient. 'Yes?'

'Well, as I mentioned, the men and Sithi were peaceful neighbors – true, there was an occasional dispute over grazing land or some such, but since mankind seemed no real threat the Fair Folk were generous. As time went on, men began to build cities, sometimes only a half a day's walk from Sithi lands. Later still a great kingdom arose on the rocky peninsula of Nabban, and the mortal men of Osten Ard began to look there for guidance. Are you still following my trail, boy?'

Simon nodded.

'Good.' A long draught. 'Well, the land seemed quite

big enough for all to share, until black iron came over the water.'

'What? Black iron?' Simon was immediately stilled by the doctor's sharp look.

'The shipmen out of the near-forgotten west, the Rimmersmen,' Morgenes continued. 'They landed in the north, armed men fierce as bears, riding in their long serpent-boats.'

'The Rimmersmen?' Simon wondered. 'Like Duke Isgrimnur at the court? On boats?'

'They were great seafarers before they settled here, the Duke's ancestors,' Morgenes affirmed. 'But when they first came they were not searching for grazing or farming land, but for plunder. Most importantly though, they brought iron – or at least the secret of shaping it. They made iron swords and spears, weapons that would not break like the bronze of Osten Ard; weapons that could beat down even the witchwood of the Sithi.'

Morgenes rose and refilled his beaker from a covered bucket standing on a cathedral of books beside the wall. Instead of returning to the table he stopped to finger the shiny epaulets of the armor suit.

'None stood against them for long – the cold, hard spirit of the iron seemed in the shipmen themselves as much as in their blades. Many folk fled south, moving closer to the protection of Nabban's frontier outposts. The Nabbanai legions, well-organized garrison forces, resisted for a while. Finally they, too, were forced to abandon the Frostmarch to the Rimmersmen. There . . . was much slaughter.'

Simon squirmed happily. 'What about the Sithi? You said they had no iron?'

'It was deadly to them.' The doctor licked his finger and rubbed away a spot on the polished wood of the breastplate. 'Even they could not defeat the Rimmersmen in open battle, *but*,' he pointed the dusty finger at Simon, as if this fact concerned him personally, 'but the Sithi knew their land. They were close to it – a part of it,

25

even – in a way that the invaders could never be. They held their own for a long time, falling slowly back on places of strength. The chiefest of these – and the reason for this whole discourse – was Asu'a. The Hayholt.'

'*This* castle? The Sithi lived in the Hayholt?' Simon was unable to keep the disbelief out of his voice. 'How long ago was it built?'

'Simon, Simon . . .' The doctor scratched his ear and returned to his perch on the table. The sunset was completely gone from the windows, and the torch light divided his face into a mummer's mask, half illumined, half dark. 'There may, for all I or any mortal can know, have been a castle here when the *Sithi* first came . . . when Osten Ard was as new and unsullied as a snow-melt brook. Sithi-folk certainly dwelled here countless years before man arrived. This was the first place in Osten Ard to feel the work of crafting hands. It is the stronghold of the country commanding the water ways, riding herd on the finest croplands. The Hayholt and its predecessors – the older citadels that lie buried beneath us – have stood here since before the memories of mankind. It was very, *very* old when the Rimmersmen came.'

Simon's mind whirled as the enormity of Morgenes' statement seeped in. The old castle seemed suddenly oppressive, its rock walls a cage. He shuddered and looked quickly around, as though some ancient, jealous thing might even at this moment be reaching out for him with dusty hands.

Morgenes laughed merrily – a very young laugh from so old a man – and hopped down from the table. The torches seemed to glow a little brighter. 'Fear not, Simon. I think – and I, of all people should know – that there is not much for you to fear from Sithi magic. Not today. The castle has been much changed, stone laid over stone, and every ell has been rigorously blessed by a hundred priests. Oh, Judith and the cooking staff may turn around from time to time and find a plate of cakes missing, but I think that can be as logically ascribed to young men as to goblins . . .'

The doctor was interrupted by a short series of raps upon the chamber door. 'Who is it?' he cried.

'It's me,' said a doleful voice. There was a long pause. 'Me, Inch,' it finished.

'Bones of Anaxos!' swore the doctor, who favored exotic expressions. 'Open the door, then . . . I am too old to run about waiting on fools.'

The door swung inward. The man framed against the glow of inner hallway was probably tall, but hung his head and hunched his body forward in such a way that it was difficult to make sure. A round, vacant face floated like a moon just above his breastbone, thatched by spiky black hair that had been cut with a dull and clumsy knife.

'I'm sorry I . . . I bothered you, Doctor, but . . . but you said come early, now didn't you?' The voice was thick and slow as dripping lard.

Morgenes gave a whistle of exasperation, and tugged on a coil of his own white hair. 'Yes, I did, but I said early after the dinner hour, which has not yet arrived. Still, no sense in sending you away. Simon, have you met Inch, my assistant?'

Simon nodded politely. He had seen the man once or twice; Morgenes had him come in some evenings to help, apparently with heavy lifting. It certainly wouldn't be for anything else, since Inch did not look as though he could be trusted to piss on the fire before going to bed.

'Well, young Simon, I'm afraid that will have to put an end to my windiness for the day,' the old man said. 'Since Inch is here, I must use him. Come back soon, and I will tell you more – if you like.'

'Certainly.' Simon nodded once more to Inch, who rolled a cowlike gaze after him. He had reached the door, almost touched it, when a sudden vision blazed into life in his head: a clear picture of Rachel's broom, lying where he had left it, on the grass beside the moat like the corpse of a strange water bird.

27

*Mooncalf!*

He would say nothing. He could collect the broom on his way back, and tell the Dragon that the chore was finished. She had so much to think about, and, although she and the doctor were two of the castle's oldest residents, they seldom spoke. It was obviously the best plan.

Without understanding why, Simon turned back. The little man was scrutinizing a curling scroll, bent over the table while Inch stood behind him staring at nothing particular.

'Doctor Morgenes . . .'

At the sound of his name the doctor looked up, blinking. He seemed surprised that Simon was still in the room; Simon was surprised, too.

'Doctor, I've been a fool.'

Morgenes arched his eyebrows, waiting.

'I was supposed to sweep your room. Rachel asked me to. Now the whole afternoon has gone by.'

'Oh. Ah!' Morgenes' nose wrinkled as if it itched him, then he broke out a wide smile. 'Sweep my chamber, eh? Well, lad, come back tomorrow and do it. Tell Rachel that I have more work for you, if she will be so good as to let you go.' He turned back to his book, then looked up again, eyes narrowing, and pursed his lips. As the doctor sat in silent thought, the elation Simon was feeling changed suddenly to nervousness.

*Why is he staring at me like that?*

'Come to think of it, boy,' the man finally said, 'I will be having many chores coming up that you could help me with – and eventually I will need an apprentice. Come back tomorrow, as I said. I will talk with the Mistress of Chambermaids about the other.' He smiled briefly, then turned back to his scroll. Simon was suddenly aware that Inch was staring across the doctor's back at him, an unreadable expression moving beneath the placid surface of his whey-colored face. Simon turned and sprinted through the door. Exhilaration caught him up as he bounded down the blue-lit hallway and emerged under dark, cloud-smeared skies. Apprentice! To the doctor!

When he reached the gatehouse, he stopped and climbed down to the edge of the moat to look for the broom. The crickets were well into the evening's chorale. When he found it at last, he sat down for a moment against the wall near the water's brink to listen.

As the rhythmic song rose around him, he ran his fingers along the nearby stones. Caressing the surface of one worn as smooth as hand-burnished cedar, he thought:

*This stone may have been standing here since . . . since before our Lord Usires was born. Perhaps some Sithi boy once sat here in this same quiet place, listening to the night. . . .*

*Where did that breeze come from?*

A voice seemed to whisper, whisper, the words too faint to hear.

*Perhaps he ran his hands across this same stone. . . .*

A whisper on the wind: *We will have it back, manchild. We will have it all back. . . .*

Clutching the neck of his coat tight against the unexpected chill, Simon got up and climbed the grassy slope, suddenly lonesome for familiar voices and light.

# 3
# Birds in the Chapel

'By the Blessed Aedon . . .'
*Whack!*
'. . . And Elysia his mother . . .'
*Whack! Whack!*
'. . . And all the saints that watch over . . .'
*Whack!*
'. . . Watch over . . . ouch!' A hiss of frustration.
'Damned spiders!' The whacking resumed, curses and
invocations laid on between. Rachel was cleaning cob-
webs from the dining hall ceiling.

Two girls sick and another with a twisted ankle. This
was the kind of day that put a dangerous glint in Rachel
the Dragon's agate eye. Bad enough to have Sarrah and
Jael down with the fluxion – Rachel was a hard task-
mistress, but she knew that every day of working a sick
girl could mean losing her three days in the longer run –
yes, bad enough that Rachel had to pick up the slack left
by their absence. As if she did not do two people's work
already! Now the seneschal said the king would dine in
the Great Hall tonight, and Elias, the Prince Regent, had
arrived from Meremund, and there was even *more* work
to do!

And Simon, sent off an hour before to pick a few
bundles of rushes, was still not back.

So, here she stood with her tired old body perched on a

30

rickety stool, trying to get the spiderwebs out of the ceiling's high corners with a broom. That boy! That, that . . .

'Holy Aedon give strength . . .'
*Whack! Whack! Whack!*
That damnable boy!

It was not enough, Rachel reflected later as she slumped red-faced and sweaty on the stool, that the boy was lazy and difficult. She had done her best over the years to thump the contrariness out of him; he was certainly a better person for it, she knew. No, by the Good Mother of God, what was worse was that *no one else seemed to care!* Simon was man-tall, and at an age when he should be doing nearly a man's work – but no! He hid and slid and mooned about. The kitchen workers laughed at him. The chambermaids coddled him, and snuck dinner to him when she, Rachel, had banished him from table. And Morgenes! Merciful Elysia, the man actually *encouraged* him!

And now he had asked Rachel if the boy could come and work for him every day, sweeping up, helping to keep things clean – hah! – and assisting the old man with some of his work. As if she didn't know better. The two of them would sit about, the old souse guzzling ale and telling the boy Heaven knew what kind of devil's stories.

Still, she couldn't help considering his offer. It was the first time anyone had asked for the boy, or wanted him at all – he was so *underfoot* all the time! And Morgenes had really seemed to think he could do the boy some good. . . .

The doctor often irritated Rachel with his fancy talk and his flowery speeches – which the Mistress of Chambermaids felt sure were disguised mockery – but he did seem to care about the boy. He had always kept an eye out for what was best for Simon . . . a suggestion here, an idea there, a quiet intercession once when the Master of Scullions had thrashed him and banished him from the kitchens. Morgenes *had* always kept a watch on the boy.

Rachel looked up at the broad beams of the ceiling, her gaze traveling off into the shadows. She blew a strand of damp hair off her face.

Starting back on that rainy night, she thought – what was it, almost fifteen years ago? She felt so old, thinking back this way . . . it seemed only a moment. . . .

The rain had been sheeting down all day and night. As Rachel went gingerly across the muddy courtyard, holding her cloak over her head with one hand, the lantern in the other, she stepped in a wide wagon rut and felt the water splash her calves. Her foot came free with a sucking sound, but without a shoe. She cursed bitterly and hurried forward. She would catch her death running around on such a night with one foot bare, but there was no time to go digging about in puddles.

A light was burning in Morgenes' study, but it seemed to take forever for the footsteps to come. When he opened the door she saw that he had been abed: he wore a long nightshirt in need of mending, and rubbed his eyes groggily in the lantern-glare. The tangled blankets of his bed, surrounded by a leaning palisade of books in the room's far corner, made Rachel think of some foul animal's nest.

'Doctor, come quick!' she said. 'You must come quick, now!'

Morgenes stared, then stepped back. 'Come in, Rachel. I have no idea what nocturnal palpitations have brought you, but since you are here . . .'

'No, no, you foolish man, it's Susanna! Her time is here, but she is very weak. I'm afraid for her.'

'Who? What? Never mind, then. Just a moment, let me get my things. What a dreadful night! Go on, I shall catch up to you.'

'But, Doctor Morgenes, I brought the lantern for you.'

Too late. The door was closed, and she was alone on the step with rain dribbling off her long nose. Cursing, she splashed back to the servant's quarters.

It was not long before Morgenes was stamping up the stairs shaking the water from his cloak. At the doorway he absorbed the scene in a single glance: a woman on the bed with her face turned away, big with child and groaning. Dark hair lay across her face, and she squeezed in a sweaty fist the hand of another young woman who kneeled beside her. At the foot of the bed Rachel stood with an older woman.

The old one stepped toward Morgenes while he shed his bulky outer clothing.

'Hello, Elispeth,' he said quietly. 'How does it look?'

'Not good, I'm afraid, sir. You know I could have dealt with it otherwise. She's been trying for hours, and she's bleeding. Her heart is very faint.' As Elispeth spoke, Rachel moved nearer.

'Hmmm.' Morgenes bent and rummaged in the sack he had brought. 'Give her some of this, please,' he said, handing Rachel a stoppered vial. 'Just a swallow, but mind she gets it.' He returned to searching his bag as Rachel gently pried open the clenched, trembling jaw of the woman on the bed and poured a little of the liquid into her mouth. The odor of sweat and blood that suffused the room was suddenly supplemented by a pungent, spicy scent.

'Doctor,' Elispeth was saying as Rachel returned, 'I don't think we can save both mother and child – if we can even save one.'

'You must save the child's life,' Rachel interrupted. 'That's the duty of the Godfearing. The priest says so. Save the child.'

Morgenes turned to her with a look of annoyance. 'My good woman, I will fear God in my own way, if you don't mind. If I save her – and I do not pretend to know I can – then she can always have another child.'

'No, she can't,' Rachel said hotly. 'Her husband's dead.' Morgenes of all people should know that, she thought. Susanna's fisherman husband had often visited the doctor before he drowned – although what they might have had to talk about, Rachel could not imagine.

'Well,' Morgenes said distractedly, 'she can always find another – what? Her husband?' A startled look came to his face, and he hurried to the bedside. He seemed to finally realize who it was lying there, bleeding her life out on the rough sheet.

'Susanna?' he asked quietly, and turned the woman's fearful, pain-clenched face toward him. Her eyes opened wide for a moment as she saw him, then another wave of agony shut them again. 'Ah, what has happened here?' Morgenes sighed. Susanna could only moan, and the doctor looked up at Rachel and Elispeth with anger on his face. 'Why didn't anyone inform me that this poor girl was ready to bear her child?'

'She was not due for two months more,' Elispeth said gently. 'You know that. We are as surprised as you.'

'And why should you care that a fisherman's widow was going to have a baby?' Rachel said. She could be angry, too. 'And why are you arguing about it now?'

Morgenes stared at her for a moment, then blinked twice. 'You are absolutely correct,' he said, and turned back to the bed. 'I will save the child, Susanna,' he told the shivering woman.

She nodded her head once, then cried out.

It was a thin, keening wail, but it was the cry of a living baby. Morgenes handed the tiny, red-smeared creature to Elispeth.

'A boy,' he said, and returned his attention to the mother. She was quiet now and breathing more slowly, but her skin was white as Harcha marble.

'I saved him, Susanna. I had to,' he whispered. The

34

corners of the woman's mouth twitched – it might have been a smile.

'I . . . know . . .' she said, voice coming ever so softly in her raw throat. 'If only . . . my Eahlferend . . . had not . . .' The effort was too much, and she stopped. Elispeth leaned down to show her the child, wrapped in blankets, still attached by the bloody umbilicus.

'He's small,' the old woman smiled, 'but that's because he arrived so early. What is his name?'

'. . . Call . . . him . . . Seoman . . .' Susanna croaked out. '. . . it means . . . "waiting" . . .' She turned to Morgenes and seemed to want to say something more. The doctor leaned closer, his white hair brushing her snow-pale cheek, but she could not make the words come. A moment later she gasped once, and her dark eyes rolled up until the whites showed. The girl holding her hand began to sob.

Rachel, too, felt tears come to her eyes. She turned away and pretended to begin cleaning up. Elispeth was severing the infant's last tie to his dead mother.

The movement caused Susanna's right hand, which had been tightly tangled in her own hair, to sag free and drop limply to the floor. As it struck, something shiny flew from her clutching palm and rolled across the rough boards to stop near the doctor's foot. From the corner of her eye Rachel saw Morgenes stoop down and pick the object up. It was small, and disappeared easily into the palm of his hand, and from there into his bag.

Rachel was outraged, but no one else seemed to have noticed. She whirled to confront him, teardrops still standing in her eyes, but the look on his face, the terrible grief, stilled her before she breathed a word.

'He will be Seoman,' the doctor said, his eyes strange and shadowed now as he moved closer, his voice hoarse. 'You must take care of him, Rachel. His parents are dead, you know.'

35

A swift intake of breath. Rachel had caught herself just before she slipped off the stool. Nodding off in bright daylight – she was ashamed of herself! Then again, it only went to show the criminal length to which she had driven herself today, all in an effort to make up for the three girls off . . . and for Simon.

What she needed was a little fresh air. Up on a stool, swatting the broom around like a madwoman – no wonder a body started in getting in the vapors. She'd just step outside for a moment. The lord knew she had every right to a little fresh air. That Simon, such a wicked boy.

They'd raised him, of course, she and the chamber-maids. Susanna hadn't any kinfolk nearby, and no one seemed to know much of anything about her drowned husband Eahlferend, so they kept the boy. Rachel had pretended to raise a fuss over it, but she would no more have let him go than she would have betrayed her King, or left beds unmade. It was Rachel who had given him the name Simon. Everyone in the service of King John's household took a name from the king's native island, Warinsten. Simon was the closest to Seoman, and so Simon it was.

Rachel went slowly down the stairs to the bottom floor, feeling just a little shaky in the legs. She wished she'd brought a cloak, as the air was bound to be nippy. The door creaked open slowly – it was such a heavy door, needed the hinges oiled, most likely – and she walked out into the entry yard. The morning sun was just nosing over the battlement, peeping like a child.

She liked this spot, just underneath the stone span that connected the dining hall building with the main body of the chapel. The little courtyard in the shadow of the span was full of pine trees and heather, all set about on small, sloping hills; the whole garden was not more than a stone's throw in length. Looking up past the stone walkway she could see the needle-slim thrust of Green Angel Tower, shining white in the sunlight like an ivory tusk.

There had been a time, Rachel remembered, long

before Simon came, when she herself had been a girl playing in this garden. How some of those maids would laugh to think of *that*: the Dragon as a little girl. Well, she *had* been, and after that a young lady – not unpleasant to look at, either, and that was only the truth. The garden then had been full of the rustle of brocade and silk, of lords and ladies laughing, with hawks on their fists and a merry song on their lips.

Now Simon, he thought he knew everything – God just made young men stupid, and that was that. Those girls had nearly spoiled him beyond redemption, and would have if Rachel hadn't kept her eye out. *She* knew what was what, even if these young ones thought otherwise.

*Things were different once*, Rachel thought . . . and as she thought it the pine smell of the shaded garden seemed to catch at her heart. The castle had been such a beautiful, stirring place: tall knights, plumed and shiny-mailed, and beautiful girls in fine dresses, the music . . . oh, and the tourney field all jewel-bright with tents! Now the castle slept quietly, and only dreamed. The towering battlements were commanded by Rachel's kind: by cooks and chambermaids, seneschals and scullions. . . .

It *was* a little chilly. Rachel leaned forward, hugging her shawl tighter, then straightened up staring. Simon stood before her, hands hidden behind his back. How on earth had he managed to slip up on her that way? And why did he have that idiot grin smeared across his face? Rachel felt the strength of righteousness come surging back into her body. His shirt – clean an hour before – was blackened with dirt and torn in several places, as were his breeches.

'*Blessed Saint Rhiap save me!*' Rachel shrieked. 'What have you done, you fool boy!?' Rhiappa had been an Aedonite woman of Nabban who had died with the name of the One God on her lips after being repeatedly violated by sea-pirates. She was a great favorite with domestics.

'Look what I have, Rachel!' Simon said, producing a tattered, lop-sided cone of straw: a bird's nest. It gave off faint chirps. 'I found it underneath Hjeldin's Tower! It must have blown off in the wind. Three of them are still alive, and I'm going to raise them!'

'Are you utterly mad?' Rachel lifted her broom on high, like the vengeful lightnings of the Lord that had surely destroyed Rhiap's ravishers. 'You are no more going to raise those creatures in my household than I am going to swim to Perdruin! Filthy things flying around, getting in people's hair – and look at your clothes! Do you know how long it will take Sarrah to patch all that?' The broomstick quivered in the air.

Simon cast his eyes down. He had not found the nest on the ground, of course: it was the one he had spotted in the Hedge Garden, partially dislodged from its seat in the Festival Oak. He had climbed up to rescue it, and in his excitement at the thought of having the young birds for his own he had not given a thought to the work he was making for Sarrah, the quiet, homely girl who did the downstairs mending. A wave of gloom and frustration washed over him.

'But Rachel, I remembered to pick the rushes!' He balanced the nest carefully and pulled from beneath his jerkin a meager, bedraggled clump of reeds.

Rachel's expression softened somewhat, but the scowl remained. 'It's just that you don't think boy, you don't think – you're like a little child. If something gets broken, or something is done late, someone has to take responsibility for it. That's the way the world is. I know you mean no real harm, but *must* you be so By-Our-Lady stupid?'

Simon looked up cautiously. Although his face still showed sorrow and contrition in proper measure, Rachel with her basilisk eye could see that he thought he was through the worst of it. Her brow re-beetled.

'I'm sorry, Rachel, truly I am . . .' he was saying when she reached out and poked his shoulder with her broom handle.

38

'Don't you come to the old "sorry" with me, lad. Just you take those birds out of here and put them back. There'll be no flapping, flying creatures 'round these parts.'

'Oh, Rachel, I could keep them in a cage! I could build one!'

'No, no, and once more means *no*. Take them and give them to your useless doctor if you want, but don't bring them 'round to trouble honest people who have *work* to do.'

Simon trudged off, the nest cupped in his hands. He had made a miscalculation somewhere – Rachel had almost given in, but she was a tough old stalk. The slightest error in dealing with her meant swift, terrible defeat.

'Simon!' she called. He whirled.

'I can keep them?!'

'Of course not. Don't be a mooncalf.' She stared at him. An uncomfortably long time passed; Simon shifted from foot to foot and waited.

'You go work for the doctor, boy,' she said at last. 'Maybe he can squeeze some sense into you. I give up.' She glowered at him. 'Mind you do what you're told, and thank him – and what little luck you have left – for this one last chance. Understand?'

'Yes, certainly!' he said happily.

'You're not escaping from me all that easily. Be back at dinner hour.'

'Yes, mistress!' Simon turned to hurry off to Morgenes, then stopped.

'Rachel? Thank you.'

Rachel made a noise of disgust and marched back towards the stairs to the dining hall. Simon wondered how she had gotten so many pine needles stuck in her shawl.

A gentle mist of snow had begun to float down from the low, tin-colored clouds. The weather had turned for good, Simon knew: it would be cold right through to Candlemansa. Rather than carry the baby birds across the windy courtyard, he decided to duck through the chapel and continue through to the western side of the Inner Bailey. Morning prayers had been over for an hour or two, and the church should be empty. Father Dreosan might not look kindly on Simon tramping through his lair, but the good father was undoubtedly entrenched at table with his usual large midmorning meal, humming ominously at the quality of the butter or the consistency of the honey-and-bread pudding.

Simon climbed the two dozen steps up to the chapel's side door. The snow had started to flurry; the gray stone of the doorway was dotted with the wet residue of dying flakes. The door swung back on surprisingly silent hinges.

Rather than leave telltale wet footprints across the tile floor of the chapel, he pushed through the velvet hangings at the back of the entry chamber and climbed another set of stairs to the choir loft.

The cluttered, stuffy loft, a steaming misery-box during high summer, was now pleasantly warm. The floor was strewn with bits of the monks' leavings: nutshells, an apple core, scraps of slate roof tiles on which messages had been written in petty contravention of the silence vows – it looked more like a cage for apes or festival bears than a room where men of God came to sing the Lord's praises. Simon smiled, threading his way quietly among the various other oddments strewn about – bolts of plaincloth, a few small, flimsy wooden stools. It was nice to know that those dour-faced, shaven-headed men could be as unruly as farm boys.

Alarmed by the sudden sound of conversation, Simon stopped and edged back into the wall hanging that blanketed the rear of the loft. Crushed into the musty fabric, he held his breath as his heart raced. If Father Dreosan or Barnabas the sexton were below, he would never make his way down and out the far door unobserved. He would have to sneak back out the way he had come, using the courtyard route after all – the master-spy in the enemy's camp.

Squatting, silent as cotton wool, Simon strained to locate those who spoke. He seemed to hear two voices; as he concentrated the birdlings peeped quietly in his hands. He balanced the nest carefully for a moment in the crook of his elbow while he pulled off his hat – more woe to him if Father Dreosan should catch him hatted in the chapel! – then slid the soft brim down over the top of the nest. The chicks went promptly silent, as if night had fallen. Parting the edges of the hanging with trembling care he leaned his head out. The voices were rising from the aisle below the altar. Their tone seemed unaltered: he had not been heard.

Only a few torches were lit. The vast roof of the chapel was almost entirely painted in shadow, the shining windows of the dome seeming to float in a nighttime sky, holes in the darkness through which the lines of Heaven could be seen. His foundlings capped and delicately cradled, Simon crept forward on noiseless feet to the rail of the choir loft. Positioning himself at the shadowy end nearest the staircase descending to the chapel proper, he poked his face between the carved rails of the balustrade, one cheek against the martyrdom of Saint Tunath, the other rubbing the birth of Saint Pelippa of the Island.

'. . . And you, with your God-be-cursed complaining!' one of the voices railed. 'I have grown unutterably tired of it.' Simon could not see the speaker's face: his back was to the loft, and he wore a high-collared cloak. His companion, however – slumped across from him on a pew-bench – was quite visible; Simon recognized him at once.

'People who are told things they do not want to hear often call such tidings "complaining," brother,' said the one on the bench, and waved a slim-fingered left hand wearily. 'I warn you about the priest out of love for the kingdom.' There was a moment's silence. 'And in memory of the affection we once shared.'

41

'You may say anything, anything you wish to!' the first man barked, his anger sounding strangely like pain, 'but the Chair is mine by law and our father's wish. Nothing you think, say, or do can change that!'

Josua Lackhand, as Simon had often heard the King's younger son called, pushed himself stiffly up from the bench. His pearl-gray tunic and hose bore subtle patterns of red and white; he wore his brown hair cropped close to his face and high upon his forehead. Where his right hand should have been, a capped cylinder of black leather protruded from his sleeve.

'I do not *want* the Dragonbone Chair – believe that, Elias,' he hissed. His words were soft-spoken, but they flew to Simon's hiding place like arrows. 'I merely warn you against the priest Pryrates, a man with . . . unhealthy interests. Do not bring him here, Elias. He is a dangerous man – *believe me*, for I know him of old from the Usirean seminary in Nabban. The monks there shunned him like a plague carrier. And yet you continue to give him your ear, as though he were trustworthy as Duke Isgrimnur or old Sir Fluiren. Fool! He will be the ruin of our house.' He composed himself. 'I seek only to offer a word of heartfelt advice to you. Please believe me. I have no designs on the throne.'

'Then leave the castle!' Elias growled, and turned his back on his brother, arms crossed on his chest. 'Go, and let me prepare to rule as a man should – free of your complaints and manipulation.'

The older prince had the same high brow and hawklike nose, but was far more powerfully built than Josua; he looked like a man who could break necks with his hands. His hair, like his riding boots and tunic, was black. His cloak and hose were a travel-stained green.

'We are *both* our father's sons, O King-to-be . . .' Josua's smile was mocking. 'The crown is yours by right. The griefs we bear against each other need not worry you. Your soon-to-be-royal self will be quite safe – my word on that. *But*,' his voice gained force, 'I will not, do you hear me, will *not* be ordered out of my sire's house by *anyone*. Not even you, Elias.'

His brother turned and stared; as their eyes met it seemed to Simon a flash of swords.

'Griefs we bear against each other?' Elias snarled, and there was something broken and agonized in his voice. 'What grief can *you* bear against *me*? Your hand?' He walked away from Josua a few steps, and stood with his back to his brother, his words thick with bitterness. 'The loss of a hand. Because of you, *I* stand a widower, and my daughter half an orphan. Do not speak to me of grief!'

Josua seemed to hold his breath for a time before replying.

'Your pain . . . your pain is known to me, brother,' he said at last. 'Do you not know, I would have given not just my right hand, but my *life*. . . !'

Elias whirled, reaching a hand to his throat, and pulled something glittering from out of his tunic. Simon gaped between the railings. It was not a knife, but something soft and yielding, like a swatch of shimmering cloth. Elias held it before his brother's startled face for a sneering moment, then threw it to the floor, pivoted on his heel and stalked away up the aisle. Josua stood motionless for a long moment, then bent, like a man in a dream, to pick up the bright object – a woman's silver scarf. As he stared, its gleam cupped in his hand, a grimace of pain or rage twisted his face. Simon breathed in and out several times before Josua at last tucked the thing into the breast of his shirt and followed his brother out of the chapel.

A lengthy interval had passed before Simon felt safe to creep down from his spying-place and make his way to the chapel's main door. He felt as though he had witnessed a strange puppet show, a Usires Play enacted for him alone. The world suddenly seemed less stable, less trustworthy, if the princes of Erkynland, heirs to all of Osten Ard, could shout and brawl like drunken soldiers.

Peering into the hall, Simon was startled by a sudden movement: a figure in a brown jerkin hurrying away up the corridor – a small figure, a youth of perhaps Simon's age or less. The stranger flicked a glance backward – a brief glimpse of startled eyes – and then was gone around the corner. Simon did not recognize him. Could this person have been spying on the princes, too? Simon shook his head, feeling as confused and stupid as a sunstruck ox. He pulled his hat off the nest, bringing daylight and chirping life back to the birds. Again he shook his head. It had been an unsettling morning.

# 4
# Cricket Cage

Morgenes was rattling about his workshop, deeply engaged in a search for a missing book. He waved Simon permission to find a cage for the young birds, then went back to his hunt, toppling piles of manuscripts and folios like a blind giant in a city of fragile towers.

Finding a home for the nestlings was more difficult than Simon had expected: there were plenty of cages, but none seemed quite right. Some had bars so widely spaced that they seemed built for pigs or bears; others were already crammed full of strange objects, none of which resembled animals in the least. Finally he found one that seemed suitable beneath a roll of shiny cloth. It was knee-high and bell-shaped, made of tightly twisted river reeds, empty but for a layer of sand on the bottom; there was a small door on the side held closed by a twist of rope. Simon worried the knot loose and opened it.

'*Stop!* Stop that this instant!'

'What?!' Simon leaped back. The doctor hopped past him and pushed the cage door shut with his foot.

'Sorry to alarm you, boy,' Morgenes panted, 'but I should have thought before sending you off to dig and muck about. This is no good for your purposes, I'm afraid.'

'But why not?' Simon leaned forward, squinting, but could see nothing extraordinary.

'Well, my grub, stand here for a bit and don't touch, and I'll show you. Silly of me not to have remembered.' Morgenes cast about for a moment until he found a long-ignored basket of dried fruit. He blew the dust off a fig as he walked to the cage.

'Now observe carefully.' He opened the door and tossed in the fruit; it landed in the sand on the cage bottom.

'Yes?' asked Simon, puzzled.

'Wait,' whispered the doctor. No sooner had the word passed his lips than something began to happen. At first it seemed that the air in the cage was shimmering; it quickly became apparent that the sand itself was shifting, eddying delicately around the fig. Suddenly – so suddenly that Simon jumped backward with a surprised grunt – a great toothy mouth opened in the sand, gulping the fruit as swiftly as a carp might break the surface of a pond to take a mosquito. There was a brief ripple along the sand, and then the cage was still again, as innocent-seeming as before.

'What's under there?' Simon gasped. Morgenes laughed.

'That's it!' He seemed very pleased. 'That's the beastie itself! There is no sand: it's just a masquerade, so to speak. The whole thing at the bottom of the cage is one clever animal. Lovely, isn't it?'

'I suppose so,' said Simon, without much conviction. 'Where does it come from?'

'Nascadu, out in the desert countries. You can see why I didn't want you poking about in there – I don't think your feathered orphans would have had a very happy time of it, either.'

Morgenes shut the cage door again, binding it closed with a leather thong, and placed it on a high shelf. Having climbed onto his table to accomplish this, he then continued along its great length, stepping expertly over the litter until he found what he wanted and hopped down. This container, made of thin strips of wood, held no suspicious sand.

'Cage for crickets,' the doctor explained, and helped the youth move the birds into their new home. A small dish of water was placed within; from somewhere else Morgenes even produced a tiny sack of seeds, which he scattered on the cage floor.

'Are they old enough for that?' Simon wondered. The doctor waved a careless hand.

'Not to worry,' he said. 'Good for their teeth.'

Simon promised his birds that he would be back soon with something more suitable, and followed the doctor across the workshop.

'Well, young Simon, charmer of finch and swallow,' Morgenes smiled, 'what can I do for you this cold forenoon? It seems to me that we had not completed your just and honorable frog transaction the other day when we were forced to stop.'

'Yes, and I was hoping . . .'

'*And* I believe there was another thing, too?'

'What?' Simon thought hard.

'A little matter of a floor in need of sweeping? A broom, lone and lorn, aching in its twiggy heart to be put to use?'

Simon nodded glumly. He had hoped an apprenticeship might start on a more auspicious note.

'Ah. A small aversion to menial labor?' The doctor cocked an eyebrow. 'Understandable but misplaced. One should treasure those humdrum tasks that keep the body occupied but leave the mind and heart unfettered. Well, we shall strive to help you through your first day in service. I have thought of a wonderful arrangement.' He did a funny little jig-step. 'I talk, you work. Good, eh?'

Simon shrugged. 'Do you have a broom? I forgot mine.'

Morgenes poked around behind the door, producing at last an object so worn and cobwebby it was scarcely recognizable as a tool for sweeping.

'Now,' the doctor said, presenting it to him with as

much dignity as if it were the king's own standard, 'what do you want me to talk to you about?'

'About the sea-raiders and their black iron, and the Sithi . . . and our castle, of course. And King John.'

'Ah, yes.' He nodded thoughtfully. 'A longish list, but if we are not once again interrupted by that cloth-headed sluggard Inch, I might be able to whittle it down a bit. Set to, boy, set to – let the dust fly! By the by, where exactly in the story was I. . . ?'

'Oh, the Rimmersmen had come, and the Sithi were retreating, and the Rimmersmen had iron swords, and they were chopping people up, and killing *everyone*, killing the Sithi with black iron . . .'

'Hmmm,' said Morgenes dryly, 'it comes back to me now. Hmm. Well, truth be told, the northern raiders were not killing quite *everybody*; neither were their expansions and assaults quite so relentless as I may have made them sound. They were many years in the north before they ever crossed the Frostmarch – even then they ran into a major obstacle: the men of Hernystir.'

'Yes, but the *Sithi-folk*. . . !' Simon was impatient. He knew all about the Hernystiri – had met many people from that pagan western land. 'You said that the little people had to flee from the iron swords!'

'Not *little people*, Simon, I . . . oh, my!' The doctor slumped down onto a pile of leather-bound books and pulled at his sparse chinwhiskers. 'I can see that I must give this story in greater depth. Are you expected back for the midday meal?'

'No,' Simon lied promptly. An uninterrupted story from the doctor seemed a fair bargain for one of Rachel's fabled thrashings.

'Good. Well, then, let us find ourselves some bread and onions . . . and perhaps a noggin of something to drink – talking is such thirsty work – then I shall endeavor to turn dross to purest Metal Absolute: in short, to teach you something.'

48

When they had provisioned themselves, the doctor once more took a seat.

'Well and well, Simon – oh, and don't be bashful about wielding that broom while you eat. The young are so flexible! – now, correct me please if I misspeak. The day today is Drorsday, the fifteenth – sixteenth? – no, fifteenth of Novander. And the year is 1164, is it not?'

'I think so.'

'Excellent. Do put that over on the stool, will you? So, the eleven-hundred and sixty-fourth year since *what?* Do you know?' Morgenes leaned forward.

Simon pulled a sour face. The doctor knew he was a mooncalf and was teasing him. How was a scullion supposed to know about such things? He continued to sweep in silence.

After some moments he looked up. The doctor was chewing, staring at him intently over a crusty chunk of dark bread.

*What sharp blue eyes the old man has!*

Simon turned away again.

'Well, then?' the doctor said around a mouthful. 'Since what?'

'I don't know,' Simon muttered, hating the sound of his own resentful voice.

'So be it. You don't know – or you think you don't. Do you listen to the proclamations when the crier reads them?'

'Sometimes. When I'm at Market. Otherwise Rachel tells me what they say.'

'And what comes at the end? They read the date at the end, do you remember? – and mind that crystal urn, boy, you sweep like a man shaving his worst enemy. What does it say at the end?'

Simon, nettled with shame, was about to throw the broom down and leave when suddenly a phrase floated up from the depths of his memory, bringing with it market-sounds – the wind-snapping of pennants and awnings – and the clean smell of spring grass strewn underfoot.

'Since the Founding.' He was sure. He heard it as though he were standing on Main Row.

'*Excellent!*' The doctor lifted his jar as if in salute and knocked back a long swallow. 'Now, the "Founding" of *what?* Don't worry,' he continued as Simon began to shake his head, 'I'll tell you. I don't expect young men these days – raised as they are on apocryphal errantry and derring-do – to know much of the real substance of events.' The doctor shook his own head, mock-sadly. 'The *Nabbanai Imperium* was founded – or declared to be founded – eleven-hundred and sixty-whatever-it-was years ago, by Tiyagaris, the first Imperator. At that time the legions of Nabban ruled all the countries of Men north and south, on both sides of the River Gleniwent.'

'But – but Nabban is small!' Simon was astonished. 'It's just a small part of King John's kingdom!'

'That, young man,' Morgenes said, 'is what we call "history." Empires have a tendency to decline; kingdoms to collapse. Given a thousand years or so, anything can happen – actually, Nabban's zenith lasted considerably less than that. What I was getting to, however, is that Nabban once ruled Men, and Men lived side by side with the Sithi-folk. The king of the Sithi reigned here in Asu'a – the Hayholt, as we call it. The Erl-king – "erl" is an old word for Sitha – refused humans the right to enter his people's lands except by special grant, and the humans – more than a little afraid of the Sithi – obeyed.'

'What *are* Sithi? You said they're not the Little Folk.'

Morgenes smiled. 'I appreciate your interest, lad – especially when I haven't put in killing or maiming once yet today! – but I would appreciate it even more if you were not so shy with the broom. Dance with her, boy, dance with her! Look, clean that off, if you will.'

Morgenes trotted over to the wall and pointed to a patch of soot several cubits in diameter. It looked very much like a footprint. Simon decided not to ask, and instead set to sweeping it loose from the white-plastered stone.

'Ahhhh, many thanks to you. I've been wanting to get that down for months – since last year's Harrow's Eve, as a matter of fact. Now, where in the name of the Lesser Vistrils was I. . . ? Oh, your questions. The Sithi? Well, they were here first, and perhaps will be here when we're gone. When we're *all* gone. They are as different from us as Man is from the Animal – but somewhat similar, too. . . .' The doctor stopped to consider.

'To be fair, Man and Animal both live a similarly brief span of years in Osten Ard, and this is not true of Sithi and Man. If the Fair Folk are not actually deathless, they are certainly much longer-lived than any mortal man, even our nonagenerian king. It could be they do not die at all, except by choice or violence – perhaps if you are a Sitha, violence *itself* might be a choice. . . .'

Morgenes trailed off. Simon was staring at him open-mouthed.

'Oh, shut that jaw, boy, you look like Inch. It's my privilege to wander in thought a little bit. Would you rather go back and listen to the Mistress of Chambermaids?'

Simon's mouth closed, and he resumed sweeping the soot off the wall. He had changed the original footprint shape to something resembling a sheep; he stopped from time to time to eye it appraisingly. An itch of boredom made itself known at the back of his neck: he *liked* the doctor, and would rather be here than anywhere else – but the old man did go on so! Maybe if he swept a little more of the top part away it would look like a dog. . . ? His stomach growled quietly.

Morgenes went on to explain, in what Simon thought was perhaps unnecessary detail, about the era of peace between the subjects of the ageless Erl-king and those of the upstart human Imperators.

'. . . so, Sithi and Man found a sort of balance,' the old man said. 'They even traded together a little . . .'

Simon's stomach rumbled loudly. The doctor smiled a tiny smile and put back the last onion, which he had just lifted from the table.

'Men brought spices and dyes from the Southern Islands, or precious stones from the Grianspog Mountains in Hernystir; in return they received beautiful things from the Erl-king's coffers, objects of cunning and mysterious workmanship.'

Simon's patience was at an end. 'But what about the shipmen, the Rimmersmen? What about the iron swords?' He looked about for something to gnaw on. The last onion? He sidled cautiously over. Morgenes was facing the window; while he gazed out at the gray noontide, Simon pocketed the papery brown thing and hurried back to the wall-spot. Much diminished in size, the splotch now looked like a serpent.

Morgenes continued without turning away from the window. 'I suppose there *has* been quite a bit of peaceful-times-and-people in my history today.' He wagged his head, walking back to his seat. 'Peace will soon give way – never fear.' He shook his head again, and a lock of thin hair settled across his wrinkled forehead. Simon gnawed furtively at his onion.

'Nabban's golden age lasted a little over four centuries, until the earliest coming of the Rimmersmen to Osten Ard. The Nabbanai Imperium had begun to turn in on itself. Tiyagaris' line had finally died out, and every new Imperator who seized power was another cast of the dice cup; some were good men who tried to hold the realm together. Others, like Crexis the Goat, were worse than any northern reavers. And some, like Enfortis, were just weak.

'During Enfortis' reign the iron-wielders came. Nabban decided to withdraw from the north altogether. They fell back across the river Gleniwent so quickly that many of the northern frontier outposts found themselves entirely deserted, left behind to join the oncoming Rimmersmen or die.

'Hmmm . . . Am I boring you, boy?'

Simon, leaning against the wall, jerked himself upright to face Morgenes' knowing smile.

'No, Doctor, no! I was just closing my eyes to listen better. Go on!'

Actually, all of these names, names, names *were* making him a bit drowsy . . . and he wished the doctor would hurry along to the parts with battles in them. But he did like to be the only one in the entire castle to whom Morgenes was speaking. The chambermaids didn't know anything about these kind of things . . . *men* things. What did maids or serving girls know about armies, and flags, and swords. . . ?

'Simon?'

'Oh! Yes? Go on!' He whirled to sweep off the last of the wall-blot as the doctor resumed. The wall was clean. Had he finished without knowing?

'So I will try and make the story a little briefer, lad. As I was saying, Nabban withdrew its armies from the north, becoming for the first time purely a southern empire. It was just the beginning of the end, of course; as time passed, the Imperium folded itself up just like a blanket, smaller and smaller until today they are nothing more than a duchy – a peninsula with its few attendant islands. What in the name of Paldir's Arrow are you *doing?*'

Simon was contorting himself like a hound trying to scratch a difficult spot. Yes, there was the last of the wall dirt: a snake-shaped smear across the back of his shirt. He had leaned against it. He turned sheepishly to Morgenes, but the doctor only laughed and continued.

'Without the Imperial garrisons, Simon, the north was in chaos. The shipmen had captured the northernmost part of the Frostmarch, naming their new home Rimmersgard. Not content with that, the Rimmersmen were fanning out southward, sweeping all before them in a bloody advance. Put those folios in a stack against the wall, will you?

'They robbed and ruined other Men, making captives of many, but the Sithi they deemed evil creatures; with fire and cold iron they hunted the Fair Folk to their death everywhere . . . careful with that one, there's a good lad.'

'Over here, Doctor?'

'Yes – but, Bones of Anaxos, don't *drop* them! Set them down! If you knew the terrible midnight hours I spent rolling dice in an Utanyeat graveyard to get my hands on them. . . ! There! Much better.

'Now the people of Hernystir – a proud, fierce people whom even the Nabbanai Imperators never really conquered – were not at all willing to bend their necks to Rimmersgard. They were horrified by what the northerners were doing to the Sithi. The Hernystiri had been of all Men the closest to Fair Folk – there is still visible today the mark of an ancient trade road between this castle and the Taig at Hernysadharc. The lord of Hernystir and the Erl-king made desperate compact, and for a while held the northern tide at bay.

'But even combined, their resistance could not last forever. Fingil, king of the Rimmersmen, swept down across the Frostmarch over the borders of the Erl-king's territory . . .' Morgenes smiled sadly. 'We're coming to the end now, young Simon, never fear, coming to the end of it all. . . .

'In the year 663 the two great hosts came to the plains of Ach Samrath, the Summerfield, north of the River Gleniwent. For five days of terrible, merciless carnage the Hernystiri and the Sithi held back the might of the Rimmersmen. On the sixth day, though, they were set on treacherously from their unprotected flank by an army of men from the Thrithings, who had long coveted the riches of Erkynland and the Sithi for their own. They made a fearful charge under cover of darkness. The defense was broken, the Hernystiri chariots smashed, the White Stag of the House of Hern trampled into the bloody dirt. It is said that ten thousand men of Hernystir died in the field that day. No one knows how many Sithi fell, but their losses were grievous, too. Those Hernystiri who survived fled back to the forest of their home. In

Hernystir, Ach Samrath is today a name only for hatred and loss.'

'*Ten thousand!*' Simon whistled. His eyes shone with the terror and grandness of it all.

Morgenes noted the boy's expression with a small grimace, but did not comment.

'That was the day that Sithi mastery in Osten Ard came to an end, even though it took three long years of siege before Asu'a fell to the victorious northerners.

'If not for strange, horrible magics worked by the Erl-king's son, there would likely have been not a single Sithi to survive the fall of the Castle. Many did, however, fleeing to the forests, and south to the waters and . . . and elsewhere.'

Now Simon's attention was fixed as though nailed. 'And the Erl-king's son? What was his name? What kind of magic did he do?' – a sudden thought – 'How about Prester John? I thought you were going to tell me about the king – our king!'

'Another day, Simon.' Morgenes fanned his brow with a sheaf of whisper-thin parchments, although the chamber was quite cool. 'There is much to tell about the dark ages after Asu'a fell, many stories. The Rimmersmen ruled here until the dragon came. In later years, while the dragon slept, other men held the castle. Many years and several kings in the Hayholt, many dark years and many deaths until John came. . . .' He trailed off, passing a hand over his face as though to brush weariness away.

'But what about the king of the Sithi's son?' Simon asked quietly. 'What about the . . . the "terrible magic"?'

'About the Erl-king's son . . . it is better to say nothing.'

'But why?'

'Enough questions, boy!' Morgenes growled, waving his hands. 'I am tired of talking!'

Simon was offended. He had only been trying to hear the whole story; why were grown people so easily upset?

However, it was best not to boil the hen who lays golden eggs.

'I'm sorry, Doctor.' He tried to look contrite, but the old scholar looked so funny with his pink, flushed monkey-face and his wispy hair sticking up! Simon felt his lip curling toward a smile. Morgenes saw it, but maintained his stern expression.

'Truly, I'm sorry.' No change. What to try next? 'Thank you for telling me the story.'

'Not a "story"!' Morgenes roared. '*History*! Now be off with you! Come back tomorrow morning ready to work, for you have still barely begun *today's* work!'

Simon got up, trying to keep his smile in check, but as he turned to go it broke loose and wriggled across his face like a ribbon-snake. As the door closed behind him he heard Morgenes cursing whatever eldritch demons had hidden his jug of porter.

Afternoon sunlight was knifing down through chinks in the heavy clouds as Simon made his way back to the Inner Bailey. On the face of it he seemed to dawdle and gape, a tall, awkward, red-haired boy in dust-caked clothes. Inside he was aswarm with strange thoughts, a hive of buzzing, murmuring desires.

*Look at this castle*, he thought – old and dead, stone pressed upon lifeless stone, a pile of rocks inhabited by small-minded creatures. But it had been different once. Great things had happened here. Horns had blown, swords had glittered, great armies had crashed against each other and rebounded like the waves of the Kynslagh battering the Seagate wall. Hundreds of years had passed, but it seemed to Simon it was happening just now only for him, while the slow, witless folk who shared the castle with him crawled past, thinking of nothing but the next meal, and a nap directly afterward.

*Idiots.*

As he came through the postern gate a glimmer of light caught his eye, drawing it up to the distant walkway that ringed Hjeldin's Tower. A girl stood there, bright and small as a piece of jewelry, her green dress and golden hair embracing the ray of sunlight as if it had arrowed down from the sky for her alone. Simon could not see her face, but he was somehow certain she was beautiful – beautiful and forgiving as the image of the Immaculate Elysia that stood in the chapel.

For a moment that flash of green and gold kindled him like a spark on dry timber. He felt all the bother and resentment that he had carried disappear, burned away in a hasty second. He was as light and buoyant as swansdown, prey to any breeze that might carry him away, might waft him up to that golden gleam.

Then he looked away from the wonderful faceless girl, down at his own ragged garments. Rachel was waiting, and his dinner had gotten cold. A certain indefinable weight climbed back into its accustomed seat, bending his neck and slumping his shoulders as he trudged toward the servants' quarters.

# 5
# The Tower Window

Novander was sputtering out in wind and delicate snow; Decander waited patiently, year's-end in its train.

King John Presbyter had been taken ill after calling his two sons back to the Hayholt, and had returned to his shadowed room, again to be surrounded by leeches, learned doctors, and scolding, fretting body servants. Bishop Domitis swept in from Saint Sutrin's, Erchester's great church, and set up shop at John's bedside, shaking the king awake at all hours to inspect the texture and heft of the royal soul. The old man, continuing to weaken, bore both pain and priest with gallant stoicism.

In the tiny chamber next to the king's own that Towser had occupied for forty years the sword Bright-Nail lay, oiled and scabbarded, wrapped in fine linens at the bottom of the jester's oaken chest.

Far and wide across the broad face of Osten Ard the word flew: Prester John was dying. Hernystir in the west and northern Rimmersgard immediately dispatched delegations to the bedside of stricken Erkynland. Old Duke Isgrimnur, John's left-hand companion at the Great Table, brought fifty Rimmersmen from Elvritshalla and Naarved, the whole company wrapped head to foot in furs and leather for the winter crossing of the Frostmarch. Only twenty Hernystiri accompanied King

58

Lluth's son Gwythinn, but the bright gold and silver they wore flashed bravely, outshining the poor cloth of their garments.

The castle began to come alive with the music of languages long unheard, Rimmerspakk and Perdruinese and Harcha-tongue. Naraxi's rolling island speech floated in the gateyard, and the stables echoed to the singsong cadences of the Thrithings-men – the grass-landers, as always, most comfortable around horses. Over these and all others hung the droning speech of Nabban, the busy tongue of Mother Church and her Aedonite priests, taking charge as always of the comings and goings of men and their souls.

In the tall Hayholt and Erchester below these small armies of foreigners came together and flowed apart, for the most part without incident. Although many of these peoples had been ancient enemies, nearly four score years beneath the High King's Ward had healed many wounds. More gills of ale were bought than harsh words traded.

There was one worrisome exception to this rule of harmony – one difficult to miss or misunderstand. Everywhere they met, under Hayholt's broad gates or in the narrow alleyways of Erchester, Prince Elias' green-liveried soldiers and Prince Josua's gray-shirted retainers jostled and argued, mirroring in public the private division of the king's sons. Prester John's Erkynguard were called upon to break up several ugly brawls. At last, one of Josua's supporters was stabbed by a young Meremund noble, an intimate of the heir-apparent. Luckily, Josua's man took no fatal harm – the blow was a drunken one, and poorly aimed – and the partisans were forced to heed the rebukes of the older courtiers. The troops of the two princes returned to cold stares and disdainful sneers; open bloodshed was averted.

These were strange days in Erkynland, and in all of Osten Ard, days freighted with equal measures of sorrow and excitement. The king was not dead, but it seemed he soon would be. The whole world was changing – how could anything remain the same once Prester John no longer sat the Dragonbone Chair?

'. . . *Udunsday: dream . . . Drorsday: better . . . Frayday: best . . . Satrinsday: marketday . . . Sunday – rest!*'

Down the creaking stairs two at a clip, Simon sang the old rhyme at the top of his voice. He almost knocked over Sophrona the Linen Mistress as she led a squadron of blanket-burdened maids in at the Pine Garden door. She threw herself back against the doorjamb with a little shriek as Simon pounded by, then waved a skinny fist at his fast-departing back.

'I'll tell Rachel!' she shouted. Her charges stifled laughter.

Who cared for Sophrona? Today was Satrinsday – market day – and Judith the cook had given Simon two pennies to buy some things for her, and a fithing piece – glorious Satrinsday! – to spend on himself. The coins made a lovely, suggestive clink in his leather purse as he spiraled out through the castle's acres of long, circular courtyards, out the Inner Bailey gate to Middle Bailey, nearly empty now since its residents, the soldiers and the artisans, were mostly on duty or at market.

In Outer Bailey animals milled in the commons yard, bumping miserably together in the cold, guarded by herders who looked scarcely more cheerful. Simon bustled along the rows of low houses, storage rooms, and animal sheds, many of them so old and overgrown with winter-naked ivy that they seemed only warty growths on the High Keep's inner walls.

The sun was glinting through the clouds on the carvings that swarmed the mighty chalcedony face of the Nearulagh Gate. As he slowed to a puddle-dodging trot, staring open-mouthed at the intricate depictions of King John's victory over Ardrivis – the battle that had brought Nabban at last under the royal hand – Simon heard the tumult of swift hooves and the shrill squeak of cart wheels. He looked up in horror to find himself faced with the white, rolling eyes of a horse, mud gouting from beneath its hooves as it plunged through the Nearulagh Gate. Simon flung himself out of the way and felt wind on his face as the horse thundered by, the cart drawn behind it pitching wildly. He had a brief glimpse of the driver, dressed in a dark hooded cloak lined with scarlet. The man's eyes raked him as the cart hurtled past – they were black and shiny, like the cruel button-orbs of a shark; although the contact was fleeting, Simon felt almost that the driver's gaze *burned* him. He reeled back, clutching at the stone facing of the gate, and watched as the cart disappeared around the track of Outer Bailey. Chickens squawked and flapped in its wake, except for those that lay crushed and bloody in the wagon's ruts. Muddied feathers drifted to the ground.

'Here, boy, not hurt are you?' One of the gatewarders peeled Simon's trembling hand from the carvings and set him back upright. 'Get on with you, then.'

Snow swirled in the air and stuck melting to his cheeks as he walked down the long hill toward Erchester. The chink of the coins in his pocket now played to a slower, wobbly-kneed rhythm.

'That priest is mad as the moon,' Simon heard the warder say to his gate companion. 'Were he not Prince Elias' man . . .'

Three little children following their toiling mother up the damp hillpath pointed at long-legged Simon as he passed, laughing at the expression on his pale face.

Main Row was roofed all over with stitched skins that stretched across the wide throughfare from building to building. At each waycrossing were set great stone fire-cairns, most – but certainly not all – of their smokes billowing up through holes in the roof-tenting. Snow fluttering down through the chimney holes sizzled and hissed in the hot air. Warming themselves by the flames or strolling and talking – all the while surreptitiously examining the goods displayed on every side – Erchester and Hayholt folk mixed with those of the outer fiefs, eddying together in and out of the wide central row which ran two full leagues from the Nearulagh Gate to Battle Square at the city's far end. Caught up in the press, Simon found his spirits reviving. What should he care for a drunken priest? After all, it was market day!

Today the usual army of marketers and shrill-voiced hawkers, wide-eyed provincials, gamblers, cutpurses, and musicians was swelled by the soldiery of the various missions to the dying king. Rimmersman, Hernystiri, Warinstenner or Perdruinese, their swagger and bright garb caught Simon's jackdaw fancy. He followed one group of blue and gold clad Nabbanai legionaries, admiring their strut and easy superiority, understanding without language the offhand way they insulted each other. He was edging up closer, hoping for a clear look at the short stabbing-swords they wore scabbarded high on their waists, when one of them – a bright-eyed soldier wearing a thin, dark mustache – turned and saw him.

'Heá, brothers!' he said with a grin, grabbing at each of his fellows' arm, 'Look now! A young sneaking thief, I wager, and one who has his eye on your purse, Turis!'

Both men squared to face Simon, and the heavy, bearded one called Turis gave the youth a grim stare. 'Did he touch it, then I would kill,' he growled. His command of the Westerling speech was not as sure as the first man's; he seemed to lack the other's humor as well.

Three other legionaries had now come back to join the first pair. They gradually closed in until Simon felt like a winded fox.

'What's here, Gelles?' one of the new arrivals asked Turis' companion. '*Hué fauge*? Did this one steal?'

'Nai, nai . . .' Gelles chuckled, 'I was but having sport with Turis. Skinny-one here did nothing.'

'I have my own purse!' Simon said indignantly. He untied it from his belt and waved it in the soldiers' smirking faces. 'I am no thief! I live in the king's household! *Your* king!' The soldiers all laughed.

'Heá, listen to him!' Gelles shouted, '*Our* king he says, so very bold!'

Simon could see now that the young legionary was drunk. Some – but not all – of his fascination turned to disgust.

'Heá, lads,' Gelles waggled his eyebrows, ' "*Mulvei-znei cenit drenisend*,' they say – let us beware this pup, then, and let him sleep!' Another round of hilarity followed. Simon, red-faced, secured his purse and turned to go.

'Goodbye, castle-mouse!' one of the soldiers called mockingly. Simon did not turn or speak, but hurried away.

He had gone past one of the fire-cairns and out from under the Main Row awnings when he felt a hand upon his shoulder. He whirled, thinking that the Nabban-men had returned to insult him further, but instead found a plump man with a weather-hardened pink face. The stranger wore the gray robe and tonsure of a mendicant friar.

'Your pardon, my young lad,' he said, with a Hernystirman's crackling burr, 'I only wished to find out if you were safe, then, if those *goirach* fellows had done you harm.' The stranger reached out to Simon and patted him, as if searching for damage. His heavy-lidded eyes, fitted round about with wrinkles marking the curves of a frequent smile, nevertheless held something back: a deeper shadow, troubling but not frightening. Simon realized he was staring, almost against his will, and shied back.

'No, thank you, Father,' he said, startled into the patterns of formality. 'They were just making sport of me. No harm.'

'Good that is, very good . . . Ah, forgive me, I have not introduced myself. I am Brother Cadrach ec-Crannhyr, of the Vilderivan Order.' He pulled a small, self-deprecatory smile. His breath smelled of wine. 'I came with Prince Gwythinn and his men. Who might you be?'

'Simon. I live in the Hayholt.' He made a vague gesture toward the castle.

The friar smiled again, saying nothing, then turned to watch a Hyrkaman walk by, dressed in bright, disparate colors and leading a muzzled bear on a chain. When the duo had passed, Cadrach returned his small, sharp eyes to Simon.

'There are some that say the Hyrkas can talk to animals, have you heard? Especially their horses. And that the animals understand perfectly.' The friar gave a mocking shrug, as if to show that a man of God naturally would not believe such nonsense.

Simon did not reply. He, of course, had also heard such tales related about the wild Hyrkamen. Shem Horsegroom swore the stories were pure truth. The Hyrkas were often seen at market, where they sold beautiful horses at outrageous prices, and befuddled the villagers with tricks and puzzles. Thinking about them – especially their less-than-honest reputation – Simon put a hand down and grabbed his leather purse, reassuring himself by the feel of the coins inside.

'Thank you for your help, Father,' he said at last – although he could not actually remember the man doing anything helpful. 'I must go now. I have spices to buy.'

Cadrach looked at him for a long moment, as if trying to remember something, a clue to which might be hidden in Simon's face. At last he said: 'I would like to ask you a favor, young man.'

'What?' Simon said suspiciously.

'As I mentioned, I am a stranger in your Erchester. Perhaps you would be good enough to guide me around for a short while, just to help me. You could then go on your way, having done a good turn.'

'Oh.' Simon felt somewhat relieved. His first impulse was to say no – it was so rarely that he got an afternoon to himself at the market. But how often did you get to talk with an Aedonite monk from pagan Hernystir? Also, this Brother Cadrach did not seem like the type who only wanted to lecture you about sin and damnation. He looked the man over again, but the monk's face was unreadable.

'Well, I suppose so – certainly. Come along . . . do you want to see the Nascadu-dancers in Battle Square. . . ?'

Cadrach was an interesting companion. Although he talked freely, telling Simon of the cold journey from Hernysadharc to Erchester with Prince Gwythinn, and made frequent jests about the passersby and their various exotic costumes, still he seemed restrained, watching always for something even as he laughed at his own stories. He and Simon wandered the market for a good part of the afternoon, looking at the tables of cakes and dried vegetables that stood against the shop walls of Main Row, smelling the warm smells of the bread bakers and chestnut vendors. Noting Simon's wistful gaze, the friar insisted they stop and buy a rough straw basket of roasted nuts, which he kindly paid for, giving the chap-faced chestnut man a half-fithing piece nimbly plucked from a pocket in his gray cassock. After burning fingers and tongues trying to eat the nut meats they conceded defeat and stood watching a comical argument between a wine merchant and a juggler blocking his wine-shop doorway while they waited for their purchase to cool.

Next they halted to watch a Usires Play being enacted for a gaggle of shrieking children and fascinated adults. The puppets bobbed and bowed, Usires in his white gown being chased by the Imperator Crexis wearing goat-horns and a beard, and waving a long, barb-headed pike. At last Usires was captured and hung upon the Execution Tree; Crexis, his voice high and shrill, leaped about poking and tormenting the tree-nailed Savior. The children, wildly excited, shouted abuse at the capering Imperator.

Cadrach nudged Simon. 'Do you see?' he asked, pointing a thick finger toward the front of the puppet-stage. The curtain that hung from the stage to the ground billowed, as if in a strong breeze. Cadrach nudged Simon again.

'Would you not say that this is a fine representation of Our Lord?' he asked, never once taking his eyes from the flapping cloth. Above, Crexis jigged and Usires suffered. 'While man plays out his show, the Manipulator remains unseen; we know Him not by sight, but by the way His puppets move. And occasionally the curtain stirs, that hides Him from His faithful audience. Ah, but we are grateful even for just that movement behind the curtain – grateful!'

Simon stared; at last Cadrach looked away from the puppet show and met his gaze. A strange, sad smile crimped the corner of the friar's mouth; for once the look in his eyes seemed to match.

'Ah, boy,' he said, 'and what should you know of religious matters, anyway?'

They strolled for some while longer before Brother Cadrach at last took his leave with many thanks to the young man for his hospitality. Simon continued to walk aimlessly long after the monk was gone, and the patches of sky that could be seen through the roof-tenting were filmed with early darkness before he remembered his errand.

At the spice-merchant's stall he discovered that his purse was gone.

His heart thumped triple-time as he thought back in panic. He knew that he had felt it swinging on his belt when he and Cadrach had stopped to buy chestnuts, but could summon no memories of having it later in the afternoon. Whenever it had disappeared, though, it was definitely gone now – along with not just his own fithing piece, but also the two pennies entrusted to him by Judith!

He searched the market vainly until the sky-holes had gone black as an old kettle. The snow that he had barely felt before seemed very cold and very wet as he returned, empty-handed, to the castle.

Worse than any beating – as Simon discovered when he came home without spices or money – was the look of disappointment that sweet, fat, flour-dusted Judith gave him. Rachel also used this most unfair of gambits, punishing him with nothing more painful than an expression of disgust at his childishness and a promise that he would 'work fingers to the nubbin' earning the money back. Even Morgenes, whom Simon went to half in hope of sympathy, seemed faintly surprised at the youth's carelessness. All in all, although spared a thrashing, he had never felt lower or more sorry for himself.

Sunday came and went, a dark, slushy day in which most of the Hayholt's staff seemed to be at chapel saying a prayer for King John – that, or telling Simon to go away. He had exactly the kind of scratchy, irritable, kick-things-across-the-floor sort of feeling that could usually be soothed by visiting Morgenes or trekking out of doors to do some exploring. The doctor, however, was busy – locked in with Inch, working on something that he said was large, dangerous, and likely to catch fire; Simon would not be needed for anything. The weather outside was so cold and dismal that even in his misery he could not convince himself to go a-roving. Instead, he spent the endless afternoon with the chandler's fat apprentice Jeremias, tossing rocks from one of the turrets of the Inner Bailey wall and arguing in a desultory way as to whether the fish in the moat froze during the winter or, if not, where they went until Spring's arrival.

The chill outside – as well as the different kind of chill in the servants' quarters – still prevailed Moonday when he arose, feeling weedy and unpleasant. Morgenes also seemed in a damp and unresponsive mood, and so when Simon had finished his chores in the doctor's chambers he filched some bread and cheese from the pantry larder and went off to be by himself.

For a while he moped by the Hall of Records in the Middle Bailey, listening to the dry, insectlike sounds of the Writing-Priests, but after an hour he began to feel as though it was his own skin on which the scribes' pens were scratching and scratching and scratching. . . .

He decided to take his dinner and climb the stairs of Green Angel Tower, something he had not done since the weather had begun to turn. Since Barnabas the sexton would as gladly chase him off as go to Heaven, he resolved to bypass the chapel route to the tower entirely, taking instead his own secret path to the upper floors. Tying his meal securely in his handkerchief, he set out.

Walking through the seemingly endless halls of the Chancelry, passing continuously from covered passage to open courtyard and back under cover again – this part of the castle was dotted with small, enclosed yards – he superstitiously avoided looking up at the tower. Eminently slender and pale, it dominated the south-western corner of the Hayholt like a birch tree in a rock garden, so impossibly tall and delicate that from ground level it almost appeared to be standing on some far hillside, miles and miles beyond the castle's wall. Standing beneath he could hear it shudder in the wind, as though it were a lute string tight-cinched on some celestial peg.

The first four stories of Green Angel Tower looked no different than any of the other hundreds of varied structures of the castle. Past masters of the Hayholt had cloaked its slim base in granite outwalls and battlements – whether out of legitimate desire for improved security or because the alienness of the tower was unsettling, no one could know. Above the level of the encircling bailey wall the armoring stopped; the tower thrust nakedly upward, a beautiful albino creature escaping its drab cocoon. Balconies and windows in strangely abstract patterns were cut directly into the stone's glossy surface, like the carved whalefish teeth Simon often saw at market. At the tower's pinnacle shimmered a distant flare of copper-gold and green: the Angel herself, one arm outstretched as if in a gesture of farewell, the other shading her eyes as she stared into the eastern distance.

The huge, noisy Chancelry was even more confounding than usual today. Father Helfcene's cassocked minions dashed back and forth from one chamber to another, or huddled for shivering discussions in the chill, snow flecked air of the courtyards. Several, bearing rolled papers and distracted expressions, tried to commandeer Simon for errands to the Hall of Records, but he bluffed his way through, protesting a mission for Doctor Morgenes.

In the throne room antechamber he halted, pretending to admire the vast mosaics while he waited for the last of the Chancelry priests to hurry through to the chapel beyond. When his moment came, he levered the door open and slid through into the throne room.

The huge hinges creaked, then went silent. Simon's own footsteps echoed and re-echoed, then stopped, fading at last into the deep, breathing quiet. No matter how many times he snuck through this room – for several years he had been, as far as he knew, the only castle resident who dared enter it – it never seemed less than awe-inspiring.

Just last month, after King John's unexpecting rising, Rachel and her crew had finally been allowed past the forbidden threshold; they had indulged themselves with a two-week assault on years of dust and grit, on broken glass and birds' nests and the webs of spiders long since gone to their eight-legged ancestors. But even thoroughly cleaned, with its flagstones mopped, its walls washed down, and some – but not all – of the banners shed of their armor of dust, despite relentless and implacable tidying, the throne room emanated a certain age and stillness. Time here seemed bound only to the measured tread of antiquity.

The dais stood at the great room's far end, in a pool of light that poured down from a figured window in the vaulted ceiling. Upon it the Dragonbone Chair stood like a strange altar – untenanted, surrounded by bright, dancing motes of dust, flanked by the statues of the Hayholt's six High Kings.

The bones of the chair were huge, thicker than Simon's legs, polished so that they gleamed dully like burnished stone. With a few exceptions they had been cut and fitted in such a way that, although their size was evident, it was difficult to guess in which part of the great fire-worm's mighty carcass they had once sheltered. Only the chair back, a great seven-cubit fan of curving yellow ribs behind the king's velvet cushions, reaching far above Simon's head, could be seen immediately for what it was – that and the skull. Perched atop the back of the great seat, jutting far enough to serve as an awning – if more than a thin film of sunlight ever penetrated the shadowed throne room – were the brain-case and jaws of the dragon Shurakai. The eye-holes were broken black windows, the teeth curving spikes as long as Simon's hands. The dragon's skull was the color of old parchment, and webbed with tiny cracks, but there was something alive about it – terribly, wonderfully alive.

In fact, there was an astonishing and holy aura about this entire room that went far beyond Simon's understanding. The throne of heavy, yellowed bones, the massive black figures guarding an empty chair in a high, deserted chamber, all seemed filled with some dread power. All eight inhabitants of the room, the scullion, the statues, and the huge eyeless skull, seemed to hold their breath.

These stolen moments filled Simon with a quiet,

almost fearful ecstasy. Perhaps the malachite kings but waited with black, stony patience for the boy to touch a blasphemous commoner's hand to the dragonbone seat, waited . . . waited . . . and then, with a horrible creaking noise, they would come to life! He shivered with nervous pleasure at his own imaginings and stepped lightly forward, surveying the dark faces. Their names had been so familiar once, when they had been strung-together nonsense in a child's rhyme, a rhyme Rachel – Rachel? Could that be right? – had taught him when he was a giggling ape of four years or so. Could he remember them still?

If his own childhood seemed so long ago, he suddenly wondered, how must it feel to Prester John, who wore so many decades? Mercilessly clear, as when Simon remembered past humiliations, or soft and insubstantial, like stories of the glorious past? When you were old, did your memories crowd out your other thoughts? Or did you lose them – your childhood, your hated enemies, your friends?

How did that old song go? Six kings . . .

> Six Kings have ruled in Hayholt's broad halls
> Six masters have stridden her mighty stone walls
> Six mounds on the cliff over deep Kynslagh-bay
> Six kings will sleep there until Doom's final day

That was it!

> Fingil first, named the Bloody King
> Flying out of the North on war's red wing
>
> Hjeldin his son, the Mad King dire
> Leaped to his death from the haunted spire
>
> Ikferdig next, the Burned King hight
> He met the fire-drake by dark of night
>
> Three northern kings, all dead and cold
> The North rules no more in lofty Hayholt

71

Those were the three Rimmersgard kings on the left of the throne. Wasn't Fingil the one Morgenes spoke of, the leader of the dreadful army? The one who killed the Sithi? So, on the right side of the yellowed bones the rest must be . . .

> *The Heron King Sulis, called Apostate*
> *Fled Nabban, but in Hayholt he met his fate*
>
> *The Herynstir Holly King, old Tethtain*
> *Came in at the gate, but not out again*
>
> *Last, Eahlstan Fisher King, in lore most high*
> *The dragon he woke, and in Hayholt he died . . .*

*Hah!* Simon stared at the Heron King's sad, pinched face and gloated. *My memory is better than most people think – better than that of most mooncalves!* Of course, now there was at last a seventh king in the Hayholt – old Prester John. Simon wondered if someone would add King John to the song someday.

The sixth statue, closest to the throne's right arm, was Simon's favorite: the only native Erkynlander who had ever sat on the Hayholt's great seat. He moved closer to look into the deep-cut eyes of Saint Eahlstan – called Eahlstan Fiskerne because he came from the fisher-people of the Gleniwent, called The Martyr because he too had been slain by the firedrake Shurakai, the creature destroyed at last by Prester John.

Unlike the Burned King on the throne's other side, the Fisher King's face was not carved in a twist of fear and doubt: rather the sculptor had brought radiant faith into the stony features, had given opaque eyes the illusion of seeing faraway things. The long-dead artisan had made Eahlstan humble and reverent, but had also made him bold. In his secret thoughts, Simon often imagined that his own fisherman father might have looked like this.

Staring, Simon felt a sudden coldness on his hand. He was touching the Chair's bone armrest! A scullion touching the throne! He snatched his fingers away — wondering all the while how even the dead substance of such a fiery beast could feel so chill — and stumbled back a step.

It seemed for a heart-seizing moment that the statues *had* begun to lean toward him, shadows stretching on the tapestried wall, and he skittered backward. When nothing resembling actual movement followed, he straightened himself with what dignity he could, bowed to Kings and Chair, and backed across the stone floor. Searching with his hand — *calmly, calmly*, he thought to himself, *don't be a frightened fool* — he at last found the door into the standing room, his original destination. With a cautious look back at the reassuringly immobile tableau, he slipped through.

Behind the standing room's heavy tapestry, thick red velvet embroidered with festival scenes, a staircase inside the wall mounted to a privy at the top of the throne room's southern gallery. Chiding himself for his nervousness of moments before, he climbed it. At the top it was a simple enough matter to squeeze out of the privy's long window-slit and onto the wall that ran beneath. The trick, however, was a little more difficult now than when he had been here last in Septander: the stones were snow-slippery, and there was a determined breeze. Fortunately the wall top was wide; Simon negotiated it carefully.

Now came the part that he liked best. The corner of this wall came out within only five or six feet of the broad lee of Green Angel Tower's fourth-floor turret. Pausing, he could almost hear the bray of trumpets, the clash of knights battling on the decks below him as he prepared to leap through the fierce wind from mast to burning mast. . . .

Whether his foot slipped a little as he jumped, or his attention was distracted by the imaginary sea-skirmish below, Simon landed badly on the edge of the turret. He caught his knee a tremendous crack on the stone, nearly sliding back and off, which would have dropped him two long fathoms onto the low wall at the tower's base or into the moat. The sudden realization of his peril spurred his heart into a terrified gallop. Instead he managed to slide down into the space between the turret's upstanding merlons, crawling forward to slip down onto the floor of long boards.

A light snow sifted down as he sat, feeling horribly foolish, and hugged his throbbing knee. It hurt like sin, betrayal, and treachery; if he had not been conscious of how childish he must already seem, he would have cried.

At last he climbed to his feet and limped into the tower. One piece of luck, anyway: no one had heard his painful landing. His disgrace was his alone. He felt in his pocket – the bread and cheese were rather nastily flattened, but still eatable. That, too, was a small solace.

Climbing stairs on his aching knee was an effort, but it was no good getting into Green Angel Tower, tallest building in Erkynland – probably in all of Osten Ard – and then not getting up any higher than the Hayholt's main walls.

The tower staircase was low and narrow, the steps made of a clean, smooth white stone unlike any other in the castle, slippery to the touch but sure beneath one's feet. The castle folk said that this tower was the only part of the original Sithi stronghold that remained unchanged. Doctor Morgenes had once told Simon that this was untrue. Whether that meant that the tower had indeed been changed, or simply that other unsullied remnants of old Asu'a still remained, the doctor – in his maddening style – would not say.

Having climbed for several minutes, Simon could see from the windows that he was already higher than Hjeldin's Tower. The somewhat sinister domed column where the Mad King had long ago met his death gazed up at Green Angel across the expanse of the throne room roof, as a jealous dwarf might stare at his prince when no one was looking.

The stone facing on the inside of the stairwell was different here: a soft fawn color, traced across with minute, puzzling designs in sky blue. Turning his attention away from Hjeldin's Tower, he stopped for a moment where the light of a high window shone on the wall, but when he tried to follow the course of one of the delicate blue scrolls it made his head dizzy and he gave up.

At last, when it seemed he had been climbing painfully for hours, the staircase opened out onto the shiny white floor of the bell tower, this, too, constructed from the unusual stair-stone. Although the tower stretched up another near-hundred cubits, tapering to the Angel herself perched on the cloudy horizon, the staircase ended here where the great bronze bells hung row by row from the vaulted rafters like solemn green fruit. The bell chamber itself was open on all sides to the cold air, so that when Green Angel's chimes sang from its high-arched windows the whole countryside might hear.

Simon stood with his back against one of the six pillars of dark, smooth, rock-solid wood that spanned floor to ceiling. As he chewed his crust of bread he looked out across the western vista, where the Kynslagh's waters rolled eternally against the Hayholt's massive sea wall. Although the day was dark, and snowflakes danced crazily before him, Simon was startled by the clarity with which the world below rose to his eyes. Many small boats rode the Kynslagh's swells, lake men in black cloaks bent stolidly over their oars. Beyond, he thought he could dimly make out the place where the river Gleniwent issued out of the lake at the start of its long journey to the ocean, a winding course of half a hundred miles, past dock-towns and farms. Out of Gleniwent, in the arms of the sea herself, Warinsten island watched the river mouth; beyond Warinsten to the west lay nothing but uncountable, uncharted leagues of ocean.

He tested his sore knee and decided for the moment against sitting down, which would necessitate rising again. He pulled his hat down over his ears, which were reddening and stinging in the wind, and started in on a piece of crumbling cheese. To his right, but far past the limits of his vision, were the meadows and jutting hills of Ach Samrath, the outermost marches of the kingdom of Hernystir, and the site of the terrible battle Morgenes had described. On his left hand, across the broad Kynslagh, rolled the Thrithings – grasslands seemingly without end. Eventually, of course, they did end: beyond lay Nabban, Firranos Bay and its islands, and the marshy Wran country . . . all places Simon had never seen and most likely never would.

Growing bored at last with the unchanging Kynslagh and imaginings of the unseeable South, he limped to the other side of the bell chamber. Seen from the center of the room, where no details of the land below were visible, the swirling, featureless cloud-darkness was a gray hole into nowhere, and the tower was momentarily a ghost-ship adrift on a foggy, empty sea. Wind howled and sang around the open window frames; the bells hummed faintly, as if the storm had driven small, frightened spirits into their bronze skins.

Simon reached the low sill and leaned out to look at the mad jumble of the Hayholt's roofs below him. At first the wind tugged as though it wished to catch him up and toss him, like a kitten sporting with a dead leaf. He tightened his grip on the wet stone, and soon the wind eased. He smiled: from this vantage point the Hayholt's magnificent hodgepodge of roofs – each a different height and style, each with its forest of chimney pots, rooftrees, and domes – looked like a yard full of odd, square animals. They sprawled half-atop one another, struggling for space like hogs at their feed.

Shorter only than the two towers, the dome of the castle chapel dominated the Inner Bailey, colorful windows draped in sleet. The keep's other buildings, the

76

residences, dining hall, throne room and chancelry, were each one of them stacked and squeezed with additions, mute evidence of the castle's diverse tenantry. The two outer baileys and the massive curtain wall, descending concentrically down the hill, were similarly cluttered. The Hayholt itself had never expanded past the outwall; the people crowding in built upward, or divided what they already had into smaller and smaller portions.

Beyond the keep the town of Erchester stretched out in street after careless street of low houses, wrapped in a mantle of white drifts; only the cathedral reared up from their midst, itself dwarfed by the Hayholt and by Simon in his sky-tower. Here and there a feather of smoke drifted upward to shred in the wind.

Past the city walls Simon could make out the dim, snow-smoothed outlines of the lich-yard – the old pagan cemetery, a place of ill repute. The downs beyond it ran almost to the forest's edge; above their humble congregation the tall hill called Thisterborg stood as dramatically as the cathedral in low-roofed Erchester. Simon could not see them, but he knew that Thisterborg was crowned with a ring of wind-polished rock pillars that the villagers called the Anger Stones.

And beyond Erchester, past the lich-yard and downs and stonecapped Thisterborg, lay the Forest. Aldheorte was its name – Oldheart – and it stretched outward like the sea, vast, dark, and unknowable. Men lived on its fringes, even maintained a few roads along its outer edges, but very few ventured inward beyond its skirts. It was a great, shadowy country in the middle of Osten Ard; it sent no embassies, and received few visitors. Placed against its eminence even the huge Circoille, the Combwood of Hernystir in the west, was a mere copse. There was only one Forest.

The sea to the West, the Forest to the East; the North and its iron men, and the land of shattered empires in the South . . . staring out across the face of Osten Ard,

Simon forgot his knee for a while. Indeed, for a time Simon himself was king of all the known world.

When the shrouded winter sun had passed the top of the sky, he moved at last to leave. Straightening his leg forced out a gasp of pain: the knee had stiffened in the long hour he had stood at the sill. It was obvious that he would not be able to take his strenuous secret route down from the bell tower. He would have to chance his luck against Barnabas and Father Dreosan.

The long stairway was a misery, but the view from the tower window had pushed away his other regrets; he did not feel nearly as sorry for himself as he otherwise might have. The desire to see more of the world glowed within him like a low-banked fire, warming him to his finger-tips. He would ask Morgenes to tell him more of Nabban and the Southern Islands, and of the Six Kings.

At the fourth level, where he had made his original entry, he heard a sound: someone moving quickly down the stairwell below him. For a moment he stood still, wondering if he had been discovered – it was not strictly forbidden to be in the tower, but he had no good reason for his presence; the sexton would presume guilt. It *was* strange, though – the footfalls were receding. Certainly Barnabas or anyone else would not hesitate to come up and get him, to lead him down by the much-handled scruff of his neck. Simon continued down the winding stairs; cautiously at first; then, despite his throbbing knee, faster and faster as his curiosity got the better of him.

The staircase ended at last in the huge entry hall of the tower. The hall was dimly lit, its walls cloaked in shadows and faded tapestries of subjects probably religious but long since obscured. He paused at the last step, still concealed in the darkness of the stairwell. There was no sound of footsteps – or of anything else. He walked as silently as possible across the flagged floor, every accidental boot-scrape hissing up toward the oak-ribbed ceiling. The hall's main door was closed; the only illumination streamed in from windows above the lintel.

How could whoever had been on the stairs have opened and closed the giant door without his knowing? He had easily heard the light footfalls, and had himself been worrying about the squeak that the large hinges would make. He turned to again scan the portal-hall.

There. From beneath the fringed trim of the stained silver tapestry hung by the stairs, two small, rounded shapes protruded – shoes. As he looked carefully now, he could see how folds of the old hanging bellied out where someone hid behind it.

Balancing on one foot like a heron, he quietly pulled off first one boot, then the other. Who could it be? Perhaps fat Jeremias had followed him here to play a trick? Well, if so, Simon would soon show *him*.

Bare feet nearly silent on the stones, he crept across the hall until he stood immediately before the suspicious bump. For a moment, reaching a hand out to the edge of the hanging, he remembered the strange thing Brother Cadrach had said about curtains while they had watched the puppet show. He hesitated, then felt ashamed of his own timidity, and swept the tapestry aside.

Instead of flying open to reveal the spy, the massive hanging tore free of its stays and billowed down like a monstrous, stiffened blanket. Simon had only a momentary glimpse of a small, startled face before the weight of the tapestry knocked him to the ground. As he lay cursing and struggling, badly tangled, a brown-clad figure shot by.

Simon could hear whoever-it-was struggling with the heavy door as he himself wrestled the dusty, enveloping fabric. At last he pulled free and rolled to his feet, moving across the room in a bound to catch the small figure before it slipped through the partially opened door. He got a firm handhold on a rough jerkin. The spy was captured, half-in and half-out.

Simon was angry now, mostly from embarrassment.

'Who are you?' he snarled. 'You spier-on-people!' His captive said nothing, but only struggled harder. Whoever he was, he was not big enough to loosen Simon's restraining grasp.

Fighting to pull the resisting figure back through the doorway – no easy task – Simon was startled to recognize the sand-colored broadcloth he was gripping. This must be the young man who had been spying at the door of the chapel! Simon gave a fierce pull and got the youth's head and shoulder back through the doorframe so he could look at him.

The prisoner was small, and his features were fine, almost sharp: there was something a shade foxlike in nose and chin, but not unpleasantly so. His hair was as dark as a crow's wing. For a moment Simon thought he might be a Sitha-man, because of his height – he tried to remember Shem's stories about not letting go of a Pookah's foot, and so winning a cauldron of gold – but before he could spend any of his dream-treasure he saw the fear-sweat and reddened cheeks and decided that this was no supernatural creature.

'What is your name, you?' he demanded. The captured youth tried to pull free again, but was obviously tiring. After a moment he stopped his struggling altogether. 'Your name?' Simon prompted, this time in a softer tone.

'Malachias.' The youth turned away panting.

'Well, Malachias, why are you following me?' He gave a little shake to the youth's shoulder, to remind him just who had captured whom.

The youth turned and stared sullenly. His eyes were quite dark.

'*I wasn't spying on you!*' he said vehemently.

As the boy averted his face once more, Simon was struck by a feeling that he had seen something familiar in this Malachias' face, something he should recognize.

'Who are you then, sirrah?' Simon asked, and reached out to turn the boy's chin toward him. 'Do you work in the stables – work somewhere here in the Hayholt?'

Before he could bring the face around to look at it once more, Malachias suddenly put both hands in the middle of Simon's chest and gave a surprisingly hard push. He lost his grip on the youth's jerkin and staggered backward, then fell on his seat. Before he could even attempt to rise, Malachias had whisked through the doorway, pulling it shut behind him with a loud, reverberating squeal of bronze hinges.

Simon was still sitting on the stone floor – sore knee, sore rump, and mortally wounded dignity clamoring for attention – when the sexton Barnabas came in out of the Chancelry hall to investigate the noise. He stopped as if stunned in the doorway, looking from Simon bootless on the floor to the torn and crumpled tapestry in front of the stairwell, then turned his stare back to Simon. Barnabas said not a word, but a vein began to drumbeat high on each temple, and his brow beetled downward until his eyes were the merest slits.

Simon, routed and massacred, could only sit and shake his head, like a drunkard who had tripped over his own jug and landed upon the Lord Mayor's cat.

# 6
# The Cairn on the Cliffs

Simon's punishment for his most recent crime was suspension from his new apprenticeship and confinement to the servants' quarters.

For days he strode the boundaries of his prison, from the scullery to the linens room and back again, restless as a hooded kestrel.

*I have done this to myself,* he sometimes thought. *I'm just as stupid as the Dragon says I am.*

*Why do they all make such trouble for me?* he fumed at other moments. *Anyone would think I was a wild animal that can't be trusted.*

Rachel, with a form of mercy in mind, found a series of petty tasks to which he could turn his hand; the days did not pass as excruciatingly slowly as they might have, but to Simon it seemed only more proof that he was to be a draft horse forever. He would fetch and haul until he was too old to labor any longer, then be taken out back and knocked on the head with Shem's splintered mallet.

Meanwhile the final days of Novander crept by, and Decander sidled in like a sneak thief.

At the end of the new month's second week Simon was given his freedom – such as it was. He was forbidden Green Angel Tower and certain other favorite haunts; he was allowed to resume service for the doctor, but given additional afternoon chores which required him to return promptly at dinnertime to the servants' quarters. Even these short visits, however, were a grand improvement. In fact, it seemed that Morgenes was more and more coming to rely on Simon. The doctor taught him many things about the uses and care of the fantastic variety of oddments littering the workshop.

He was also, painfully, learning to read. It was infinitely more laborious than sweeping floors or washing dusty alembics and beakers, but Morgenes drove him through it with a determined hand, saying that without letters Simon could never be a useful apprentice.

On Saint Tunath's Day, Decander the twenty-first, the Hayholt was bustling with activity. The saint's day was the last high holiday before Aedonmansa, and a mighty feast was being laid on. Serving girls set sprigs of mistletoe and prickly holly around dozens of slender white beeswax candles – these were all to be lit at sunset, when their flames would pour light from every window, summoning wandering Saint Tunath in from the midwinter darkness to bless the castle and its occupants. Other servants stacked pitchy, new-split logs in the fireplaces, or strewed fresh rushes on the floor.

Simon, who had done his best all afternoon to remain unnoticed, was nevertheless discovered and deputed to go to Doctor Morgenes and find if he had any oil suitable for polishing things – Rachel's troops had used up all the available supply putting a blinding gloss on the Great Table, and work had barely begun on the Main Hall.

Simon, who had already spent an entire morning in the doctor's rooms reading aloud word by boggling word from a book entitled *The Sovran Remedys of the Wranna Healers*, still infinitely preferred anything Morgenes might want of him to the horrors of Rachel's steel-glint gaze. He practically flew from the Main Hall, down the long Chancelry hall, and out into the Inner Commons beneath Green Angel. He was across the moat-bridge seconds later like a spar-hawk on the wing; only moments passed before he was at the doctor's doors for the second time that day.

The doctor did not answer his knock for some time, but Simon could hear voices within. He waited as patiently as he could, picking long splinters from the weathered doorframe, until at last the old man came. Morgenes had seen Simon only a short while earlier, but made no comment on his reappearance. He seemed distracted as he ushered the young man in; sensing his strange mood, Simon followed quietly down the lamplit corridor.

Heavy draperies cloaked the windows. At first, as his eyes adjusted to the darkness of the chamber, Simon could see no sign of any visitor. Then he made out a dim shape sitting on a large sea-chest in the corner. The gray-cloaked man was gazing at the floor, face concealed, but the boy knew him.

'Forgive me, Prince Josua,' Morgenes said, 'this is Simon, my new apprentice.'

Josua Lackhand looked up. His pale eyes – were they blue? . . . gray? – flicked over him with an air of detachment, as a Hyrka trader might examine a horse he did not intend to buy. After a moment's inspection the prince turned his attention back to Morgenes as completely as if Simon had just winked out of existence. The doctor motioned for the boy to go and wait at the far end of the room.

'Highness,' he said to the prince, 'I am afraid there is nothing further I can do. My skills as a doctor and apothecary have been exhausted.' The old man rubbed his hands together nervously. 'Forgive me. You know that I love the king, and hate to see him suffering, but . . . but some things are not to be meddled in by such as I – too many possibilities, too many unforeseeable consequences. One of those things is the passing of a kingdom.'

Now Morgenes, whom Simon had not seen in this sort

of mood, plucked an object on a golden chain out of his robe and handled it agitatedly. In Simon's knowledge, the doctor – who loved to scorn pretension and show – had never worn jewelry of any kind, either.

'But, God curse it, I am not asking you to interfere with the succession!' Josua's quiet voice was taut as a bowstring. Having to overhear such a conversation embarrassed Simon tremendously, but there was nowhere for him to go without making himself even more conspicuous.

'I ask you to "meddle" with nothing, Morgenes,' Josua continued, ' – only give me something that will make the old man's last moments easier. If he dies tomorrow or next year, Elias is still the High King, and I am still liege-lord only of Naglimund.' The prince shook his head. 'At least think of the ancient bond you and my father share – you, who have been his healer, and have studied and chronicled his life for scores of years!' Josua swept his hand across his body to point at a pile of loose book-leaves stacked on the doctor's worm-bored writing desk.

*Writing about the life of the king?* Simon wondered. This was the first *he* had heard of such a work. The doctor seemed very full of secrets this morning.

Josua was still trying. 'Can you not take pity? He is like an aged lion at bay, a great beast being dragged down by jackals! Sweet Usires, the unfairness . . .'

'But, Highness . . .' Morgenes had painfully begun when all three in the room became aware of the sound of running feet and voices in the courtyard outside. Josua, pale-faced and fever-eyed, was on his feet with his sword drawn so quickly it seemed to have simply appeared in his left hand. A loud pounding shook the door. Morgenes, starting forward, was restrained by a hiss from the prince. Simon felt his heart racing – Josua's obvious fear was contagious.

'Prince Josua! Prince Josua!' someone called. The rapping resumed. Josua scabbarded his sword with a flick and moved past Doctor Morgenes into the workshop corridor. He flung the door open to reveal four figures standing on the courtyard porch. Three were his own gray-liveried soldiers; the last, who dropped to one knee before the prince, was dressed in a shining white robe and sandals. Dreamily, Simon recognized him as Saint Tunath, long-dead subject of countless religious paintings. What could this mean. . . ?

'Oh, your Highness . . .' said the kneeling saint, and stopped to catch his breath. Simon's mouth – which had begun to quirk upward in a grin as he realized that this was only another soldier, dressed up to enact the saint's part in tonight's festivities – now froze as he saw the stricken look on the young man's face. 'Your Highness . . . Josua . . .' the soldier repeated.

'What is it, Deornoth?' the prince demanded. His voice was strained.

Deornoth looked up, dark, rough-cut soldier's hair framed in the white gleam of his hood. He had in that moment true martyr's eyes, blasted and knowing.

'The king, Lord, your father the king . . . Bishop Domitis said . . . that he is dead.'

Soundlessly, Josua pushed past the kneeling man and was gone across the courtyard, the soldiers trotting behind. After a moment Deornoth rose too and followed, hands clasped monkishly before him as if the breath of tragedy had changed imposture to reality. The door swung listlessly in a cool wind.

When Simon turned to Morgenes, the doctor was staring after them, his old eyes shining and brimful.

So it was that King John Presbyter died at last on Saint Tunath's Day, at an exceedingly advanced age: beloved, revered, and as thoroughly a part of his people's lives as the land itself. Although it had been long expected, still the sorrow of his passing reached out and touched all the countries of Men.

Some of the very oldest remembered that it had been Tunath's Day in the Founding-year 1083 – exactly eighty years before – when Prester John had slain the devilworm Shurakai and ridden back in triumph through the gates of Erchester. When this tale was retold, not without some embellishing, heads nodded wisely. Anointed by God as King – they said – as revealed by that great deed, then taken back to the bosom of the Redeemer on its anniversary. It should have been foreseen, they said.

It was a sad midwinter and Aedontide, although people flocked to Erchester and the High Castle from all the lands of Osten Ard. Indeed, many of the local folk began to growl about the visitors who came to take up the best benches in church, and the same in the taverns. There was more than a little resentment of outlanders making such a fuss over *their* king: although he had been master of all, John had been more like a simple fiefholder to the townsmen of Erchester. In younger, haler days he had loved to go out among the people, cutting a beautiful figure all gleaming-armored and a-horseback. The citizens of the town, in the poor quarters at least, often spoke with familiar, possessive pride of 'our old man up to th' Hayholt.'

Now he was gone, or at least out of the reach of such simple souls. He belonged to the history-scribes, the poets, and priests.

In the forty days mandated between the death and burial of a king, John's body went to the Hall of Preparing in Erchester, where the priests bathed it in rare oils, rubbed it with pungent herbal resins from the southern islands, then bound it up from ankle to neck in white linen, saying all the while prayers of overmastering piety. King John was next clothed in a simple gown of the type used by young knights at their first vows, and gently laid on a bier in the throne room, slender black candles burning all around.

As Prester John's body lay in state, Father Helfcene, the king's chancellor, ordered the Hayefur kindled atop the rock-fortress at Wentmouth, something done only in times of war and great happenings. Few living could remember the last time the mighty torch-tower had been fired.

Helfcene also commanded a great pit to be dug at Swertclif, on the headlands east of Erchester overlooking the Kynslagh – the windy hilltop, where stood the six snow-thatched barrows of the kings who had held the Hayholt before John. It was miserable weather for digging, the ground winter-frozen, but the Swertclif laborers were proud, and suffered the biting air and bruises and broken skin for the honor of the task. Much of the chill month of Jonever passed before the excavation was completed and the pit was covered with a vast tent of red and white sailcloth.

Preparations at the Hayholt proceeded at a less deliberate pace. The castle's four kitchens glowed and smoked like busy foundries as a horde of perspiring scullions prepared the funeral baked goods, the meats and bread and festival wafers. The seneschal Peter Gilded-Bowl, a small, fierce man with yellow hair, was everywhere at once like an avenging angel. With equal facility he tasted the broth billowing in giant vats, looked for dust in the cracks of the Great Table – thin chance, since that was Rachel's province – and threw imprecations after scurrying servitors. It was, all agreed, his finest hour.

The mourning-party gathered at the Hayholt from all the nations of Osten Ard. Skali Sharp-nose of Kaldskryke, Duke Isgrimnur's unloved cousin, arrived from Rimmersgard with ten suspicious, deep-bearded kinsmen. From the three clans that among them ruled the wild, grassy Thrithings came the Marchthanes of their reigning houses. Oddly enough, the clansmen put enmity aside for once and arrived together – a token of their respect for King John. It was even said that when news of John's death reached the Thrithings the Randwarders of the three clans had met at the borders they guarded so jealously against each other; weeping together, they had drunk to John's spirit all through the night.

From the Sancellan Mahistrevis, the ducal palace in Nabban, Duke Leobardis sent his son Benigaris with a column of legionaries and mail-clad knights numbering almost a hundred head. As they disembarked from the warships, each of the three with Nabban's golden kingfisher on its sail, the crowd at wharfside oohed appreciatively. A few respectful cheers were even raised for Benigaris as he passed, mounted on a tall gray palfrey, but many people whispered that if this was the nephew of Camaris, greatest knight of the age of John, then he was a cutting from his father's tree and not his uncle's. Camaris had been a mighty, towering man – or so said those old enough to have remembered him – and Benigaris, truth to tell, looked to run a little to fat. But it *had* been almost forty years since Camaris-sá-Vinitta had been lost at sea: many of the younger folk suspected that his stature had grown somewhat in the memories of gaffers and gossips.

Another great delegation also came from Nabban, one only slightly less martial than Benigaris': the Lector Ranessin himself sailed into the Kynslagh on a beautiful white ship, upon whose azure sail gleamed the white Tree and golden Pillar of Mother Church. The wharfside crowd, which had greeted Benigaris and the Nabbanai soldiers mildly – as if in dim remembrance of days when Nabban had striven with Erkynland for mastery – hailed the lector with a loud, welcoming cry. Those gathered on the quay surged forward, and it took the combined force of the king's and lector's guardsmen to hold them back; still, some two or three were crowded so that they fell into the bone-cold lake, and only swift rescue saved them from freezing.

'This is not as I would have wanted it,' the lector whispered to his young aide, Father Dinivan. 'I mean, just look at this gawdy thing they have sent me.' He gestured at the litter, a splendid creation of carved cherry wood and blue and white silks. Father Dinivan, robed in homely black, grinned.

Ranessin, a slender, handsome man of nearly seventy years, frowned down in annoyance at the waiting litter, then gently beckoned over a nervous Erkynguard officer.

'Please take this away,' he said. 'We appreciate Chancellor Helfcene's thought, but we prefer to walk near the people.'

The offending conveyance was hustled away, and the lector moved toward the crowded Kynslagh stairs. As he made the sign of the Tree – thumb and small finger as hooked branches, then a vertical stroke with the middle fingers – the jostling crowd slowly opened an aisle up the length of the great steps.

'Please don't walk so fast, Master,' said Dinivan, pushing past reaching, waving arms. 'You'll outpace your guardsmen.'

'And what makes you think,' – Ranessin allowed a mischievous smile to cross his face so quickly none but Dinivan saw – 'that this is not what I am trying to achieve?'

Dinivan cursed quietly, then immediately regretted his weakness. The lector had gained a step on him, and the crowd was pushing in. Luckily, the dockside wind now sprang to life and Ranessin was forced to slow down, clutching with his unoccupied hand at his hat, which seemed nearly as tall, thin, and pale as His Sacredness himself. Father Dinivan, seeing the lector begin to tack slightly into the wind, struggled forward. When he caught up with the older man, he took a firm grip on an elbow.

'Forgive me, Master, but Escritor Velligis would never understand it if I were to let you fall into the lake.'

90

'Of course, my son,' Ranessin nodded, continuing to trace the Tree in the air on either side of their progress up the long, wide staircase. 'I was thoughtless. You know how much I despise this unnecessary pomp.'

'But Lector,' Dinivan argued gently, lifting his bushy eyebrows in a look of mock-surprise, 'you are Usires Aedon's worldly voice. It won't do to have you scrambling up stairs like a seminary boy.'

Dinivan was disappointed when this raised only a faint smile. For a while they climbed in silent lockstep, the young man retaining his protective grasp on the older's arm.

*Poor Dinivan*, Ranessin thought. *He tries so hard, and is so careful. Not that he doesn't treat me – the Lector of Mother Church, after all – with a certain lack of respect. Of course he does, because I have allowed it – for my own good. But I am not in a light mood today, and he knows it.*

It was John's death, of course – but not merely the loss of a good friend and fine king: it was change, and the Church, in the person of Lector Ranessin, could not afford to trust change too easily. Of course it was also the parting – in this world only, the lector reminded himself firmly – from a man of good heart and intention, although John certainly had been at times over-direct in the fulfilling of those intentions. Ranessin owed much to John, not least that the king's influence had played a large part in the elevation of the former Oswine of Stanshire to the heights of the church, and eventually to the Lectorship that no other Erkynlander had held in five centuries. The king would be much missed.

Fortunately, Ranessin held hope for Elias. The prince was undoubtedly courageous, decisive, bold – all traits rare in the sons of great men. The king-to-be was also short-tempered and somewhat careless, but – *Duos wulstei* – these were faults often cured, or at least softened by responsibility and good counsel.

As he reached the top of the Kynslagh stairs and entered with his struggling retinue onto the Royal Walk that circumscribed the walls of Erchester, the lector promised himself that he would send a trustworthy advisor to help the new king – and of course to keep a wary eye out for the Church's welfare – someone like Velligis, or even young Dinivan . . . no, he wouldn't part with Dinivan. Anyway, Ranessin would find somebody to counteract Elias' bloody-minded young nobles, and that blowing idiot, Bishop Domitis.

The first of Feyever, the day before Elysiamansa – Lady Day – dawned bright, chill, and clear. The sun had barely scaled the steepled peaks of the far mountains when a slow, solemn crowd began to file into the Hayholt's chapel. The king's body was already lying before the altar on a bier draped in cloth-of-gold and black silk ribbons.

Simon watched the nobles in their rich, somber dress with resentful fascination. He had come to the unused choir loft straight from the kitchens, still wearing his gravy-stained shirt; even crouched hidden in the shadows he felt ashamed to be so poorly clad.

*And me the only servant here*, he thought. *The only one of all who lived in the castle with our king. Where are all these fancy lords and ladies from? I recognize only a few – Duke Isgrimnur, the two princes, some others.*

There was certainly something wrong, that those seated in the chapel below should be so splendid in their funeral silks while he carried the stink of the scullery on him like a blanket – but wrong in what way? Should the castle serving help be welcomed in among the nobles? Or was he himself at fault for daring to intrude?

*What if King John is watching?* He felt a chill as he thought it. *What if he is somewhere, watching? Will he tell God that I snuck in wearing a dirty shirt?*

Lector Ranessin entered at last, arrayed in the full circumstance of his holy office robes of black, silver, and

92

gold. On his head he wore a wreath of sacred ciyan leaves, and he held a censer and wand crafted from black onyx. Motioning the crowd to their knees, he began the opening prayers of the *Mansa-sea-Cuelossan*: the Death Mass. As he called out the lines in his rich, but still ever-so-slightly accented Nabbanai, and censed the body of the dead king, it seemed to Simon that a light shone on Prester John's face, that he could see for a moment how the king must have looked when he had first ridden, bright-eyed and battle-stained, out of the gates of the new-conquered Hayholt. How he wished he could have seen him then!

When the numerous prayers were finished, the company of nobles rose to sing the *Cansim Falis*; Simon contented himself with mouthing the words. As the mourners sat down again, Ranessin began to speak, surprising everyone by abandoning Nabbanai to use the country-plain Westerling speech that John had made the common tongue of his kingdom.

'It may be remembered,' Ranessin intoned, 'that when the last nail had been driven into the Execution Tree, and our Lord Usires was left to hang in terrible agony, a noble woman of Nabban named Pelippa, daughter of a mighty knight, saw him and her heart was filled with pity for His suffering. As the darkness fell that First Night, while Usires Aedon hung dying and lone – for His disciples had been scourged from the Temple courtyard – she came to Him with water, which she gave to Him by dipping her rich scarf in a golden bowl and then bringing it to His dry lips.

'As she gave Him to drink, Pelippa wept to see the Ransomer's pain. She said to Him: "Poor man, what have they done to you?" Usires answered her: "Nothing that poor Man is not born to."

'Now Pelippa wept afresh, saying: "But terrible enough that they kill you for words, without also they hang you heels-high for the sake of humiliation." And Usires the Reclaimer said: "Daughter, it matters not

93

which way I hang, top-first or the opposite – I am still looking full into the face of God my Father."

'So, then . . .' the lector lowered his gaze to the assemblage, '. . . as was said by our Lord Usires, so may we say it is with our beloved John. The common people in the city below us say that John Presbyter is not gone, but remains to watch over his people and his Osten Ard. The Book of the Aedon promises that even now he has ascended to our beautiful Heaven of light and music and blue mountains. Others – our brethren, John's subjects in Hernystir – will say that he has gone to join the other heroes in the stars. It matters not.

'Whatever he is, he who was once young John the King, be he enthroned in bright mountains or stellar fields, we know this: he is happily gazing full into the face of God. . . .'

When the lector had finished speaking, tears standing in even his eyes, and the final prayers had been recited, the assembled company left the chapel.

Simon watched in reverent silence as King John's black-clad body servants began their final services on his behalf, stalking like beetles around a fallen dragonfly, dressing him in his royal raiment and war-gear. He knew he should leave – this was beyond sneaking and spying; it bordered on blasphemy – but he could not make himself move. Fear and sorrow had been replaced by a strange sense of unreality. Everything seemed a pageant or mummer's play, the characters moving stiffly through their parts as though their limbs were freezing and thawing and then freezing once more.

The dead king's servants dressed him in his ice-white armor, tucking his folded gauntlets into his baldric but leaving his feet bare. They drew a tunic of sky blue over John's corselet, and pulled a shiny crimson cloak about his shoulders, moving all the while as slowly as fever victims. His beard and hair were knotted up in war-braids, and the iron circlet that signified mastery of the

Hayholt was set upon his brow. At last Noah, the king's aged squire, brought out the iron ring of Fingil which he had been keeping back; the sudden sounds of his grief shattered the enveloping silence. Noah sobbed so bitterly that Simon wondered how he could see through his tears to slip the ring onto the king's white finger.

Finally the black-cloth beetles lifted King John back onto his bier. Draped in the cloth-of-gold mantle, he was carried out of his castle for the last time, three men on each side. Noah followed behind carrying the king's dragon-crested war helmet.

In the shadows of the loft overhead, Simon released what seemed an hour's worth of prisoned breath. The king was gone.

As Duke Isgrimnur saw Prester John's body pass out through the Nearulagh Gate, and the procession of nobility began to fall into place behind, a slow, fog-shrouded feeling overtook him, like a dream of drowning.

*Don't be such an ass, old man,* he told himself. *No one lives forever – even if John did take a mighty swipe at it.*

The funny thing was, even when they had stood side to side in the screeching hell of battle, the black-fletched Thrithings arrows whistling past like Udun's own – damn, *God's* own – lightning, Isgrimnur had always known that John Presbyter would die abed. To see the man at war was to see a man anointed by Heaven, untouchable and commanding, a man who laughed as the blood-mist darkened the sky. If John had been a Rimmersman, Isgrimnur smiled inwardly, he would have been a bear-shirt for certain.

*But he is dead, and that's the hard thing to understand. Look at them, knights and lords . . . they thought he'd last forever, too. Frightened, the greater part of them.*

Elias and the lector had taken their places directly

behind the king's bier. Isgrimnur, Prince Josua, and fair-haired Princess Miriamele – Elias' only child – followed closely. The other high families had taken their places as well, with none of their usual elbowing for favorable position. As the body was carried down the Royal Walk toward the headlands, the common people fell into step at the rear, a huge crowd quieted and overawed by the procession.

Resting on a bed of long poles at the base of the Royal Walk lay the king's boat *Sea-Arrow*, in which it was said he had long ago come to Erkynland out of the Westerling islands. It was but a small vessel, no more than five ells in length; Duke Isgrimnur was glad to see that its woods had been new-lacquered until they glimmered in the dim Feyever sunlight.

*Gods, but he loved that boat!* Isgrimnur remembered. Kingship had left him scant time for the sea, but the duke recalled one wild night, thirty years or more ago, when John had been in such a mood that nothing would do but that he and Isgrimnur – a young man then – must get *Sea-Arrow* rigged and go out upon the windlashed Kynslagh. The air had been so cold it stung. John, almost seventy years old, had whooped and laughed as *Sea-Arrow* bucked on the high swells. Isgrimnur, whose ancestors had taken to land long before his time, had held on tightly to the gunwale and prayed to his many old gods and his one new one.

Now the king's servants and soldiers were laying John's body into the boat with great tenderness, lowering it onto a platform that had been prepared to hold the bier. Forty soldiers of the king's Erkynguard picked up the long poles and placed them on their shoulders, bearing the boat up and carrying it forward.

The king and *Sea-Arrow* led the vast company half a league along the headlands above the bay; at last they reached Swertclif, and the grave. The covering tent had been removed, and the hole was like an open wound beside the six solemn, rounded barrows of the Hayholt's earlier masters.

On one side of the pit stood a massive pile of cut turves and a heap of stones and undressed timbers. *Sea-Arrow* was laid down on the grave's far side, where the earth had been dug down at a shallow angle. When the boat came to rest, the noble houses of Erkynland and the Hayholt's servants filed by to place some small thing in boat or barrow as a token of love. Each of the lands beneath his High Ward had also sent some thing of mighty craft, that Prester John might carry it with him to Heaven – a robe of precious Risa-island silk from Perdruin, a white porphyry Tree from Nabban. Isgrimnur's party had brought from Elvritshalla in Rimmersgard a silver axe of Dverning-make with mountain-blue gems in its haft. Lluth, the Hernystiri king, had sent from the Taig at Hernysadharc a tall ashwood spear all inlaid with red gold, and with a golden point.

The noon sun seemed to hang too high in the sky, Duke Isgrimnur thought as he made his way forward at last: though it rolled unhindered across the gray-blue dome of the sky, it seemed to hold back its warmth. The wind blew harder, skirling across the clifftop. Isgrimnur carried John's battered black war-boots in his hand. He could not find it in his heart to look up at the white faces that peered from the crowd like glimmers of snow in the deep forest.

As he approached *Sea-Arrow*, he looked one last time at his King. Although paler than a dove's breast, still John looked so stern and fine and full of sleeping life that Isgrimnur caught himself worrying for his old friend, lying out in the wind this way with no blanket. For a moment he almost smiled.

*John always said I had the heart of a bear and the wit of an ox*, Isgrimnur chided himself. *And if it be cold up here, think how chill it will be for him in the frozen earth. . . .*

Isgrimnur moved carefully but nimbly around the

steep ramp of earth, using a hand to steady himself when necessary. Although his back hurt him fiercely, he knew no one suspected it; he was not too old to find some pride in that.

Taking John Presbyter's blue-veined feet in his hands one at a time, he slipped the boots on. He silently commended the skilled hands in the House of Preparing for the ease with which his task was accomplished. Without looking again at his friend's face he quickly took the hand and kissed it, then walked away, feeling stranger still.

Suddenly it seemed to him that this was not his king's lifeless husk that was being condemned to the soil, the soul fluttered free like a newly-unfurled butterfly. The suppleness of John's limbs, the so-familiar face in repose – as Isgrimnur had seen it countless times when the king snatched an hour or two of sleep in the lull of battle – all these things made him feel as though he deserted a living friend. He *knew* John was dead – he had held the king's hand as the last breaths fluted out of him – still, he felt a traitor.

So possessed was he by his thoughts that he nearly stepped into Prince Josua, who moved nimbly around him on his path to the barrow. Isgrimnur was shocked to see that Josua carried John's sword Bright-Nail on a gray cloth.

*What happens here?* Isgrimnur wondered. *What is he doing with the sword?*

As the Duke reached the first row of the crowd and turned to watch, his unease deepened: Josua had laid Bright-Nail on the king's chest, and was clasping John's hands about the hilt.

*This is madness*, the duke thought. *That sword is for the king's heir – I know John would have wanted Elias to have it! And even if Elias chose to bury it with his father, why does he not lay it in the grave himself? Madness! Does no one else marvel at such a thing?*

Isgrimnur looked from side to side, but saw nothing on the faces around him but sorrow.

Now Elias walked down, passing his younger brother slowly, like a participant in a stately dance – as in fact he was. The heir to the throne bent over the gunwale of the boat. What he sent with his father no one could see, but it was noted by all that although a tear sparkled on Elias' cheek when he turned, Josua's eyes were dry.

The company now made one more prayer. Ranessin, robes billowing in the lake-breeze, sprinkled *Sea-Arrow* with holy oils. Then the boat was gently lowered down the sloping pitfall, soldiers laboring in silence with their heavy staves until it lay at last a fathom deep in the earth. Above, timbers were raised into a great arch and workmen laid the turves about, one atop the other. Finally, as stones were being lifted into place to complete John's cairn, the mourning party turned and made its slow way back along the cliffs above the Kynslagh.

The funeral feast that night in the castle's great hall was not a solemn gathering, but rather a brave and merry occasion. John was dead, of course, but his life had been long – far beyond that of most men – and he had left behind a kingdom wealthy and at peace, and a strong son to rule.

The fireplaces were banked high; the leaping flames threw strange, capering shadows on the walls as sweating servants hurried in and out. The feasters waved their arms and shouted toasts to the old king gone, and the new one to be crowned in the morning. The castle hounds, large and small, barked and scrabbled over discarded scraps and rooted in the straw that covered the floor. Simon, pressed into service bearing one of the heavy wine ewers from table to table, shouted at and splashed by roaring merrymakers, felt as though he served wine in some noisy hell from Father Dreosan's sermons; the bones scattered across the tables and crunching underfoot could be the remains of sinners, tormented and then cast aside by these laughing demons.

Not yet crowned, Elias already had the look of a warrior-king. He sat at the main table surrounded by the young lords in his favor: Guthwulf of Utanyeat, Fengbald the Earl of Falshire, Breyugar of the Westfold, and others – each wearing some bit of Elias' green on the mourning black, each vying to make the loudest toast, the sharpest jest. The king-to-be presided over all their striving, rewarding the favorites with his loud laughter. From time to time he leaned over to say something to Skali of Kaldskryke, Isgrimnur's kinsman, who sat at Elias' table by special invitation. Although he was a large man, hawk-faced and blond-bearded, Skali seemed a little overwhelmed at the crown prince's side – especially when Duke Isgrimnur had received no similar honor. Something Elias now said, though, struck home; Simon saw the Rimmersman smile, then break out into a great guffaw and clang his metal goblet against the prince's. Elias, grinning wolfishly, turned and said something to Fengbald; he, too, joined the merriment.

By comparison, the table at which Isgrimnur sat with Prince Josua and several others was much more subdued, seeming to match in mood the prince's gray raiment. Although the other nobles were doing their best to make conversation, Simon could see as he passed by that the two chief figures were having none of it. Josua stared into space, as though fascinated by the tapestries that lined the walls. Duke Isgrimnur was just as unresponsive to the table talk, but his reasons were no mystery. Even Simon could see the way the old duke glowered at Skali Sharp-nose, and how his huge, gnarled hands plucked distractedly at the fringe of his bear-skin tunic.

Elias' slight to one of John's most faithful knights was not going unnoticed at other tables: some of the younger nobles, although courteous enough not to make a show of it, seemed to find the duke's discomfiture amusing.

They whispered behind their hands, eyebrows raised to signal the magnitude of the scandal.

As Simon swayed in place, amazed by the din and the smoke and his own confused observations, a voice rang out from a back table, cursing him and calling for more wine, stirring him into scurrying life once more.

Later in the evening, when Simon finally found a chance to snatch a moment's rest in an alcove beneath one of the giant tapestries, he noticed that a new guest was seated at the head table, wedged in between Elias and Guthwulf on a tall stool. The newcomer was robed in most unfunereal scarlet, with black and gold piping wound about the hem of his voluminous sleeves. As he leaned forward to whisper in Elias' ear, Simon watched him with helpless fascination. The man was completely hairless, without even eyebrows or lashes, but his features were those of a youngish man. His skin, tight-stretched on his skull, was notably pale even in the flaring orange rushlight; his eyes were deep-sunken, and so dark that they seemed only shiny black spots below his naked brows. Simon knew those eyes – they had glared out at him from the hooded cloak of the cart-driver who had nearly run him down at Nearulagh Gate. He shuddered and stared. There was something sickening but enthralling about the man, like a swaying serpent.

'He's a nasty looking one, isn't he?' said a voice at his elbow. Simon jumped. A young man, dark-haired and smiling, stood in the alcove behind him, an ashwood lute cradled against his pigeon-gray tunic.

'I . . . I'm sorry,' Simon stuttered. 'You took me by surprise.'

'I didn't mean to,' the other laughed, 'I was just coming to see if you could give me a bit of a help.' He pulled his other hand from behind his back and showed Simon an empty wine cup.

'Oh . . .' said Simon, 'I'm so sorry – I was resting, master . . . I'm very sorry. . . .'

'Peace, friend, peace! I did not come to cause trouble for you, but if you do not stop apologizing, then I *will* be upset. What's your name?'

'Simon, sir.' He hastily upended the ewer and filled the young man's flagon. The stranger set his cup down in a niche, readjusting his grip on the lute, and reached into his tunic to produce another cup. He proffered it with a bow.

'Here,' he said, 'I was going to steal this, Master Simon, but instead I think we shall drink each other's health, and the old king's memory – and please don't call me "sir," for that I am not.' He bumped the cup against the ewer until Simon poured again. 'There!' said the stranger. 'Now, call me Sangfugol – or, as old Isgrimnur mangles it, "Zong-vogol." '

The stranger's excellent imitation of the Rimmersgard accent brought a tiny smile to Simon's face. After looking around furtively for Rachel he set the ewer down and tipped back the flagon that Sangfugol had given him. Strong and sour, still the red wine rolled down his parched throat like spring rain; when he lowered the cup, his smile had widened.

'Are you part of Duke Isgrimnur's . . . retinue?' Simon asked, wiping his lips with his sleeve.

Sangfugol laughed. Mirth seemed to come quickly to him.

'Retinue! Quite a word for a bottle boy! No, I am Josua's harper. I live at his keep at Naglimund, in the North.'

'Does Josua like music?!' For some reason this thought astounded Simon. He poured himself another cupful. 'He seems so serious.'

'And serious he is . . . but that doesn't mean he dislikes harping or lute playing. True, it is my melancholy songs that are most often to his liking, but there are times when he calls for the Ballad of Three-Legged Tom or some such.'

Before Simon could ask another question, there was a

great whoop of hilarity from the high table. Simon turned to see that Fengbald had knocked a flagon of wine into the lap of another man, who was drunkenly wringing out his shirt while Elias and Guthwulf and the other nobles jibed and shouted. Only the bald stranger in the scarlet robe was aloof, with cold eyes and a tight, tooth-baring smile.

'Who is that?' Simon turned back to Sangfugol, who had finished his wine and was holding his lute up to his ear, plucking at the strings as he delicately turned the pegs. 'I mean the man in red.'

'Yes,' said the harper, 'I saw you looking at him when I came up. Frightful fellow, eh? That is Pryrates — a Nabbanai priest, one of Elias' counselors. People say that he is a marvelous alchemist — although he does look rather young for it, doesn't he? Not to mention that it doesn't quite seem a fitting practice for a priest. Actually, if you listen closely, you may also hear it whispered that he is a warlock: a black magician. If you listen closer still . . .' Here, as if to demonstrate, Sangfugol's voice dropped dramatically; Simon had to lean forward to hear. He realized, as he swayed slightly, that he had just drunk a third flagon of wine.

'If you listen very, very carefully . . .' the harper continued, 'you will hear people say that Pryrates' mother was a witch, and his father . . . *a demon*!' Sangfugol loudly twanged a lute-string, and Simon leaped back, surprised. 'But Simon, you cannot believe everything you hear — especially from drunken minstrels,' Sangfugol finished with a chuckle and extended his hand. Simon stared at it stupidly.

'To clasp, my friend,' the harper grinned. 'I have enjoyed speaking with you, but I fear I must return to table, where other diversions impatiently await me. Farewell!'

'Farewell . . .' Simon grasped Sangfugol's hand, then watched as the harper wound his way across the room with the nimbleness of an experienced drunkard.

As Sangfugol took his seat again, Simon's eyes came to rest on two of the serving girls leaning against a wall in the hallway at the room's far side, fanning themselves with their aprons and talking. One of them was Hepzibah, the new girl; the other was Rebah, one of the kitchen maids.

There was a certain warmth in Simon's blood. It would be so easy to walk across the room and speak to them. There was something about that Hepzibah, a sauciness in her eyes and mouth when she laughed. . . . Feeling more than a little lightheaded, Simon stepped out into the room, the roar of voices rising around him like a flood.

*A moment, a moment,* he thought feeling suddenly flushed and frightened, *how can I just walk up and speak – won't they know I've been watching them? Wouldn't they* . . .

'Hi there, you lazy clodpoll! Bring us some more of that wine!'

Simon turned to see red-faced Earl Fengbald waving a goblet at him from the king's table. In the hallway the serving girls were sauntering away. Simon ran back to the alcove to get his ewer, and fetched it out from a tangle of dogs fighting over a chop. One pup, young and scrawny, with a splotch of white on its brown face, whined piteously at the fringe of the mob, unable to compete with the larger dogs. Simon found a scrap of greasy skin on a deserted chair and tossed it to the little dog. It wagged its stub of tail as it bolted the treat, then followed at Simon's heels as he carried the ewer across the room.

Fengbald and Guthwulf, the long-jawed Earl of Utanyeat, were involved in some kind of wrist-wrestling contest, their draggers drawn and plunged into the tabletop on either side of the combatants' arms. Simon stepped around the table as nimbly as he could, pouring wine from the heavy ewer into the cups of the shouting spectators and trying not to trip over the dog, which was darting in and out between his feet. The king was watching the contest with amusement, but he had his own page at his shoulder so Simon left his goblet alone. He poured Pryrates' wine last, avoiding the priest's glance, but could not help noticing the strange scent of the man, an inexplicable amalgam of metal and over-sweet spices. Backing away, he saw the little dog rooting in the straw near Pryrates' shiny black boots, on the track of some fallen treasure.

'Come!' Simon hissed, backing farther away and slapping his knee, but the dog paid no heed. It began to dig with both paws, its back bumping against the priest's red-robed calf. 'Come along!' Simon whispered again.

Pryrates turned his head to look down, shiny skull pivoting slowly on his long neck. He lifted his foot and brought his heavy boot down on the dog's back – a swift, compact movement finished in a heartbeat. There was a crack of splintered bone, and a muffled squeal; the little dog writhed helplessly in the straw until Pryrates lifted his heel again and crushed its skull.

The priest stared for a disinterested moment at the body, then lifted his gaze, his eyes alighting on Simon's horrified face. That black stare – remorseless, uncon-cerned – caught and held him. Pryrates' flat, dead eyes flicked down again to the dog, and when they returned to Simon a slow grin stretched across the priest's face.

*What can you do about it, boy?* the smile said. *And who cares?*

The priest's attention was drawn back to the table; Simon, freed, dropped the ewer and stumbled away, looking for a place to throw up.

It was just before midnight; fully half the revelers had staggered, or been carried, off to bed. It was doubtful many of them would be present for the morrow's coronation. Simon was pouring into a drunken guest's cup the heavily watered wine that was all Peter Gilded-Bowl would serve at this late hour, when Earl Fengbald, the only one remaining of the king's party, staggered into the hall from the commons outside. The young noble was disheveled and his breeches were half-undone, but he wore a beatific smile on his face.

'Come outside, everybody!' he shouted, 'Come outside now! Come see!' He lurched back out the door. Those who could do it pulled themselves to their feet and followed him, elbowing and jesting, some singing drunkenly.

Fengbald stood in the commons, head tilted backward, black hair hanging unbound down the back of his stained tunic as he stared up into the sky. He was pointing; one by one, the faces of the followers turned up to look.

Across the sky a strange shape was painted, like a deep wound that spurted blood against the nightblack: a great, red comet, streaming across the sky from north to south.

'A bearded star!' someone shouted. 'An omen!'

'The old king is dead, dead, dead!' cried Fengbald, waving his dagger in the air as if daring the stars to come down and fight. 'Long live the new king!' he shouted, 'A new age is begun!'

Cheers rang out, and some of those present stamped their feet and howled. Others began a giddy, laughing dance, men and women holding hands as they whirled in a circle. Above them the red star gleamed like a smoldering coal.

Simon, who had followed the merrymakers outside to see the cause of the ruckus, turned back to the hall; the shouts of the dancers floated up behind him. He was surprised to see Doctor Morgenes standing in the shadows of the bailey wall. The old man, wrapped in a heavy robe against the chill air, did not notice his apprentice – he, too, was staring up at the bearded star, the scarlet slash across the vault of Heaven. But unlike the others, there was no drunkenness or glee upon his face. He looked fearful and cold and small.

He looked, Simon thought, like a man alone in the wilderness listening to the hungry song of wolves. . . .

# 7

# The Conqueror Star

The spring and summer of Elias' first regnal year were magical, sun-bright with pomp and display. All Osten Ard seemed reborn. The young nobility came back to fill the Hayholt's long-quiet halls, and so marked was the difference that they might have brought color and daylight with them to what had been a dark place. As in John's young days the castle was full of laughter and drinking, and the swagger of shining battle-blades and armor. At night music was heard in the hedged gardens once more, and the splendid ladies of the court flitted to — or fled from — assignations in the warm darkness like graceful, flowing ghosts. The tourney field sprang back to life, sprouting multicolored tents like a bank of flowers. To the common people it seemed as though every day was holiday, and that the merrymaking would have no end. King Elias and his friends made furious sport, in the manner of children who must soon be put to bed, and know it. All of Erkynland seemed to roister and tumble like a summer-drunken dog.

Some of the villagers muttered darkly — it was hard to get the spring crop sowed with such heedlessness in the air. Many of the older, sourer priests grumbled at the spread of licentiousness and gluttony. But most people laughed at these doomsayers. Elias' monarchy was but newly-coined, and Erkynland — all of Osten Ard, it seemed – had come out of a long winter of age into a season of headlong youth. How could that be unnatural?

Simon felt his fingers cramping as he laboriously traced the letters onto the gray parchment. Morgenes was at the window, holding a long, fluted piece of glass pipe up to the sunlight as he examined it for dirt.

*If he says one word about the thing not being properly cleaned, I'll walk out,* Simon thought. *The only sunshine I see anymore is what's reflected in the beakers I polish.*

Morgenes turned from the window and brought the piece of glass pipe over to the table where Simon slaved at his writing. As the old man approached, Simon prepared himself for the scolding, feeling a swelling of resentment that seemed to lodge between his shoulder blades.

'A lovely job, Simon!' Morgenes said as he laid the pipette down beside the parchment. 'You take much better care of things around here then I ever could by myself.' The doctor gave him a pat on the arm and leaned over. 'How are you coming there?'

'Terribly,' Simon heard himself say. Even though the resentful knot was still there, he was disgusted by the petty tone of his own voice. 'I mean, I'll never be good at this. I can't make the letters cleanly without the ink blobbing up, and I can't read any of what I'm writing anyway!' He felt a little better for having said it, but he still felt stupid.

'You're worrying about nothing, Simon,' the doctor said, and straightened up. He seemed distracted: as he spoke his eyes darted about the room. 'First of all, everybody's writing "blobs up" at first; some folk spend their whole lives blobbing up – that doesn't mean they have nothing important to say. Secondly, *of course* you can't read the things you're writing – the book is written in Nabbanai. You can't read Nabbanai.'

'But why should I copy words that I don't understand?' Simon growled. 'That's foolish.'

Morgenes turned sharp eyes back to Simon. 'Since I told you to do it, I suppose I'm foolish, too?'

'No, I didn't mean that . . . it's just that . . .'

'Don't bother to explain.' The doctor pulled up a stool and sat by Simon's side. His long, bent fingers scrabbled aimlessly in the rubbish of the tabletop. 'I want you to copy these words because it's easier to concentrate on the form and shape of your letters if you're not distracted by the subject matter.'

'Hmmmph.' Simon felt only partially satisfied. 'Can't you tell me what book it is, anyway? I keep looking at the pictures, but I still can't figure it out.' He flipped the page back to an illustration that he had stared at many times in the past three days, a grotesque woodcut of an antlered man with huge staring eyes and black hands. Cringing figures huddled at his feet; above the horned man's head a flaming sun hung against an ink-black sky.

'Like this,' Simon pointed at the strange picture, 'here at the bottom it says "*Sa Asdridan Condiquilles*" – what does that mean?'

'It means,' Morgenes said as he closed the cover and picked the book up, ' "The Conqueror's Star," and it is not the kind of thing that you need to know about.' He placed the book on a precariously balanced stack against the wall.

'But I'm your apprentice!' Simon protested. 'When are you going to teach me something?'

'Idiot boy! What do you think I'm doing? I'm trying to teach you to read and to write. That's the most important thing. What do you *want* to learn?'

'Magic!' Simon said immediately. Morgenes stared at him.

'And what about reading. . . ?' The doctor asked ominously.

Simon was cross. As usual, people seemed determined to balk him at every turn. 'I don't know,' he said. 'What's so important about reading and letters, anyway? Books

109

are just stories about things. Why should I want to read books?'

Morgenes grinned, an old stoat finding a hole in the henyard fence. 'Ah, boy, how can I be mad at you . . . what a wonderful, charming, perfectly stupid thing to say!' The doctor chuckled appreciatively, deep in his throat.

'What do you mean?' Simon's eyebrows moved together as he frowned. 'Why is it wonderful and stupid?'

'Wonderful because I have such a wonderful answer,' Morgenes laughed. 'Stupid because . . . because young people are made stupid, I suppose – as tortoises are made with shells, and wasps with stings – it is their protection against life's unkindnesses.'

'Begging your pardon?' Simon was totally flummoxed, now.

'Books,' Morgenes said grandly, leaning back on his precarious stool, ' – books *are* magic. That is the simple answer. And books are traps as well.'

'Magic? Traps?'

'Books are a form of magic – ' the doctor lifted the volume he had just laid on the stack, ' – because they span time and distance more surely than any spell or charm. What did so-and-so think about such-and-such two hundred years agone? Can you fly back through the ages and ask him? No – or at least, probably not.

'But, ah! If he wrote down his thoughts, if somewhere there exists a scroll, or a book of his logical discourses . . . he speaks to you! Across centuries! And if you wish to visit far Nascadu, or lost Khandia, you have also but to open a book. . . .'

'Yes, yes, I suppose I understand all that.' Simon did not try to hide his disappointment. This was not what *he* had meant by the word "magic". 'What about traps, then? Why "traps"?'

Morgenes leaned forward, waggling the leather-bound volume under Simon's nose. 'A piece of writing *is* a trap,' he said cheerily, 'and the best kind. A book, you

110

see, is the only kind of trap that keeps its captive – which is knowledge – alive forever. The more books you have,' the doctor waved an all-encompassing hand about the room, 'the more traps, then the better chance of capturing some particular, elusive, shining beast – one that might otherwise die unseen.' Morgenes finished with a grand flourish, dropping the book back on the pile with a loud thump. A tiny cloud of dust leaped up, the flecks milling in the banded sunlight leaking past the window bars.

Simon stared at the shimmering dust for a moment, collecting his thoughts. Following the doctor's words was like trying to catch mice while wearing mittens.

'But what about *real* magic?' he said at last, a stubborn crease between his brows. 'Magic like they say Pryrates does up in the tower?'

For a brief instant a look of anger – or was it fear? – contorted the doctor's face.

'No, Simon,' he said quietly. 'Do not throw Pryrates up to me. He is a dangerous, foolish man.'

Despite his own horrid memories of the red priest, Simon found the intensity of the doctor's look strange and a little frightening. He nerved himself to ask another question. '*You* do magic, don't you? Why is Pryrates dangerous?'

Morgenes stood suddenly, and for a wild moment Simon feared that the old man might strike him, or shout. Instead Morgenes walked stiffly to the window and stared out for a moment. From where Simon sat, the doctor's thin hair was a bristly halo above his narrow shoulders.

Morgenes turned and walked back. His face was grave, troubled by doubt. 'Simon,' he said, 'it will probably do me no good at all to say this, but I want you to keep away from Pryrates – don't go near him, and don't talk about him . . . except to me, of course.'

'But why?' Contrary to what the doctor might think, Simon had already decided to stay far away from the alchemist. Morgenes was not usually so forthcoming, though, and Simon was not going to waste the opportunity. 'What is so bad about him?'

'Have you noticed that people are afraid of Pryrates? That when he comes down from his new chambers in Hjeldin's Tower people hurry to get out of his way? There is a reason. He is feared because he himself has none of the right kinds of fear. It shows in his eyes.'

Simon put the pen nib to his mouth and chewed, thoughtfully, then took it out again. 'Right kinds of fear? What does that mean?'

'There is no such thing as "fearless," Simon — not unless a man is mad. People who are called fearless are usually just good at hiding it, and that is quite a different thing. Old King John knew fear, and both his sons certainly have known it . . . I have, too. Pryrates . . . well, people see that he doesn't fear or respect the things that the rest of us do. That is often what we mean when we call someone mad.'

Simon found this fascinating. He wasn't sure that he could believe either Prester John or Elias had ever been afraid, but the subject of Pryrates was itself compelling.

'*Is* he mad, doctor? How could that be? He is a priest, and one of the king's counselors.' But Simon remembered the eyes and toothy smile, and knew Morgenes was right.

'Let me put it another way.' Morgenes twined a curl of snowy beard around his finger. 'I spoke to you of traps, of searching for knowledge as though hunting an elusive creature. Well, where I and other knowledge-seekers go out to our traps to see what bright beast we may have been lucky enough to capture, Pryrates throws open his door at night and waits to see what comes in.' Morgenes took the quill pen away from Simon, then lifted the sleeve of his robe and dabbed away some of the ink that had smeared on Simon's cheek. 'The problem with Pryrates' approach,' he continued, 'is that if you do not like the beast that comes to call, it is hard – very, *very* hard – to get the door closed again.'

'Hah!' Isgrimnur growled. 'A touch, man, a touch! Admit it!'

'The barest whisper across my vest,' Josua said, raising an eyebrow in feigned surprise. 'I'm sorry to see that infirmity has driven you to such desperate devices . . .' In mid-sentence, without altering tone, he lunged forward, Isgrimnur caught the wooden blade on his own hilt with a clack, and skewed the thrust aside.

'Infirmity?' the older man hissed through bared teeth. 'I'll give you an infirmity that will send you crying back to your wet nurse!'

Still swift for all his years and bulk, the Duke of Elvritshalla pressed forward, his two-handed grip enabling him to keep good control as he swung the wooden sword in wide arcs. Josua leaped backward, parrying, thin hair hanging in sweat-dampened points across his forehead. At last he saw an opening. As Isgrimnur brought the practice sword around in another whistling sweep, the prince ducked down, using his own blade to help angle the duke's cut past his head, then hooked a foot behind Isgrimnur's heel and pulled. The duke crashed backward onto the ground like an old tree. A moment later Josua, too, had slumped to the grass at Isgrimnur's side. With his single hand he nimbly unlaced his thick, padded vest and rolled onto his back.

Isgrimnur, puffing like a bellows, said nothing for several long moments. His eyes were closed; sweat-beads in his beard gleamed in the strong sunlight. Josua leaned over to stare. Then, a look of worry crossing his face, he reached over to undo Isgrimnur's vest. As he got his fingers under the knot the duke's great pink hand came up and buffeted him on the side of the head, rolling him again onto his back. The prince lifted a hand to his ear and winced.

113

'Hah!' Isgrimnur wheezed. 'That'll learn you . . . Young pup . . .'

Another stretch of silence followed as the two men lay gasping, staring up into the cloudless sky.

'You cheat, little man,' Isgrimnur said at last, levering himself into a sitting position. 'The next time you wander back here to the Hayholt I will have some revenge. Besides, had it not been so gods-cursed hot, and me so damnably fat, I would have staved in your ribs an hour ago.'

Josua sat up, shading his eyes. Two figures were approaching across the yellow grass of the tourney field. One was draped in a long robe. 'It *is* hot,' Josua said.

'And in Novander!' Isgrimnur grunted, pulling off the dueling-vest. 'The Days of the Hound are long behind us, and still this by-the-Mother heat! Where is the rain?'

'Frightened away, perhaps.' He squinted at the two figures as they drew nearer.

'Ho, my young brother!' one of the two figures called. 'And old Nuncle Isgrimnur! It looks like you have worn yourselves out at your play!'

'Josua and the heat have damn near killed me, Your Majesty,' Isgrimnur called out as the king approached. Elias was garbed in a rich tunic of sea green. Dark-eyed Pryrates walked at his side in flapping red robe, a comradely scarlet bat.

Josua stood, extending his hand to Isgrimnur as the older man clambered to his feet. 'Duke Isgrimnur, as usual, exaggerates,' the prince said softly. 'I was forced to knock him to the ground and sit on him to save my own life.'

'Yes, yes, we were watching your horseplaying from Hjeldin's Tower,' Elias said, waving a careless hand back to where the tower's bulk loomed over the Hayholt's outwall, ' – weren't we, Pryrates?'

'Yes, Sire.' Pryrates' smile was thin as thread, his voice a dry rasp. 'Your brother and the duke are mighty men indeed.'

114

'By the way, Your Majesty,' Isgrimnur said, 'may I ask you about something? I hate to trouble you with state business at such a time.'

Elias, who had been staring out across the field, turned to the old duke with a look of mild annoyance. 'I *am*, as it happens, discussing some important matters with Pryrates. Why do you not come to see me when I am holding court on such things?' He turned back again. Across the tourney field Guthwulf and Count Eolair of Nad Mullach – a kinsman of Hernystir's King Lluth – were chasing a fractious stallion that had broken its traces. Elias laughed at the sight and elbowed Pryrates, who favored him with another perfunctory smile.

'Um, your pardon, Majesty,' Isgrimnur resumed, 'but I have been trying to take this matter up with you for a fortnight. Your chancellor Helfcene keeps telling me that you're too busy – '

' – At Hjeldin's Tower,' Josua added curtly. For a moment the brothers locked eyes, than Elias turned to the duke.

'Oh, very well, then. What is it?'

'It's the royal garrison at Vestvennby. They have been gone for well over a month now, and remain unreplaced. The Frostmarch is still a wild place, and I do not have enough men to keep the northern Wealdhelm Road open without the Vestvennby garrison. Will you not send another troop?'

Elias had returned his gaze to Guthwulf and Eolair, two small figures shimmering in the heat as they chased the diminishing stallion. He answered without turning. 'Skali of Kaldskryke says that you have more than enough men, old Uncle. He says you are hoarding your soldiers at Elvritshalla and Naarved. Why is that?' His voice was deceptively light.

Before the startled Isgrimnur could reply, Josua spoke up. 'Skali Sharp-nose is a liar if he says that. You are a fool if you believe him.'

Elias whirled, his lip curling. 'Is that right, brother

115

Josua? Skali is a liar? And I should take your word for that, you who have never tried to hide your hatred of me?'

'Now then, now then . . .' Isgrimnur interrupted, flustered and more than a little frightened. 'Elias . . . Your Majesty, you know my loyalty – I was the firmest friend your father ever had!'

'Oh, yes, my *father!*' Elias snorted.

'. . . And please do not take your displeasure over these scandalous rumors – for that is all they are – out on Josua. He does not hate you! He is as loyal as I am!'

'Of that,' said the king, 'I have no doubt. I shall garrison Vestvennby when I am ready to, and not before!' For a moment Elias stared at them both, eyes wide. Pryrates, long-silent, reached up a white hand to tug at Elias' tunic sleeve.

'Please, my lord,' he said, 'this is not the time or place for such things . . .' he flicked an impudent, heavy-lidded glance at Josua, '. . . or so I humbly submit.'

The king stared at his minion, and then nodded once. 'You are right. I have allowed myself to become angered over nothing. Forgive me, Uncle,' he said to Isgrimnur, 'for as you said, it is a hot day. Forgive my temper.' He smiled.

Isgrimnur bobbed his head. 'Of course, Sire. It is easy to let ill-humors get the best of us in such stifling weather. It is strange, this late in the year, is it not?'

'That it is.' Elias turned and grinned broadly at the red-cloaked priest. 'Pryrates, here, for all his holy standing in the Church, cannot seem to convince God to give us the rain we are praying for – can you, counselor?'

Pryrates looked at the king strangely, ducking his head back into the collar of his robe like an albino tortoise. 'Please, my Lord . . .' he said, 'let us resume our talk and leave these gentlemen to their swordplay.'

'Yes.' The king nodded. 'I suppose so.' As the pair began to move off, Elias stopped. He wheeled slowly around to face Josua, who was picking the wooden practice swords up from the dry grass.

'You know, brother,' the king said, 'it has been a long time since the two of us crossed staves. Watching you has put me in mind of those old times. What do you say we make a few passes, as long as we are all here upon the field?'

A quiet moment passed. 'As you wish, Elias,' Josua replied at last, and tossed one of the wooden blades to the king, who caught the hilt deftly in his right hand.

'. . . As a matter of fact,' Elias said, a half-smile playing across his lips, 'I don't believe we have engaged since your . . . accident.' He put on a look of greater solemnity. 'Lucky for you it was not your sword-wielding hand that was lost.'

'Lucky, indeed.' Josua measured himself a pace and a half, then turned to face Elias.

'On the other hand,' Elias began, ' – ah, that was a poor choice of words, wasn't it? My apologies. *Alternately*, it is unlucky that we must fence with these poor wooden oars.' He waggled the practice sword. 'I do so enjoy watching you use – what do you call that thin blade of yours? – ah, *Naidel*. It is a pity you do not have it here.' Without warning Elias leaped forward, swinging a hard backhand toward Josua's head. The prince caught the blow, allowing it to slide by, then thrust forward. Elias trapped the oncoming lunge and deftly turned it aside. The two brothers backed apart, circling.

'Yes.' Josua leveled his sword before him, his thin face slick with sweat. 'It is too bad that Naidel is not with me. It is also too bad that you do not have Bright-Nail.' The prince made a swift downward cut, and slid into another looping thrust. The king backpedaled swiftly, then counter-attacked.

'Bright-Nail?' said Elias, breathing a little heavily. 'What do you mean by that? You know that it is buried with our father.' He ducked an arching backhand and pushed Josua back.

'Oh, I know,' said Josua, parrying, 'but a king's sword – just like his kingdom – should be wisely,' – a thrust –

117

'and proudly,' – a counter-thrust – '. . . should be wisely and carefully used . . . by his heir.'

The two wooden blades slid together with a noise like an axe cleaving timber. The pressure moved down until the hilts locked together, and Elias' and Josua's faces were merely inches apart. Muscles bunched beneath the brothers' shirts; for a moment they were nearly still, the only movement a slight trembling as they strained against each other. Finally Josua, who could not grip his hilt with two hands as the king could, felt his blade begin to slide. With a supple shrug he disengaged and sprang backward, lowering the blade before him again.

As they faced each other across the expanse of grass, chests heaving, a loud, deep tolling rang out across the tourney field: the bells of Green Angel Tower marking the noontide.

'There you are, gentlemen!' cried Isgrimnur, a sickly smile on his face. There had been no mistaking the naked hatred that flowed between the two. 'There're the bells, and that means dinnertime. Shall we call it a draw? If I don't get out of the sun and find a flagon of wine, I'm afraid I won't make it to Aedonmansa this year. These old northern bones weren't meant to stand such cruel heat.'

'The duke is right, my lord,' Pryrates rasped, laying his hand on Elias' wrist, which still held the upraised sword. A reptilian smile tightened the priest's lips. 'You and I can finish our business as we walk back.'

'Very well,' Elias grunted, and tossed the sword over his shoulder where it struck the ground and cartwheeled once, then fell flat. 'Thank you for the exercise, brother.' He turned and offered his arm to Pryrates. They moved away, scarlet and green.

'What do you say, Josua?' Isgrimnur asked, taking the wooden sword from the prince's hand. 'Shall we go and have some wine?'

'Yes, I suppose so,' Josua replied, bending to pick up the vests as Isgrimnur retrieved the sword the king had

118

flung away. He straightened, staring into the distance. 'Do the dead always stand between the living, Uncle?' he asked quietly, then drew his hand across his face. 'Never mind you. Let us go and find someplace cool.'

'Really, Judith, it's all right. Rachel won't mind . . .'

Simon's questing hand was captured mere inches away from the mixing bowl. Judith's grip, for all her pinkness and plumpness, was quite strong.

'Get on with you. "Rachel wouldn't mind," indeed! Rachel would break every bone in this frail old body of mine.' Pushing Simon's hand back into his lap, Judith blew a strand of hair out of her eyes and wiped her fingers on her stained apron. 'I should have known that the merest whiff of the Aedontide bread a-baking would bring you 'round like an Inniscrich camp-dog.'

Simon traced sad patterns in the flour-strewn counter. 'But Judith, you've got mounds and mounds of dough – why can't I have a taste from the bowl?'

Judith levered herself up from the stool and moved gracefully to one of the kitchen's hundreds of shelves, like a barge on a placid river. Two young scullions scattered before her like startled seagulls. 'Now, where . . .' she mused, '. . . where is that crock of sweet butter?' As she stood, finger to mouth in a thoughtful pose, Simon edged nearer to the mixer bowl.

'Don't you dare, laddie.' Judith cast the words over her shoulder without even turning to look at him. Did she have eyes on all sides? 'It's not that there's not dough to spare, Simon. Rachel doesn't want you spoiling your supper.' She continued her perusal of the orderly shelves stacked with goods as Simon sat back and glowered.

Despite the occasional frustrations, the kitchen was a fine place. Longer even than Morgenes' chambers, it seemed nevertheless small and intimate, full of the pulsing warmth of the ovens and the scents of good things. Lamb stew seethed in iron pots, Aedontide breads were rising in the oven, and papery brown onions hung like copper bells in the fogged window. The air was thick with the smells of spices, tangy ginger and cinnamon, saffron, cloves, and scratchy pepper. Scullions rolled barrels of flour and pickled fish through the door, or pulled loaves from the baking ovens with flat wooden paddles. One of the chief apprentices was boiling rice paste over the fire in a pot of almond milk, making a blanchesweet for the king's dessert. And Judith herself, a huge, gentle woman who made the giant kitchen seem as intimate as a farmer's cot, directed all without once raising her voice, a kindly but sharp-eyed sovereign in her kingdom of bricks and pots and firelight.

She returned with the missing crock, and as Simon regretfully watched she took a long-handled brush and dabbed the butter over the braided Aedontide loaves.

'Judith,' Simon asked at last, 'if it's almost Aedonmansa, why is there no snow? Morgenes said he's never seen it wait this late in the year.'

'That I don't know, I'm sure,' Judith said briskly. 'We had no rain in Novander, either. I expect it's just a dry year.' She frowned, and brushed again at the nearest loaf.

'They have been watering the sheep and cows from the town in the Hayholt's moat,' Simon said.

'Have they, then?'

'Yes. You can see the brown rings around the edges where the water's gone down. There are places you can stand where the water doesn't even reach your knees!'

'And you've found them all, I don't doubt.'

'I think so,' Simon replied proudly. 'And last year this time it was all frozen. Think of it!'

Judith looked up from her loaf-glazing to fix Simon with her pale, kind blue eyes. 'I know it's exciting when things like this happen,' she said, 'but just remember, laddie, we need that water. There'll be no more fine meals if we get neither rain nor snow. You can't drink the

Kynslagh, you know.' The Kynslagh, like the Gleniwent that fed it, was as salty as the sea.

'I know that,' Simon said. 'I'm sure it will snow soon – or rain, since it's so warm. It's just that it will be a very strange midwinter.'

Judith was about to say something else when she stopped, looking over Simon's shoulder at the doorway.

'Yes, girl, what is it?' she asked. Simon turned to see a familiar curly-haired serving girl standing a few feet away – Hepzibah.

'Rachel sent me to find Simon, mum,' she replied, giving a lazy half-curtsy. 'She needs him to get something down from a high shelf.'

'Well, dearie, you don't need to ask me. He's just sitting here mooning over my baking, not being any help or anything.' She made a shooing gesture at Simon. He did not see it, as he was admiring Hepzibah's tight-cinched apron, and the wavy hair which her cap could neither control nor contain. 'Lysia's mercy, boy, get on with you.' Judith leaned over and poked him with the handle of the brush.

Hepzibah had already turned and was nearly out the door. As Simon scrambled down off his stool to follow, the kitchen-mistress laid a warm hand on his arm.

'Here,' she said, 'I seem to have spoiled this one – see, it's all crooked.' She handed him a loaf of warm bread, twisted like a piece of rope and smelling of sugar.

'Thank you!' he said, tearing off a piece and pushing it into his mouth as he hurried to the door. 'It's good!'

'Of course it is!' Judith called after him. 'If you tell Rachel, I'll skin you!' By the time she had finished, she was shouting at an empty doorway.

It only took a few paces before Simon caught up with Hepzibah, who was not walking very quickly.

*Was she waiting for me?* he wondered, feeling oddly breathless, then decided it was more likely that anyone given an errand which took them out of Rachel's clutches would dawdle all they could.

'Would you . . . would you like some of this?' he asked, gasping slightly. The serving-girl took a piece of the sweet bread and sniffed it, then popped it into her mouth.

'Oh, that's good, that is,' she said, then gifted Simon with a dazzling smile, eyes crinkling at the corners. 'Give me another, won't you?' He did.

They passed out of the hall and into the courtyard. Hepzibah crossed her arms as if to hug herself. 'Ooh, it's cold,' she said. It was actually fairly warm – blazing hot, considering it was Decander-month – but now that Hepzibah had mentioned it, Simon was sure that he could detect a breeze.

'Yes, it *is* cold, isn't it?' he said, and fell silent again.

As they walked past the corner of the inner keep that housed the royal residences, Hepzibah pointed up to a small window just below the upper turret. 'See there?' she asked. 'Just the other day I saw the princess standing there, combing her hair . . . oh, my, but hasn't she got nice hair?'

A dim memory of gold catching the afternoon sunlight floated up in Simon's mind, but he was not to be distracted.

'Oh, I think you have much nicer hair,' he said, then turned away to look at one of the guardtowers in the Middle Bailey wall, a treacherous blush stealing up his cheeks.

'Do you really?' laughed Hepzibah. 'I think it's the worst tangle. Princess Miriamele has ladies to brush hers. Sarrah – you know her, the fair-haired girl? – knows one of them. Sarrah says that this lady told her the princess is very sad, sometimes, and that she wants to go back to Meremund where she grew up.'

Simon was looking with great interest at Hepzibah's neck, wreathed by the sprays of curly brown hair that hung down from her cap. 'Hmmm,' he said.

'You want to know something else?' Hepzibah asked, turning away from the tower. ' – What are you staring at?' she squealed, but her eyes were merry. 'Stop it, I told you my hair was in a strew. Do you want to know something else about the princess?'

'What?'

'Her father wants her to marry Earl Fengbald, but she doesn't want to. The king is very angry with her, and Fengbald is threatening to leave the court and go back to Falshire – although why he'd want to do that, who knows. Lofsunu says he never will, since no one in his earldom has enough money to appreciate his horses and clothes and things.'

'Who's Lofsunu?' Simon wanted to know.

'Oh.' Hepzibah looked coy. 'He's a soldier I know. He's with Count Breyugar's household force. He's very handsome.'

The last of the Aedontide bread turned to wet ashes in Simon's mouth. 'A soldier?' he said quietly. 'Is he . . . a relative of yours?'

Hepzibah giggled, a sound that Simon was beginning to find a little irritating. 'A relative? Merciful Rhiap, no, I should say not! Mooning around after me all the time!' She giggled again. Simon liked it even less. 'Maybe you've seen him,' she continued, ' – he's a guard in the eastern barracks? Big shoulders and a beard?' She sketched in the air a man in whose shadow two Simons could comfortably have sat on a summer day.

Simon's feelings were at war with his more sensible nature. His feelings won. 'Soldiers are stupid,' he grunted.

'They are not!' said Hepzibah. 'You take that back! Lofsunu is a fine man! Someday he's going to marry me!'

'Well, you'll make a fine couple,' Simon snarled, then felt sorry. 'I hope you'll be happy,' he finished, hoping that the reasons for his resentment were not as crystal-linely clear as he felt sure they were.

'Well, we will be,' said Hepzibah, mollified. She stared

at a pair of yeomen warders walking on the battlements above their heads, long pikes couched on shoulders. 'Someday Lofsunu will be a sergeant, and we shall have a house of our own in Erchester. We'll be happy as . . . as can be. Happier than that poor princess, anyway.'

Grimacing, Simon picked up a round stone and rattled it off the bailey wall.

Doctor Morgenes, pacing the battlements, looked down as Simon and one of the young serving girls passed beneath him. A dry breeze blew his hood back from his head as the couple passed below. He smiled and silently wished Simon good luck – the boy appeared to need it. His awkward carriage and bouts of sullenness made him seem more child than man, but he had the height, and showed the promise of growing into it some day. Simon was straddling the borderline, and even the doctor, whose age no one in the castle now could guess, remembered what *that* was like.

There was a sudden whirring of wings in the air behind him; Morgenes turned, but slowly, as if it was no surprise. Anyone watching would have seen a fluttering gray shadow that hung in the air before him for the span of a few heartbeats, then disappeared into the spacious folds of his gray sleeves.

The doctor's hands, which had been empty a moment earlier, now held a small roll of fine parchment bound with a slender blue ribbon. Cupping it in one palm, he unrolled it with a gentle finger. The message upon it was in the southern tongue of Nabban and the Church, but the letters were stark Rimmersgard runes.

*Morgen –*

*The fires of Stormspike have been lit. From Tungoldyr I have seen their smokes nine days, and their flames eight nights. The White Foxes are awake again, and in the darkness they trouble the children. I have also sent winged words to our smallest friend, but I doubt they*

124

*will find him unawares. Someone has been knocking at*
*dangerous doors.*

— Jarnauga

Beside the signature the author had drawn a crude feather in a circle.

'Odd weather, is it not?' a dry voice said. 'And yet so pleasant for walking on the battlements.'

The doctor whirled, crumpling the parchment in his hand. Pryrates stood at his shoulder, smiling.

'The air is full of birds today,' the priest said. 'Are you a student of birds, doctor? Do you know much of their habits?'

'I have some small knowledge of them,' Morgenes said quietly. His blue eyes were narrowed.

'I myself have thought of studying them,' Pryrates nodded. 'They are easily captured, you know . . . and they hold so many secrets that the inquiring mind would find valuable.' He sighed and rubbed his smooth chin. 'Ah, well, merely another thing to consider – my time is so full already. Good day, doctor. Enjoy the air.' He moved off down the battlement, boots clicking on the stone.

For a long while after the priest had gone Morgenes stood quietly, staring at the blue-gray northern sky.

# 8
# Bitter Air and Sweet

It was late in the month of Jonever. The rains had still not come. As the sun began to sink behind the western walls, and insects gossiped in the tall dry grass, Simon and Jeremias the chandler's boy sat back to back and panting.

'Come on, then.' Simon forced himself to his feet. 'Let's have another go.' Jeremias, now unsupported, slumped backward until he lay out-stretched in the scratchy grass like an upended tortoise.

'You go on,' he wheezed. 'I'll never be a soldier.'

'Of course you will,' said Simon, annoyed at such talk. 'We both will. You were much better last time. Come on, get up.'

With a groan of pain Jeremias allowed himself to be tugged upright. He reluctantly took the barrel stave Simon handed to him.

'Let's go in, Simon. I hurt all over.'

'You think too much,' Simon responded, and lifted his own stave. 'Have at you!' Stave smacked on stave.

'Ouch!' Simon yelped.

'Ho, ho!' chortled Jeremias, much heartened. 'A mortal blow!' The clicking and smacking resumed.

It had not been just his unsuccessful flirtation with Hepzibah that reawakened Simon's old fascination with the glories of the military life. Before Elias had come to the throne Simon had felt sure that his true desire – the one for which he would give anything – was to be Morgenes' apprentice, and to learn all the secrets of the doctor's muddled, magical world. But now that he had it, and had replaced plodding Inch as the doctor's helper, the glory had begun to pale. There was so much *work*, for one thing, and Morgenes was so damnably rigorous about everything. And had Simon learned to do any magic at all? He had not. Placed against hours of reading and writing and sweeping and polishing in the doctor's dark chamber, great deeds on the battlefield and the admiring glances of young women were not to be sneered at.

Deep in Jakob the Chandler's tallow-scented den, fat Jeremias had also been caught up in the martial splendor of the king's first year. During the week-long pageants that Elias seemed to hold virtually every month, all the color of the realm settled on the jousting lists, the knights like shiny butterflies of silk and gleaming steel, far more beautiful than any mortal thing. The glory-spiced wind that blew across the tournament field awakened deep longings in the breasts of young men.

Simon and Jeremias went to the cooper for long slats to fashion into swords, just as they had in childhood. They traded blows together for hours after chores were finished, at first staging their mock battles in the stables until Shem Horsegroom threw them out for the peace of his wards, then moving to the unmowed grass just south of the tourney field. Night after night Simon came limping back to the servants' quarters, breeches snagged and shirt torn, and Rachel the Dragon turned up her eyes and prayed aloud for Saint Rhiap to save her from the blockheadedness of boys, then rolled up her sleeves and added some bruises to those Simon had already garnered.

'I think . . .' Simon puffed, 'that's . . . enough.' Jeremias, pink-faced and doubled over, could only nod his agreement.

As they trooped back toward the castle in the fading light, sweating and huffing like plow oxen, Simon noted with approval that Jeremias was beginning to lose some of his lumpishness. Another month or so and he would begin to resemble a soldier. Before their regular dueling began, he had looked more like something his master might put a wick into.

'That was good today, wasn't it?' Simon asked. Jeremias rubbed his head through his cropped hair and gave Simon a look of disgust.

'I don't know how you talked me into this,' he grumbled. 'They will never let folk like us be anything but cook-fire boys.'

'But on the field of battle anything can happen!' Simon said. 'You might save the king's life from Thrithingsmen or Naraxi raiders – and be knighted on the spot!'

'Hmmm.' Jeremias was not impressed. 'And how are we going to get them to take us in the first place, with no families, nor horses, nor swords even?' He waggled his stave.

'Yes,' said Simon, 'well . . . well then, I'll think of something.'

'Hmmm,' agreed Jeremias, and mopped his flushed face with the hem of his tunic.

The flare of torchlight sprang up before them in a score of places as they neared the castle walls. What had been open, grassy space in the shadow of the Hayholt's outwall was now an infestation of wretched huts and tents, piled together and overlapping each other like the scales of an old, sick lizard. The grass was long gone, cropped to the soil by sheep and goats. As the ragged shanty dwellers milled about, setting up their campfires for the night and calling their children in ahead of the darkness, the dust kicked into gritty plumes that swirled briefly before settling, dyeing clothes and tent-fabric alike a dusky gray-brown.

'If it doesn't rain soon,' said Jeremias, frowning at a pack of shrieking children who tugged at the faded garments of a faded-looking woman, 'the Erkynguard will have to drive them away. We don't have enough water to keep giving it to them. Let them go and dig their own wells.'

'But where . . .' Simon started to ask, then broke off, staring. Down at the end of one of the squatter-town byways he saw what seemed a familiar face. It had appeared for only a moment in a crowd, then disappeared, but he was sure it was that of the boy he had caught spying, the one who had left him to the wrath of the sexton Barnabas.

'It's that one I told you about!' he hissed excitedly. Jeremias looked back without comprehension. 'You know, Mal . . . Malachias! I owe him something!' Simon reached the knot of people where he felt sure he had seen the spy's sharp-featured face. They were mostly women and young children, but a few older men stood among them, bent and withered like old trees. They had surrounded a young woman crouching on the ground before the opening to a half-tumbled hovel, which backed directly onto the stone of the great outwall. She held the pale body of a tiny child in her lap as she rocked herself from side to side, weeping. Malachias was nowhere in sight.

Simon looked at the impassive, battered faces around him, and then down at the crying woman.

'Is the child sick?' he asked someone next to him. 'I am Doctor Morgenes' apprentice. Should I go and fetch him?'

An old woman turned her face up to him. Her eyes, set in an intricate net of dirty wrinkles, were as harsh and dark as a bird's.

'Get away from us, castle man,' she said, and spat into the dirt. 'King's man. Just get away.'

'But I want to help . . .' Simon began, when a strong hand gripped his elbow.

'Do what she says, lad.' It was a wiry old man with a matted beard. The look on his face was not unkind as he

129

tugged Simon away from the circle. 'You can do nought here, and people are bad angry. The child is dead. Go on with you.' He gave Simon a gentle but firm push.

Jeremias was still standing in the same spot when Simon returned. The campfires all around outlined his worried expression in flickering light.

'Don't do that, Simon,' he whined. 'I don't like it out here, especially after the sun has gone down.'

'They looked at me like they *hated* me,' Simon murmured, puzzled and upset, but Jeremias was already hurrying ahead.

*None of the torches were lit, but strange, smoky light filled the long hall. He could see not a soul stirring anywhere in the Hayholt, but down every passageway echoed the sound of voices lifted in song and laughter.*

*Simon moved from one room to another, pulling aside curtains, opening pantry doors, but still could find no one. The voices seemed almost to mock him as he searched – now swelling in volume, now diminishing, chanting and singing in a hundred different languages not one of them his own.*

*At last he stood before the door of the throne room. The voices were louder than ever, all seeming to cry out from inside the great chamber. He reached a hand down; the door was not locked. As he pushed it open the voices stilled, as though startled into silence by the creak of the hinges. The misty light poured out past him like shimmering smoke. He stepped inside.*

*The yellowing throne, the Dragonbone Chair, stood in the room's center. Around it danced a linked circle of figures, hands clasped, moving as slowly as though they were in deep, deep water. He recognized several; Judith, Rachel, Jakob the Chandler and other castle folk, their faces stretched with wild merriment as they bowed and capered. Among them moved dancers more grand: King Elias, Guthwulf of Utanyeat, Gwythinn of Hernystir; these, like the castle folk, wheeled as slowly and deliberately as ageless ice grinding mountains down* to dust. *Scattered about the silent circle were looming figures, shiny-black as beetles – the malachite kings come down from their pedestals to join the sluggish festivity. And in the middle bulked the great chair, a skull-peaked mountain of dull ivory that seemed somehow full of vitality, suffused with an ancient energy that held the circling dancers by taut, invisible reins.*

*The throne room was silent but for a thin thread of melody that wavered in the air: the Cansim Falis, the Hymn to Joy. The tune was stretched and discomforting, as if the invisible hands that plucked it out were not made to handle earthly instruments.*

*Simon felt himself drawn toward the terrible dance, as to a whirlpool; he dragged his feet, but still moved inexorably inward. The dancers' heads turned toward his approach with a slow twisting motion like the unwinding of crumpled stems of grass.*

*In the center of the ring, on the Dragonbone Chair itself, a darkness was coalescing – a darkness of many flittering parts, like a cloud of flies. Near the top of this swarming, rolling dark, two smoldering sparks of crimson began to brighten, as though fanned by a sudden breeze.*

*The dancers were staring at him now as they swam by, mouthing his name:* Simon, Simon, Simon . . . *On the far side of the ring, beyond the crawling obscurity on the throne, a gap opened: two clasped hands sliding apart like the tearing of a rotted rag.*

*As the opening moved around to him, one of the hands fluttered out in fishlike undulation. It was Rachel's, and as she neared she beckoned to him. Instead of her usual look of suspicion, her face was set in lines of desperate cheerfulness. She reached out: across from her fat Jeremias held the gap open, a dull smile on his pale features.*

'Come boy . . .' *Rachel said, or at least it was her lips that moved – the voice soft and hoarse, was a man's.* 'Come, can you not feel the place we have left for you? A place especially prepared?'

*The grasping hand caught at his collar and began to pull him into the dance's orbit. He struggled, slapping at the clammy fingers, but his arms were strengthless. Rachel's and Jeremias' lips split in wide grins. The voice deepened.*

'Boy! Don't you hear me?! Come on, boy!'

'No!' The cry came out at last, leaping from the prison of Simon's constricted throat. 'No! I won't! No!'

'Oh, Frayja's Garters, boy, wake up! You've woken everyone else!' The hand shook him again, roughly, and there was a sudden gleam of light. Simon sat up, tried to scream and fell back in a coughing fit. A dark shape leaned over him, starkly outlined by an oil lamp.

*Actually the boy hasn't really wakened anyone,* Isgrimnur realized. *The rest of 'em have been tossing and moaning since I walked in – like they were all having the same nightmare. What a gods-cursed strange night!*

The duke watched as the restless shapes around him slowly lapsed back into quietude, then returned his attention to the boy.

*Look there – the little puppy is coughing something fierce. Truthfully, though, he's not so little – just thin as a starveling colt.*

Isgrimnur put the lantern down in a niche, then pulled the sheet of homespun stretched across the alcove to one side, so he could get a good grip on the youth's shoulder. He pulled the boy upright in bed and gave him a firm swat on the back. The boy coughed once more and then stopped. Isgrimnur patted him a few more times with a wide, hairy hand.

'Sorry, fellow, sorry. Take your time, there.'

While the youth regained his breath the Duke looked around the curtained-off alcove in which the boy's slat bed was set. From beyond the drooping cloth came the murmuring night-sounds of the dozen or so scullions bedded nearby.

Isgrimnur picked up the lantern again, peering at the odd shapes pegged on the shadowed wall: an unraveling bird's nest, a silky streamer – it looked green in the poor lamplight – that had probably come from some knight's festival gear. Nearby, also hanging from nails driven into cracks, were a hawk feather, a crude wooden Tree, and a picture whose ragged edge showed it to be torn from a book. Squinting, Isgrimnur thought he could make out a staring man with wild hair standing out from his head . . . or were they antlers. . . ?

When he looked down again, smiling to himself at the unholy clutter of younglings, the boy had regained his breath. He was looking up at the duke with wide, nervous eyes.

*With that nose and thatch of – what is it, red? – hair, the boy looks like a be-damned marsh bird*, Isgrimnur thought.

'Sorry to startle you,' the old duke said, 'but you were closest to the door. I need to speak to Towser – the jester. Do you know who he is?' The boy nodded, watching his face intently. *Good*, thought the Rimmersman, *at least he isn't simple-minded*. 'I was told that he dossed down here tonight, but I don't see him. Where is he?'

'You're . . . you're . . .' The youth was having trouble coming out with it.

'Yes, I'm the Duke of Elvritshalla – and don't start in bowing and "sir"-ing. Just tell me where the jester is and I'll let you back to sleep.'

Without another word the boy slid off his pallet and stood up, pulling his blanket free and wrapping it about his shoulders. The hem of his shirt hung down below, flapping against bare legs as he stepped over the slumbering men around him, some of whom lay wrapped in their cloaks in the middle of the floor as though they had not been able to make it all the way to their beds. Isgrimnur followed with the lamp, stepping carefully over the dark forms as though he followed one of Udun's ghost-maidens through a field of battle-slain.

They went through two more rooms this way, the big spirit and the small, the larger just as silent for all his bulk. In the last room a few dim coals sparkled in the fireplace. On the bricks before the grate, curled in a nest of coats and with a sheepskin winebag still gripped in his horny old fist, Towser the jester lay snoring and mumbling.

'Ah,' Isgrimnur grunted. 'Well, thanks then, boy. Go back to your bed with my apologies – although I think you were dreaming a dream you'd be just as happy to wake from. Go on now.'

The youth turned and went back past Isgrimnur toward the doorway. As he brushed by, the duke was mildly surprised to note that the youth was nearly as tall as he was – and Isgrimnur was not a small man. It was the boy's slenderness, and the way he hunched when he walked, that made his size less evident.

*It's a pity nobody's taught that one to stand up*, he thought. *And most likely he never will learn in the kitchens, or wherever.*

When the youth had disappeared a moment later, Isgrimnur bent and shook Towser – gently at first, then with increasing vigor as it became apparent that the little man was well and truly swotted; even the firmest agitation produced only faint noises of protest. At last Isgrimnur's patience ended. He bent down, clutching one of the older man's ankles in each hand, and pulled them up in the air until Towser dangled upside down, only the crown of his bald head touching the floor. Towser's grumbling turned to gurgles of discomfort, and at last became good, understandable Westerling words.

'What. . . ? . . . Down! Put . . . down, Aed'n damn you . . .'

'If you don't wake up, old souse, I shall knock your head against the ground until you think wine is poison forever!' Isgrimnur wedded word to deed, lifting the jester's ankles a few hand-spans, then setting his head back down none too gently on the cold stone.

'Desist! Demon, I . . . surrender! Turn me 'round, man, turn me 'round – I am not Usires, to hang heels-o'er-head for the instruction of . . . of the masses!'

Isgrimnur lowered him gently until the little jester lay stretched full length on his back.

'Don't add blasphemy to besottedness, old fool,'

134

Isgrimnur growled. Watching Towser roll painfully onto his stomach, the duke failed to see a slender shadow take up a position in the doorway behind him.

'Oh, merciful, merciful Aedon,' Towser groaned as he levered himself into a sitting position, 'did you have to use my head for a digging stick? If it is a well you wish to scrape, I could have told you the ground is too stony here in the servant's chambers.'

'Enough, Towser. I didn't wake you two hours before sunrise to bandy jokes. Josua is gone.'

Towser rubbed his crown, searching blindly with the other hand for his wineskin. 'Gone where, Isgrimnur? For pity's sake, man, have you broken *my* pate because Josua failed to meet you somewhere? I had nothing to do with it, I promise you.' He took a long, self-pitying swig from the bag.

'Idiot,' Isgrimnur said, but his tone was not harsh. 'I mean the prince is *gone*. Left the Hayholt.'

'Impossible,' said Towser firmly, recovering some of his self-possession with his second trembling swallow of malmsey. 'He is not leaving until next week. He said so. He told me I could go with him if I wished then, and be his jester at Naglimund.' Towser leaned his head to the side and spat. 'I told him I would give him my answer tomorrow – today, I suppose now – since Elias doesn't seem to care if I stay or I go.' He shook his head. 'And me his father's dearest companion . . .'

Isgrimnur shook his head impatiently, his gray-shot beard wagging. 'No, man, he is gone. Left sometime after middle-night, as far as I can tell – or so said the Erkynguardsman I found at his empty chamber when I went to keep a meeting-time with him. He had asked me to come so late, though I would have rather been abed, but he said it was something that would not wait. Does that sound like a man who would leave without even a message for me?'

'Who knows?' said Towser, his wrinkled face screwed up as he pondered. 'Mayhap that is why he wished to speak to you – because he was leaving secretly.'

'Then why did he not wait till I arrived? I do not like it.' Isgrimnur squatted down and poked at the coals with a stick lying there. 'There is a queer air in the halls of this house tonight.'

'Josua is often strange in his actions,' said Towser with calm assurance. 'He is moody – by the Lord, is he moody! He has probably gone out to hunt owls by moonlight, or some other tricksy pastime. Fear not.'

After a long moment of silence, Isgrimnur let out a long breath. 'Ah, I am sure you're right,' he said, and his tone was quite nearly convincing. 'Even were he and Elias at open odds, nothing could ever happen here in his father's house, before God and the court.'

'Nothing but you thumping me on the head in the middle-night. God seems to be a bit slow in doling out punishments tonight.' Towser grinned a wrinkly grin.

As the two men carried on their talking, voices hushed near the dull embers, Simon stole quietly back to his bed. He lay awake for some long time wrapped in his blanket, staring up into the darkness; but by the time the cock in the court yard below finally saw the sun's first rising glow, he had fallen back into sleep.

'Now you just remember,' Morgenes cautioned, wiping the sweat from his forehead with a bright blue kerchief, ' – don't eat anything until you've brought it back and asked me. *Especially* if it has red spots. Understood? Many of the articles I've asked you to gather are direst poison. Avoid stupidity, if such a thing is possible. Simon, you are in charge, boy. I hold you responsible for the safety of the others.'

The others were Jeremias the chandler's lad and Isaak, a young page from the upstairs residence. The doctor had picked this hot Feyever afternoon to organize a mushroom and herb-hunting expedition to the Kynswood, a small forest of less than a hundred acres that huddled on

136

the high bank of the Kynslagh along the Hayholt's western wall. Because of the drought, Morgenes' supplies of important commodities had dwindled alarmingly, and the Kynswood, standing as it did beside the great lake, seemed a good place to search for the doctor's moisture-loving treasures.

As they fanned out through the forest, Jeremias hung back, waiting until the sound of Morgenes' crunching footsteps had diminished into the crackly brown undergrowth.

'Have you asked him yet?' Jeremias' clothes were already so wet with perspiration that they clung.

'No.' Simon had squatted down to watch a press-gang of ants hurrying single file up the trunk of a Vestivegg pine. 'I'm going to do it today. I just have to think of the right way to do it.'

'What if he says no?' Jeremias eyed the procession with some distaste. 'What will we do then?'

'He won't say no.' Simon stood up. 'And if he does . . . well, I'll think of something.'

'What are you two whispering about?' Young Isaak had reappeared in the clearing. 'It's not right to keep secrets.' Though he was some three or four years younger than Simon and Jeremias, Isaak had already developed an 'upstairs' tone. Simon scowled at him.

'Never you mind.'

'We were looking at this tree,' Jeremias offered, quick to feel guilt.

'I should have thought,' Isaak said archly, 'that there were plenty of trees to look at without skulking and telling secrets.'

'Oh, but this one,' Jeremias began, 'This one is . . .'

'Forget the stupid tree,' said Simon in disgust. 'Let's go. Morgenes has gotten the jump on us, and will let us know if he outgathers us.' He ducked a branch and waded into the ankle-high tangle of undergrowth.

It was hard work; when they stopped to drink water and

rest in the shade some hour and a half later, all three of the boys were covered in fine red dust up to their elbows and knees. Each carried a small bundle of goods wrapped in his kerchief: Simon's the largest, Isaak's and Jeremias' of more modest size. They found a large spruce which they shared as a backrest, dusty legs fanning out around it like the spokes on a wheel. Simon tossed a stone across the clearing; it thumped into a pile of broken branches, setting dead leaves a–tremble.

'Why is it so hot?' moaned Jeremias, swabbing his brow. 'And why is my handkerchief full of ridiculous mushrooms, so that I have to wipe the sweat away with my hands?' He held up slick, wet palms.

'It's hot because it's hot,' Simon grumbled. 'Because there's no rain. And that's that.'

A longish stretch of time passed in silence. Even the insects and birds seemed to have disappeared, gone to dark places to sleep the dry, still afternoon away in silence.

'I suppose we should be glad we are not at Meremund,' said Jeremias at last. 'They say that a thousand have died there from the plague.'

'A thousand?' said Isaak, scornful. The heat had brought high color to his thin, pale face. 'Thousands! It is the talk of the residence. My master goes about the Hayholt with a kerchief doused in holy water clapped to his face, and the plague has not come within a hundred leagues of here.'

'Does your master know what is happening in Meremund?' Simon asked, interested – Isaak did have his uses. 'Does he speak of it to you?'

'All the time,' The young page was smug. 'His wife's brother is the mayor. They were among the first to flee the plague. He has gotten much news from them.'

'Elias made Guthwulf of Utanyeat the King's Hand,' said Simon. Jeremias groaned and slid away from the trunk, stretching out full-length on the pine needle-matted ground.

138

'That's right,' Isaak replied, scratching in the dirt with a long twig. 'And he has kept the plague there. It has not spread.'

'What caused it, this pestilence?' Simon asked. 'Do any of the residence people know?' He felt stupid asking questions of a child so much younger than himself, but Isaak did hear the upstairs gossip and was not reticent in sharing it.

'Nobody knows for sure. Some people say that jealous Hernystir merchants from Abaingeat across the river poisoned the wells. Many people in Abaingeat have died, too.' Isaak said this with a certain air of satisfaction – after all, the Hernystiri were not Aedonites but heathens, however noble an ally the House of Lluth might be under the High King's Ward. 'Others say that the drought has cracked the earth with dryness, and poisonous airs have escaped from the ground. Whatever it is, my master says that it spares nobody, rich man, priest, or peasant. You first become hot and feverish . . .' – Jeremias, on his back, groaned and mopped at his forehead – '. . . then you blister up, like you had laid on hot coals. Then the blisters begin to ooze . . .' He emphasized this last word with a childish grimace, fine blond hair hanging in his flushed face. 'And then you die. Painfully.'

The forest breathed heat around them as they sat without speaking.

'My master Jakob,' Jeremias said at last, 'fears that the plague shall come to the Hayholt, on account of all the dirty peasants living by the walls.' The Kynswood took another slow breath. 'Ruben the Bear, the blacksmith, told my master that he had gotten news from a mendicant friar that Guthwulf has taken very harsh measures in Meremund.'

'Harsh measures?' Simon asked, eyes closed. 'What does that mean?'

'The friar told Ruben that Guthwulf, when he arrived in Meremund as King's Hand, took the Erkynguard and went to the homes of the sick. They took hammers, nails, and boards, and sealed the houses up.'

'With the people inside?' Simon asked, horrified but fascinated.

'Of course. To stop the spread of plague. They boarded up the houses so families of the diseased could not run away and spread the plague to others.' Jeremias raised his sleeve and mopped again.

'But I thought the plague came from bad airs, from the ground?'

'Even so, it can be spread. That is why so many priests and monks and leeches have died. The friar said that at night, for many weeks, the streets of Meremund were . . . were . . . what did he say. . . ? "Like the Halls of Hell." You could hear the people howling like dogs in the boarded-up houses. Finally, when they all went silent, Guthwulf and the Erkynguard burned them. Unopened.'

As Simon marveled at this last detail, there was a sound of breaking branches.

'Ho there, you lazy lumps!' Morgenes appeared from a knot of trees, his robes festooned with twigs and leaves, a fringe of moss clinging to the brim of his wide hat. 'I should have known I would find you flat on your backs.'

Simon struggled to his feet. 'We have only been sitting a short while, Doctor,' he said. 'We gathered for a long time.'

'Don't forget to ask him!' hissed Jeremias, pulling himself up.

'Well,' Morgenes said, eyeing their bundles critically. 'I suppose you have not done badly, considering the conditions. Let me see what you have found.' He squatted like a farmer weeding a hedgerow and began sifting through the boys' collections. 'Ah! Devil's Ear!' he cried, holding a scalloped mushroom up to the shaft of sunlight. 'Excellent!'

'Doctor,' Simon said, 'I wanted to ask you a favor.'

'Hmmm?' Morgenes was poking through bits of fungus, using an unrolled kerchief as a table.

'Well, Jeremias is interested in joining the guards – or

140

trying to. The problem is, Count Breyugar knows us castle folk hardly at all, and Jeremias has no connection into such circles.'

'That,' said Morgenes dryly, 'is no surprise.' He emptied out the next kerchief.

'Do you think you could write him a letter of introduction? You are well known to all.' Simon tried to keep his voice calm. Isaak looked at sweating Jeremias with a mixture of respect and amusement.

'Hmmm.' The doctor's tone was neutral. 'I suspect I am only too well known to Breyugar and his friends.' He looked up, fixing Jeremias with a sharp eye. 'Does Jakob know?'

'He . . . he knows my feelings,' stammered Jeremias.

Morgenes bundled all the gatherings together in a sack and returned the boys' kerchiefs. The doctor stood, shaking the clinging leaves and tree needles from his robe.

'I suppose I could,' he said, as they started back toward the Hayholt. 'I don't think I approve – and I don't think a note from me will quite bring them to respectful attention – but I suppose if Jakob knows, then it's all right.' They waded single file through the scratching thicket.

'Thank you, Doctor,' said Jeremias breathlessly, struggling to keep up.

'I doubt they shall want you.' Isaak sounded a little envious. As they moved closer to the castle, his haughtiness seemed to return apace.

'Doctor Morgenes,' Simon said, mustering as best he could a tone of benign unconcern, 'why don't *I* write the letter, and then you can look at it and sign it? It would be good practice for me, don't you think?'

'Why, Simon,' the doctor said, stepping over a fallen tree trunk, 'that's an excellent idea. I'm glad to see you take such initiative. Maybe I will make a true apprentice of you yet.'

The doctor's cheerful statement, his tone of pride,

weighed Simon down like a cape of lead. He hadn't done *anything* yet, let alone anything bad, and already he felt like a murderer or some worse thing. He was about to say something else when the stifling forest air was ripped by a scream.

Simon turned around to see Jeremias, his face white as wheat paste, pointing at something in a thicket beside the fallen log. Isaak stood beside him, frozen in shock. Simon hurried back, Morgenes only a step behind him.

It was a corpse, lying tumbled half-in and half-out of the thicket. Although the face was mostly covered by bushes, the near-fleshless state of the exposed parts showed that the body had been dead for some time.

'Oh, oh, oh,' gasped Jeremias, 'he's dead! Are there outlaws here? What shall we do?'

'Oh, hush,' snapped Morgenes. 'That will be a start. Let me have a look.' The doctor picked up the hem of his robe and waded forward into the thicket, then stopped and gingerly lifted the branches that masked much of the body.

From the tendrils of beard that still clung to his bird and insect-gnawed face, he seemed to have been a northerner – a Rimmersman perhaps. He wore un-remarkable traveling clothes, a light wool cloak and tanned leather boots, rotting now so that bits of the fur lining showed through.

'How did he die?' asked Simon. The eyeless sockets, dark and secretive, unnerved him. The toothy mouth, flesh shrunken and pulled away, seemed to be grinning, as though the cadaver had been lying here for weeks enjoying a bleak joke.

Morgenes used a stick to pull the tunic aside. A few flies rose lazily and circled. 'Look,' he said.

From a puckered hole in the corpse's desiccated trunk rose the stump of an arrow, broken off a handsbreadth above the ribs.

'Done by someone in a hurry, perhaps – someone who did not want their arrow recognized.'

They had to wait a moment for Isaak to finish being noisily ill before they could hurry on to the castle.

# 9
# Smoke on the Wind

'Did you get it? Did he guess?' Still pale for all his hours in the sun, Jeremias bobbed along at Simon's side like the sheep's-bladder float on a fisherman's net.

'I've got it,' Simon growled. Jeremias' agitation irritated him; it seemed out of keeping with the masculine gravity of their mission. 'You think too much.'

Jeremias took no offense. 'As long as you've got it,' he said.

Main Row, open to the harsh noontide sky, tent roofing skinned back, was nearly deserted. Here and there the constabulary guard – yellow-liveried to show their immediate allegiance to Count Breyugar, bearing sashes of Elias' royal green – lounged in the doorways or diced with one another against the walls of shuttered shops. Even though the morning market was long over, still it seemed to Simon that there were fewer common people in the streets than was usual. Those to be seen were mostly the homeless who had been flooding into Erchester in the recent winter months, driven out of the countryside by drying streams and failing wells. They stood or sat in the shadows of stone walls and buildings, knots of indifference, their movements slow and purposeless. The constables pushed past or stepped over them as though they were dogs in the street.

The pair turned right off of Main Row onto Tavern Way, the largest of the thoroughfares running perpendicular to the Row. Here there was more activity, although still the largest number of folk in sight were soldiers. The heat had driven most of them indoors; they leaned out of the low windows with flagons in their hands, watching Simon and Jeremias and the half a dozen or so other pedestrians with beery disinterest.

A peasant girl in a homespun skirt – some ostler's daughter most likely, by the jug she balanced on her shoulder – hurried past up the street. A few soldiers whistled and called out to her, spilling great sloshes of beer into the dust below the tavern windowsills. The girl did not look up as she trotted by, chin on chest. Her haste, combined with the heavy jug, kept her steps short. Simon watched the fluid sway of her hips appreciatively, even turning completely around to keep her in view until she swooped abruptly into an alleyway and disappeared.

'Simon, come *on!*' Jeremias called. 'There it is!'

In the middle of the block of buildings, standing up from Tavern Row like a rock in a rutted road, stood Saint Sutrin's cathedral. The stone of its great face dully reflected the patient sun. Its tall arches and vaulting buttresses cast thin shadows over the nests of gargoyles, whose lively, twisted faces peered down happily, cackling and joking over the shoulders of the humorless saints. Three limp pennants hung from the flagpole over the high double doors: Elias' green dragon, the Pillar and Tree of the church, and at the bottom the gold coronet of Erchester-town on a white field. A pair of constabulary guards leaned on the open doors, their pikes point down in the wide stone doorway.

'Well, here's for it,' said Simon grimly, and with Jeremias trotting at his heels he made his way up the two dozen marble steps. At the top one of the guards lifted his pike lazily and barred their entrance. His chain mail hood was pulled back, hanging like a veil across his shoulders.

'What do you want, then?' he asked, narrowing his eyes.

'A message for Breyugar.' Simon was embarrassed to hear his voice break. 'For Count Breyugar, from Doctor Morgenes at the Hayholt.' A little defiantly, he thrust out the rolled parchment. The guardsman who had spoken took it and gave the seal a cursory glance. The other was staring intently up at the carved door-lintel, as if hoping to see written there his dismissal from duty for the day.

The first guard handed the parchment back with a shrug. 'Inside and to the left. Don't be scamping about.'

Simon drew himself up to his full height, indignant. When *he* was a guardsman, he would carry himself with a great deal more style than these bored, unshaven idiots. Didn't they know what an honor it was to wear the king's green? He and Jeremias climbed past them into Saint Sutrin's cool interior.

Nothing moved in the antechamber, not even the air, but Simon could see the play of light on figures in motion beyond the far doorway. Instead of going directly to the door on the left, he looked back to see if the guards were watching – they weren't, of course – then strode forward to look into the cathedral's grand chapel.

'*Simon!*' Jeremias hissed, alarmed. 'What are you *doing?!* They said over there!' He pointed to the leftmost doorway.

Ignoring his companion, Simon leaned his head through the doorway. Jeremias, muttering nervously, came up behind.

*It's like one of those religious pictures*, Simon thought. *Where you see Usires and the Tree way in the back, and the faces of Nabbanai peasants and all very close up front.*

Indeed, the chapel was so large and high-ceilinged that it seemed a whole world. Sunlight, softened by the colored windows as though by clouds, streamed down from the uppermost reaches. White-robed priests moved around the altar, cleaning and polishing like shaven-headed chambermaids. Simon supposed they were preparing for the Elysiamansa services only a week or two away.

Closer to the door, moving equally busily but with no other common reference, Breyugar's yellow-tunicked constables milled back and forth on various errands, dotted here and there with the green of one of the castle's Erkynguard, or the dun or black clothes of some Erchester notable. The two groups seemed completely separated; it took a moment for Simon to see the row of boards and stools that had been mounted between the front and back of the cathedral. In a flash of insight, Simon realized that it was not a fence to keep the scurrying priests *in*, as was the first impression – no, rather it was to keep the soldiers *out*. It seemed that Bishop Domitis and the priests had still not given up hope that the Lord Constable's occupation of their cathedral would be less than permanent.

As they climbed the stairs, they had to show their parchment to three more guards in turn, all of these more alert than those at the massive front door – either because they were inside out of the sun, or else due to their increased proximity to the object of protection. At last they stood in a crowded guardroom before a seam-faced, gap-toothed veteran whose belt full of keys and air of harried disinterest bespoke authority.

'Yes, the Lord Breyugar's here today. Give me the letter, and I'll be passing it on.' The sergeant scratched his chin impassively.

'No, sir, we must give it to him. It's from Doctor Morgenes.' Simon tried to sound firm. Jeremias was staring at the floor.

'Oh, is it then? Well, think of that.' The man spat on the sawdust-covered floor. Here and there the gleam of marble tiles showed through. 'Aedon bite me, what a day. Wait here, then.'

'So. What have we here?' Count Breyugar, sitting at the table beside the bony remnants of a meal of small birds, raised an eyebrow. He had delicate features, nearly lost in jowly flesh, and the hands of a musician – fine, long-fingered hands.

'A letter, my Lord.' Simon, on one knee, extended the tube of parchment.

'Well give it to me, then, boy. Can't you see I'm at dinner?' The count's voice was high-pitched and effeminate, but Simon had heard that Breyugar was a terrifying swordsman – those slender hands had killed many men.

As the count read the message, lips moving, shiny with grease, Simon tried to keep his shoulders straight and his back stiff as a pike handle. Out of the corner of his eye he thought he saw the grizzled sergeant looking at him, so he tilted his chin back and stared straight ahead, thinking about what a favorable comparison he must make to the slouching dullards on watch at the cathedral doors.

'. . . Please consider the . . . *bearers* . . . for service under your Lordship's guidance . . .' Breyugar read aloud. His emphasis gave Simon a panicky moment – had he noticed the 's' Simon had added to 'bearer'? He *had* made it a bit squeezy so it would fit.

Count Breyugar, his eyes on Simon, handed the letter to the staff sergeant. As the sergeant read, slower even than Breyugar, the nobleman looked the youth up and down, then flicked a brief glance to the still-kneeling Jeremias. When the sergeant handed the letter back, he wore a smile that showed two teeth missing, and a pink tongue probing in the dark gulf.

'So.' Breyugar fluted the sound like a sorrowful breath. 'Morgenes, the old apothecary, wants me to take on a couple of castle-mice and turn them into men.' He picked up a tiny haunch from his plate and chewed on the bone. 'Impossible.'

Simon felt his knees buckle and his stomach push up toward his throat. 'But . . . but why?' he stammered.

'Because I don't need you. I have fighting men

148

enough. I can't afford you. No one can plant if it doesn't rain, and I have men lined up already looking for a job of work that will feed them. But most important, I don't *want* you – a couple of suet-soft castle boys who have felt nothing more painful in their lives than a smack on their pink arses for stealing cherries. Go on with you. If war comes, if those sneering heathen in Hernystir continue to resist the king's will, or treacherous Josua turns up, then you can carry a pitchfork or scythe with the rest of the peasants – maybe you can even follow the army and water the horses, if manpower gets short enough. But you'll *never* be soldiers. The king didn't make me Lord Constable to nursemaid groundlings. Sergeant, show these castle-mice a hole to scamper out.'

Neither Simon or Jeremias said a word all the long journey back to the Hayholt. When Simon was alone in his curtained alcove he broke his barrel-stave sword over his knee. He did not cry. He *would not* cry.

*There is something strange in the north wind today*, thought Isgrimnur. *Something that smells like an animal, or a storm about to happen, or both . . . some scratchy thing that puts the hair on my neck right up.*

He rubbed his hands together as though the air were cold, which it was not, and pushed the sleeves of his light summer tunic – worn months early in this oddest of years – up over his corded old forearms. He went again to the doorway and looked out, feeling embarrassed that an old soldier like himself should be playing such stripling's games.

*Where is that damned Hernystirman?*

Turning to pace again he nearly tripped over a stack of writing boxes, instead catching a boot buckle in the bottommost of a small pyramid of parchment scrolls that hemmed in his confined walking space. Cursing roundly, he bent in time to keep the arrangement from toppling. Certainly the deserted room in the Hall of Records, emptied so that the writing-priests could make their Elysiamansa observances, was as good a place as could be found on short notice for a clandestine meeting – but why couldn't they leave enough room among their damned daubings for a grown man to move around?

The door latch rattled. Duke Isgrimnur, relieved of waiting at last, sprang forward. Instead of peering out cautiously he flung the door open to find not two men, as expected, but one.

'Praise Aedon you're here, Eolair!' he barked. 'Where's the escritor?'

'Sshh.' The Count of Nad Mullach held two fingers to his lips as he entered, pulling the door closed behind him. 'More quiet. The archive-master is nattering about just up the hall.'

'And why should I care?' the duke exclaimed, but not so loudly as the first time. 'Are we children, to hide from that leathery old eunuch?'

'If you wanted a meeting that all know about,' Eolair asked, settling himself on a stool, 'then why are we hiding in a closet?'

'It's no closet,' the Rimmersman grumbled, 'and you know perfectly well why I told you to come here, and why no secret is safe in the Inner Keep. Where's Escritor Velligis?'

'He felt that a closet was no place for the lector's right-hand man.' Eolair laughed. Isgrimnur did not. He thought the Hernystirman drunk by his flushed face, or at least a little so. He wished he were the same.

'I thought it important that we meet somewhere we could talk freely.' Isgrimnur said, a little defensively. 'We have been much seen in deep conversation lately.'

'No, Isgrimnur, it's you that's right.' Eolair waved a hand reassuringly. He was dressed for the Lady Day celebrations, playing the part of respectful outsider – a part which the pagan Hernystiri had learned well. His festival tunic of white was belted three times, each belt

150

covered in gold or enameled metals, and his long mane of black hair was pulled back behind his head and tied with golden ribbon. 'I was only making a joke, and a sad joke it is,' he resumed, 'when King John's loyal subjects must meet in secret to speak of things which are no treason.'

Isgrimnur moved slowly to the door and juggled the latch, making sure it had closed. He turned, putting his wide back against the wood, and crossed his arms across his substantial chest. He, too, was dressed for the festivities in a fine, light-weight blue tunic and hose, but the braids of his beard had already been frayed loose by nervous tugging, and the hose bagged at the knee. Isgrimnur hated dressing up.

'Well,' he growled at last, tilting his head defiantly, 'should I speak first, or will you?'

'There is no need to worry who will speak first,' the count said.

For a moment the flush of Eolair's face, the color on his high, thin cheekbones, reminded the older man of something he had seen once, years ago; a haunting figure glimpsed across fifty yards of Rimmersgard snow.

*One of the 'white foxes,' my father called that one.*

Isgrimnur wondered if the old stories were true – was there really Sithi blood in the Hernystiri noble houses?

Eolair ran a hand across his forehead as he continued speaking, blotting away the tiny droplets of sweat, and the momentary likeness was gone. 'We have spoken enough to know that things have gone fiercely wrong. What we need to speak on – and what we need privacy to speak on,' he waved his hand at the cluttered archive room, a dark nest of paper and parchment lit by a high triangular window, ' – is what we can do about it. If anything. But that is it: *What can be done?*'

Isgrimnur was not yet willing to jump so boldly into talk that, whatever Eolair might say, had already the faint, sickening tang of treason.

'It's this way,' he said. 'I would be the last to hold Elias to blame for this bedamned weather. I should know:

151

while it's hot as the Devil's breath and dry as a bone here, in my land in the north we're having a terrible winter: snows and ice that beat anything remembered. So weather here is no fault of the king's, any more than the roofs collapsed and the cattle frozen in the barn halls in Rimmersgard are mine.' He tugged fiercely, and another beard-braid raveled loose, the ribbon hanging limply down from the gray tangle. 'Of course, Elias *is* to blame for keeping me here while my kinsfolk and people suffer, but that is another line and another hook. . . .

'No, it's that the man doesn't seem to care! The wells drying up, the farms lying fallow, starving people sleeping in the fields and cities a-choke with the plague – and he seems not to notice. The taxes and levies go up, those bedamned arse-licking pups of the nobility he has befriended ring him 'round all day drinking and singing and fighting and . . . and . . .' The old duke grunted in disgust. 'And the *tournaments!* Udun's red spear, I was as much for the tourney as any man in my day, but Erkynland is crumbling to dust beneath his father's throne, the countries of the High Ward are restless as a spooked colt – and *still* the tournaments go on! And the barge parties on the Kynslagh! And the jugglers, and the tumblers, and the bearbaitings! It's as bad as what they say of the worst days of Crexis the Goat!' Red in the face himself now, Isgrimnur balled his fists and stared at the floor.

'In Hernystir,' – Eolair's voice was soft and musical after the Rimmersman's hoarse tirade – 'we say: "A shepherd, not a butcher," meaning a king should preserve his land and people like a flock, taking from them only what he needs to get by – not use them up until there's nothing left to do but eat what remains.' Eolair stared at the small window and the particles of parchment dust that eddied in its diffuse light. 'That's what Elias is doing: eating his land bite by bite, as surely as did the giant Croich-ma-Feareg once devour the mountain at Crannhyr.'

'He was a good man once, Elias was,' Isgrimnur said wonderingly, ' – far easier to deal with than his brother. Surely, not all men are meant for kingship, but it seems more is wrong than just a man made ill by power. Something is damnably wrong – and it is not only Fengbald and Breyugar and those that are leading him to the cliff.' The duke had somewhat regained his breath. 'You know it is that vicious bastard Pryrates who fills his head with strange notions, and keeps him up nights in that tower with lights and unholy noises, until sometimes it seems that the king does not know where he is when the sun is up. What could Elias want from such a creature as that whoreson priest? He is king of the known world – what could Pryrates possibly have to offer him?'

Eolair stood, still with eyes fixed to the light above, and dampened his sleeve against his forehead. 'I wish I knew,' he said at last. 'So. What then is there to do?'

Isgrimnur narrowed his old, fierce eyes. 'What said Escritor Velligis? It is, after all, Mother Church's cathedral that is confiscate at Saint Sutrin's. It is Duke Leobardis' Nabbanai ships, along with your King Lluth's, that Guthwulf has stolen under the lie of "plague danger" at the sovereign harbor of Abaingeat. Leobardis and Lector Ranessin are close; they rule Nabban like one two-headed monarch. Surely Velligis must have had *something* to say on his master's behalf.'

'He has much to say, but little of substance, my friend.' Eolair slumped back on his stool. The bright shaft of sunlight was diminished now, its source partially blocked as the sun sank, the little room in even denser shadow. 'Of what Duke Leobardis thinks of this act of piracy – three grain ships thieved outright in a Hernystir harbor – Velligis professes not to know. On his master's behalf he is, as ever, vague. His Sacredness Ranessin, I think, has designs to be a peacemaker between Elias and Duke Leobardis, and perhaps at the same time improve the position of your Aedonite Church here at court. My master King Lluth has directed me next to travel to

153

Nabban, and perhaps I will find out the truth of that when I am there. I fear, however, that if such is the case, the lector has misjudged: if the snubbing that Elias and his sycophants have given Velligis is any indication, the King is more restless even than his father was under Mother Church's broad shadow.'

'So many plots!' Isgrimnur groaned. 'So many intrigues! It makes my head swim. I am not a man for such things. Give me a sword or an axe and let me deal blows!'

'Is that why you have taken to closets?' Eolair smiled, and produced from beneath his cloak a skin of sour-honey mead. 'There does not seem anyone to swing at here. I think you are taking rather well to intrigue late in life, my good Duke.'

Isgrimnur frowned, and took the offered skin. *He's a born intriguer himself, our Eolair,* he thought. *I should be grateful, if nothing else, to have someone to talk to. For all that Hernystiri poetry-talk I've heard him trot out for the ladies, he's hard as shield-steel underneath – a good ally for treacherous times.*

'There's something else.' Isgrimnur handed the skin back to Eolair and wiped his mouth. The count took a long swallow and then nodded his head.

'Out with it. I'm all ears like a Circoille hare.'

'That dead man old Morgenes found out in the Kynswood?' Isgrimnur said, ' – the arrowshot one?' Eolair nodded again. 'He was mine. Bindesekk by name, although by the time he was discovered I would never have known him but for a broken bone in his face that was got in an earlier service for me. Of course I said nothing.'

'Yours?' Eolair cocked an eyebrow. 'And doing what? Do you know?'

Isgrimnur laughed, a short, barking sound. 'Certainly. That is why I kept quiet. I sent him out when Skali of Kaldskryke took his kinsmen and departed north. Sharp-nose has been making too many new friends among Elias' court for my liking, so I send Bindesekk out with a message to my son Isorn. As long as Elias is keeping me here with these ridiculous errands, these shows of mock-diplomacy that he claims are so important – and if they *were* so important, why entrust them to a blunt old war-dog like me? – then I wanted Isorn to be on especial close watch. I don't trust Skali any more than I would a starving wolf, and my son has troubles enough at home already, from what I hear. All the reports that have trickled down across the Frostmarch are bad – raging storms in the north, the roads unsafe, villagers forced to huddle together in the main halls. It makes for troubled times, and Skali knows that.'

'Do you think, then, it was Skali killed your man?' Eolair leaned forward, passing the skin back.

'I don't know, to be sure.' The duke tipped back his head for another long swallow, the muscles in his thick neck pulsing; a thin drizzle of mead spattered down his blue tunic. 'What I mean is: it's the most obvious thing, but I have many doubts.' He wiped at the stain absently for a moment. 'First of all, even if he caught Bindesekk, it's an act of treason to kill him. For all his contempt, Skali is my liege-man and I am his liege-lord.'

'But the body was hidden.'

'Not well. And why so close to the castle? Why not wait until they had reached the Wealdhelm Hills – or the Frostmarch Road if it's even passable – and kill him there, where I'd never find out? Also, the arrow doesn't strike me as Skali's way. I could see him chopping Bindesekk up in a rage with that great axe of his, but shooting him and then dropping him in the Kynswood? It doesn't sit right, somehow.'

'Then who?'

Isgrimnur shook his head, feeling the mead at last. 'That's what worries me, Hernystirman,' he said at last. 'I just don't know. There are strange things afoot. Travelers' tales, castle rumors . . .'

Eolair went to the door and unlatched it, pushing it open to allow fresh air into the small room.

'These are indeed strange times, my friend,' he said, and took a deep breath. 'And, perhaps the most important question of all – where in this strange world is Prince Josua?'

Simon picked up a small piece of flint and sent it spinning into space. After describing a graceful arc through the morning air the stone descended with a muffled snap into a leafless topiary animal in the garden below. Crawling to the edge of the chapel roof, Simon marked its impact point like a skilled catapult man, noting the quiver at the haunches of the hedge-squirrel. He rolled back from the roof gutter and into the shadow of a chimney, savoring the cool solidity of the stones beneath his spine. Overhead the fierce eye of the Marris sun glared down, nearing its noon apex.

It was a day to evade responsibility, to escape Rachel's chores and Morgenes' explanations. The doctor had not yet found out – or had not mentioned – Simon's thwarted foray into the military arts, and Simon was content to keep it that way.

Spread-eagled and squint-eyed in the morning brightness, he heard a faint ticking noise near his head. He opened one eye in time to see a tiny gray shadow whisk past. Rolling slowly over onto his stomach, he scanned the rooftop.

The great chapel roof spread before him, a field of humped and irregular slate tiles in whose cracks sprouted tight-coiled hanks of brown and pale green moss that had somehow miraculously survived the drought, clinging to life as grudgingly as they clung to the splintered tiles. The plain of slates marched uphill from the guttered edge to the chapel's dome, which pushed up through the roof like a sea turtle's shell breaching the shallow wavelets of a quiet cove. Seen from this angle the dome's colorful glass panels – which shone inside the chapel with magical pictures of the lives of saints – looked dark and flat, a parade of crude figures across a dun-colored world. At the dome's apex an iron knob held aloft a golden Tree, but from Simon's viewpoint it was merely gilded, the gold leaf peeling in slender, shimmering strips that revealed the corrosion beneath.

Beyond the castle chapel the sea of roofs spread out in all directions: the Great Hall, the throne room, the archives and servants' quarters, all pitched and uneven, repaired or replaced many times as the seasons in their passing licked at gray stone and lead shingle, then nibbled them away. To Simon's left loomed the slender white arrogance of Green Angel Tower; farther back, protruding above the arch of the chapel dome, the gray, squat bulk of Hjeldin's Tower sat up like a begging dog.

As Simon surveyed the expanse of the roof-world, a flirt of gray appeared again at the edge of his vision. Turning swiftly, he saw the hindquarters of a small soot-colored cat disappear into a hole at the roof's edge. He crawled across the slates to investigate. When he was close enough to observe the hole, he dropped back down onto his stomach, balancing his chin onto the back of his hands. There was no sign of movement now.

*A cat on the roof*, he thought. *Well, someone might as well live up here besides flies and pigeons – I suppose he eats those scrabbling roof rats*.

Simon, despite having seen only its tail and back legs thus far, felt a sudden affinity with this outlaw roof cat. Like him, the cat knew the secret passages, the angles and crannies, and went where it would without leave. Like himself, this gray hunter made its way without the concern or charity of others. . . .

Even Simon knew that this was a terrible exaggeration of his own situation, but he rather liked the comparison.

For example, hadn't he crept unsuspected onto this same rooftop four days ago, the day after Elysiamansa, to watch the mustering out of the Erkynguard? Rachel the Dragon, irritated by his infatuation with everything except maintenance of the household, which she felt was his true – and neglected – duty, had earlier forbidden him to go down and join the crowd at the main gate.

Ruben the Bear, the hump-shouldered, slab-muscled master of the castle smithy, had told Simon that the Erkynguard was going to Falshire, up the River Ymstrecca to the east of Erchester. The wool merchant's guild there was causing trouble, Ruben had explained to the youth as he dropped a red-hot horseshoe into a bucket of water. Waving away the hissing steam, Ruben had then tried to describe the complicated situation: it seemed that the drought had caused such distress that the sheep of Falshire's farmers – their main livelihood – must now be appropriated by the crown to feed the starving, dispossessed masses crowding into Erchester. The wool merchants, crying that this would ruin them – that they, too, would be made to starve – were swarming in the streets, inflaming the local folk against the unpopular edict.

So Simon had climbed secretly onto the chapel roof Tiasday-last to watch the Erkynguard ride out, several hundred well-armed foot soldiers and a dozen knights under the command of Earl Fengbald, whose fief Falshire was. As Fengbald rode out at the front of the Guard, helmed and corseleted, splendid in his red tunic and silver-stitched eagle, several of the more cynical in the watching crowd suggested the Earl was taking so many soldiers for fear that his Falshire subjects would not recognize him, owing to his extended absences. Others suggested he might fear that they *would* recognize him – Fengbald had not exactly been tireless in the interests of his hereditary domain.

Simon thought back warmly on Fengbald's impressive helmet, a gleaming silver casque crested with a pair of spreading wings.

*Rachel and the others are right*, he thought suddenly. *Here I am daydreaming again. Fengbald and his noble friends will*

158

*never know if I live or die. I must make something of myself. I don't want to be a child forever, do I?* He scratched at a slate tile with a piece of gravel, trying to draw an eagle. *Besides, I would probably look foolish in armor . . . wouldn't I?*

The memory of the soldiers of the Erkynguard marching so proudly out the great Nearulagh Gate touched him in sore spots, but it warmed him, too; he kicked his feet lazily as he watched the cat's cave for sign of its denizen.

It was an hour past noon before a suspicious nose appeared at the front of the hole. By this time Simon was riding a stallion through the gates of Falshire, flowers raining down from the windows above. Tugged back to attention by the sudden movement, he held his breath as the nose was followed by the rest of the beast: a small, short-furred gray cat with a patch of white running from right eye to chin. The youth stayed stock-still as the cat – a mere half a fathom from his own position – took momentary fright at something and arched its back, eyes narrowing. Simon feared it had seen him, but as he remained motionless it suddenly moved forward, bounding out of the shadow of the roof's upcurved edge and into the broad path of the sun's passage. As Simon watched, delighted, the gray catling found a loose piece of flint and batted it skittering across the tiles, following to hook it with an agile paw and begin the game anew.

He watched the roof cat's antics for some time, until a particularly ridiculous pratfall – the catling had skidded to a stop with both front paws on the slate chip, tumbled head over heels into a crack between the tiles, then lay there with its tail wriggling in exasperation – forced him to reveal his position. His long-suppressed snort of laughter broke forth; the little beast leaped tumbling into the air, landed, and bolted for its hole with no more than a brief glance in Simon's direction. This scrambling exit convulsed him again.

'Scatter, cat!' he called after the vanished creature. 'Scatter, you catter! Scatter-scatter!'

As he was crawling toward the hole-mouth to sing a little song of shared outlook on roofs and stones and solitude to the gray cat – who he was somehow certain would be listening – something else caught his eye. He put his hands on the roof edge and poked his head up to look. The beginnings of a breeze traced subtle designs through his hair.

Away to the southeast, far beyond the limits of Erchester and the headlands above the Kynslagh, a deep gray mark was smeared across the clear Marris sky, as if a dirty thumb had been dragged across a newly-painted wall. The wind shredded the dark smudge even as he watched, but darker billows were rising from below, a turbulent darkness too thick for any wind to diffuse. A regular black cloud was mounting upward on the eastern horizon.

It took him a long, puzzled moment before he realized that what he was seeing was smoke, a dense plume of it besmirching the pale, clean sky.

Falshire was burning.

# 10
# King Hemlock

Two days later, on the morning of Marris' last day, Simon was going down to breakfast with the other scullions when he was brought up short by a heavy black hand on his shoulder. For an unreal, terrifying moment his thoughts skipped back to his throne room dream, and the ponderous dancing of the malachite kings.

This hand, though, proved to be wearing a cracked, fingerless black glove. Neither was its owner made of dark stone – although as Simon stared up in surprise at the face of Inch, it did seem that God had somehow neglected to provide enough living stuff while this Inch-person was being made, and that last-minute substitutions of some inert, imperturbable matter had been necessary.

Inch leaned down until his whiskered face was very close to Simon's; even his breath seemed to smell more of stone than of wine or onions or anything ordinary.

'Doctor wants to see you.' He rolled his eyes from side to side. 'Right away, like.'

The other scullions had scattered past Simon and the hulking Inch with curious looks and continued on their way. Simon, trying to squirm out from underneath the weighty hand, watched them go despairingly.

'Very well. I'll be right there,' he said, and with a wiggle tugged free. 'Just let me get a crust of bread that I can eat as I go.' He trotted on down the corridor toward the servants' eating room, stealing a backward glance; Inch was still standing in the same place, following his retreat with the tranquil eyes of a bull in a meadow.

When he emerged in a short while with a heel of bread and a wedge of chewy white cheese, he was dismayed to find that Inch had waited for him. The large man fell into step alongside as he headed towards Morgenes' chambers. Simon offered him some food, trying to smile as he did so, but Inch only stared at it incuriously and said nothing.

As they walked across the dry-rutted open ground of the Middle Bailey, threading through the flocks of writing-priests making their daily pilgrimages between the Chancelry and the Hall of Archives, Inch cleared his throat as if to speak. Simon, who felt so uncomfortable around this person that even silence made him nervous, looked up expectantly.

'Why . . .' Inch at last began, '. . . why do you take my place?' He did not turn his waxy eyes away from the priest-clogged pathway before them.

It was Simon's heart that now took on the qualities of stone: cold, heavy, and burdensome. He was sorry for this farm animal that thought itself a man, but frightened by him, too.

'I . . . I haven't taken your place.' His protestations sounded false even to his own ears. 'Doesn't the doctor still have you in to help out with carrying things, and setting things up? He is teaching me to do other things, things that are very different.'

They walked on in silence. At last Morgenes' chambers were in view, crouched in choking ivy like the nest of a small but resourceful beast. When they were perhaps ten paces away, Inch's hand clutched Simon's shoulder once more.

'Before you came,' Inch said, his wide, round face moving down toward Simon's like a basket being

162

lowered from an upstairs window, '. . . before you came, *I* was his helper. *I* was going to be next.' He frowned, pushing his lower lip out and knitting his single bar of eyebrow into a steeper angle, but his eyes were still mild and sad. 'Doctor Inch, I would have been.' He focused his gaze on Simon, who half-feared he would be crumpled beneath the weight of the paw on his collar-bone. '*I don't like you*, little kitchen boy.'

Turning him loose, Inch shuffled away, the back of his head barely visible above the mountainous rise of his bowed shoulders. Simon, rubbing his neck, felt a little sick.

Morgenes was ushering a trio of young priests out of his chambers. They were conspicuously – and somewhat shockingly, as far as Simon was concerned – drunk.

'They came for my contribution to the All Fool's Day celebration,' Morgenes said as he shut the door behind the trio, who had already burst into ragged song. 'Hold this ladder, Simon.'

A bucket of red paint was perched on the ladder's topmost step, and when the doctor reached it he fished out a brush that had fallen in and began daubing strange characters above the doorframe – angular symbols, each one a tiny, puzzling picture. They looked to Simon a little like the ancient writings contained in some of Morgenes' books.

'What are those for?' he asked. The furiously painting doctor did not reply. Simon took his hand off the rung to scratch his ankle and the ladder began to sway ominously. Morgenes had to grasp the door lintel to keep from toppling.

'No, no, no!' he barked, trying to keep the ebb and flow of the paint from overtopping the bucket's edge. 'You know better, Simon. The rule is: all questions written out! But wait until I'm down from here – if I fall off and die, there'll be no one to answer you.' Morgenes went back to his painting, sputtering quietly to himself.

'Sorry, Doctor,' Simon said, a touch indignantly, 'I just forgot.'

A few moments passed with no other sounds than the whiskery swish of Morgenes' brush.

'Will I always have to write down my questions? I can't hope to write as fast as I think up things I want to know about.'

'That,' said Morgenes, squinting at his last stroke, 'was the general idea behind the rule. You, boy, devise questions like God makes flies and poor people – in droves. I am an old man, and prefer to set my own pace.'

'But,' Simon's voice took on a despairing tone, 'I shall be writing the rest of my days!'

'I can think of many less worthwhile ways you might spend your life,' Morgenes responded, beetling down the ladder. He turned to survey the complete effect, the arch of strange letters all along the top of the door frame. 'For instance,' he said, casting a sharp, knowing eye over to Simon, 'you might forge a letter and join Breyugar's guardsmen, then spend your time having little bits of you hacked off by men with swords.'

*Curses*, thought Simon, *caught like a rat.*

'So you . . . heard, did you?' he asked at last. The doctor nodded, retaining his tight, angry smile.

*Usires save me, but he has such eyes!* Simon thought. *Like needles. He has a stare worse than Rachel's dragon-voice.*

The doctor continued to watch him. Simon's gaze dropped to the floor. At last, in a sullen voice that sounded years younger than he would have preferred, Simon said it.

'I'm sorry.'

Now the doctor, as if a restraining cord had been cut, began to pace. 'If I'd had any idea of what you were going to use that letter for . . .' he fumed. 'What were you thinking of? And why, *why* did you feel you had to lie to *me!?*'

Somewhere deep inside, a part of Simon was pleased to see the doctor upset – a part that enjoyed the attention.

Another part, however, felt ashamed. Somewhere else inside him – how many Simons were there? – was a calm, interested observer who waited to see which part would speak for all.

Morgenes' pacing was beginning to make him nervous. 'Besides,' he called to the old man, 'why should you care? It's my life, isn't it? A kitchen boy's stupid life! They didn't want me, anyway . . .' he finished in a mutter.

'And you should be grateful!' Morgenes said sharply. 'Grateful that they don't want you. What kind of life is it? Sitting around the barracks playing dice with know-nothing louts during time of peace; getting hacked, arrow-pierced and stallion-stamped in time of war. You don't know, you stupid boy – to be a simple kern while all of these high-living, peasant-cudgeling knights are on the battlefield is no better than being a shuttle-cock at the Lady's Day games.' He whirled to face Simon. 'Do you know what Fengbald and his knights did at Falshire?'

The youth did not answer.

'They put the entire wool district to the torch, that's what they did. Burned women and children along with the rest – just because they didn't want to give up their sheep. Fengbald had the sheep-dipping vats filled with hot oil and scalded the leaders of the wool merchants' guild to death. Six hundred of Earl Fengbald's own subjects slaughtered, and he and his men marched back to the castle singing! And this is the company you wish to join!?'

Simon was truly angry, now. He felt his face getting hot, and was terrified that he might burst into tears. The dispassionate observer-Simon had disappeared entirely. 'So?' he shouted. 'What does it matter to anyone!?' Morgenes' apparent surprise at this unusual outburst made him feel worse. 'What is to become of *me?*' he asked, and slapped at his thighs in frustration. 'There is no glory in the scullery, no glory among the chamber-maids . . . and no glory here in a dark room filled with stupid . . . *books*!'

The hurt look on the old man's face burst the straining dikes at last; Simon fled in tears to the far part of the doctor's chamber to huddle sobbing on the sea-chest, his face pressed against the cold stone wall. Outside, somewhere, the three young priests were singing hymns in distracted, drunken harmony.

The little doctor was at his side in a moment, patting with an awkward hand at the youth's shoulder.

'Now, boy, now . . .' he said bewilderedly, 'what is all this talk of glory? Have *you* caught the sickness, too? Curse me for a blind beggar, I should have seen. This fever has cankered even your simple heart, hasn't it, Simon? I'm sorry. It takes a strong will or practiced eye to see through the glitter to the rotten core.' He patted Simon's arm again.

Simon had no idea what the doctor was talking about, but the tone of Morgenes' voice was soothing. Despite himself, he felt his anger begin to slip away – but the feeling of what seemed like weakness that followed made him sit up and shake off the doctor's hand. He wiped his wet face roughly with his jerkin sleeve.

'I don't know why you're sorry, Doctor,' he began, trying to keep his voice from shaking. '*I* am sorry . . . for acting like a child.' He stood up, and the little man's eyes followed him as he crossed the room to the long table, where he stood drawing a finger across a scatter of open books. 'I have lied to you, and I have made a fool of myself,' he said, not looking up. 'Please forgive the stupidity of a kitchen boy, Doctor . . . a kitchen boy who thought he could be more than that.'

In the silence that followed this brave speech, Simon heard Morgenes make a strange sound – was he actually *crying?* But a moment later it became all too clear: Morgenes was chuckling – no, laughing, trying to muffle it behind his billowing sleeve.

Simon whirled, ears burning like coals. Morgenes caught his eye for a moment, then looked away, shoulders heaving.

166

'Oh, lad – oh, lad,' he wheezed at last, putting a restraining hand out toward the outraged Simon, 'don't go! Don't be angry. You would be wasted on the field of battle! You should be a great lord, and win the victories at treaty-table that always outweigh victories of the field – or an escritor of the Church, and wheedle the eternal souls of the rich and dissolute.' Morgenes snickered again, and chewed on his beard until the fit passed. Simon stood stone-still, face a-frown, unsure if he was being paid compliment or insult. Finally the doctor regained his composure; he vaulted to his feet and made his way to the ale butt. A long swallow completed the calming procedure, and he turned to the youth with a smile.

'Ah, Simon, bless you! Don't let the clanking and boasting of King Elias' goodfellows and bravos impress you so much. You have a keen wit – well sometimes, anyway – and you have gifts you know nothing about yet. Learn what you can from me, young hawk, and those others you find who can also teach you. Who knows what your fate will be? There are many kinds of glory.' He upended the butt for another frothy mouthful.

After a moment's careful inspection of Morgenes, to make sure that the last speech was not just another tease, Simon at last permitted himself a shy grin. He liked being called 'young hawk.'

'Very well, then. And I *am* sorry that I told you a lie. But if I have keen wit, why will you not show me anything important?'

'Like what?' Morgenes asked, his smile fading.

'Oh, I don't know. Magic . . . or something.'

'*Magic!*' Morgenes hissed. 'Is that all you think about, boy? Do you think I am some hedge-wizard, some cheap-cloth court conjuror, that I should show you tricks?' Simon said nothing. 'I am still angry with you for lying to me,' the doctor added. 'Why should I reward you?'

'I will do any chores you want, at any hour,' Simon said. 'I'll even wash the ceiling.'

167

'Here now,' Morgenes responded, 'I will not be bullied. I tell you what, boy: leave off this endless fascination with magic and I will answer all your other questions for a month entire, and you shall not have to write down a one! How's that, hey?'

Simon squinted, but said nothing.

'Well then, I shall let you read my manuscript on the life of Prester John!' the doctor offered. 'I remember you asked about that once or twice.'

Simon squinted harder. 'If you'll teach me magic,' he suggested, 'I'll bring you one of Judith's pies every week, and a barrel of Stanshire dark from the larder.'

'There now!' Morgenes barked triumphantly. 'See?! Do you see, boy? So convinced are you that magical tricks will bring you power and good luck that you are quite willing to steal and bribe me into teaching you! No, Simon, I cannot make bargains with you over this.'

Simon was angry again, but took a deep breath and pinched his arm. 'Why are you so set against it, Doctor?' he asked when he felt calmer. 'Because I am a scullion?'

Morgenes smiled. 'Even if you still labor in the scullery, Simon-lad, you are no scullion. You are my apprentice. No, there is no deficiency in you – except for your age and immaturity. You simply do not comprehend what you are asking.'

Simon slumped onto a stool. 'I don't understand,' he murmured.

'Exactly.' Morgenes downed another gulp of ale. 'What you call "magic" is really only the action of things of nature, elemental forces much like fire and wind. They respond to natural laws – but those laws are very hard to learn and understand. Many may never be understood.'

'But why don't you *teach* me the laws!?'

'For the same reason I wouldn't give a burning torch to an infant sitting on a pile of straw. The infant – and no insult is meant, Simon – is not prepared for the responsibility. Only those who have studied many years in many other subjects and disciplines can begin to master the Art that fascinates you so. Even then they are not necessarily fit to wield any power.' The old man drank again, wiped his lips and smiled. 'By the time most of us are capable of using the Art, we are old enough to know better. It is too dangerous for the young, Simon.'

'But . . .'

'If you say: "But Pryrates . . ." I shall kick you,' Morgenes said. 'I told you once, he is a madman – or as good as. He sees only the power to be gained from wielding the Art, and ignores the consequences. Ask me about the consequences, Simon.'

He asked dully: 'What about the con . . .'

'You cannot exert force without paying for it, Simon. If you steal a pie, someone else goes hungry. If you ride a horse too fast, the horse dies. If you use the Art to open doors, Simon, you have little choice of houseguests.'

Simon, disappointed, glared around the dusty room. 'Why do you have those signs painted over *your* door, Doctor?' he asked at last.

'So no one else's houseguests come a-visiting *me*.' Morgenes stooped to put his flagon down, and as he did so something gold and shining fell out of the collar of his gray robe, tumbling down to dangle swinging on its chain. The doctor seemed not to notice. 'I should send you back, now. But remember this lesson, Simon, one fit for kings . . . or the sons of kings. *Nothing is without cost.* There is a price to all power, and it is not always obvious. Promise me you will remember that.'

'I promise, doctor.' Simon, feeling the effects of the earlier crying and shouting, was as lightheaded as if he had run a race. 'What is that thing?' he asked, bending forward to watch the golden object pendulum back and forth. Morgenes held it out on his palm, giving Simon a brief look.

'It's a feather,' the doctor said shortly. As he dropped the gleaming thing back into his robe, Simon saw that the quill end of the golden feather was attached to a writing scroll carved of pearly white stone.

169

'No, it's a pen,' he said wonderingly, ' – a quill pen, isn't it?'

'Very well, it's a pen.' Morgenes growled. 'Now if you have nothing better to do than interrogate me about my personal ornaments, be off with you! And don't forget your promise! Remember!'

Wandering back to the servants' quarters across the hedged courtyard gardens, Simon wondered at the events of a strange morning. The doctor had found out about the letter, but didn't punish him, or throw him out, never to return. However, he had also refused to teach Simon anything about magic. And why had his assertion about the quill-pendant irritated the old man so?

Pondering, plucking absently at the dry, unbudded rosebushes, Simon pricked his finger on a hidden thorn. Cursing, he held up his hand. The bright blood was a red bead on his fingertip, a single crimson pearl. He stuck his finger in his mouth and tasted salt.

In the darkest part of the night, on the very cusp of All Fool's Day, a tremendous crash reverberated through the Hayholt. It rattled sleepers awake in their beds and drew a long, sympathetic hum from the dark bell clusters in Green Angel Tower.

Some of the young priests, gleefully ignoring midnight prayers on this, their once-yearly night of freedom, were struck from their stools as they sat swilling wine and insulting Bishop Domitis; the concussive force of the blow was so great that even the drunkest felt a wave of terror run through them, as though in a deep-sunken part of themselves they had known all along that God would eventually make his displeasure felt.

But when the ragged, startled crew milled out to the courtyard to see what had happened, shaven acolyte heads like so many pale mushrooms in the silky moon-light, there was no shape of the universal cataclysm they had all expected. Except for a few faces of other recently-wakened castle-dwellers peering curiously from the windows, the night was untroubled and clear.

Simon was dreaming in his spare, curtained bed, nested among the treasures he had so carefully collected; in his dream he climbed a pillar of black ice, every straining inch upward eroded by a nearly identical slip backward. He clutched a parchment in his teeth, a message of some sort. At the topmost point of the cold-burning pillar was a door; in the doorway a dark presence crouched, waiting for him . . . waiting for the message.

As he finally reached the threshold a hand snaked out, grasping the parchment in an inky, vaporous fist. Simon tried to slide back, to fall away, but another dark claw jabbed out from the doorway and caught his wrist. He was drawn upward toward a pair of eyes, red-bright as paired crimson holes in the belly of an infernal black oven. . . .

As he woke gasping from sleep he heard the sullen voices of the bells, moaning their displeasure as they descended back into cold, brooding sleep.

Only one person in all the great castle claimed to have seen anything. Caleb the horse-boy, Shem's slow-witted assistant, had been terribly excited and unable to sleep all night. The next morning he was to be crowned King of Fools, and carried on the shoulders of the young priests as they marched through the castle singing bawdy songs and tossing oats and flower petals. They would take him to the refectory hall where he would preside over the All Fool's banquet from his mock throne built of Gleniwent river reeds.

Caleb had heard the great roar, he told any who would listen, but he had also heard *words*, a booming voice speaking a language that the stable boy could only say was 'bad.' He also seemed to think he had seen a great snake of fire leap from the window of Hjeldin's Tower, looping itself around the spire in flaming coils and then splintering into a shower of sparks.

No one paid Caleb's story much heed – there was a reason the simple-minded boy had been chosen King of Fools. Also, the dawn brought something to the Hayholt that eclipsed any thunder in the night, and even the prospects of Fool's Day.

Daylight revealed a line of clouds – rain clouds – crouching on the northern horizon like a flock of fat, gray sheep.

'By Dror's becrimsoned mallet, Udun's one dread eye, and . . . and . . . and our Lord Usires! Something must be done!'

Duke Isgrimnur, nearly forgetting his Aedonite piety in his wrath, brought his scarred, fur-knuckled fist down on the Great Table hard enough to make the crockery jump six feet away. His broad body swayed like an over-cargoed ship in a squall as he cast his eyes from one end of the table to the other, then brought his fist down again. A goblet teetered briefly, then surrendered to gravity.

'Steps must be taken, sire!' he roared, and tugged angrily at his belt-length whiskers. 'The Frostmarch is in a state of bedamned anarchy! While I sit here with my men like so many knots on a log, the Frostmarch Road has become a byway for bandits! And I have had no word from Elvritshalla for two months or more!' The duke blew out a great gust of air that made his mustache flutter. 'My son is in dread need, and I can do nothing! Where is the High King's ward of safety, my Lord?'

Reddening like a beet the Rimmersman dropped back into his chair. Elias raised a languid eyebrow and surveyed the other knights scattered about the

172

circumference of the table, far outnumbered by the empty chairs between them. The torches in the wall sconces threw long wavering shadows onto the high tapestries.

'Well, now that the aged but honorable Duke has made himself known, would anyone else like to join his suit?' Elias toyed with his own gold goblet, scuffing it along the crescent-shaped scars in the oak. 'Is there anyone else who feels that the High King of Osten Ard had deserted his subjects?' At the king's right hand Guthwulf smirked.

Isgrimnur, smarting, began to climb back to his feet, but Eolair of Nad Mullach laid a restraining hand on the old duke's arm.

'Sire,' Eolair said, 'neither Isgrimnur nor anyone else who has spoken is accusing you of anything.' The Hernystirman placed his palms flat on the table. 'What we are all saying then, is that we are asking – *entreating*, my lord – that you pay more heed to the problems of those of your subjects who live outside your view here at the Hayholt.' Perhaps thinking his words too harsh, Eolair summoned a smile onto his mobile face. 'The problems, they *are* there,' he continued. 'Outlawry is everywhere in the north and west. Starving men have few scruples, and the drought just ended has brought out the worst . . . in everyone.'

Elias, unspeaking, continued to stare at Eolair after the westerner had finished. Isgrimnur couldn't help noticing how pale the king looked. It reminded the older man of the time in the southern islands that he had nursed Elias' father John through a bout of fever.

*That bright eye*, he thought, *that nose like a hunting bird. Odd how these bits, these brief expressions and reminders, go on generation after generation – long after the man and his works are dead.*

Isgrimnur thought of Miriamele, Elias' pretty, melancholy child. He wondered what baggage of her father's she would carry on, what disparate images of her beautiful haunted mother, dead ten years now – or was it twelve?

Across the table Elias shook his head slowly, as if waking from a dream or trying to dispel the wine fumes from his head. Isgrimnur saw Pryrates, seated at the king's left side, quickly withdraw his pale hand from Elias' sleeve. There was something abhorrent about the priest, Isgrimnur thought, not for the first time, something far deeper than merely his hairlessness and scratchy voice.

'Well, Count Eolair,' the king said, an elusive smile briefly twitching on his lips, 'as long as we are speaking of "obligations" and such, what does your kinsman King Lluth have to say about the message I sent him?' He leaned forward with apparent interest, his powerful hands folded on the table.

Eolair replied in measured tones, choosing his words with care. 'As always, Lord, he sends his respect and love to noble Erkynland. He does feel, though, that he cannot afford to send more in the way of taxes . . .'

'Tribute!' snorted Guthwulf, picking his nails with a slim poniard.

'. . . In the way of taxes right now,' Eolair finished, ignoring the interruption.

'Is that so?' Elias asked, and smiled again.

'Actually, my lord,' Eolair deliberately misread the smile's import, 'he sent for me to ask you for royal help. You know the troubles the drought has caused, and the plague. The Erkynguard must work with us to keep the trade roads open.'

'Oh, they must, must they?' King Elias' eyes glinted, and a tiny throb began between the strong cords of his neck. 'It is "must" now, is it?' He leaned farther forward, shaking off Pryrates' serpent-swift restraining hand. 'And who are you,' he growled, 'the weanling stepcousin of a sheepherder-king – who is only a king at all by my father's weak-willed forebearance! – who are you to tell me "*must*"!?'

'My Lord!' cried old Fluiren of Nabban in horror, flapping his spotted hands – mighty hands once, now bent and curled like a hawk's feet. 'My Lord,' he panted, 'your anger is kingly, but Hernystir is a trusted ally under your father's High Ward – not to mention his country was the birth-land of your saintly mother, rest her soul! Please, sire, do not speak so of Lluth!'

Elias swung his emerald gaze to Fluiren, and seemed about to focus his wrath on that diminished hero, but Pryrates tugged the king's dark sleeve again and leaned close to mouth a few words in Elias' ear. The king's expression softened, but the line of his jaw remained taut as a bowstring. Even the air over the table seemed pulled tight, a grinding net of awful possibility.

'Forgive me for the unforgivable, Count Eolair,' Elias said at last, a strange, stupid grin stretching the corners of his mouth wide. 'Forgive me my harsh, causeless words. It has been less than a month since the rains began, and it was a difficult twelvemonth for us all before that.'

Eolair nodded, his clever eyes uneasy. 'Of course, Highness. I understand. Please, you'll grant me your pardon for provoking you.' Across the oval table Fluiren folded his mottled hands with a satisfied nod.

Isgrimnur now rose to his feet, ponderous as a brown bear climbing an ice floe. 'I, too, Sire, shall try to speak in a gentle fashion, though you all know it is clean against my soldier's nature.'

Elias' cheerful grimace remained. 'Very good, Uncle Bear-skin – we will all practice gentility together. What would you of your king?'

The Duke of Elvritshalla took a deep breath, nervously finger-tangling his beard. 'Mine and Eolair's people are in dire need, Lord. For the first time since the earliest part of John Presbyter's reign, the Frostmarch Road has again become impassable – blizzards in the north, highway robbers further south. The royal North Road past Wealdhelm is not much better. We need these roads open, and kept so.' Isgrimnur leaned to the side and spat

175

on the floor. Fluiren winced. 'Many of the clan-villages, according to my son Isorn's last letter, are suffering for lack of food. We cannot trade our goods, we cannot keep contact with the more remote clans.'

Guthwulf, carving at the table's edge, yawned conspicuously. Heahferth and Godwig, two younger barons wearing prominent green sashes, quietly tittered.

'Surely, Duke,' Guthwulf drawled, leaning back against the arm of his chair like a sun-warmed cat, 'you don't blame us for that. Has our lord the king powers like God Almighty – to stop the snows and storms with a wave of his hand?'

'I do not suggest that he should!' Isgrimnur rumbled.

'Perhaps,' Pryrates said from the head of the table, his wide smile strangely inappropriate, 'you also blame the king for his brother's disappearance, as we have heard it rumored?'

'Never!' Isgrimnur was genuinely shocked. Beside him Eolair narrowed his eyes, as if seeing something unexpected. 'Never!' the duke repeated, looking helplessly at Elias.

'Now, men, I know Isgrimnur would never think such a thing,' the king said, waving a listless hand. 'Why, old Uncle Bear-skin dandled both Josua and myself on his knees. I hope, of course that Josua has suffered no harm – the fact that he has not appeared at Naglimund in all this time is troubling – but if anything foul is afoot it is not *my* conscience that will need soothing.' But as he finished, for a moment Elias *did* look troubled, staring at nothing as though he wandered through a confusing memory.

'Let me get back to the point, Lord,' Isgrimnur said. 'The northern roads are not safe, and weather is not the only factor. My carls are spread too thin. We need more men – strong men to make the Frostmarch safe again. The marchland is aswarm with robbers and outlaws and . . . and worse things, some say.'

Pryrates leaned forward interestedly, chin perched on long-fingered hands like a child watching rain through a window, sunken eyes catching the torches' gleam. '*What* "worse things," noble Isgrimnur?'

'It's not important. People think . . . things, that is all. You know how the marchdwellers are . . .' The Rimmersman trailed off, taking an embarrassed draft of his wine.

Eolair rose. 'If he will not voice his thoughts, what we have heard in the markets and among the servants, I will. The northern people are afraid. There are things going about that cannot be explained by deadly weather and bad harvests. In my land we do not need to name things angels and devils. We of Hernystir – we of the West – know that things walk upright on this earth that are not men . . . *and* we know whether to fear them or not. We Hernystiri knew the Sithi when they still lived in our fields, when the high mountains and wide meadows of Erkynland were theirs.'

The torches were guttering now, and Eolair's high forehead and cheeks seemed to shine with a faint scarlet radiance. 'We have not forgotten,' he said quietly. His voice carried even to half-sleeping Godwig, who lifted his drunken head like a hound hearing a distant call. 'We, the Hernystiri, remember the days of the giants, and the days of the northern curse, the White Foxes, so now we speak plainly: evil is abroad in this ill-omened winter and spring. It is not only the bandits that prey on travelers, and who cause the disappearance of isolated farmers. The people of the North are afraid . . .'

' "We the Hernystiri"!' Pryrates' mocking voice lanced out through the silence, skewering the spell of otherworldliness. ' "We the Hernystiri!" Our noble pagan friend claims to speak plainly!' Pryrates traced an exaggerated Tree on the breast of his unpriestly red vestments. Elias' expression turned to sly good humor. 'Very well!' the priest continued. 'He has delivered us the plainest pack of riddles and shadow-talk I have ever heard! Giants and elves!' Pryrates flicked his hand, and his sleeve fluttered above the dinner plates. 'As if his majesty the king did not have enough to worry about – his brother vanished, his subjects hungry and frightened – as if even the king's great heart was not near-to-breaking! And you, Eolair, you bring him pagan ghost stories from the mouths of old wives!'

'He be pagan, yes,' growled Isgrimnur, 'but there be more Aedonite good will in Eolair than in the pack of lazy pups I have seen lolling around this court . . .' – Baron Heahferth barked, drawing drunken laughter from Godwig – 'lolling around while the people have been living on meager hope and less harvest!'

'It's all right then, Isgrimnur,' said Eolair wearily.

'My lords!' Fluiren flapped.

'Well, I will not hear you insulted so for your honesty!' Isgrimnur rumbled at Eolair. He lifted his fist to hammer the table again, then thought better of it, bringing it instead to his breast where it enfolded the wooden Tree hanging there. 'Forgive my outburst, my king, but Count Eolair tells the truth. Whether their fears have substance or no, the people *do* fear.'

'And what do they fear, dear old Uncle Bear-skin?' asked the king as he held his goblet for Guthwulf to refill.

'They fear the dark,' the old man said, all dignity now. 'They fear the winter's dark, and they fear the world will grow darker still.'

Eolair turned his empty cup upside-down on the table. 'In Erchester's market the few merchants who have been able to come south fill the people's ears with news of a strange vision. I have heard the same story so many times that I do not doubt everyone in the town has heard it, too.' Eolair paused and looked at the Rimmersman, who nodded once, gravely, creasing the gray-shot beard.

'Well?' said Elias impatiently.

'In the Frostmarch wastes at night, a wonderful thing has been seen – a cart, a black cart, drawn by white horses . . .'

'How unusual!' Guthwulf sneered, but Pryrates and

Elias locked eyes of a sudden. The king raised an eyebrow as he rechanneled his gaze to the westerner.

'Go on.'

'Those who have seen it say it appeared a few days after All Fool's Day. They say the cart bears a casket, and that black-robed monks walk behind it.'

'And to what heathen nature-sprite do the peasants attribute this vision?' Elias leaned slowly backward in his chair, until he was looking down the bridge of his nose at the Hernystirman.

'They say, my king, that it is your father's death-cart – begging your pardon, sire – and that as long as the land suffers, he shall not sleep peacefully in his barrow.'

After an interval the king spoke, his voice barely louder than the hissing of the torches.

'Well, then,' he said, 'we will have to make sure my father gets his well-earned rest, will we not?'

*Look at them,* old Towser thought as he dragged his bent leg and tired body up the aisle of the throne room. *Look at them, all lollying and smirking – they look more like heathen chiefs of the Thrithings than Aedonite knights of Erkynland.*

Elias' courtiers hooted and called out as the jester limped by, wagging their heads at him as though he were a Naraxi ape on a chain. Even the king and the King's Hand, Earl Guthwulf, whose chair was pulled up next to the throne, contributed to the rough jests; Elias sat with a leg up on the arm of the Dragonbone Chair like a farm lout on a gate. Only the king's young daughter Miriamele sat stiffly silent, pretty face solemn, shoulders pulled back as if she were expecting a blow. Her honey-colored hair – which came from neither her dark father nor raven-haired mother – hung down on either side of her face like curtains.

*She looks like she's trying to hide behind that hair,* thought Towser. *What a shame. They say that the freckled darling is*

*stubborn and forward, but all I see in her eyes is fear. She
deserves better, I suspect, than the swaggering wolves who
prowl our castles these days, but they say her father's promised
her already to that be-damned drunken strutter Fengbald.*

He did not make swift progress, his path to the throne
hindered by the hands that reached out to pat or lightly
slap at him. It was said to be good luck to touch the head
of a dwarf. Towser was not one, but he was old, very
old, and bent, it amused the courtiers to treat him as if he
were.

He reached Elias' throne at last. The king's eyes were
red-rimmed with too much drink or too little sleep, or –
most likely – both.

Elias turned his green gaze downward to the little man.
'So, my dear Towser,' he said, 'you grace us with your
company.' The jester noticed that the buttons of the
King's white blouse were undone, and that there was a
gravy stain on the beautiful doeskin gloves tucked into
his belt.

'Yes, sire, I have come.' Towser assayed a bow,
difficult with his stiff leg; a sputter of mirth came from
the lords and ladies.

'Before you entertain us, oldest jester,' Elias said,
swinging his leg down off the throne arm and fixing the
old man with his most sincere stare, 'may I perhaps beg
of you a small favor? A question I have long wanted to
ask?'

'Of course, my king.'

'Then tell me, Towser dear, however did you happen
to be given a *dog's name?*' Elias raised his eyebrows in
mock puzzlement, turning first to look at Guthwulf,
who grinned, and then to Miriamele, who looked away.
The rest of the courtiers laughed and whispered behind
their hands.

'I was not given a dog's name, sire,' said Towser
quietly. 'I chose it for myself.'

'What!' said Elias, turning to the old man once more. 'I
don't think that I heard you properly.'

180

'I gave *myself* a dog's name, sire. Your noble father used to tease me for being so faithful, because I would always go with him, would be at his side. As a jest he named one of his hounds "Cruinh," the which was my given name.' The old man turned slightly, so as to play to the crowd more fully. ' "So then," quoth I, "if the dog be given my name by John's will, then I shall take the dog's in turn." I have never answered since to any name but Towser, and never shall.' Towser permitted himself a tiny smile. 'It is possible that your revered father regretted somewhat his joke thereafter.'

Elias did not seem altogether pleased with this answer, but laughed sharply anyway and slapped his knee. 'A saucy dwarf, is he not?' he said, looking around. The others assembled, trying to take the king's mood, laughed politely – all but Miriamele, who looked down on Towser from her high-backed chair, her face caught in an intricate expression whose meaning he could not unpuzzle.

'Well,' said Elias, 'If I were not the good king that I am – were I, say for instance, a pagan king like Hernystir's Lluth – I might have thy minuscule, wrinkled head off for speaking so of my late father. But, of course, I am not such a king.'

'Of course not, sire,' Towser said.

'Are you come to sing for us, then, or to tumble – we hope not, since you appear over-frail for such antics – or what? Come, tell us.' Elias eased himself back in his throne and clapped for more wine.

'To sing, Majesty,' the jester replied. He took the lute from off his shoulder and began to turn the pegs, bringing it into tune. As a young page scurried over to fill the king's cup, Towser looked up to the ceiling where the banners of Osten Ard's knights and nobles hung before the rain-splashed upper windows. The dust was now gone and the cobwebs dispersed, but to Towser the bright colors of the pennoncels seemed false – too bright, like the painted skin of a drab who hopes to mimic her

181

own younger days, thus destroying what true beauty remains.

As the nervous page finished filling the goblets of Guthwulf, Fengbald, and the others, Elias waved his hand at Towser.

'My lord,' he nodded, 'I will sing of another good king – this one an unfortunate and sad monarch, however.'

'I do not like sad songs,' said Fengbald; he was, predictably, well into his cups. Beside him, Guthwulf smirked.

'Hush.' The King's Hand made a show of elbowing his companion. 'If we do not like the tune when he has finished, *then* we can make the dwarf hop.'

Towser cleared his throat and strummed, singing then in his thin, sweet voice:

> 'Old King Juniper
> Mickle old was he
> Snowy-white his beard that hung
> From chin to bony knee.
>
> Noble old King Juniper
> Sitting on his throne
> Called: "Now bring my sons to me,
> For soon I will be gone."
>
> They brought him then his princely sons
> They came with hounds and hawks
> The younger hight Prince Holly
> The older Prince Hemlock.
>
> "We have heard thy summons, sire,
> And left our hunt withal."
> So Hemlock said, "What wouldst thou
> That thou biddest us to thy hall?"
>
> "I soon must die, my princely sons,"
> The aged king he said.
> "And would see peace between thou twain
> When I at last am dead . . ." '

182

'I do not think I like the sound of this song,' growled Guthwulf. 'It has a mocking tone.'

Elias bade him be silent; his eyes gleamed as he signaled Towser to continue.

> ' "But father dear, why dost thou fear?
> Prince Hemlock has the right."
> Said Holly, "I could not counter him
> And be a Godly knight."
>
> His mind thus eased, the King did bid
> His sons go out again
> And thanked merciful Aedon
> That they were such goodly men.
>
> But in the heart of Hemlock
> Who was the king-to-be
> Prince Holly's words so gentle
> Sparked a fire of infamy.
>
> "That speaks so sweet a princely tongue
> Must wicked heart disguise."
> Thought Hemlock, "Gainst my crafty kin
> I must some scheme devise."
>
> So fearing then the gentle heart
> That beat in Holly's breast
> He took a draught of poison
> From out the lining of his vest.
>
> And when the brothers sate at meat
> He poured it in a cup
> And bade Prince Holly drink it down . . .'

'Enough! This is treason!' roared Guthwulf as he leaped up, knocking his chair back among the startled courtiers; his long sword hissed free of its scabbard. Had Fengbald not sprung up in befuddlement, entangling his arm, Guthwulf would have lunged at the quailing Towser.

Elias, too, was quickly on his feet. 'Sheathe that

183

bodkin, you lackwit!' he shouted. 'No one draws sword in the king's throne room!' He turned from the snarling Earl of Utanyeat to the jester. The old man, having recovered somewhat from the alarming spectacle of Guthwulf enraged, struggled to put on dignity.

'Do not think, dwarfish creature, that we are amused by your little song,' the king snarled, 'or that your long service for my father makes you untouchable – but do not think either that you can prickle the royal skin with such dull barbs. Get you out of my sight!'

'I confess, sire, that the song was a new-minted one,' began the jester shakily. His belled hat was askew. 'But it was not . . .'

'*Get you hence!*' Elias spat, all pale face and beast's eyes. Towser hobbled quickly out of the throne room, shuddering at the king's last, wild look, and the caged, hopeless face of his daughter, Princess Miriamele.

# 11

# An Unexpected Guest

Middling afternoon on the last day of Avrel; Simon was sunk in the stable's dark hayloft, comfortably adrift in a scratchy yellow sea, only his head above the dusty billows. The haydust sparkled down past the wide window as he listened to his own measured breath.

He had just come down from the shadowed gallery of the chapel, where the monks had been singing the noon rites. The clean, sculpted tones of their solemn prayers had touched him in a way that the chapel, and the dry doings within its tapestried walls, seldom did – each note so carefully held and then lovingly released, like a woodcarver putting delicate toy boats into a stream. The singing voices had wrapped his secret heart in a sweet, cold net of silver; the tender resignation of its strands still clutched him. It had been such a strange sensation: for a moment he had felt himself all feathers and racing heartbeat – a frightened bird cupped in the hands of God.

He had run down the gallery steps, feeling suddenly unworthy of such solicitousness and delicacy – he was too clumsy, too foolish. It seemed that he might, with his chapped scullion's hands, somehow mishandle the beautiful music, as a child might unwittingly trample a butterfly.

Now, in the hayloft, his heart began to slow. He buried himself deep in the musty, whispering straw, and with his eyes closed listened to the gentle snorting of the horses in their stalls below. He thought he could feel the almost insensible touch of the dust motes as they drifted down onto his face in the still, drowsy darkness.

He might have dozed – he couldn't be sure – but the next thing Simon noticed was the sudden, sharp sound of voices below him. Rolling over, he swam through the tickling straw to the loft's edge, until he could see down to the stable below.

There were three: Shem Horsegroom, Ruben the Bear, and a little man that Simon thought might be Towser, the old jester – he couldn't be sure because this one wore no motley, and had a hat that covered much of his face. They had all come in through the stable doors like a trio of comic fools; Ruben the Bear swung a jug from a fist as broad as a leg of spring lamb. All three were drunk as birds in a berry-bush, and Towser – if it was he – was singing an old tune:

> 'Jack take a maid
> Up on the cheery hill
> Sing a way-o, hey-o
> Half-a-crown day . . .'

Ruben handed the jug to the little man. The weight over-balanced him in midchorus so that he staggered a step and then tumbled over, his hat flying off. It was indeed Towser; as he rolled to a stop Simon could see his seamed, purse-mouthed face begin to wrinkle up at his eyes, as though he would cry like a baby. Instead he began to laugh helplessly, leaning against the wall with the jug between his knees. His two companions tromped unsteadily over to join him. They sat all in a row, like magpies on a fence.

Simon was wondering if he should announce himself; he didn't know Towser well, but he had always been friendly with Shem and Ruben. After a moment's consideration he decided against it. It was more fun watching them unsuspected – perhaps he would be able to think of a trick to play! He made himself comfortable, secret and silent in the high loft.

'By Saint Muirfath and the Archangel,' Towser said with a sigh after a few sodden moments had passed, 'I had sore need of this!' He ran his forefinger around the lip of the jug, then put the finger in his mouth.

Shem Horsegroom reached to him across the smith's broad stomach and took the jug for a swallow. He wiped his lips with the back of a leathery hand. 'Whur will ye go, then?' he asked the jester. Towser vented a sigh. The life suddenly seemed to drain out of the little drinking party; all stared glumly at the floor.

'I have some kinfolk – distant kinfolk – in Grenefod, at the river's mouth. Mayhap I will go there, although I doubt they'll be too happy with another mouth to feed. Mayhap I will go north to Naglimund.'

'But Josua is gone,' said Ruben, and belched.

'Aye, goon away,' added Shem.

Towser closed his eyes and bumped his head back against the rough wood of the paddock door. 'But Josua's people still hold Naglimund, and they will have sympathies for someone chased out of his home by Elias' churls – even more sympathy now, when people say that Elias has murdered poor Prince Josua.'

'But other'uns say that *Joosua* has turn traitor,' Shem offered, rubbing his chin sleepily.

'Pfagh.' The little jester spat. In the loft above, Simon, too, felt the warmth of the spring afternoon, the drowsy, dragging weight of it. It lent the conversation below an air of unimportance, of distance – murder and treachery seemed the names of faraway places.

During the long pause which followed, Simon felt his eyelids creeping inexorably downward . . .

'Mayhap it been not sich a wise thing t'do, brother Towser . . .' – Shem was speaking now, skinny old

187

Shem, as gaunt and weathered as something hung in a smokehouse – '. . . baitin' the king, I mean. Did ye need to sing sich a goadin' song?'

'Hah!' Towser scratched his nose busily. 'My western ancestors, they were *true* bards, not limping old tumblers like me. They would have sung him a song to curl his ears up rightly! They say that the poet Eoin-ec-Cluias once made an anger-song so mighty that all the golden bees of the Grianspog descended on the chieftain Gormhbata and stung him to death . . . *that* was a song!' The old jester leaned his head back once more against the stable wall. 'The king!? God's teeth, I cannot stand even to call him such. I was with his sainted father man and boy – *there* was a king you could call a king! This one is no better than a brigand . . . not half the man that his . . . father John was. . . .'

Towser's voice wavered sleepily. Shem Horsegroom's head slowly fell forward onto his breast. Ruben's eyes were open, but it was as though he looked into the darkest spaces between the rafters. Beside him Towser stirred once more.

'Did I tell you,' the old man abruptly said, 'did I tell you about the king's sword? King John's sword – Bright-Nail? He gave it to me, you know, saying: "Towser, only you can pass this to my son Elias. Only you. . . !" ' A tear winked on the jester's furrowed cheek. ' "Take my son to the throne room and give him Bright-Nail," he told me – and I did! I brought it to him the night his dear father died . . . put it in his hand just the way his father told me to . . . and he dropped it!. *Dropped it!*' Towser's voice rose in anger. 'The sword that his father carried into more battles than a brachet has fleas! I could scarce believe such clumsiness, such . . . disrespect! Are you listening Shem? Ruben?' Beside him the smith grunted.

'Hist! I was horrified, of course. I picked it up and wiped it with the linen wrappings and gave it to him; this time he took it with two hands. "It twisted," he said, like an idiot. Now as he held it again the strangest look passed over his face, like . . . like . . .' The jester trailed off. Simon was afraid he had fallen asleep, but apparently the little man was merely thinking, in a slow, wine-addled way.

'The look on his face,' Towser resumed, 'was like a child caught doing something very, very wicked – that was it exactly! Exactly! He turned pale, and his mouth went all slack – and he handed it back to me! "Bury this with my father," he said. "It is his sword; he should have it with him." – "But he wanted it given to *you*, my lord!" I said . . . but would he listen? Would he? No. "This is a new age, old man," he told me, "we do not need to dote on these relics of the past." Can you imagine the thundering gall of such a man!?'

Towser searched around with his hand until he found the jug and lifted it up for a long drink. Both his companions now had closed their eyes and were breathing hoarsely, but the little old man paid no notice, lost in indignant reverie.

'And then he would not even do his poor dead father the courtesy of . . . placing it in the grave himself. Wouldn't . . . wouldn't even touch it! Made his younger brother do it! Made Josua . . .' Towser's bald head nodded. 'You'd have thought it burned him . . . to see him hand it back . . . so swift . . . damned puppy . . .' Towser's head bobbed once more, sank to his breast, and did not come up again.

As Simon came quietly down the hayloft ladder, the three men were already snoring like old dogs before a fireplace. He crept past them on his toe-tips, kindly halting to stopper the jug lest one of them knock it over with a sleep-flung arm. He moved out into the slanting sunlight on the commons.

*So many strange things have happened this year,* he thought as he sat dropping pebbles into the well in the center of the commons yard. *Drought and sickness, the*

*prince disappeared, people burned and killed in Falshire . . .*
But somehow none of it seemed very serious.

*Everything happens to someone else,* Simon decided,
half-glad, half-regretful. *Everything happens to strangers.*

She was curled up in the window seat, staring down
through the delicately etched panes at something below.
She did not look up when he entered, although the scuff
of his boots on the flagstones announced him clearly; he
stood for a moment in the doorway, arms folded across
his breast, but still she did not turn. He strode forward
and then stopped, looking over her shoulder.

There was nothing to see in the commons but a kitchen
boy sitting on the rim of the stone cistern, a long-legged,
shock-haired youth in a stained smock. The yard was
otherwise empty of anything but sheep, dirty bundles of
wool searching the dark ground for patches of new grass.

'What is wrong?' he asked, laying a broad hand on her
shoulder. 'Do you hate me now, that you should stalk
away without a word?'

She shook her head, briefly netting a stripe of sunlight
in her hair. Her hand stole up to his and grasped it with
cool fingers.

'No,' she said, still staring at the deserted acre below.
'But I hate the things I see around me.' He leaned
forward, but she quickly pulled her hand free and lifted it
to her face, as if to shade it from the afternoon sun.

'What things?' he asked, a measure of exasperation
creeping into his voice. 'Would you rather be back in
Meremund, living in that drafty prison of a place my
father gave me, with the smell of fish poisoning the air of
even the highest balconies?' He reached down and
cupped her chin, turning it with firm gentleness until he
could see her angry, tearful eyes.

'Yes!' she said, and pushed his hand away, but now she

190

held his gaze. 'Yes, I would. You can smell the wind there, too, and you can see the ocean.'

'Oh, God, girl, the ocean? You are mistress of the known world and yet you cry because you can't see the damnable water? Look! Look there!' He pointed out past the Hayholt's walls. 'What, then, is the Kynslagh?'

She looked back with scorn. 'That is a bay, a king's bay, which waits passively for the king to boat on it, or swim in it. No king owns the sea.'

'Ah.' He dropped onto a hassock, his long legs splayed on either side. 'And the thought behind this all, I suppose, is that you are prisoned here too, eh? What nonsense! I know why you are upset.'

She turned fully away from the window, her eyes intent. 'You do?' she asked, and beneath the scorn fluttered a tiny breath of hope. 'Tell me why, then, Father.'

Elias laughed. 'Because you are about to be married. It is not surprising at all!' He slid nearer. 'Ah, Miri, there's nothing to be afraid of. Fengbald is a swaggerer, but he's young and still foolish. With a woman's patient hand at work he'll learn manners soon enough. And if he doesn't – well, it would show him a fool indeed were he to mistreat the king's daughter.'

Miriamele's face hardened into a look of resignation. 'You don't understand.' Her tone was flat as a tax collector's. 'Fengbald is of no more interest to me than a rock, or a shoe. It's you who I care about – and it's you who has something to fear. Why do you show off for them? Why do you mock and threaten old men?'

'Mock and threaten?!' For a moment Elias' broad face curled into an ugly snarl. 'That old whoreson sings a song that as much as accuses me of doing away with my brother, and you say I mocked him?' The king stood up suddenly, giving the hassock an angry push with his foot that sent it spinning across the floor. 'What do I have to fear?' he asked suddenly.

'If you don't know, Father – you who spend so much

191

time around that red snake Pryrates and his deviltry – if you can't feel what's happening . . .'

'What in Aedon's name are you saying?' the king demanded. 'What do you know?' He struck his hand against his thigh with a crack. 'Nothing! Pryrates is my able servant – he will do for me what no one else can.'

'He is a monster and a necromancer!' the princess shouted. 'You are becoming his tool, Father! What has happened to you? You have changed!' Miriamele made an anguished sound, trying to bury her face in her long blue veil, then leaped up to dash past on velvet-slippered feet into her bedchamber. A moment later she had pushed the heavy door closed behind her.

'Damn all children!' Elias swore. 'Girl!' he shouted, striding to the door, 'you understand *nothing!* You know nothing about what the king is called on to do. And you have no right to be disobedient. I have no son! *I have no heir!* There are ambitious men all around me, and I need Fengbald. You will not thwart me!'

He stood for a long moment, but there was no reply. He struck the heel of his hand against the door and the timbers shuddered.

'Miriamele! Open the door!' Only silence answered him. 'Daughter,' he said at last, leaning his head forward until it touched the unyielding wood, 'only bear me a grandson, and I will give you Meremund. I will see that Fengbald does not hinder your going. You may spend the rest of your life staring at the ocean.' He brought up his hand and wiped something from his face. 'I do not like to look at the ocean myself . . . it makes me think of your mother.'

One more time he struck the door. The echo bloomed and died. 'I love you, Miri . . .' the king said softly.

The turret at the corner of the western wall had taken the first bite out of the afternoon sun. Another pebble rattled down the cistern, following a hundred of its fellows into oblivion.

*I'm hungry,* Simon decided.

It would not be a bad idea, he reflected, to wander over to the pantry and beg something to eat from Judith. The evening meal would not be served for at least an hour, and he was uncomfortably aware that he hadn't had a bite since early morning. The one problem was that Rachel and her crew were cleaning out the long refectory hallway and chambers alongside the dining hall, the latest battle in Rachel's strenuous spring campaign. It would certainly be better, if possible, to circumvent the Dragon and any words she might have to offer on the subject of begging food before supper.

After a moment's consideration, during which time he sent three more stones tick-tack-ticking down the well, Simon decided it would be safer to go under the Dragon than around her. The refectory hall took up the entire length of the upper story along the seawall of the castle's central keep; it would take a very long time to go all the way around by the Chancelry to come at the kitchens on the far side. No, the storage rooms were the only route.

He took a chance on a quick dash from the commons yard across the western portico of the refectory, and made it through unobserved. A whiff of soapy water and the distant slosh of mops hastened his steps as he ducked into the darkened lower floor, and the rooms of stored goods that took up most of the area below the dining halls.

Since this floor was a good six or seven ells below the top of the Inner Bailey walls, only the faintest gleam of reflected light made its way in through the windows. The deep shadows reassured Simon. Because of many combustibles, torches were almost never brought down to these rooms – there was little chance he would be discovered.

In the large central chamber great piles of iron-banded casks and butts were stacked to the ceiling, a murky

193

landscape of rounded towers and close-hemmed passages. Anything might be stored in these barrels: dried vegetables, cheeses, bolts of fabric from years long past, even suits of armor like shining fish in casks of midnight-dark oil. The temptation to open some and see what treasures lay hidden privily inside was very strong, but Simon had no prybar to unlid the heavy, tight-nailed barrels – neither did he dare make too much noise with the Dragon and her legions dusting and polishing away just above like the charwomen of the damned.

Midway across the long, shadowed room, threading his way between barrel-towers that leaned like cathedral buttresses, Simon nearly fell down a hole into darkness.

Dancing back in heart-thumping surprise, he quickly saw that rather than a mere hole it was a hatchway that gaped in the floor before him, its door flung open and back. With care he could step around it, despite the narrowness of the path . . . but why was it open? Obviously, heavy hatch-doors did not swing open unaided. Doubtless one of the housekeepers had brought something up from a storeroom farther below, and been unable to both manage the burden and close the door.

With only an instant's hesitation, Simon scrambled down the ladder into the hatchway. Who could say what strange, exciting things might be hiding in the room below?

The space beneath was darker than the room above, and at first he could see nothing at all. His groping foot encountered something below him; as he gingerly lowered his weight it took on the solidity of familiar board flooring. When he took the other foot off the ladder, however, it met no resistance at all – only his tight grip on the ladder-rung kept him from toppling off balance. There was still open space immediately below the ladder – another hatchway to a floor even further below. He maneuvered his swinging foot until it found the lip of the lower hatch, then moved off onto the security of this middle room's floor.

The hatch-door above him was a gray square in the wall of darkness. By its faint light he saw with disappointment that this area was little more than a closet: the roof was far lower than that of the upper room, and the walls extended back only a few arm's lengths from where he stood. This small room was crowded to the rafters with barrels and sacks, with only a small aisle that reached back to the far wall separating the leaning dry goods.

As he surveyed the closet with disinterest a board creaked somewhere, and he heard the measured sound of footsteps in the blackness below him.

*Oh, God's Pain, who's that?! And what have I done now?*

How stupid of him not to think that the hatchway might be open because someone was still down in the rooms below! He had done it *again*! Silently cursing himself for an idiot, he slid into the narrow aisle between the packed goods. The footfalls below approached the ladder. Simon wedged himself back off the aisle into a space between two musty plaincloth sacks that smelled and felt like they might be full of old linen. Realizing that he would still be visible to anyone who stepped away from the hatch and into the pathway, he sank into a half-crouch, resting his weight carefully on an oak-ribbed trunk. The steps halted, and the ladder began to creak as someone climbed up. He held his breath. He had no idea why he was suddenly so frightened; if he was caught it would only mean more punishment, more of Rachel's hard looks and peppery remarks – why then did he feel like a rabbit scented by hounds?

The sound of climbing continued, and for the moment it seemed that whoever it was would continue up to the large room above . . . until the steady creaking stopped. The silence sang in Simon's ears. There was a creak, then another – but he realized with a heavy feeling in his stomach that the noises were coming back down. A muffled bump as the unseen figure stepped off the ladder onto the floor of the closet, and again there was silence, but this time the very stillness seemed to throb. The slow tread moved closer down the slender aisle, until it halted directly across from Simon's hastily-chosen hiding place. In the dim light he could see pointed black boots, almost close enough to touch; above hung the black-trimmed hem of a scarlet robe. It was Pryrates.

Simon crouched back among the dry goods and prayed that Aedon would stop his heart, which seemed to be beating like thunder. He felt his gaze drawn upward against his will until he stared out between the sagging shoulders of the sacks that hid him. Through the narrow gap he could see the alchemist's bleak face; for a moment it seemed Pryrates looked right at him, and he nearly squealed in terror. An instant later he saw it was not so: the red priest's shadow-shrouded eyes were focused on the wall above Simon's head. He was listening.

*Come out.*

Pryrates' lips had not moved, but Simon heard the voice as plainly as if it had whispered in his ear.

*Come out. Now.*

The voice was firm but reasonable. Simon found himself ashamed at his conduct: there was nothing to fear; it was childish foolishness to crouch here in the dark when he could stand up and reveal himself, admit the little joke he had played . . . but still . . .

*Where are you? Show yourself.*

Just as the calm voice in his ear had finally convinced him that nothing would be simpler than to stand and speak – he was reaching for the sacks to help himself up – Pryrates' black eyes swept for a scant moment across the dark crack through which Simon peered, and the glancing touch killed any thought of rising as a sudden frost shrivels a rose blossom. Pryrates' gaze touched Simon's hidden eyes and a door opened in the boy's heart; the shadow of destruction filled that doorway.

This *was* death – Simon knew it. He felt the cold

crumble of grave soil beneath his scraping fingers, the weight of dark, moist earth in his mouth and eyes. There were no more words now, no dispassionate voice in his head, only a pull – an untouchable something that was dragging him forward by fractions of inches. A worm of ice clasped itself around his heart as he fought – this was death waiting . . . *his* death. If he made a sound, the merest tremble or gasp, he would never see the sun again. He shut his eyes so tightly that his temples ached; he locked teeth and tongue against the straining need for breath. The silence hissed and pounded. The pull strengthened. Simon felt as though he were sinking slowly down into the crushing depths of the sea.

A sudden yowl was followed by Pryrates' startled curse. The intangible, throttling grip was gone; Simon's eyes popped open in time to see a sleek gray shape skitter past, leap over Pryrates' boots and streak to the hatchway, where it bounded down into darkness. The priest's surprised laughter scraped out, echoing dully in the cluttered room.

'A *cat*. . . ?'

After a pause of half a dozen heartbeats, the black boots turned away and moved back up the aisle. In a moment Simon heard the ladder-thongs squeaking. He continued to sit rigidly, his breathing shallow, all of his senses alarmed. Chill sweat was running into his eyes, but he did not lift his hand to wipe it away – not yet.

At last, after many minutes had passed and the ladder-sounds had faded, Simon rose from the sheltering sacks, balancing on weak, trembling legs. Praise Usires and bless that little gray scattercat! But what to do? He had heard the upper hatchway close, and the sound of booted footfalls on the floor overhead, but that did not mean that Pryrates had gone very far. It would be a risk even to lift the heavy door and look; if the priest were still in the storeroom the chances were good that he would hear. How could he get out?

He knew he should just stay where he was, waiting in the dark. Even if the alchemist were in the upper room now, eventually he must finish his business and depart. This seemed by far the safest plan – but part of Simon's nature rebelled. It was one thing to be frightened – and Pryrates frightened him witless – it was another thing to spend the whole evening locked in a dark closet, and suffer the attendant punishments, when the priest was almost certainly on his way back to his eyrie in Hjeldin's Tower.

*Besides, I don't think he* really *could have made me come out . . . could he? Likely I was just scared nearly to death. . . . .*

The memory of the broken-backed dog rose in his mind. He gagged and spent long moments breathing deeply.

And what of the cat who had saved him from being caught – *caught*: the image of Pryrates' pit-black eyes would not leave him: *they* were no fear-fantasy. Where had the cat gone? If it had jumped down to the lower floor it was doubtless trapped, and would never find its way back without Simon's assistance. That was a debt of honor.

As he moved quietly forward he could see a dim glow from the doorway in the floor. Was there a torch lit down there? Or perhaps there was some other way out, a doorway opening into one of the lower baileys?

After a few moments of listening silently at the open hatchway, making sure that no one would surprise him this time, Simon stepped cautiously onto the ladder and began to climb down. A breath of cold air ruffled his tunic and goosebumped his arms; he bit the inside of his lip and hesitated, then continued.

Instead of being halted by another landing directly below, Simon's careful descent continued for some moments. At first the only light rose from below him, as though he were climbing down some sort of bottle-neck. At last the illumination became more general, and soon after that his downward-groping exploration met with resistance. He touched wood with his toes to one side of the ladder: he had found the floor. Stepping down he saw that there was no further passageway below, that the bottom rung of the ladder rested here. The only source of light in the chamber – and with the topmost hatchway now closed, the only source of illumination at all – was a strange, glowing rectangle that shone against the far wall, a misty door painted on the wall in fitful yellowish light.

Simon superstitiously made the sign of the Tree as he looked around. The rest of the room contained only a broken quintain and a few other pieces of discarded jousting furniture. Although the room's elongated shadows left many corners obscure, Simon could see nothing that would interest a man like Pryrates. He moved toward the gleaming design on the wall with hands extended, five-fingered silhouettes outlined in amber. The glowing rectangle flared suddenly, then quickly faded, dropping a shroud of absolute black over all.

Simon was alone in darkness. There was no sound except for that of his own blood booming in his ears like a distant ocean. He took a cautious step forward; the sound of his shoe scraping the floor filled the emptiness for a moment. He took another step, and then one more: his outstretched fingers felt cold stone . . . and something else: strange, faint lines of warmth. He slumped to his knees beside the wall.

*Now I know what it's like to be at the bottom of a well. I only hope no one starts pitching stones down at me.*

As he sat, pondering what to do next, he heard a faint whisper of movement. Something struck him in the chest, and he gave a shout of surprise. At his cry the touch was gone, but it returned a moment later. Something was butting gently at his tunic . . . and purring.

'Cat!' he whispered.

*You saved me, you know.* Simon rubbed at the invisible shape. *Slow down, there. It's hard to tell which end is which when you squirm around so. That's right, you saved me, and I'm going to get you out of this hole you've gotten into.*

'Of course, I've gotten myself into the same hole,' Simon said aloud. He picked the furry shape up and lifted it into his tunic. The cat's purring took a deeper note as it settled itself against his warm stomach. 'I know what that glowing thing was,' he whispered. 'A door. A magic door.'

It was also *Pryrates'* magic door, and Morgenes would skin him for even going near it, but Simon felt a certain stubborn indignation: this was *his* castle too, after all, and the storage rooms did not belong to any upstart priest, no matter how fearsome. In any case, if he went back up the ladder and Pryrates was still there . . . well, even Simon's returning pride did not permit him to delude himself about what would happen then. So, it was sit at the bottom of a pitch-black well all evening, or . . .

He flattened his palm on the wall, sliding it across the chill stones until he found the streaks of warmth again. He traced them with his fingers and found they corresponded roughly with the rectangular shape he had first seen. Laying his hands flat in the middle he pushed, but met only the stolid resistance of unmortared stone. He pushed again, as hard as he could; the cat stirred uneasily beneath his shirt. Again nothing happened. As he leaned panting against the spot, he felt even the warm spots growing chill beneath his hands. A sudden vision of Pryrates – the priest waiting in the dark overhead like a spider, a grin stretching his bony face – sent Simon's heart a-pounding.

'Oh, Elysia Mother of God, open!' he murmured hopelessly, fear-sweat making his palms slippery. 'Open!'

The stone became suddenly warm, then hot, forcing Simon to lean away. A thin golden line formed on the wall before him, running like a stream of molten metal along the horizontal until both ends dropped down and then ran back together. The door was there, shimmering, and Simon had only to lift his hand and touch it with a finger for the lines to grow brighter: actual cracks became visible, running the length of the silhouette. He placed his fingers carefully in one edge and pulled; a stone door swung silently outward, spilling light into the room.

It took a moment for his eyes to adjust to the wash of brilliance. Behind the door a stone corridor sloped away and disappeared around a corner, carved directly into the rough rock of the castle. A torch burned brightly in a sconce just inside; it was this that had dazzled him so. He climbed to his feet, the cat a comfortable weight inside his shirt.

Would Pryrates have left a torch burning if he didn't plan to return? And what was this strange passageway? Simon recalled Morgenes saying something of old Sithi ruins beneath the castle. This was certainly old stonework, but crude and raw, completely unlike the polished delicacy of Green Angel Tower. He resolved to make a quick inspection: if the corridor led nowhere, he would have to climb the ladder after all.

The coarse stone walls of the tunnel were damp. As Simon padded down the walkway he could hear a dull booming sound through the very rock.

*I must be below the level of the Kynslagh. No wonder the stones, even the air, everything is so damp.* As if to punctuate this thought, he felt water coming in at the seams of his shoes.

Now the corridor turned again, continuing its downward slope. The dimming light from the entranceway torch was supplemented by some new source. As he turned one last corner he came onto a leveled, widened floor that ended some ten paces away in a wall of craggy granite. Another torch guttered in its bracket there.

Two dark holes loomed in the wall at his left; at the end just beyond them was what looked to be another door, seated almost flush with the corridor's end. Water splashed near his shoe-tops as he moved forward.

The first two spaces seemed to have once been chambers of some kind – cells, most likely – but now splintered doors hung lazily off their hinges; the flickering torchlight revealed nothing inside but shadows. A damp odor of decay hung in these untenanted holes, and he quickly passed them by to stand before the door at the end. The hidden cat pricked him with gentle claws as he examined the blank, heavy timbers in the wavering light. What might lie beyond? Another rotting chamber, or a corridor leading still farther into the sea-bitten stone? Or was it perhaps Pryrates' secret treasure room, concealed from all spying eyes . . . well, *most* spying eyes. . . ?

Midway up the door was fixed a plate of metal: Simon could not tell if it was a latch or a peephole cover. When he tried it the rusty metal did not budge, and he came away with red flecks covering his fingers. Casting about, he saw a bit of broken hinge lying beside the open doorway to his left. He picked it up and pried at the metal until, with a begrudging squeak, the plate tilted upward on a rust-and-salt stiffened hinge. After a quick look up the corridor and a moment of silence listening for footfalls, he leaned forward and put his eye to the hole in the door.

To his great surprise there was a handful of rushes burning in a wall bracket in the chamber, but any heady and terrifying thought of having found Pryrates' secret hoard-room was quickly dashed by the dank, straw-covered floor and bare walls. There was *something* at the back of the chamber, though . . . some dark bundle of shadow.

A clanking noise pulled Simon around in surprise. Fear washed through him as he looked frantically about, expecting any moment to hear the thump of black boots in the corridor. The noise came again; Simon realized with astonishment that it sounded from the chamber beyond the door. Putting his eye cautiously back to the hole, he stared into the shadows.

Something was moving at the back wall, a dark shape,

and as it slowly swayed to one side the harsh, metallic sound echoed again in the small space. The shadow-shape raised its head.

Choking, Simon jumped back from the spy-hole as though slapped across the face. In a whirling moment he felt the firm earth totter beneath him, felt that he had turned over something familiar to find crawling corruption beneath. . . .

The chained thing that had stared out at him – the thing with the haunted eyes – was Prince Josua.

# 12
# Six Silver Sparrows

Simon stumbled across the commons yard, his thoughts shouting in his head like a great crowd. He wanted to hide. He wanted to run away. He wanted to bellow the terrible truth and laugh, to bring the castlefolk tripping and tumbling out of doors. How sure they were, sure about everything, guessing and gossiping – but they knew nothing! *Nothing!* Simon wanted to howl and knock things over, but he could not free his heart from the spell of fear cast by Pryrates' carrion-bird eyes. What could be done? Who would help to turn the world right side up again?

*Morgenes.*

Even as Simon ran shamble-jointed across the dusky commons, the doctor's calm, quizzical face appeared in his thoughts, pushing back the priest's deathly countenance and the chained shadow in the dungeon below. Without another conscious thought he fled past the chained, black-painted gate of Hjeldin's Tower and up the stairs to the Chancelry. In mere moments he was through the long hallways and pulling open the door to forbidden Green Angel Tower. So violent was his need to reach the doctor's chambers that had Barnabas the sexton been waiting there to catch him, Simon might have turned to quicksilver in the man's hands. A great wind rushed through him, filling him with wild haste, pushing him on. Before the tower's side door had swung shut behind him he was on the drawbridge; seconds later he was pounding on Morgenes' door. A pair of Erkynguardsmen looked up incuriously, then went back to their dice.

'Doctor! Doctor! Doctor!' Simon shouted, banging away like a demented cooper. The doctor quickly appeared, feet bare and eyes alarmed.

'Horns of snorting Cryunnos, boy! Are you mad!? Have you eaten bumblebees?!'

Simon pushed past Morgenes without a word of explanation and headed down the corridor. He stood panting before the inner door as the little man came up behind. After a moment of shrewd inspection Morgenes let himself and Simon in.

No sooner had the door closed than Simon began the story of his expedition and its results. The doctor fussed up a small fire and poured a jar of spicy hippocras into a pan to warm. As he worked Morgenes listened, carefully poking an occasional question into Simon's tirade as a man might reach a stick into a bear cage. He shook his head grimly, handing the youth a cup of mulled wine, then sat down with his own cup in a scarred highback chair. He had put slippers on his thin white feet; as he sat cross-legged on the chair cushion, his gray robe rucked up above his bony shins.

'. . . And I *know* I shouldn't have touched a magic door, Doctor, I know it, but I did – and it *was* Josua! I'm sorry, I'm getting things out of order, but I'm sure I saw him! He had a beard, I think, and he looked terrible . . . but it was him!'

Morgenes sipped his wine and dabbed at his chin-whiskers with a long sleeve. 'I believe you, lad,' he said. 'I wish that I didn't, but it makes an evil kind of sense. It confirms some strange information I received.'

'But what will we do?!' Simon almost shouted. 'He's dying! Did Elias do that to him? Does the king know?'

'I really can't say – it is certain, however, that *Pryrates* knows.' The doctor put down his wine cup and stood. Behind his head the last of the afternoon sun reddened the narrow windows. 'As for what to do, the first thing is for you to go and eat supper.'

'*Supper?!*' Simon choked, spattering hippocras down his tunic. 'With Prince Josua. . . ?'

'Yes, boy, that's what I said. Supper. There's nothing we can do right this instant, and I need to think. If you miss your supper, it will just raise a hue and cry – albeit a small one – and it will help to do just what we don't want to do: attract attention. No, go now and eat supper . . . and between bites, keep your mouth shut, will you?'

Mealtime seemed to pass as slowly as spring thaw. Wedged between loudly chewing scullions, his heart beating double time, Simon resisted the wild impulse to lash out and knock cups and crockery spinning to the rush-strewn floor. The conversation infuriated him with its irrelevance, and the shepherd's pie that Judith had prepared especially for Belthainn Eve was as tasteless and unchewable in his mouth as wood.

Rachel watched his fidgeting with displeasure from her seat at the head of the table. When Simon had sat still as long as he could and leaped up to make his excuses, she followed him to the door.

'I'm sorry, Rachel, I'm in a hurry!' he said, hoping to stave off the lecture she seemed primed to deliver. 'Doctor Morgenes has something very important he wants me to help him with. Please?'

For a moment the Dragon looked as though she were going to get that fearful grip on his ear and bring him forcibly back to table, but something in his face or tone caught at her; for a moment she almost smiled.

'All right, boy, just this once – but you thank Judith for that nice bit of pie before you go. She worked on it the whole afternoon.'

Simon bolted over to Judith, pitched like a huge tent at her own table. Her plump cheeks colored prettily while he praised her exertions. As he hurried back to the door, Rachel leaned out and captured his sleeve. He stopped and turned, mouth already open to complain, but Rachel only said: 'Now just calm yourself and be careful, you mooncalf boy. Nothing's so important that you should kill yourself getting there.' She patted his arm and released him; he was through the door and gone as she watched.

Simon had pulled on his vest and coat by the time he reached the well. Morgenes had not yet arrived, so he paced impatiently in the deeper shadow of the dining hall until a soft voice at his elbow made him start in surprise.

'Sorry to make you wait, lad. Inch came by, and I had a devilish time convincing him that I didn't need him after all.' The doctor pulled his hood forward, hiding his face.

'How did you come up so quietly?' Simon asked, his whisper an imitation of the doctor's.

'I *can* still get about a little, Simon,' the doctor said in an injured tone. 'I am old, but not yet moribund.'

Simon did not know what 'moribund' meant, but he caught the general idea. 'Sorry,' he whispered.

The two made their way silently down the dining room stairs and into the first storage room, where Morgenes produced a crystal sphere the size of a green apple. When he rubbed it, a small spark flickered into being at the center, gradually brightening until it limned the encircling casks and bundles with soft honey-colored light. Morgenes shrouded the nether half of it in his sleeve and held it before them as they paced carefully through the stacked dry goods.

The hatchway was closed; Simon did not remember whether or not he had shut it himself in his mad dash out. They went down the ladder carefully, Simon leading, Morgenes above him casting about this way and that with the shining globe. Simon pointed out the closet where Pryrates had almost captured him. They passed on, down to the bottom floor.

The lowermost room was as untenanted as before, but the door leading to the stone passageway was shut. Simon was almost positive that he had not done this, and told Morgenes so, but the little man just waved his hand and strode to the wall, finding the spot where the crack had been according to Simon's directions. The doctor rubbed his hand in a circular movement across the wall, muttering something under his breath, but no crevice appeared. After Morgenes had squatted by the wall talking to himself for some time, Simon grew tired of bouncing from one foot to the other and crouched down at the doctor's side.

'Can't you just say some magic and make it open?'

'No!' Morgenes hissed. 'A wise man never, I repeat, *never* uses the Art when he doesn't need to – especially when dealing with another adept, like our Father Pryrates. We might as well sign my name to it.'

As Simon sat back on his heels and scowled, the doctor placed his left hand flat in the middle of the area where the door had been; after a moment's light palpation of the surface he hit it smartly with the heel of his right hand. The door popped open, pouring torchlight into the room. The doctor peeked through, then dropped his lamp–crystal into the hem of his voluminous sleeve and pulled out a stitched leather bag.

'Ah, Simon–lad,' he chuckled quietly, 'what a thief I would have made. It was not a "magic door" – only hidden by use of the Art. Come on, now!' They stepped through into the damp stone corridor.

Their footfalls made syrupy echoes as they slipped and stepped down the walkway to the corridor's end and the locked door. After a moment's examination of the lock Morgenes stepped to the peephole and peered inside.

'I think you're right, lad,' he hissed. 'Nuanni's Shinbone! But I wish you weren't.' He returned to the scrutiny of the lock. 'Run up to the end of the corridor and keep an ear open, won't you?'

As Simon stood guard, Morgenes fished around in his

leather bag, at last extracting a long, needle-thin blade set in a wooden handle. He waved it merrily at Simon.

'Naraxi pig-sticker. Knew it would come in useful one day!'

He tested it against the keyhole; it slid into the aperture with room to spare. He removed it and shook a tiny jar from his bag which he uncorked with his teeth. As Simon watched, fascinated, Morgenes upended the jar and poured a dark, sticky substance onto the needle blade, then quickly poked the tip back into the keyhole; it left glistening traces as it passed into the lock.

Morgenes wiggled the pig-sticker for a moment, then stepped back and counted on his fingers. When he had tallied both hands three times each, he grasped the slender handle and twisted. He grimaced and let go.

'Come here, Simon. We need your strong young arms.'

At the doctor's direction Simon grasped the strange tool by the butt end and began to twist. For a moment his sweaty palms slipped on the polished wood; he tightened his grip, and after a short interval felt something catch inside the lock. An instant later he heard the bolt slide back. Morgenes nodded his head, and Simon shouldered the door open.

The smoldering rushes in the wall socket threw only faint light. As Simon and the doctor approached they saw the shackled figure at the rear of the cell look up, and his eyes widen slowly, as if in some kind of recognition. His mouth worked, but only a scratchy huff of breath came out. The smell of wet, foul straw was overwhelming.

'Oh . . . oh . . . my poor Prince Josua . . .' Morgenes said. As the doctor gave a quick inspection to Josua's manacles, Simon could only look on, feeling as helpless to affect the rush of events as if he dreamed. The prince was achingly thin, and bearded like a roadside doom-crier; the parts of his skin that showed through the miserable sacking were covered with red sores.

Morgenes was whispering in Josua Lackhand's ear. He

had again produced his bag, and held in his hand a shallow pot, the sort that ladies kept for their lip-paint. Briskly rubbing something from the pot on first one palm, then the other, the little doctor once more looked over Josua's restraints. Both arms were shackled to a massive iron ring in the wall, one manacled about the wrist, the handless other by a cuff about the prince's thin upper arm.

Morgenes finished smearing his hands and passed pot and bag to Simon. 'Now be a good lad,' he said, 'and cover your eyes. I traded a silk-bound volume of Plesinnen Myrmenis – the only one north of Perdruin – for this muck. I just hope – Simon, *do* cover your eyes . . .'

As the youth raised his hands he saw Morgenes reaching for the ring that bound the prince's chains to the stone. An instant later a flash of light glared pinkly through Simon's meshed fingers, accompanied by a crack like hammer on slate. When the youth looked again Prince Josua lay with his chains in a heap on the floor and Morgenes kneeled beside him, palms smoking. The wall-ring was blackened and twisted like a burnt bannock.

'Faugh!' the doctor gasped, 'I hope . . . I hope I . . . never have to do that again. Can you pick up the prince, Simon? I am very weak.'

Josua rolled stiffly over and looked around. 'I . . . think . . . I can . . . walk. Pryrates . . . gave me something.'

'Nonsense.' Morgenes took a deep breath and climbed shakily to his feet. 'Simon is a strong lad – come on, boy, don't gape! Pick him up!'

After some maneuvering Simon managed to wrap the hanging strands of Josua's chains, still attached at wrist and arm, into a loop around the prince's waist. Then, with Morgenes' assistance, he somehow hoisted Josua up like a pickaback child. He stood and sucked in a great draught of air. For a moment he feared he could not bear

210

up, but with a clumsy hop he moved Josua higher on his back and found that even with the added weight of the chains it was not impossible.

'Wipe that silly smile off your face, Simon,' the doctor said, 'we still have to get him up the ladder.'

Somehow they managed – Simon grunting, almost weeping with the exertion, Josua pulling weakly at the rungs, Morgenes pushing behind and whispering encouragement. It was a long, nightmarish climb, but at last they reached the main storeroom. Morgenes scurried past as Simon leaned against a bale to rest, the prince still clinging to his back.

'Somewhere, somewhere . . .' Morgenes muttered, pushing his way between the close-stacked goods. When he reached the southern wall of the room, shining his crystal before him, he began to search in earnest.

'What. . . ?' Simon started to ask, but the doctor silenced him with a gesture. As they watched Morgenes appear and disappear behind piles of barrels, Simon felt a delicate touch on his hair. The prince was patting gently at his head.

'Real. *Real!*' Josua breathed. Simon felt something wet run down his neck.

'Found it!' came Morgenes' hushed but triumphant cry. 'Come along!' Simon rose, staggering a little, and carried the prince forward. The doctor was standing beside the blank stone wall, gesturing toward a pyramid of large casks. The lamp–crystal gave him the shadow of a looming giant.

'Found what?' Simon adjusted the prince and stared. 'Barrels?'

'Indeed!' the doctor cackled. With a flourish he twisted the round rim of the topmost cask a half-turn. The whole side of the barrel swung open as if it were a door, revealing cavernous darkness beyond.

Simon stared suspiciously. 'What's that?'

'A passageway, you foolish boy.' Morgenes took his

elbow and guided him toward the open-sided barrel, which stood scarcely more than chest-high. 'This castle is honeycombed with such secret byways.'

With a frown Simon stooped, peering at the black depths beyond. 'In there?'

Morgenes nodded. Simon, realizing he could not walk through, got down on his knees to inch inside, the prince riding his back as if he were a festival pony. 'I didn't know there were such passages in the storerooms,' he said, his voice echoing in the barrel. Morgenes leaned down to guide Josua's head under the low entrance.

'Simon, there are more things you *don't* know than there are things that I *do* know. I despair of the imbalance. Now close your mouth and let's hurry.'

They were able to stand again on the far side: Morgenes' crystal revealed a long, angled corridor, unremarkable but for a fabulous accumulation of dust.

'Ah, Simon,' Morgenes said as they hurried along, 'I only wish I had time to show you some of the rooms past which this hallway creeps – some were the chambers of a very great, very beautiful lady. She used this passage to keep her secret assignations.' The doctor looked up at Josua, whose face lay against Simon's neck. 'Sleeping, now,' Morgenes murmured. 'All sleeping.'

The corridor climbed and dipped, turning one way and another. They passed many doors, some whose locks were rusted shut, some whose handles were as shiny as a new fithing piece. Once they passed a series of small windows; in a brief glance Simon was startled to see the sentries on the western wall, silhouetted against the sky. The clouds were tinted a faint rose where the sun had gone.

*We must be above the dining hall*, Simon marveled. *When did we do all the climbing?*

They were stumbling in exhaustion when Morgenes finally stopped. There were no windows in this part of the winding corridor, only tapestries. Morgenes lifted one, revealing gray stone beneath.

'Wrong tapestry,' the doctor panted, lifting the next one to reveal a door of rough wood. He laid his ear against it and listened for a moment, then pulled it open.

'Hall of Records.' He gestured at the torchlit hallway beyond. 'Only a few . . . hundred paces from my chambers . . .' When Simon and his passenger had come through, he let the door swing shut behind; it closed with an authoritative bump. Looking back, Simon could not distinguish it from other wooden panels that lined the corridor wall.

There was only one last dash to be made in the open, a relatively rapid sprint from the easternmost door of the archive rooms, across the open commons. As they lurched across the shadowed grass, staying as close to the walls as they could without tripping through the ivy, Simon thought he saw a movement in the shadows of the wall across the yard: something large that shifted slightly as though to watch their passage, a familiar, stoop-shouldered form. But the light was dying fast and he could not be sure – it was only one more black spot moving before his eyes.

He had a stitch in his side that felt as though someone had caught his rib with Ruben's foundry-tongs. Morgenes, who had limped ahead, held the door open. Simon tottered through, carefully put his burden down, then pitched full-length on the cool flagstones, sweaty and breathless. The world spun about him in a giddy dance.

'Here, your Highness, drink this – go on,' he heard Morgenes say. After some little while he opened his eyes and lifted himself on one elbow. Josua sat propped against the wall; Morgenes crouched over him holding a brown ceramic jug.

'Better?' the doctor asked.

The prince nodded weakly. 'Stronger already. This liquor feels like what Pryrates gave me . . . but not so bitter. Said that I was weakening too fast . . . that they needed me tonight.'

'Needed you? I don't like the sound of that, not at all.' Morgenes brought the jug over to Simon. The drink was busy and sour to the taste, but warming. The doctor peered out the door, then dropped the bolt.

'Tomorrow is Belthainn Day, the first of Maia,' he said. 'Tonight is . . . tonight is a very bad night, my prince. Stoning Night, it is called.'

Simon felt the doctor's liquor burning pleasantly as it moved down to his stomach. The ache in his joints lessened, as though a twisted length of cloth had been slackened a turn or two. He sat up, feeling dizzy.

'I find it ominous, their "needing" you on such a night,' Morgenes repeated. 'I fear worse things even than the imprisoning of the king's brother.'

'The imprisoning itself was bad enough for me.' A wry grimace stretched Josua's gaunt features, then disappeared. Deep lines of sorrow took its place. 'Morgenes,' he said a moment later, his voice cracking, 'those . . . those whoreson bastards killed my men. They ambushed us.'

The doctor raised his hand as though to grasp the prince's shoulder, then put it awkwardly back down. 'I'm sure, my lord, I'm sure. Do you know for certain whether your brother was responsible? Could it have been Pryrates acting alone?'

Josua shook his head wearily. 'I don't know. The men who attacked us wore no insignia, and I never saw anyone but the priest once I was brought here . . . but it is astonishing to consider Pryrates doing such a thing *without* Elias.'

'True.'

'But why?! Why, damn them? I do not covet power – the reverse, if anything! You know that, Morgenes. Why should they do this?'

'My prince, I am afraid I do not have the answers right this instant, but I must say this goes far toward confirming my suspicions about . . . other things. About . . . northern matters. Do you remember hearing of the *white*

214

*foxes?*' Morgenes' tone was significant, but the prince only cocked an eyebrow and said nothing. 'Well, there is no time to spend talking of my fears at this moment. Our time is short, and we must attend to more immediate matters.'

Morgenes helped Simon up from the floor, then went puttering off in search of something. The youth stood looking shyly at Prince Josua, who remained slumped against the wall, eyes closed. The doctor returned with a hammer, its head rounded by much use, and a chisel.

'Strike off Josua's chains, will you, lad? I have a few things left to attend to.' He scuttled off again.

'Your Highness?' Simon said quietly, approaching the prince. Josua opened bleary eyes and stared first at the youth, then at the tools he carried. He nodded.

Kneeling at the prince's side he burst the lock on the band that encircled Josua's right arm with a pair of sharp blows. As he moved round to the prince's left, Josua opened his eyes again and laid a restraining hand on Simon's arm.

'Take only the chain from this side, young one.' A ghostly smile flickered across his face. 'Leave me the shackle to remember my brother by. Leave me his band.' He displayed the puckered stump of his right wrist. 'We have a sort of tally system, you see.'

Simon, suddenly chilled, trembled as he braced Josua's left forearm against the stone flags. With a single stroke he sliced through the chain, leaving the cuff of blackened iron above the hand.

Morgenes appeared, carrying a bundle of dark clothing. 'Come, Josua, we must hurry. It is almost an hour after dark, and who knows when they will go looking for you? I broke my lock-pick off in the door, but that will not long prevent them discovering your absence.'

'What will we do?' asked the prince, standing unsteadily on his feet as Simon helped him into the musty peasant gear. 'Who in the castle can we trust?'

'Nobody at present – not on such short notice. That is why you must make your way to Naglimund. Only there will you be safe.'

'Naglimund . . .' Josua seemed bemused. 'I have dreamed so often of my home there in these horrible months – but no! I must show the people my brother's duplicity. I will find strong arms to aid me!'

'Not here . . . not now.' Morgenes' voice was firm, his bright eyes commanding. 'You will find yourself back in a dungeon, and this time you will go quickly to a private beheading. Don't you see? You must get to a strong place where you are safe from treachery before you can press any claim. Many kings have imprisoned and killed their relatives – most got away with it. It takes more than familial infighting to excite the populace.'

'Well,' said Josua reluctantly, 'even if you are correct, how would I escape?' A fit of coughing shook him. 'The castle gates . . . are . . . are doubtless closed for the night. Should I walk up to the inner gate dressed as a traveling minstrel and try to sing my way out?'

Morgenes smiled. Simon was impressed by the spirit of the grim prince, who an hour before had been chained in a damp cell with no hope of rescue.

'As it happens, you have not caught me unprepared with that question,' the doctor said. 'Please observe.'

He walked to the back of the long chamber, to the corner where Simon had once cried against the rough stone wall. He gestured to the star chart whose connected constellations formed a four-winged bird. With a little bow he swept the chart aside. Behind it lay a great square hole cut into the rock, set with a wooden door.

'As I demonstrated already, Pryrates is not the only one with hidden doors and secret passages.' The doctor chuckled. 'Father Red-Cape is a newcomer, and has much yet to learn about the castle that has been *my* home for longer than you two could guess.'

Simon was so excited that he could hardly stand still, but Josua's expression was doubtful. 'Where does it go,

Morgenes?' he asked. 'It will do me scant good to escape Elias' dungeon and rack only to find myself in the Hayholt's moat.'

'Never fear. This castle is built on a warren of caves and tunnels – not to mention the ruins of the older castle beneath us. The whole maze is so vast that even I do not know the half of it – but I know it well enough to give you safe-passage out. Come with me.'

Morgenes led the prince, who went leaning on Simon's arm, over to the chamber-spanning table; there he spread out a rolled parchment whose edges were gray and feathery with age.

'You see,' said Morgenes. 'I have not been idle while my young friend Simon here was at supper. This is a plan of the catacombs – of necessity only a partial one, but with your route marked. If you follow this carefully, you will find yourself above ground at last in the lich-yard beyond the walls of Erchester. From there I am sure you can find your way to safe haven for the night.'

After they had studied the map, Morgenes pulled Josua aside and the two of them engaged in whispered conversation. Simon, feeling more than a little left out, stood and examined the doctor's chart. Morgenes had marked the path with bright red ink; his head swam following the twists and turns.

When the two men finished their discussion, Josua collected the map. 'Well, old friend,' he said, 'if I am to go, then I should go quickly. It would be unwise for another hour to find me still here in the Hayholt. I shall think carefully on these other things you have told me.' His gaze swept around the cluttered room. 'I only fear what your brave acts might bring down on you.'

'There is nothing you can do about that, Josua,' Morgenes replied. 'And I am not without some defenses of my own, a few feints and tricks I can employ. As soon as Simon told me about finding you, I began to make some preparations. I have long feared that my hand

217

would be forced; it has only been hastened slightly by this. Here, take this torch.'

So saying, the little doctor removed a brand from the wall and gave it to the prince, next handing him a sack that hung next to it on a hook.

'I have put some food in here for you, and some more of the curative liquor. It is not much, but you must travel light. Please hurry.' He held the star chart up and away from the doorway. 'Send word to me soon as you are safe at Naglimund and I will have more things to tell.'

The prince nodded, limping slowly into the corridor mouth. The torch's flame pushed his shadow far down the dark shaft as he turned back.

'I will never forget this, Morgenes,' he said. 'And you, young man . . . you have done a brave thing today. I hope it will be the making of your future, someday.'

Simon knelt, embarrassed by the emotions he felt. The prince looked so haggard and grim . . . He felt pride, sorrow, and fear all pulling at him, his thoughts stirred and muddied.

'Fare you well, Josua,' Morgenes said, resting a hand on Simon's shoulder. Together they watched the prince's torch recede down the low passageway until it was swallowed by the murk. The doctor pulled the door shut and dropped the hanging back into place.

'Come, Simon,' he said then, 'we still have much to do. Pryrates is missing his guest this Stoning Night, and I cannot think he will be pleased.'

An interval crept by in silence. Simon dangled his feet from his perch on the tabletop, frightened but nevertheless savoring the excitement that charged the room – that now hung over all of the staid old castle. Morgenes fluttered back and forth past him, hurrying from one incomprehensible task to another.

'I did most of this while you were eating, you see, but there are still a few things left, a few unknotted ends.'

The little man's explanation enlightened Simon not

one whit, but things had been happening fast enough to satisfy even his impatient nature. He nodded and dangled his feet some more.

'Well, I suppose that's all I can do tonight,' Morgenes said at last. 'You had better wander back and go to bed. Come here early in the morning, perhaps right after you do your chores.'

'Chores?' gasped Simon. 'Chores? Tomorrow?'

'Certainly,' snapped the doctor. 'You don't think anything out of the ordinary is going to happen, do you? Do you suppose that the king is going to announce: "Oh, by the way, my brother escaped from the dungeon last night, so we'll all have a holiday and go look for him," – you don't think that, do you?'

'No, I . . .'

'And *you* would certainly not say: "Rachel, I can't do my chores because Morgenes and I are plotting treason," – *would you*?'

'Of course not. . . !'

'Good. Then you will do your chores and come back as soon as you can, and then we will assess the situation. This is far more dangerous than you realize, Simon, but I am afraid you are now a part of things, for good or for ill. I had hoped to keep you out of all this . . .'

'Out of all what? Part of *what*, Doctor?'

'Never mind, boy. Isn't your plate full enough already? I'll try to explain what I safely can tomorrow, but Stoning Night is not the best occasion to speak of things like . . .'

Morgenes' words were chopped short by a loud pounding at the outer door. For a moment Simon and the doctor stood staring at one another; after a pause the knocking was repeated.

'Who's there?' Morgenes called, in a voice so calm Simon had to look again at the fear showing on the little man's face.

'Inch,' came the reply. Morgenes visibly relaxed.

'Go away,' he said. 'I told you I didn't need you tonight.'

There was a brief silence. 'Doctor,' Simon whispered, 'I think I saw Inch earlier . . .'

The dull voice came again. 'I think I left something . . . left it in your room, Doctor.'

'Come back and get it another time,' Morgenes called, and this time the irritation was genuine. 'I'm far too busy to be disturbed right now.'

Simon tried again. 'I think I saw him when I was carrying Jos . . .'

*'Open this door immediately – in the king's name!!'*

Simon felt cold despair grip his stomach: this new voice did not belong to Inch.

'By the Lesser Crocodile!' Morgenes swore in soft wonderment, 'the cow-eyed dullard has sold us out. I didn't think he had the sense – *I will be disturbed no longer!*' he shouted then, jumping to the long table and straining to push it in front of the bolted inner door. 'I am an old man, and need my rest!' Simon leaped to help, his terror mixed with an inexplicable rush of exhilaration.

A third voice called from the hallway, a cruel, hoarse voice: 'Your rest will be a long one indeed, old man.' Simon stumbled and nearly fell as his knees buckled beneath him. Pryrates was here.

A hideous crunching noise began to echo through the inner hallway as Simon and the doctor finally slid the heavy table into place. 'Axes,' said Morgenes, and sprang along the table in search of something.

'Doctor!' Simon hissed, bouncing up and down in fright. The sound of splintering wood reverberated outside. 'What can we do?' He whirled to find himself confronted with a scene of madness.

Morgenes was up on his knees on the table top, crouching beside an object that Simon recognized after an instant as a birdcage. The doctor had his face pressed close against the slender bars; he was cooing and muttering to the creatures within even as Simon heard the outer door crash down.

'*What are you doing?*' Simon gasped. Morgenes hopped down carrying the cage, and trotted across the room to the window. At Simon's yelp he turned to look calmly at the terrified youth, then smiled sadly and shook his head.

'Of course, boy,' he said. 'I must make provision for you, too, just as I promised your father. How little time we had!' He set the cage down and scuttled back to the table, where he groped about in the clutter even as the chamber door began to rock with the impact of heavy blows. Harsh voices could be heard, and the clatter of men in armor. Morgenes found what he sought, a wooden box, and upended it, dumping some shining golden thing into his palm. He began to move back to the window, then stopped and retrieved also a sheaf of thin parchments from the chaos of the tabletop.

'Take this, will you please?' he said, handing the bundle to Simon as he hurried back to the window. 'It's my life of Prester John, and I begrudge Pryrates the pleasure of criticism.' Stupefied, Simon took the papers and tucked them into his waistband beneath his shirt. The doctor reached into the cage and removed one of its small inhabitants, cupping it in his hand. It was a tiny, silver-gray sparrow; as Simon watched in numb astonishment the doctor calmly tied the shiny bauble – a ring? – to the sparrow's leg with a bit of twine. A tiny scrap of parchment was bound already to its other leg. 'Be strong with this heavy burden,' he said quietly, speaking, it seemed, to the little bird.

The blade of an axe crashed through the heavy door just above the bolt. Morgenes bent over and picked a long stick up off the floor and broke the high window, then lifted the sparrow to the sill and let it go. The bird hopped along the frame for a moment, then took wing and disappeared into the evening sky. One by one, the doctor released five more sparrows that way, until the cage stood empty.

221

A large piece had been bitten from the door's center; Simon could see the angry faces and the flare of torchlight on metal beyond.

The doctor beckoned. 'The tunnel, boy, and quickly!' Behind them another ragged chunk of wood tore loose and clattered to the floor. As they sped across the room the doctor handed Simon something small and round.

'Rub this and you will have light, Simon,' he said. 'It is better than a torch.' He swept the hanging aside and pulled the door open. 'Go on, hurry! Look for the Tan'ja Stairs, then climb!' As Simon entered the corridor mouth the great door sagged on its hinges and collapsed. Morgenes turned.

'But, Doctor!' Simon shouted. 'Come with me! We can escape!'

The doctor looked at him and smiled, shaking his head. The table before the doorway was overturned with a smash of glass, and a group of armed men in green and yellow began to push past the wreckage. In the midst of the Erkynguard, crouched like a toad in a garden of swords and axes, was Breyugar, the Lord Constable. In the littered hallway stood the bulky form of Inch; behind him Pryrates' cloak flashed scarlet.

'*Stop!*' a voice thundered through the room – Simon was still able to marvel, in the midst of all his fear and confusion, that such a sound could come from Morgenes' frail body. The doctor stood now before the Erkynguard, fingers splayed in a strange gesture. The air began to bend and shimmer between the doctor and the startled soldiers. The very substance of nothingness seemed to grow solid as Morgenes' hands danced strange patterns. For a moment the torches outlined the scene before Simon's eyes as if it were frozen on an ancient tapestry.

'Bless you, boy,' Morgenes hissed, '*Go! Now!*' Simon retreated another step down the corridor.

Pryrates pushed past the stunned guards, a blurry red shadow behind the wall of air. One of his hands stabbed

222

forth; a seething, coruscating web of blue sparks marked where it touched the thickening air. Morgenes reeled, and his barrier began to melt like a sheet of ice. The doctor bent and swept up a pair of beakers from a rack on the floor.

'Stop that youth!' Pryrates shouted, and suddenly Simon could see his eyes above the scarlet cloak . . . cold black eyes, serpentine eyes that seemed to hold him . . . transfix him . . .

The shimmering pane of air dissolved. 'Take them!' spat Count Breguyar, and the soldiers surged forward. Simon watched in sick fascination, wanting to run but unable to, nothing between him and the Erkynguards' swords but . . . Morgenes.

'*ENKI ANNUKHAI SHI'IGAO!*' The doctor's voice boomed and tolled like a bell made of stone. A wind shrieked through the chamber, flattening and extinguishing the torches. In the center of the maelstrom Morgenes stood, a flask in each outstretched hand. In the brief instant of darkness there was a crash, then a flare of incandescence as the glass beakers shattered into flame. In a heartbeat fiery streams were running down the arms of Morgenes' cloak, and then his head was haloed in leaping, crackling tongues of fire. Simon was buffeted by terrible heat as the doctor turned to him once more; Morgenes' face seemed already to shift and change behind the blazing mist that enveloped it.

'Go, my Simon,' he breathed, and he was voiced in flame. 'It is too late for me. Go to Josua.'

As Simon staggered backward in horror, the doctor's frail form leaped with burning radiance. Morgenes wheeled. Taking a few halting steps, he threw himself with outspread arms onto the screeching, quailing guardsmen, who tore at each other in their desperation to escape back through the broken doorway. Hellish flames billowed upward, blackening the groaning roofbeams. The very walls began to shudder. For a brief moment Simon heard the harsh choking voice of Pryrates inter-

223

twined with the sounds of Morgenes' final agonies . . .
then there was a great crack of light and an ear-thumping
roar. A hot whip of air flung Simon down the passageway, blowing the door shut behind him with a noise like
the Hammer of Judgment. Stunned, he heard the grinding, splintering shriek of the roof timbers collapsing. The
door shuddered, wedged shut by many thousandweight
of scorched oak and stone.

For a long time he lay wracked with sobs, the tears of his
eyes sucked away by the heat. At last he crawled to his
feet. He found the warm stone wall with his hand and
went stumbling down into darkness.

# 13

# Between Worlds

Voices, many voices – whether birthed in his own head or in the comfortless shadows that surrounded him, Simon could not tell – were his only companions in that first terrible hour.

*Simon mooncalf! Done it again, Simon mooncalf!*

*His friend is dead, his only friend, be kind, be kind!*

*Where are we?*

*In darkness, in darkness forever, to bat-flitter like a lost shrieking soul through the endless tunnels . . .*

*He is Simon Pilgrim now, doomed to wander, to wonder . . .*

*No*, Simon shuddered, trying to rein in the clamoring voices, *I will remember. I will remember the red line on the old map, and to look for the Tan'ja Stairs – whatever they might be. I will remember the flat black eyes of that murderer Pryrates: I will remember my friend . . . my friend Doctor Morgenes . . .*

He sank down onto the gritty tunnel floor, weeping with helpless, strengthless anger, a barely beating heart of life in a universe of black stone. The blackness was a choking thing that pressed down on him, squeezing out his breath.

*Why did he do it? Why didn't he run?*

*He died to save you, idiot boy – and Josua. If he had run, they would have followed; Pryrates had the stronger magic. You would have been caught, and they would have been free to follow the prince, to hunt him down and drag him back to his cell. Morgenes died for that.*

Simon hated the sound of his own crying, the hacking, sniveling sound echoing on and on. He pushed it all up from inside him, sobbing until his voice was a dry rasp – a sound he could live with, not the weepy bleat of a lost mooncalf in the dark.

Lightheaded and sick, wiping his face with his shirt-sleeve, Simon felt the forgotten weight of Morgenes' crystal sphere in his hand. Light. The doctor had given him light. Along with the papers crimped uncomfortably in the waistband of his breeches, it was the last gift the doctor had given him.

*No*, a voice whispered, *the second-to-last, Simon Pilgrim*.

Simon shook his head, trying to dispel the licking, murmuring fear. What had Morgenes said as he tied the glinting bauble to the sparrow's slender leg? To be strong with its heavy burden? Why was he sitting in the pitch dark, mewling and dribbling – wasn't he Morgenes' apprentice, after all?

He clambered to his feet, dizzy and trembling. He felt the glassy surface of the crystal warm beneath his stroking fingers. He stared into the darkness where his hands must be, thinking of the doctor. How could the old man laugh so often, when the world was so full of hidden treachery, of beautiful things with rot inside of them? There was so much shadow, so little . . .

A pinprick of light flared before him – a needle hole in the sun-shrouding curtain of night. He rubbed harder and stared. The light bloomed, folding back the shadows; the passageway's walls leapt out on either side, brushed with glowing amber. Air seemed to rush into his lungs. He could see!

The momentary elation evaporated as he turned to look up and down the corridor. A pain in his head made the walls waver before his gaze. The tunnel was nearly featureless, a lonely hole burrowing down into the

226

underbelly of the castle, festooned with pale cobwebs. Back up the passage he could see a crossway he had already passed, a gaping mouth in the wall. He walked back. A quick shine of the crystal revealed nothing beyond the opening but tailings and rubble, a sloping pile of debris leading down out of reach of the sphere's thin light. How many other cross-paths had he missed? And how would he know which ones were the right ones? Another wave of choking hopelessness washed over him. He was hopelessly alone, hopelessly lost. He would never find himself back in the world of light.

*Simon Pilgrim, Simon mooncalf . . . family dead, friend dead, see him wander and wander forever . . .*

'Silence!' he growled out loud, and was startled to hear the word caroming down the path before him, a messenger carrying a proclamation from the king of Under-the-ground: 'Silence . . . silence . . . silen . . . si . . .'

King Simon of the Tunnels began his staggering progress.

The passageway squirmed downward into the stone heart of the Hayholt, a smothering, winding, cob-webbed track lit only by the gleam of Morgenes' crystal sphere. Broken spiderwebs performed a slow, ghostly dance in the wake of his passage; when he turned to look back the strands seemed to wave after him, like the clutching, boneless fingers of the drowned. Hanks of silky thread stuck to his hair and draped stickily across his face, so that he had to hold his hand before his eyes as he walked. Often he would feel some small, leggy thing scuttling away across his fingers as he broke through its netting, and would have to stop for a moment, head down, until the shivers of disgust subsided.

It was becoming colder, and the close-cramped walls of the passageway seemed to breathe with moisture. Parts of the tunnel had crumbled; in some places dislodged dirt and stone were piled so high in the center of the path that he had to push his back against the damp walls and edge around them.

He was doing just that – squeezing around an obstruction, the light-wielding hand held over his head, the other feeling before him for a way past – when he felt a searing pain like a thousand needle-pricks run up his questing hand and onto his arm. A flash of the crystal brought a vision of horror – hundreds, no, *thousands* of tiny white spiders swarming up his wrist and under his shirt sleeve, biting like a thousand burning fires. Simon shrieked and slammed his arm against the tunnel wall, bringing a shower of clotted dirt down into his mouth and eyes. His terrified shouts echoed down the passageway, quickly failing. He fell to his knees in damp soil, smacking his stinging arm up and down into the dirt until the flaring pain began to subside, then crawled forward on his hands and knees, away from whatever horrible nest or den he had disturbed. As he crouched and frantically scrubbed his arm with loose soil the tears came again, racking him like a whipping.

When he could stand to look at his arm, the crystal's light revealed only reddening and swelling skin beneath the dirt, instead of the bloody wounds he had been sure he would find. The arm throbbed, and he wondered dully if the spiders were poisonous – if the worst was yet to come. When he felt the sobs climbing once more in his chest, shortening his breath, he forced himself to his feet. He must go on. He must.

*A thousand white spiders.*

He *must* go on.

He followed the sphere's dim light downward. It gleamed on moisture-slick stone and earth-choked cross-corridors, twining with pallid roots. Surely he must be far below the castle by now – far down into the black earth. There was no sign of Josua's passage, or of anyone's. He was sickeningly certain he had missed some turning-place in the darkness and confusion, and was even now spiraling downward into an inescapable pit.

He had trudged on so long, making so many twists and turns, that the memory of the narrow red line on Morgenes' old parchment was now useless. There was nothing remotely like stairs anywhere in these narrow, strangling wormholes. Even the glowing crystal was beginning to flicker. The voices escaped his control again, surrounding him in the crazy shadows like a shouting throng.

*Dark and getting darker. Dark and getting darker.*

*Let us lie down for a while. We want to sleep, just for a while, sleep . . .*

*The king has an animal inside him, and Pryrates is its keeper . . .*

*'My Simon.' Morgenes called you 'my Simon' . . . he knew your father. He kept secrets.*

*Josua is going to Naglimund. The sun shines there all day and night. Naglimund. They eat sweet cream and drink clear, shining water at Naglimund. The sun is bright.*

*Bright and hot. It is hot. Why?*

The damp tunnel was suddenly very warm. He stumbled on, hopelessly sure that he felt the first fever of spider-poison. He would die in the dark, the terrible dark. He would never again see the sun, or feel its . . .

The warmth seemed to push into his lungs. It *was* getting hotter!

Stifling air enfolded him, sticking his shirt to his chest and his hair to his forehead. He felt a moment of even greater panic.

*Have I circled round? Have I walked for years only to come back to the ruins of Morgenes' chamber* – the burned, blackened remains of his life?

But it was not possible. He had been going downward steadily, never once mounting back to anything more than a moment's level going. Why was it so hot?

The memory of one of Shem Horsegroom's stories pushed forward, a story of young Prester John wandering through darkness toward a great, brooding heat – the dragon Skurakai in its lair beneath the castle . . . *this* castle.

*But the dragon is dead! I've touched its bones, a yellow chair in the throne room. There is no dragon anymore* – no sleepless, deep-breathing red hulk the size of the tourney field, waiting in the darkness with claws like swords and a soul as old as the stones of Osten Ard – *the dragon is dead.*

But did dragons never have brothers?

And what was that sound? That dull, grumbling roar?

The heat was oppressive, and the air was thick with itching smoke. Simon's heart was a lump of dull lead in his chest. The crystal began to dim as broad smears of reddish light blotted out the sphere's weaker radiance. The tunnel flattened, turning now neither left nor right, leading down a long, eroded gallery to an arched doorway that danced with a flickering orange radiance. Shivering despite the sweat streaming down his face, Simon felt himself drawn toward it.

*Turn and* run, *mooncalf!*

He could not. Each step was a labor, but he moved closer. He reached the archway and craned his neck fearfully around the portal's rim.

It was a great cavern, awash in leaping light. The rock walls seemed to have melted and set like wax at the base of a candle, the stone smoothed in long, verticle ripples. For a moment Simon's light-stunned eyes opened wide in amazement: at the cavern's far side a score of dark figures were kneeling before the shape of . . . *a monstrous, flame-blazing dragon!*

An instant later he saw that it was not so: the huge shape crouched against the stone was a great furnace. The dark-clad figures were forking logs into its flaming maw.

*The foundry! The castle foundry!*

All around the cavern heavily dressed and scarf-masked men were smithying the tools of war. Massive buckets of glowing liquid iron were pulled from the flames on the ends of long poles. Molten metal jumped and hissed as it drizzled into plate-shaped molds, and

230

above the groaning voice of the furnace reverberated the clang of hammer on anvil.

Simon shrank back from the doorway. For a heartbeat he had felt himself about to leap forward and run to these men – for men they were, despite their strange dress. It had seemed in that instant that anything was better than the dark tunnel, and the voices – but he knew better. Did he think these foundrymen would help him to escape? Doubtless they knew only one route from the blazing cavern: up and back into the clutches of Pryrates – if he had survived the inferno of Morgenes' chambers – or the brutal justice of Elias.

He sank down onto his haunches to think. The noise of the furnace and his own painful head made it difficult. He could not remember passing any cross-tunnels for some time. He *could* see what looked like a row of holes along the far wall of the foundry-cavern; it could be that they were nothing but storage chambers . . .

*Or dungeons . . .*

But it seemed just as likely that they were other routes in and out of the chamber. To retreat back up the tunnel seemed foolish . . .

*Coward! Scullion!*

Numb, battered, he balanced on the knife-edge of indecision. To go back, and wander through the same dark, spider-haunted tunnels, his only light flickering into extinction . . . or to make his way across the roaring inferno of the foundry floor – and from there, who could know? Which should it be?

*He will be King of Under-ground, Lord of the Weeping Shades!*

*No, his people are gone, let him be!*

He smacked himself on the head, trying to dispel the chittering voices.

*If I'm going to die*, he decided, wresting back the mastery of his speeding heart, *at least let it be in the light*.

He bent over, head throbbing, to stare at the cupped gleam of the crystal sphere. Even as he looked, the light died, then throbbed back into tenuous life. He slipped it into his pocket.

The furnace flame and the dark shapes that passed before them laid pulsing stripes of red, orange and black along the wall; he dropped down from the archway to huddle beside the downsloping ramp. The nearest hiding place was a shabby brick structure some fifteen or twenty ells from where he crouched, a disused kiln or oven that squatted on the chamber's fringe. After a few deep breaths he bolted for it, half-running, half-crawling. His head ached from the motion, and when he reached the bulky kiln he had to lower his face between his knees until the black spots went away. The harsh roar of the feeding furnace rang like thunder inside his head, silencing even his voices with its painful clamor.

He made his way from dark place to dark place, little islands of shadowed safety in the ocean of smoke and red noise. The foundrymen did not look up and see him; they barely communicated among themselves, limited in the crushing din to broad gestures, like armored men in the chaos of battle. Their eyes, points of reflected light above the masking cloth, seemed instead to stare at one thing only: the bright, compelling glow of hot iron. Like the red map-line that still snaked a wistful course through Simon's memory, the radiant metal was everywhere and all the same, like a dragon's magical blood. Here it splashed over the edge of a vat, spattering in gemlike drops; over there it wound serpentlike away across the rock to flow hissing into a pool of brackish water. Great tongues of incandescence sluiced down from buckets, coloring the bundled foundrymen in demonic scarlet.

Creeping, scuttling, Simon made his slow way around the rim of the smelting-cave until he reached the nearest ramp leading out of the chamber. The oppressive, breathing heat and his own sickened spirit urged him to climb up, but the packed earth of the ramp showed a deep, crisscrossing scrawl of cartwheel tracks. This was a much-used doorway, he reasoned, thoughts blurry and slow. It was not a place he should try.

At last he reached a mouth in the cavern wall that had no ramp. It was a difficult scrabble up the smooth – fire-melted? *Dragon-melted?* – rock, but his flagging strength held up long enough for him to pull himself over the lip and collapse full length in the sheltering shadows just inside, the unpocketed sphere glowing weakly in his hand like a trapped firefly.

When he knew who he was once more, he was crawling.

*On your knees again, mooncalf?*

The blackness was virtually complete, and he was moving blindly downward. The tunnel floor was dry and sandy beneath his hands.

He crawled for a long, long time; even the voices began to sound as if they felt sorry for him.

*Simon lost . . . Simon lost lost los . . .*

Only the slowly diminishing heat behind convinced him he was actually moving – but toward what? Where? He crept like a wounded animal, through solid shadow, heading down, always down. Would he crawl downward to the very center of the world?

Scuttling, leggy things beneath his fingers meant nothing now. The darkness was complete, inside and outside. He felt himself almost bodiless, a bundle of frightened thoughts bumping down into the cryptic earth.

Somewhere, sometime later, the darkened sphere he had clutched for so long that it seemed a part of him began to glow again, this time with a strange azure light. From a core of pulsing blue the light expanded until he had to hold the sphere away from him, squinting. He climbed slowly to his feet and stood panting, his hands and knees tingling where they no longer touched sand.

The tunnel walls were covered in fibrous black growths, tangled as uncombed wool, but through the twining strands gleamed shining patches, reflecting the new-flowered light. Simon hobbled closer to investigate, drawing his hand back with a thin wheeze of disgust as he touched the greasy black moss. Some of his self had come back with the light, and as he stood swaying he thought about what he had crawled through, and trembled.

The wall beneath the moss was covered in some kind of tile, chipped and scored in many places, missing in others so that the dull earth showed through. Behind him the tunnel sloped upward, the rut of his passage stopping where he now stood. Before him the darkness led on. He would try walking on two legs for a while.

The passage soon widened. The arched entrances of scores of other corridors joined the one he traveled, most of them filled with soil and stone. Soon there were also flagstones beneath his shambling feet, uneven, fractured stone that nonetheless caught the light of the lantern-sphere with strange opalescence. The ceiling gradually angled away above him, out of reach of the blue light; the corridor continued downward into the earth. Something that might have been the beat of leathery wings fluttered in the emptiness above.

*Where am I now? How could Hayholt run so deep? Doctor said castles under castles, down into the world's bones. Castles under castles . . . under castles . . .*

He had stopped without knowing it, and had turned to stand before one of the cross-passages. In some part of his head he could see himself and how he must look – tattered, dirt-smeared, head wagging from side to side like a half-wit. A strand of spittle dangled from his lower lip.

The doorway before him was unblocked; a strange scented air like dried flowers hung in the black arch. He stepped forward, dragging an arm that felt like heavy, useless meat across his mouth, holding aloft the crystal sphere in his other hand.

*. . . ! Beautiful! Beautiful place. . . !*

It was a chamber, perfect in the blue glow, as perfect as

if someone had left it only a moment before. The ceiling was high-vaulted, covered in a tracery of delicate painted lines, a pattern suggesting thorn bushes, or flowering vines, or the meandering of a thousand meadow streams. The rounded windows were choked with rubble, and dirt had poured down from them to silt the tiled floor beneath, but all else was untouched. There was a bed – a miracle of subtle, curving wood – and a chair as fine as the bones of a bird. In the room's center stood a fountain of polished stone that looked as if it might fill with singing water at any moment.

*A home for me. A home beneath the ground. A bed to sleep in, sleep and sleep until Pryrates and the king and the soldiers have all gone away . . .*

A few dragging steps forward and he stood beside the bed, the pallet as clean and unsmirched as the sails of the blessed. There was a face staring down at him from a niche above it, a splendid, clever woman's face – a statue. Something about it was wrong, though: the lines were too angular, the eyes too deep and wide, the cheekbones high and sharp. Still it was a face of great beauty, captured in translucent stone, forever frozen in a sad, knowing smile.

As he reached out to gently touch the sculpted cheek his shin nudged the bedframe, a touch delicate as a spider's step. The bed crumbled into powder. A moment later, as he stared in horror, the bust in the niche dissolved into fine ash beneath his fingertips, the woman's features melting away in an instant. He took a stumbling step back and the light of the sphere glared and then waned to a dim glow. The thump of his foot on the floor leveled the chair and delicate fountain, and a moment later the ceiling itself began to sift down, the twining branches moldering into soft dust. The sphere flickered as he lurched for the door, and as he plunged back out into the corridor the blue light guttered out.

Standing in the darkness again, he heard someone crying. After a long minute he reeled forward, down into

235

the never-ending shadows, wondering who it was that could still have tears left to shed.

The passage of time had become a thing only of fits and starts. Somewhere behind him he had dropped the spent crystal to lie forever in darkness, a pearl in the blackest trenches of the secret sea. In a last, sane part of his wandering thoughts, thoughts now unbounded by the hedge of light, he knew that he was moving still further downward.

*Going down. Into the pit. Going down.*

*Going where? To what?*

*From shadow to shadow, as a scullion always travels.*

*Dead mooncalf. Ghost mooncalf . . .*

Drifting, drifting . . . Simon thought of Morgenes with his wispy beard curling in flame, thought of the shining comet glaring redly down on the Hayholt . . . thought of himself, descending – mounting? – through the black nothing spaces like a small, cold star. Drifting.

The emptiness was complete. The darkness, at first just an absence of light and life, began to assume qualities of its own: narrow, choking dark when the tunnels narrowed, Simon clambering over drifts of rubble and tangling roots, or the lofty, airy darkness of invisible chambers, full of the parchment scrape of bat wings. Feeling his way through these vast, underground galleries, hearing his own muffled footfalls and the hissing patter of dirt shaken loose from the walls, any remaining sense of direction fell away. He might be walking straight up the walls, for all he could tell, or staggering across the ceiling like a maddened fly. There was no left or right; when his fingers found solid walls again, and doors leading to other tunnels, he groped mindlessly on through more constricted passageways and into other bat-squeaking, measureless catacombs.

*Ghost of a mooncalf!*

The odor of water and stone was everywhere. His sense of smell, like his hearing, seemed to have grown more acute in the blind, black night, and as he fumbled his way ever downward the scents of this midnight world washed over him – damp, loamy earth, nearly as rich as bread dough, and the bland but harsh fragrance of rocks. He was awash in the vibrant, breathing odors of moss and roots, the busy, sweet rottenness of tiny things living and dying. And floating through everything, permeating and complicating all, was the sour, mineral tang of seawater.

Seawater? Sightless, he listened, hunting the booming sounds of the ocean. How deep had he come? All he heard were the minute shufflings of digging things and his own ragged breathing. Had he tunneled beneath even the unsounded Kynslagh?

There! Faint musical tones, chiming in the farther depths. Water dripping.

Down he went. The walls were moist.

*You are dead, Simon Mooncalf. A spirit, doomed to haunt a void.*

*There is no light. There never was such a thing. Smell the darkness? Hear the resounding nothing? This has ever been.*

The fear was all he had left, but even that was something – he was afraid, so he must be alive! There was darkness, but there was Simon, too! They were not one and the same. Not yet. Not quite . . .

And now, so slowly he did not perceive the difference for a long time, light came back. It was a light so faint, so dim, that at first it was less than the points of color hovering before his useless eyes. Then, curiously, he saw a black shape before him, a deeper shadow. A clot of worms, wriggling? No. Fingers . . . a hand . . . *his* hand! It was silhouetted before him, bathed in a faint glow.

The close-bending tunnel walls were thick with twining moss, and it was the moss itself that gleamed – a pale, green-white shimmer that threw only enough light to show the greater darkness of the tunnel before him, and the light-blocking shadow of his own hands and

237

arms. But it was light! Light! Simon laughed sound-lessly, and his nebulous shadows criss-crossed the passageway.

The tunnel opened out into another open gallery. As he looked up, astounded at the constellation of radiant mosses sprouting on the faraway ceiling, he felt a drop of cold water on his neck. More water drizzled slowly from above, each drop striking the rocks below with a sound like a tiny mallet falling on glass. The vaulting chamber was full of long pillars of stone, fat on either end, narrow in the middle; some were as slender as a hair's-breadth, like strands of oozing honey. As he trudged forward he realized, in some remote part of his battered mind, that most of this was the work of stone and dripping water, not of laboring hands. But still, there were lines in the dimness that did not seem natural: right-angled creases on the moss-girdled walls, ruined pillars among the stalagmites too orderly to be accidental. He was moving through a place that had once known something other than the ceaseless rhythm of water pattering in stone pools. Once it had echoed to other footsteps. 'But 'once' only meant something if Time was still a barrier. So long had he been crawling in dark places, he might have dug through into the misty future or the shadowed past, or into unmapped realms of madness – how was he to know. . . ?

Putting his foot down, Simon felt a moment of shocking emptiness. He plunged into cold, wet black-ness. His hands lit on the far edge as he fell, and the water proved only as deep as his knees. He thought some clawed thing clutched at his leg as he yanked himself back out onto the passageway, shaking from more than the cold.

*I don't want to die. I want the sun again.*

*Poor Simon*, his voices responded. *Mad in the dark.*

Dripping, shivering, he limped on through the green-glimmered chamber, watching carefully for the empty blacknesses that next time might not be so shallow. Faint flickers, glowing pink and white, darted to and fro in the

238

holes as he stepped across or made his way carefully around them. Fish? Shining fish in the deeps of the earth?

Now, as one large chamber opened into another, and another, the lines of hand-wrought things began to show more clearly beneath the cloak of moss and stone-drip. They made strange silhouettes in the dim half-light: crumbled spans that might once have been balconies, arched depressions matted in pallid moss that could have been windows or gateways. As he squinted, trying to make out details in the near-darkness, he began to feel his vision was slipping sideways, somehow – the overgrown shapes, smothered in shadow, seemed to simultaneously flicker with the lineaments they had once worn. From the corner of his eye he saw one of the shattered columns lining the gallery suddenly standing straight, a shining white thing carved with trains of graceful flowers. When he turned to stare, it was only a clump of broken stone once more, half-shrouded in moss and encroaching earth. The deep gloom of the chambers bent crazily at the corners of his sight, and his head pounded. The ceaseless sound of falling water now began to feel like hammer-blows to his reeling mind. His voices came chittering back, revelers excited by wild music.

*Mad! The boy is mad!*

*Have pity, he's lost, lost, lost. . . !*

*We will have it back, manchild! We will have it all back!*

*Mad mooncalf!*

And as he passed down yet one more sloping tunnel he began to hear other voices in his head, voices he had not heard before, somehow both more real and more unreal than those which had long been his unwanted companions. Some of these shouted in languages that he did not know, unless he had glimpsed them in the doctor's ancient books.

*Ruakha, ruakha Asu'a!*

*T'si e-isi'ha as'-irigú!*

*The trees are burning! Where is the prince?! The witchwood is in flames, the gardens are **burning**!*

The half-darkness was contorting around him, bending, as though he stood at the center of a spinning wheel. He turned and stumbled blindly down a passageway and into one more lofty hall, holding his agonized head in his hands. There was other, different light here: thin blue beams angling down from cracks in the unseen ceiling above, light that pierced the darkness but illuminated nothing where it fell. He smelled more water, and strange vegetation; he heard men running, shouting, women crying and the ring of metal on metal. In the strange almost-blackness the sound of some terrible battle raged all around, but did not touch him. He screamed – or thought he did – but could not hear his own voice, only the ghastly din in his head.

Then, as if to confirm his already certain madness, dim figures began to rush past in the blue-lanced darkness, bearded men with torches and axes chasing others more slender who bore swords and bows. All of them, pursuers and pursued, were as transparent and ill-defined as mist. None touched or saw Simon, although he stood squarely in their midst.

*Jinguzu! Aya'ai! O Jingizu!* came a wailing cry.

*Kill the Sithi demons,* harsher voices shouted. *Put fire to their nest!*

Hands clutched tight over his ears could not keep the voices away. He stumbled forward, trying to escape the swirling shapes, and fell through a doorway, coming to rest at last on a flat landing of gleaming white stone. He could feel cushioning moss beneath his groping hands, but his eyes saw nothing but polished blankness. He crawled forward on his stomach, still trying to escape the horrible voices shrieking in pain and anger. His fingers felt cracks and pits, but still the stone looked as flawless as glass. He reached the lip and stared out across a great, level field of black emptiness which smelled of time and death and the patient ocean. An invisible pebble rolled from beneath his hand to fall silently for long moments and then splash in the depths below.

Something large and white gleamed beside him. He lifted his heavy, aching head from the lip of the dark tarn and looked up. Scant inches from where he lay jutted the bottom steps of a great stone staircase, an upward-sweeping spiral that climbed away, mounting the side of the cavern and circling the underground lake to disappear at last into upper darkness. He gaped as an urgent, fractured memory pushed through the clamor in his head.

*Stairs. Tan'za Stairs. Doctor said look for stairs. . . .*

He clambered forward, pulling himself up onto the cool, polished stone, and knew that he was mad beyond salvation, or had died and was trapped in some terrible netherworld. He was beneath the earth in final darkness: there could be no voices, no phantom warriors. There would be no light making the steps gleam before him like moonlit alabaster.

He began to climb, pulling himself up to the next high step with trembling, sweat-slippery fingers. As he mounted higher, sometimes standing, sometimes clawing his way up in a scrabbling crouch, he peered out from the stairs. The silent lake, a vast pool of shadow below him, lay at the bottom of a great circular hall, bigger by far than the foundry. The ceiling stretched immeasurably upward, lost in the blackness above with the top of the slender, beautiful white pillars ringing the chamber. A foggy, directionless light glinted on the sea-blue and jade-green walls, and touched the frames of high-vaulting windows that flickered now with an ominous crimson glare.

In the middle of the pearly mists, hovering above the silent lake, sat a dark, wavering shape. It cast a shadow both of wonder and of terror, and it filled Simon with inexpressible, pitying dread.

*Prince Ineluki! They come! The Northerners come!*

As this last impassioned cry echoed in the dark walls of Simon's skull, the figure at the room's center lifted its head. Gleaming red eyes bloomed in its face, cutting through the fog like torches.

*Jingizu*, a voice breathed. *Jingizu. So much sorrow.*

The crimson light flared. The shriek of death and fear rose from below like a great wave. At the center of it all, the dark figure lifted a long slender object and the beautiful chamber shuddered, shimmering like a shattered reflection, then fell away into nothingness. Simon turned away in horror, enveloped in a strangling pall of loss and despair.

Something was gone. Something beautiful had been destroyed beyond retrieval. A world had died here, and Simon felt its failing cry embedded in his heart like a gray sword. Even his consuming fear was driven out by the terrible sadness that cut through him bringing painful shuddering tears from reservoirs that should have been long dry. Embracing the darkness, he lurched on up the endless climb, winding around the mighty chamber. The shadows and silence swallowed the dream-battle and the dream-chamber below him, bringing a black shroud to pull over his fevered mind.

A million steps passed beneath his blind touch. A million years slid past as he traveled in the void, drowning in sorrow.

Darkness without and darkness within. The last thing he felt was metal beneath his fingers and fresh air on his face.

# 14
# The Hill Fire

He awakened in a long, dark room, surrounded by still, sleeping figures. It had all been a dream, of course. He was back in his bed among the other slumbering scullions, the only light a thin film of moonglow sliding in through a crack in the door. He shook his aching head.

*Why am I sleeping on the floor? These stones are so cold.* . . .

And why did the others lie so unmovingly, their shadowy shapes fantastic with helmets and shields, laid out on their beds in neat rows, like . . . like the dead awaiting judgment. . . ? It *had* all been a dream . . . hadn't it. . . ?!

With a gasp of terror Simon crawled away from the black mouth of the tunnel toward the blue-white chink in the doorway. The images of the dead, fixed in immobile stone atop their ancient tombs, did not stay his passing. He shouldered open the heavy door of the crypt and fell forward into the long, damp grass of the lich-yard.

After what had seemed countless years in the black places below, the round ivory moon that ranged high in the darkness above looked like yet another hole, this one leading to a cool, lamplit place beyond the sky, a country of shining rivers and forgetfulness. He lowered his cheek to the ground and felt the wet strands bend beneath his face. Fingers of time-worn rock thrust up on either side through the prisoning grass, or stretched headlong in

243

broken segments, etched by the moon in bone-white light, nameless and uncaring as the ancient dead whose graves they marked.

In Simon's mind the dark span of hours from the last fiery moments in the doctor's chambers to the night-damp grass of the present was as unreachable as the nearly invisible clouds threading the sky. The shouting and the cruel flames, Morgenes' burning face, Pyrates' eyes like punch-holes into ultimate darkness – these were as genuine as the breath he had just taken. The tunnel was only dwindling, half-remembered pain, a fog of voices and empty madness. He knew there had been rough walls, and cobwebs, and endlessly forking tunnels. It seemed there had also been vivid dreams of sadness and the death of beautiful things. Altogether he felt drained dry like an autumn leaf, fragile and without strength. He thought he had crawled at the end – his knees and arms were certainly sore enough, and his clothing was torn – but his memory seemed cloaked in darkness. None of it was quite *real*. Not like the lich-ground where he now lay, the moon's quiet commons yard.

Sleep was pushing at the back of his neck with soft, heavy hands. He fought it, rising to his knees with a slow shake of the head. It would not do to doze off here: there had been, as far as he knew, no pursuit through the blocked doorway of the doctor's chamber, but that didn't mean a great deal. His enemies had soldiers, and horses, and the king's authority.

Drowsiness was pushed aside by fear, and not a little anger. They had stolen all else from him: his friends, his home – they would not take his life and freedom, too. He climbed carefully to his feet and looked around, steadying himself on the leaning stones of the tomb as he wiped away tears of exhaustion and fear.

The town wall of Erchester loomed some half a league away, a moonlit belt of stone separating the sleeping citizens from the lich-yard and the world beyond. Before the outer gates sprawled the pale band of the Wealdhelm

Road; on Simon's right it meandered gradually north to the hills; on his left it companioned the river Ymstrecca through the farmlands below Swertclif, past Falshire on the far bank, and ultimately to the grasslands of the East.

It seemed likely that these towns along the great road would be the first places that the Erkynguard would search for a fugitive. Also, much of the road's length wandered through the valley farms of Hasu Vale, where he would be hard-pressed to find a hiding place if forced off the path.

Turning his back on Erchester, and the only home he had yet known, Simon hobbled out across the lich-yard toward the far downs. His first steps set off a flair of pain at the base of his skull, but he knew it would be best to ignore the aches of body and spirit for a while longer, fleeing as far away from the castle as possible while it was still dark; he could worry about the future when he had found a safe place to lie up.

As the moon scudded across the warm sky toward midnight, Simon's steps grew heavier and heavier. The lich-yard seemed to have no ending – indeed, the grounds had begun to rise and fall over the gentle humps of the outer downs while he still walked among the weathered stone teeth, some solitary and upright, others leaning together like old men in senile colloquy. He wove in and out among the buried pillars, stumbling across the uneven, tussocky ground. Every step became a struggle, as though he waded in high waters.

Staggering with weariness, he tripped over yet one more concealed stone and fell heavily to the ground. He tried to rise, but his limbs felt like sacks of wet sand. After crawling forward a short distance he curled up on the sloping shoulder of a grassy mound. Something dug into his back and he rolled clumsily to one side; this made him almost equally uncomfortable, since he was now lying on Morgenes' folded manuscript, tucked under his belt. Staring, eyes half-shut with exhaustion, he reached out to find the original source of irritation. It was a piece of metal, thick with corrosion and perforated like worm-gnawed wood. He tried to pull it free, but it was stuck fast in the earth. Perhaps the rest of it, whatever it might be, lay deep in the soil of a moon-frosted mound, anchored by dirt – a spear point? A belt buckle or greave from some costume whose owner had long since gone to feed the grass on which he lay? Simon thought for a bleary moment of all the bodies lying deep beneath the earth, the flesh that had once been quick with life but now moldered in silence and darkness.

As sleep captured him at last, it seemed that he was again on the roof of the chapel. Below him sprawled the castle . . . but this castle was made of damp, crumbling soil and blind white roots. The people in the castle slept on and on, tossing uneasily as in their dreams they heard Simon walking on the rooftop above their beds. . . .

He walked now – or dreamed he did – along a black river that splashed noisily but reflected no light, like fluid shadow. He was surrounded by mist, and could discern nothing of the land he walked on but a certain dimness. He heard many voices in the obscurity behind him; their murmurs intermixed with the slurring voice of the black water, coming closer, rushing like wind through the leaves.

No mist or fog shrouded the far side of the river. The grass on the nether bank stretched out before his gaze, and beyond it a somber grove of alder trees sloped up to the skirts of the hills. All the country beyond the river was dark and moist, as though it stood at dawn or twilight; after a moment it seemed clear that it must be evening, for the close-leaning hills echoed with the distant, solitary song of a nightingale. Everything seemed fixed and unchanging.

He peered across the burbling water and saw a figure standing by the river's edge on the far shore: a woman dressed all in gray, long straight hair shadowing the sides

246

of her face; in her arms she held something close-cradled. When she turned her eyes up to him he saw that she was weeping. It seemed that he knew her.

'Who are you?' he cried. His voice died out as the words left his mouth, swallowed up by the damp hiss of the river. The woman stared at him as if to memorize every feature with her wide dark eyes. At last she spoke.

'Seoman.' Her words came as down a long corridor, faint and hollow. 'Why have you not come to me, my son? The wind is drear and chill, and I have been such a long time waiting.'

'Mother?' Simon felt a terrible coldness. The soft rush of the water seemed everywhere. She spoke again.

'We have not met for so long, my beautiful child. Why do you not come to me? Why do you not come and dry a mother's tears? The wind is cold, but the river is warm and gentle. Come . . . will you not cross over to me?' She held her arms outstretched; her mouth below her black eyes opened in a smile. Simon moved toward her, his lost mother who called to him, walking down the soft riverbank toward the laughing black river. Her arms were open for him . . . for her son. . . .

And then Simon saw that what she had cradled, that which now dangled from an outflung hand, was a doll . . . a doll made from reeds and leaves and twining stems of grass. But the doll was blackened, the shriveled leaves curling back from their stems, and Simon knew suddenly that nothing alive crossed that river into the twilight country. He stopped at the water's edge and looked down.

Down in the inky water there was a faint gleam of light; as he watched, it rose toward the surface, becoming three slender, shining shapes. The sound of the river changed, became a kind of prickling, unearthly music. The water leaped and boiled, obscuring the objects' true forms, but it seemed that if he desired to, he could reach down and touch them. . . .

'Seoman. . . !' his mother called again. He looked up

to see her farther away, receding swiftly, as though her gray land were a torrent rushing away from him. Her arms were held wide, and her voice was a thing of vibrant loneliness, of the cold's lust for the warm, and the darkness' hopeless desire for the light.

'Simon . . . Simon. . . !' It was a wail of despair.

He sat stock-upright on the grass, in the lap of the ancient cairn. The moon still hung high, but the night had gone cold. Tendrils of mist caressed the broken stones around him as he sat, heart working madly.

'. . . *Simon* . . .' The cry came whispering up from the blackness beyond. It was a gray figure, surely, and a woman's voice calling faintly to him from the misty lich-yard he had crossed – only a tiny, wiggling gray shape, a faraway flicker in the ground-clutching fog that wound through the barrows, but seeing it Simon felt his heart would burst in his chest. He began to run across the downs, running as though the very Devil chased him with grasping hands. The dark bulk of Thisterborg rose on the shrouded horizon, and the downs were all around him, and Simon ran and ran, and ran. . . .

A thousand speeding heartbeats later he slowed at last to a ragged walk. He could not have run farther even if he *had* been the arch-demon's quarry: he was exhausted, limping, and hungry beyond belief. His fear and confusion hung on him like a mantle of chains; the dream had frightened him so that he felt even weaker than before his sleep.

Plodding forward, always with the castle at his back, he felt the memories of better times raveling away, leaving him with nothing but the thinnest of strands still tied to the world of sunlight and order and safety.

*What did it feel like when I used to lie in the hayloft, in the quiet? There's nothing in my head now, only words. Did I like to be there in the castle? Did I sleep there, run there, eat and talk and. . . ?*

*I don't think so. I think I have always walked these downs beneath the moon – that white face – walked and walked like the pitiful, lonely ghost of a mooncalf, walked and walked . . .*

A sudden shiver of flame on the hilltop halted his gloomy imaginings. For some time the ground had been sloping steadily upward, and he had nearly reached the base of shadowy Thisterborg; its mantle of tall trees was a solid, impenetrable darkness against the obscurity of the hill itself. Now a fire bloomed along the hill's crest, a sign of life amidst the downs and damp and centuries of death. He broke into a slow trot, the most he could manage in his present condition. Perhaps it was a shepherd's campfire, a merry blaze to keep the night at bay.

*Perhaps they have food! A shank of mutton . . . a knob of bread . . .*

He had to lean forward. His innards twitched and cramped at the thought of eating. How long had it been? Only supper last. . . ? It was astonishing to consider.

*Even if they have no food, how wonderful it will be just to hear voices, to warm myself before a fire . . . a fire . . .*

A memory of hungry flames leaped before his mind's eye, bringing a different kind of hollowness.

He climbed upward through the trees and tangled brush. The base of Thisterborg was ringed all around by mist, as if the hill was an island upthrust from a cobweb-gray sea. As he approached the summit he saw the blunt shapes of the Anger Stones crowning the final rise, etched in red relief against the sky.

*More stones. Stones and more stones. What did Morgenes say this was, this night – if it was still the same moon, the same darkness cradling the same dim stars – what did he call it?*

Stoning Night. As though the very stones celebrated. As if while Erchester lay sleeping behind shuttered window and latched door the stones made a holiday. In his weary thoughts Simon could see them ponderously a-step, the merrymaking stones bowing and wheeling . . . slowly turning. . . .

*Stupid!* he thought. *Your mind is wandering – and no*

*surprise. You need food and sleep: otherwise, you'll go truly mad* – whatever going mad meant . . . angry all the time? Frightened of nothing? He had seen a mad woman in Battle Square, but she had merely clutched a bundle of rags and rocked herself to and fro, keening like a gull.

*Mad beneath the moon. A mad mooncalf.*

He had reached the last stand of trees that surrounded the hill-crown. The air was still, as though expectant; Simon felt his hairs go all a-prickle. It suddenly seemed a good idea to walk quietly, to have a cautious look at these night-shepherds instead of crashing suddenly from the underbrush like an angry boar. He worked his way closer to the light, ducking beneath the twisted limbs of a wind-wracked oak. Just above him jutted the Anger Stones, concentric rings of tall, storm-sculpted pillars.

Now he saw a cluster of man-shapes huddled about the leaping fire at the center of the stone rings, cloaks hunched up at their shoulders. Something about them seemed stiff and uneasy, as though they waited on something expected but not necessarily desired. To the northeast, past the stones, the cap of Thisterborg narrowed. The windswept grass and heather there clung closely to the downsloping ground, which stretched away from the stones to sink at last out of the firelight at the hill's northern edge.

Staring at the statue-still figures around the fire, Simon again felt the weight of his fear drag at him. Why did they stand so unmoving? Were they living men at all, or some eerie carvings of hill-demons?

One of the shapes moved to the fire and poked it with a stick. As the flames jumped, Simon saw that this one at least was a mortal man. He crawled stealthily forward, stopping just beyond the outer circle of stones. The firelight caught and reddened a momentary glimpse of metal beneath the cloak of the nearest figure – this shepherd wore a mail shirt.

The vast night sky seemed to shrink down, a prisoning blanket. *All* the half-a-score of shrouded men were

250

armored: it was the Erkynguard – he was sure of it. He cursed himself bitterly: he had come straight to their fire, like a moth flinging itself into the candleflame.

*Why am I always such a damnable, damnable fool?!*

A thin night-wind sprang up, setting the high flames whipping like a burning pennant. The cloaked and hooded guardsmen turned their heads in unison, slowly and almost reluctantly, gazing out into the darkness at the hill's northern rim.

Then Simon heard it, too. Above the hissing wind that riffled the grass and gently shook the trees there came a faint sound, growing ever so gradually louder: the aching creak of wooden cart wheels. A bulky shape was climbing upward out of the obscurity of the north edge. The guardsmen moved away from the approach, circling the fire to cluster together on the side nearest Simon; no word had yet been uttered by any of them.

Dim, pale shapes that slowly became horses appeared at the fringe of the fireglow; following behind, growing distinct from the night, was a great black wagon. Black-hooded figures walked on either side, four in all, matching the wagon's stately, funeral pace. The flickering light revealed a fifth atop the wagon, hunched over the team of ice-white stallions. This last figure was somehow larger than the others, and darker, as if it wore some cloak of obscurity; its very stillness seemed to speak of a hidden, brooding power.

The guards still did not move, but stood rigidly watching. Only the thin mewing of the wagon wheels punctured the silence. Simon, transfixed, felt cold pressure in his head, a gnawing clutch in his vitals.

*A dream, a bad dream . . . Why can't I move?!*

The black cart and its attendants drew to a halt just within the circle of firelight. One of the four standing figures raised an arm, the black sleeve falling away to reveal a wrist and hand as thin and white as bone.

It spoke, voice silvery-cold, toneless as ice cracking.

'We are here to fulfill the covenant.'

251

There was a stir among those who had been waiting. One of them stepped foward.

'As are we.'

Watching helplessly as this mad fancy progressed, Simon was not at all surprised to recognize the voice of Pryrates. The priest pulled back his hood; firelight traced the high arc of his forehead and emphasized the skeletal depths of his eyes. 'We are here . . . as agreed,' he continued. Was there a faint quaver in his voice? 'Have you brought that which was promised?'

The bone-white arm swept back, gesturing to the looming wagon. 'We have. Have you?'

Pryrates nodded his head. Two of the guardsmen bent and wrestled some burden up from the grass where it lay, dragging it forward to be dropped urgently at the alchemist's booted feet. 'It lies here,' he said. 'Bring forth your master's gift.'

Two of the robed figures moved to the wagon, carefully lifting down a long, dark object. As they brought it forward, one holding either end, a biting wind sprang up and whistled over the hilltop. The black robes billowed, and the hood on the nearest blew back, spilling a flurry of gleaming white hair. The face revealed in the brief moment was delicate as a mask of the thinnest, most exquisite ivory. An instant later the hood flapped back.

*Who are these creatures? Witches? Ghosts?* Behind the shielding rocks Simon brought a trembling hand up to make the sign of the Tree.

*The white foxes . . . Morgenes said 'white foxes' . . .*

Pryrates, these demons – or whatever they might be – it was all too much. He *must* still be dreaming in the graveyard. He prayed it was so, and closed his eyes to block out the unholy imaginings . . . but the ground beneath him was pungent with the unmistakable smell of wet earth, and the fire crackled in his ears. Opening his eyes he found the nightmare unchanged.

*What is* happening?

The two shadowy figures reached the edge of the fire-circle; as the soldiers edged even farther away they set their burden down and stepped back. It was a coffin, or at least coffin-shaped, but only three hands high. A ghastly bluish light smoldered along its edge.

'Bring forth that which you have promised,' said the first dark-robed creature. Pryrates gestured and the bundle at his feet was dragged forward. When the soldiers stepped back, the alchemist pushed the object over with the toe of his boot. It was a man, gagged and bound at the wrists. Simon only slowly recognized the round, pale face of Count Breyugar, the Lord Constable.

The robed figure regarded Breyugar's bruised features for a long interval. Its expression was hidden in the hood's shadowed folds, but when it spoke there was a twist of anger in the clear, unearthly tones.

'This does not seem to be what was promised.'

Pryrates tilted his body a little to the side, as if narrowing his exposure to the hooded thing. 'This one allowed the promised one to escape,' he said, seeming to betray some apprehension. 'He will take the promised one's place.'

Another figure shouldered its way out from between a pair of guardsmen, moving forward to loom at Pryrates' side.

'Promised? What is this "promised"? *Who* was promised?'

The priest raised his hands placatingly, but his expression was stern. 'Please, my king, I think you know. Please.'

Elias snapped his head around to stare at his counselor. '*Do* I know, priest? What did you promise on my behalf?'

Pryrates leaned toward his master; his harsh voice slipped into a wounded tone. 'Lord, you bade me do what I must for this meeting. I did it . . . or would have, had not this – *cenit*,' he dug a toe into bound Breyugar, 'failed in his duty to his sovereign.' The alchemist looked over to the dark-robed figure, whose impassivity carried nonetheless a hint of impatience. Pryrates frowned.

253

'Please, my king, the one we speak of is gone; the point is moot. Please.' He laid a light hand on Elias' cloaked shoulder. The king shook it off, staring out of the shadows of his hood at the priest, but saying nothing. Pryrates turned to the black-robed figure once more.

'This one we offer you . . . his blood, too, is noble. His lineage is high.'

'Of high lineage?' the dark thing asked, and then its shoulders shook as though it laughed. 'Oh, yes, that is very important. Does its family go back many generations of men?' The dark hood turned and met the shrouded gaze of its fellows.

'Certainly,' said Pryrates, seemingly disconcerted. 'Hundreds of years.'

'Well, our master will certainly be pleased.' And then it did laugh, a blade-edged trill of merriment that made Pryrates take a step backward. 'Proceed.'

The priest looked to Elias, who pulled back his hood. Simon felt the looming sky crouch still closer. The king's face, pale even in the ruddy firelight, seemed to float in midair. The night swirled, and the king's impassive gaze drew light like a mirror in a torchlit hallway. Finally, Elias nodded.

Pryrates stepped forward and grasped Breyugar by the collar, dragging him to the coffin-box where he let him slump to the earth. The priest then unclasped his cloak, revealing a dull flare of red robe, and reached into the inner folds to withdraw a long, curved blade like a sickle. He raised it before his eyes as he faced the northernmost point of the rings of stones, then began to chant, his voice rising in volume and authority:

> 'To the Dark One, who is master of this world:
> Who bestrides the Northern Sky:
> **Vasir Sombris, feata concordin!**
>
> To the Black Huntsman,
> Possessor of the icy Hand:
> **Vasir Sombris, feata concordin!**

*To the Storm King, the Outreaching
The Dweller in the Stony Mountain,
The Frozen and Burning,
The Sleeping but Awakened:*
**Vasir Sombris, feata concordin!'**

The black-robed figures swayed – all but the one atop
the wagon, who sat as still as the Anger Stones – and a
hiss went up from their midst, mingling with the new-
risen wind.

> *'Hear now Your supplicant!'*
> Pryrates cried,

> *'The beetle beneath Your black heel;
> The fly between Your cold fingers;
> The whispering dust in Your endless shadow –
> Oveiz mei! Hear me!
> Timior cuelos exaltat mei!*
> **Shadow-Father – let the bargain be struck!'**

The alchemist's hand snaked down and grasped
Breyugar's head. The count, who had been lying limp at
his feet, suddenly lurched forward and away, leaving the
startled Pryrates holding nothing but a hank of bloodied
hair.

Simon watched helplessly as the pop-eyed Lord
Constable stumbled directly toward his hiding place; he
dimly heard Pryrates' angry shouting. The close-leaning
night tightened around him, choking his breath and
blackening his vision as a pair of guards leaped after
Breyugar.

The count was only a few paces away, running
awkwardly because of his tied hands, when he tripped
and fell. His legs kicked, and his breath sawed noisily
behind the gag as the guardsmen bore down on him.
Simon had risen to a half-crouch behind the concealing
stone, and his weary heart was hammering as though it

might rupture. He tried desperately to still his trembling legs. The guards, close enough to touch, yanked Breyugar to his feet with fearful curses. One of them raised a sword and struck the count with the flat of his blade. Simon could see Pryrates staring out from the circle of light, and the king's ashen, fascinated face beside him. Even as Breyugar's limp form was wrestled back toward the fire, Pryrates continued to squint at the place where the count had fallen.

*Who is there?*

The voice seemed to fly on the back of the wind straight into Simon's head. Pryrates was staring right at him! He *must* see him!

*Come out, whoever you are. I command you to come forward.*

The black-robed figures began a strange, ominous humming, and Simon struggled against the alchemist's will. He remembered what had almost happened to him in the storeroom, and braced himself against the compelling force, but he was weakened, wrung dry like a piece of cloth.

*Come out*, the voice repeated, and a questing something reached out to touch his mind. He fought, trying to hold shut the doors of his soul, but the probing thing was stronger than he by far. It had only to find him, to grasp him. . . .

'If the covenant no longer suits you,' a thin voice said, 'then let it be broken off now. It is dangerous to leave the ritual half-spoken – *very* dangerous.'

It was the hooded figure speaking, and Simon could feel the red priest's questing thoughts shaken.

'Wh . . . What?' Pryrates spoke like a man new-wakened.

'Perhaps you do not understand what you are doing here,' the black shape hissed. 'Perhaps you do not comprehend who and what is involved.'

'No . . . yes, I do . . .' the priest stammered; Simon could somehow sense his nervousness, as if it were an odor. 'Quickly,' he turned to the guardsmen, 'bring that sack of offal here before me.' The guards dragged their burden back to lie again at his feet.

'Pryrates . . .' the king began.

'Please, your majesty, please. It is only a moment now.'

Horribly, a part of Pryrates' thought had not left Simon's mind, some clinging tag-end that the priest had not pulled back: he could almost taste the alchemist's quivering expectancy as Pryrates pulled up Breyugar's head, could sense the priest responding to the low murmuring of the hooded ones. And now he felt something deeper, too, a chill wedge of horror driving into his raw and sensitive mind. Some inexplicable *other* was there in the night – a terrible *something-else*. It hovered over the hilltop like a choking cloud, and burned inside the seated figure on the wagon like a hidden black flame; it dwelt also in the bodies of the standing stones, infusing them with its greedy attention.

The sickle rose. For a moment the flashing crimson curve of the blade was a second moon against the sky, an old, red crescent moon. Pryrates cried out in a high-pitched language Simon could not understand.

*'Aí Samu'sitech'a! – Aí Nakkiga!'*

The sickle descended and Breyugar sagged forward. Purplish blood pumped from his throat, spattering down onto the coffin. For a moment the Lord Constable twitched violently beneath the priest's hand, then went limp as an eel; the dark flow continued to drizzle on the black lid. Enmeshed in the bizarre intermixture of thought, Simon helplessly experienced Pryrates' panicky exhilaration. Behind that he felt the *something-else* – a cold, dark, horribly vast thing. Its ancient thoughts sang with obscene joy.

One of the soldiers was throwing up; but for the flabby numbness that unmanned and silenced him, Simon would have done the same.

Pryrates pushed the count's body aside; Breyugar

tumbled in a disordered heap, oyster-pale fingers curled toward the sky. The blood smoked on the dark box, and the blue light flickered more brightly. The line it described around the edge became more pronounced. Slowly, dreadfully, the lid began to open, as if forced up from within.

*Holy Usires Who loves me, Holy Usires Who loves me* – Simon's thoughts were a rush, a panicked tangle – *help me, help me help it's the Devil in that box, he's coming out help save me oh help* . . .

*We have done it, we have done it!* – other thoughts, foreign, not his – *Too late to turn back. Too late.*

*The first step* – the coldest, most terrible thoughts of all – *How they will pay and pay and pay* . . .

As the lid tilted up the light within burst forth, throbbing indigo touched with smoky gray and sullen purple, a terrible bruised light that pulsed and glared. The lid fell open, and the wind tightened its pitch as if frightened, as if sickened by the radiance of the long black box. At last what was inside could be seen.

*Jingizu*, a voice whispered in Simon's head. *Jingizu* . . .

It was a sword. It lay inside the box, deadly as an adder; it might have been black, but a floating sheen mottled the blackness, a crawling gray like oil on dark water. The wind shrieked.

*It beats like a heart – the heart of all sorrow* . . .

Calling, it sang inside Simon's head, a voice both horrible and beautiful, seductive as claws gently scraping his skin.

'Take it, Highness!' Pryrates urged through the hiss of the wind. Enthralled, helpless, Simon suddenly wished he had the strength to take it himself. Could he not? Power was singing to him, singing of the thrones of the mighty, the rapture of desire fulfilled.

Elias took a dragging step forward. One by one the soldiers around him stumbled back, turning to run sobbing or praying down the hill, lurching into the darkness of the girdling trees. Within moments only Elias, Pryrates, and hidden Simon remained on the hilltop with the hooded ones and their sword. Elias took another step; now he stood over the box. His eyes were wide with fear; he seemed stricken by wrenching doubt, his lips working soundlessly. The unseen fingers of the wind plucked at his cloak, and the hill grasses twined about his ankles.

'You must take it!' Pryrates said again, and Elias stared at him as though seeing the alchemist for the first time. 'Take it!' Pryrates' words danced frantically through Simon's head like rats in a burning house.

The king bent, reaching out his hand. Simon's lust turned to sudden horror at the wild, empty nothingness of the sword's dark song.

*It's wrong! Can't he feel it?! Wrong!*

As Elias' hand neared the sword, the wail of the wind subsided. The four hooded figures stood motionless before the wagon; the fifth seemed to sink into deeper shadow. Silence fell on the hilltop like a palpable thing.

Elias grasped the hilt, lifting the blade out of the coffin in one smooth movement. As he held it before him the fear was suddenly wiped from his face, and his lips parted in a helpless, idiot smile. He lifted the sword high; a blue shimmer played along the edge, marking it out from the blackness of the sky. Elias' voice was almost a whimper of pleasure.

'I . . . will take the master's gift. I will . . . honor our pact.' Slowly, the blade held before him, he sank to one knee. *'Hail to Ineluki Storm King!'*

The wind sprang up anew, shrieking. Simon reeled back from the flapping, whirling hill-fire as the four robed figures lifted their white arms, chanting: *'Ineluki, aí! Ineluki, aí!'*

*No!* Simon's thoughts flurried, *the king . . . all is lost! Run, Josua!*

*Sorrow . . . Sorrow on all the land . . .*

The fifth hooded shape began to writhe atop the wagon. The black robe fell away, and a shape of fire-crimson light was revealed, flapping like a burning sail. A ghastly, heart-gnawing fear beat outward from the thing as it began to grow before Simon's terror-fixed eyes – bodiless and billowing, larger and larger until the empty, wind-snapping bulk of it loomed over all, a creature of howling air and glowing redness.

*The Devil is here! Sorrow, his name is sorrow. . . ! The king has brought the Devil! Morgenes, Holy Usires, save me save me save me!!*

He ran mindlessly down through black night, away from the red thing and the exulting *something-else*. The sound of his flight was lost in the screaming wind. Branches tore at his arms and hair and face like claws. . . .

*The icy claw of the North . . . the ruins of Asu'a.*

And when he fell at last, tumbling, and his spirit fled from such horror, fled away into deeper darkness, it seemed that in the final instant he could hear the very stones of the earth moaning in their beds beneath him.

# PART TWO

---

# SIMON
# PILGRIM

THE DIMMERSKOG

ST. SKENDI'S

HAETHSTAD

THE
FROSTMARCH

DA'AL
CHIKIZA

NAGLIMUND

ST. HODERUND'S

THE KNOCK

GELOË'S
LAKE

ALDHEORTE

SISTAN

FLETT

THISTERBORG

ERCHESTER

THE HAYHOLT

SWERTCLIFF

STANSHIRE

FALSHIRE

RIVER
STEFFLOD

GRENEFOD

RIVER GLENIWENT

RIVER
YMSTRECCA

MEREMUND

WENTMOUTH

# 15
# A Meeting at the Inn

The first thing Simon heard was a humming noise, a dull buzz that pushed insistently against his ear as he struggled toward wakefulness. Half-opening an eye, he found himself staring at a monstrosity – a dark, indistinct mass of squirming legs and glittering eyes. He sat up with a startled yelp and a great flailing of arms; the bumblebee that had been guilelessly exploring his nose leaped away in a whir of translucent wings to search for a less excitable perch.

He lifted a hand to shade his eyes, startled by the vibrant clarity of the world around him. The daylight was dazzling. The spring sun, as if on imperial procession, had scattered gold on all sides across the grassy downs; everywhere he looked the gentle slopes were rich with dandelions and long-stemmed marigolds. Bees hurried among them, nipping from flower to flower like little doctors discovering – much to their surprise – all their patients getting well at the same time.

Simon slumped back down into the grass, clasping his hands behind his head. He had slept a long while: the rich sun was almost straight overhead. It made the hairs on his forearms glow like molten copper; the tips of his ragged shoes looked so far away he could almost imagine them the peaks of distant mountains.

A sudden cold sliver of memory pierced his drowsiness. How had he gotten here? What. . . ?

A dark presence at his shoulder brought him quickly onto his knees; he turned to see the tree-mantled mass of Thisterborg looming behind him, not half a league away. Every detail was stunningly clear, a pattern of precise edges; but for the troubling throb of memory it might have seemed comfortable and cool, a placid hill rising through encircling trees, banded with shade and bright green leaves. Along its crest were the Anger Stones, faint gray points against the blue sky.

The vivid spring day was now corrupted by a mist of dream – what had happened last night? He had fled the castle, of course – those moments, his last with Morgenes, were burned into his very heart – but after? What were these nightmarish memories? Endless tunnels? Elias? A fire, and white-haired demons?

*Dreams – idiot, bad dreams. Terror and tiredness and more terror. I ran through the graveyard at night, fell down at last, slept and dreamed.*

But the tunnels, and . . . a black casket? His head still hurt, but there was also an odd sense of numbness, as if ice had been laid on an injury. The dream had seemed so real. Now it was distant, slippery and meaningless – a dark pang of fear and pain that would drift away like smoke if he allowed it to – or, at least, he hoped it would. He pushed the memories down, burying them as deeply as he could, and closing his mind over them like the lid of a box.

*It's not as though I don't have enough things to worry about. . . .*

The bright sun of Belthainn Day had smoothed some of the kinks from his muscles, but he was still sore . . . and very hungry. He clambered stiffly to his feet and brushed the clinging grass from his tattered, mud-smeared clothes. He stole another look at Thisterborg. *Did* the ashes of a great fire still smolder among the stones there? Or had the shattering events of the day before pushed him for a while into madness? The hill stood, impassive; whatever secrets might lurk beneath the cloak

264

of trees, or nestle in the crown of stones, Simon did not want to know. There were already too many hollows that needed filling.

Turning his back on Thisterborg, he faced across the downs to the dark breakfront of the forest. Staring across the vast expanse of open land, he felt a deep sorrow welling up within him, and pity for himself. He was so alone! They had taken everything from him, and left him without home or friends. He slapped his hands together in anger and felt the palms sting. Later! Later he would cry; now he had to be a man. But it was all so horribly unfair!

He breathed in and out deeply, and looked again to the distant woods. Somewhere near that thin line of shadow, he knew, ran the Old Forest Road. It rolled for miles along Aldheorte's southern perimeter, sometimes at a distance, sometimes sidling up close to the old trees like a teasing child. In other places it actually passed beneath the forest's eaves, winding through dark bowers and silent, sun-arrowed clearings. A few small villages and an occasional roadhouse nestled in the forest's shadow.

*Perhaps I can find some work to do — even to earn a meal, anyway. I feel hungry as a bear . . . a just-woken bear, at that. Starved! I haven't eaten since before . . . before . . .*

He bit his lip, hard. There was nothing else to do but start walking.

The touch of the sun felt like a benediction. As it warmed his sore body, it seemed also to cut a little way through the clinging, troubling pall of his thoughts. In a way he felt new-born, like the colt Shem had brought him to see last spring, all shaky legs and curiosity. But the new strangeness of the world was not all innocent; something strange and secretive lurked behind the bright tapestry laid out before him; the colors were almost too bright, the scents and sounds over-sweet.

He was soon uncomfortably aware of Morgenes' manuscript tucked into his waistband, but after he had tried carrying the sheaf of parchment in his sweating palms for a few hundred paces he gave up and slipped it back under his belt. The old man had asked him to save the thing, and save it he would. He pushed his shirttail behind it to ease the rubbing.

When he tired of searching patiently for places to ford the small streams that webbed the meadows he took off his shoes. The smell of the grasslands and the moist Maia air, untrustworthy indicators though they were, nevertheless went some way toward keeping his thoughts from straying toward the black, hurting places; the feel of mud between his toes helped, too.

Before long he reached the Old Forest Road. Instead of continuing along the road itself, which was wide and muddy and scored with the rain-filled ruts of wagon wheels, Simon turned west and accompanied its passage atop the high grass bank. Below him white asphodels and blue gillyflowers stood abashed and unprotected between the wheelmarks, as though surprised in the midst of a slow pilgrimage from one bank to the other. Puddles caught the sky's afternoon blue, and the humble mud seemed studded with shining glass.

A furlong away across the road the trees of Aldheorte stood in endless formation like an army asleep on its feet. Darknesses so complete that they might have been portals into the earth gaped between some of the trunks. In other places were things that must be woodcutters' huts, noticeably angular against the forest's graceful lines.

Walking, staring at the interminable forest porch, Simon tripped over a berry-bush and painfully scratched both his feet. As soon as he realized what he had stumbled over, he stopped cursing. Most of the berries were still green, but enough had ripened that his cheeks and chin were thoroughly stained with berry juice when he continued on some minutes later, chewing contentedly. The berries were not quite sweet yet, but still they seemed the first serious argument he had found in a long time for the benevolent ordering of Creation. When he finished, he wiped his hands on his ruined shirt.

As the road, with Simon for company, began to mount a long track of rising ground, definite evidence of human habitation finally appeared. Here and there in the southerly distance the rough spines of split-wood fences pushed up from the high grass; beyond these weathered boundary wardens were indistinct figures moving in the slow rhythms of planting, putting down the spring peas. Somewhere nearby, others would be moving deliberately down the rows plying the weed hooks, doing their best to save the fruits of a bad year. The younger folk would be up on the cottage roofs, turning back the thatch, beating it down firmly with long sticks and pulling off the moss that had grown during the rains of Avril. He felt a strong urge to head out across the fields toward those calm, ordered farms. Someone would surely give him work, take him in . . . feed him.

*How stupid can I be?* he thought. *Why don't I just walk back to the castle and stand shouting in the commons yard?!* Country folk were notoriously suspicious of strangers – especially these days, with rumors of banditry and worse drifting down from the north. The Erkynguard would be looking for him, Simon felt sure. These isolated farms would be very likely to remember a red-haired young man who had recently passed by. Besides, he was in no hurry to speak to strangers, anyway – not so close to the Hayholt. Perhaps he would be better off in one of the inns that bordered the mysterious forest – if one would have him.

*I do know something about working in kitchens, don't I? Someone will give me work . . . won't they?*

Topping a rise, he saw the road before him intersected by a dark swath, a crease of wagon tracks that emerged from the forest and meandered south across the fields: a woodsman's road, perhaps, a route from the wood-chopper's harvesting-place to the farmlands west of Erchester. Something dark stood, angular and erect, at the meeting point of the two roads. A brief twinge of fear passed through him before he realized that it was too tall an object to be someone waiting for him. He guessed it to be a scarecrow, or a roadside shrine to Elysia, the Mother of God – crossroads were infamously strange places, and the common folk often mounted a holy relic to keep away loitering ghosts.

As he neared the crossing he decided that he had been right about it being a scarecrow – the object seemed to be hanging from a tree or pole, and swayed softly, breeze-blown. But as he came closer he saw it was no scarecrow. Soon he could no longer convince himself that it was anything other than what it was: the body of a man swinging from a crude gibbet.

He reached the crossroad. The wind subsided; thin roadway dust hung about him in a brown cloud. He stopped to stare helplessly. The road grit settled, then leaped into swirling motion once more.

The hanged man's feet, bare and swollen black, dangled at the height of Simon's shoulder. His head lolled to one side, like a puppy picked up by the neck-scruff; the birds had been at his eyes and face. A broken shingle of wood with the words '*M THE KINGS LAND*' scratched upon it bumped gently against his chest; in the road below lay another piece. On it was scrawled: '*POACHED FRO.*'

Simon stepped back; an innocent breeze twisted the sagging body so that the face tipped away to stare sightlessly across the fields. He hurried across the lumber-road, tracing the four-pointed Tree on his chest as he passed through the thing's shadow. Normally such a sight would be fearful but fascinating, as dead things were, but now all he could feel was sick terror. He himself had stolen – or helped to steal – something far greater than this poor sneak thief could ever have dreamed of: he had stolen the king's brother from the king's own dungeon. How long would it be until they caught him, as they had caught this rook-eaten creature? What would *his* punishment be?

He looked back once. The ruined face had swung again, as if to watch his retreat. He ran until a dip in the road had blocked the crossing from view.

It was late afternoon when he reached the tiny village of Flett. It was truthfully not much of a village, just an inn and a few houses crouching beside the road within a stone's-throw of the woods. No people were about except a thin woman standing in the doorway of one of the rude houses, and a pair of solemn, round-eyed children that peered out past her legs. There were, however, several horses – farm nags, mostly – tied to a log before the town's inn, the *Dragon and Fisherman*. As Simon walked slowly past the open door, looking cautiously all around, men's loud voices rolled out from the beery darkness, frightening him. He decided to wait and try his luck later, when there might be more customers stopping off the Old Forest Road for the night, and his dirty, tattered appearance would be less notable.

He followed the road a little farther. His stomach was rumbling, making him wish he had saved some of his berries. There were only a few more houses and a little one-room cottage-church, then the road swerved up and under the forest's eaves and Flett, such as it was, ended.

Just past the edge of town he found a small stream gurgling along over the black, leafy soil. He knelt and drank. Ignoring the brambles and the dampness as best he could, he took his shoes back off again to use for a pillow and curled up at the base of a live oak, just out of sight of the road and the last house. He fell asleep quickly beneath the trees, a grateful guest in their cool hall.

Simon dreamed . . .

He found an apple lying on the ground at the foot of a great white tree, an apple so shiny and round and red that he hardly dared to bite it. But his hunger was strong, and soon he lifted it to his mouth and set his teeth in it. The taste was wonderful, all crunch and sweetness, but when he looked where he had bitten he saw the thin, slippery

269

body of a worm coiled beneath the bright surface. He could not bear to throw the apple away, however – it was such a beautiful fruit, and he was famished. He turned it around and bit into the other side, but as his teeth met he pulled away and saw once more the sinuous body of the worm. Over and over he bit, each time in a different place, but each time the slithering thing lay beneath the skin. It seemed to have no head or tail, but only endless coils wound around the core, spreading through the apple's cool, white flesh. . . .

Simon awoke beneath the trees with an aching head and a sour taste in his mouth. He went to the streamlet to drink, feeling faint and weak of spirit. When had anyone ever been so alone? The slanting afternoon light did not touch the sunken surface of the creek; as he kneeled for a moment staring down into the murmuring dark water, he felt he had been in a place like this before. As he wondered, the soft wind-speech of the trees was over- whelmed by a rising murmur of voices. For a moment he feared he was dreaming again, but as he turned he saw a crowd of people, a score at least, coming up the Old Forest Road toward Flett. Still in the shadow of the trees, he moved forward to watch them, drying his mouth with the arm of his shirt.

The marchers were peasant folk, dressed in the rough cotsman's cloth of the district, but with a festive air. The women had ribbons twined in their unpinned hair, blue and gold and green. Skirts twirled about bare ankles. Some who ran in front carried flower petals in their aprons which they cast fluttering to the ground. The men, some young and lightfooted, some limping gaffers, carried on their shoulders a felled tree. Its branches were as ribbon-festooned as the women, and the menfolk held it high, swinging it jauntily as they came up the road.

Simon smiled weakly. The Maia-tree! Of course. It was Belthainn Day today, and they were bringing the Maia-tree. He had often watched the tree go up in

Erchester's Battle Square. Suddenly his smile felt too wide. He was lightheaded. He crouched lower among the concealing brush.

Now the women were singing, their sweet voices mixing unevenly as the throng danced and whirled.

> *'Come now to the Breredon,*
> *Come to the Hill of Briars!*
> *Put on your merry flower-crown!*
> *Come dance beside my fire!'*

The men replied, voices ragged and cheerful:

> *'I'll dance before your fire, lass,*
> *Then, in the forest's shadow*
> *We'll lay a bed of blossoms down*
> *And put an end to sorrow!'*

Both together sang the refrain:

> *'So stand beneath this Yrmansol*
> *Sing hey-up! Hey-yarrow!*
> *Stand beneath the Maia-pole*
> *Sing hey-up! God is growing!'*

The women were beginning another verse, one about hollyhock and lily-leaves and the King of Flowers, as the noisy band drew abreast of Simon. Caught up for a moment in the high spirits, his dizzy head full of the exuberant music, he began to push forward. Not ten paces away on the sun-blotted road one of the men nearest him stumbled, a trailing ribbon coiled about his eyes. A companion helped him to disentangle himself, and as he pulled the gold streamer loose his whiskery face creased in a broad grin. For some reason the flash of laughing teeth held Simon a step short of leaving the concealment of the trees.

*What am I doing!?* he berated himself. *The first sound of*

271

*friendly voices and I go bounding out into the open? These
people are merrymakers, but a hound will play with his master,
too – and woe to the stranger that comes up unannounced.*

The man he had been watching shouted something to
his companion which Simon could not hear over the din
of the crowd, then turned and held up a ribbon, shouting
to someone else. The tree jounced along, and when the
procession's last stragglers had passed, Simon slipped out
on to the road and followed – a thin, rag-wrapped figure,
he might have been the tree's mournful spirit wistfully
pursuing its stolen home.

The lurching parade turned up a small hill behind the
church. Across the broad fields the last splinter of sun
was vanishing fast; the shadow of the church's rooftop
Tree lay across the hillock like a long, curve-hilted knife.
Not knowing what was planned, Simon hung well back
of the group as they carried the tree up the slight rise,
stumbling and catching on the new-sprung briars. At the
top the men gathered, sweaty and full of loud jests, and
levered the trunk upright into a hole dug there. Then,
while some held the swaying bulk steady, others shored
up the base with stones. At last they stepped back. The
Maia-tree tottered a bit, then tipped slightly to one side,
drawing a gasp of apprehensive laughter from the crowd.
It held, only slightly out of plumb; a great cheer went up.
Simon, in the tree-shadows, gave voice himself to a
small, happy noise, then had to retreat into hiding as his
throat tightened. He coughed until blackness fluttered
before his eyes: it had been nearly a full day since he had
uttered a spoken word.

Eyes watering, he crept back out. A fire had been
kindled at the hill's foot. With its highest point painted by
the sunset, and the flames jigging down below, the tree
seemed a torch fired at both ends. Irresistibly drawn by
the scent of food, Simon moved near to the gaffers and
gossips who were spreading cloths and laying supper by
the stone wall behind the little church. He was surprised
and disappointed to see how meager the stores were –

272

slim rewards for a festival day, and, dreadful luck, an even slimmer chance of him making off with any unnoticed.

The younger men and women had begun to dance around the base of the Maia-tree, trying to make a ring. The circle, with drunken tumbling-down-the-hill and other impediments, never became completely joined; the spectators whooped to see the dancers vainly reaching for a hand to close on as they whirled giddily by. One by one the merrymakers reeled away from the dance, staggering, sometimes rolling down the low hill to lie at the bottom laughing helplessly. Simon ached to join them.

Soon knots of people were sitting all about the grass and along the wall. The highest tip of the tree was a ruby spearhead, capturing the sun's final rays. One of the men at the base of the hill brought out a shinbone flute and began to play. A gradual silence descended as he piped, touched only by whispers and an occasional squeak of muffled laughter. At last the breathing blue darkness surrounded them all. The plaintive voice of the flute soared above, like the spirit of a melancholy bird. A young woman, black-haired and thin-faced, got to her feet, steadying herself on the shoulder of her young man. Swaying gently, like a slim birch tree in the wind's path, she began to sing; Simon felt the great hollowness inside himself open up to the song, to the evening, to the patient, contented smell of the grass and other growing things.

> *'O faithful friend, O Linden tree.'*

she sang,

> *'That sheltered me when I was young,*
> *O tell me of my faithless one*
> *Be friend again to me.*
>
> *The one who was my heart's desire*
> *Who promised all for all in turn*

*Has left me lorn, my heart has spurned*
*And made of Love a liar.*

*Where has he gone, O Linden tree?*
*Into the arms of what sweet friend?*
*What call will bring him back again?*
*O spy him out for me!*

*Ask me not that, my mistress fair*
*I'd fain not make answer to you.*
*For I could only answer true*
*And I would your feelings spare.*

*Deny me not, O Linden tall*
*Tell me who holds him close tonight!*
*What woman has o'erthrown my right?*
*Who keeps him from my call?*

*O mistress fair, then truth I'll tell*
*He'll not to you come anymore.*
*Tonight he walked the river shore*
*And stumbled there and fell.*

*The river-woman now he holds*
*And she in turn holds fast to him.*
*But she will send him back again.*
*All river-wet and cold.*

*Thus will he come from there again.*
*All river-wet and cold . . .'*

As the black-haired girl sat down again the fire
crackled and spat, as if in mockery of such a damp, tender
song.

Simon hurried away from the fire, his eyes filling with
tears. The woman's voice had awakened in him a fierce
hunger for his home: for the joking voices of the
scullions, the offhand kindnesses of the chambermaids,
his bed, his moat, the long, sun-speckled expanse of
Morgenes' chambers, even – he was chagrined to realize
– the stern presence of Rachel the Dragon.

274

The murmurs and laughter behind him filled the spring darkness like the whir of soft wings.

A score or so of people were in the street before the church. Most of them, in knots of two or three or four, seemed headed through the settling darkness toward the *Dragon and Fisherman*. Firelight glowed within the door there, stippling the loiterers on the porch with yellow light. As Simon approached, still wiping at his eyes, the odors of meat and brown ale rolled over him like an ocean wave. He walked slowly, several paces behind the last group, wondering if he should ask for work right off, or just wait in the sociable warmth until later, when the innkeeper might have a moment to speak with him and see that he was a trustworthy lad. It made him fearful just to think about asking a stranger to take him in, but what else could he do? Sleep in the forest like a beast?

As he squirmed through a clump of drunken farmers arguing the merits of late-season shearing, he nearly tripped over a dark figure huddled against the wall beneath the inn's swinging sign. A round pink face with small dark eyes turned up to stare at him. Simon mumbled noises of apology, and was moving on when he remembered.

'I know you!' he said to the crouching figure; the dark eyes widened as if in alarm. 'You're the friar I met in the Main Row! Brother . . . Brother Cadrach?'

Cadrach, who for a brief moment had looked as though he might scramble away on hands and knees, narrowed his eyes to stare in turn.

'Don't you remember me?' he said excitedly. The sight of a familiar face was as heady as wine. 'My name is Simon.' A couple of the farmers turned to look blearily and incuriously in their direction, and he felt a stab of fright, remembering that he was a fugitive. 'My name is Simon,' he repeated in a softer voice.

A look of recognition, and something else, passed over the monk's plump face. 'Simon! Ah, of course, boy! What brings you, then, up from the great Erchester to dismal little Flett?' With the aid of a long stick that had been leaning against the wall beside him, Cadrach climbed to his feet.

'Well . . .' Simon was nonplussed.

*Yes, what have you been doing, you idiot, that you should strike up conversation with near-strangers.* Think, *stupid! Morgenes tried to tell you that this was no game.*

'I have been on an errand . . . for some people at the castle . . .'

'And you decided to take the small bit of money left to you and stop at the famous *Dragon and Fisherman,*' Cadrach made a wry face, 'and have a bit of something to eat.' Before Simon could correct him, or decide if he wanted to, the monk continued. 'What you should be after, then, is taking your supper with me, and let me pay your count – no, no, lad, I insist! It is only a fairness, after the kindly ways you showed to a stranger.' Simon could not utter a word before Brother Cadrach had his arm, pulling him into the public room.

A few faces turned as they entered, but no one's eyes lingered. The room was long and low-ceilinged, lined along both walls with tables and benches so wine-stained, hacked, and carved-upon that they seemed held together only by the dried gravy and suet with which they were so generously splattered. At the end nearest the door a roaring fire burned in a wide stone fireplace. A sooty, sweating peasant lad was turning a joint of beef on a spit; he winced as the dripping fat made the flames sizzle. To Simon it all suddenly looked and smelled like heaven.

Cadrach dragged him to a spot along the back wall; the tabletop was so cracked and pitted that it hurt to rest his skinned elbows on its surface. The monk took the seat across from him, leaning back against the wall and extending his legs down the length of the bench. Instead of the sandals that Simon would have expected, the friar wore ragged boots, splitting from weather and hard use.

'Innkeeper! Where are you, worthy publican?!'

Cadrach called. A pair of beetle-browed, blue-jawed locals that Simon would have sworn were twins looked over from the opposite table with annoyance written in every facial furrow. After a little wait the owner appeared, a barrel-chested, bearded man with a deep scar across his nose and upper lip.

'Ah, there you are,' said Cadrach. 'Bless you, my son, and bring us each a mug of your best ale. Then, will you be so good as to carve us off some of that joint – that, and two trenchers of bread to sop with. Thanks to you, laddie.'

The owner frowned at Cadrach's words, but nodded his head curtly and walked away. As he left, Simon heard him grumble: '. . . Hernystiri buggerer . . .'

The ale came soon, and then the meat, then more ale. At first Simon ate like a starving dog, but after easing his initial, desperate hunger, and looking about the room to make sure no one was paying them undue attention, he slowed his pace and began to attend to Brother Cadrach's meandering conversation.

The Hernystirman was a wonderful storyteller, despite the burr of his accent that sometimes made him a little difficult to understand. Simon was vastly amused by the tale of the harper Ithineg and his long, long night, despite being a bit shocked to hear such a story told by a man of the cloth. He laughed so hard at the adventures of Red Hathrayhinn and the Sithi woman Finaju that he sprayed ale over his already stained shirt.

They had lingered a long while; the inn was half-empty when the bearded innkeeper finished filling their mugs for the fourth time. Cadrach, with broad gesticulation, was telling Simon of a fight he had once witnessed on the docks of Ansis Pelippé in Perdruin. Two monks, he explained, had cudgeled each other into near-unconsciousness during an argument about whether or not the Lord Usires had magically freed a man from a pig-spell on the island of Grenamman. Just at the most exciting point – brother Cadrach was waving his arms so enthusiastically in the description that Simon feared he would fall off the bench – the tavernkeeper thumped an ale jug loudly down in the middle of the table. Cadrach, caught in mid-exclamation, looked up.

'Yes, my good sir?' he asked, cocking a bushy brow. 'And how can we be helping you?'

The innkeeper stood with arms folded, a look of suspicion pinching his face. 'I've let you stand credit so far 'cause you're a man of the faith, father,' he said, 'but I must be closing up soon.'

'Is *that* all that's afflicting you?' A smile raced across Cadrach's round face. 'We'll be right over to reckon up with you, good fellow. What was your name, then?'

'Freawaru.'

'Well, never fear then, goodman Freawaru. Let the lad and me be finishing these noggins and then we'll let you get your sleep.' Freawaru nodded in his beard, more or less satisfied, and stumped off to yell at the turnspit boy. Cadrach emptied his mug with a long and noisy swallow, then turned his grin on Simon.

'Drink up, now, lad. We must not keep the man waiting. I am of the Granisian order, you know, and have a feeling for the poor fellow. Among other things, good Saint Granis is the patron of innkeepers and drunkards – a natural enough pairing!'

Simon chuckled and drained his cup, but as he put it down a finger of memory tugged at him. Hadn't Cadrach told him when they first met in Erchester that he was of some *other* order? Something with a 'v'? Vilderivan?

The monk was fishing about the pockets of his robe with a look of great concentration on his face, so Simon let the question pass. After a moment Cadrach pulled out a leather purse and dropped it on the table; it made no sound – no clink, no jingle. Cadrach's shining forehead wrinkled in a look of concern, and he held the purse up to his ear and slowly shook it. There was still no sound. Simon stared.

278

'Ah, laddie, laddie,' said the friar mournfully, 'will you look at that, now? I stopped to help a poor beggar-man today – carried him down to the water I did, and washed his bleeding feet – and look what he has done to repay my kindness.' Cadrach turned the purse over so that Simon could see the gaping hole slit across the bottom. 'Can you wonder why I sometimes fear for this wicked world, young Simon? I helped the man, and, why, he must have robbed me even as I was carrying him.' The monk heaved a great sigh. 'Well, lad, I'm afraid I'll have to prevail on your human kindness and Aedonite charity to lend me the money that we are owing here – I can soon pay you back, never fear. *'Tch, tch,'* he clucked, waving the slit wallet at the gape-eyed Simon, 'oh, but this world is sick with sin.'

Simon heard Cadrach's words only vaguely, a babble of sounds in his ale-muddled head. He was looking not at the hole, but at the seagull worked on the leather in heavy blue thread. The pleasant drunkenness of a minute before had turned heavy and sour. After a moment he raised his stare until his eyes met Brother Cadrach's. The ale and the warmth of the commons room had flushed Simon's cheeks and ears, but now he felt a tide of blood that was hotter still mounting up from his fast-beating heart.

'That's . . . my . . . purse!' he said. Cadrach blinked like an undenned badger.

'What, lad?' he asked apprehensively, sliding slowly away from the wall to the middle of the bench. 'I'm afraid I was not hearing you well.'

'That . . . purse . . . is *mine*.' Simon felt all the hurt, all the frustration of losing it come welling up – Judith's disappointed face, Doctor Morgenes' sad surprise – and the shocked sickness of trust betrayed. All the red hairs on his neck stood up like boar's bristles. *'Thief!'* he shouted suddenly, and lunged, but Cadrach had seen it coming: the little monk was off the bench and skittering backward up the length of the inn toward the door.

'Now wait, boy, it's a mistake you're making!' he

shouted, but if he really thought so, he did not seem to have much faith in his ability to convince Simon. Without pausing for a moment he grabbed his stick and sprang out of the doorway. Simon was after him at a sprint, but was barely through the doorjamb when he felt himself grappled around the waist by a pair of bearlike arms. A moment later he was up off the floor, breath pressed out, legs helplessly dangling.

'Now what do you think you're doing, hey?' Freawaru grunted in his ear. Turning in the doorway, he flipped Simon back into the fire-painted commons room. Simon landed on the wet floor and lay gasping for a moment.

'It's the monk!' he groaned at last. 'He stole my purse! Don't let him get away!'

Freawaru poked his head briefly outside the door. 'Well, if that's true he's long gone, that one – but how do I know this isn't all part of the plan, hey? How do I know that you two don't play this monk–and–catamite trick in every inn between here and Utanyeat?' A couple of late drinkers laughed behind him. 'Get up, boy,' he said, grasping Simon's arm and yanking him roughly onto his feet. 'I'm going to see if Deorhelm or Godstan has heard of you pair before.'

He hustled Simon out the door and around the side of the building, holding his arm prisoned in a firm grip. The moonlight picked out the stable's roof of pallid thatch, and the first tree-sentinels of the forest a stone-throw away.

'I don't know why you didn't just ask for work, you donkey,' Freawaru growled as he propelled the stumbling youth before him. 'With my Heanfax just quit I could have used a good-sized young fellow like you. Bloody foolishness – and just you keep your mouth shut.'

Alongside the stable was a small cottage, standing out but still connected to the main body of the inn. Freawaru banged his fist on the door.

'Deorhelm!' he called. 'Are you up? Come look at this

lad and tell me if you've seen him before.' The sound of footsteps could be heard within.

'S'bloody Tree, is that you, Freawaru?' a voice grumbled. 'We have to be on the road at cockcrow.' The door swung open. The room behind was lit by several candles.

'Lucky for you we were dicing, and not abed yet,' said the man who'd opened the door. 'What is it?'

Simon's eyes went wide, and his heart exploded into horrified pounding. This man, and the one polishing his sword on one of the bed sheets, wore the green livery of Elias' Erkynguard!

'This young ruffian and thief of a . . .' Freawaru had just time to say, when Simon turned and butted his head into the innkeeper's stomach. The bearded man went down with a startled outrush of breath. Simon sprang over his kicking legs and headed for the shelter of the forest; in a few leaping steps he had disappeared. The two soldiers gazed after him in mute surprise. On the ground in front of the candlelit doorway Freawaru the tavern-keeper cursed and rolled and kicked and cursed.

# 16

# The White Arrow

'It's not fair!' Simon sobbed for perhaps the hundredth time, fisting the wet ground. Leaves stuck to his reddened knuckles; he did not feel the least bit warmer. 'Not fair!' he murmured, curling back into a ball. The sun had been up for an hour, but the thin light brought no heat. Simon shivered and wept.

And it *wasn't* fair – it wasn't at all. What had he done that he should be lying damp, miserable and homeless in the Aldheorte forest while others were alseep in warm beds, or just risen to bread and milk and dry clothes? Why should he be hunted and chased like some filthy animal? He had tried to do what was right, to help his friend and the prince, and it had made of him a starveling outcast.

*But Morgenes got far worse, didn't he?* a part of him pointed out contemptuously. *The poor doctor would probably shift places with you gladly.*

Even that, though, was beside the point: Doctor Morgenes at least had possessed some idea of what was involved, of what might happen. He himself had been, he thought disgustedly, as innocent and stupid as a mouse who goes out of doors to play tag with the cat.

*Why does God hate me so?* Simon wondered, sniffling. How could Usires Aedon, who the priest said watched over everyone, have left him to suffer and die in the wilderness like this? He burst out in fresh weeping.

Rubbing his eyes some time later, he wondered how long he had been lying there staring at nothing. He pulled himself up, moving away from the sheltering tree to shake the life back into his hands and feet. He returned to the tree long enough to empty his bladder, then stalked sullenly down to the tiny stream to drink. The merciless ache in his knees, back, and neck rebuked him with every step.

*Damn everyone to Hell. And damn the bloody forest. And God, too, for that matter.*

He looked up fearfully from his chill handful of water, but his silent blasphemy went unpunished.

When he had finished he moved upstream a short distance to a place where the stream eddied out into a pool, and the turbulent waters were smoothed. As he crouched, staring at his tear-rippled reflection, he felt a resistance at his waist that made it difficult to bend over without steadying himself with his hands.

*The doctor's manuscript!* he remembered.

He half-stood, pulling the warm, flexible mass out from between pants and shirt-front. His belt had smashed a crease the length of the whole bundle. He had carried them so long that the pages were molded to the curve of his belly like a piece of armor; in his hand they lay bowed like a wind-breasted sail. The top page was smeared and caked with dirt, but Simon recognized the doctor's small, intricate script: he had been wearing the thin armor of Morgenes words. He felt a sudden fierce pang like hunger, and put the papers gently aside, returning his gaze to the pool.

It took a moment to separate his own reflection from the bands and blotches of shadow cast on the water's surface. The light was behind him; his image was largely silhouette, a dark figure with only the suggestion of features along the illuminated temple, cheek, and jaw. Twisting his head to catch the sun, he looked from the corner of his eye to see a hunted animal mirrored in the water, its ear tilted as though listening for pursuit, hair a tangled hedge of tufts, neck angled in a way that spoke not of civilization, but of watchfulness and fear. He quickly gathered up the manuscript and walked up the stream bank.

*I'm completely alone. No one will take care of me ever again. Not that anyone ever did.* He thought he could feel his heart breaking within his chest.

After searching for a few minutes he found a patch of sunlight, and settled down to dry his tears and think. It seemed obvious, as he listened to the echoing speech of birds in the otherwise soundless forest, that he *must* find warmer clothes if he was going to spend nights out of doors – and that he would certainly have to do until he got farther away from the Hayholt. He also needed to decide where he was going.

He began to leaf absently through Morgenes' papers, each one dense with words. Words – how could anyone think of so many words at one time, let alone write them down? It made his brain hurt just thinking about it. And what good were they, he thought, his lip trembling with bitterness, when you were cold, and hungry . . . or when Pryrates was at your door? He pulled two pages apart. The bottom one tore, and he felt as though he had unwittingly insulted a friend. He stared at it for a moment, solemnly tracing the familiar calligraphy with a scratched finger, then held it up to catch the light, squinting his eyes to read.

'. . . *it is strange, then, to think how those who wrote the songs and stories that entertained John's glittering court made of him, in an effort to construct him larger than life, less than he truly was.*'

Reading it through the first time, puzzling it word by word, he could make nothing of it; but as he read it again the cadences of Morgenes' speech came out. He almost smiled, forgetting for a moment his horrible situation. It

284

still made little sense to him, but he recognized the voice of his friend.

*'Consider for example,'* it continued, *'his coming to Erkynland out of the island of Warinsten. The balladeers would have it that God summoned him to slay the dragon Shurakai; that he touched shore at Grenefod with his sword Bright-Nail in his hand, his mind set only on this great task.*

*'While it is possible that a benevolent God called him to free the land from the fearsome beast, it remains to be explained why God allowed said dragon to lay waste to the country for long years before raising up its nemesis. And of course, those who knew him in those days remembered that he left Warinsten a swordless farmer's son, and reached our shores in the same condition; nor did he even think on the Red Worm until he had the better part of a year in our Erkynland . . .'*

It was vastly comforting to hear Morgenes' voice again, even if it was only in his own head, but he was puzzled by the passage. Was Morgenes trying to say that Prester John had *not* killed the Red Dragon, or only that he had not been chosen by God to do so? If he hadn't been chosen by the Lord Usires in heaven, how had he killed the arch-beast? Didn't the people of Erkynland say he was the king anointed by God?

As he sat thinking, a cold wind kited down through the trees and raised gooseflesh on his arms.

*Aedon curse it, I must find a cloak, or something warm to wear,* he thought. *And decide where I am going, instead of sitting here mooning like a half-wit over old writings.*

It seemed obvious now that his plan of the previous day – that of covering himself with a shallow layer of anonymity, becoming a turnspit or a scrubber at some rural hostel – was an impossible notion. Whether the two guardsmen he had escaped would have known him was not the issue: if they hadn't recognized him, someone eventually would. He felt sure that Elias' soldiers were already beating the countryside for him: he was not just a runaway servant, he was a criminal, a terrible criminal. Several deaths had already been paid out over the issue of Josua's escape; there would be no mercy for Simon if he fell into the hands of the Erkynguard.

How could he escape? Where would he go? He felt the panic rising again, and tried to suppress it. Morgenes' dying wish had been that he follow Josua to Naglimund. It seemed now that was the only useful course. If the prince had made good his escape, surely he would welcome Simon. If not, then doubtless Josua's liegemen would trade sanctuary for news of their lord. Still, it was a dismally long way to Naglimund; Simon knew the route and distance only by repute, but no one would call it short. If he continued to follow the Old Forest Road west, eventually it would cross the Wealdhelm Road, which ran northward along the base of the hills from which it took its name. If he could find the Wealdhelm way, he would at least be headed in the right direction.

With a strip torn from the hem of his shirt he bound the papers up, rolling them into a cylinder and wrapping the cloth around it, tying it with a careful twist of the ends. He noticed that he had neglected a page; it lay to one side, and as he picked it up he saw that it was the one his own sweat had smeared. In the blur of ruined letters one sentence had escaped; the words leaped out at him.

'. . . If he was touched by divinity, it was most evident in his comings and goings, in his finding the correct place to be at the most suitable time, and profiting thereby . . .'

It was not exactly a fortune-telling or a prophecy, but it strengthened him a little, and hardened his resolve. Northward it would be – northward to Naglimund.

A prickly, painful, miserable day's journey in the lee of the Old Forest Road was salvaged in part by a fortuitous discovery. As he stilted through the brush, skirting the occasional cottage that crouched within hailing distance of the road, he caught a glimpse through the chink in the forest cover of a treasure beyond price: someone's untended washing. As he crept toward the tree, whose branches were festooned with damp clothes and one rank, sodden blanket, he kept his eye on the shabby, bramble-thatched cabin that stood a few paces away. His heart beat swiftly as he pulled down a wool cloak so heavy with moisture that he staggered when it slid free into his arms. No alarm was raised from the cottage; in fact, no one seemed to be about anywhere. For some reason this made him feel even worse about the theft. As he scrambled back into the tangled trees with his burden, he saw again in his mind's eye a crude wooden sign bumping against an unbreathing chest.

The thing of it was, Simon quickly realized, living the outlaw life was nothing at all like the stories of Jack Mundwode the Bandit that Shem had told him. In his imaginings Aldheorte Forest had been a sort of endless high hall with a floor of smooth turf and tall tree-trunk pillars propping a distant ceiling of leaves and blue sky, an airy pavilion where knights like Sir Tallistro of Perdruin or the great Camaris rode prancing chargers and delivered ensorcelled ladies from hideous fates. Stranded in an uncompliant, almost malevolent reality, Simon found that the trees of the forest fringe huddled close together, branches intertwining like slip-knotted snakes. The undergrowth itself was an obstacle, an endless humped field of brambles and fallen trunks that lay nearly invisible beneath moss and moldering leaves.

In those first days, when he occasionally found himself in a clearing and could walk unencumbered for a short while, the sound of his own footfalls drumming on the loose-packed soil made him feel exposed. He caught himself hurrying across the dells in the slanting sunlight, praying for the security of the undergrowth again. This failure of nerve so infuriated him that he forced himself to cross these clearings slowly. Sometimes he even sang brave songs, listening to the echo as though the sound of his voice quailing and dying in the muffling trees was the most natural thing in the world, but once he had regained the brambles he could seldom remember what he had sung.

Although memories of his life at the Hayholt still filled his head, they had become wisps of remembrance that seemed increasingly distant and unreal, replaced by a growing fog of anger and bitterness and despair. His home and happiness had been stolen from him. Life at the Hayholt had been a grand and easeful thing: the people kind, the accommodations wonderfully comfortable. Now, he crashed through the tortuous forest hour after bleak hour, awash in misery and self-pity. He felt his old Simon-self vanishing away, and more and more of his waking thought revolving around only two things: moving forward and eating.

At first he had pondered long over whether he should take the open roadway for speed and risk discovery, or try and follow it from the safety of the forest. The last had seemed the better idea, but he quickly discovered that the two, road and forest fringe, diverged widely at certain points, and in the thick tangle of Oldheart it was often frighteningly difficult to find the road again. He also realized with painful embarrassment that he did not have the slightest idea of how to make a fire, something he had never thought about as he listened to Shem describing droll Mundwode and his bandit fellows feasting on roast venison at their woodland table. With no torch to light his way, it seemed that the only possible thing to do was to follow the road at night, when moonlight permitted it. He would then sleep by daylight, and use the remaining hours of sun to slog through the forest.

No torch meant no cook-fire, and this was in some ways the hardest blow of all. From time to time he found clutches of speckled eggs deposited by the mother grouse in hiding-holes of matted grass. These provided some nourishment, but it was hard to suck out the sticky, cold yolks without thinking of the warm, scented glories of Judith's kitchen, and to reflect bitterly on the mornings when he had been in such a tearing hurry to see Morgenes or get out to the tourney field that he had left great chunks of butter and honey-smeared bread untouched on his plate. Now, suddenly, the thought of a buttered crust was a dream of riches.

Incapable of hunting, knowing little or nothing about what wild plants might be eaten without harm, Simon owed his survival to pilferage from the gardens of local cotsmen. Keeping a wary eye out for dogs or angry residents, he would swoop down from the shelter of the forest to rifle the pitifully sparse vegetable patches, scraping up carrots and onions or hurriedly plucking apples from lower branches – but even these meager goods were few and far between. Often as he walked, the hunger pains were so great that he would shout out in anger, kicking savagely at the tangling shrubbery. Once he kicked so hard and screamed so loudly that when he fell down on his face in the undergrowth he could not get up for a long time. He lay listening to the echoes of his cries disappear, and thought he would die.

No, life in the forest was not a tenth so glorious as he had imagined it in those long-ago Hayholt afternoons, crouching in the stables smelling hay and tack leather, listening to Shem's stories. The mighty Oldheart was a dark and miserly host, jealous of doling comforts out to strangers. Hiding in thorny brush to sleep away the hours of sun, making his damp, shivering way through the darkness beneath the tree-netted moon, or scuttling furtively through the garden plots in his sagging, too-large cloak, Simon knew he was more rabbit than rogue.

Although he carried the rolled pages of Morgenes' life of John wherever he went, clutching them like a baton of office or a priest's blessed Tree, less and less often as the days passed did he actually read them. At the thin end of the day, between a pathetic meal — if any — and the frightening, close-leaning darkness of the world out of doors, he would open the bundle and read a part of a page, but every day the sense of it seemed harder to grasp. One page, on which the names of John, Eahlstan the Fisher King, and the dragon Shurakai were prominent, caught his mayfly attention, but after he had read it through four times, struggling, he realized that it made no more sense to him than would the year-lines on a piece of timber. By his fifth afternoon in the forest he only sat, crying softly, with the pages spread on his lap. He absently stroked the smooth parchment, as he had once scratched the kitchen cat uncountable years ago, in a warm, bright room that smelled of onions and cinnamon. . . .

A week and a day out from the *Dragon and Fisherman* he passed within shouting distance of the village of Sistan, a settlement only slightly larger than Flett. The twin clay chimneys of Sistan's roadhouse were smoking, but the road was empty, the sun bright. Simon peered down a hillside from the clump of silvery birches and the memory of his last hot meal struck him like a physical blow, weakening his knees so that he almost fell. That long-lost evening, despite its conclusion, seemed almost like Doctor Morgenes' onetime description of the pagan paradise of the old Rimmersgarders: eternal drinking and storytelling; merrymaking without end.

He crept down the hill toward the quiet roadhouse, hands trembling, forming wild plans of stealing a meat pie from an unguarded windowsill, or slipping in a back door to pillage the kitchen. He was out of the trees and halfway down the slope when he suddenly realized what he was doing: walking out of the woods at unshadowed noon, a sickened, feverish animal that had lost its self-protective instincts. Feeling suddenly naked despite his bramble-studded wool cloak he froze in place, then

290

whirled and scrambled away, back up to the swan-slim birch trees. Now even they seemed too exposed; cursing and sobbing, he clambered past to the thicker shadows, drawing Oldheart around him like a cloak.

Five days west of Sistan the begrimed and famished youth found himself crouched on another slope, peering down into a forest dell at a rough split-log hut. He was sure – as sure as he could be with his thoughts so piteously scattered and fragmented – that another day without real food or another solitary night spent in the chill, uncaring forest would leave him really and finally deranged: he would become completely the beast he more and more frequently felt himself to be. His thoughts were turning foul and brutish: food, dark hiding-places, weary forest tramping, these were his all-consuming preoccupations. It was increasingly difficult to remember the castle – had it been warm there? Had people spoken to him? – and when a branch had lanced his tunic and scored his ribs the day before he had only been able to growl and flail at it – a beast!

*Somebody . . . somebody lives here . . .*

The woodsman's cottage had a front path lined with tidy stones. A stack of halved timbers nestled beneath the eaves against the side wall. Surely, he reasoned, sniffling quietly, surely somebody here would take pity on him if he walked to the door and calmly asked for some food.

*I'm so hungry. It's not fair. It's not right! Somebody must feed me . . . somebody . . .*

He went slowly down the hill on stiff legs, his mouth gaping open and closed. A flagging recollection of the social contract told him that he must not frighten these rustic people, these suspicious woodsfolk in their tree-tiered hollow. He held his empty palms before him as he walked, pale fingers thrust wide apart in a dumb show of harmlessness.

The cottage was empty, or else the inhabitants were simply not responding to his sore-knuckled knocking. He walked around the little hut, dragging his fingertips along the rough wood. The single window was shuttered with a wide plank. He rapped again, harder; only hollow echoes answered.

As he sank into a crouch beneath the boarded window, wondering desperately if he could batter it open with a piece of firewood, a rustling, snapping noise from the stand of trees before him brought him back upright so quickly that his vision momentarily narrowed to a core of light surrounded by blackness; he wavered, feeling sick. The tree-fence bulged outward as though struck by a huge hand, then sprang back with a quiver. A moment later the silence was skewered again, this time by a strange, staccato hiss. The noise was transmuted into a rapid stream of words – in no language that Simon knew, but words nonetheless. After a percussive instant the glade was quiet again.

Simon was stone-struck; he could not move. What should he do? Perhaps the cottager had been attacked by an animal on his way home . . . Simon could help him . . . then they would *have* to give him food. But how could he help? He could barely walk. And what if it was a beast, only a beast – what if he had only imagined hearing words in that abrupt spatter of sound?

And what if it was something worse? The king's guardsmen with bright sharp swords, or a starvation-slender, white haired witch? Perhaps it was the very Devil himself, with ember-red robes and nightshade eyes?

Where he found the courage, even the strength, to unbend his rigid knees and walk forward into the trees Simon could not say. If he had not felt so ill and so desperate he might not have . . . but he *was* ill, and starved, and as dirty and lonely as a Nascadu jackal. Wrapping his cloak tightly about his chest, holding the

292

furl of Morgenes' writings before him, he limped toward the copse.

In the trees the sunlight fell unevenly, strained through a sieve of spring leaves, dotting the forest floor like a scatter of fithing pieces. The air seemed taut as held breath. For a moment he saw nothing but dark tree-shapes and slivers of lancing daylight. In one spot the shafts of light were jigging fitfully; he realized a moment later that they shone on a struggling figure. As he took a step forward, the leaves whispered beneath his foot, and with that sound the struggling ceased. The hanging thing – it dangled fully a yard off the spongy ground – lifted its head and stared at him. It had the face of a man, but the merciless topaz eyes of a cat.

Simon leaped back, his heart tipping in his chest; he flung out his hands, fingers spread wide as though to block out the sight of this bizarre gallows bird. Whatever or whoever he was, he was not like any man Simon had seen. Still, there was something achingly familiar about him, as from a half-remembered dream – but so many of Simon's dreams were now bad ones. What a strange apparition! Although caught in a cruel trap, piniomed at waist and elbows by a noose of snaky black rope and hanging from a bobbing branch out of reach of the earth, still this prisoner looked fierce, unhumbled: a treed fox who would die with his teeth in a hound's throat.

If he was a man, he was a very slender man. His high-cheeked, thin-boned face reminded Simon for a moment – a horrifyingly cold moment – of the black-robed creatures on Thisterborg, but where they had been pale, white-skinned as blindfish, this one was golden brown like polished oak.

Trying to get a better look in the dim light, Simon took a step forward; the prisoner narrowed his eyes, then skinned back his lips, baring his teeth in a feline hiss. Something in the way he did it, something inhuman about the way his quite-human face moved, told Simon in an instant that this was no man trapped here like a weasel . . . this was something different. . . .

Simon had moved closer than was prudent, and as he stared into the flecked-amber eyes the prisoner lashed out, bringing cloth-booted feet up into the youth's ribcage. Simon, though he had seen the momentary backswing and anticipated the assault, still received a painful blow in the side, so swift was the prisoner's movement. He stumbled back, glowering at his attacker, who scowled horribly in return.

As he faced the stranger across the span of a man's height, Simon watched the somehow unnatural muscles draw the mouth open in a sneer, and the Sitha – for Simon had realized suddenly, as if someone had told him, that this hanging creature was exactly that – the Sitha spat out a single awkward word in Simon's Westerling tongue.

*'Coward!'*

Simon was so angered by this that he nearly charged forward, starvation and fear and aching limbs notwithstanding . . . until he realized that this was just what the Sitha's oddly-accented jibe had been meant to accomplish. Simon pushed down the pain of his kicked ribs, folded his hands over his chest, and stared at the trapped Sitha-man; he had the grim satisfaction of seeing what he felt sure was a squirm of frustration.

The Fair One, as Rachel had always superstitiously referred to the race, wore a strange, soft robe and pants of a slithery brown material only a shade darker than his skin. Belt and ornaments of shiny green stone contrasted most wonderfully with his hair – lavender-blue like mountain heather, pulled back close against his head by a bone ring, dangling in a horse-tail behind one ear. He seemed only slightly shorter, although much thinner, than Simon – but the youth had not seen himself recently in any reflection but murky forest pools; perhaps now he, too, looked this scrawny and wild. But even so, still there were differences, not-quite-definable things: birdlike

294

motions of the head and neck, an odd fluidity in the pivoting of joints, an aura of power and control that was discernible even while its possessor hung like an animal in the crudest of traps. This Sitha, this dream-haunter, was unlike anything Simon had known. He was terrifying and thrilling . . . he was alien.

'I don't . . . don't want to hurt you,' Simon said at last, and realized he was speaking as though to a child. 'I didn't set the trap.' The Sitha continued to regard him with baleful crescent eyes.

*What terrible pain he must be hiding,* Simon marveled. *His arms are pulled up so far that . . . that I would be screaming . . . if it were me!*

Protruding above the prisoner's left shoulder was a quiver, empty but for two arrows. Several more arrows and a bow of slim, dark wood lay strewn on the turf beneath his dangling feet.

'If I try to help you, will you promise not to hurt me?' Simon asked, forming his words slowly. 'I'm very hungry, myself,' he lamely added. The Sitha said nothing, but as Simon took another step he coiled his legs up before him to kick; the youth retreated.

'Be damned!' Simon shouted. 'I only want to help you!' But why *did* he? Why let the wolf out of the pit? 'You must . . .' he began, but the rest of his words were snuffed out as a large dark form came swishing and crackling out of the trees toward them.

'Ah! Here it be, here it be. . . !' a deep voice said. A man, bearded and dirty, waded into the little clearing. His clothes were heavy and much mended: in his hand he swung an axe.

'Now then, you . . .' he stopped when he saw Simon huddled against a tree. 'Here,' he growled, 'who be *you*? What are you about?'

Simon looked down at the pitted axe-blade. 'I'm . . . I'm just a traveler . . . I heard a noise here in the trees . . .' He waved his hand toward the odd tableau. 'I found *him* here, in . . . in this trap.'

'*My* trap!' the woodsman grinned. 'My damned trap —and there he be, too.' Turning his back on Simon the man looked the dangling Sitha over coolly. 'I promised I'd stop their sneakin' and spyin' and sourin' the milk, that I did.' He reached out a hand and pushed the prisoner's shoulder, swinging him helplessly back and forth in a slow arc. The Sitha hissed, but it was an impotent sound. The woodsman laughed.

'By the Tree, they got fight in 'em they do. Got fight.'

'What . . . what are you going to do with him?'

'What do *you* think, boy? What do you think God'd have us do with sprites an' imps an' devils when we catch 'em? Send 'em back to hell with my good chopper, that'll tell you.'

The prisoner slowly stopped swinging, revolving in a lazy circle at the end of the black rope like a webbed fly. His eyes were downcast, his body limp.

'Kill him?' Simon, ill and weak as he was, still felt a cold wash of shock. He tried to marshal his straggling thoughts. 'You're going to . . . but you can't! You can't! He's . . . he's a . . .'

'What he's not is no natural creature, that's sure! Get away from here, stranger. You're in my bit o' garden, as it were, an' you got no call to be. *I* know what these creatures are a-gettin' up to.' The woodsman contemptuously turned his back on Simon and moved toward the Sitha, axe raised as though to split timber. *This* timber, though, suddenly heaved, became a struggling, kicking, snarling beast fighting for its life. The cotsman's first blow went awry, grazing the bony cheek and digging a jagged furrow down the arm of the strange, shiny garment. A ribbon of all too human-looking blood dribbled down the slender jaw and neck. The man advanced again.

Simon dropped down to his sore knees, looking for something to stop this ghastly struggle, to halt the man's grunting and cursing, and the scratchy snarl of the beleaguered prisoner that punished his ears. Groping, he found the bow, but it was even lighter than it had looked, as though strung on marsh reed. An instant later his hand closed on a half-buried rock. He heaved, and it broke free from the clinging soil. He held it over his head.

'Stop!' he shouted. 'Leave him be!' Neither combatant gave him a flicker of notice. The woodsman now stood at arm's length, swiping at his swirling target, landing only glancing blows but continuing to draw blood. The Sitha's thin chest was heaving like a bellows; he was weakening quickly.

Simon could not stand the cruel spectacle any longer. Setting free the howl that had been coiling itself within him through all the interminable, terrifying days of his exile, he sprang forward, crossing the tiny clearing in a bound to bring the rock down on the back of the cotsman's head. A dull smack reverberated through the trees; the man seemed to go boneless in an instant. He pitched heavily forward onto his knees and then his face, a surge of red welling up through his matted hair.

Staring down at the bloody wreckage, Simon felt his insides heave; he fell to his knees retching, bringing up nothing but a sour strand of spittle. He pressed his dizzy head against the damp ground and felt the forest sway and rock about him.

When he was able, he stood and turned to the Sithi-man, who again dangled quietly in the noose. The snaky tunic was laced with streamers of blood, and the feral eyes were dimmed, as though some internal curtain had rolled down to block the light within. As haltingly as a sleepwalker, Simon picked up the fallen axe and traced the taut rope up from the prisoner to where it wrapped around a high limb of the tree – a limb too high to reach. Simon, too numb for fear, worked the nicked blade-edge against the knot behind the Sitha's back. The Fair One winced as the noose pulled tighter, but made no sound.

After a long moment of scraping and rubbing, the slippery knot parted. The Sitha fell to the ground, legs buckling, and tumbled forward onto the motionless woodsman. He rolled away from the mute hulk immediately, as though burned, and began gathering up his scattered arrows. Holding them like a clutch of long-stemmed flowers, he picked up his bow in the other hand and paused to stare at Simon. His cold eyes glinted, stopping the words in Simon's mouth. For an instant the Sitha, injuries forgotten or ignored, stood poised and tense as a startled deer; then he was gone, a flash of brown and green that vanished into the trees, leaving Simon gape-jawed and deserted.

The spotted sunlight had not finished rippling on the leaves where he had passed when Simon heard a buzz like an angry insect and felt a shadow flit across his face. An arrow stood out from a tree trunk beside him, quivering gradually back into visibility less than an arm's length from his head. He stared at it dully, wondering when the next one would strike him. It was a white arrow, shaft and feathers alike bright as a gull's wing. He waited for its inevitable successor. None came. The stand of trees was silent and motionless.

After the strangest and most terrible fortnight of his life, and after a particularly bizarre day, it should not have surprised Simon to hear a new and unfamiliar voice speaking to him from the darkness beyond the trees, a voice that was not the Sitha's, and certainly did not come from the woodsman, who lay like a felled tree.

'Go ahead to take it,' the voice said. 'The arrow. Take it. It is yours.'

Simon should not have been surprised, but he was. He dropped helplessly to the ground and began to cry – great choking sobs of exhaustion and confusion and total despair.

'Oh, Daughter of the Mountains,' the strange new voice said. 'This does not seem good.'

# 17

# Binabik

When Simon at last looked up to the source of the new voice, his tearful eyes widened in surprise. A child was walking toward him.

No, not a child, but a man so small that the top of his black-haired head would probably not reach much higher than Simon's navel. His face did have something of the childish about it: the narrow eyes and wide mouth both stretched toward the cheekbones in an expression of simple good humor.

'This is not a good place for crying,' the stranger said. He turned from kneeling Simon to briefly survey the fallen cotsman. 'It is also my feeling that it will not accomplish much – at least for this dead fellow.'

Simon wiped his nose on the sleeve of his coarse shirt and hiccoughed. The stranger had moved forward to examine the pale arrow, which stood from the tree trunk near Simon's head like a stiff ghost-branch.

'You should take this,' the little man said, and again his mouth widened in a froggy smile, baring for an instant a palisade of yellow teeth.

He was not a dwarf, like the fools and tumblers Simon had seen at court and in the Main Row of Erchester – although big-chested, he seemed otherwise well-proportioned. His clothes looked much like a Rimmersman's: jacket and leggings of some thick animal

299

hide stitched with sinew, a fur collar turned up below his round face. A large skin bag hung bulging from a shoulder strap, and he held a walking stick that looked to be carved from some long, slender bone.

'Please excuse my suggestions, but you should be taking this arrow. It is a Sithi White Arrow, and it is very precious. It signifies a debt, and the Sithi are conscientious folk.'

'Who . . . are you?' Simon asked around another hiccough. He was wrung out, beaten flat like a shirt pounded dry on a rock. If this little man had come out of the trees snarling and waving a knife, he did not think he could have reacted any differently.

'Me?' the stranger asked, pausing as though giving the question much thought. 'A traveler like yourself. I will be happy to explain more things at a later time, but now we should go. This fellow,' he indicated the woodsman with a sweep of his stick, 'will reliably not become more alive, but he may have friends or family who will be unsettled to find him so extremely dead. Please. Take the White Arrow and come with me.'

Mistrustful and wary, Simon nevertheless found himself rising to his feet. It was too much effort to *not* trust, for the moment; he no longer had the strength to stay on guard – a part of him wanted only to lie down and quietly die. He levered the arrow loose from the tree. The tiny man was already on the march, climbing back up the hillside above the cottage. The little house crouched as silently and tidily as if nothing had happened.

'But . . .' Simon gasped as he scrambled up after the stranger, who moved with surprising quickness, '. . . but what about the cottage? I am . . . I am *so* hungry . . . and there might be food . . .'

The small man turned on the hillcrest to stare down at the struggling youth. 'I am very shocked!' he said. 'First you make him dead, then you wish to rob his larder. I fear I have fallen in with a desperate outlaw!' He turned and continued into the close-knit trees.

300

The far side of the crest was a long, gradual down-slope. Simon's limping strides finally brought him abreast of the stranger; in a few moments he had caught his breath.

'Who are you? And where are we going?'

The strange little man did not look up, but kept his eyes moving from tree to tree, as though looking for some landmark in the unremitting sameness of the deep woods. After twenty silent paces he turned his eyes up to Simon's and pulled his stretchy smile.

'My name is *Binbiniqegabenik*,' he said, 'but around the cookfire I am called Binabik. I hope you will honor me by using the shorter version of friendship.'

'I . . . I will. Where are you from?' He hiccoughed again.

'I am of the troll-folk of Yiqanuc,' Binabik replied. 'High Yiqanuc in the snowing and blowing northern mountains . . . and *you* are?'

He stared suspiciously for a moment before answering. 'Simon. Simon of the . . . of Erchester.' This was all happening rather quickly, he thought . . . like a market-place meeting, but in the middle of a forest after a bizarre slaying. Holy Usires, did his head hurt! And his stomach, too. 'Where . . . where are we going?'

'To my camp. But first I must find my mount . . . or rather, she must find me. Please, do not be startled.'

So saying, Binabik put two fingers in his wide mouth and blew a long, trilling note. After a moment he did it again. 'Remember, do not be startled or anxious.'

Before he could ponder the troll's words there was a crackle like wildfire in the underbrush. A moment later a huge wolf burst into the clearing, bounding past a shocked Simon to leap like a shaggy thunderbolt onto little Binabik, who tumbled end over end beneath his growling attacker.

'Qantaqa!' The troll's cry was muffled, but there was amusement in his voice. Master and mount continued to wrestle across the forest floor. Simon distractedly

301

wondered if the world outside the castle was always like this – was the entirety of Osten Ard but a playing field for monsters and lunatics?

Binabik at last sat up, Qantaqa's great head cradled in his lap. 'I have left her alone all the day, today,' he explained. 'Wolves have much affection, and they become easily lonely.' Qantaqa grinned hugely and panted. Much of her girth was heavy gray fur, but still she was immense.

'Make yourself free,' Binabik laughed. 'Scratch upon her nose.'

Despite the continuing unreality of his situation, Simon did not yet feel quite ready for that; instead he asked: 'I'm sorry . . . but did you say you had food at your camp, sir?'

The troll clambered to his feet, laughing, and retrieved his stick. 'Not sir – Binabik! And as for food: yes. We will eat together – you, I, even Qantaqa. Come along. Being deferential to your weak and hungry feeling, I will walk and not ride.'

Simon and the troll were on the march for some time. Qantaqa accompanied them for stretches, but more often trotted ahead, disappearing in a few bounds into the dense undergrowth. Once she came back licking her muzzle with her long pink tongue.

'Well,' Binabik said cheerfully, 'one is fed already!'

At last, when it seemed to the aching, dragging Simon that he could walk no farther, when he lost the thread of Binabik's every sentence within a couple of words, they reached a little dell, empty of tree trunks but roofed overhead with a lattice of intertwined branches. Beside a fallen log lay a ring of blackened stones. Qantaqa, who had been pacing along beside them, bounded ahead to make a sniffing circuit of the dingle.

' *"Bhojujik mo qunquc,"* as my people say.' Binabik made an expansive gesture around the clearing. ' " – If the bears do not eat you, it is home." ' He led Simon to a log; the youth collapsed, breathing heavily. The troll looked him up and down with concern. 'Oh,' Binabik said, 'you are not going to be crying again, are you?'

'No.' Simon smiled weakly. His bones felt cumbersome as dead stone. 'I . . . I don't think so. I'm just very hungry and tired. I promise not to cry.'

'Look you. I shall make a fire. Then, I shall produce a supper.' Binabik swiftly gathered a pile of sticks and twigs, hayricking them in the middle of the ring of stones. 'These are spring wood, and damp,' he said, 'but luckily that is a matter easily dealt with.'

Sliding the skin bag from his shoulder, the troll placed it on the ground and began to rummage determinedly through it. To Simon, in his fatigue-born whimsy, the small squatting figure looked more than ever like that of a child: Binabik stared into his sack with lips pursed and eyes narrowed in concentration – a six year old studying a limping beetle with high seriousness.

'Hah!' said the troll at last, 'it is found.' He pulled from the sack a smaller sack, about the size of Simon's thumb. Binabik took a pinch of some powdery substance from it and sprinkled it on the green wood, then took two pieces of stone from his belt and struck them together. The spark that leaped down sputtered for a moment, then a slender curl of yellow smoke spiraled up. A moment later the wood puffed into flame, and within instants it was a merry, crackling fire. The pulsing warmth lulled Simon, despite the pangs of his empty stomach. His head was nodding, nodding . . . But wait – a rush of fear swept over him – how could he just fall asleep, all unguarded in a stranger's camp!? He ought to . . . he should . . .

'Sit and be warm, friend Simon.' Binabik dusted off his hands as he stood. 'I will return very quickly.'

Although a deep unease was fighting to make itself known in the back of his thoughts – where was the troll going? To get confederates? Fellow bandits? – still Simon could not muster the effort to watch Binabik leave. His eyes were again fixed on the wavering flames, the

tongues like the petals of some shimmering flower . . . a
fire-poppy quivering in a warm summer wind. . . .

He awakened from a great cloudy emptiness to find the
gray wolf's massive head lying across his thighs. Binabik
crouched over the fire, fussing at some project. Simon
felt there was something slightly wrong about having a
wolf in one's lap, but could not find the proper puppet
strings in his mind to do anything about it . . . it didn't
seem truly important, anyway.

The next time he woke, Binabik was shooing Qantaqa
from his lap to offer him a large cup of something warm.

'It is cool enough now for drinking,' the troll said, and
helped Simon raise the vessel to his lips. The broth was
musky and delicious, tangy as the smell of autumn
leaves. He drank it all; it seemed he could feel it flowing
directly into his veins, the molten blood of the forest,
warming and filling him with the secret strength of trees.
Binabik gave him a second cupful and he drank that, too.
A dense, leaden clutch of worry at the juncture of his
neck and shoulders melted away, swept aside by the rush
of good feelings. A new airiness coursed through him,
bringing with it a paradoxical heaviness, a warm, diffuse
drowsiness. As he slipped away he heard his own cradled
heartbeat, muffled though it was in the tickling wool of
exhaustion.

Simon was almost certain that when he came to Binabik's
camp it had been at least an hour short of sunset, but
when he opened his eyes again the forest glade was bright
with new-smithied morning. As he blinked he felt the
last strands of dream pulling free – a bird. . . ?

*A bright-eyed bird in a sun-catching golden collar . . . an old,
strong bird whose eyes were full of the wisdom of high places and
broad vision . . . from his chitinous claw hung a beautiful
rainbow-shimmering fish . . .*

Simon shivered, pulling his heavy cloak nearer about him. As he stared up at the overarching trees, their budding spring leaves picked out by the sun in emerald filigree, he heard a moaning sound and rolled over on his side to look.

Binabik sat cross-legged beside the firepit, swaying gently from side to side. Before him an assortment of odd, pale shapes were spread on a flat rock – bones. The troll was making the unusual noise – was he singing? Simon stared for a moment, but could not puzzle out what the little man might be doing. What a strange world!

'Good morning,' he said at last. Binabik jumped guiltily.

'Ah! It is friend Simon!' The troll grinned over his shoulder and quickly swept the objects into his open skin bag, then stood up and hastened to Simon's side. 'How are you now feeling?' he asked, bending over to place a small, rough hand on Simon's forehead. 'You must have needed a great sleep.'

'I did.' Simon moved closer to the small fire. 'What's that . . . that smell?'

'A pair of wood pigeons who have stopped to dine with us this morning,' Binabik smiled, pointing out two leaf-wrapped bundles in the coals at the edge of the campfire. 'Keeping their company are some berries and nuts recently gathered. I would have been waking you up soon to help entertain them all. They are very good-tasting, I think. Oh, a moment please.' Binabik walked back to his skin bag, drawing forth two thin packages.

'Here.' He handed them across. 'Your arrow, and something else,' – that was Morgenes' papers – 'you had placed them in your belt, and I feared they would then be broken when you were sleeping.'

Suspicion flared in Simon's breast. The idea of some-one handling the doctor's writings while he slept made him covetous, distrustful. He snatched the proffered bundle from the troll's hand and replaced it in his belt.

305

The little man's cheerful look changed to one of dismay. Simon felt ashamed – although one couldn't be *too* careful – and took the arrow, which had been wound in thin cloth, more gently.

'Thank you,' he said stiffly. Binabik's expression was still that of a man whose kindness had been scorned. Guilty and confused, Simon unwrapped the arrow. Although he had not yet had a chance to study it closely, at the moment he was most concerned with finding something to do with his hands and eyes.

The arrow was not painted, as Simon had assumed: rather it was carved from some wood as white as birch bark, and fletched with snow-white feathers. Only the arrowhead, carved from some milky blue stone, had any color. Simon hefted it, weighing its surprising lightness against its amazing flexibility and solidity, and the memory of the day before came back in a rush. He knew he could never forget the feline eyes and disturbingly swift movements of the Sitha. All the stories that Morgenes had told were true.

All along the shaft of the arrow slender whorls, curlicues, and dots were pressed into the wood with infinite care. 'It's all thick with carvings,' Simon mused aloud.

'They are very important things,' the troll replied, and shyly reached out his hand. 'Please, if I may?' Simon felt another wash of guilt and quickly handed him the arrow. Binabik tilted it back and forth, catching the sunlight and firelight just so. 'This is an old-fellow.' He squinted his narrow eyes until the dark pupils disappeared altogether. 'It has been around for quite some long time. You are the holder now of a quite-honorable thing, Simon: the White Arrow is not given in lightness. It seems that this one was affletched in Tumet'ai, a Sithi stronghold long since gone below the blue ice east of my homeland.'

'How do you know all that?' Simon asked. 'Can you read those letters?'

'Some. And there are things an eye that is trained can see.'

Simon took it back, handling it with a good deal more care than before. 'But what should I do with it? You said it was payment for a debt?'

'No, friend. It is a mark of a debt that is owing. And what you should be doing is to keep it safe. If it has nothing else to be, it will be a beautiful thing to look on.'

A thin mist still clung to the clearing and forest floor beyond. Simon propped the arrow point-downward against the log and slid closer to the fire. Binabik pulled the pigeons from the embers, pincering with a pair of sticks; he put one bundle down on the warm rock before Simon's knees.

'Remove the folded leaves,' the troll instructed, 'then wait for a short passing-time so the bird will slightly cool.' It was very difficult to obey the last, but somehow Simon managed.

'How did you get these?' he asked at one point, mouth full and fingers sticky with grease.

'Later I will show you,' the troll replied.

Binabik was picking his teeth with a bowed rib bone. Simon leaned back against the log and belched contentedly.

'Mother Elysia, that was wonderful.' He sighed, feeling for the first time in a long while that the world was not an entirely hostile place. 'A little food in your stomach changes everything.'

'I am glad your cure was so simple for effecting,' the troll smiled around the slender bone.

Simon patted his middle. 'I don't care about anything right this moment.' His elbow brushed the arrow, which began to topple. As he caught it and straightened it a flicker of memory came to him. 'I don't even feel bad anymore about . . . about that man yesterday.'

Binabik turned his brown eyes to Simon. Although he continued to probe his teeth, his forehead creased above the bridge of his nose. 'You do not feel bad about him *being* dead, or about *making* him dead?'

307

'I don't understand,' said Simon. 'What do you mean? What's the difference?'

'There is as much difference as between a big rock and a little, little bug – but I shall leave the pondering to you.'

'But . . .' Simon was confused again. 'Well, but . . . he was a bad man.'

'Hmmmm . . .' Binabik nodded his head, but the gesture carried no suggestion of agreement. 'This world is certainly filling itself with bad men, of that there can be no doubts.'

'He would have killed the Sitha-man!'

'That is also a truth.'

Simon stared sullenly at the plundered heap of bird bones piled before him on the rock. 'I don't understand. What do you want me to tell you?'

'Where it is that you are going to.' The troll tossed his toothpick into the fire and stood up. He was so small!

'What?' Simon stared suspiciously as the import of the little man's words caught up at last.

'I wish to know where you are going, so that perhaps we can be traveling together for a while.' Binabik spoke slowly and patiently, as though to a beloved but stupid old dog. 'I think that perhaps the sun is too young in the sky for the other questions to be troubled with. We trolls say: "Make Philosophy your evening guest, but do not let her stay the night." Now, if my question is not of a too-much inquiring nature, where do you go to?'

Simon rose, knees stiff as unoiled hinges. Again he felt doubt. Could the little man's curiosity really be as innocent as it seemed? He had made the mistake of trusting at least once already, with that damnable monk. But what choice did he have? He did not have to tell the troll everything, and it was certainly preferable to have a companion versed in woodcraft. The little man seemed to know just what to do, and suddenly Simon longed to have someone to rely on again.

'I am going north,' he said, and then took a calculated

risk. 'To Naglimund.' He watched the troll carefully. 'And yourself?'

Binabik was packing his few implements into his shoulder bag. 'Ultimately, I expect to be traveling far north,' he replied without looking up. 'It seems that we have a coincidence of paths.' Now he raised his dark eyes. 'How strange that you should be traveling toward the Naglimund, which stronghold's name I have heard much in recent weeks.' His lips quirked in a tiny, secret smile.

'You have?' Simon had picked up the White Arrow, and tried to look studiously unconcerned as he pondered how to carry it. 'Where?'

'Time there will be for talking as we take to the road.' The troll grinned, a full, friendly yellow grin. 'I must call Qantaqa, who is without doubt spreading horror and despair among the rodents of this vicinity. Feel yourself welcome to empty your bladder now, so that we may swiftly walk.'

Simon had to hold the White Arrow between clenched teeth as he followed Binabik's advice.

# 18
# A Net of Stars

Blistered, sore-footed, and clothed in rags, Simon never-theless felt the pall of despair begin to lift a little. Both mind and body were badly bruised by mischance, and he had developed a startled eye and reflexive flinch – neither of which escaped the sharp gaze of his new companion – but the brooding horror had been pushed back a short way; it had become, for the moment, just another painful half-memory. The unexpected companionship helped to ease the ache of lost friends and lost home – at least to the extent that he allowed it. A large, secret part of his thoughts and feelings he continued to hold back. He was still suspicious, and also unwilling to invest again and risk further loss.

As they trekked through the cool, bird-trilling halls of the morning forest, Binabik explained to Simon that he had come down from his lofty home of Yiqanuc, as he apparently did once a year, on 'business' – a series of errands that carried him to eastern Hernystir and Erkynland. Simon gathered that it involved some sort of trading.

'But, oh! my young friend, what disturbances I find this spring-tide! Your peoples are very upset, very frightened!' Binabik waved his hands in mock-agitation. 'In the outlying provinces the king is not popular, is he? And they are fearful of him in Hernystir. Elsewhere there is anger and there is starving. People are afraid to travel; the roads are no longer safe. Well,' he grinned, 'if you wish truth to be told, the roads never *were* safe, at least in the areas of isolation – but it *is* real that there is a change for the worse in the north of Osten Ard.'

Simon was observing how the noon sun had set vertical columns of light among the tree trunks. 'Have you ever traveled to the South?' he asked at last.

'If by "South" you mean south of Erkynland, my answering is: yes, once or twice. But please remember: among my people almost any leaving of Yiqanuc is "travel to the South." '

Simon was not paying very close attention. 'Did you travel by yourself? Did . . . did . . . did Qantaqa go with you?'

Binabik wrinkled another smile. 'No. It was long ago, before my wolf-friend was born, when I was . . .'

'How did you . . . how did you get this wolf?' Simon interrupted. Binabik gave an exasperated hiss.

'It is a difficult thing answering questions when one is having continual interruptions with more questions!'

Simon tried to look penitent, but he was feeling the spring as a bird feels wind in its feathers. 'Sorry,' he said. 'I've been told before . . . by a friend . . . that I ask too many questions.'

'It is not "too many." ' Binabik said, using his stick to push a low-hanging branch away from their path. ' – it is "piled on top of one and another." ' The troll barked a short laugh. 'Now, which do you want for my answering?'

'Oh, whichever you want. You decide,' Simon replied meekly, then jumped as the troll smacked him lightly on the wrist with his walking stick.

'It would please me your not being obsequious. That is a trait of marketplace people who are selling shoddy goods. I am sure to prefer endless stupid questions to that.'

'Ob . . . obseek. . . ?'

311

'Obsequious. Flattering with oiliness. It is not liked by me. In Yiqanuc we say: "Send the man with the oily tongue to go and lick the snowshoes." '

'What does that mean?'

'It means that we do not like flatterers. Never mind, then!' Binabik threw back his head and laughed, black hair swinging, eyes nearly disappearing as his round cheeks rose toward his brows. 'Never mind! We have wandered as far as the wandering of Lost Piqipeg – wandered in our conversing, I mean. No, do not ask anything. We will stop here for a rest, and I will tell you now about how I met my friend Qantaqa.'

They chose a huge stone, an outcropping of granite thrusting up from the forest floor like a speckled fist, its upper half painted by a swath of sunlight. The young man and the troll climbed up to perch on top. The forest was silent around them; the dust of their passage slowly settled. Binabik reached into his bag and produced a stick of dried meat and a goatskin of thin, sour wine. As Simon chewed, he kicked off his shoes and wiggled his sore toes in the warming sun. Binabik looked at the shoes critically.

'We shall have to be finding something else.' He poked the tattered, blackened leather. 'A man's soul is in peril when his feet are hurting.'

Simon grinned at this thought.

They spent a while in silent contemplation of the surrounding forest, the living greenery of Oldheart. 'Well,' said the troll at last, 'the first thing that needs understanding is that my people do not shun the wolf – although we are not usually having friendships with them, either. Trolls and wolves have lived side by side for many thousands of years, and we are leaving each other alone most times.

'Our neighbors, if so polite a term can be used, the hairy men of the Rimmersgard, think the wolf a dangerous animal of great treachery. You are familiar with the men of Rimmersgard?'

312

'Oh, yes.' Simon was pleased to be in the know. 'They were all about in the Hay – ' he caught himself, 'in Erchester. I have talked to many of them. They wear their beards long,' he added, demonstrating his familiarity.

'Hmmm. Well, since we live in the high mountains, we Qanuc – we trolls – and we do not kill these wolves, the Rimmersmen think we are wolf-demons. In their frost-crazy, blood-feuding brains,' Binabik put on a look of comical disgust, 'it is their thought that troll-folk are magical and evil. There have been bloody fights, very many many, between Rimmersmen – *Croohok* we call them – and my Qanuc-folk.'

'I'm sorry,' said Simon, thinking guiltily of the admiration he had felt for old Duke Isgrimnur – who, on reflection, did not seem like the type to massacre innocent trolls, testy though he was reputed to be.

'Sorry? You should not be. Now myself, I am thinking that men – and women – of Rimmersgard are clumsy, stupid, and suffer with excessive tallness – but I do not think they are then evil, or deserving of being made dead. Ahhh,' he sighed, shaking his head like a philosopher-priest in a dead-end tavern, 'Rimmersmen are a puzzlement to me.'

'But what about the wolves?' Simon asked, then silently chided himself for interrupting. This time Binabik did not seem to mind.

'My people live on craggy Mintahoq, in the mountains called Trollfells by the Rimmersmen. We ride the shaggy, nimble-footed rams, raising them up from tiny lambkins until they have enough bigness to bear us through the mountain passes. There is nothing, Simon, that is in this world quite like being a ram-rider of Yiqanuc. To sit your steed, to be wending the pathways of the Roof of the World . . . to be leaping in a single bound of greatness across mountain chasms so very deep, so exquisitely deep that if a rock was dropped by you it would take half a day to strike bottom. . . .'

Binabik smiled and squinted in happy reverie. Simon, trying to visualize such heights, suddenly felt a little dizzy and put his palms flat on the reassuring stone. He looked down. This perch, at least, stood only a man's height above the earth.

'Qantaqa was a pup when she was found by me,' Binabik continued at last. 'Her mother had been probably killed, or from starvation had died. She snarled at me when I discovered her, a ball of white fur given away in the snow by black nose.' He smiled. 'Yes, she is gray now. Wolves, like people are doing, often change their colors as they grow. I found myself . . . touched by her effort at defending. I brought her back with me. My master . . .' Binabik paused. The harsh cry of a jay filled the moment. 'My master said if I would be taking her from the arms of Qinkipa the Snow Maiden, then I was assuming duties of a parent. My friends had thought that I was not being sensible. Aha! I said. I will teach this wolf to carry me just like a ram with horns. It was not believed – it was not a thing that had been done before. So many things are things not done before . . .'

'Who is your master?' Below then Qantaqa, who had been napping in a splash of sun, rolled onto her back and kicked, the white fur of her belly thick as a king's mantle.

'That, Simon-friend, is another tale to tell: not today. To finish, though, I will say that I did teach Qantaqa to carry me. The teaching was a very . . .' – he wrinkled his upper lip – 'diverting experience. But there is no regret in me for this. I travel often, farther than my tribesmen. A ram is a wonderful jumping animal, but their minds are very small. A wolf is clever-clever-clever, and they are faithful as a debt unpaid. When they take a mate, do you know, they are taking only one for their entire lives? Qantaqa is my friend, and I think her much preferable to any sheep. Yes, Qantaqa? Yes?'

The great gray wolf sat up, her wide yellow eyes fixed on Binabik. She dipped her head and uttered a short bark.

'You see?' the troll grinned. 'Come now, Simon. I

think we should be to marching while this sun stands high.' He slid down the rock, and the boy followed, hopping as he pulled on his ruined shoes.

As the afternoon passed, and they tramped on through the crowding trees, Binabik answered questions about his travels, displaying an enviable familiarity with places Simon had trod only in daydreams. He spoke of the summer sun revealing the gleaming inner facets of icy Mintahoq like a jeweler's deft hammer; of the northernmost regions of this same Aldheorte Forest, a world of white trees and silence and the tracks of strange animals; of the cold outer villages of Rimmersgard that had barely heard of the Court of Prester John, where wild-eyed, bearded men huddled over fires in the shadows of high mountains, and even the bravest of them feared the shapes that walked the howling darkness above. He spun tales of the hidden gold mines of Hernystir, secret, serpentine tunnels that wound down into the black earth among the bones of the Grianspog mountains, and he spoke of the Hernystiri themselves, artful, dreamy pagans whose gods inhabited the green fields and the sky and stones – the Hernystiri, who of all men had known the Sithi best.

'And the Sithi are real . . .' Simon said quietly, with wonder and more than a little fear as he remembered. 'The doctor was right.'

Binabik cocked an eyebrow. 'Of course Sithi are real. Do you suppose they sit here in the forest wondering if men are real? What nonsense! Men are but a recentness compared to them – although a recentness that has terribly damaged them.'

'It's just that I had never seen one before!'

'You had never seen me or my people, either,' Binabik replied. 'You have never seen Perdruin or Nabban or the Meadow Thrithing . . . is this, then, meaning that *they* do not have existence? What a fund of superstitious silliness is owned by you Erkynlanders! A man whose wisdom is true does not sit in waiting for the world to come at him piece by piece for proving its existence!' The troll stared straight ahead, eyebrows knotted; Simon was afraid he might have offended him.

'Well, what *does* a wise man do, then?' he asked, a little defiantly.

'The wise man is not waiting for the realness of the world to prove itself to him. How can one be an authority before the experiencing of this realness? My master taught me – and to me it seems *chash*, meaning correct – that you must not defend against the entering of knowledge.'

'I'm sorry, Binabik,' Simon kicked at an oak boll and sent it tumbling, 'but I'm just a scullion – a kitchen boy. That kind of talk makes no sense to me.'

'Aha!' Quick as a snake, Binabik leaned over and whacked Simon on the ankle with his stick. 'That is being an example, exactly! Aha!' The troll shook his small fist. Qantaqa, thinking herself summoned, came galloping back to dart in circles around the pair, until they had to halt to avoid tripping over the frisking wolf.

'*Hinik*, Qantaqa!' Binabik hissed. She bounded off, tail bobbing like any tame castle hound. 'Now, friend Simon,' the troll said, 'please forgive my squeaking, but you have made my point.' He held his hand up to stall Simon's question. The youth felt a smile twitching his lips at the sight of the little troll so rapt and serious. 'First,' said Binabik, 'scullion boys are not from fish spawned, or chicken eggs hatched. They can be thinking like the wisest wise folk, if only they *do not fight entering knowledge*: if they do not say "can't" or "won't." Now, it was explaining that I was going to do about this – do you mind?'

Simon was amused. He didn't even mind being struck on the ankle – it hadn't really hurt, anyway. 'Please, explain to me.'

'Then, let us be considering knowledge like a river of water. If you are a piece of cloth, how are you finding out

316

more about this water – if someone dips in your corner and then pulls it out again, or if you are having yourself thrown in without resistance, so that this water is flowing all through you, around you, and you are becoming soaking wet? Well, then?'

The thought of being flung into a cold river made Simon shiver a little. The sunlight had begun to take a sideways angle: the afternoon was dwindling. 'I suppose . . . I suppose getting soaked might make you know more about water.'

'With *exactness*!' Binabik was pleased. 'With exactness! Thus, you are seeing my lesson-point.' The troll resumed walking.

In truth, Simon had forgotten the original question, but he cared little. There was something quite charming about this little person – an earnestness beneath the good humor. Simon felt himself to be in good, although small, hands.

It was hard not to notice that they were now headed in a westerly direction: as they tramped along, the slanting rays of the sun were nearly full in their eyes. Sometimes a dazzling bolt would find its way through a chink in the trees and Simon would stumble for a moment, the forest air suddenly full of glittering pinpricks of light. He asked Binabik about their westward turn.

'Oh, yes,' the troll replied, 'we are heading ourselves toward the Knock. We shall not get there today, though. Soon we will stop to make some camp and eat.'

Simon was glad to hear this, but could not forgo asking another question – it was, after all, his adventure too. 'What is the Knock?'

'Oh, it is not a dangerous thing, Simon. It is the point at which the southern foothills of Wealdhelm dip down with a saddle-like air, and one can easily be leaving the thick and not-too-safe forest and cross to the Wealdhelm Road. As I was saying, though, we shall not reach it this day. Let us cast around for a camp.'

317

Within a few furlongs they found a site that looked promising: a cluster of large rocks on a gently sloping bank beside a forest stream. The water splashed quietly along a course of round, dove-colored stones, eddying noisily around the twisted branches that had tumbled into the stream, disappearing at last into a thicket a few yards below. A stand of aspens, green coins for leaves, rattled softly in the beginnings of an evening breeze.

The pair quickly built a fire circle with dry stones found by the water-course. Qantaqa seemed fascinated by their project, darting close at intervals to growl and lightly snap at the rocks as they were carried laboriously into place. A short while later the troll had a campfire flickering, pale and spectral in the last potent sunbeams of the fading afternoon.

'Now, Simon,' he said, elbowing the intrusive Qantaqa into an unwilling crouch, 'we find it hunting time. Let us discover some suitable supper-bird and I will show you clever tricks.' He rubbed his hands together.

'But how will we catch them?' Simon looked at the White Arrow clutched in his own sweat-grimed paw. 'Will we have to throw this at them?'

Binabik chortled, slapping his hide-suited knee. 'You have some funniness for a scullion boy! No, no, I said I will show you clever tricks. Do you see, where I live there is only a short season for the hunting of birds. In the cold winter there are not any birds at all, except for the cloud-high-flying snow geese who pass our mountain homes on their way to the Northeastern Wastes. But in some of the southern lands I have traveled, they are hunting and eating *only* birds. There I learned some cleverness. I will show you!'

Binabik picked up his walking staff and signed for Simon to follow. Qantaqa leaped up, but the troll waved her off.

'*Hinik aia*, old friend,' he told her kindly. Her ears twitched, and her gray brow furrowed. 'We are going on a mission of stealthiness, and your big paws will not be a

318

help.' The wolf turned and slouched back to stretch by the campfire. 'Not that she cannot be deadly quiet,' the troll told Simon, 'but it is when *she* wants to only.'

They crossed the stream and waded into the underbrush. Within a short time they were into deep woods again; the noise of the water behind them had faded to a murmur. Binabik squatted down, inviting Simon to join him.

'Now we are going to work,' he said. He gave his walking stick a quick twist; to Simon's surprise it separated into two segments. The short one, he now saw, was the handle of a knife whose blade had been concealed within the hollow length of the longer section. The troll upended the longer segment and shook it, and a leather pouch slid out onto the ground. He then removed a small piece from the other end; the long segment was now a hollow tube. Simon laughed with pure delight.

'That's wonderful!' he exclaimed. 'Like a conjuring trick.'

Binabik nodded sagely. 'Surprises in small packages – the Qanuc credo, that is!' He took the knife up by its cylindrical bone handle and poked for a moment in the hollow tube. Another bone tube slid partway out, and he finished the removal with his fingers. When he held it up for inspection, Simon could see that this tube had a row of holes along one side.

'A . . . flute?'

'A flute, yes. Of what good is supper without music following?' Binabik put the instrument aside and poked the leather pouch with the knife tip. Unfolded, it revealed a pressed clump of carded wool and yet one more slim tube, this one no longer than a finger.

'Smaller and smaller we go, yes?' The troll twisted this open to show Simon the contents, tiny needles of bone or ivory, packed close together. Simon reached out a hand to touch one of the delicate slivers, but Binabik hastily pulled the container away.

'Please, no,' he said. 'Be observing.' He plucked one of

319

the needles out with thumb and arched forefinger, holding it up to catch the dying afternoon light; the dart's sharp tip was smeared with some black and sticky substance.

'Poison?' breathed Simon. Binabik nodded seriously, but his eyes showed a certain excitement.

'Of course,' he said. 'Not all are so poisoned – it is not a necessity for the killing of small birds, and it has an unpleasant tending to ruin the meat – but one cannot stop a bear or other large, angered creature with only a tiny dart.' He slid the envenomed needle down among its fellows and selected another, unstained dart.

'You've killed a bear with one?' Simon asked, extremely impressed.

'Yes, I have done it – but the wise troll does not stay in the area while waiting for the bear to know he is dead. The poison is not finishing its work immediately, you see. Very big are bears.'

While talking, Binabik had torn off a piece of the coarse wool and unraveled the fibers with the point of his knife, fingers working as quickly and competently as Sarrah the upstairs maid going at the mending. Before this homely memory could summon any companions, Simon's attention was captured again as Binabik began wrapping the threads rapidly around the base of the dart, weaving them over one another until the butt end was a soft globe of wool. When it was finished he pushed the whole thing, needle and wad, into one end of the hollow walking stick. He wrapped the other needles in their pouch, tucked it in his belt, and handed the rest of the dismantled staff to Simon.

'Carry these, if you will please,' he said. 'I do not see many birds here, although quite often they are emerging now for feeding on the insects. It is perhaps we shall have to be settling for a squirrel – not that they are not tasting good,' he hastened to explain as they stepped over a fallen tree, 'but there is a certain more delicate touch and experience in the hunting of small birds. When the dart

320

hits, you will be understanding. I think it is their flying that touches me so, and how quickly their tiny hearts are beating.'

Later, in the leaf-whisper of the spring evening, as Simon and the little troll lazed by the fire digesting their meal – two pigeons *and* a fat squirrel – Simon thought on what Binabik had said. It was strange to realize how little you understood someone that you had grown to like. How could the troll feel such affection toward something he was going to kill?

*I certainly don't feel that way about that bloody woodsman,* he thought. *He probably would have killed me as quickly as he would have killed the Sitha-man.*

But would he have? Would he have taken the axe to Simon? Maybe not: he had thought the Sitha a demon. He had turned his back on Simon, something he would not have done had he feared him.

*I wonder if he had a wife?* Simon suddenly thought. *Did he have children? But he was a wicked man! Still, bad men can have children – King Elias has a daughter. Would she feel bad if her father died? I certainly wouldn't. And I don't feel bad that the woodsman is dead – but I would feel sad for his family if they found him dead in the forest that way. I hope he didn't have any family, that he was alone, that he lived all alone in the forest by himself . . . alone in the forest. . . .*

Simon started upright, full of fear. He had nearly drifted off, alone by himself and helpless . . . but no. There was Binabik sitting back against the bank, humming to himself. Simon felt suddenly very grateful for the little man's presence.

'Thank you . . . for the supper, Binabik.'

The troll turned to look at him, an indolent smile tugging at the corners of his mouth. 'It is happily given. Now you have seen what the sourthern blow-darts can do, perhaps you would like to learn their using yourself?'

'Certainly!'

'Very good. Then I will be showing you tomorrow –

perhaps then *you* can be hunting our supper, hmm?'

'How long . . .' Simon found a twig and stirred the embers, 'how long will we be travelling together?'

The troll closed his eyes and leaned back, scratching his head through his thick black hair. 'Oh, a while at least, I am thinking. You are going to Naglimund, correct? Well, I have sureness I will travel at least the great part of the way there. Is that a fair thing?'

'Yes! . . . ummm, yes.' Simon felt much better. He, too, leaned back, wiggling his unshod toes before the coals.

'*However,*' Binabik said beside him, 'I am still not understanding why you are wishing to go there. I am hearing reports that the Naglimund stronghold is being garrisoned for war. I am hearing rumors that Josua the prince – whose disappearing became known even in the remote places of my travels – may be hiding there to make war on his brother the king. Do you not know these sayings? Why, if I may so presume, are you going there?'

Simon's moment of nonchalance evaporated. *He's just small*, he chided himself, *not stupid!* He forced himself to breathe deeply several times before answering. 'I don't know much about these things, Binabik. My parents are dead, and . . . and I have a friend at Naglimund . . . a harper.' *All true, more or less – but convincing?*

'Hmmmm.' Binabik had not opened his eyes. 'There are perhaps better destinations than a fortress in caparison for a sieging. Still, you show quite the bravery for setting out alone, although, "Brave and Foolish often live in the same cave," as we say. Perhaps if your destination proves not likable to you, you may come and be living with we Qanuc. It is a great, towering troll you would be!' Binabik laughed, a high, silly giggle like a scolding squirrel. Simon, despite a certain rawness of nerves, could not help but join in.

The fire had burned down to a dull glow, and the

surrounding forest was an indeterminate, undistinguished clump of darkness. Simon had pulled his cloak tightly about him. Binabik was absently running his fingers across the holes of his flute as he stared up into the velvety patch of sky visible through a gap in the trees.

'Look!' he said, extending his instrument to point up into the night. 'Do you see?'

Simon tilted his head closer to the little man's. Nothing was in view above but a thin train of stars. 'I don't see anything.'

'Don't you see the Net?'

'What net?'

Binabik looked strangely at him. 'Are they teaching you nothing in that boxy castle? *Mezumiiru's Net*.'

'Who's that?'

'Aha.' Binabik let his head fall back. 'The stars. That drift that you are seeing above you there: it is *Mezumiiru's Net*. They say that she spreads it to catch her husband Isiki, who has run away. We Qanuc call her *Sedda*, the Dark Mother.'

Simon stared up at the dim points; it looked as though the thick black fabric separating Osten Ard from some world of light was wearing thin. If he squinted he could make out a certain fan shape to the arrangement.

'They're so faint.'

'The sky is not clear, you are right. It is said that Mezumiiru prefers it that way, that otherwise the bright light that the jewels of her net are making warns Isiki away. Still, there are often cloudy nights, and she is not catching him yet . . .'

Simon squinted. 'Mezza . . . Mezo . . .'

'Mezumiiru. Mezumiiru the Moon Woman.'

'But you said that your people call her . . . Sedda?'

'That is right. She is the mother of all, as the Qanuc believe.'

Simon thought for a moment. 'Then why do you call *that*,' – he pointed up – ' "*Mezumiiru's Net*." Why not "*Sedda's Net*"?'

Binabik smiled and lifted his eyebrows. 'A good question. My people *do* call it that – or, actually, they are saying *"Sedda's Blanket."* I travel more, however, and am learning other names, and, after all is said, it is the Sithi who were here first. It is the Sithi who were long ago naming all the stars.'

The troll sat for a moment, staring with Simon up at the black roof of the world. 'I know it,' he said suddenly. 'I will go to singing you the song of Sedda – or a little part, perhaps. It is song of great length, after all. Should I assay this singing?'

'Yes!' Simon snuggled himself even deeper in his cloak. 'Sing, please!'

Qantaqa, who had been snoring softly across the troll's legs, now woke up, raising her head to look this way and that, giving a low growl. Binabik, too, stared around, narrowing his eyes as he tried to pierce the gloom outside the campfire. A moment leter Qantaqa, apparently satisfied that all was well, poked Binabik into a more pleasing configuration with her huge head, then settled back down and closed her eyes. Binabik patted her, took up his flute, and blew several preparatory notes.

'Be understanding,' he said, 'that this can only be a shortness of the whole song. I will be explaining things. Sedda's husband, by the Sithi named Isiki, my people are calling Kikkasut. He is the Lord of all Birds . . .'

Solemnly, the troll began to chant in a high-pitched voice – strangely tuneful, like wind in a high place. He paused at the end of each line to pipe skirling notes on his flute.

> '*Water is flowing*
> *By Tohuq's cave*
> *Shining sky-cave*
> *Sedda is spinning*
> *Sky-lord's dark daughter*
> *Pale, black-haired Sedda.*

324

*Bird-king is flying*
*On the star path*
*Gleaming bright path*
*Now he sees Sedda*
*Kikkasut sees her*
*Vows she'll be his.*

*"Give me your daughter.*
*Your daughter who spins.*
*Spins slender thread."*
*Kikkasut calls then.*
*"I'll clothe her finely*
*All in bright feathers!"*

*Tohuq he listens*
*Hears these fine words*
*Rich bird-king's words*
*Thinks of the honor —*
*Sedda he'll give up*
*Old, greedy Tohuq.'*

'So,' Binabik explained in his speaking voice, 'old Tohuq the sky-lord is selling his daughter to Kikkasut for a beautiful cape of feathers, which he will use to make the clouds. Sedda is then going with her new husband to his country beyond the mountains, where she is becoming the Queen of Birds. But the marriage has not much happiness. Soon Kikkasut, he begins to ignore her, coming home only to eat and curse at Sedda.' The troll laughed quietly, wiping the end of his flute on his fur collar. 'Oh, Simon, this is always being *such* a length of story . . . Well, Sedda goes to a wise woman, who tells that she could gain back Kikkasut's wandering heart if she will be giving him children.

'With a charm the wise woman has given, made from bones and mockfoil and black snow, Sedda is able to then conceive, and she gives birth to nine children. Kikkasut is hearing, and sends word that he is coming to take them

325

from her, so that it is properly raised as birds they will be, and not by Sedda raised as useless moon–children.

'When she is hearing this, Sedda takes the two most young and hides them. Kikkasut comes for taking away the others, and he asks of her the happenstances of the missing two. Sedda tells him they had become sick and dead. He goes away from her, and she curses him.'

Again he sang.

> 'Kikkasut winging
> Sedda she weeps
> Weeps for her lost
> Her children all taken
> But for the hidden pair
> Lingit and Yana.
>
> Sky-lord's grandchildren
> Moon-woman's twins
> Secret and pale
> Yana and Lingit
> Hid from their father
> Deathless she'll keep them . . .'

'You are seeing,' Binabik interrupted himself, 'Sedda did not want her children to have mortalness and be dying, as the birds and the beasts of the fields. They were her all and onlyness . . .

> 'Sedda is mourning
> Lone and betrayed
> Vengeance she plots
> Takes her bright jewels
> Kikkasut's love gift
> Weaves them together.
>
> Mountain-top lofty
> Dark Sedda climbs
> Blanket new-woven
> She spreads on night's sky

A trap for her husband
Thief of her children . . .'

Binabik trilled a melody for a while, wagging his head slowly from side to side. At last he put the flute down. 'It is a song of strenuous length, Simon, but it speaks of most important things. It goes on to tell of the children Lingit and Yana, and their choosing between the Death of the Moon and the Death of the Bird – the moon, you are seeing, dies, but then has return as itself. The birds die, but leave their egged young to survive them. Yana, we trolls think, chose the way of the Moon-death, and was being the matriarch – a word meaning grandmother – the matriarch of the Sithi. The mortals, myself and yourself, Simon-friend, are of the descent of Lingit. But it is a long, very long song . . . would you like to be hearing more some time?'

Simon made no reply. The song of the moon and the gentle brush of night's feathered wing had sent him swiftly down to sleep.

# 19
# The Blood of Saint Hoderund

It seemed that every time Simon opened his mouth to speak, or even to breathe deeply, it was immediately filled with leaves. No matter how often he bobbed and ducked, he could not avoid the branches that seemed to grab for his face like the greedy hands of children.

'Binabik!' he wailed, 'why can't we go back to the road? I'm being torn to pieces!'

'Do not complain so much. We will soon be returning toward the road.'

It was infuriating to watch the tiny troll threading his way between the tangling twigs and branches. Easy for *him* to say "don't complain!" The denser the forest got the more slippery Binabik seemed to become, slithering gracefully through the thick, clutching underbrush while Simon crashed on behind. Even Qantaqa bounded lightly along, leaving barely a ripple in the foliage behind her. Simon felt as though half of Oldheart must be clinging to him in the form of broken twigs and scratching thorns.

'But why are we doing this? Surely it wouldn't take any longer to follow the road around the edge of the forest than it's taking me to burrow through it inch by inch!?'

Binabik whistled for the wolf, who was momentarily out of sight. She soon loped back into view, and as the

328

troll waited for Simon to catch up he ruffled the thick collar of fur around her neck.

'You are most correct, Simon,' he said as the youth dragged up. 'It is just as good time we might be making the longer way about. But,' he held up a stubby, admonitory finger, 'there are other considerations.'

Simon knew he was supposed to ask. He didn't, but stood panting beside the small man and inspected the most recent of his lacerations. When the troll realized Simon would not rise to the bait, he smiled.

' "Why?", you are asking curiously? What "considerations"? The answer is being all around, up every tree and beneath all rocks. Feel! Smell!'

Simon stared miserably around him. All he could see were trees. And brambles. And even more trees. He groaned.

'No, no, is it no senses you have left at all?' Binabik cried. 'What manner of teachings did you have in that lumpish stone anthill, that . . . castle!?'

Simon looked up, 'I never said I lived in a castle.'

'It is having great obviousness in all your actions.' Binabik turned quickly around to face the barely-visible deer trail they had been following. 'You see,' he said in a dramatic voice, 'the land is a book that you should be reading. Every small thing,' – a cocky grin – 'is having a story to tell. Trees, leafs, mosses and stones, all have written on them things of wonderful interest . . .'

'Oh, Elysia, no,' Simon moaned and sank to the ground, dropping his head forward to rest on his knees. 'Please don't read me the books of the forest right this moment, Binabik. My feet ache and my head hurts.'

Binabik leaned forward until his round face was inches from Simon's. After a moment's scrutiny of the youth's bramble-matted hair the troll straightened up again.

'I suppose we may quietly rest,' he said, trying to hide his disappointment. 'I will tell you of these things in a later moment.'

'Thank you,' Simon mumbled into his knees.

Simon avoided the task of hunting for supper that night by the simple expedient of falling asleep the moment they made camp. Binabik only shrugged, took a long draught from his water bag and a similar one from his wineskin, then made a short walking tour of the area, Qantaqa sniffing sentry at his side. After an undistinguished but filling meal of dried meat, he cast the knucklebones to the accompaniment of Simon's deep breathing. On the first pass he turned up *Wingless Bird*, *Fish-Spear*, and *The Shadowed Path*. Unsettled, he closed his eyes and hummed a tuneless tune for a while as the sound of night-insects slowly rose about him. When he threw again, the first two had changed to *Torch at the Cave-Mouth* and *Balking Ram*, but *The Shadowed Path* turned up again, the bones propped against each other like the leavings of some fastidious carnivore. Not the sort to follow the bones to hasty decisions – his master had taught him too well – Binabik nonetheless slept, when he finally could, with his staff and bag cradled close.

When Simon awakened, the troll presented him with a satisfying meal of roasted eggs – quail he said – some berries, and even the pale orange buds of a flowering tree, which proved quite edible and rather sweet in an odd, chewy way. The morning's walking also went considerably easier than the previous day's: the country was gradually becoming more open, the trees more distantly spaced.

The troll had been rather quiet all morning. Simon felt sure that his disinterest in Binabik's woodlore was the reason. As they were coming down a long, gentle slope, the sun high in its morning climb, he felt driven to say something.

'Binabik, do you want to tell me about the book of the forest today?'

His companion smiled, but it was a smaller, tighter grin than Simon was used to seeing. 'Of course, friend Simon, but I am afraid I have given you a wrong thinking. You see, when I am speaking of the land as a book, I am not suggesting you should be reading it to improve your spiritual well-feeling, like a religious tome – although paying attention to your surroundings for that reason is certainly possible. No, I am speaking of it more as a book of physic, something one learns for the sake of health.'

*It is truly amazing,* Simon thought, *how easy it is for this little fellow to confuse me. And without trying!*

Aloud, he said, 'Health? Book of physic?'

Binabik's face took on a sudden look of seriousness. 'For your living or dying, Simon. You are not in your home, now. You are not in *my* home, although I am undoubtedly being an easier guest than you here. Even the Sithi, for all the ages they have watched the sun as it is rolling around and around the skies, even they do not claim Aldheorte as theirs.' Binabik stopped, and laid his hand on Simon's wrist, then squeezed. 'This place where we stand, this great forest, is the *oldest place*. That is why it is called, as your people say, Aldheorte: it is always the old heart of Osten Ard. Even these trees of younger age,' he poked with his stick on all sides, 'were pitting themselves against flooding, wind, and fire before your great King John was first drawing baby-breath on the Warinsten Island.'

Simon looked around, blinking.

'Others,' Binabik continued, 'others there are, some that *I* have seen, whose roots are growing into the very rock of Time; older they are than all the kingdoms of Man and Sithi that were thrown up in glory and were then crumbling in obscurity.'

Binabik squeezed his wrist again, and Simon, looking down the slope into the vast bowl of trees, felt suddenly small: infinitesimal, like an insect crawling up the sheer side of a cloud-lancing mountain.

'Why . . . why are you saying these things to me?' he asked at last, sucking breath and fighting back something that felt like tears.

'Because,' said Binabik, reaching up and patting his arm, 'because you must not think that the forest, the wide world, is anything like the alleyways and such of Erchester. You must watch, and you must be *thinking* and *thinking*.

A moment later the troll was off again. Simon stumbled after him. What had brought all this on? Now the crowding trees seemed a hostile, whispering throng. He felt like he had been slapped.

'Wait!' he called. 'Thinking about what?' But Binabik did not slow down or turn.

'Come now,' he called over his shoulder. His voice was even but curt. 'We must be making better time. With luck we will reach the Knock before darkness is falling.' He whistled for Qantaqa. 'Please, Simon,' he said.

And those were his last words for the morning.

'There!' Binabik finally broke his silence. The pair stood atop a ridge, the treetops a humped blanket of green below. 'The Knock.'

Two more strands of trees were stair-stepped below them, and beyond these a sloping ocean of grass stretched out to the hills, which stood profiled by the afternoon sun. 'That is Wealdhelm, or at least its foothills.' The troll pointed with his staff. The shadowed, silhouetted hills, rounded like the backs of sleeping animals, seemed only a stone's toss away across the expanse of green.

'How far are they . . . the hills?' Simon asked. 'And how did we get so high up? I don't remember climbing.'

'Climbing we did not do, Simon. The Knock is a dipping-down place, sunken low like someone has been pushing at it. If you could be looking backward,' he waved back up the ridge, 'you would see that where we

332

now stand, we are a little lower than the Erchester Plain. And, to give your second question answering, the hills are being quite some far ways, but your sight is deceiving you to make them close. In truth, we had better be at climbing if we wish to make my stopping-place with sun still on us.'

The troll trotted a few paces along the ridge. 'Simon,' he said, and as he turned the boy could see some of the tightness had left his jaw and mouth, 'I must tell you that even though those Wealdhelm Hills are babies only compared to my Mintahoq, still to be near high places again will be . . . like wine.'

*Suddenly childlike again,* Simon thought, watching Binabik's short legs carrying him rapidly down the slope between the trees . . . *No,* he thought then, *not childlike, that's just the size, but young, very young.*

*How old is he, anyway?*

The troll was in fact becoming smaller and smaller even as he watched. Simon cursed mildly and hurried after him.

They went fairly quickly down the broad and well-forested ridges, even though actual climbing was necessary in some places. Simon was not at all surprised by the dexterity which Binabik could exercise – leaping softly as a feather, kicking up less dust than a squirrel, showing a sureness of foot that Simon was sure the rams of Qanuc themselves would not scorn. Binabik's nimbleness did not surprise him, but his own did. He was recovering a little from his earlier deprivations, it seemed, and a few good meals had gone far toward restoring the Simon who had once been known around the Hayholt as 'the ghost-boy,' – the fearless scaler-of-towers and tumbler-off-of-walls. While no match for his mountain-born companion, he nevertheless felt he made a good account of himself. It was Qantaqa who had a few problems, not because she was not surefooted, but instead because of the few steep downward climbs – childishly easy with handholds – that were too far to jump. Faced with these situations she growled a little, sounding more annoyed than upset, and trotted off to find some longer way down, rejoining them usually within a short time.

When they finally found a winding deer track down the last hummock, the afternoon sun had fallen below the middle of the sky, warm on their necks and bright in their faces. A tepid breeze riffled the leaves but failed to dry the sweat on their brows. Simon's cloak, tied around his waist, made him as middle-heavy as if he had eaten a large meal.

To his surprise, when they at last reached the upper slopes of the meadow – the beginnings of the Knock – Binabik elected to bear north-east, hugging the line of the forest, rather than striking out directly across the whispering, gently undulating ocean of grass.

'But the Wealdhelm Road is on the other side of the hills!' Simon said. 'It would be so much faster to . . .'

Binabik held up a stubby paw, and Simon lapsed into sullen silence. 'There is faster, Simon-friend, and then there is being *faster*,' he said, and the cheerful knowingness of his tone almost – but not quite – incited Simon to say something mocking and childish, but temporarily satisfying. When he had carefully shut his already opened mouth, Binabik continued. 'Do you see, I thought it might be nice – be a niceness? . . . a nicety? – to take some respite tonight in a place where you may be sleeping in a bed, and eating at a table. What are you thinking about *that*, hmmm?'

All his resentment boiled away at that, like a steam from beneath a raised pot lid. 'A bed? Are we going to an inn?' Recalling Shem's story of the Pookah and the Three Wishes, Simon knew how a person felt seeing his first wish made real . . . until he abruptly remembered the Erkynguard, and the hanged thief.

'Not an inn.' Binabik laughed at Simon's eagerness. 'But just as good it is – no, it is a better thing. It is a place where you are being fed, and rested, and no one is asking who you are or where you come from.' He pointed out across the Knock, toward where the far side of the forest bowed back around until its perimeter at last ended at the base of the Wealdhelm's foothills. 'Across there, it is, although it cannot be seen from where we are standing. Come now.'

*But why can't we walk straight down across the Knock?* Simon wondered. *It's as though Binabik doesn't want to be so out in the open, so . . . exposed.*

The troll had indeed taken the northeasterly path, skirting the wide meadow to travel in Aldheorte's shadow.

*And what did he mean about a place where no one asks . . . whatever all that was. . . ? Is **he** hiding, too?*

'Slow down, Binabik!' he called. At intervals Qantaqa's white rump bobbed up from the grass, like a seagull floating on the choppy Kynslagh. 'Slow down!' he called again, hurrying now. The wind caught at his words and gently carried them away up the rippling slope behind him.

When Simon had drawn abreast of him at last, the sun on both of their backs, Binabik reached up and patted his elbow.

'Earlier I was being very sharp, very abrupt with you. It was not my place to so speak. Apologies.' He squinted up at the youth, then turned his eyes ahead to where Qantaqa's tail was waving above the swaying grass, now here, now there, the banner of a tiny but swiftly moving army.

'There is nothing . . .' Simon began, but Binabik interrupted.

'Please, please, friend Simon,' he said, a note of embarrassment clear in his voice, 'it was not being my place. Say no more.' He lifted both hands up by his ears and waggled them in a strange gesture. 'Rather, let me tell you something of where we go – Saint Hoderund's of the Knock.'

'What is that?'

335

'It is the place we will stay. Many times I have been there myself. It is a retreating place – a "monastery" as you Aedonites say. They are kind to travelers.'

That was enough for Simon. Immediately visions of long, high halls, roasting meat, and clean pallets swarmed through his head – a delirium of comforts. He began to walk faster, accelerating almost to a trot.

'Running is not needed,' Binabik admonished him. 'It will be waiting there still, regardless.' He cast a look back at the sun, still several hours above the western horizon. 'Do you want me to tell you of Saint Hoderund's? Or are you knowing already?'

'Tell me,' Simon replied. 'I know about such places. Someone I know stayed at the abbey in Stanshire once.'

'Well, this is an abbey of specialness. It has a history.'

Simon raised his eyebrows, willing to listen.

'A song there is,' Binabik said, 'the Lay of Saint Hoderund. It is much more popular in the south than it is in the north – north, by which I am saying Rimmersgard, not Yiqanúc my home – and it is obvious why. Are you knowing anything about the battle of Ach Samrath?'

'That's where the northerners, the Rimmersmen, beat the Hernystirmen and the Sithi.'

'Oho? Then it was some educating you received after all? Yes, Simon-friend, it was Ach Samrach that saw the Sithi and Hernystir armies driven from the field by Fingil Redhand. But there were other, earlier battles, and one of them was here.' He spread his hand to encompass the waving field beside them. 'This land was differently named, then. The Sithi, who were, I suppose, those who knew it best, called it *Ereb Irigú* – Western Gate, that means.'

'Who named it the Knock? It's a funny name.'

'I do not know with certainty. Myself, I am thinking that the Rimmersmen's name for the battle is the root. This place they called *Du Knokkegard* – the Boneyard.'

Simon looked back across the rustling grass, watching as row after row bowed in turn beneath the footsteps of

the wind. 'Boneyard?' he asked, and a chill of premonition ran through him.

*The wind is always moving out here*, he thought. *Restless
–like it's looking for something lost . . .*

'Boneyard, yes. There were many underestimations
made on both sides for that battle. These grasses are
growing above the graves of many thousands of men.'

*Thousands, like the lich-yard.* Another city of the dead
beneath the feet of the living. *Do they know?* he suddenly
wondered. *Do they hear us and hate us for . . . for being in the
sun? Or are they happier being through with it all?*

*I remember when Shem and Ruben had to put down old Rim
the plow horse.* Just before Ruben the Bear's mallet had
fallen, Rim had looked up at Simon – eyes mild but
knowing, Simon had thought. Knowing, and yet not
caring.

*Did King John feel that way at last, old as he was? Ready to
go to sleep, like old Rim?*

'And it is a song any harper south of the Frostmarch
will sing,' Binabik said. Simon shook his head and tried
to concentrate, but the sighing of the grass, the drawn
whisper of wind, was loud in his ears. 'I, and you may be
thanking me for it, will sing no song,' Binabik continued, 'but about Saint Hoderund I should explain, since
it is to his house, as it were, we are going.'

Boy, troll, and wolf reached the easternmost end of the
Knock and turned again, left sides to the sun. As they
waded through the high grass Binabik pulled off his
jacket of hide and knotted the sleeves about his waist.
The shirt that he wore beneath was white wool, loose-
woven and baggy.

'Hoderund,' he began, 'was a Rimmersman by birth
who, after many experiences, became converted to the
Aedonite religion. Eventually he was by the church made
a priest.

'As it is said, no single stitch is interesting until the
cloak has fallen apart. We would not have a care what
Hoderund did, I am quite sure, had not King Fingil

Redhand and his Rimmersmen crossed the Greenwade River and for the first time moved themselves into the lands of the Sithi.

'This, as with most tales of importance, is too long for describing in an hour of walking. I will avoid those explainings and tell this: the Northmen had driven all before them, winning for themselves several battles in their southern movement. The Hernystiri, under their Prince Sinnach, decided to meet the Rimmersmen here,' Binabik again waved an all encompassing hand across the breadth of the sun-tipped prairie, 'to put a stop to their onslaught for all and once.

'All people and Sithi were fleeing from the Knock, fearing to be crushed between two armies – all were fleeing but Hoderund. Battle, it is seeming, draws priests like it does flies, and Hoderund it drew. He went to Fingil Redhand in his tent and then was begging that king to withdraw, so by sparing the thousands of lives that would be lost. He preached, in his – if I may say – silliness and bravery to Fingil, telling him of the words of Usires Aedon to take your enemy to breast and make him brother.

'Fingil, it is not surprising, thought him a madman, and was much disgusted to be hearing such words from a fellow Rimmersman . . . *Oho*, is that *smoke*?'

Catching Simon by surprise with the change of subject – Binabik's narrative had lulled him into a sort of sunstruck, walking dream – the troll pointed up the far side of the Knock. Indeed, from behind a series of gentle hills, the farthest of which looked to bear the marks of cultivation, a thin tendril of smoke was rising. 'Supper, I am thinking,' Binabik grinned. Simon's mouth fell open in anticipatory longing. This time the troll quickened his steps as well. They turned back toward the sun as the forest's dark edge curved around.

'As told,' the troll resumed, 'Fingil was finding Hoderund's new Aedonite ideas most offensive. He commanded the priest be executed, but a merciful soldier instead let him go.

'But go away Hoderund did not do. When the two armies met at last, he rushed out onto the battlefield, between directly the Hernystiri and Rimmersgarders, brandishing his Tree and calling down on to them all the peace of Usires God. Caught between two angry pagan armies, he was quickly killed very dead.

'So,' Binabik waved his stick, beating down a high tussock of grass, 'a story whose philosophy is difficult, hmmm? At least for we Qanuc, who prefer both being what *you* call pagan, and being what *I* call alive. The Lector in Nabban, however, called Hoderund a martyr, and in the early days of Erkynland named this place a church and abbey for the Order Hoderundian.'

'Was it a terrible battle?' Simon asked.

'The Rimmersgard men called this place Boneyard. The later battle at Ach Samrath was perhaps bloodier, but there was treachery there. Here at the Knock it was breast to breast, sword on sword, and blood running like the streams of first thaw.'

The sun, sliding low in the sky, beat full in their faces. The afternoon breeze, which had sprung up in earnest, bent the long grasses and tossed the hovering insects so that they danced in the air, tiny flashes of golden light. Qantaqa came charging back through the field, obliterating in her approach the sawing, hissing music of stem on stem. As they began to trudge up a long incline she circled them, waggling her wide head in the air and yipping excitedly. Simon shielded his eyes, but could see nothing beyond the rise but the treetops of the forest's edge. He turned to ask Binabik if they were almost there, but the troll was staring down as he walked, brows knit in concentration, paying no heed to Simon or the capering wolf.

After some time had passed in silence, sullied only by the swish of their passage through the heavy grass and an occasional agitated bark from Qantaqa, Simon's empty stomach steeled him to ask again. He had no sooner opened his mouth when Binabik astonished him by breaking into high, keening song.

> *'Ai-Ereb Irigú.*
> *Ka'ai shikisi aruya'a*
> *Shishei. shishei burusa'eya*
> *Pikuuru n'dai-tu.'*

As Simon climbed that light-soaked, wind-rippled hill, the words and the strange tune seemed a lament of birds, a desolate call from the high, lonely, unforgiving spaces of the air.

'A Sithi song.' Binabik gave Simon an odd, shy look. 'I am not singing it well. It is about this place, where the first Sithi died at the hands of Man, where blood was first spilled by the warring of men on the lands of the Sithi.' As he finished speaking he flapped a hand at Qantaqa, who was bumping his leg with her broad muzzle. *'Hinik aia!'* he told her. 'She is smelling people now, and food cooking,' he muttered apologetically.

'What did the song say?' Simon asked. 'The words, I mean.' The strangeness still chilled him, but at the same moment it reminded him how big the world truly was, and how little he had seen even in the busy Hayholt. Small, small, small he felt, smaller than the little troll climbing beside him.

'I doubt, Simon, whether the Sithi words can truly be made for singing in mortal languages – whether their thought is being properly passed on, do you see? Even worse, it is not the language of my birthplace that *we* are speaking, you and I . . . but I can try.'

They strode on some moments longer. Qantaqa had grown bored at last, or had thought better of sharing her lupine enthusiasms with these cloddish humans, and had disappeared over the top of the rise.

'This, I am thinking, is near in meaning,' Binabik said at last, and then chanted, rather than sang:

'At the Gate of the West
Between the sun's eye and the hearts
Of the ancestors
Falls a tear
Track of light, track of earthward-falling light
Touches iron and becomes smoke . . .'

Binabik laughed self-consciously. 'Do you see, in the woodcrafty hands of a troll, the song of air is becoming words of lumpish stone.'

'No,' Simon said, 'I don't understand it, exactly . . . but it makes me . . . *feel* something . . .'

'That is then good,' Binabik smiled, 'but no words of mine can be matching the Sithi's own songs, especially this one. It is one of the longest, I am told, and saddest. It is also said that the Erl-king Iyu'unigato made it himself, in the last hours before he was killed by . . . by . . . Ah! Look, we are now at the top!'

Simon raised his eyes; in truth, they had almost reached the summit of the long rise, the endless sea of Aldheorte's huddling treetops stretching before them.

*But I don't think he stopped talking because of that,* Simon thought. *I think he was about to say something he didn't want to say. . . .*

'How did you learn to sing Sithi songs, Binabik?' he asked as they clambered the last few steps to stand on the hill's wide bask.

'We will speak of it, Simon,' the troll replied, staring around. 'But now, look! There is the way down to Saint Hoderund's!'

Starting barely more than a long stone's throw beneath them, clinging to the hill's sloping side like moss growing on an ancient tree, twined rows and rows of evenly spaced, carefully tended vines. They were separated one from the other by horizontal terraces cut into the hillside, edges rounded as though the soil had been shaped long ago. Paths ran between the vines, winding down the slope as sinuously as the plants

341

themselves. In the valley below, sheltered on one side by this first, small cousin of the Wealdhelm Hills, and on the other by the dark border of the forest, a whole basket-weave pattern of farming plots could be seen, laid out with the meticulous symmetry of an illuminated manuscript. Farther along, just visible around the jut of the hill, were the small outbuildings of the abbey, a rough but well-tended collection of wooden sheds and a fenced-in field, empty now of sheep or cows. A gate, the one small moving object in the massive tapestry, swung slowly back and forth.

'Follow the paths, Simon, and it is soon we shall be eating, and perhaps also imbibing a small of the monasterial vintage.' Binabik started down at a quick walk. Within moments he and Simon were threading their way among the grapevines while Qantaqa, scornful of the slow traverse of her companions, sprang down the hillside, leaping over the curling vines without touching a stake or crushing a single grape beneath her great paws.

Watching his feet as he hurried down the steep path, feeling his heels skid a little on every long stride, Simon suddenly felt rather than saw a presence before him. Thinking that the troll had halted to wait for him, he looked up with a sour expression, about to say something about showing some mercy for folk who did not grow up on a mountain. Instead, when his eyes met the nightmare shape before him, he shouted in fear and lost his footing, tumbling back onto his rump and sliding two arm's lengths down the path.

Binabik heard him and turned, racing back up the hill to find Simon sitting in the dirt beneath a large, tattered scarecrow. The little man looked at the scarecrow, hanging off-center on a wide stake, its crude, painted face all but wiped away by wind and rain, then looked down to Simon sucking his scuffed palms in the path. Binabik suppressed his laughter until he had helped the boy up, grabbing with his small, strong hands at Simon's elbow and levering him to his feet, but then could hold back no longer. He turned and started back down, leaving Simon frowning angrily as the smothered sounds of the little man's mirth floated up to him.

Simon bitterly knocked the worst of the dirt off his breeches and checked the two packages tucked in his belt, arrow and manuscript, to make sure neither was damaged. It was obvious Binabik couldn't know about the thief hanged at the crossroads, but he *had* been there to see the Sithi strung up in the woodsman's trap. So why should it be so laughable for Simon to be startled?

He felt very foolish, but as he looked again at the scarecrow he still felt a tremor of foreboding. He reached up to it, grasped the hollow sack of a head – rough and cool to the touch – and folded it over, tucking the top into the shapeless, tattered cloak that flapped at its shoulders so that the blurry sightless eyes would be hidden. Let the troll laugh.

Binabik, composed now, was waiting farther down. He did not apologize, but patted Simon on the wrist and smiled. Simon returned the smile, but his was smaller than Binabik's.

'When I was here three moons ago,' Binabik said, 'on my trip passing southward, I ate the most wonderful venison! The brothers are permitted to take a very few deer from the king's forest for the succoring of wayfarers – and themselves, it needs no saying. Oho, there it is . . . and smoke is rising!'

They had rounded the last curve of the hill; the mournful sound of the squeaking gate was directly below them. Just ahead and down the slope were the clustered thatch roofs of the abbey. Smoke was indeed rising, a thin plume floating up to whirl and dissipate in the wind off the hilltop. But it was not coming from chimney or smoke hole.

'Binabik . . .' Simon said, surprise not quite turned to alarm.

'Burned,' Binabik whispered. 'Or burning. Daughter

of the Mountains. . .!' The gate banged shut and immediately popped open again. 'It is a terrible guest who has come to Saint Hoderund's house.'

To Simon, who had never seen the abbey before, the smoking waste below seemed Binabik's very story of the Boneyard come to life. As in the terrible, mad hours beneath the castle, he felt the jealous claws of the past pushing through to drag present time down into a dark place of regret and fear.

The chapel, the main abbey, and most of the out-buildings had been reduced to steaming husks. The charred roof beams, their burdens of wattle and thatch burned away, lay exposed to the ironic spring sky like the blackened ribs of a hungry god's feast. Scattered about the surroundings, as if dice-thrown by the selfsame god, were the bodies of at least a score of men, as rag-jointed and lifeless as the scarecrow on the hilltop.

'Chukku's Stones . . .' Binabik breathed, still staring, and tapped himself lightly on the chest with the heel of his hand. He moved forward, pulling his bag from his shoulder, and hurried down the hill. Qantaqa, vindi-cated, barked and capered joyfully.

'Wait,' Simon said, barely a whisper. 'Wait!' he called, and lurched after, 'Come back! What are you doing? You'll be killed!'

'Hours old this is!' Binabik called without turning. Simon saw him halt briefly to lean over the first body he reached. A moment later he trotted on.

Gasping, heart racing with fear despite the obvious truth of the little man's words, Simon looked at the same body as he passed. It was a man in a black robe, a monk by his appearance – his face was hidden, pressed into the grass. An arrowhead had pushed violently out through the back of his neck. Flies walked daintily on the dried blood.

A few steps later Simon tripped and fell, catching himself painfully with the palms of his hands on the gravel path. When he saw what he had tripped over, and saw the flies resettling on the upturned eyes, he was violently, excruciatingly sick.

When Binabik found him, Simon had crawled into the shade of a chestnut tree. The youth's head nodded bonelessly as Binabik, like a tender but efficient mother, wiped the bile from his chin with a hank of grass. The carrion stench was everywhere.

'Bad it is. Bad.' Binabik touched Simon's shoulder gently, as if to reassure himself that the youth was real, then squatted on his haunches, narrowing his eyes against the last red rays of sunshine. 'I can find no one that is living here. Monks for the greatest part, all dressed in abbey robes, but there are others, too.'

'Others. . . ?' It was a gurgle.

'Men in traveler's clothes . . . Frostmarch men, stopping here for a night perhaps, although there is a goodish quantity of them. Several are wearing beards, and to me have the looking of Rimmersmen. It is a puzzlement.'

'Where's Qantaqa?' Simon asked weakly. He found himself strangely worried for the wolf, although she of all of them was probably least in danger.

'Running. Smelling. She is very excited.' Binabik, Simon noticed, had his stick pulled apart, and had tucked the knife section into his belt. 'I wonder,' the troll said, staring at the rising smoke as Simon finally sat up, 'what was bringing this on? Bandits? A kind of battling for religious matters – I hear that is not uncommon with you Aedonites – or what? Most curious . . .'

'Binabik . . .' Simon hawked and spat. His mouth tasted like a pig-keeper's boots. 'I'm frightened.' Somewhere in the distance Qantaqa barked, a surprisingly high-pitched sound.

'Frightened.' Binabik's smile was thin as twine. 'Frightened is what you should be.' Though his face appeared clear and unworried, a kind of stunned defenselessness lurked behind the troll's eyes. That scared Simon

345

more than had anything else. There was something more: a hint of resignation, as if the awful thing had not been entirely unexpected.

'I am thinking . . .' Binabik began, when Qantaqa's yipping suddenly rose into a snarling crescendo. The troll sprang to his feet. 'She has found something,' he said, and pulled the startled youth to his feet with a strong tug on the wrist. 'Or something finds her . . .' With Simon staggering behind him, impulses of flight and fear twittering through his skull like bats, Binabik dug away in the direction of the sounds. As he ran, he reached his finger into his blowpipe to push something into place. Simon knew – a heavy, forbidding realization – that this dart was black-tipped.

They ran across the abbey grounds, away from the wreckage and through the orchard, following the sounds of Qantaqa's distress. A blizzard of apple blossoms fell all around; the wind prodded and pushed along the edge of the forest.

Less than ten running steps into the wood they saw Qantaqa, hackles upraised, her growl so deep that Simon could feel it in his stomach. She had caught a monk, and had backed him against a poplar trunk. The man held his pectoral Tree on high, as if to call heavenly lightning down on the offending beast. Despite his heroic stance, the sick pallor of his face and his trembling arm showed that he expected no lightning to come. His pop-eyes, exaggerated by fear, were fixed on Qantaqa: he had not yet seen the two newcomers.

'. . . *Aedonis Fiyellis extulanin mei* . . .' His wide lips worked convulsively; the shadows of leaves mottled his pink skull.

'Qantaqa!' Binabik shouted, *'Sosa!'* Qantaqa growled, but her ears twitched. *'Sosa aia!'* The troll whacked his hollow stick against his thigh. The crack echoed. With a last hacking snarl Qantaqa dropped her head and trotted back toward Binabik. The monk, staring at Simon and the troll as though they were quite as terrifying as the

346

wolf, swayed slightly and then toppled backward to land sitting on the ground with the stunned expression of a child who has hurt himself but has not yet realized that he wants to cry.

'Usires the merciful,' he gabbled at last as the pair hurried toward him, 'Usires the merciful, the merciful . . .' A wild look came into his bulging eyes. 'Leave me alone, you pagan monsters!' he shouted, and tried to struggle to his feet. 'Murdering bastards, pagan bastards!' His heel skidded from beneath him and he sat down again, mumbling. 'A troll, a murdering troll . . .' He began to pinken, his color coming back. He sucked in a great convulsive breath, then looked as if at last he truly would cry.

Binabik stopped. Grabbing Qantaqa by the neck, he gestured Simon forward, saying: 'Help him.'

Simon walked slowly, trying with some difficulty to compose his face into something befitting a friend coming to help – his own heart, after all, was drumming at his ribcage like a woodpecker. 'It's all well, now,' he said, 'all well.'

The monk had covered his face with his sleeve. 'Killed them all, now you want us, too,' he cried, his voice, though muffled, sounding more of self-pity than fear.

'A Rimmersman, he is,' said Binabik, 'as if you would not be guessing already to hear him at slandering the Qanuc. *Pfah.*' The troll made a disgusted noise. 'Help him up, friend Simon, and let us take him out into the light.'

Simon got the man's bony, black-robed elbow and laboriously steered him onto his feet, but when he tried to guide him toward Binabik the man pulled away.

. 'What are you doing?!' he shouted, feeling on his chest for his Tree. 'Making me desert the others? No, you just get away from me!'

'Others?' Simon turned questioningly to Binabik. The troll shrugged and scratched the wolf's ears. Qantaqa seemed to grin as if the spectacle amused her.

'Are there others alive?' the boy asked gently. 'We will

347

help you, and them, too, if we can. I am Simon, and that is my friend Binabik.' The monk stared at him suspiciously. 'I believe you met Qantaqa already,' Simon added, and immediately felt sorry for the poor joke. 'Come, who are you? Where are these others?'

The monk, whose composure was beginning to return, gave him a long, mistrustful look, then turned to stare briefly at the troll and wolf. When he turned back to Simon, some of the tension had left his face.

'If you are indeed . . . a good Aedonite acting in charity, then I ask your forgiveness.' The monk's tone was stiff, as in one unused to apologizing. 'I am Brother Hengfisk. Does that wolf . . .' he turned his gaze sideways, 'does he accompany you?'

'She does,' Binabik said sternly before Simon could answer. 'Too bad it is that she frightened you, Rimmersman, but you must notice that she did you no harm.'

Hengfisk did not reply to Binabik. 'I have left my two charges for too long a time,' he told Simon. 'I must go to them now.'

'We'll come with you,' Simon replied. 'Perhaps Binabik can help. He is very gifted with herbs and things.'

The Rimmersman briefly raised his eyebrows, which made his eyes seem to bulge all the more. His smile was bitter. 'It is a kind thought, boy, but I am afraid Brother Langrian and Brother Dochais are not going to be helped by any . . . woodland poultices.' He turned on his heel and struck off, rather unsteadily, into the deeper forest.

'But wait!' called Simon. 'What happened to the abbey?'

'I do not know,' Hengfisk said without turning, 'I was not here.'

Simon looked to Binabik for help, but the troll made no immediate move to follow. Instead, he called after the limping monk.

'Oh, Brother Hangfisk?'

The monk whirled, furious. 'My name is Hengfisk, troll!' Simon noted how quickly color came to his face.

348

'I was merely making translation for my friend,' Binabik grinned his yellow grin, 'who is not speaking the language of Rimmersgard. You say you are not knowing what happened. Where *were* you when your brethren were being so very slaughtered?'

The monk seemed about to spit back a reply, but instead reached his hand up to his Tree and clutched it. A moment later, in a quieter voice, he said: 'Come, then, and see. I have no secrets from you, troll or from my God.' He stalked away.

'Why were you making him mad, Binabik?' Simon whispered. 'Haven't enough bad things happened here already?'

Binabik's eyes were slits, but he had not lost his grin. 'Perhaps I am being unkind, Simon, but you heard his speaking. You have been seeing his eyes. Do not let yourself be fooled by the wearing of a holy robe. We Qanuc have wakened too many times in the night, finding eyes like this Hengfisk's looking down on us, and torches and axes close by. Your Usires Aedon has not burned with success that hatred from his northern heart.' With a cluck for Qantaqa to follow, the troll moved after the stiff-backed priest.

'But, listen to you!' Simon said, holding Binabik's eye. 'You're full of hatred, too.'

'Ah.' The troll lifted a finger before his now-expressionless face. 'But I am not claiming to believe in your – forgive the saying – upside-down God of Mercy.'

Simon took a breath to say something, then thought better of it.

Brother Hengfisk turned once, silently taking notice of their presence. He did not speak again for some time. The light that filtered through the leaves was fast diminishing; within a short time his angular, black-robed form was little more than a moving shadow before them. Simon was startled when he turned and said: 'Here.' He led them around the base of a great fallen tree whose exposed roots resembled more than anything else a huge broom – a broom that would have fired the imagination of Rachel the Dragon toward heroic, legendary feats of sweeping.

Simon's wry thought of Rachel, coupled with the day's events, brought on a pang of homesickness so intense that he stumbled, catching himself with a hand against the scaly bark of the fallen tree. Hengfisk was kneeling, throwing branches into a small fire that glowed in a shallow pit. Lying beside the fire, one on either side in the shelter of the tree's toppled length, were two men.

'This is Langrian,' Brother Hengfisk said, indicating the one on the right, whose face was largely obscured by a bloody bandage made of sacking. 'I found him, the only one alive at the abbey when I returned. I think Aedon will take him back soon.' Even in the fading light Simon could see that Brother Langrian's skin, that which showed, was pale and waxy. Hengfisk threw another stick on the fire as Binabik, without meeting the Rimmersman's eyes once, kneeled down beside the injured man and began to gently examine him.

'That one is Dochais,' Hengfisk said, gesturing to the other man, who lay as limply as Langrian, but without visible injury. 'It was him I went out to find when he did not come back from his vigil. When I brought Dochais back – carried him – ' there was bitter pride in Hengfisk's tone, 'I returned to find . . . to find all dead.' He made the sign of the Tree on his breast. 'All but Langrian.'

Simon moved close to Brother Dochais, a thin, young man with a long nose and the blue chin-stubble of the Hernystiri. 'What happened to him? What's wrong?'

'I do not know, boy,' Hengfisk said. 'He is mad. He has caught up some fever of the brain.' He returned to his search for firewood.

Simon watched Dochais for a moment, noting the man's labored breathing and the slight trembling of his thin eyelids. As he turned to look over to Binabik, who was delicately unwinding the bandage around Langrian's head, a white hand came up like a snake from the black robe before him and caught his shirt-front in a horrific-ally powerful grip.

Dochais, eyes still shut, had stiffened, his back so bowed that his waist rose from the ground. His head was thrown back, and snapped from side to side.

'Binabik!' Simon shouted in terror, 'he's . . . he's . . .'

'*Aaaahhhh!*' The voice that pushed up from Dochais' straining throat was harsh with pain. 'The *black wagon!* See, it is coming for me!' He thrashed again, like a landed fish, and his words brought Simon a thrill of reawaken-ing horror.

*The hilltop . . . I remember something . . . and the creak of black wheels . . . oh, Morgenes, what am I doing here?!*

A moment later, while Binabik and Hengfisk stared in amazement from the far side of the fire pit, Dochais had pulled Simon forward until the youth's face was almost touching the Hernystirman's own fear-stretched features.

'They are taking me back!' the monk hissed, ' – back to . . . back to . . . *that terrible place!*' Shockingly, his eyes popped open and stared blindly into Simon's own, a handsbreadth away. Simon could not struggle out of the monk's grip, even though Binabik was now at his side trying to help pull him free.

'*You* know!' Dochais cried, 'you know who it is! You have been marked! Marked like I was! I saw them as they passed – the white foxes! They walked in my dream! The *white foxes*! Their master has sent them to put ice on our hearts, and take away our souls on their black, black wagon!'

And then Simon was loose, gasping and sobbing. Binabik and Hengfisk held the twitching monk until he finally stopped thrashing. The silence of the black forest returned, surrounding the tiny campfire as the gulfs of night embrace a dying star.

351

# 20
# The Shadow of the Wheel

He was standing on the open plain at the center of a vast, shallow bowl of grass, a speck of pale upright life in the midst of an endless riot of green. Simon had never felt quite so exposed, so naked to the sky. The fields sloped up and away from him; the horizon on all sides made a tight seal of grass and stone-gray sky.

After a span that could have been moments or years in such impersonal, fixed timelessness, the horizon was breached.

With the ponderous creak of a ship of war under heavy wind, a dark object appeared above the rim that was the outermost limit of Simon's view. It rose and rose, impossibly tall, until its shadow fell across Simon at the valley's depth – the shadow's impact was so sudden that it seemed almost to resound as it struck, a deep, reverberating hum that shook Simon's bones.

The great bulk of the thing came clear against the sky as it stood for a long moment poised on the valley's edge. It was a wheel, a huge black wheel as tall as a tower. Sunk into the twilight of its shadow, Simon could only gape as it began to turn with excruciating deliberateness, to slowly roll down the long green slope, spouting flayed gouges of sod behind it. Simon stood frozen in its awful path as it ground on, as inexorable as the millstones of Hell.

Now it was over him, rim foremost, a black trunk stretching to the firmament, raining turf down all round. The ground beneath Simon's feet pitched forward as the weight of the wheel tipped the bed of the earth. He stumbled, and as he found his balance the black rim was upon him. As he stared, mute and horrified, a gray shadow passed before his eyes, a gray shadow with a flashing core . . . a sparrow, flying madly past, with some bright thing caught up in its curling grip. He flicked his eyes to follow, and then, as if it had somehow caught at his heart in its swift passage, he flung himself after it, out of reach of the plunging wheel . . .

But even as he dove, and the wall-wide rim smashed down, Simon's pants leg was snagged by a burning cold nail protruding from the great wheel's outer edge. The sparrow, only inches away, fluttered free, spiraling up gray on gray against the slate sky like a moth, its glinting burden disappearing with it into the twilight. A great voice spoke.

*You have been marked.*

The wheel took Simon and tumbled him, shook him like a hound breaking a rat's neck. Then it rolled on, yanking him high up into the air. Dangling, he was pulled skyward, the ground rocking and pitching beneath his head like a pulsing green sea. The wind of the wheel's passage was all around him as he rose, circling toward the apex; the blood sang in his ears.

Scrabbling with his hands in the grass and mud that clotted the broad rim, Simon pulled himself painfully upright, riding the wheel as though it were the back of some cloud-tall beast. He rose ever nearer to the arching sky.

He reached the top, and for a moment sat perched at the world's summit. All the spreading fields of Osten Ard were visible beyond the rim of the valley. The sunlight lanced through the dim sky to touch on the battlements of a castle, and onto a beautiful shining spire, the only thing in the world that seemed as tall as the black

353

wheel. He blinked, seeing something familiar in its sweeping line, but even as it began to come clear the wheel ground on, pushing him over the top, then pulling him swiftly toward the ground so far below.

He struggled with the nail, ripping at his pants leg to work himself loose, but somehow he and the nail became one; he could not break free. The ground leaped up. The two, Simon and the virgin green earth, were rushing together with a noise like the horns of the final day booming through the valley. He struck – the two came together – and the wind and the light and the music blew away like a candle flame.

Suddenly:

Simon was in darkness, deep in earth which parted before him like water. There were voices around him, slow halting voices that issued from mouths full of choking dirt.

*Who enters our house?*

*Who comes to disturb our sleep, our long sleep?*

*They will steal from us! The thieves will take from us our quiet and our dark beds. They will drag us up again through the Bright Gate . . .*

As the mournful voices cried Simon felt hands clutch at him, hands as cold and dry as bone, or as wet and soft as burrowing roots, stretching, twining fingers reaching out to catch him up to empty breasts . . . but they could not stop him. The wheel rolled, rolled, grinding him downward, ever farther, until the voices died behind him and he was sliding through gelid, silent darkness.

Darkness . . .

*Where are you, boy? Are you dreaming? I can almost touch you.* It was Pryrates' voice that suddenly spoke, and he felt the malevolent weight of the alchemist's thoughts behind it. *I know now who you are – Morgenes' boy, a scullion, a meddler. You have seen things you should not have* seen, kitchen boy – trifled with things beyond you. You know far too much. I will search you out.

*Where **are** you?*

And then there was a greater darkness, a shadow beneath the shadow of the wheel, and deep in that shadow two red fires bloomed, eyes that must have gazed from a skull horribly full of flame.

*No, mortal*, a voice said, and in his head it had the sound of ashes and earth, and the mute, unvoiced end of things. *No, this is not for you.* The eyes flared, full of curiosity and glee. *We will take this one, priest.*

Simon felt Pryrates' hold slipping away, the alchemist's power withering before the dark thing.

*Welcome*, it said. *This is the Storm King's house, here beyond the Darkest Gate . . .*

*What . . . is . . . your . . . name?*

And the eyes fell in, like crumbling embers, and the emptiness behind them burned colder than ice, hotter than any fire . . . and darker than any shadow. . . .

'No!' Simon thought he shouted, but his mouth, too, was full of earth. '*I won't tell you!*'

*Perhaps we will give you a name . . . you **must** have a name, little fly, little dust speck . . . so that we will know you when we meet . . . you must be marked . . .*

'No!' He tried to struggle free, but the weight of a thousand years of earth and stone were upon him. '*I don't want a name! I don't want a name! I don't . . .*'

'. . . want a name from *you!*' Even as his last cry echoed out through the trees, Binabik was crouching over him, a look of real concern etched on his face. The weak morning sunlight, sourceless and directionless, filled the glade.

'A madman, and one near death I have already to nurse,' Binabik said as Simon sat up, 'and now you must start shouting in your sleep as well?' He wanted it to be a joke, but the morning was too cold and thin to support the attempt. Simon was shivering.

'Oh, Binabik, I . . .' He felt a trembling, sickly smile

355

come to his face, forced out by the simple fact of being in the light, of being on top of the ground. 'I had a terrible, terrible dream.'

'I am not very surprised,' the troll said, and squeezed Simon's shoulder. 'A terrible day yesterday would not by chance alone lead to less-than-restful sleeping.' The little man straightened up. 'If you like, be free to find something to eat in my bag. I am at tending the two monks.' He pointed to the dark shapes on the far side of the campfire. The nearer one, who Simon guessed was Langrian, was wrapped in a dark green cloak.

'Where is . . .' Simon remembered the name after a few moments, '. . . Hengfisk?' His head was pounding, and his jaw throbbed as though he had been cracking nuts with his teeth.

'The unpleasant Rimmersman – who, in fairness it is necessary to say, *did* give his cloak for warming Langrian – is off searching in the wreckage of his home for food and such things. I must be returning to my wards, Simon, if you are feeling better.'

'Oh, certainly. How are they?'

'Langrian, I have pleasure to say, is much improved.' Binabik gave a little nod of satisfaction. 'He has been sleeping quietly for some long time – a claim you cannot also be making, hmmm?' The troll smiled. 'Brother Dochais, sadly, is beyond my help, but he is not sick except in his fearful thoughts. Him I have given something to help sleep also. Now please forgive, I must look at Brother Langrian's dressings.'

Binabik stood and stumped off around the fire pit, stepping over Qantaqa who lay sleeping near the warm stones, and whose back Simon had previously taken for another large rock.

The wind lightly fingered the leaves of the oak tree above his head as Simon riffled through Binabik's bag. He pulled out one small sack that felt as though it might contain breakfast, but even before he opened it a clinking noise told him it held the strange bones he had seen before. A further search turned up smoked, dried meat wrapped in a rough cloth, but as soon as he had the package open he realized that the last thing he wanted to do was put food of any kind into his churning stomach.

'Is there any water, Binabik? Where's your skin?'

'Better, Simon,' the troll called from his crouch over Brother Langrian. 'A stream there is just a short walk down this way.' He pointed, then reached down and tossed Simon the skin bag. 'Filling this will be a help for me.'

As Simon picked up the skin, he saw his twin bundles lying nearby. On an impulse, he caught up the rag-wrapped manuscript and brought it with him as he walked down to the stream.

The streamlet moved sluggishly, and its eddies were clogged with twigs and leaves. Simon had to clear a space before he could lean down and bring up handfuls of water to splash his face. He scrubbed hard with his fingers – it felt as though the smoke and blood of the ruined abbey's ending had worked its way into his every pore and wrinkle. Afterward he drank several great swallows, then filled Binabik's bag.

He sat down on the bank, and his mind turned to the dream that had cloaked his thoughts like a dank mist since he had arisen. Like Brother Dochais' wild words of the night before, the dream had raised dreadful shadows in Simon's heart, but the daylight was even now melting them away like unquiet ghosts, leaving only a residue of fear. All he remembered was the great black wheel as it had borne down upon him. All else was gone, leaving black, empty spots in his mind, doors of forgetfulness he could not open.

Still, he knew that he was caught up in something larger than just the struggle of royal brothers – greater even than the death of that good old man Morgenes, or the slaughter of a score of holy men. These were all but eddies of some larger, deeper current – or, rather, small things crushed by the heedless turning of a mighty wheel. His mind could not grasp what it all might mean, and the more he thought, the more elusive such ideas became. He only understood that he had fallen beneath the wheel's broad shadow, and if he were to survive, he must harden himself to its dreadful revolutions.

Slumped on the bank, the thin fizz of the insects who hovered over the stream filling the air, Simon unwrapped the pages of Morgenes' life of Prester John and began to leaf through it. He had not looked at it in some time, due to long marching and early bedtime once camp was made. He pulled apart some of the pages where they had stuck to each other, reading a sentence here, a handful of words there, not caring so much what it said as indulging in the comforting memory of his friend. Staring at the script, he remembered the old man's slender, blue-veined hands, nimble and clever as nest-building birds.

A passage caught his eye. It was on a page following a crude, hand-drawn map that the doctor had titled at the bottom: *'The Battle-field at Nearulagh.'* The sketch itself was of little interest, as for some reason the old man had not bothered to label any of the armies or landmarks, nor had he included an explanatory caption. The subsequent text, however, leaped out at him, an answer of a sort to thoughts that had been plaguing him since the awful discovery of the day before.

*'Neither War nor Violent Death,'* Morgenes had written, *'have anything uplifting about them, yet they are the candle to which Humanity flies again and again, as complacently as the lowly moth. He who has been upon a battlefield, and who is not blinded by popular conceptions, will confirm that on this ground Mankind seems to have created a Hell on Earth out of sheer impatience, rather than waiting for that original to which – if the priests are correct – most of us will eventually be ushered.*

'Still, it is the field of war that determines those things that God has forgotten – accidentally or not, what mortal can know? – to order and arrange. Hence, it is often the arbiter of Divine Will, and Violent Death is its Law Scribe.'

Simon smiled, and drank a little water. He remembered very well Morgenes' habit of comparing things to other things, like people to bugs, and Death to a wrinkly old archive-priest. Usually these comparisons had been beyond Simon, but sometimes, as he strained to follow the twists and turns of the old man's thoughts, a meaning had come clear all of a sudden, like a curtain drawn from in front of a sunny window.

'John Presbyter,' the doctor had also written, 'was without doubt one of the greatest warriors of the age, and without that ability would never have risen to his final, royal state. But it was not his battling that made him a great king; rather it was his use of the tools of kingship that battling brought into his hands, his statecraft and his example to the common people.

'In fact, his greatest strengths on the field of combat were his worst failings as High King. In the pitch of battle he was a fearless, laughing killer, a man who destroyed the lives of those who came against him with the cheerful enjoyment of an Utanyeat hedge-baron arrow-feathering a buck deer.

'As a king he was sometimes prone to quick action and heedlessness, and it was in that way he very nearly lost the Battle of Elvritshalla Dale, and did lose the good will of the conquered Rimmersgarders.'

Simon frowned as he traced along the passage. He could feel sunlight slipping down through the trees to heat the back of his neck. He knew he really should get the water skin back to Binabik . . . but it had been so long since he had sat quietly by himself, and he was most curiously surprised to read Morgenes apparently

359

speaking ill of the golden, indomitable Prester John, a man who figured in so many songs and stories that only the name of Usires Aedon was better known in all the world, and that not by a long measure.

> 'By contrast,' the passage continued, 'the one man who was John's match on the field of war was his virtual opposite. Camaris-sá-Vinitta, last prince of the Nabbanai royal house, and brother of the current duke, was a man to whom war seemed only another fleshly distraction. Astride his horse Atarin, and with the great sword Thorn in his hand, he was probably the most deadly man in our world – yet he took no pleasure from battle, and his great skill was only a burden, in that his mighty reputation brought many against him who would otherwise have had no cause, and forced him to kill when he would not.
>
> 'It is said in the book of the Aedon that when the priests of Yuvenis came to arrest Holy Usires he went willingly, but when they purposed to take also His acolytes Sutrines and Granis, Usires Aedon would not have it, and slew the priests with a touch of His hand. He wept at the slaying, and blessed their bodies.
>
> 'So it was with Camaris, if so sacrilegious a comparison can be made. If anyone approached the terrible power and universal love which Mother Church imputes to Usires, Camaris was that one, a warrior who killed with no hatred for his enemies, and yet was the most terrifying fighter of this, or probably any other . . .'

'Simon! Will you please come quickly! I need water, and I am needing it now!'

The sound of Binabik's voice, harsh with urgency, made Simon jump guiltily. He scrambled up the bank toward the camp.

But Camaris was a great fighter! All the songs described him laughing heartily as he hewed the heads from the wild men of the Thrithings.

*Shem used to sing one, how did it go. . . ?*

*'. . . He gave them the left side*
*He gave them the right side.*
*He shouted and he sang*
*As they ran and showed their backside.*

*Camaris came a-laughing*
*Camaris came a-fighting*
*Camaris came a-riding*
*Through the Battle of the Thrithings . . .'*

As he emerged from the brush Simon saw in the bright
sunlight – how had the sun gotten so high? – that
Hengfisk had returned, and that he and Binabik were
crouching over the supine form of Brother Langrian.

'Here, Binabik.' Simon handed the skin bag to the
kneeling troll.

'It was a fine long time you were . . .' Binabik began,
then broke off, shaking the water bag. 'Half full?' he said,
and the look on his face made Simon blush with shame.

'I had just drunk some when you called,' he offered.
Hengfisk turned a reptilian eye on him and scowled.

'Well,' Binabik said, returning to Langrian, who
looked much rosier than Simon remembered.
' "Climbed is climbed, fallen is fallen." I think our friend
here is to be improving.' He lifted the bag and squirted a
few drops of water into Langrian's mouth. The unconscious monk coughed and sputtered for a moment, then
his throat moved convulsively as he swallowed.

'Do you see?' Binabik asked proudly, 'it is the wound
on the head that I believe I am . . .'

Before Binabik could finish his explanation,
Langrian's eyes fluttered open. Simon heard Hengfisk
suck in a sharp breath. Langrian's gaze wandered blearily
over the faces that hovered above him, then his eyes fell
shut again.

'More water, troll,' hissed Hengfisk.

'What am I doing here is what I know, Rimmersman,'
Binabik replied with icy dignity. 'You were already

361

performing your duty when you pulled him from the ruins. Now I am at performing mine, and need no suggestions.' As he spoke the little man trickled water past Langrian's cracked lips. After some moments the monk's thirst-swollen tongue pushed out of his mouth like a bear coming up from a winter's sleep. Binabik moistened it with the bag, then dampened a cloth and draped it across Langrian's forehead, which was traced with healing cuts.

Finally he opened his eyes again, and seemed to focus on Hengfisk. The Rimmersman took Langrian's hand in his.

'Heh . . . Hen . . .' Langrian croaked. Hengfisk pressed the damp cloth against the skin.

'Don't speak, Langrian. Rest.'

Langrian turned his eyes slowly from Hengfisk to Binabik and Simon, then back to the monk. 'Others. . . ?' he managed to say.

'Rest, now. You must rest.'

'This man and I are agreeing at last on something.' Binabik smiled at his patient. 'You should take sleep.'

Langrian appeared to want to speak more, but before he could his eyelids slid down, as if heeding advice, and he slept.

Two things happened that afternoon. The first occurred while Simon, the monk, and the troll were eating a sparse meal. Since Binabik had not wanted to leave Langrian there was no fresh game; the trio made do with dried meat and the products of Simon's and Hengfisk's foraging, berries and a few greenish nuts.

As they sat, chewing silently, each wrapped in his own very different thoughts – Simon's an equal mixture of the horrid dream-wheel and the triumphant battlefield figures of John and Camaris – Brother Dochais suddenly died.

362

One moment he was sitting quietly, awake but not eating – he had refused the berries Simon offered him, staring like a mistrustful animal until the boy took them away – and a moment later he had rolled over on his face, quivering at first and then pitching violently. By the time the others could turn him over his eyes had rolled up, showing a ghastly white in his dirt-smeared face; a moment later he had quit breathing, although his body remained as rigid as a spar. Shaken as he was, Simon was certain that just before the final passion he had heard Dochais whisper *'Storm King.'* The words burned in his ears and troubled his heart, although he did not know why, unless he had heard them in his dream. Neither Binabik nor the monk said anything, but Simon was sure they had both heard.

Hengfisk, to Simon's surprise, wept bitterly over the body. He himself, in some strange way, felt almost relieved, a bizarre emotion that he could neither understand nor quell. Binabik was as unreadable as stone.

The second thing happened as Binabik and Hengfisk were arguing, an hour or so later.

'. . . And I am agreeing we will help, but you are upon the wrong ledge if you think to order me.' Binabik's anger was tightly controlled, but his eyes had narrowed to black slashes beneath his brows.

'But you will only help bury Dochais! Would you leave the others to be food for wolves?' Hengfisk's anger was not at all controlled, and his eyes pushed out, wide and staring in his reddening face.

'I tried to help Dochais,' the troll snapped. 'I failed. We will bury him, if that is what you wish. But it is not my plan to be spending three days to bury *all* of your dead brethren. And there are worse purposes they could serve than "food for wolves" – and perhaps did while living, some of them!'

It took a moment for Hengfisk to work out Binabik's

tangled speech, but when he did his color grew even brighter, if such was possible.

'You . . . you heathen monster! How can you speak ill of unburied dead, you . . . poisonous dwarf!'

Binabik smiled, a flat, deadly smile. 'If your God loves them so, then he has taken their . . . souls, yes? . . . up to Heaven, and to be lying around will do harm only to their mortal bodies . . .'

Before another word could be spoken, both combatants were startled out of their dispute by a deep growl from Qantaqa, who had been napping on the far side of the fire pit, beside Langrian. In a moment it became clear what had startled the gray wolf.

Langrian was talking.

'Someone . . . someone warn the . . . the abbot . . . treachery! . . .' The monk's voice was a harsh whisper.

'Brother!' Hengfisk cried, limping quickly to his side. 'Save your strength!'

'Let him speak,' Binabik replied. 'It might be saving our lives, Rimmersman.'

Before Hengfisk could respond, Langrian's eyes were open. Staring first at Hengfisk, then at his surroundings, the monk shuddered as though with a chill, despite being wrapped in a heavy cloak.

'Hengfisk . . .' he grated, '. . . the others . . . are they. . . ?'

'All dead,' said Binabik plainly.

The Rimmersman shot him a hateful glance. 'Usires has taken them back, Langrian,' he said. 'Only you were spared.'

'I . . . I feared it . . .'

'Can you tell us what happened?' The troll leaned forward and put another damp cloth on the monk's forehead. Simon could see now for the first time, behind the blood and scars and sickness, that Brother Langrian was quite young, perhaps not yet twenty years of age. 'Do not tire yourself too much,' Binabik added, 'but tell us what you know.'

Langrian closed his eyes again, as if falling back into sleep, but he was only marshaling his strength. 'There were . . . a dozen or so men who came . . . came in, sheltering from . . . off the Road.' He licked his lips; Binabik brought the water bag. 'Many large . . . parties are traveling these days. We gave them to eat, and Brother Scenesefa . . . put them up in Traveler's Hall.'

As he drank water and talked, the monk seemed to slowly gain strength. 'They were a strange lot . . . didn't come down to the main hall that night, except the leader – a pale-eyed man who bore . . . an evil-looking helm . . . and dark armor – he asked . . . asked if we had heard word of a party of Rimmersmen coming North . . . from Erchester. . . .'

'Rimmersmen?' said Hengfisk, frowning.

*Erchester?* thought Simon, wracking his brain. *Who could it be?*

'Abbot Quincines told the man we had heard of no such party . . . and he seemed . . . satisfied. The abbot seemed troubled, but of course he did not share his worry with . . . we younger brothers. . . .

'The next morning one of the brothers came in from the hill-fields to report a company of riders from the south . . . the strangers seemed . . . very interested, saying that it was . . . the rest of their original party come to meet them. Their pale-eyed leader . . . took his men out to the great courtyard, to greet the new arrivals – or so we thought. . . .

'Just as the new company had crested Vine Hill and been sighted from the abbey – they looked to be only a . . . head or two fewer than our current guests. . . .'

Here Langrian had to stop for a moment's rest, panting slightly. Binabik would have given him something to make him sleep, but the injured monk waved away the troll's offer.

'Not much . . . more to tell. One of the other brothers . . . saw one of the guests come running out, late, from Traveler's Hall. He had not finished donning his cloak –

they were all cloaked, 'though the morning was warm – and beneath it there was the flash of a sword blade. The brother ran to the abbot, who had feared something of the like. Quincines went to confront the leader. Meanwhile, we could see the men riding down the hill – Rimmersmen all, bearded and braided. The abbot told the leader he and his men must put up, that Saint Hoderund's would not be the site of some bandit struggle. The leader pulled his sword out and put it to Quincines' throat.'

'Merciful Aedon,' breathed Hengfisk.

'A moment later we heard hoofbeats. Brother Scenesefa suddenly ran to the courtyard gate and shouted a warning to the approaching strangers. One of the . . . "guests" . . . put an arrow in his back, and the leader slit the abbot's throat.'

Hengfisk stifled a sob and made the sign of the Tree over his heart, but Langrian's face was solemn, emotionless; he continued his narrative without pausing.

'Then there was carnage, the strangers leaping onto the brothers with knife and sword, or pulling bows and arrows from places of hiding. When the new arrivals came through the gate it was with their own swords drawn . . . I suppose they heard Scenesefa's warning, and saw him shot down in the gateway arch.

'I do not know what happened then, for all was madness. Someone threw a torch upon the chapel roof, and it caught afire. I ran for water as people screamed and horses screamed and . . . and something hit me on the head. That is all.'

'So you do not know who was in either of these two warring bands?' Binabik asked. 'Did they fight with each other, or were they being partners?'

Langrian nodded seriously. 'They fought. The ambushers had a much more difficult time with them than they did with unarmed monks. That is all I can say – all I know.'

'May they burn!' hissed Brother Hengfisk.

'They shall.' Langrian sighed. 'I think I must sleep again.' He closed his eyes, but his breathing did not change.

Binabik straightened up. 'I think I will be walking a short ways,' he said. Simon nodded. '*Ninit*, Qantaqa,' he called, and the wolf leaped up, stretched, and followed him. He had vanished into the woods within moments, leaving Simon with the three monks, two living, one dead.

The services for Dochais were brief and spare. Hengfisk had found a winding sheet in the ruins of the abbey. They wrapped it around Dochais' thin body and lowered him into a hole the three able-bodied folk had dug in the abbey's cemetery, while Langrian slept in the forest with Qantaqa for a guardian. The digging had been hard work – the fire in the great barn had burned the wooden handles from the shovels, leaving only the blades to be wielded by hand – straining, sweaty work. By the time Brother Hengfisk had completed his impassioned prayers, coupling them with promises of divine justice – seeming to forget in his fervor that Dochais had been far away from the abbey when the murderers had done their work – it was the darkling tag-end of afternoon. The sun had dropped until there was nothing left but a bright residue along the crest of Vine Hill, and the grass of the churchyard was dark and cool. Binabik and Simon left Hengfisk crouching at the graveside, goggle-eyes tightly shut in prayer, and went to forage and explore around the abbey lands.

Although the troll was careful to avoid as much as possible of the scene of the tragedy, its results were so widespread that Simon quickly began to wish he had returned to the forest camp to wait with Langrian and Qantaqa. A second hot day had done nothing to improve the condition of the bodies: in their bloated, swollen pinkness Simon saw an unpleasant similarity to the roast pig that crowned the Lady Day table at home. A part of

367

him was scornful of his weakheartedness – hadn't he already seen violent death, a battlefield-full in a few short weeks? – but he realized as he walked . . . trying to keep his eyes ahead, to avoid the sight of other eyes, glazed and cracked by the sun . . . that death, at least for him, was never the same, no matter how veteran an observer he had become. Each one of these ruined sacks of bone and sweetbreads had been a life once, a beating heart, a voice that complained or laughed or sang.

*Someday this will happen to me,* he thought as they threaded their way around the side of the chapel, – *and who will remember me?* He could find no ready answer, and the sight of the tiny field of grave markers, their tidiness cruelly lampooned by the sprawled bodies of slain monks, offered him little comfort.

Binabik had found the charred remnants of the chapel's side door, areas of sound wood showing through the coal-black surface like streaks of new-cleaned brass on an old lamp. The troll poked at the door, knocking loose burned fragments, but the structure held. He gave it a more vigorous poke with his stick, but still it stuck closed, a sentry who had died on watch.

'Good,' Binabik said. 'It is suggesting we may wander inside without the whole structure crashing upon our heads.' He took his stick and poked it in through a fissure between door and frame, then used it like a mason's prybar, pushing and levering until, with a little help from Simon, it sprang open in a shower of black dust.

After working so hard to open a door, it was truly strange to enter and find the roof gone, the chapel as open to the air as an unlidded cask. Simon looked up to see the sky framed above him, going red at the bottom and gray at the top with the onset of evening. Around the top of the walls the windows were blackened in their frames, the leading twisted outward, spilling its sooty glass as though a giant hand had pulled off the roof, reached down through the beams and poked out each window with a titan finger.

A quick survey turned up nothing of use. The chapel, perhaps because of its rich draperies and hangings, had burned to the walls. Crumbled ash sculptures of benches and stairs and an altar stood in place, and the stone altar steps bore the ghost of a floral wreath, a perfect, impossibly delicate crown of paper-thin leaves and diaphanous gray ash-flowers.

Next, Simon and Binabik made their way across the commons to the residences, a long low hall of tiny cells. The damage here was moderate – one end had caught fire, but for some reason had burned out before the conflagration had spread.

'Be looking especially for boots,' Binabik said. 'It is sandals these abbey men wear mostly, but some of them may occasionally need to ride or travel in cold weather. Some that are fitting you are best, but in necessity settle for too large rather than too small.'

They started at opposite ends of the long hall. None of the doors were locked, but they were distressingly bare little rooms, a Tree on the wall the only decoration in most. One monk had hung a flowering rowan branch above his hard pallet; its jauntiness in such spare surroundings cheered Simon immensely, until he remembered the fate of the room's resident.

On the sixth or seventh, Simon was startled when his pulling open the cell door was followed by a hissing noise and a blur of something whisking past his ankle. At first he thought an arrow had been shot at him, but one look at the tiny, empty cell showed the impossibility of such a thing. A moment later he realized what it was, and quirked his mouth in a half-smile. One of the monks, no doubt in direct contravention of abbey rules, had kept a pet – a cat, no less, just like the little gray scattercat he had befriended at the Hayholt. After two days locked in the cell, waiting for the master who would not return, it was hungry, angry, and frightened. He went back down the hall looking for it, but the animal was gone.

Binabik heard him clomping about. 'Is all well, Simon?' he called, out of sight in one of the other cells.

'Yes,' Simon yelled back. The light in the tiny windows above his head was quite gray now. He wondered if he should head back to the door, finding Binabik on the way, or go back and look some more. He was interested at least in examining the cell of the monk with the contraband cat.

A few moments later Simon was reminded about the problems of keeping animals shut in too long. Holding his nose, he looked quickly around the cell, and spotted a book, small but nicely bound in leather. He tiptoed across the suspect floor, hooked it off the low bed, and stilted out again.

He had just sat down in the next cell to have a look at his prize when Binabik appeared in the doorway.

'I am having small luck here. You?' the troll asked.

'No boots.'

'Well, it is fast becoming evening. I think I should be having a look around the Traveler's Hall where the murderous strangers were sleeping, in case there is some object there that will tell us anything. Wait for me here, hmmm?'

Simon nodded and Binabik left.

The book was, as Simon had expected, a Book of Aedon, although it was a very expensive and finely-made book for a poor monk to have in his possession; Simon guessed it was a gift from a rich relative. The volume itself was unremarkable, although the illuminations were very nice – at least as far as Simon could tell in the fading light – but there was one thing that caught his attention.

On the first page, where people often wrote their names, or words of salutation if the book was a gift, there was a phrase, carefully but shakily written:

*Piercing My Hearte there is A Golden Dagger;*
*That is God*
*Piercing God's Hearte there is a Golden Needle;*
*That is me*

370

As Simon sat looking at the words his newfound resolve was tested; he felt a wave wash through him, a staggering ocean breaker of remorse and fear, and a feeling of things that, though unseen, were nonetheless slipping heartbreakingly away.

In the midst of his staring reverie Binabik popped his head through the door and tossed a pair of boots onto the floor beside him with a muffled clatter. Simon did not look up.

'Many interesting things there are at Traveler's Hall, your new boots not least. But dark is coming, and I may take only a moment more. Meet with me before this hall, soon.' And he was gone again.

After long, silent moments in the troll's wake, Simon set the book down – he had planned to take it, but had changed his mind – and tried the boots on his feet. At other moments he would have been pleased to find how well they fitted, but now he just left his tattered shoes on the floor and walked down the hall toward the front entrance.

The muted light of evening had descended. Across the commons stood the Traveler's Hall, a twin to the building he had just left. For some reason the sight of the door across from him swinging listlessly to and fro filled him with vague fear. Where was the troll?

Just as he remembered the swinging paddock gate that had been the first signal that all was not well at the abbey, Simon was startled by a rough hand grasping at his shoulder, pulling him backward.

'Binabik!' he managed to shout, and then a thick palm was clamped over his mouth, and he was crushed back against a rock-hard body.

'*Vawer es do kunde?*' a voice growled at his ear in the stony accents of Rimmersgard.

'*Im tosdten-grukker!*' another voice sneered.

In a blind panic Simon opened his mouth behind the shielding hand and bit. There was a grunt of pain, and for a moment his mouth was free.

'Help me! Binabik!' he screeched, then the hand covered him again, crushingly painful now, and a second later he felt a black impact behind his ear.

He could still hear the echoes of his cry dissipating as the world turned to water before his eyes. The door of Traveler's Hall swung, and Binabik did not come.

# 21
# Cold Comforts

Duke Isgrimnur of Elvritshalla had put a little too much pressure on the blade. The knife leaped from the wood and nicked his thumb, freeing a sudden stripe of blood just below the knuckle. He fumed a curse, dropped the piece of heartwood to the ground and stuck his thumb in his mouth.

*Frekke is right*, he thought, – *damn him. I'll never have the knack of this. I don't even know why I try.*

He *did* know, though: he had convinced old Frekke to show him the rudiments of carving during his virtual imprisonment at the Hayholt. Anything, he had reasoned, was preferable to pacing about the castle's halls and battlements like a chained bear. The old soldier, who had served the Duke's father Isbeorn as well, had patiently shown Isgrimnur how to choose the wood, how to spy out the natural spirit that lurked inside, and how to release it, chip by chip, from the prisoning grain. Watching Frekke at work – his eyes nearly shut, his scarred lip quirked in an unconscious smile – the demons and fish and lively beasts that climbed into being from beneath his knife had seemed the inevitable solutions to the questions the world put forth, questions of randomness and confusion in the shape of a tree limb, the position of a rock, the vagaries of rain clouds.

Sucking on his wounded thumb, the duke toyed in a

disordered way with such thoughts – for all Frekke's claims, Isgrimnur found it damnably hard to think about anything at all while he was carving: the knife and wood seemed at odds, in pitched battle that might elude his vigilance at any moment to slide over into tragedy.

*Like now,* he thought, sucking and tasting blood.

Isgrimnur sheathed his knife and stood up. All around him his men were hard at work, cleaning a brace of rabbits, tending the fire, getting camp ready for the evening. He moved toward the blaze, turned, and stood with his broad backside to the flames. His earlier thought of rainstorms came back to him as he looked up at the rapidly-graying sky.

*So here it is Maia-month,* he mused. *And here we are, less than twenty leagues north of Erchester . . . and where did that storm come from?*

At the time, some three hours gone, Isgrimnur and his band had been in hot pursuit of the brigands who had waylaid them at the abbey. The Duke still had no idea who the men had been – some of them had been countrymen, but none had familiar faces – or why they had done what they had. Their leader had worn a helmet in the form of a snarling hound's face, but Isgrimnur had never heard of such an emblem. He might not have even survived to wonder, but for the black-robed monk who had screamed a warning from the St. Hoderund's gateway just before toppling with an arrow between his shoulder blades. The fighting had been fierce, but the monk's death . . . God's mercy to him, whoever he was . . . had served notice, and the Duke's men had been ready for the attack. They had lost only young Hove on the initial charge; Einskaldir had been wounded, but killed his man anyway, and another beside. The enemy had not been looking for a fair fight, Isgrimnur thought sourly. Faced by Isgrimnur and his guard, fighting men all and itching for action after months in the castle, the would-be ambushers had fled across the abbey commons to the stables, where their horses were apparently saddled and waiting.

374

The duke and his men, after a quick inspection found none of the monks alive to explain what had occurred, had resaddled and followed. It might have been more politic to stay and bury Hove and the Hoderundans, but Isgrimnur's blood had been fired. He wanted to know who, and he wanted to know why.

It was not to be, however. The brigands had gotten a start of some ten minutes on the Rimmersmen, and their horses were fresh. The Duke's men had sighted them once, a moving shadow sweeping down off Vine Hill onto the plain, heading through the low hills toward the Wealdhelm Road. The sight had filled Isgrimnur's company with new life, and they had spurred their horses down the slope into the valleys of the Wealdhelm foothills. Their mounts seemed to have caught some of their excitement, drawing up reserves of strength; for a brief while it had seemed that they might run the waylayers down, coming on them from behind like a vengeful cloud rolling across the plain.

Instead, a strange thing had happened. One moment they had been rolling along in the sunlight, then the world had grown perceptibly darker. When it did not change, when half a mile later the hills around them were still lifeless and gray, Isgrimnur had looked up to see a knot of steel-colored clouds swirling in the sky overhead, a fist of shadow over the sun. A dim, grumbling crack, and suddenly the sky was spilling rain – a splatter at first, then torrents.

'Where did this come from?' Einskaldir had shouted across to him, a hissing mist now pulled like a curtain between them. Isgrimnur had no idea, but it had troubled him greatly – he had never seen a storm come up so fast out of a relatively clear sky. When a moment later one of the men's horses had slipped on the wet, matted grass and stumbled, throwing its rider – who, thank Aedon, landed safely – Isgrimnur raised his voice and bellowed his troops to a halt.

So it was that they had elected to make camp, here only

a league or so from the Wealdhelm road. The duke had briefly considered going back to the abbey, but the men and horses were tired, and the blaze that had been roaring from the main buildings when they rode off suggested there would probably be little to go back for. Wounded Einskaldir, however – who, though Isgrimnur knew better, sometimes seemed to possess no emotions save a general fierceness – had ridden right back to the abbey for Hove's body, and to pick up anything else that might give a clue to the attackers' identities or motivations. Knowing Einskaldir and his ways, the duke had given in quickly, stipulating only that he must take Sludig along, who was a slightly less ardent spirit. Sludig was a fine soldier, but nevertheless valued his own skin enough to provide · some counterweight to bright-burning Einskaldir.

*So here I stand,* Isgrimnur thought in tired disgust, *baking my bum in front of the campfire while the young men do the work. Curse age, curse my aching back, curse Elias, curse these damnable times!* He looked down at the dirt, then stooped and took up a piece of wood lying there which he had hoped some miracle would help him shape into a Tree, to lie against his wife Gutrun's breast when he returned to her.

*And curse carving!* He gave it to the flames.

He was tossing rabbit bones into the fire, feeling a little better for having eaten, when there came a sudden roll of hoofbeats. Isgrimnur dropped his hands to wipe grease on his kirtle, and his liegemen did the same – it would not do to have a slippery hand on axe or sword. It sounded like a very small company of riders, two or three at most; still, no one relaxed until Einskaldir and his white horse came clear against the twilight. Sludig rode just behind, leading a third mount across whose pommel were draped . . . *two* bodies.

Two bodies, but, as Einskaldir explained in his terse manner, only one a corpse.

'A boy,' Einskaldir grunted, his dark beard already shining with rabbit fat. 'Found him nosing about. Thought we should bring him along.'

'Why?' Isgrimnur rumbled. 'He doesn't look like anything but a scavenger.'

Einskaldir shrugged. Fair-haired Sludig, his companion, grinned affably: it hadn't been *his* idea.

'No houses around. We saw no boy at the abbey. Where did he come from?' Einskaldir cut loose another piece with his knife. 'When we grabbed him, he yelled for someone. "Bennah," or "Binnock," couldn't say for sure.'

Isgrimnur turned away to briefly survey Hove's body, now laid out on a cloak. He was kin, the cousin of his son Isorn's wife – not close kin, but close enough by the customs of the cold north that Isgrimnur felt a deep pang of remorse as he stared down at the young man's snow-pale face, at his thin yellow beard.

From there he turned to the captive, still bound at the wrists, but lowered from the horse to lie propped against a rock. The boy was only a year or two younger than Hove, thin but wiry, and the sight of his freckled face and shock of reddish hair tugged at Isgrimnur's memory. He could not summon the reminder forth. The youth was still stunned from the tap Einskaldir had given him, eyes closed and mouth slack.

*Looks like any poor peasant lout,* the duke thought, *except for those boots – which I'll wager he found at the abbey. Why in the name of Memur's Fountain did Einskaldir bring him? What am I supposed to do with him? Kill him? Keep him? Leave him to starve?*

'Let's get to finding rocks,' the duke said at last. 'Hove will need a cairn – this looks like wolf country to me.'

Night had come down; the outcroppings of rock that

dotted the desolate plain below Wealdhelm were only clumps of deeper shadow. The fire had been stoked high, and the men were listening to Sludig sing a bawdy song. Isgrimnur knew only too well why men who had been blooded, who had lost one of their own – Hove's undistinguished pile of stones was one of the shadow-clumps out beyond the firelight – might feel the urge to indulge in such foolishness. As he himself had said months ago, standing across the table from King Elias, there were frightening rumors on the wind. Here on the open plain, dwarfed but not protected by the looming hills, things that were travelers' tales in the Hayholt or Elvritshalla, ghost-fables to enliven a dull evening, were no longer so easy to brush aside with a laughing remark. So the men sang, and their voices made an off-key but very human sound in the night wilderness.

*And ghost-tales aside*, Isgrimnur thought, *we were attacked today, and for no reason I can fathom. They were waiting for us. Waiting! What in the name of sweet Usires does that mean?!*

It could have been that the brigands were merely waiting for the next group of travelers who might stop at the abbey – but why? If they were only after robbing and whatnot, why not pillage the abbey itself, a place likely to have at least a fine reliquary or two? And why wait for chance travelers at an abbey in the first place, where there would naturally be witnesses to any act of thievery?

*Not that we've got many witnesses left, damn their eyes. One, maybe if that boy proves to have seen anything.*

It just did not make good sense. Waiting to waylay a company of travelers who, even in these times, might prove to be king's guardsmen – who had, in fact, turned out to be armed, battle-honed northerners.

So the possibility had to be entertained that he and his men had been the targets. Why? And just as importantly, who? Isgrimnur's enemies, Skali of Kaldskryke being a prime example, were well known to him, and none of the bandits had been recognized as members of Skali's clan.

Besides, Skali was gone back to Kaldskryke long ago, and how could he have known that Isgrimnur, sick to death of inactivity and fearing for the safety of his duchy, would decide at last to confront Elias and, after an argument, receive his reluctant royal permission to take his men north?

*'We need you here, Uncle,' he told me. He knew I had stopped believing that long ago. Just wanted to keep his eye on me, that's what I think.*

Still, Elias had not resisted anywhere near as strongly as the duke had anticipated; the argument had seemed to Isgrimnur only a matter of form, as though Elias had known the confrontation was coming, and had decided to accede already.

Frustrated by the circles his thoughts were following, Isgrimnur was about to lever himself up and off to his bedroll when Frekke came to him, the fire at the aged soldier's back making him a gaunt, shambling shadow.

'A moment, your Lordship.'

Isgrimnur suppressed a grin. The old bastard must be drunk. He only got formal when he was in his cups.

'Frekke?'

'It's that boy, sire, the one Einskaldir brought back. He's awake. Thought your Lordship might like to chat with him.' He swayed a little, but quickly turned it into a gesture of pulling up his breeches.

'Well, I suppose.' The breeze was up. Isgrimnur pulled his kirtle tighter and started to turn, then stopped. 'Frekke?'

'Lordship?'

'I threw another damned carving in the fire.'

'I 'spected you would, sire.'

As Frekke wheeled around to head back to the beer jug, Isgrimnur was positive the old man wore a tiny smile.

*Well, damn him and his wood, anyway.*

The boy was sitting up, chewing the meat from a bone.

Einskaldir sat on a rock beside him looking deceptively relaxed – Isgrimnur had *never* seen the man relax. The firelight could not reach Einskaldir's deep-set stare, but the boy, when he looked up, was as wide-eyed as a deer surprised at a forest pond.

At the duke's approach the boy stopped chewing and regarded Isgrimnur suspiciously for a moment, mouth half-open. But then, even by fireglow, Isgrimnur saw something pass across the boy's face . . . was it relief? Isgrimnur was troubled. He had expected, despite Einskaldir's suspicions – the man, after all, was as prickly with mistrust as a hedgehog – to find a frightened peasant boy, terrified or at least dully apprehensive. This one *looked* like a peasant, an ignorant cotsman's son in tattered clothes, covered in dirt, but there was a certain alertness to his gaze that made the duke wonder if perhaps Einskaldir hadn't been right.

'Here now, boy,' he said gruffly in the Westerling speech, 'what were you doing poking about the abbey?'

*'I think I'm going to slit his throat now,'* Einskaldir said in Rimmerspakk, pleasant tone in horrid contrast to his words. Isgrimnur scowled, wondering if the man had lost his mind, then realized as the boy continued to stare blandly up at him that Einskaldir was only probing to find if the boy spoke their tongue.

*Well, if he does, he's one of the coolest wits I've ever seen,* Isgrimnur thought. No, it beggared imagination to think a boy this age in the camp of armed strangers could have understood Einskaldir's chilling words and not reacted at all.

'He doesn't understand,' the duke said to his liegeman in their Rimmersgard tongue. 'But he is a calm one, isn't he?' Einskaldir grunted an affirmative and scratched his chin through his dark beard.

'Now, boy,' the duke resumed, 'I asked you once. Speak! What brought you to the abbey?'

The youth lowered his eyes and set the bone he had

been gnawing on the ground. Isgrimnur again felt a tug at his memory, but still could summon nothing.

'I was . . . I was looking for . . . for some new shoes to wear.' The boy gestured to his clean, well-cared-for boots. The duke picked him out by his accent as an Erkynlander, and something more . . . but what?

'And you found some, I see.' The duke squatted, so that he was at eye level. 'Do you know you can be *hanged* for stealing from the unburied dead?'

Finally, a satisfying reaction! The boy's heartfelt flinch at the threat could not have been studied, Isgrimnur felt sure. Good.

'I'm sorry . . . master. I didn't mean any harm. I was hungry from walking, and my feet hurt . . .'

'Walking from where?' He had it now. The boy spoke too well to be a woodsman's brat. He was a priest's boy, or a shopkeeper's son, or some such. He'd run away, no doubt.

The youth held Isgrimnur's stare for a moment; again the duke had the feeling the boy was calculating. A runaway from a seminary, perhaps, or a monastery? What was he hiding?

The boy spoke at last. 'I . . . I have left my master, sir. My parents . . . my parents apprenticed me to a chandler. He beat me.'

'What chandler? Where? Quickly!'

'Mo . . . Malachias! In Erchester!'

*It makes sense, mostly,* the duke decided. *Except for two details.*

'What are you doing here, then? What brought you to Saint Hoderund's? And who,' Isgrimnur lanced in, now, 'is *Bennah?*'

'Bennah?'

Einskaldir, who had been listening with half-closed eyes, leaned forward. *'He knows, Duke,'* he said in Rimmerspakk, *'he said "Bennah" or "Binnock." That's sure.'*

'How about "Binnock," then?' Isgrimnur dropped a

381

wide hand on the captive's shoulder, and felt only a twinge of regret when the boy winced.

'Binnock. . . ? Oh, Binnock's . . . my dog sir. Master's, actually. He ran away, too.' And the boy actually smiled, a lopsided grin that he quickly suppressed. Despite his misgivings the old duke found himself liking the lad.

'I'm heading for Naglimund, sir,' the boy continued quickly. 'I heard the abbey fed travelers like me. When I saw the . . . the bodies, the dead men, I was scared – but I needed some boots, sir, I truly did. Those monks were good Aedonites, sir – they wouldn't have minded, would they?'

'Naglimund?' The duke's eyes narrowed, and he sensed Einskaldir grow a little more taut, if such a thing was possible, at the boy's side. 'Why Naglimund? Why not Stanshire, or Hasu Vale?'

'I have a friend there.' Behind Isgrimnur Sludig's voice rose, careening through a final drunken chorus. The boy made a gesture in the direction of the fire circle. 'He's a harper, sir. He told me if I ran away from . . . Malachias, to come to him and he would help me.'

'A harper? At Naglimund?' Isgrimnur stared intently, but the boy's face, though shadowed, was as innocent as cream. Isgrimnur suddenly felt disgusted with the whole business. *Look at me! Questioning a chandler's boy as if he had single-handedly led the ambush at the abbey! What a damnable day it has been!*

Einskaldir was still not satisfied. He bent his face close to the boy's ear and asked, in his heavily-accented speech, 'What is the Naglimund harper's name?'

The youth turned, alarmed, but seemingly from the sudden proximity of Einskaldir rather than the question, for a moment later he blithely responded.

'Sangfugol.'

'Frayja's Paps!' Isgrimnur cursed, and climbed heavily to his feet. 'I know him. That's enough. I believe you, boy.' Einskaldir had turned away, pivoting on his rocky

382

seat to watch the men laughing and arguing at the fire. 'You may stay with us, boy, if you like,' the duke said. 'We will be stopping at Naglimund, and thanks to those whoreson bastards we have Hove's horse going riderless. This is hard country for a stripling to cross alone, and these days it's near as much as slitting your own throat to travel out of company. Here.' He walked to one of the horses and pulled a saddle blanket down, tossing it to the youth. 'Bed down wherever you like, as long as it's close in. Easier for the man standing sentry if we're not strung out like a flock of straying sheep.' He stared at the thistledown hair starting out in all directions, and the bright eyes. 'Einskaldir fed you. Do you need aught?'

The boy blinked – where *had* he seen him? In the town, probably. 'No,' the boy replied, 'I was just hoping that . . . that Binnock will not get lost without me.'

'Trust me, boy. If he doesn't find you, he'll find someone else, and that's a fact.'

Einskaldir had already slipped away. Isgrimnur stumped off. The boy curled himself in the blanket and lay down at the foot of the rock.

*I haven't really seen the stars for a while,* Simon thought as he stared up from his blanket. The bright points seemed to hang like frozen fireflies. *It's just not the same looking up through the trees as it is out here in the open – like being on a tabletop.*

He thought of Sedda's Blanket, and doing so thought of Binabik.

*I hope he's safe – then again, it was him who left me to the Rimmersmen.*

It had been a stroke of luck that his captor had turned out to be Duke Isgrimnur, but still, there had been moments of real terror, waking up in the camp surrounded by hard-looking, bearded men. He supposed that, knowing the ill-will between Binabik's people and the Rimmersmen, he did not really hold it against the troll for having disappeared – if he had even known of Simon's abduction. Still, it hurt to lose a friend that way. He would have to harden himself: he had begun to depend on the little man to know what was right, what had to be done, just as he had once listened raptly to Doctor Morgenes. Well, the lesson was clear: he would be his own man, keep his own counsel, and make his way.

In truth, he had not wanted to tell Isgrimnur his true destination, but the duke was sharp, and Simon had felt several times that the old soldier was balancing him on the blade of a knife – one false step would have tipped him over.

*Besides, that dark one who sat beside me all the time, he looked like he would kill me just like drowning a kitten if it suited him.*

So, he had given the duke all the truth he comfortably could, and it had worked.

The question, then, was what to do now. Should he stay with the Rimmersmen? It would seem foolish not to, but still . . . Simon was not yet totally sure of where the duke stood. Isgrimnur was going to Naglimund, but what if it was to arrest Josua? Everybody at the Hayholt was forever talking about how loyal Isgrimnur had been to old King John, how he held the High King's Ward more sacred than his own life. Where did he fit in with Elias? Under no circumstances did Simon intend to tell what part he had played in Josua's departure from the Hayholt, but things had a way of slipping out, sometimes. Simon was dying to hear some news of the castle, of what had happened after Morgenes' last gambit – had Pryrates lived? Inch? What had Elias told the people had happened? – but it was exactly those kind of questions, no matter how guilefully asked, that could drop him into boiling water.

He was too wound up to sleep. As he stared up at the scattered stars, he thought of the bones he had seen

Binabik cast that morning. The wind brushed his face, and suddenly the stars themselves were bones – a wild array strewn across the dark field of the sky. It was lonely out here among strangers, under the limitless night. He longed for his homely bed in the servants' quarters, for the days when none of these things had happened. His longing was like the piercing music of Binabik's flute: a cool pain that was nevertheless the only thing he could cling to in the wide, wild world.

He had dozed a little, but when the noise awakened him, heart thumping, the stars still burned deep in the blackness. A momentary panic constricted his throat as a dark shape loomed over him, impossibly tall. Where was the moon?

It was only the man on watch, he saw an instant later, stopping for a moment with his back to Simon's blanket. The sentry had his own saddle blanket, and had wrapped it high on his shoulders, the dome of his unhelmeted head poking up through the folds.

The watchman wandered past without looking down. He had an axe tucked in his broad belt, a wickedly sharp, heavy weapon. He also carried a spear longer than he was tall; as he paced, the butt end dragged in the dirt.

Simon pulled the blanket closer, huddling himself against the sharp wind that was moving across the plain. The sky had changed: where before it had been clear, the stars picked out in brilliant detail against its unfathomable blackness, now it was sullied by streamers of clouds, milky tendrils reaching out like fingers from the north. At the far side of the sky they had covered the lowest stars like sand poured over the coals of a fire.

*Maybe Sedda will catch her husband tonight,* Simon thought sleepily.

The second time he awoke it was to a splash of water in his eyes and nose. He opened his eyes, gasping, to see the stars had been snuffed above him as neatly as a top closing on a jewel chest. It was raining, the clouds now directly overhead. Simon grunted, wiping water from his face, and turned on his side, pulling the blanket up to make a hood for his head. He could see the sentry again, a little farther away now, shielding his face and staring up into the rain.

Simon's eyes were just drifting closed when the man made an odd grunting noise and dropped his head to look down. Something in the man's stance, something that suggested that though he stood rock-still he was nevertheless struggling, made Simon open his eyes wider. The rain began to sheet down, and thunder growled distantly. Simon strained to see the sentry through the boiling downpour. The man was still standing in the same place, but something was moving now at his feet, something active that had pulled free from the general blackness. Simon sat up, and the raindrops pounded and splashed on the ground all about.

A flash of lightning abruptly lit the night, making the rocks glare forth like painted wooden props from a Usires Play. Everything in the camp came clear – the steaming remains of the fire, the huddled, sleeping forms of the Rimmersmen – but what leaped to Simon's eye in that split instant was the sentry, whose face was stretched in a hideous, silent mask of absolute terror.

Thunder crashed, and then the sky was smeared with lightning again. The ground around the sentry was seething, gouting up in great sprays of dirt. Simon's heart lurched in his breast as the man fell to his knees. The thunder cannoned again; lightning flared three times in succession. The earth continued to fountain up, but now there were hands everywhere, and long thin arms, glinting slickly in the rain as they crawled up the body of the kneeling man, pulling him down, face forward into the black soil. The sky-glare caught a greater surge of movement as a horde of dark things pushed up from the earth, thin, ragged things with waving arms, staring white eyes, and – horribly revealed as the lightning leaped across the sky and the rain hissed down – matted whiskers and tattered clothes. As the thunder died out Simon shouted, choking on water, then shouted again.

It was worse than any vision of Hell. The Rimmersmen, startled awake by Simon's terrified cry, were beset from all sides by hopping, flailing bodies. The things were boiling up from the ground like rats – indeed, as they scrambled through the camp the night was filled with thin, mewling squeals that rang of tunnels and blindness and cowardly malice.

One of the northerners was on his feet, the creatures swarming over him. They were none of them as tall as Binabik, but their numbers were prodigious, and even as the northerner unsheathed his sword they pulled him down. Simon thought he saw the flash of sharp things in their hands, rising and falling.

'*Vaer! Vaer Bukkan!*' one of the Rimmersmen shouted from the other side of the camp. The men were up now, and in the intermittent flashes Simon could see the pale fire of their swords and axes. Kicking away the blanket, he climbed to his feet, searching desperately for a weapon. The things were everywhere, prancing on their thin legs like insects, calling out, shrieking thinly when the axe of a Rimmersman bit. Their cries almost sounded like a language, and that, in the midst of nightmare, was one of the most horrible things of all.

Simon ducked behind the rock that had sheltered him, circling around as he looked frantically for something to protect himself with. A figure hurtled toward him, tumbling to the ground only a pace away – one of the northerners, half of his face a wet ruin. Simon bolted forward to pull the axe from his convulsive grasp; not yet dead, the man gurgled as Simon dragged the weapon free. A moment later Simon felt a bony clutch at his knee, and whirled to see a hideous little manlike face behind the grasping claw, eyes staring whitely. He swung the axe down at the face, as hard as he could, and felt a crunch like a beetle ground underfoot. The stiff fingers fell away, and Simon leaped free, gagging.

With the light from the sky alternately blooming and dying, it was nearly impossible to tell what was happening. The swaying figures of the Rimmersmen stood all around, but there was a far greater number of hopping, piping demons. It seemed that the best place to . . .

Simon was knocked to the ground without warning, a gripping paw around his neck. He felt the side of his face go down into the mud, tasted it, then heaved up against the thing on his back. A crude blade whickered past his eyes and stuck with a sucking noise in the earth. Simon clambered to his knees, but another hand reached around his face, covering his eyes. It stank of mud and foul water, the fingers squirming like nightcrawlers.

*Where is the axe? I've dropped the axe!*

He clambered shakily to his feet, legs wide on the slippery ground, and tried to pry loose the clamping fingers around his windpipe. He stumbled forward, nearly falling again, unable to dislodge the awful, strangling thing from his back. The bony hand was cutting off his air, the sharp knees digging at his ribs; he thought he heard the ropy thing squealing in triumph. He managed a few more steps before he dropped to his knees, the din of battle growing fainter behind him. His ears roared; strength flowed out of his arms and body like meal from a torn sack.

*I'm dying* . . . was all he could think. Before his eyes there was nothing but dull red light.

Then the crushing, scratching grip on his throat was suddenly gone. Simon fell heavily on his chest and face and lay gasping.

Wheezing, he looked up. Painted against the black sky by a sheet of crackling lightning was a mad silhouette . . . a man on a wolf.

*Binabik!*

Sucking air into his ragged throat, Simon tried to pull himself upright, but could get no farther than his elbows before the little man was at his side. A pace away the body of the earth-creature lay curled like a singed spider, blind eyes to the sky.

'Say nothing!' Binabik hissed, 'We must go! Quickly!' He helped Simon to a sitting position, but the boy waved him away, batting at the little man with baby-weak hands.

'Have to . . . have to . . .' Simon wagged a shaking hand toward the chaos that raged around the campsite, some twenty paces away.

'Ridiculous!' Binabik snapped. 'The Rimmersmen can fight their own battles. My duty is to get you to safety. Now come!'

'No,' Simon said stubbornly. Binabik held his hollowed stick in his hand; Simon knew what had felled his attacker. 'We ha – have to he – help them.'

'They will survive.' Binabik was grim. Qantaqa had followed her master, and now sniffed solicitously at Simon's wound. 'You are my charge.'

'What do you . . .' Simon began. Qantaqa growled, a deep, threatening sound of alarm; Binabik looked up. 'Daughter of the Mountains!' he groaned. Simon followed his gaze.

A clot of the greater darkness had broken off from the swirling melee and was rapidly moving toward them. It was hard to tell how many creatures might be in the bounding tangle of arms and eyes, but it was more than a few.

'*Nihut,* Qantaqa!' Binabik shouted; an instant later the wolf sprang toward them; they squealed in whistling terror as she struck.

'We have no more time to waste, Simon,' the troll snapped. Thunder caromed across the plain as he pulled his knife from his belt and dragged Simon up. 'The duke's men are holding their own, now, and I have no way to afford your being killed in the last struggling.'

In the midst of the earth-burrowers Qantaqa was a gray-furred engine of death. As her great jaws bit, and she shook and bit again, thin black bodies hurtled away on all sides to fall in broken heaps. More were swarming over, and the wolf's buzzling snarl rose above the storm's rumble.

'But . . . but . . .' Simon held back as Binabik moved toward his mount.

'It was my bound promise to protect you,' Binabik said, tugging Simon along. 'That was Doctor Morgenes' wish.'

'Doctor. . . !? *You* know Doctor Morgenes. . . !?'

As Simon stared, mouth working, Binabik stopped and whistled twice. Qantaqa, with a last ecstatic shiver, flung two of the creatures aside and bounded toward them.

'Now, run, foolish boy!' Binabik shouted. They ran – Qantaqa first, leaping like a hart, her muzzle black with blood, Binabik after. Simon followed, tripping and staggering across the muddy plain as the storm shouted unanswerable questions.

RIVER
YMSTRECCA
HIGH
THRITHING
ERKYNLAND
MEADOW
THRITHING
WARINSTEN
PERDRUIN
ANSIS PELLIPE
LAKE
THRITHING
NEARULAGH
BAY OF
EMETTIN
LAKE
CLODU
CITY OF
NABBAN
NABBAN
THE
LAKELANDS
VINITTA
LAKE
EADNE
LAKE
MYRME
DEVA
KWANITUPUL
BAY OF FIRANNOS
THE SPITE
NARAXI
HARCHA
NASCADU

# 22

# A Wind from the North

'No, I don't want a damned thing!' Guthwulf, Earl of Utanyeat spat citril juice on the tile floor as the wide-eyed page went scurrying away. Watching him go, Guthwulf regretted his hasty words — not out of any sympathy for the boy, but because he had suddenly realized that he might indeed want something. He had been nearly an hour waiting outside the throne room without a drop of anything to drink, and only Aedon Himself knew how much longer he might sit here rotting.

He spat again, the pungent citril stinging his tongue and lips, and cursed as he wiped a line of spittle off his long jaw. Unlike many of the men in his command, Guthwulf was not accustomed to having a piece of the bitter southern root always tucked in his cheek, but during this strange, damp spring — one that had found him confined for days at a time in the Hayholt, waiting on the king's bidding — he had found that any distraction, even that of burning one's palate, was welcome.

Also, and undoubtedly because of the wet weather, the halls of the Hayholt seemed to reek of mold, mold and . . . no, corruption was too melodramatic a word. Anyway, the strongly aromatic citril seemed to help.

Just as Guthwulf had climbed to his feet, deserting the stool to resume the frustrated pacing that had occupied most of his waiting time, the throne room door creaked and swung inward. Pryrates' blunt head appeared in the gap, black eyes flat and shiny as a lizard's.

'Ah, good Utanyeat!' Pryrates showed his teeth. 'How long we have kept you waiting! The king is ready to see you now.' The priest pulled the door farther in, revealing his scarlet robe and a glimpse of the high hall behind. 'Please,' he said.

Guthwulf had to pass very close to Pryrates as he entered, sucking in his chest to minimize the contact. Why was the man standing so close? Was it to make Guthwulf uncomfortable – there was no love lost between King's Hand and the king's counselor – or was he trying to keep the door as nearly shut as he possibly could? The castle *was* cold this spring, and if anyone deserved to keep warm it was Elias. Perhaps Pryrates was only trying to conserve heat in the spacious throne room.

Well, if that was what he was up to, he had failed utterly. The moment Guthwulf stepped over the threshold and past the door he felt the chill descend upon him, turning the skin on his strong arms into chicken-flesh. Looking past the throne, he saw that several of the upper windows were open, propped with sticks. The cold northern air that swirled down tugged at the torch flames, making them dance in their cressets.

'Guthwulf!' Elias boomed, half-rising from his chair of yellowed bone. The massive dragon skull leered over his shoulder. 'I am ashamed to have kept you waiting. Come here!'

Guthwulf strode forward up the tiled walkway, trying not to shiver. 'You have much on your mind, Majesty. I do not mind waiting.'

Elias sat back in his throne as the Earl of Utanyeat dropped to a knee before him. The king wore a black shirt trimmed with green and silver, and his boots and breeks were also black. The iron crown of Fingil sat high on his pale brow, and in a sheath at his side was the sword with the strange crossed hilt. He had not been without it in weeks, but Guthwulf had no idea whence it came. The king had never mentioned it, and there was something queer and unsettling about the blade that prevented Guthwulf from asking.

' "Do not mind waiting," ' Elias smirked. 'Go on, sit down.' The king indicated a bench a pace or two back of where the Earl kneeled. 'Since when do you not mind waiting, Wolf? Just because I am king, do not think I have gone blind and stupid as well.'

'I am sure that when you have something for your King's Hand to do, you will inform me.'

Things had changed between Guthwulf and his old friend Elias, and the Earl of Utanyeat did not like that. Elias had never been secretive, but now Guthwulf felt vast, hidden currents moving beneath the surface of daily events, currents that the king pretended did not even exist. Things had changed, and Guthwulf felt sure he knew who was to blame. He looked past the king's shoulder at Pryrates, who was watching him fixedly. When their eyes met, the red-robed priest lifted a hairless eyebrow, as if in mocking question.

Elias rubbed at his temples for a moment. 'You will have work enough and more soon, I promise you. Ah, my head. A crown is indeed a heavy thing, friend. I sometimes wish I could lay it down and go off somewhere, like we once did so often. Free companions of the road!' The king turned his grim smile from Guthwulf to his counselor. 'Priest, my head aches again. Bring me some wine, will you?'

'At once, my Lord.' Pryrates moved off to the back of the throne room.

'Where are your pages, Majesty?' Guthwulf asked. The king looked dreadfully tired, he thought. The whiskers on his unshaven cheeks stood out, black against his wan skin. 'And why, with respect, are you shut up in this freezing cave of a hall? It is colder than the Devil's black arse in here, and smells of mildew beside. Let me light a fire in the grate.'

'No.' Elias waved a broad hand dismissively. 'I don't

want it any warmer. I'm warm already. Pryrates says it is just an ague. Whatever it is, the cool air feels good to me. And there is plenty of breeze, so no need to fear stagnancy or bad humors.'

Pryrates had returned with the king's goblet; Elias drained it with a swallow and dried his lips with his sleeve.

'Plenty of breeze indeed, Majesty,' Guthwulf grinned sourly. 'Well, my king, you . . . and Pryrates . . . know best, and doubtless have nothing to learn from a fighting man. Is there some other way I can serve you?'

'I think perhaps you can, although the task may not be much to your liking. First, though, tell me: has Earl Fengbald returned?'

Guthwulf nodded. 'I spoke with him this morning, sire.'

'I have summoned him.' Elias held out his cup for more wine, and Pryrates brought the ewer and poured. 'But since you have seen him, tell me now: is his news good?'

'I'm afraid not, sire. The spy you seek, Morgenes' henchman, is still at large.'

'God's curses!' Elias rubbed at a spot just beside his eyebrow. 'Did he not have the hounds I gave him? And the master-huntsman?'

'Yes, Majesty, and he left them still on the hunt, but in fairness to Fengbald I must say that you have set him a nearly impossible task.'

Elias narrowed his eyes, staring, and for a moment Guthwulf felt he faced a stranger. Then the bumping of ewer against goblet broke the tension, and Elias relaxed. 'Welladay,' he said, 'you are most likely right. I shall have to be careful not to take any frustrations out on Fengbald. He and I . . . share a disappointment.'

Guthwulf nodded, watching the king. 'Yes, sire, I was alarmed to hear of your daughter's illness. How is Miriamele?'

The king looked briefly to Pryrates, who finished

pouring and backed away. 'It is kind of you to ask, Wolf. We do not think she is in any danger, but Pryrates feels sure that the sea air of Meremund will be the best remedy for her ailments. It is a pity to put off the marriage, though.' The king stared into his wine cup as though it were the mouth of a well down which he had just dropped something valuable. The wind whistled in the open windows.

After some long moments had passed, the Earl of Utanyeat felt compelled to speak. 'You said that there was some small task I could do for you, my king?'

Elias looked up. 'Ah. Of course. I wish you to go to Hernysadharc. Since I was forced to raise the taxes to make up for the cursed, miserable drought, that old hill–gopher Lluth has defied me. He sent that prancing Eolair to soothe me with honeyed words, but the time for words is over.'

'Over, my Lord?' Guthwulf raised an eyebrow.

'Over,' Elias growled. 'I wish you to take a dozen knights – any more and Lluth would have no choice but to resist – and hie you to the Taig to beard the old miser in his den. Tell him to refuse me my rightful due is to slap my face . . . to spit on the very Dragonbone Chair. But be subtle, say nothing in front of his knights that will shame him into resistance – nevertheless, make it clear that to deny me further will risk his walls falling in flames about his head. Make him *fear*, Guthwulf.'

'I can do that, Lord.'

Elias smiled tightly. 'Good. And while you're there, keep an eye open for any sign of Josua's whereabouts. There is no news from Naglimund, though my spies have it ringed 'round. It is possible my treacherous brother might have gone to Lluth. It may even be he who is fueling Hernystir's obstinance!'

'I will be your Eye as well as your Hand, my King.'

'If I may, King Elias?' At the king's elbow, Pryrates lifted a finger.

'Speak, priest.'

397

'I would also like to suggest that our lord of Utanyeat keep an eye out for the boy, Morgenes' spy. It would help to supplement Fengbald's effort. We *need* that boy, Majesty – what good to slay the serpent if the hatchlings go free?'

'If I find the young viper,' Guthwulf grinned, 'I will happily grind him beneath my heel.'

'No!' Elias shouted, startling Guthwulf with his vehemence. 'No! The spy must live, and any of his companions, until we have them here in the Hayholt safe. There are questions we must ask them.' Elias, as if embarrassed by his outburst, turned strangely pleading eyes to his old friend. 'You understand that, surely?'

'Of course, Majesty,' Guthwulf answered quickly.

'They need only be brought to us with the breath still quick in their bodies,' said Pryrates, calm as a baker talking of flour. 'Then we shall discover *everything*.'

'Enough.' Elias slid farther back on his seat of bone. Guthwulf was surprised to see drops of sweat beading his forehead, even as the Earl of Utanyeat was shivering in the chill air. 'Go now, old friend. Bring me Lluth's full allegiance, or if not, I will send you back to bring me his head. Go.'

'God keep you, Majesty.' Guthwulf dropped off the bench onto one knee, then rose to his feet and backed down the aisle. The banners above his head swung, wind-whipped; in the fluid shadows thrown by the flickering torches the clan-animals and heraldic beasts seemed engaged in an eerie, fitful dance.

Guthwulf met Fengbald in the antechamber hall. The Earl of Falshire had bathed the grit of the road from his face and hair since their meeting that morning, and was dressed in a red velvet jerkin with the silver eagle of his family chased on the breast, its feathers twining in a fanciful pattern.

'Ho, Guthwulf, have you seen him?' he asked.

The Earl of Utanyeat nodded. 'Yes, and you will, too.

God curse it, he is the one who should be taking salt air at Meremund instead of Miriamele. He looks . . . I don't know, he looks damned ill. And the throne chamber is cold as frost.'

'So it's true?' Fengbald asked sullenly. 'About the princess? I was hoping he'd changed his mind.'

'Gone west to the sea. Your great day will have to wait a bit, it looks.' Guthwulf smirked. 'I'm sure you'll find something to keep your interest up until the princess returns.'

'That's not the problem.' The Earl of Falshire's mouth twisted as though he tasted something sour. 'I just fear he's trying to back out of his promise. I have heard that nobody knew she was ill until she was gone.'

'You worry too much,' Guthwulf said. 'It's womanish. Elias needs an heir. Be grateful that you fit his bill of particulars for a son-in-law better than I do.' Guthwulf showed his teeth in a mocking smile. 'I would go to Meremund and get her.' He gave a mock salute and sauntered away, leaving Fengbald standing before the high oak doors of the throne room.

She could tell from far away up the corridor that it was Earl Fengbald, and that he was in a foul temper. His arm-swinging walk, like a young boy sent away from the supper table, and the loud, deliberate banging of his boot heels on the floor stones trumpeted his mood before him.

She reached forward and tugged at Jael's elbow. When the cow-eyed girl looked up, already sure she'd done something else wrong, Rachel made a gesture toward the approaching Earl of Falshire.

'Better move that bucket, girl.' She took the scrubbing broom from Jael's hand. The pail of soapy water stood in the center of the hallway, directly in the path of the oncoming nobleman.

'Hurry up, you stupid girl!' Rachel hissed, a touch of

alarm tingeing her voice. The moment the words were out Rachel knew she should not have uttered them. Fengbald was cursing to himself, his face set in a petulant snarl. Jael, in a frenzy of ill-coordinated haste, let the bucket slide through her wet fingers. It struck the floor with a loud thump, and a gout of sudsy water slopped over the rim to splatter onto the hallway. Fengbald, upon them now, stepped squarely in the spreading puddle. He lost his balance for a moment, throwing his arms up as he slid, then clutched at a tapestry on the wall for support as Rachel watched in helpless, anticipatory horror. It was a stroke of luck that the hanging held Fengbald's weight long enough for him to regain his equilibrium; nonetheless, a moment later the tapestry itself pulled free at an upper corner and slid gently down the wall to sag into the soapy pool.

Rachel looked at the Earl of Falshire's reddening face for only a moment before turning to Jael. 'Go, you clumsy cow. Get on with you. Now!' Jael, with a hopeless glance at Fengbald, turned and ran, her fat rump wagging pitifully.

'Come back here, you slut!' Fengbald screamed, jaw trembling with rage. His long black hair, disarranged, hung in his face. 'I'll have my due, my due for . . . for this . . . this. . . !'

Rachel, keeping an eye cocked toward the Earl, bent and lifted the sodden corner of the tapestry out of the water. There was no way she could re-hang it; she stood holding it, watching it drip as Fengbald raged.

'Look! Look at my boots! I'll have that filthy bitch's throat slit for this!' The Earl turned his eye onto Rachel. 'How dare you send her away?'

Rachel cast her eyes down, not hard to do since the young nobleman stood at least a foot taller than she. 'I'm sorry, Lord,' she said, and her honest fear put a convincing tone of respect into her voice. 'She is a stupid girl, Master, and she will be beaten for it, but I am the Mistress of Chambermaids and I take the blame, you see. I'm very, very sorry.'

Fengbald stared down at her for a moment, and his eyes narrowed. Then, as swiftly as an arrow strikes, he reached out and slapped Rachel across the face. Her hand flew up to the red mark spreading across her cheek, spreading as the puddle had across the flagstones.

'Then give that to the fat slut,' Fengbald spat, 'and if I run into her again, you tell her I'll break her neck.' He stared at the Mistress of Chambermaids for a moment, then walked on down the hall, leaving a trail of heel-and-toe boot prints shimmering wetly on the flags.

*And he could do it, too.* Rachel thought to herself later as she sat on her bed holding a wet washrag to her burning cheek. Across the hall, in the maid's dormitory, Jael was sobbing. Rachel had not had the heart even to shout at her, but the sight of Rachel's swelling face had been punishment enough to send the lumpy, soft-hearted girl into a paroxysm of tears.

*Sweet Rhiap and Pelippa. I'd rather be slapped twice than listen to her blubbering.*

Rachel rolled over onto the hard pallet – she kept it on a board because of her always-aching back – and pulled the blanket up over her head to dull the sound of Jael's weeping. Wrapped in the blanket she could feel her own warm breath wreathing her face.

*This must be what it's like to be laundry in the basket,* she thought, and then childed herself for such simple-mindedness. *You're getting old, old woman . . . old and useless.* Suddenly she found tears coming, the first she had cried since the news about Simon.

*I'm just so tired. Sometimes I think I'm going to drop where I stand, fall over like a broken broom at the feet of these young monsters – stamping around my castle, treating us like we were dirt – and they'd probably just push me out with the dust. So tired . . . if only . . . if . . .*

The air beneath the blanket was thick and warm. She had finished crying – what good were tears anyway? Leave them to her stupid, flighty girls – and now she felt herself falling into sleep, succumbing to its heaviness as though drowning in warm, sticky water.

And in her dream Simon was not dead, had not died in the terrible fire that had also taken Morgenes, and several of the guardsmen who had rushed to put it out. Even Count Breyugar, they said, had perished in the catastrophe, crushed beneath the collapse of the flaming roof . . . No, Simon was alive, and healthy. Something about him was different, but Rachel could not say what – the look in his eye, the harder line of his jaw? – but that did not matter. It was Simon, alive, and as she dreamed Rachel's heart was full again. She saw him, the dead boy – *her* dead boy, really: hadn't she raised him like a mother until he was taken away? – and he was standing in a place of near-absolute whiteness, staring up at a great, white tree that stretched into the air like a ladder to the Throne of God. And though he stood resolutely, his head flung back and his eyes upon the tree, Rachel could not help noticing that his hair, that thick reddish tangle, was badly in need of cutting . . . well, she would see to that soon, right enough . . . the boy needed a firm hand. . . .

When she woke, pulling the smothering blanket aside in a panic to find more darkness around her – this time the darkness of evening – the weight of loss and grief came sliding back down like a wet tapestry. As she sat up on the bed and climbed slowly to her feet the washrag tumbled free, dry as an autumn leaf. There was no call for her to be laying about, pining like some fluttery girlchild. There was work that needed doing, Rachel reminded herself, and no rest this side of Heaven.

The tabor rattled, and the lute player plucked a gentle chord before beginning the last verse

402

> '. . . And now dost thou come, my lady fair
> In Khandery-cloth and silks withal?
> Then if thou wouldst rule o'er my heart
> Take foot now and follow to Emettin's Hall!'

The musician finished with a flurry of delicate notes, then bowed as Duke Leobardis applauded.

'Emettin's Hall!' the duke said to Eolair, Count of Nad Mullach, who followed Leobardis' example with his own dutiful applause. Secretly, the Hernystirman felt sure that he had heard better. He was not much taken by the love ballads that were so popular here in the Nabbanai court.

'I *am* fond of that song,' the duke smiled. His long white hair and pink cheeks gave him the look of a favorite old great-uncle, the sort who drank too much stout at the Aedontide feasts and then tried to teach the children how to whistle. Only the flowing white robe trimmed in lapis and gold, and the golden circlet on his head with its mother-of-pearl kingfisher, proclaimed him as different than ordinary men. 'Come, Count Eolair, I thought that music was the lifeblood of the Taig. Does not Lluth count himself Osten Ard's greatest patron of harpers, and your Hernystir the natural home of musicians?' The duke leaned across the arm of his sky-blue chair to pat Eolair's hand.

'King Lluth does indeed keep his harpers beside him at all times,' Eolair agreed. 'Please, Duke, if I seem preoccupied, it is in no way due to any stinting on your part. Your kindness had been indeed a thing to remember. No, I must admit I am still bothered about the matters we discussed earlier.'

A look of concern came to the duke's mild blue eyes. 'I have told you, my Eolair, that there is time for such things. It is very wearing to have to wait, but there you are.' Leobardis motioned to the lute player, who had been waiting patiently on one knee. The musician rose, bowed, and moved off. His fantastically intricate garment flounced around him as he joined a group of courtiers similarly garbed in sumptuously embroidered robes and tunics. The ladies had supplemented their outfits with exotic hats winged like seabirds, or crested like the fins of bright fish. The colors in the throne room, like those of the courtiers' costumes, were muted: tasteful blues, yellow beiges, pinks, whites, and foam greens. The impression was that of a palace built from delicate sea-stones, everything smoothed and softened by the clutch of the ocean.

Beyond the gentlemen and ladies of the court, taking up the whole southwest wall facing the duke's chair, were the high arched windows that looked out over the active, sun-tipped green sea. The ocean, which threw itself ceaselessly against the rocky headland on which the ducal palace perched, was a vibrant, living tapestry. Watching through the day as the moving light danced on its surface, or revealed patches of still sea as heavy and translucent as jade, Eolair frequently wished to sweep the courtiers from the way, send them tumbling and squeaking from the room so that nothing would obscure his view.

'Perhaps you are right, Duke Leobardis,' Eolair said at last. 'One must stop talking sometime, even when the subject is á vital one. I suppose, sitting here, I should be taking a lesson from the ocean. It doesn't need to work hard to get what it wants; eventually it wears the rock away, the beaches . . . even the mountains.'

Leobardis liked this sort of conversation better. 'Ah, yes, the sea never changes, does it? And yet, it is always changing.'

'That's true, my lord. And it is not always quiet. Sometimes there are storms.'

As the duke cocked his head toward the Hernystirman, unsure whether this remark meant something more than was immediately obvious, his son Benigaris strode into the room, nodding briefly to some of the courtiers who greeted him as he moved toward the duke's chair.

404

'The duke my father; Count Eolair,' he said, bowing once to each. Eolair smiled, and put out a hand to clasp Benigaris'.

'It's good to see you,' the Hernystirman said, Benigaris was taller then when he had last seen him, but the duke's son had then been only seventeen or eighteen. Nearly two decades had passed, and Eolair was not displeased to see that despite his being a good eight years the elder, it was Benigaris who had thickened around the waist, not he. Nonetheless, the duke's son was tall and broad-shoudered, with intent dark eyes beneath thick black brows. He made quite an imposing figure in his belted tunic and quilted vest – an energetic contrast to his affable father.

'Héa, it has been a long time,' Benigaris agreed. 'We shall talk at supper tonight.' Eolair did not think he sounded very excited at the prospect. Benigaris turned to his father. 'Sir Fluiren is here to see you. He is with the chamberlain at the moment.'

'Ah, good old Fluiren! There is irony for you, Eolair. One of the greatest knights Nabban has ever produced.'

'Only your brother Camaris was ever called greater,' Eolair interrupted, not adverse to resurrecting the memories of a more martial Nabban.

'Yes, my dear brother.' Leobardis smiled a sad smile. 'Well, to think that Fluiren should be coming to see me as an emissary of Elias!'

'There is a certain irony,' Eolair said lightly.

Benigaris curled his lip with impatience. 'He's waiting for you. I think you should see him quickly, as a gesture of respect to the High King.'

'My, my!' Leobardis turned an amused glance toward Eolair. 'Do you hear my son order me?' When the duke turned back to Benigaris, Eolair thought there might be something in Leobardis' gaze beside amusement – anger? Worry? 'Yes, then, tell my old friend Fluiren I will see him . . . let me think . . . yes, in the Council Hall. Will you join us, Eolair?'

Benigaris leaped in. 'Father, I do not think you should invite even so trusted a friend as the count in to hear secret communications from the High King!'

'And what need, may I ask, is there for secrets to be kept from Hernystir?' the duke asked. Anger had crept into his voice.

'Please, Leobardis, I have things I must do anyway. I shall walk in later to say hello to Fluiren.' Eolair rose and bowed.

As he stopped on his way across the throne room to look one more time on the splendid view, he heard the voices of Leobardis and his son raised behind him in muffled argument.

*Waves make more waves as these Nabbanai say*, thought Eolair. *It looks as though Leobardis' balance is more delicate than I thought. Doubtless that is why he is so unwilling to talk frankly with me about his troubles with the king. A good thing it is that Leobardis is a tougher stalk than he appears to be.*

He heard the courtiers whispering behind him, and turned to see several of them looking in his direction. He smiled and nodded. The women blushed, covering their mouths with their flowing sleeves; the men nodded gravely and quickly looked away. He knew what they were thinking – he was a curiosity, a rustic and untutored westerner, even if he was an old friend of the duke's. No matter what he wore, or how perfectly he spoke, still they would feel the same. Suddenly, Eolair felt a deep longing for his home in Hernystir. He had been too long in foreign courts.

The waves rushed against the rocks below, as though the sea would not be satisfied until its monstrous patience had at last brought the palace tumbling down into its watery grasp.

Eolair spent the rest of the afternoon strolling the high, airy hallways and meticulous gardens of the Sancellan Mahistrevis. Although it was now the duke's palace and the capitol of Nabban, once it had been the seat of Man's whole empire in Osten Ard; diminished in importance now, still its glories were many.

Perched on the rocky knob of the Sancelline Hill, the palace's western walls overlooked the sea which had always been Nabban's lifeblood – indeed, all of Nabban's noble houses used water birds as the symbols of their power: the Benidrivine kingfisher of the current duke's line, the Prevan osprey and Ingadarine albatross; even the Heron of Sulis that had once, briefly, flown over the Hayholt in Erkynland.

East of the palace the city of Nabban itself spread down the peninsula's neck, a crowded, swarming city of hills and close quarters, thinning at last as the peninsula widened out into the meadows and farms of the Lakeland. From the known world to this peninsular duchy and bridal-veil of island possessions, Nabban's vistas had narrowed, and its rulers had turned in on themselves. But once, not too long ago, the mantle of the Nabbanai Imperators had covered the world, from the brackish Wran to the farthest reaches of icy Rimmersgard; in those days the wrangling of osprey and pelican and the strivings of heron and gull had carried as their reward a prize worth any risk.

Eolair walked in the Hall of Fountains, where jets of glimmering spray arched up to commingle as fine mist beneath the open latticework of the stone roof, and wondered if there was yet the will left in the Nabbanai to fight, or whether they had simply come to terms with their own gradual diminution, so that Elias' provocations only served to drive them further into their beautiful, delicate shell. Where now were the men of greatness like those who had carved Nabban's empire out of the rough stone of Osten Ard – men like Tiyagaris or Anitulles. . . ?

*Of course*, he thought, *there was Camaris* – a man who, had he not found in himself a stronger call to serve than to be served, might have held the willing world in the palm of his hand. Camaris had been a mighty man indeed.

*And who are we Hernystirmen to speak?* he wondered. *Since Hern the Great, what mighty men have risen up in our western lands? Tethtain, who took the Hayholt from Sulis? Perhaps. But who else? Where is Hernystir's Hall of Fountains, where are our great palaces and churches?*

*But of course, that is the difference.* He looked out past the streaming fountains to the cathedral spire of the Sancellan Aedonitis, the palace of the Lector and Mother Church. *We of the Hernystiri do not look at the hill streams and say: how can I bring that to my home? We build our homes beside the stream. We do not have a faceless God to glorify with towers taller than the trees of the Circoille. We know that the gods live in the trees and in the bones of the earth, and in the rivers that splash high as any fountain, racing down from the Grianspog mountains.*

*We never wanted to rule the world.* He smiled to himself, remembering the Taig at Hernysadharc, a castle made not of stone but wood: oak-hearted to match the hearts of his people. *Really, now, all we want is to be left alone. Still, with all their years of conquest, perhaps these Nabban folk have forgotten sometimes you have to fight for that, too.*

As he left the room of fountains, Eolair of Nad Mullach brushed past two legion guardsmen coming in.

'Bloody hillman,' he heard one of them say, eyeing his garb and horsetail of black hair.

'Heá, you know,' the other replied, 'every now and then the sheep-herders need to come and see what a city looks like.'


'. . . And how is my little niece Miriamele, Count?' the duchess asked. Eolair was seated at her left hand near the head of the long table. Fluiren, as a more recent arrival and a distinguished son of Nabban, had the place of honor on the right of Duke Leobardis.

'She seemed well, my lady.'

'Did you see much of her while you were at the High King's court?' The Duchess Nessalanta leaned toward him, raising an exquisitely drawn eyebrow. The duchess was a sternly beautiful older woman, although how much of that beauty was due to the skilled manipulations of her hairdressers, seamstresses, and lady's maids, Eolair had no way of guessing. Nessalanta was exactly the kind of woman who made Eolair – no stranger to the company of the fairer sex – feel completely out of his depth. She was younger than her husband the duke, but she was the mother of a man well into his prime. What here was lasting beauty and what was artifice? Then again, what did it matter? Nessalanta was a powerful woman, and only Leobardis himself held greater sway over the affairs of the nation.

'I was not often in the princess' company, Duchess, but we had several chances to speak at supper. She was as delightful as ever, but I'm thinking she was already very homesick for Meremund.'

'Hmmm.' The duchess popped a corner of her trencher-bread into her mouth and then delicately licked her fingers. 'It was interesting you should mention that, Count Eolair. I have just had news from Erkynland that she has returned to the castle at Meremund.' She raised her voice. 'Father Dinivan?'

A few seats down a young priest looked up from his meal. Although his scalp was shaved in a monasterial style, the hair that remained was curly and rather long. 'Yes, my lady?' he asked.

'Father Dinivan is His Sacredness the Lector Ranessin's private secretary,' Nessalanta explained. The Herny-stirman made an impressed face, and Dinivan laughed.

'I don't think it's accreditable to any great wit or talent on my part,' he said. 'The lector also takes in stray dogs. Escritor Velligis gets very upset. "The Sancellan Aedonitis is not a kennel," he tells the lector, but His Sacredness smiles and says: "Neither is Osten Ard a nursery, but the Benevolent Lord lets His children remain, for all their mischief." ' Dinivan waggled his bushy brows. 'It's hard to argue with the lector.'

'Isn't it true,' the Duchess said as Eolair laughed, 'that

when you saw the king he said his daughter was gone to Meremund?'

'Yes, yes he did,' Dinivan said, more serious now. 'He said she had taken ill, and the court physicians recommended sea air.'

'I am sorry to hear that.' Eolair looked past the duchess to the duke and old Sir Fluiren, who were conversing quietly amidst the uproar of supper – for a refined people, he reflected, the Nabbanai certainly enjoyed loud table talk.

'Well,' Nessalanta pronounced, sitting back in her chair as a page scurried up with a finger basin, 'it just proves that you can't force people to be what they're not. Miriamele has Nabbanai blood, of course, and our blood is salty as the sea. We are not meant to be taken away from the coast. People should stay where they belong.'

*And what,* the count wondered to himself, *are you trying to tell me, my gracious lady? To stay in Hernystir and leave your husband – and your duchy – alone? To, in effect, go back to my own kind?*

Eolair watched Leobardis' and Fluiren's discussion wistfully. He had been maneuvered, he knew: there was no gracious way he could ignore the duchess and insinuate himself into their conversation. Meanwhile, old Fluiren was at work on the duke, transmitting Elias' blandishments. And threats? No, probably not. Elias would not have sent the dignified Fluiren for that. He had Guthwulf the King's Hand ready for use whenever such a tool was called for.

Resigned, he made light talk with the duchess, but his heart was not in it. He was sure now that she knew his mission and was hostile to it. Benigaris was the apple of her eye, and he had been avoiding Eolair all evening. Nessalanta was an ambitious woman, and doubtless felt the fortunes of Nabban would be better assured if they were yoked to the power of Erkynland – even a domineering, tyrannical Erkynland – instead of the pagans of Hernystir.

*And,* Eolair realized suddenly, *she has a marriageable daughter herself, the Lady Antippa. Perhaps her interest in Miriamele's health is not just that of a kindly aunt's for her niece.*

The duke's daughter Antippa was pledged already, he knew, to one Baron Devasalles, a foppish-looking young nobleman who at this precise moment was arm wrestling with Benigaris in a pool of wine at the far end of the table. But maybe Nessalanta had her eye on greater things.

*If Princess Miriamele will not – or cannot – marry . . .* Eolair mused, *then perhaps the duchess has eyes for Fengbald to marry her daughter instead. The Earl of Falshire would be a much finer catch than any back-row Nabbanai baron. And Duke Leobardis would then be tied to Erkynland with cords of steel.*

So now, the count realized, there was not only Josua's whereabouts to worry over, but Miriamele's as well. What a tangle!

*Just think how old Isgrimnur would see this, with all his complaints about intriguing! His beard would catch fire!*

'Tell me, Father Dinivan,' the count said, turning to the priest, 'what does your holy book have to say on the art of politicking?'

'Well,' a look of concentration momentarily clouded Dinivan's homely, intelligent face, 'the Book of the Aedon speaks often of the trials of nations.' He thought a moment more. 'One of my favorite passages has always been: *"If your enemy comes to speak bearing a sword, open your door to him and speak, but keep your own sword at hand. If he comes to you empty-handed, greet him the same way. But if he comes to you bearing gifts, stand on your walls and cast stones down on him."* ' Dinivan wiped his fingers on his black cassock.

'A wise book, indeed,' nodded Eolair.

# 23
# Back into the Heart

The wind flung rain into their faces as they ran eastward through the darkness toward the hidden foothills. The clamor of Isgrimnur's camp receded, muffled in a blanket of thunder.

Coursing across the wet plain, Simon's panicked exhilaration began to recede as well; the ecstatic sensation of energy, the feeling that he could run and run through the night like a deer, was gradually cooled by the rain and relentless pace. Within half a league his gallop had slowed to a fast walk; soon even that was an effort. Where a bony hand had clutched his knee he felt the joint stiffening like a rusty hinge; bands of pain around his throat throbbed at every deep breath.

'Morgenes . . . sent you?' he shouted.

'Later, Simon,' Binabik gasped. 'All told later.'

They ran and ran, tripping and splashing over the sodden turf.

'Then . . .' Simon panted, 'then what . . . were those things. . . ?'

'The . . . attacking things?' Even as he ran the troll made an odd hand-to-mouth gesture. 'Bukken – "diggers" they are . . . also called.'

'What are they?' Simon asked, and nearly slipped on a patch of mud, skidding for a moment flat-footed.

'Bad.' He grimaced. 'There is no more needs telling now.'

When they could run no longer they walked, trudging on until the sun edged up behind the wash of clouds, a candle behind a gray sheet. The Wealdhelm stood before them, thrown up in relief against the pallid dawn like the bowed backs of monks at prayer.

In the meager shelter of a cluster of rounded granite boulders, set starkly in the sea of grass as though in imitation of the hills beyond, Binabik made a sort of camp. After walking around the rocks to find the spot most sheltered from the shifting rains, he helped Simon down into a space where two boulders leaned together, forming an angle in which the boy could recline with some minimal comfort. Simon fell quickly into limp, exhausted sleep.

Flying raindrops skipped from the tops of the boulders as Binabik crouched, tucking in the boy's cloak – which the troll had brought with their other things all the way from Saint Hoderund's – then rooted in his pack for some dried fish to chew, and his knucklebones. Qantaqa returned from an investigatory tour of her new territory to curl up on Simon's shins. The troll took the bones out and tossed them, using his pack bag for a table.

*The Shadowed Path.* Binabik grinned a bitter grin. Then, *Masterless Ram*, and again, *The Shadowed Path.* He cursed, quietly but lengthily – only a fool would ignore such a clear message. Binabik knew himself to be many things, and foolish was occasionally one of them, but here, now, there was no room to take such chances.

He pulled his fur hood back up around his face and curled in beside Qantaqa. To any passing by – if they could have seen anything at all in the faint light, and with rain in their faces – the three companions would have looked like nothing so much as an unusual, dun-colored lichen on the lee-side of the rocks.

'So, what kind of a game have you been playing with me, Binabik?' Simon asked sullenly. 'How do you know of Doctor Morgenes?' In the few hours he had slept the pale dawn had turned into a cold, gloomy morning, un-redeemed by campfire or breakfast. The sky, swollen with clouds, hung close overhead like a low ceiling.

'It is no game I am playing, Simon,' the troll replied. He had cleaned and bandaged Simon's neck and leg wounds, and was patiently seeing to Qantaqa's. Only one of the wolf's injuries was serious, a deep slash on the inside of her foreleg. As Binabik picked grit from the skin, Qantaqa sniffed at his fingers, trusting as a child.

'I have no regret for not telling you; if I had not felt forced, still you would not know.' He rubbed a fingerful of salve into the cut and then turned his mount loose. She promptly bent and began licking and biting at the leg. 'I knew that she would do that,' he said in mild reproach, then mustered a careful smile. 'Like you, she is not thinking I know my work.'

Simon, realizing he had been unconsciously plucking at his own bandages, sat forward. 'Come, Binabik, just *tell* me. How do you know of Morgenes? Where do you *really* come from?'

'I am from exactly where I say,' the troll replied indignantly. 'I am a Qanuc. And I am not merely knowing *of* Morgenes, once I met him. He is a good friend of my master. They are . . . colleagues, I think the learned men say.'

'What do you mean?'

Binabik sat back against the rock. Although at the moment there was no rain to shelter from, the cutting wind alone was reason enough to stay close to the outcropping. The little man seemed to be considering his words carefully. He looked tired to Simon, his dark skin loose and a shade paler than normal.

414

'First,' the troll said at last, 'you must be knowing something of my master. He was named Ookequk. He was the . . . Singing Man, you would call him, of our mountain. When we say Singing Man, we mean not someone who is just singing, but someone who is remembering the old songs and old wisdom. Like doctor and priest joined together, it seems to me.

'Ookequk was my master because of certain things the elders thought they were seeing in me. It was a great honor to be the one to share in Ookequk's wisdom – I went three days without eating food when I was told, just to make myself of the right pureness.' Binabik smiled. 'When I announced this pridefully to my new master, he hit me on my ear. "You are too young and stupid to be starving yourself on purpose," he said to me. "It has presumptuousness. You may only starve by accident." '

Binabik's grin split open into a laugh; when Simon thought about it for a moment, he laughed a little, too.

'In any way,' he continued, 'I will be telling you someday about my years learning from Ookequk – he was a great, fat troll, Simon; he weighed more than you, and he was being my height only – but now the point must be reached sooner.

'I do not know with exactness where my master first met Morgenes, but it was long before I came to his cave. They were friends, though, and my master taught Morgenes the art of making birds carry messages. They had much talk in letters, my master and your doctor. They shared many . . . ideas about the world's ways.

'Just two summers gone my parents were killed. Their death came in the dragon-snow of the mountain we call Little Nose, and once they were no more, I devoted all my thinking – well, almost all – to learning from master Ookequk. When he told me this thaw that I was to be accompanying him on a great journey south, I was filled with excitement. It was clear-seeming to me that this would be my test of worthiness.

'What I was not knowing,' the troll said, poking up the

415

muddy grass before him with his walking stick – almost angrily, Simon thought, but there was no anger to hear in his voice – 'what I was not told, was that Ookequk had more important reasons for traveling than the finish of my apprenticeship. He had been receiving words from Doctor Morgenes . . . and some others . . . of things that disturbed him, and he felt it was time to be returning the visit Morgenes had made on him long years before, when I first was with him.'

'What "things"?' Simon asked. 'What did Morgenes tell him?'

'If you are not yet knowing,' Binabik said serious, 'then perhaps there are still truths you can do without. On that I must think, but for now let me say what I can – what I must.'

Simon nodded stiffly, rebuked.

'I will not either burden you with all the long story of our southward trip. I was realizing quite early on that my master had not given *me* all the truth, either. He was worried, much worried, and when he cast the bones or read certain signs in the sky and wind he became even more so. Also, some of our experiences were very bad. I have traveled by myself, as you know, much of it before becoming a servant of my master Ookequk, yet never have I seen times so bad for travelers. An experience much like yours of last night we were having just below the lake Drorshullvenn, on the Frostmarch.'

'You mean those . . . Bukken?' Simon asked. Even with daylight around them, the thought of the clasping hands was terrifyingly vivid.

'Indeed,' Binabik nodded, 'and that was . . . *is* . . . being a bad sign, that they should attack so. It is not in the memory of my people that the *Boghanik*, which is our name for them, should assault a group of armed men. Bold it is, and frighteningly so. Their usual way is to be preying on animals and solitary travelers.'

'What *are* they?'

'Later, Simon, there is much that you will learn if you

416

have patience with me. My master did not tell me all, either – which is not saying, please notice, that I am *your* master – but he was very much upset. In our whole journeying down the Frostmarch I did not see him sleeping. When I would sleep, still he would be awake, and the morning would find him up before me. He was not young, either: he was old before I came to him, and several years I was by him studying.

'One night, when first we had crossed down into the northern parts of Erkynland, he asked me to be standing watch so that he could walk the Road of Dreams. We were in a place much like this,' Binabik gestured around at the bleak plain below the hills, 'spring arrived, but not yet broken through. This would have been, oh, perhaps around the time of your All Fool's Day or the day before.'

*All Fools Eve* . . . Simon tried to think back, to remember. *The night that terrible noise awakened the whole castle. The night before . . . the rains came . . .*

'Qantaqa was off hunting, and the old ram One-eye – a great, fat, patient thing he was to carry Ookequk! – was sleeping by the fire. We were alone with just the sky. My master ate of the dream-bark that came to him from the marshy Wran in the south. He crossed over into a kind of sleeping. He had not told me why he was doing this, but I could guess he was searching for answers that he could find no other way. The Boghanik had frightened him, because there was wrongness in their actions.

'Soon he was mumbling, as he was usually doing as his heart walked the Road of Dreams. Much was not understandable, but one or two things that he said were *also* said more lately by Brother Dochais, which is why you may have seen me show surprise.'

Simon had to restrain a sour smile. And he had thought that it had been his own fear which was so obvious, sparked by the Hernystirman's delirious words!

'Suddenly,' the troll continued, still poking fixedly with his stick at the spongy turf, 'it seemed to me that something had caught at him – again, with likeness to Brother Dochais. But my master was strong, stronger in his heart, I think, than nearly anyone, man or troll, and he fought. Struggled and struggled, he did, all the afternoon long and into the evening, as I was standing beside him with no help to give but to wet his brow.' Binabik pulled a handful of grass, tossing it into the air to bat at it with his staff. 'Then, a little past the middle of the night, he said some words to me – quite calmly, as if he were at drinking with the other elders in the Clan cave – and died.

'It was for me, I am thinking, worse than my parents, because they were lost – just vanished in a snowslide, gone with no trace. I buried Ookequk there on a hillside. None of the proper rituals were correctly done, and that is a shame for me. One-eye would not leave without his master; for all I can know, he may be there still. I am hoping so.'

The troll was quiet for a while, staring fiercely at the scuffed hide on the knee of his breeches. His pain was so close to Simon's own sorrow that the boy could think of no words to say that would make sense to anyone but himself.

After a while Binabik silently opened his bag and proffered a handful of nuts. Simon took them, along with the waterskin.

'Then,' Binabik began again, almost as if he had not stopped, 'a strange thing happened.'

Simon huddled in his cloak and watched the troll's face as he talked.

'Two days I had spent beside my master's burial place. A nice enough place it was, lying beneath unblocked sky, but my heart was sore because I knew he would be more happy up high in the mountains. I was thinking of what I should be doing, whether to continue on to Morgenes in Erchester, or return to my people and tell them the Singing Man Ookequk was dead.

'I decided on the afternoon of the second day that I

should return to Qanuc. I had no understanding of the importance of my master's talk with Doctor Morgenes – I am still not understanding much, sadly to say – and I had other . . . responsibilities.

'As I was calling Qantaqa, and scratching a last time between the horns of faithful One-eye, a small gray bird fluttered down, landing on Ookequk's mound. I recognized it as one of my master's messenger birds; it was very tired from carrying a heavy burden, a message and . . . and another thing. As I approached to capture it, Qantaqa came crashing up along the underbrush. The bird, it is not surprising, was frightened and leaped into the air. I barely caught it. It was a nearness, Simon, but I caught it.

'It was written by Morgenes, and the subject of the note was you, my friend. It told to the reader – who should have been my master – that you would be in danger, and traveling alone from the Hayholt toward Naglimund. It asked my master to be helping you – without your knowing, if such was possible. It said a few things more.'

Simon was riveted: this was a missing part of his own story. 'What other things?' he asked.

'Things only for my master's eyes.' Binabik's tone was kindly, but firm. 'Now, it needs no saying that here was a difference. My master was asked a favor by his old friend . . . but only I could do that favor. This was also difficult, but from the moment I read Morgenes' note, I knew I must fulfill his request. I set out that day before evening toward Erchester.'

*The note said I would be traveling alone. Morgenes never thought he would escape.* Simon felt tears coming, and covered the effort of suppressing them with a question.

'How were you supposed to find me?'

Binabik smiled. 'By the use of Qanuc hard work, friend Simon. I had to pick up your trail – the signs of passing of a young man, no set destination, things of this kind. Qanuc hard work and a largeness of luck led me to you.'

A memory flared in Simon's heart, gray and fearful even in distant retrospect. 'Did you follow me across the lich-yard? The one outside the city walls?' It had not *all* been a dream, he knew. *Something* had called his name.

The troll's round face, however, was unreassuringly blank. 'No, Simon,' he said carefully, thinking. 'I was not discovering your track until, I think, upon the Old Forest Road. Why?'

'It's not important.' Simon rose and stretched, looking around the damp flatland. He sat again, and reached for the waterskin. 'Well, I guess I understand, now . . . but I have much to think about. It seems we should continue to Naglimund, I suppose. What do you think?'

Binabik looked troubled. 'I am not sure, Simon. If the Bukken are active in the Frostmarch, the road to Naglimund-keep will be too dangerous for a pair of travelers alone. I must admit I am much worried about what to do now. I am wishing we had your Doctor Morgenes here to advise us. Are you in so much peril, Simon, that we could not risk even a message to him somehow? I am not thinking he wants me to take you through such terrible dangers.'

It took a moment for Simon to realize that the 'he' Binabik was talking about was still Morgenes. A second later the astonishing realization struck: *the troll did not know what had happened.*

'Binabik,' he began, and even as he spoke he felt he was inflicting a kind of wound, 'he's dead. Doctor Morgenes is dead.'

The little man's eyes flared wide for a moment, the white around the brown visible for the first time. An instant later Binabik's expression froze in a dispassionate mask.

'Dead?' he said at last, his voice so cold that Simon felt a strange defensiveness, as though it was somehow his fault – he, who had cried so many tears over the doctor!

'Yes,' Simon considered for a moment, then took a calculated risk. 'He died getting Prince Josua and me out

420

of the castle. King Elias killed him – well, he had his man Pryrates do it, anyway.'

Binabik stared into Simon's eyes, then looked down. 'I had knowledge of Josua's captivity. In the letter it was mentioned. The rest is . . . tidings that are very bad.' He stood, and the wind plucked at his straight black hair. 'Let me walk now, Simon. I must think what these things are meaning . . . I must think . . .'

His face still emotionless, the little man stepped away from the clutch of rocks. Qantaqa immediately leaped up to follow, and Binabik started to shoo her off, then shrugged. She circled him in wide, lazy arcs as he moved slowly away, head bowed and small hands hidden in his sleeves. Simon thought he looked far too small for the burdens that he carried.

Simon was half-hoping that when the troll returned he might be carrying a fat wood pigeon or something similar. In this he was disappointed.

'I am sorry, Simon,' the little man said, 'but it would have been of small use anyway. We cannot have a smokeless fire with nothing around but wet brush, and a smoke-beacon I do not think is good at the moment. Have some dried fish.'

The fish, itself in short supply, was neither filling nor tasty, but Simon chewed morosely at his piece: who knew when he would next get a meal on this miserable adventure?

'I have been thinking, Simon. Your news, with no fault of yours, is hurtful. So soon after my master's death, to hear of the ending of the doctor, that good old man . . .' Binabik trailed off, then bent and began shoving things back into his pack, after first separating out several articles.

'These are your things – see, I was saving them for

you.' He handed Simon the two familiar cylindrical bundles.

'This other . . .' Simon said, accepting the packages, '. . . not the arrow, but this . . .' He handed it back to Binabik. 'It's writing by Doctor Morgenes.'

'Truthfully?' Binabik skinned back a corner of the rag wrappings. 'Things that will help us?'

'I don't think so,' Simon said. 'It's his life of Prester John. I read some of it – it's mostly about battles and things.'

'Ah. Yes.' Binabik passed it back over to Simon, who pushed it through his belt. 'Too bad, that is. We could use his more specific words at this moment.' The troll bent and continued pushing objects into his pack. 'Morgenes and Ookequk my master, they were belonging together to a very special group.' He scooped something out of his belongings and held it up for Simon to see. It gleamed faintly in the overcast afternoon light, a pendant of a scroll and quill pen.

'Morgenes had one of those!' Simon said, leaning close to look.

'Indeed,' Binabik nodded. 'This was my master's. It is a sigil belonging to those who join the League of the Scroll. There are, I was told by him, never more than seven members. Your and my masters are dead – there can be no more than five left, now.' He snapped his small hand shut on the pendant and dropped it into the sack.

'League of the Scroll?' Simon wondered. 'What is it?'

'A group of learned people who share knowledge, I have heard my master saying. Perhaps something more, but he would never tell me.' He finished the last of his packing and straightened up. 'I am sorry to be saying this, Simon, but I am afraid we must walk again.'

'Again?' Aches he had forgotten suddenly flared in Simon's muscles.

'I am afraid it is needed. As I was telling, I have been much in thought. I have thought these things . . .' He tightened his walking stick at the join and whistled for Qantaqa.

'Firstly, I am bound for getting you to Naglimund. This has not been changed, it was unhappily only my resolution that was slipping. The problem is: I do not trust the Frostmarch. You saw the Bukken – it is likely you would prefer not to see them again. But it is northward we must travel. I am thinking, then, that we must go back to Aldheorte.'

'But Binabik, how will we be any safer there? What's to keep those digger-things from coming after us in the forest, where we probably can't even run?'

'A good question to ask. I spoke to you once of the Oldheart – of its age and . . . and . . . I cannot think of a word in your language, Simon, but "soul" and "spirit" may be giving you an idea.

'The Bukken can pass beneath the old forest, but not easily. There is power in the Aldheorte's roots, power that is not to be lightly broached by . . . such creatures. Also, there is someone there I must see, someone who must hear the telling of what happened to my master and yours.'

Simon was already tired of hearing his own questions, but asked anyway. 'Who is that?'

'Her name is Geloë. A wise woman she is, one known as a *valada* – a Rimmersgard word, that. Also, she can perhaps help us to reach Noglimund, since we will have to be crossing from the forest side on the east over the Wealdhelm, a route that is not known to me.'

Simon pulled his cloak on, hooking the worn clasp beneath his chin. 'Must we leave today?' he asked. 'It's so late in the afternoon.'

'Simon,' Binabik said as Qantaqa jogged up, tongue lolling, 'please believe me. Even though there are things that I cannot yet tell to you, we must be true companions. I need your trust. It is not only the business of Elias' kingship that is at stake. We have lost, both of us, people who we were holding dearly – an old man and an old troll who knew much more than we are knowing. They were both afraid. Brother Dochais, I am thinking, *died* of fright. Something *evil* is waking, and we are foolish if we spend more time in open ground.'

'*What* is waking, Binabik? *What* evil? Dochais said a name – I heard him. Just before he died he said . . .'

'You need not. . . !' Binabik tried to interrupt, but Simon paid him no heed. He was growing tired of hints and suggestions.

'. . . *Storm King,*' he finished resolutely.

Binabik looked quickly around, as though he expected something terrible to appear. 'I know,' he hissed. 'I heard, too, but I do not know much.' Thunder tolled beyond the distant horizon; the little man looked grim. 'The Storm King is a name of dread in the dark north. Simon, a name out of legends to frighten with, to conjure with. All I have are small words my master was giving me sometimes, but it is enough to make me sick with worry.' He shouldered his bag and started off across the muddy plain, toward the blunt, crouching line of hills.

'That name,' he said, his voice incongruously hushed in the midst of such flat emptiness, 'is of itself a thing to wither crops, to bring fevers and bad dreaming . . .'

'. . . Rain and bad weather. . .?' Simon asked, looking up at the ugly, lowering sky.

'And other things,' Binabik replied, and touched his palm to his jacket, just above his heart.

# 24
# The Hounds of Erkynland

Simon dreamed that he was walking in the Pine Garden of the Hayholt, just outside the Dining Hall. Above the gently swaying trees hung the stone bridge that connected hall and chapel. Although he felt no sensation of cold – indeed, he was not aware of his body at all except as something to move him from one place to another – gentle flakes of snow were filtering down around him. The fine, needled edges of the trees were beginning to blur beneath blankets of white and all was quiet: the wind, the snow, Simon himself, all moved in a world seemingly without sound or swift motion.

The unfelt wind blew more fiercely now, and the trees of the sheltered garden began to bend before Simon's passage, parting like ocean waves around a submerged stone. The snow flurried, and he moved forward into the opening, into a tree-lined hallway of swirling white. On he went, the trees leaning back before him like respectful soldiers.

The garden was never this long, was it?

Suddenly Simon felt his eyes drawn upward. At the end of the snowy path stood a great white pillar, looming far over his head into the dark skies.

*Of course*, he thought to himself in dreamy half-logic, *it's Green Angel Tower*. He could never walk directly from the garden to the base of the tower before, but

425

things had changed since he'd been gone . . . things had changed.

*But if it's the tower*, he thought, staring upward at the immense shape, *why does it have branches? It's not the tower . . . or at least it isn't any more . . . it's a* **tree** *– a great white tree . . .*

Simon sat upright, staring.

'*What* is a tree?' asked Binabik, who sat close by, restitching Simon's shirt with a bird–bone needle. He finished a moment later, and handed it back to the youth, who extended a freckled arm from beneath his sheltering cloak to claim it. 'What is a tree, and was your sleeping good?'

'A dream, that's all,' Simon said, muffled for a moment as he pulled the shirt over his head. 'I dreamed that Green Angel Tower turned into a tree.' He looked at Binabik quizzically, but the troll only shrugged.

'A dream,' Binabik agreed.

Simon yawned and stretched. It had not been particularly comfortable, sleeping in a protected crevice on the side of a hill, but it was eminently preferable to spending a night unprotected on the plain. He had seen the logic of that quickly enough, once they had gotten moving.

Sunrise had come while he slept, inconspicuous behind the blanket of clouds, just a smear of pinkish gray light across the sky. Looking back from the hillside perch it was difficult to tell where the sky left off and the misty plains began. The world seemed a murky and unformed place this morning.

'I saw fires in the night, while you were sleeping,' the troll said, startling Simon out of his reverie.

'Fires? Where?'

Binabik pointed with his left hand, southward along the plain. 'Back there. Do not be worrying, I think they are a far way off. It is quite the possibility they have nothing to do with us.'

'I suppose so.' Simon squinted into the gray distance.

'Do you think it might be Isgrimnur and his Rimmers-garders?'

'It is doubtful.

Simon turned to look at the little man. 'But you said they would get away! That they'd survive. . . .'

The troll gave him an exasperated look. 'If you would wait, you would hear. I am sure they survived, but *they* were traveling *north*, and I am doubting they would turn back. Those fires were farther toward south, as though . . .'

'. . . As though they were traveling up from Erkynland,' Simon finished.

'Yes!' Binabik said, a little testily. 'But it could be they are traders, or pilgrims . . .' He looked around. 'Where has Qantaqa now gone to?'

Simon grimaced. He knew a dodge when he saw one. 'Very well. It could be anything . . . but *you* were the one counseling speed yesterday. Are we to wait so we can see first hand if these are merchants or . . . or *diggers*?' The joke felt more than a little sour. The last word had not tasted good in his mouth.

'Not being stupid is important,' Binabik grunted in disgust. 'Boghanik – the Bukken – light no fires. They *hate* things that are bright. And no, we will not be waiting for these fire builders to reach us. We are heading back to the forest, as I was telling you.' He gestured back over his head. 'On the hill's far side we will be within sight of it.'

The brush crackled behind them, and troll and boy jumped in surprise. It was only Qantaqa, traversing erratically down the hillside, nose held tight to the ground. When she reached their campsite, she butted Binabik's arm until he scratched her head.

'Qantaqa has a cheerful mood, hmmm?' The troll smiled, showing his yellow teeth. 'Since we have the advantage of a day with heavy clouds, which will be covering the smoke of a campfire, I am thinking we can

427

at least have a decent meal before we again take to our feet. Are you in favor?'

Simon tried to make his expression a serious one. 'I . . . *suppose* I could eat something . . . if I must,' he said. 'If you really think it's important . . .'

Binabik stared, trying to decide if Simon actually disapproved of breakfast, and the boy felt laughter trying to bubble free.

*Why am I acting like a mooncalf?* he wondered. *We're in terrible danger, and it won't get any better soon.*

Binabik's puzzled look was finally too much, and the laughter burst forth.

*Well*, he answered himself, *a person can't worry all the time*.


Simon sighed, contented, and allowed Qantaqa to take the few remaining bits of squirrel meat from his fingers. He marveled at the delicacy the wolf could exhibit with those great jaws and gleaming teeth.

The fire was a small one, since the troll did not believe in unnecessary risks. A thin stream of smoke curled sinuously in the wind sliding along the hillside.

Binabik was reading Morgenes' manuscript, which he had unwrapped with Simon's permission. 'It is my hope you understand,' the troll said without looking up, 'that you will not be trying that with any other wolf beside my friend Qantaqa.'

'Of course not. It's amazing how tame she is.'

'Not *tame*.' Binabik was emphatic. 'She has a bond of honor with me, and it is including those who are my friends.'

'Honor?' Simon asked lazily.

'I am sure you know that term, much as it is bandied about in southern lands. Honor. Are you thinking such a thing cannot exist between troll and beast?' Binabik glanced over, then went back to leafing through the manuscript.

'Oh, I don't think much about anything these days,'

428

Simon said airily, leaning forward to scratch Qantaqa's deep-furred chin. 'I'm just trying to keep my head down and reach Naglimund.'

'You are making a gross evasion,' Binabik muttered, but did not pursue the subject. For a while there was no sound on the hillside but the riffling of parchment. The morning sun climbed up through the sky.

'Here,' Binabik said at last, 'listen, now. Ah, Daughter of the Mountains, but I am missing Morgenes more just from reading his words. Do you know of Nearulagh, Simon?'

'Certainly. Where King John beat the Nabbanai. There's a gate at the castle all covered with carvings of it.'

'You are right. So then, here Morgenes is writing of the Battle of Nearulagh, where John was first meeting the famous Sir Camaris. May I read to you?'

Simon suppressed a twinge of jealousy. The doctor had not intended that his manuscript be for Simon and no one else, he reminded himself.

' ". . . *So after Ardrivis' decision – a brave one, some said, arrogant said others – to meet this upstart northern king in the flat plain of the Meadow Thrithing before Lake Myrme, proved a disaster. Ardrivis pulled the bulk of his troops back into the Onestrine Pass, a narrow way between the mountain lakes Eadne and Clodu . . .*" '

'What Morgenes speaks of,' Binabik explained, 'is that Ardrivis, the Imperator of Nabban, did not believe Prester John could come against him with great force, so far from Erkynland. But the Perdruinese islanders, who were always being in the Nabbanai shadow, made secret treaty with John and helped to supply his forces. King John cut Ardrivis' legions in ribbons near the Meadow Thrithing, a thing unsuspected as possible by the proud Nabbanai. Do you see?'

'I think so.' Simon was not sure, but he had heard

429

enough ballads about Nearulagh to recognize most of the names. 'Read some more.'

'I shall do so. Let me only be finding the part I wanted to read for you . . .' He scanned down the page. 'Ho!'

' ". . . And so, as the sun sank behind Mount Onestris, the last sun for eight thousand dead and dying men, young Camaris, whose father Benidrivis-sá Vinitta had taken the Imperator's Staff from his dying brother Ardrivis only an hour before, led a charge of five hundred horse, the remainder of the Imperial Guard, in quest of vengeance . . ." '

'Binabik?' Simon interrupted.

'Yes?'

'Who took what from which?'

Binabik laughed. 'Forgive me. It is a net full of names to capture at once, is it not? Ardrivis was the last Imperator of Nabban, although his empire was no larger, you are seeing, than what is the duchy of Nabban today. Ardrivis fell out with Prester John, likely because Ardrivis knew that John had designs on a united Osten Ard, and that eventually there would have to be conflict. In any way, I will not bore you with all the fighting, but this was their last battle, as you know. Ardrivis the Imperator was killed by an arrow, and his brother Benidrivis became the new Imperator . . . for the rest of that day, only, ending with Nabban's surrendering. Camaris was the son of Benidrivis – and being young, too, perhaps fifteen years – and so for that afternoon he was the last prince of Nabban, as songs are sometimes calling him . . . understood, now?'

'Better. It was all those "arises" and "ivises" that left me behind for a moment.'

Binabik picked up the parchment and continued reading.

' "Now, with the coming of Camaris onto the field, the

430

*tired armies of Erkynland were much distraught. The young prince's troops were not fresh, but Camaris himself was a whirlwind, a storm of death, and the sword Thorn that his dying uncle had given him was like a fork of dark lightning. Even at that late moment, the records say, the forces of Erkynland might have been routed, but Prester John came onto the field, Bright-Nail clutched in his gauntleted fist, and cut a path through the Nabbanai Imperial Guard until he was face to face with the gallant Camaris."* '

'This is the part I wanted you especially to hear,' Binabik said as he leafed forward to the next sheet.

'This is very good,' Simon said. 'Will Prester John cleave him in twain?'

'Ridiculous!' snorted the troll. 'How, then, would they come to be the fastest and most famous of friends? – "cleave him in twain"!' He resumed.

' *"The ballads say that they fought all day and into the night, but I doubt greatly that was so. Certainly they fought a long while, but doubtless the twilight and darkness had nearly arrived anyway, and it only **seemed** to some of the tired observers that these two great men had battled all the day long . . ."* '

'What thinking your Morgenes does!' Binabik chortled.

' *"Whatever the truth, they traded blow after blow, clanging and hammering on each other's armor as the sun sank and the ravens fed. Neither man could gain an upper hand, even though Camaris' guard had long since been defeated by John's troop. Still, none of the Erkynlanders dared to interfere.*

*"By chance at last, Camaris' horse stepped in a hole, breaking its leg, and fell with a great scream, trapping the prince beneath it. John could have ended it there, and few*

*would have blamed him, but instead — observers uni-
formly swear — he helped the fallen knight of Nabban out
from under his steed, gave him back his sword, and when
Camaris proved sound, continued the fight." '*

'Aedon!' breathed Simon, impressed. He had heard the
story, of course, but it was a different thing entirely to
hear it confirmed in the doctor's wry, confident words.

*' "So they struggled on and on until Prester John —
who was, after all, over twenty years Camaris' senior —
grew weary and stumbled, falling to the ground at the feet
of the Prince of Nabban."
"Camaris, moved by the power and honor of his
opponent, forewent slaying him and instead held Thorn
at John's gorget and asked him to promise to leave
Nabban in peace. John, who had not expected his mercy
to be repaid in kind, looked around at the field of
Nearulagh, empty but for his own troops, thought for a
moment, and then kicked Camaris-sá-Vinitta in the fork
of his legs." '*

'No!' said Simon, taken aback; Qantaqa raised a sleepy
head at the exclamation. Binabik only grinned and
continued to read from Morgenes' writings.

*' "John then stood in his turn over the sorely wounded
Camaris, and told him: 'You have many lessons to learn,
but you are a brave and noble man, I will do your father
and family every courtesy, and take good care of your
people. I hope in turn you will learn the first lesson, the
one I have given you today, and that is this: Honor is a
wonderful thing, but it is a means, not an end. A man
who starves with honor does not help his family, a king
who falls on his sword with honor does not save his
kingdom.'
"When Camaris recovered, so awed was he by his new*

432

*king that he was John's most faithful follower from that day forward . . ." '*

'Why did you read that to me?' Simon said. He felt more than a little insulted by the glee that Binabik had displayed while reading about the foul practices of the greatest hero of Simon's country . . . still, they *had* been Morgenes' words, and when you thought about them, they made old King John seem more like a real person, and less like a marble statue of Saint Sutrin catching dust on the cathedral facade.

'It seemed to be interesting,' Binabik smiled impishly. 'No, that was not the reason,' he explained quickly as Simon frowned, 'truly, I was wanting you to take a point, and I thought Morgenes could do it with more ease than I.

'You did not want to leave the men of Rimmersgard, and I understand your feeling – it was not, perhaps, the most honorable way of behaving. Neither, however, was it honorable for me to leave *my* duties unfulfilled in Yiqanuc, but sometimes we must go against honor – or, it is to say, against what is *obviously* honorable . . . are you understanding me?'

'Not particularly.' Simon's frown turned into a mocking, affectionate smile.

'Ah.' Binabik gave a philosophical shrug. '*Ko muhuhok na mik aqa nop*, we say in Yiqanuc: "When it falls on your head, then you are knowing it is a rock." '

Simon pondered this stoically as Binabik returned his cooking things to his bag.

Binabik had certainly been right about one thing. As they crested the hill they could see virtually nothing but the great, dark sweep of Aldheorte stretching illimitably before them – a green and black ocean frozen a moment before its waves crashed at the feet of the hills. Oldheart, however, looked like a sea that the land itself might break against and fail.

Simon could not help sucking in a deep breath of wonderment. The trees rolled off and away into the distance until the mist swallowed them, as if the forest might somehow pass beyond the very boundaries of the earth.

Binabik, seeing him staring, said: 'Of all times when it is important to be listening to me, this will be it. If we lose each other out there, there may be no finding again.'

'I was in the forest before, Binabik.'

'The fringes, only, friend. Now we are going deeply in.'

'All the way through?'

'Ha! No, that would take months – a year, who is knowing? But we are going far past her borders, so we must hope we are permitted guests.'

As Simon stared down he felt his skin tingle. The dark, silent trees, the shadowy pathways that had never known the sound of a footfall . . . all the stories of a town and castle-dwelling people were just at the fringes of his imagination, and all too easy to summon.

*But I must go,* he told himself. *And anyway, I don't think the forest is evil. It's just old . . . very old. And suspicious of strangers – or at least it makes me feel that way. But not evil.*

'Let's go,' he said in his clearest, strongest voice, but as Binabik started down the hill before him Simon made the sign of the Tree on his breast, just to be on the safe side of things.

They had made their way down the hill and onto the league of grassy downs that sloped to Aldheorte's edge when Qantaqa suddenly stopped, shaggy head cocked to one side. The sun was high in the sky now, past noon, and much of the ground-hugging mist had burned away. As Simon and the troll walked toward the wolf, who crouched motionless as a gray statue, they looked all around. No movement broke the land's static undulation on either side.

Qantaqa whined as they approached and tilted her

434

head to the other side, listening. Binabik gently lowered his shoulder bag to the ground, stilling the quiet clinking of the bones and stones inside, then cocked an ear himself.

The troll opened his mouth to say something, his hair hanging lank in his eyes, but before he spoke Simon heard it too: a thin, faint noise, rising and falling as though a flight of honking geese were passing leagues overhead, far above the clouds. But it did not seem to come from the sky above – rather, it sounded as though it rolled down the long corridor between the forest and the hills, whether from north or south Simon could not say.

'What. . . ?' he began to ask. Qantaqa whined again and shook her head, as though she did not like the sound in her ears. The troll raised his small, brown hand and listened a moment more, then shouldered his bag again, beckoning Simon to follow him toward the murky breakfront of the forest.

'Hounds, I am thinking,' he said. The wolf trotted around them in erratic ovals, moving close and then bounding out again. 'I think they are far away, still, south of the hills . . . upon the Frostmarch. The sooner we are entering the forest, though, the better. . . .'

'Perhaps,' Simon said, making good time as he strode along beside the little man, who was going at a near-trot, 'but they didn't sound like any hounds that I've heard. . . .'

'That,' Binabik grunted, 'is my thought, also . . . and it is also why we are going quickly as we can.'

As he thought about what Binabik had said, Simon felt a cold hand clutch his innards.

'Stop,' he said, and did.

'What are you doing?' the little man hissed. 'They are still far behind, but . . .'

'Call Qantaqa.' Simon stood patiently. Binabik stared at him for a moment, then whistled for the wolf, who was already trotting back.

'I hope that you will soon explain . . .' the troll began, but Simon pointed at Qantaqa.

'Ride her. Go on, now, get up. If we need to hurry, I can run – but your legs are too short.'

'Simon,' Binabik said, anger crinkling his eyes, 'I was running on the slender ridges of Mintahoq when I had only baby-years . . .'

'But this is flat ground, and downhill. Please, Binabik, you said we needed to go quickly!'

The troll stared at him for a moment, then turned and clucked at Qantaqa, who sank to her stomach in the sparse grass. Binabik threw a leg over her broad back and pulled himself into place using the thick fur of her hackles for a pommel. He clucked again and the wolf rose, front feet and then hind, Binabik swaying on her back.

'*Ummu*, Qantaqa,' he snapped; she started forward. Simon lengthened his pace and began to lope along beside them. They could hear no sound now beside the noise of their own passage, but the memory of the distant howling made the back of Simon's neck prickle, and the dark face of Aldheorte look more and more like the welcoming smile of a friend. Binabik leaned low over Qantaqa's neck, and for a long time would not meet Simon's eye.

Side by side they ran down the long slope. At last, as the flat gray sun was tipping down toward the hills behind them, they reached the first line of trees, a cluster of slim birches – pale serving girls ushering visitors into the house of their dark old master.

Although the downs outside were bright with slanting sunlight, the companions found themselves passing quickly into twilit gloom as the trees rose above them. The soft forest floor cushioned their footfalls, and they ran silently as ghosts through the sparse outer woods. Columns of light speared down through the branches, and the dust of their passage rose behind them to hang sparkling between the shadows.

Simon was tiring rapidly, sweat running down his face and neck in dirty rivulets.

'Farther we must go,' Binabik called to him from the pitching platform of Qantaqa's back. 'Soon enough the way will be too tangled for speed, and the light too dim. Then we will rest.'

Simon said nothing but only dug on, his breath burning in his lungs.

When the boy slowed at last to an unsteady canter, Binabik slipped down from the wolf's back and ran at his side. The angling sun was sliding up the tree trunks around them, the forest floor darkening even as the upper branches took on shining haloes, like the colored windows of the Hayholt's chapel. At last, as the ground before them disappeared in darkness, Simon tripped over a half-buried stone; when Binabik caught him up at the elbow, he held on.

'Sit, now,' the troll said. Simon slid to the ground without a word, feeling the loose soil give slightly beneath him. A moment later Qantaqa circled back. After sniffing the immediate area, she sat down and began to lick the perspiration from the back of Simon's neck; it tickled, but Simon was too exhausted to do much of anything about it.

Binabik crouched on his haunches, examining their stopping place. They were partway down a small slope, at the bottom of which snaked a muddy streambed with a dark trickle of water at its center.

'When you are again breathing,' he said, 'I think we might be moving just there.' With his finger he indicated a spot slightly uphill where a great oak stood, its tangle of roots warding off the encroachment of other trees so that there was a stone's throw of clear ground on all sides of its massive, gnarled trunk. Simon nodded, still laboring for breath. After a while, he dragged himself to his feet and moved with the little man up the slope to the tree.

'Do you know where we are?' Simon asked as he sank down to place his back against one of the looping, half-buried roots.

'No,' said Binabik cheerfully. 'But tomorrow when

437

the sun is up and I have time for doing certain things . . . then I will. Now help me find some stones and sticks and we will be having a bit of fire. And later,' Binabik rose from his crouch and began foraging for deadwood in the fast-fading daylight, 'later there will be a pleasant surprise for you.'

Binabik had built a sort of three-sided box of stones around the fire pit to shield its light, but still it crackled in a most heartening manner. The red gleam cast odd shadows as Binabik rooted in his bag. Simon watched a few lonely sparks spiral upward.

They had made themselves a meager dinner of dried fish, hard cakes, and water. Simon did not feel he had treated his stomach as well as he would have liked, but it was still better to be lying here warming the dull ache in his legs than to be running. He could not remember a time when he had ever run so long or so far without stopping.

'Ha!' Binabik chortled, lifting his firelight-tinted face from his bag in triumph. 'A surprise I was promising you, Simon, and a surprise I have!'

'A *pleasant* surprise, you said. I've had enough of the other kind to last for my whole life.'

Binabik grinned, his round face seeming to stretch back toward his ears. 'Very well, it is for you to decide. Have a try of this.' He handed Simon a small ceramic jar.

'What is it?' Simon held it up to the fire. It felt solid, but the jar had no markings. 'Some troll-thing?'

'Open it.'

Simon stuck his finger into the top and found it was sealed with something that felt like wax. He scraped a hole through, then brought it up to his nose for a tentative sniff. A moment later he pushed his finger in, pulled it out, and stuck it in his mouth.

'Jam!' he said, delighted.

'Made from grapes, I am sure,' Binabik said, pleased by Simon's response. 'Some I found at the abbey, but the excitement of late had driven it from my mind.'

After eating several dollops, Simon reluctantly passed it to Binabik, who also found it rather pleasant. Within a short while they had finished it off, leaving Qantaqa the sticky jar to lick.

Simon curled himself in his cloak beside the warm stones of the dying fire. 'Could you sing a song, Binabik?' he asked, 'or tell a story?'

The troll looked over. 'I am thinking not a story, Simon, for we need to sleep and rise early. Perhaps a short song.'

'That would be fine.'

'But, after thinking again,' Binabik said, tugging his hood up around his ears, 'I would like to be hearing *you* sing a song. A quiet singing, of course.'

'Me? A song?' Simon pondered. Through a chink in the trees he thought he could see the faint glimmer of a star. A star . . . 'Well, then,' he said, 'since you sang your song for me, about Sedda and the blanket of stars . . . I suppose I can sing one that the chambermaids taught me when I was a child.' He moved around a bit, making himself more comfortable. 'I hope I remember all the words. It's a funny song.'

*'In the Oldheart's deep dell,'*

Simon began softly,

*'Jack Mundwode did yell*
*To his men of the woods near and far,*
*He offered a crown, and the forest's reknown*
*To the one who could catch him a star.*

*Beornoth stood first time, and he shouted: "I'll climb*
*To the top of the highest of trees!*
*And I'll snatch that star down for the fair golden crown*
*That will soon belong only to me."*

*So he climbed up a birch to the highest high perch*
*Then he leaped to an old, tall yew.*

439

But as much as he jumped, and he leaped and he bumped
Reach the star, that he never could do.

Next gay Osgal stood, and he promised he would
Loose an arrow up into the sky.
"I will knock that star free so it falls down to me
And the crown will be mine by and by . . ."

Twenty arrows he shot. Not a single one caught
On the star that hung mocking above.
As the arrows fell back Osgal hid behind Jack
Who chuckled and gave him a shove.

Now all the men sought, and they quarreled and fought
And they had not a pinch of success,
Till the fair Hruse rose, and she looked down her nose
At the men as she smoothed out her dress.

"'Tis a small enough task for Jack Mundwode to ask,"
She said with a gleam in her eye,
"But if none of you here hold a gold crown that dear
I will seek Mundwode's knot to untie."

Then she took up a net which she'd bade the men get
And she cast it full into the lake.
So the water did roil, and it almost did spoil
The reflection the bright star did make.

But then after a while she turned 'round with a smile,
Said to Jack: "Do you see what's about?
It is there in my net, all caught up and quite wet
If you want it, then **you** pull it out."

Old Jack laughed and he shouted to all those who crowded
"Here's the woman I must take to wife.
For she's taken my crown, and she's brought my star down
So I might as well give her my life."
Yes, she's taken the crown, and she's brought the star down
So Jack Mundwode has took her to wife . . . '

From the darkness he could hear Binabik laugh, quietly and easily.

'A song of enjoyment, Simon. Thanks to you.'

Soon the hissing of the embers quieted, and the only sound was the soft breathing of the wind through the endless trees.

Before he opened his eyes he was aware of a strange droning noise, rising and falling close to where he lay. He lifted his head, feeling sticky with sleep, to see Binabik sitting cross-legged before the fire. The sun had not been up long; the forest around them was draped in tendrils of pale mist.

Binabik had carefully placed a circle of feathers around the fire pit, feathers of many different birds, as though he had scavenged them from the surrounding woods. Eyes closed, he leaned toward the small fire and chanted in his native language, the sound that had pulled Simon to wakefulness.

'. . . *Tutusik-Ahyuq-Chuyuq-Qachimak, Tutusik- Ahyuk-Chuyuq-Qaqimak* . . .' On and on he went. The slender ribbon of smoke that rose from the campfire began to waver, as though in a strong breeze, but the tiny feathers lay flat on the ground, unmoving. With his eyes still closed, the troll began to move the palm of his hand in a flat circle over the fire; the ribbon of smoke bent as though pushed, and began to stream steadily away across one corner of the pit. Binabik opened his eyes and looked for a moment at the smoke, then stopped the circling movement of his small hand. A moment later the smoke resumed its normal motion.

Simon had been holding his breath. He let it out. 'Do you know where we are now?' he asked. Binabik turned and smiled, pleased.

'Morning greetings. Yes, I think I am knowing to a nicety. We should be having little trouble – but much walking – to get to Geloë's house . . .'

'House?' Simon asked. 'A house in the Aldheorte? What's it like?'

'Ah,' Binabik straightened his legs and rubbed his calves, 'it is not like any house you . . .' He stopped, and sat staring over Simon's shoulder, transfixed. The youth whirled in alarm, but there was nothing to see.

'What is it?'

'Hush . . .' Binabik continued to gaze out. 'There. Are you hearing?'

After a moment, he did hear it: the distant baying they had marked in their journey across the downs to the forest. Simon felt his skin crawl.

'The hounds again. . . !' he said. 'But it sounds as though they're still far away.'

'You are not understanding yet.' Binabik looked down at the fire pit, then up at the morning light bleeding down through the treetops. 'They have passed us in the night. They have run all night! And now, unless my ears are playing tricks at me, they have turned back toward us.'

'*Whose* hounds?' Simon felt his palms go moist with sweat, and rubbed them on his cloak. 'Are they following us? They can't hunt us in the forest, can they?'

Binabik scattered the feathers with a scuff of his small boot and began packing his shoulder bag. 'I do not know,' he said. 'I am not knowing the answer to any of those questions. There is power in the forest that might confuse hunting hounds – *ordinary* hounds. It is doubtful, however, that any local baron out for sport would be running his dogs through all the night, and I have not heard of dogs that could do so.'

Binabik called Qantaqa. Simon sat up and hurriedly pulled his boots on. He felt sore all over, and now he felt sure he would be running again.

'It's Elias, isn't it?' he said grimly, wincing as he pushed his blistered foot down into the boot heel.

'Perhaps.' Qantaqa trotted up, and Binabik threw a leg over her back, pulling himself up. 'But what is making a doctor's helper so important to him – and where is the

442

king finding hounds that can run twenty leagues between dusk and sunrise?' Binabik put the pack on Qantaqa's shoulders before him, and handed Simon his walking stick. 'Do not lose this, please. I wish we had found a horse for your riding.'

The pair started down the slope to the gulley, then up the far side.

'Are they close?' Simon asked. 'How far is . . . this house?'

'Neither hounds nor house are nearby,' Binabik said. 'Well, I shall be running beside you as soon as Qantaqa is tiring. *Kikkasut!*' he swore, 'how I am wishing for a horse!'

'Me, too,' Simon panted.

They trekked on through the morning, eastward into deeper forest. As they went up and down the rocky dells the baying behind them faded for long minutes, then returned seemingly louder than ever. As good as his word, Binabik jumped down from Qantaqa when the wolf began to flag and trotted along beside, his short legs carrying him two steps for Simon's every one, his teeth bared as his cheeks puffed in and out.

They stopped to drink water and rest as the sun neared midmorning. Simon tore strips from his two packages to bandage his blistered heels, then handed the bundles to Binabik so he could put them in the pack: Simon could no longer stand to feel them rattling against his thigh as he walked and ran. As they sloshed the last musky drops from the waterbag in their cheeks and tried to regain their straining breath, the sounds of the pursuit came up again. This time the unmistakable clamor of the hounds was so much nearer that they immediately lurched into motion once more.

Within a short while they began to ascend a long rise. The ground was becoming increasingly rocky as it mounted upward, and even the types of trees seemed to be changing. Staggering up the hilly slope, Simon felt a

443

sickening sense of defeat spread through his body like a poison. Binabik had told him it would be late in the afternoon at least before they reached this Geloë, yet they were already losing the race, with the sun not risen to noon above the sheltering trees. The noise of their pursuers was constant, an excited howling so loud that Simon could not help wondering, even as he stumbled up the daunting slope, where they found the breath to run and bark at once. What kind of hounds *were* they? Simon's heart beat as fast as a bird's wings. He and the troll would get to face the hunters soon enough. The thought made him feel sick.

At last a slender patch of sky could be seen through the standing trunks on the horizon: the top of the rise. They limped past the final line of trees. Qantaqa, who ran before them, stopped abruptly and barked, a sharp, high pitched sound from deep in her throat.

'Simon!' Binabik shouted and threw himself to the ground, knocking the boy's legs from beneath him so he tumbled down with a huff of punched-out breath. When the black tunnel of Simon's vision widened a moment later, he was lying on his elbows looking down a craggy rock face into a deep canyon. A cluster of fragments broke loose from the stone beneath his hand and hopped and tumbled down the sheer wall to disappear into the green treetops far below.

The baying was like the brazen flare of war trumpets. Simon and the troll edged themselves away from the canyon's edge, a few feet back down the slope, and stood.

'Look!' Simon hissed, his bleeding hands and chin of no import now. 'Binabik, look!' He pointed back down the long slope they had just climbed, through the clinging blanket of trees.

Passing in and out of the clearings, far, far less than a half a league behind, was a flurry of low white shapes: the hounds.

Binabik took his stick from Simon and twisted it into

halves. He shook out his darts and handed the knife end to Simon.

'Quickly,' he said. 'Cut yourself a tree branch, a cudgel. If selling our lives we must be, let us keep the price high.'

The throaty voices of the dogs boiled up the hillside, a rising song of the closing and the kill.

# 25
# The Secret Lake

He hacked and chipped frantically, bending the limb down with his full weight, the knife slippery in his trembling fingers. It took Simon many costly seconds to cut loose a branch that would suit him – pathetic defense though it would be – and every second brought the hounds nearer. The limb that he finally snapped off was as long as his arm, knobbled at one end where another branch had fallen away.

The troll was rummaging in his backpack, one hand clutching the heavy fur at Qantaqa's neck.

'Hold her!' he called to Simon. 'If she is let go now, she will attack too soon. They will drag her down and be quickly killing her.' Simon crouched with an arm around the wolf's broad neck. She was trembling with excitement, heart beating beneath his arm. Simon felt his own heart speeding in tandem – this was all so unreal! Just this morning he and Binabik had been sitting calmly beside the fire. . . .

The cry of the pack intensified; they came surging up the hill like white termites fleeing a crumbling nest. Qantaqa lunged forward, dragging Simon to his knees.

'Hinik Aia!' Binabik shouted, and flicked at her nose with his hollow bone tube, then dropped it as he pulled a length of rope from the bottom of his bag and began to make a noose. Simon, thinking he understood, looked over the canyon's edge behind them and shook his head despairingly. It was much too far to the bottom, more than twice as far as Binabik's rope could reach down the sheer rock face. Then he saw something, and felt hope still struggling inside him.

'Binabik, look!' he pointed. The troll, despite the impossibility of a climb down, was looping his rope around a stump anchored not a yard from the canyon's edge. As he finished he looked up to follow Simon's pointing finger.

Less than a hundred paces from where they crouched a huge old hemlock lay tipped downward, its bottom end balanced on the near lip, the tip lodged halfway down the far canyon wall, caught on a jutting ledge.

'We can climb across to the far side!' Simon said. But the troll shook his head.

'If we can climb down it with Qantaqa, then they can be doing it as well. And it goes to nowhere.' He gestured. The ledge where the tree had caught was no more than a wide shelf in the rock face. 'But it will be some help.' He stood up and tugged at the rope, testing the knot around the stump. 'Take Qantaqa down onto it, if you can. Not far, perhaps ten cubits only. Hold her *until I am calling*, understood!?'

'But . . .' Simon began, then looked back down the slope. The white shapes, perhaps a dozen in all, were almost upon them. He grabbed the balking Qantaqa by the scruff of the neck and urged her toward the fallen hemlock.

Enough of the tree had remained on the canyon's edge that there was space between the twisting roots and the rock rim. It was not easy to keep balance while clinging to the wolf. She shivered and pulled back, growling; the noise was almost subsumed in the clamor of the approaching hounds. He could not coax her up onto the broad trunk, and turned to Binabik in despair.

'*Ummu!*' the troll called hoarsely, and a moment later she jumped up onto the hemlock, still growling. Simon straddled the trunk as best he could, his club a hindrance in his belt. He slid backward on his rump, keeping a grip on Qantaqa, until he was well out from the canyon's rim. Just then the troll cried out, and Qantaqa whirled toward the sound of his voice. Simon hung on to her neck with both arms as his knees gripped the rough bark. He was suddenly cold, so cold! He lowered his face into her fur, smelled her thick, wild smell, and whispered a prayer.

'. . . *Elysia, mother of our Ransomer, give mercy, protect us . . .*'

Binabik was standing with a coil of rope in his hand just a step before the rim. '*Hinik*, Qantaqa!' he called, and then the hounds were out of the trees and up the final slope.

Simon could not really see much of them from where he sat holding the straining wolf – only long, thin white backs and sharp ears. The beasts moved toward the troll at a gallop, making a noise like metal chains dragged on a slate floor.

*What is Binabik doing?* Simon thought, panic making it hard for him to breathe. *Why doesn't he run, why doesn't he use his darts – something?!*

It was like the recurrence of his worst nightmare, like Morgenes in flames standing between Simon and the deadly hand of Elias. He couldn't sit and watch Binabik killed before his eyes. As he started to pull himself forward, the dogs leaped toward the troll.

Simon had only a moment's impression of long, pale snouts, of empty, pearl-white eyes, and a flare of red curving tongues and red mouths . . . then Binabik jumped backward, down into the canyon.

'*No!*' Simon shrieked, horrified. The five or six creatures that had been nearest lunged forward, unable to stop, and tumbled over the cliff in a squealing tangle of white legs and tails. Helpless, Simon watched the clot of whinnying dogs bounce against the steep rock face and plummet down into the trees far below with an explosive popping of broken branches. He felt another choking scream rise in his breast . . .

'*Now, Simon! Let her go!*'

Mouth agape, Simon looked down to see Binabik's feet braced against the canyon wall, the troll hanging suspended from the rope about his waist not two dozen feet below the spot where he had jumped. 'Let her go!' he called again, and Simon finally uncurled his restraining arm from Qantaqa's neck. The remainder of the dogs were milling at the rim above Binabik's head, sniffing the ground and staring down, barking savagely at the little man who hung so frustratingly near.

As Qantaqa made her cautious way back up the hemlock's broad back, one of the white hounds turned tiny eyes like fogged mirrors toward the tree and Simon, letting out a great rasping snarl as he hurried forward; the other quickly followed.

Before the yammering pack reached the hemlock, the gray wolf negotiated the last steps, reaching the rim with a magnificent leap. The first dog was on her in a heartbeat, two more right behind. The snarling battle song of the wolf rose, a deeper note among the barking and howling of the hounds.

Simon, frozen for a moment of indecision, began inching forward toward the edge of the rim. The trunk was so broad that his spread legs ached, and he considered getting up to his knees to crawl forward, sacrificing his clutch on the tree for speed. For the first time he turned his gaze straight down. The tops of the trees were a bumpy green carpet far below. The distance was dizzying, much farther than the leap from the wall to Green Angel Tower. His head reeled and he looked away, deciding to keep his knees right where they were. As he looked up, a white shape bounded from the canyon's edge onto the wide hemlock.

The hound growled and drove forward, talons catching at the bark. Simon had only an instant to pull out his knotted branch before the beast crossed the dozen or so feet and dove for his throat. For a moment the branch caught in his belt, but he had pushed it in narrow-end-down, which saved his life.

As the club came free, the dog was upon him. Yellow teeth gleamed as it bit at his face. He got the branch up high enough to strike a glancing blow, turning the dog's lunge so that the teeth snapped on air an inch from his left ear, spraying him with saliva. Its paws were on his chest, and the awful carrion-stench of its breath blew in his face; he was losing his hold. He tried to pull the club back up, but it caught between the animal's extended front legs. He leaned back as the long, snarling muzzle once more snaked toward his face, and tried to twist the branch free. There was a moment of resistance, then one of the white hound's paws was knocked from his shoulder and the beast overbalanced. It squealed and tumbled away, scrabbling for a moment at the bark, then pulling the club from his hand as it slid from the tree trunk to fall end over end down into the canyon.

Simon sank forward, catching at the tree with his hands, and coughed, trying to drive the fetid breath of the thing out of his nostrils. He was cut short by a low growl. He lifted his head slowly to see another hound standing on the log just below the roots, milky eyes glinting like a blind beggar's. It bared its teeth in a frothing, crimson-tongued grin. Simon hopelessly lifted his empty hands as the beast padded slowly down the trunk, ropy muscles bunching beneath the short fur.

The hound turned to nip at its flank, worrying the skin for a moment, then returned its eerie, vacant gaze to Simon. It took another step, wobbled, took one shaky step more, then folded in place to slide off the hemlock into oblivion.

'The black dart seemed the safest,' Binabik called. The little man stood a few yards down slope from the tree's ball of dried roots. A moment later Qantaqa limped up to stand at his side, her muzzle dripping with dark red blood. Simon stared, slowly realizing that they had survived.

'Go slowly, now,' the troll called. 'Here, I will throw the rope. It would be bad sense to lose you after all we were going through . . .' The rope arced out and fell slithering across the log where Simon sat. He took it gratefully, his hands shaking as though with palsy.

Binabik laboriously turned the dog over with his foot. It was one he had killed with a dart: the cotton wadding sprouted from the smooth white fur of the creature's neck like a tiny mushroom.

'See there,' the troll said. Simon leaned a little closer. It was not like any hunting hound *he* had ever seen: the slender muzzle and underslung jaw reminded him more of the sharks that fishermen pulled thrashing from the Kynslagh. The opalescent white eyes, now staring sightlessly, seemed windows of some inner disease.

'No, look there.' Binabik pointed. On the dog's chest, burned black through the short hairs, was a slender triangle with a narrow base. It was a branded mark, like the kind that the Thrithings-men burnt into the flanks of their horses with flame-heated spears.

'That sign is for *Stormspike*,' Binabik said quietly. 'It is the mark of the Norns.'

'And they are. . . ?'

'A strange people. Their country is north even of Yiqanuc and Rimmersgard. A great mountain is there – very tall and with a covering of snow and ice – called Stormspike by the Rimmersmen. The Norns do not travel in the fields of Osten Ard. Some are saying that they are Sithi, but I do not know if that is truth.'

'How can that be?' Simon asked. 'Look at the collar.' He leaned down, gingerly pushing a finger under the white leather to lift it away from the stiffening flesh of the dead hound.

Binabik smiled sheepishly. 'Shame to me! I over-looked the collar, white against white as it is – me, taught since child-age to hunt in snow!'

'But look at it,' Simon urged. 'See the buckle?'

The buckle of the collar was indeed an interesting thing: a piece of hammered silver in the shape of a coiling dragon.

'That's the dragon of Elias' kennels,' Simon said firmly. 'I should know – I used to visit Tobas the houndkeeper often.'

Binabik crouched, staring at the carcass. 'I believe you. And as for the mark of Stormspike, it is only necessary to look for seeing that these dogs are not things raised in your Hayholt.' He stood up and stepped back a pace; Qantaqa moved in to sniff at the body, then quickly backed away with a rumbling growl.

'A mystery whose solving must wait,' the troll said. 'Now we are very lucky to have our lives, with all of our limbs as well. We should be moving again. I have no wish to meet this hound's master.'

'Are we close to Geloë?'

'Somewhat we have been driven off our route, but not beyond repairing. If we leave now, we should still outrun the darkness.'

Simon looked down at the long snout and vicious jaw of the hound, at its powerful body and filming eye. 'I hope so,' he said.

They could find no way to cross the canyon anywhere, and reluctantly decided to move back down the long slope and look for another, easier descent than the sheer rock face before them. Simon was almost childishly happy not to have to climb down: his knees still felt as weak as if he'd had a fever. He had no wish to look down into the canyon's maw again with nothing beneath him but a long, long fall. It was one thing to climb the walls and towers of the Hayholt, with their square corners and mason's cracks – a tree trunk suspended like a frail twig over nothingness was another story entirely.

At the base of the long slope an hour later they turned to their right hand and began to track around to the northwest. They had not gone more than five furlongs when a high-pitched, wailing cry knifed through the afternoon air. They both stopped short; Qantaqa pricked her ears and growled. The sound came again.

'It sounds like a child screaming,' Simon declared, turning his head to locate the noise's source.

'The forest is often playing such tricks,' Binabik began. The keening noise rose again. Quickly afterward came an angry baying that they knew all too well.

'Qinkipa's Eyes!' Binabik cursed. 'Will they chase us all the way to Naglimund!?' The baying rose again, and he listened. 'It has the sound of one dog only, however. That is something lucky.'

'It sounds like it's coming from down there.' Simon pointed to where the trees grew more densely some distance away. 'Let's go and see.'

'Simon!' Binabik's voice was harsh with surprise. 'What thing are you saying? We are fleeing to keep our lives!'

'You said it sounded like only one. We have Qantaqa. Someone is being *attacked*. How can we run away?'

'Simon, we do not know if that crying is a trick . . . or an animal it could be.'

'What if it isn't?' Simon demanded. 'What if that thing has caught some woodsman's child . . . or . . . or something?'

'A woodsman's child? This far from the forest's edge?' Binabik stared at him in frustration for a moment. Simon returned the gaze defiantly. 'Ha!' Binabik said heavily. 'So it will be, then, as you are wishing.'

Simon turned and began jogging down toward the thickening trees.

' "*Mikmok hanno so gijiq*," we say in Yiqanuc!' Binabik called. ' "If you wish to carry a hungry weasel in your pocket, it is your choice!" ' The youth did not look back. Binabik slapped the ground with his walking stick, then trotted after him.

He caught up to Simon within a hundred paces; within twenty more he had opened his staff to shake loose his

453

dart bag. He hissed a command to bring the racing Qantaqa back, then deftly rolled coarse wool around one of the dark-tipped darts as he ran.

'Couldn't you get poisoned if you tripped and fell?' Simon asked. Binabik shot him a sour, worried look as he struggled to keep up.

When they came upon the scene at last, its appearance was deceptively innocent: a dog crouching before a spreading ash tree, staring up at a dark shape huddled on a branch overhead. It might have been one of the Hayholt castle hounds with a treed cat, except that both dog and quarry were far larger.

They were less than a hundred paces away when the dog turned toward them. It skinned back its lips and barked, a vicious, raw bray of sound. It looked back at the tree for a moment, then straightened long legs and loped toward them. Binabik slowed and stopped, raising his hollow tube to his lips; Qantaqa trotted past him. As the hound closed the gap, the troll puffed out his cheeks and blew. If the dart struck, the dog gave no sign; instead it sped forward, growling, and Qantaqa charged to meet it. This hound was even bigger than the others, as large or even a little larger than Qantaqa herself.

The two animals did not circle, but flung themselves together, jaws snapping; a moment later they tumbled to the ground snarling, a heaving, spinning ball of gray and white fur. At Simon's side Binabik cursed sharply; his leather packet fell from his hand in his haste to wind another dart. The ivory needles scattered into the leaves and moss underfoot.

The snarls of the combatants had risen to a higher pitch. The long white head of the hound lunged in and out: once, twice, thrice, like a striking viper. The last time it came back with blood on its pale muzzle.

Simon and the troll were trotting toward them when Binabik made a strange choking noise.

'Qantaqa!' he cried, and sped forward. Simon saw the flash of Binabik's bone-handled blade, then a moment

454

later, incredibly, the troll cast himself onto the writhing, snapping animals and brought the knife down, raised it, and struck again. Simon, fearing for the lives of both his companions, snatched the hollow tube from where Binabik had dropped it and ran forward. He arrived in time to see the troll brace himself, grab the thick gray fur of Qantaqa's back, and pull. The two animals slid apart; there was blood on each of them. Qantaqa slowly stood, favoring a leg. The white hound lay silent.

Binabik crouched and put an arm around the wolf's neck, pressing his forehead to hers. Simon, oddly touched, walked away from them to the tree.

The first surprise was that there were two figures up in the branches of the white ash: a wide-eyed youth who held a smaller, silent figure in his lap. The second surprise was that Simon knew the larger of the two.

'It's *you!*' He stared up in astonishment at the grime-streaked and bloody face. 'You! Mal . . . Malachias!'

The boy said nothing, but gazed down with haunted eyes, gently rocking the small figure in his lap. For a moment the forest copse was silent and unmoving, as though the afternoon sun above the trees had been arrested in its progress. Then the blare of a horn shattered the quiet.

'Quickly!' Simon called up to Malachias. 'Down! You must come down!' Binabik came up behind him with the limping Qantaqa.

'Huntsman's horn, I am sure,' was all he said.

Malachias, as if comprehending at last, began sliding up the long branch toward the trunk, holding his small companion carefully. When he reached the crotch, he hesitated a moment, then handed the limp burden down to Simon. It was a little dark-haired girl, aged no more than ten years. She was unmoving, eyes closed in her too-pale face; when Simon took her, he felt something sticky all across the front of her rough dress. A moment later Malachias lowered himself down from the branch,

455

falling the last few feet and tumbling, getting up almost immediately.

'What now?' Simon asked, trying to balance the little girl against his chest. The horn echoed again somewhere on the canyon rim they had left behind, and now there rose the excited squalling of more hounds as well.

'We cannot fight men, and dogs along with them,' the troll said, exhaustion plain on his slack face. 'Horses we cannot outrun. We must hide ourselves.'

'How?' Simon demanded. 'The dogs will smell us.'

Binabik leaned forward and took Qantaqa's injured paw in his small hand, bending it back and forth. The wolf resisted for a moment, then sat, panting, as the little man finished his manipulations.

'Painful it is, but not broken,' he told Simon, then turned to speak to the wolf. Malachias lifted his gaze from Simon's burden to stare. '*Chok*, Qantaqa my brave friend,' the troll said, '*ummu chok Geloë!*'

The wolf rumbled deep in her chest, then leaped away at once to the northwest, away from the rising clamor behind them. Favoring the bloodied front leg, she was gone from view among the trees in a matter of moments.

'I am hoping,' Binabik explained, 'that the confusion of scents here,' he gestured to the tree, and then to the huge hound lying nearby, 'will distract them, and that the scent they will follow may be Qantaqa's. I think they cannot catch her, even lamed – too smart she is.'

Simon looked around. 'How about there?' he asked, pointing to a crevice on the hillside formed by a great rectangle of streaked stone that had broken loose and fallen back, as though split by a vast wedge.

'Except that we do not know which direction they will take,' Binabik said. 'If they come down the hillside, that will be luck for us. If they are descending farther back, they will ride past the hole there. Too much risk.'

Simon found it hard to think. The din of the approaching hounds was fearsome. Was Binabik right? Were they to be chased all the way to Naglimund? Not that they could run much longer, weary and battered as they were.

'There!' he said, suddenly. Another finger of rock thrust up through the forest floor some distance away, three times the height of a man. Trees grew close about its base, surrounding it like young children helping their grandfather hobble to the supper table.

'If we can climb up that,' Simon said, 'we will be above even the ones on horses!'

'Yes,' Binabik said, nodding his head. 'Right, you are right. Come, let us climb.' He made for the outcropping, the silent Malachias just behind him. Simon readjusted the little girl against his body and hurried after.

Binabik scrambled up partway, and clung to the branch of a close-leaning tree as he turned. 'Pass the little one to me.'

Simon did, extending his arms to their full reach, then turned to put a guiding hand on the elbow of Malachias, who was looking for an initial toehold. The boy shook off Simon's helpful gesture and climbed carefully upward.

Simon was last. When he got to the first ledge he picked up the still figure of the little girl and gently slung her over his shoulder, then made his way up to the rock's rounded top. He lay down with the others among the leaves and twigs, hidden from the ground by a screen of branches. His heart thudded from exhaustion and fear. He had, it seemed, been running and hiding forever.

Even as they squirmed, trying to find comfortable positions for all four bodies, the yammering of the dogs rose to a hideous pitch; a moment later the woods below were full of darting white shapes.

Simon left the little girl clutched in Malachias' arms and quietly pulled himself forward until he could join Binabik at the outcropping's edge, peering with the troll through a gap in the foliage. The dogs were everywhere, sniffing, barking; there were at least a score of them running excitedly back and forth between the tree, the body of their fellow, and the base of the outcropping.

One of them even seemed to stare directly up at Simon and Binabik, empty white eyes gleaming, red mouth grinning fiercely. A moment later it trotted back to join its lathered companions.

The horn sounded nearby. Within a minute a line of horses appeared, picking their way down the densely wooded hillside. Now the dogs had a fourth corner to their circuit, and ran braying between the stone-gray legs of the lead horse, who walked on as calmly as if they were moths. The trailing horses were not quite so sanguine; one immediately behind shied a little, and its master cut it out of line, spurring it down the last short slope to bring it to a pacing, sputtering halt near the outcropping.

This rider was young and clean-shaven, with a strong chin and curling hair the color of his chestnut horse. He wore a blue and black surcoat over his silvery armor, with a design of three yellow flowers set diagonally from shoulder to waist. His expression was sour.

'Another one dead,' he spat. 'What do you make of this, Jegger?' his voice took on a sarcastic tone. 'Oh, pardon me, I meant *Master Ingen*.'

Simon was amazed at how clear the man's words were, as though he spoke directly to the hidden listeners. He held his breath.

The armored man was staring at something out of their view, and his profile suddenly seemed very familiar. Simon felt sure he had seen this man somewhere, most likely at the Hayholt. He was certainly an Erkynlander, by his accent.

'It is not important what you call me,' another voice said, a deep, smooth, cold voice. 'You did not make Ingen Jegger master of this hunt. You are here as . . . courtesy, Heahferth. Because these are your lands.'

Simon realized that the first man was Baron Heahferth, a regular at Elias' court and a crony of Earl Fengbald. The second speaker rode his gray horse into the gap through which Simon and Binabik stared. Agitated white dogs twined in and out around the horse's hooves.

The man called Ingen was dressed all in black, his surcoat, breeches and shirt all the same bleak, lusterless shade. At first he looked to be white-bearded; a moment later it was apparent that the close-cropped whiskers on the hard face were a yellow so light as to be nearly colorless – as colorless as his eyes, faint pale spots in his dark face. They might be blue.

Simon stared at the cold face framed in the black coif, at the powerful, thick-muscled body, and felt a fear different than any he had felt this whole dangerous day. Who was this man? He looked like a Rimmersman, his name was a Rimmersgard name, but he spoke strangely, with slow, strange accents Simon had never heard.

'My lands ended at the forest's edge,' Heahferth said, and turned his balking mount back into place. Half a dozen men in light armor had filed down into the clearing behind and sat their horses, waiting. 'And where my lands ended,' Heahferth continued, 'my patience did, too. This is a farce. Dead dogs scattered about like chaff . . .'

'And two prisoners escaped,' Ingen finished heavily.

'Prisoners!' Heahferth scoffed. 'A little boy and girl! Do you think these are the traitors Elias is so anxious to get? Do you think such a pair,' he tipped his head toward the carcass of the great hound, 'did *that?*

'The dogs have been chasing *something*.' Ingen Jegger stared down at the dead mastiff. 'Look. Look at the wounds. This was no bear, no wolf that did this. It is our quarry, and he is still running. And now, thanks to your stupidity, our prisoners are running, also.'

'How dare you?!' Baron Heahferth said, his voice rising. 'How dare you?! With one word I could have you sprouting arrows like a hedgehog.'

Ingren looked slowly up from the body of the hound. 'But you will not,' he said quietly. Heahferth's horse shied back, rearing, and when the baron had mastered him the two men stared at each other for a moment.

'Oh . . . very well, then,' Heahferth said. A different

459

note had crept into his voice as he looked away from the black-clad man to stare out across the forest. 'What now?'

'The dogs have a scent,' Ingen said. 'We will do what we must do. Follow.' He raised the horn that swung at his side and winded it once. The dogs, who had been swarming about at the edge of the clearing gave throat and sped off in the direction Qantaqa had disappeared; Ingen Jegger spurred his tall gray horse after them without a word. Baron Heahferth, cursing, waved to his men and followed. Within the course of a hundred heartbeats the woods below the outcropping were empty and silent once more, but Binabik kept them all in place for some time before he would let them climb down.

Once on the ground, he quickly examined the little girl, opening her eyes with a delicate, stubby finger, leaning close to listen to her breathing.

'Very bad she is, this one. What is her name, Malachias?'

'Leleth,' the boy said, staring at the pale face. 'My sister.'

'Our only hope is to quickly get her to the house of Geloë,' Binabik said. 'And hope also that Qantaqa has led those men astray, so that we are reaching it alive.'

'What are you *doing* out here, Malachias!?' Simon demanded. 'And how did you get away from Heahferth?' The boy did not answer, and when Simon asked again he turned his head away.

'Questions for later,' Binabik said, standing. 'Quickness we need now. Can you carry this girlchild, Simon?'

They made their way northwest through the dense forest, the lowering sun lancing through the branches. Simon asked the troll about the man named Ingen and his odd way of speaking.

'Black Rimmersman, I am thinking,' Binabik said. 'They are a rare lot, not often seen except at northern-most settlements where they sometimes come to trade. They do not speak the language of Rimmersgard. It is

460

said they live on the fringes of the lands belonging to the Norns.'

'The Norns again,' Simon grunted, ducking beneath a branch that had sprung from Malachias' careless hand. He turned to confront the troll. '*What is going on?!* Why should such people be concerned with us?'

'Perilous times, friend Simon,' Binabik said. 'Through perilous times we are passing.'

Several hours went by and the shadows of afternoon grew longer and longer. The patches of sky that glimmered through the treetops turned slowly from blue to shell pink. The three walked on. The land was mostly level, from time to time sloping away like a shallow beggar's bowl. In the branches above, squirrels and jays carried on their endless arguments; crickets droned in the leaf-tangle at their feet. Once Simon saw a large gray owl scudding like a phantom through the twining branches overhead. Later he saw another, so like the first as to have been its twin.

Binabik watched the sky carefully when they passed through clearings, and jogged them a little to the east; soon they reached a small forest stream that gurgled past a thousand tiny breakwaters of fallen branches. They walked through the thick grasses that lined its banks for a while; when the bulk of a tree blocked their passage, they stepped out and made their way past on the backs of the stones dotting the stream's gentle course.

The streambed became wider as another small waterway entered, and within moments Binabik raised a hand to bring them to a stop. They had just rounded a bend in the watercourse; here the stream suddenly dropped away, rushing in a tiny waterfall down a series of rock slabs.

They stood on the rim of a great bowl, a sloping expanse of trees leading down to a wide, dark lake. The sun had dipped out of sight, and in the insect-humming twilight the water looked purple and deep. Tree roots

461

twisted down into the water like snakes. There was an air of stillness about the lake, of quiet secrets whispered only to the endless trees. At the far side, dim and difficult to see in the gathering darkness, a tall thatched hut stood over the water in such a way that at first it seemed to float on air; a moment later Simon could see that it was raised above the lake's surface on stilts. Buttery light gleamed in the two small windows.

'The house of Geloë,' Binabik said, and they started down into the tree-lined bowl. With a soundless rush of wings a gray shape tore loose from the trees above them and glided out to circle low over the lake two times, then vanish into the darkness beside the cottage. For a moment Simon thought he saw the owl pass *into* the cottage, but his eyelids were heavy from exhaustion and he could not see clearly. The crickets' nightsong rose about them as the shadows deepened. A bounding shape came speeding around the lake's rim toward them.

'Qantaqa!' Binabik laughed, and ran down to meet her.

# 26

# In the House of Geloë

The figure that stood framed in the warm light of the doorway did not move or speak as the companions mounted the long board-bridge that slanted from the doorstep to the lake's edge. As Simon followed Binabik up, carefully cradling the child Leleth, he could not help wondering why this Geloë woman did not have an entranceway of a more permanent nature, something at least with a rope handrail. His weary feet were having trouble keeping to the narrow bridge.

*I suppose she doesn't get many visitors, for one thing,* he thought, looking out across the rapidly darkening forest.

Binabik pulled up short of the front step and bowed, almost bumping Simon off into the still waters.

'Valada Geloë,' he announced, 'Binbines Mintahoqis requests your aid. I bring travelers.'

The figure in the doorway stepped back, leaving the way open.

'Spare me the Nabbanai constructions, Binabik.' It was a harshly musical voice, heavily and strangely accented, but unmistakably a woman's. 'I knew it was you. Qantaqa has been here an hour.' At the shore end of the ramp the wolf pricked her ears forward. 'Of course you are welcome. Do you think I would deny you?'

Binabik entered the house. Simon, a step behind, spoke up.

'Where shall I put the little girl?' He ducked through the door, getting a quick impression of a high roof and long, fluttering shadows cast by the flames of many candles, then Geloë stepped in front of him.

She was dressed in a rough robe of dun cloth, clumsily tied with a belt. Her height was somewhere between Simon's and the troll's, her face wide and sunbrowned, seamed with wrinkles at both the eyes and mouth. Her dark hair was shot all through with gray and cut short, so that she looked almost like a priest. But it was her eyes that caught him – round, heavy-lidded yellow eyes with large, jet-black pupils. They were old, knowing eyes, as though they belonged to some ancient bird of the heights, and there was a power behind them that fixed him in his tracks. She seemed to measure him completely, to turn him inside out and shake him like a sack, all in a moment. When her gaze at last flicked down to the injured girl, he felt drained like an empty wineskin.

'This child is hurt.' It was not a question.

Simon helplessly let her take Leleth from his arms as Binabik came forward.

'She has been attacked by dogs,' the troll said. 'Dogs with the brand of Stormspike.'

If he expected a look of surprise or fear, he was disappointed. Geloë pushed briskly past to a straw pallet on the floor, where she laid the girl down. 'Find food if you are hungry,' she said. 'I must work now. Were you followed?'

Binabik was hurriedly telling her of the most recent events, Geloë all the while undressing the unresponsive body of the child, when Malachias finally entered. He squatted down near the pallet, hovering as Geloë cleaned Leleth's wounds. When Malachias leaned too close, blocking her movements, the valada gently touched the boy's shoulder with a sun-freckled hand. She held the contact, staring at him for a moment, until Malachias glanced up and flinched. After a moment he raised his eyes to Geloë's once more, and something seemed to pass

464

silently between them before Malachias turned away and sat back against the wall.

Binabik poked up the fire, ingeniously set in a deep well in the floor. The smoke – there was surprisingly little – rose up to the ceiling; Simon imagined there must be a chimney hidden in the shadows overhead.

The cottage itself, which was really one large room, reminded him in many ways of Morgenes' study chambers. Many strange objects were hung on the clay-plastered walls: leafy branches tied in careful sheaves, bags of dried flowers spilling their petals, and stalks, reeds, and long, slippery roots that looked as though they had come grudgingly from the lake below. The firelight also flickered across a multitude of tiny animal skulls, limning their bright, polished surfaces without penetrating the darkness of the eyes.

One entire wall was divided between floor and ceiling by a waist-high shelf of frame-stretched bark; it, too, was covered with curious objects: animal pelts and tiny bundles of sticks and bones, beautiful water-smoothed rocks of every shape and color, and a carefully stacked aggregation of scrolls, handles facing out like a cord of firewood. It was so cluttered that it took Simon a moment to realize it was not really a shelf at all, but a writing table; beside the scrolls was a stack of vellum, and a quill pen in an inkwell made from another animal skull.

Qantaqa whined softly and nosed against his thigh. Simon scratched her muzzle. There were cuts on her face and ears, but the fur had been carefully cleaned of dried blood. He turned from the table to the wide wall that faced out on the lake with its two small windows. The sun was gone now, and the candlelight streaming out made two long, irregular rectangles on the water; Simon could see his own gangly silhouette in one of them, like the pupil of a bright eye.

'I have warmed some soup,' Binabik said behind him, and offered a wooden bowl. 'I have need of it myself,' the

465

troll smiled, 'and so do you and everyone else. I hope to never have another day the like of this.'

Simon blew on the hot liquid, then sucked a little past his lips. It was tangy and a little bitter, like mulled Elysiamansa cider.

'It's good,' he said, and sipped a little more. 'What is it?'

'Better that you are not asking, perhaps,' Binabik grinned mischievously. Geloë looked up from the pallet, eyebrows slanting down to the bridge of her sharp nose, and fixed Binabik with a penetrating glance.

'Stop that, troll, you'll give the boy stomach pains,' she snorted irritably. 'Honeylock, dandelion, and stone-grass is all that's in it, boy.'

Binabik seemed chastened. 'Apologies, Valada.'

'I like it,' Simon said, worried that he had somehow offended her, even if only as the recipient of Binabik's teasing. 'Thank you for taking us in. My name is Simon.'

'Ah,' grunted Geloë, then turned back to cleansing the little girl's injuries. Nonplussed, Simon finished his broth as quietly as he could. Binabik took the bowl and refilled it; he finished that one almost as quickly.

Binabik began combing Qantaqa's thick pelt with his stubby fingers, tossing the burrs and twigs he worked loose into the fire. Geloë was silently applying dressings to Leleth while Malachias looked on, lank black hair hanging in his face. Simon found a relatively uncluttered place to lean against the cottage wall.

A legion of crickets and other night singers filled the night's hollow spaces as Simon slid into exhausted sleep, his heart beating along in slow time.

It was still night when he awoke. He bobbed his head stupidly, trying to clear away the sticky residue of a too-short sleep; it took a moment of peering around the unfamiliar room until he remembered where he was.

Geloë and Binabik were quietly talking, the woman on a high stool, the troll cross-legged at her feet, like a

466

student. Behind them on the pallet lay a dark, bumpy shape that Simon at last recognized as Malachias and Leleth huddled together in sleep.

'It doesn't matter whether you were clever or not, young Binabik,' the woman was saying. 'You have been lucky, which is a better thing.'

Simon decided to let them know he was awake. 'How is the little girl?' he asked, yawning.

Geloë turned her hooded stare toward him. 'Very bad. Badly wounded and feverish. The Nornhounds . . . well, it is not good to be bitten. They eat unclean flesh.'

'The valada has done all things that can be done, Simon,' Binabik said. He had something in his hands: a new pouch that he was stitching out of skin even as he spoke. Simon wondered where the troll might find new darts. Oh, for a sword . . . even a knife! People on adventures always had swords or sharp wits. Or magic.

'Did you tell her . . .' Simon hesitated. 'Did you tell her about Morgenes?'

'I already knew.' Geloë stared at him, firelight reddening her bright eyes. When she spoke, it was with powerful deliberateness. 'You were with him, boy. I know your name, and I felt Morgenes' mark upon you when I touched you as I took the child.' As if to demonstrate, she held out her own wide, callused hand.

'You knew my name?'

'Where the doctor is concerned, I know many things.' Geloë leaned over and poked up the fire with a long, blackened stick. 'A great man has been lost, a man we can ill afford to lose.'

Simon hesitated. Curiosity at last won out over awe. 'What do you mean?' He crawled across the floor to sit near the troll. 'That is, what does *we* mean?'

' "We" means all of us,' she said. ' "We" means: those who do not welcome darkness.'

'I have told Geloë what happened to us, friend Simon.' Binabik spoke quietly. 'There is no secret that I have few explanations.'

467

Geloë made a wry face and pulled her coarse robe tighter around her body. 'And I have none to add . . . yet. It is clear to me now, however, that the weather signs I have seen even here on my isolated lake, the north-flying geese that should have gone clattering overhead a fortnight ago, all of the things that have given me pause in this strange season,' she pushed her palms together, as in a gesture of prayer, 'they are real – and the change they augur is real, also. Terribly real.' She dropped her hands heavily to her lap and stared at them.

'Binabik is right,' she said at last. Beside her the troll nodded his head gravely, but Simon thought he saw a satisfied glint in the little man's eyes, as though he had been paid a great compliment. 'This is far more than the striving of a king and his brother,' she continued. 'The contendings of kings can beat down the land, can uproot trees and bathe the fields in blood,' a log collapsed with a pop of sparks, and Simon jumped, 'but the wars of men do not bring dark clouds from the north, or send the hungry bears back to their dens in Maia-month.'

Geloë stood up and stretched, the wide sleeves of her robe hanging like the wings of a bird. 'Tomorrow I will try and find some answers for you. Now all should sleep while they can, for I fear the child's fever will return strongly during the night.'

She moved to the far wall and began putting small jars back on the shelves. Simon spread his cloak on the floor near the edge of the fire well.

'Perhaps you should not sleep so closely,' Binabik cautioned. 'A spark leaping out may set you on fire.'

Simon looked at him carefully, but the troll did not appear to be joking. He pulled his cloak back several feet and lay on top of it, rolling the hood into a cushion beneath his head, then carefully pulled the sides up and over himself. Binabik moved away toward the corner, and after a moment of rustling and thumping made himself comfortable as well.

The song of the crickets had died out. Simon stared

into the shadows that flickered in the rafters, and listened to the gentle hiss of the wind passing endlessly through the branches of the circling trees and out across the lake.

No lanterns were burning, and no fire; only the mushroom-pale light of the moon filtered in through the high windows, painting the cluttered room with a kind of frost-sheen. Simon stared around him at the curious, unrecognizable silhouettes that littered the tabletops, and the blocky, inert shapes of books stacked in crooked piles, sprouting up from the floor like grave markers in a churchyard. His eyes were drawn to one particular book that lay spread open, gleaming white like the flesh of a bark-stripped tree. In the middle of the open page there was a familiar face – a man with burning eyes, whose head wore the branching antlers of a stag.

Simon looked up at the room, then back to the book. He was in Morgenes' chambers, of course. Of course! Where had he thought he was?

Even as the realization came to him, as the silhouettes took on the familiar shapes of the doctor's flasks and racks and retorts, there was a cautious scraping noise at the door. He started at the unexpected sound. Diagonal stripes of moonlight made the wall seem to lean crazily. The scraping came again.

'. . . Simon. . . ?'

The voice was very quiet, as though the speaker did not wish to be heard, but he recognized it instantly.

'Doctor?!' He leaped to his feet and crossed to the door in a few steps. Why hadn't the old man knocked? And what was he doing coming back so late? Perhaps he had been away on some mysterious journey, and had foolishly locked himself out – that was it, of course! Lucky that Simon was there to let him in.

He fumbled with the shadowy latch. 'What have you been up to, Doctor Morgenes?' he whispered. 'I have been waiting for you for such a long time!' There was no answer.

Even as he worked the bolt from the slot, he was filled with a sudden sense of unease. He stopped with the door half-unbarred, standing on his tiptoes to peer down through a crack between the boards.

'Doctor?'

In the inner passageway, splashed in the blue light of the hall lamps, the old man's hooded, cloaked form stood before the door. His face was shadowed, but there was no mistaking his tattered old cloak, his slight build, the wisps of white hair that straggled from his hood, blue-tinted in the lampglow. Why wouldn't he answer? Was he hurt?

'Are you all right?' Simon asked, swinging the door inward. The small, bowed figure did not move. 'Where have you been? What have you found out?' He thought he heard the doctor say something, and bent forward.

'What?'

The words that rose up to him were full of air, painfully harsh. '. . . False . . . messenger . . .' was all he understood – the dry voice seemed to labor at speech – and then the face tilted up, and the hood fell back.

The head that wore the ragged fringe of white hair was a burnt, blackened ruin: a knob with cracked, empty pits for eyes, the spindly neck on which it wobbled a charred stick. Even as Simon staggered away, an unfreeable scream lodged in his throat, a thin red line spread across the front of the black, leathery ball; an instant later the mouth yawned open, a split grin of pink meat.

'. . . The . . . false . . . messenger . . .' it said, each word a rustling gasp. '. . . Beware . . .'

And then Simon did scream, until the blood pounded in his ears, for the burned thing spoke, beyond a doubt, with the voice of Doctor Morgenes.

His speeding heart took a long time to slow. He sat, breathing raggedly, and Binabik sat beside him.

'There is nothing of harm here,' the troll said, then pressed his palm against Simon's forehead. 'You are chilled.'

470

Geloë strode back from the pallet where she had replaced Malachias' blanket, kicked free when Simon's cry had startled him awake.

'You had powerful dreams like this when you lived at the castle, boy?' she asked, fixing him with a stern eye as if daring him to deny it.

Simon shivered. Faced with that overwhelming gaze, he felt no urge to tell anything but the truth. 'Not until . . . until the last few months before . . . before . . .'

'Before Morgenes died,' said Geloë flatly. 'Binabik, unless the learning I have has deserted me completely, I cannot believe this is chance, for him to dream of Morgenes in my house. Not a dream like that.'

Binabik ran a hand through his own sleep-tousled hair. 'Valada Geloë, if *you* do not know, how can I? Daughter of the Mountains! I feel that I am listening to noises in the dark. I cannot make out the dangers that surround us, but dangers I know they are. Simon dreams of a warning against "false messengers" . . . but that is one only of too many mysterious things. Why the Norns? The Black Rimmersman? The filthy Bukken?'

Geloë turned to Simon and gently but forcefully pushed him back onto his cloak. 'Try and go back to sleep,' she said. 'Nothing will enter the house of the witch woman that can harm you.' She turned to Binabik. 'I think, if the dreaming he has described is as coherent as it seems, he will be of use in our search for answers.'

Lying on his back, Simon saw the valada and the troll as black shapes against the firefly gleam of the embers. The smaller shadow leaned close to him.

'Simon,' Binabik whispered, 'are there any other dreamings that have been left out? That you have not told?'

Simon slowly wagged his head from side to side. There was nothing, nothing but shadows, and he was tired of talking. He could still taste the fear from the burned thing in the doorway; he only wanted to surrender to the sucking pull of oblivion, to sleep, to sleep. . . .

But it did not come so easily. Although he held his eyes tightly closed, still the images of fire and catastrophe rose before him. Tossing in place, unable to find a position that would encourage his tight muscles to loosen, he heard the quiet talk of the troll and the witch woman scratch away like rats in the walls.

Finally even that noise ceased, and the solemn breathing of the wind rose again in his ears; he opened his eyes. Geloë was sitting alone before the fire, shoulders up like a bird huddling from the rain, eyes half-open; he could not tell if she was sleeping or watching the fire smolder out.

His last waking thought, which rose slowly up from deep inside him, flickering as it came like a fire beneath the sea, was of a tall hill, a hill crowned with stones. That had been in a dream, hadn't it? He should have remembered . . . should have told Binabik.

A fire sprang up in the darkness of the hilltop, and he heard the creaking of wooden wheels, the wheels of dream.

When morning came, it did not bring the sun with it. From the window of the cottage Simon could see the dark treetops at the far edge of the bowl, but the lake itself wore a thick cloak of fog. Even directly below the window the water was hard to see, slowly swirling mist making all things hazy and insubstantial. Above the top of the murky treeline the sky was a depthless gray.

Geloë had marched the boy Malachias out with her to gather a certain healing moss, leaving Binabik behind to tend to Leleth. The troll seemed faintly encouraged about the child's condition, but when Simon looked at her pale face and the faint movements of her small chest he wondered what difference the little man could see that he could not.

Simon rebuilt the fire from a pile of dead branches that

Geloë had stacked neatly in the corner, then went to help change the girl's dressings.

As Binabik peeled the sheet back from Leleth's body and lifted away the bandages Simon winced, but would not let himself turn away. Her whole torso was blackened by bruises and ugly toothmarks. The skin had been torn from under her left arm to her hip, a ragged slash a foot long. As Binabik finished cleaning the wound and bound her up again with broad strips of linen, little roses of blood bloomed through the cloth.

'Does she really have a chance to live?' Simon asked. Binabik shrugged, his hands engaged in the making of careful knots.

'Geloë thinks she may,' he said. 'She is a woman of a stern and direct mind, who places people not above animals in her esteem, but that is still esteem most high. She would not struggle against the impossible, I am thinking.'

'Is she really a witch woman like she said?'

Binabik pulled the sheet up over the little girl, leaving only her thin face exposed. Her mouth was partly open; Simon could see that she had lost both her front teeth. He felt a sudden, bitter ache of empathy for the child – lost with only her brother in the wild forest, captured and tormented, frightened. How could the Lord Usires love such a world?

'A witch woman?' Binabik stood up. Outside, Qantaqa clattered up the front door bridge: Geloë and Malachias would be close behind. 'A *wise* woman she certainly is, and a being of rare strength. In your tongue I understand "witch" to mean a bad person, one who is of your Devil and does her neighbors harm. That the valada is certainly not. Her neighbors are the birds and the forest dwellers, and she tends them like a flock. Still, she was leaving Rimmersgard many years ago – many, *many* years ago – to come here. Possible it is that the people who once lived around her thought some nonsense as that . . . perhaps that was the cause of her coming to this lake.'

Binabik turned to greet the impatient Qantaqa, scratching through the deep fur of her back as she wriggled in pleasure, then took a pot out to the front door and lowered it down into the water. Returning, he hung it on a hooked chain over the fire.

'You have known Malachias from the castle, you said?'

Simon was watching Qantaqa: the wolf had trotted back down to the lake and was standing in the shallows, lunging at the water with her snout. 'Is she trying to catch fish?' he asked, laughing.

Binabik smiled patiently and nodded. 'And catch them she can do, too. Malachias?'

'Oh. Yes, I knew him there . . . a little. I caught him once, spying on me. He denied it, though. Did he speak to you? Did he tell you what he and his sister were doing in Aldheorte, how they were captured?'

Qantaqa had indeed caught a fish, a shining silver thing that fluttered wildly but pointlessly as the wolf mounted onto the lake's edge, streaming with water.

'More luck I would be having trying to teach a rock to sing.' Binabik found a bowl of dried leaves on one of Geloë's shelves and crumbled a handful into the pot of boiling water. Instantly, the room was full of warm, minty smells. 'Five or six words I have heard from his mouth since we found them up in that tree. He remembers you, though. Several times I have seen him at staring at you. I think he is not dangerous – in fact, I have a real sureness of it – but still, he is in need of watching.'

Before he could speak, Simon heard Qantaqa give a short bark down below. He looked out the window in time to see the wolf spring up, her mostly-devoured catch left on the lakeshore, and bound away up the path; within a moment she had disappeared into the mist. She soon came trotting back, followed by two dim shapes that gradually became Geloë and the odd, fox-faced boy Malachias. The two of them were talking animatedly.

'Qinkipa!' Binabik snorted as he stirred the pot of water. 'Now he is speaking.'

As she scraped her boots at the doorway, Geloë leaned her head inside. 'Fog everywhere,' she said. 'The forest is sleepy today.' She entered shaking out her cloak, followed by Malachias, who again looked wary. The color was high in his cheeks.

Geloë went promply to her table and began sorting out the contents of a pair of sacks. Today she was dressed like a man, in thick wool breeches, a jerkin, and a pair of worn but sturdy boots. She exuded an air of calm force, like a war captain who had made all possible preparations, and now waited only for the battle to commence.

'Is the water ready?' she asked.

Binabik leaned over the pot and sniffed. 'It is seeming to be,' he said after a moment.

'Good.' Geloë untied a small cloth bag from her belt and removed a handful of dark green moss, still shiny with beads of water. After dumping it unceremoniously into the pot she stirred it with the stick Binabik had given her.

'Malachias and I have been talking,' she said, squinting down into the steam. 'We have spoken of many things.' She looked up, but Malachias only ducked his head, his pink cheeks even reddening a bit further, and went to sit beside Leleth on the pallet. He took her hand and stroked her pale, damp forehead.

Geloë shrugged. 'Well, we shall speak when Malachias is ready. For now, we have tasks enough, anyway.' She lifted some of the moss on the end of the stirring stick, poked it with her finger, then plucked a bowl from a small wooden table and scooped the whole sticky mess out of the pot. She carried the steaming bowl over to the mattress.

While Malachias and the witch woman made poultices of the moss, Simon walked down to the lakeside. The outside of the witch woman's cottage looked quite as odd by daylight as the inside seemed by night; the thatched roof came to a point, like a strange hat, and the dark wood of the walls was covered all over in black and blue rune-paintings. As he walked around the house and down to the shore the letters disappeared and reappeared as the angle of the sun changed. Mired in the dark shadows beneath the hut, the twin stilts on which it stood also seemed covered with some kind of unusual shingles.

Qantaqa had returned to the carcass of her fish, delicately worrying the last bits of meat loose from the slender bones. Simon sat beside her on a rock, then moved a bit farther away in response to her warning growl. He threw pebbles out into the swallowing mist, listening for the splash, until Binabik came down to join him.

'Break your fasting?' the troll asked, handing him a knob of crusty dark bread liberally smeared with pungent cheese. Simon ate it quickly, then they sat and watched a few birds picking in the sand of the lake shore.

'Valada Geloë would like you to join us, to be part of the thing we are to be doing this afternoon,' Binabik said at last.

'What thing?'

'Searching. Searching answers.'

'Searching how? Are we going somewhere?'

Binabik looked at him seriously. 'In some way, yes – no, do not be looking so cross! I will explain.' He cast a pebble. 'There is a thing that is done sometimes, when ways of finding things out are closed. A thing that the wise can do. My master Ookequk called it walking the Road of Dreams.'

'But that killed him!'

'No! That is to say . . .' the troll's expression was worried as he searched for words. 'It is to say, yes, he died while on the road. But a man may die on any road. That is not meaning that anyone who walks upon it will be dying. People have been crushed by carts in your Main Row, but hundreds of others walk upon it every day without harm.'

'What exactly *is* the Road of Dreams?' Simon asked.

'I must first admit,' Binabik said with a sad half-smile,

'that the dream-road is more dangerous than Main Row. I was taught by my master that this road is like a mountain path higher than any others.' The troll lifted his hand in the air above his own head. 'From this road, although the climbing of it has great difficulty, you can see things that never otherwise would you have seen – things that from the road of every-day would be invisible.'

'And the dream part?'

'I was taught that by dreaming is one way to mount up to this road, one any person can do.' Binabik furrowed his brow. 'But when a person reaches to the road by ordinary night dreaming, he cannot then be walking along the road: he sees from one spot only, and then must come back down. So – Ookequk told to me – this one does not often know what he is looking at. Sometimes,' he gestured out at the mist that clung to the trees and lake, 'it is only fog that he sees. The wise one, though, can be walking *along* the road, once he has mastered the art of climbing to it. He can be walking and looking, seeing things as they are, as they change.'

He shrugged. 'Explaining is difficult. The dream-road is a place to go and see things that cannot be seen clearly where we stand beneath the waking sun. Geloë is a veteran of this journey. I have been given some experience of it myself, although I am no master.'

Simon sat staring quietly out across the water for a while, thinking about Binabik's words. The lake's other shore was invisible; he wondered idly how far away across the water it was. His tired memories of their arrival the day before were as hazy as the morning air.

*Now that I come to think of it*, he realized, *how far have I come? A long way, farther than I thought I would ever travel. And still have many leagues to go, I'm sure. Is it worth the risk to better our chances of reaching Naglimund alive?*

Why had such decisions fallen on him? It really was horribly unfair. He wondered bitterly why God had picked him out for such mistreatment – if indeed it was true, as Father Dreosan used to say, that He kept His eye on everyone.

But there was more to think about than just his anger. Binabik and the others seemed to be counting on him, and that was something Simon was not used to. Things were expected of him now.

'I'll do it,' he said finally. 'But tell me one thing. What really happened to your master? Why did he die?'

Binabik slowly nodded his head. 'I am told that there are two ways that things can happen on the road . . . things that are dangerous. The first, and it is usually happening only to the unskilled, is that if one tries to walk the road without proper wisdom, it is possible to miss the places where the dream-road and the track of earthbound life go separate ways.' He skewed the palms of his hands. 'The walker then cannot locate the way back. But Ookequk, I am thinking, was far too wise for that.'

Going lost and homeless in those imagined realms touched a responsive point in Simon, and he sucked in a breath of damp air. 'Then what happened to Ook . . . Ookequk?'

'The other danger, he was teaching me,' Binabik said as he stood up, 'was that there are other things beside the wise and the good that roam upon the Road of Dreams, and other dreamers of a more dangerous sort. It is my thinking that he met one of these.'

Binabik led Simon up the little ramp into the cottage.

Geloë unstoppered a wide pot and stuck two fingers in, bringing them out covered with a dark green paste even stickier and stranger smelling than the moss poultice.

'Lean forward,' she said, and wiped a gob of it on Simon's forehead just above his nose, then did the same for herself and Binabik.

'What is it?' Simon asked. It felt strange on his skin, both hot and cold.

Geloë settled herself before the sunken fire and

478

gestured for the boy and troll to join her. 'Nightshade, mockfoil, whitewood bark to give it the proper consistency . . .' She ranged the boy, the troll, and herself around the fireplace in a triangle, placing the pot on the floor by her knee.

The sensation on his forehead was most curious, Simon decided as he watched the valada throw green twigs onto the fire. White streamers of smoke went writhing upward, turning the space between them into a misty column through which her sulfurous eyes glowed, reflecting the firelight.

'Now rub this on both your hands,' she said, scooping out another gobbet for each of them, 'and a dab on your lips – but not in your mouth! Just a dab, there . . .'

When all was finished, she had them reach out and join hands. Malachias, who had not spoken since Simon and the troll had returned, watched from the pallet beside the sleeping child. The strange boy looked tense, but his mouth was set in a grim line, as though he willed himself to keep his nervousness hidden. Simon stretched his arms out on both sides, clasping Binabik's small dry paw in his own left hand and Geloë's sturdy one in his right.

'Hold tightly,' the witch woman said. 'There is nothing terrible that will happen if you let go, but it will be better if you hold on.' She cast her eyes down and began to speak softly, the words inaudible. Simon stared at her moving lips, at the drooping lids of her wide eyes; again he was struck by how much she resembled a bird, a proud, steep-soaring bird at that. As he continued to gaze through the column of smoke, the tingling on his palms, forehead, and lips began to bother him.

Darkness was suddenly all around, as though a dense cloud had passed before the sun. In a moment he could see nothing but the smoke and the red fireglow beneath it, all else had disappeared into the walls of blackness that loomed up on either side. His eyes were heavy, and at the same time he felt as though someone had pushed his face down in snow. He was cold, very cold. He fell backward, toppling, and the blackness was all around him.

After a time – and Simon had no idea how long it might have been, only that through it all he could still faintly feel the grip on both his hands, a very reassuring sensation – the darkness began to glow with a direction-less light, a light that gradually resolved itself into a field of white. The whiteness was uneven: some parts of it shone like sunlight on polished steel; other places were almost gray. A moment later the field of white became a vast, glittering mountain of ice, a mountain so impos-sibly tall that its head was hidden in the swirling clouds lining the dark sky. Smoke belched from crevices in its glassy sides and streamed upward to join the cloud-halo.

And then, somehow, he was *inside* the great mountain, flying as rapidly as a spark through tunnels that led ever inward, dark tunnels that were nevertheless lined with mirroring ice. Uncountable thousands of shapes made their way through the mists and shadows and frostgleam – pale-faced, angular shapes who marched the corridors in moving thickets of glimmering spears, or tended the strange blue and yellow fires whose smokes crowned the heights above.

The spark that was Simon still felt two firm hands grasping his own, or rather felt something else that told him he was not alone, for certainly a spark could have no hands to hold. He was at last in a great chamber, a vast hollow in the mountain's center. The roof was so high above the ice-glazed tiles of the floor that snow flurried down from its upper reaches, leaping, whirling clouds of snow like armies of tiny white butterflies. In the center of the immense chamber was a monstrous well, whose mouth flickered with pale blue light, and which seemed the source of a hideous, heart-squeezing fear. Some heat must have been floating up from its unguessable depths, for the air above it was a roiling pillar of fogs, a misty column gleaming with diffuse colors like a titan icicle catching the sun's light.

Hanging somehow in the fog above the well, its shape not quite clear or its dimensions entirely guessable, was an inexplicable *something*: a thing made up of many things and many shapes, all colorless as glass. It seemed – as its lineaments appeared here and there in the swirling mist-pillar – a creation of angles and sweeping curves, of subtle, frightening complexity. In some not quite definable way it seemed an instrument of music. If so, it was an instrument so huge, alien, and frightening that the spark that was Simon knew he could never hear its awful music and live.

Facing the well, in an angular seat of rime-crusted black rock, a figure sat. He could see it clearly, as though suddenly he hovered directly over the terrible, blue-burning well. It was cloaked in a white and silver robe of fantastic intricacy. Snowy hair streamed down over its shoulders to blend almost invisibly with the immaculate white garments.

The pale form lifted its head, and the face was a mass of shining light. A moment later, as it turned away again, he could see that it was only a beautiful, expressionless sculpture of a woman's face . . . a mask of silver.

The dazzling, exotic face turned back toward him. He felt himself pushed away, brusquely disconnected from the scene like a clinging kitten being pulled free from the hem of a dress.

A vision swam up before him that was somehow a part of the wreath of fogs and the grim white figure. At first it was only another patch of alabaster whiteness; gradually it became an angular shape crisscrossed with black. The black shapes became lines, the lines became symbols; at last an open book hung before him. On its opened page were letters Simon could not read, twisting runes that wavered and then came clear.

A timeless instant passed, then the runes began to shimmer once more. They pulled apart and reformed themselves into black silhouettes, three long, slender shapes . . . three swords. One had a hilt shaped like the

Tree of Usires, another a hilt like the right-angle crossbeams of a roof. The third had a strange double guard, the cross pieces making, with the hilt, a sort of five-pointed star. Somewhere, deep in Simon's self, he recognized this last sword. Somewhere, in a memory black as night, deep as a cave, he had seen such a blade.

The swords began to disappear, one by one, and when they were gone only gray and white nothingness was left.

Simon felt himself falling back – away from the mountain, away from the well chamber, away from the dream itself. A part of him welcomed this falling away, horrified by the terrible, forbidden places where his spirit had flown, but another part of him did not want to let go.

Where were the *answers?!* His whole life had been caught up, snagged by the passage of some damnable, remorseless, uncaring wheel, and deep in the part of himself that was most private, he was desperately angry. He was frightened, too, trapped in a nightmare that would not end, but what he felt now was the anger; at that moment, it was the stronger.

He resisted the pull, fighting with weapons he did not understand to retain the dream, to wring from it the knowledge he wanted. He seized the fast-diminishing whiteness and furiously tried to mold it, to make it into something that would tell him why Morgenes had died, why Dochais and the monks of Saint Hoderund's had perished, why the little girl Leleth lay close to death in a hut in the depths of the wild forest. He struggled and he hated. If a spark could weep, he wept.

Slowly, painfully, the ice mountain formed again from the blankness before him. Where was the truth? He wanted answers! As Simon's dream-self struggled, the mountain grew taller, grew more slender, began sprouting branches like an icy tree as it reached into the heavens. Then the branches fell away, and it was only a smooth white tower – a tower that he knew. Flames burned at its summit. A great, booming sound came, like the tolling

482

of a monstrous bell. The tower wavered. The bell thundered again. This was something of dreadful importance, he knew, something ghastly, something secret. He could feel an answer almost within reach. . . .

*Little fly!* **You** *have come to* **us***, have you?*

A horrible, searing black nothingness reached up and engulfed him, blocking out the tower and the sounding bell. He felt the breath of life burning away inside his dream-self as infinite coldness closed around him. He was lost in the screamingly empty void, a tiny speck at the bottom of a sea of infinite black depths, cut free from life, breath, thought. Everything had vanished . . . everything except the horrible, crushing hatred of the thing that gripped him . . . smothered him.

And then, beyond all hope, he was free.

He was soaring, dizzyingly high above the world of Osten Ard, clutched in the strong talons of a large gray owl, flying like the wind's own child. The ice mountain was disappearing behind him, swallowed up in the immensity of the bone-white plain. In impossibly swift moments the owl carried him away, over lakes and ice and mountains, winging toward a dark line on the horizon. Just as it came clear to him, as the line became a forest, he felt himself beginning to slip from the owl's claws. The bird clutched him tighter, and dropped earthward in a whistling dive. The ground leaped up, and the owl spread her wide wings. They flattened out, gliding, and whirled across the snowfields toward the security of the forest.

And then they were under the eaves, and safe.

Simon groaned and rolled over onto his side. His head was pounding like Ruben the Bear's anvil during tournament time. His tongue seemed swollen to twice its normal size; the air he breathed tasted of metal. He pulled himself into a crouch, moving his heavy head as slowly as possible.

Binabik was lying nearby, his wide face pale; Qantaqa

nosed at the troll's side, whimpering. Across the smoking fireplace dark-haired Malachias was shaking Geloë, whose mouth hung slack, her lips gleaming wetly. Simon groaned again as his head throbbed, hanging down between his shoulders like a bruised fruit. He crawled to Binabik. The little man was breathing; even as Simon leaned over him the troll began to cough, gasped for air, and opened his eyes.

'We . . .' he rasped, 'we . . . are . . . all here?'

Simon nodded, looking over to Geloë, still motionless despite Malachias' attentions. 'A moment . . .' he said, and slowly got to his feet.

He walked gingerly out the hut's front door, carrying a small, empty pot. He was faintly surprised to see that, despite the pall of fog, it was still full afternoon: the time on the dream-road had seemed much longer than that. He also had the nagging feeling that something else had changed outside the cottage, but could not put his finger on what the difference was. The view seemed slightly off. He decided it must be some effect of his experience. After filling the pot with lake water and washing the sticky green paste from his hands, he returned to the house.

Binabik drank thirstily, then gestured that Simon should take the container to Geloë. Malachias watched, half-hopeful, half-jealous, as Simon carefully took the witch woman's jaw in one hand and splashed a little water into her open mouth. She coughed, then swallowed, and Simon gave her a little more.

As he held her head Simon was suddenly aware that, in some way, Geloë had saved him while they were all walking in dream. As he looked down at the woman, who was breathing more regularly now, he remembered the gray owl who had caught him up when his dream-self had been at its final gasp, and had borne him away.

Geloë and the troll had not expected quite such a circumstance, he sensed; in fact, it was Simon who had put them in such danger. For once, though, he had no feelings of shame over his actions. He had done what needed doing. He had been fleeing the wheel long enough.

'How is she?' Binabik asked.

'I think she will be well,' Simon replied, looking at the witch woman carefully. 'She saved me, didn't she?'

Binabik stared for a moment, hair hung in sweaty spikes on his brown forehead. 'It is likely that she did,' he said finally. 'She is a powerful ally, but even her strength has been by this taxed to the limit.'

'What did it mean?' Simon asked now, releasing Geloë to the supporting arms of Malachias. 'Did you see what I saw? The mountain, and . . . and the lady with the mask, and the book?'

'I wonder if we saw all things the same, Simon,' Binabik answered slowly. 'But I am thinking it is important we wait until Geloë can share her thoughts with us. Perhaps later, when we have eaten. I am full of terrible hunger.'

Simon gave the troll a shaky half-smile, and turned to find Malachias staring at him. The boy started to turn away, then seemed to find some internal resolution and held his stare, until it was Simon who began to feel uncomfortable.

'It was as if the whole house was shaking,' Malachias said abruptly, startling Simon more than a little. The boy's voice was strained, high-pitched and hoarse.

'What do you mean?' Simon asked, fascinated as much by the fact of Malachias speaking as by what he said.

'The whole cottage. While you three sat and stared at the fire, the walls began to . . . to quiver. Like someone picked it up and set it down again.'

'Most likely it was only the way we were moving while we were . . . I mean . . . oh, I don't know.' Simon gave up in disgust. The truth was, he didn't really know anything right at this moment. His brains felt as though they'd been stirred with a stick.

Malachias turned away to give more water to Geloë.

Raindrops suddenly began to patter down onto the windowsill; the gray sky could hold back its burden of storm no longer.

The witch woman was grim. They had pushed aside the soup bowls and sat facing each other on the bare floor: Simon, the troll, and the mistress of the cottage. Malachias, although obviously interested, remained on the bed beside the little girl.

'I saw evil things moving,' Geloë said, and her eyes flashed. 'Evil things that will shake the roots of the world we know.' She had recovered her strength, and something else: she was solemn, and grave as a king in judgment. 'I almost wish we had not taken the dream-path – but that is an idle wish, from the part of me that wants just to be left alone. I see darker days coming, and I fear to be drawn in by events so ill-omened.'

'What do you mean?' Simon asked. 'What was all that? Did you see the mountain, too?'

'Stormspike.' Binabik's voice was strangely flat. Geloë looked over at him, nodded, then turned back to Simon.

'True. It was *Sturmrspeik* we saw, as they call it in Rimmersgard, where it is a legend, as far as Rimmersmen are concerned. Stormspike. The mountain of the Norns.'

'We Qanuc,' Binabik said, 'know Stormspike to be real. But still, the Norns have not been intruding on the affairs of Osten Ard since time beyond time. Why now? It looked to me as if, as if . . .'

'As if they were preparing for war,' Geloë finished for him. 'You are right, if the dream is to be trusted. Whether it was true-seeing, of course, would take a better-trained eye than even mine. But you said the hounds that pursue you wear the brand of Stormspike; that is real evidence in the waking world. I think we can trust this part of the dream, or at least I think we ought to.'

'Preparing for war?' Simon was already confused.

'Against who? And who was the woman in the silver mask?'

Geloë looked very tired. 'The mask? Not a woman. A creature out of legend, you could say, or a creature out of time beyond time, as Binabik put it. That was *Utuk'ku*, the Queen of the Norns.'

Simon felt a chill sweep over him. The wind outside sang a cold and lonely song. 'But what *are* these Norns? Binabik said they were Sithi.'

'The old wisdom says that they were part of the Sithi once,' Geloë responded. 'But they are a lost tribe, or renegades. They never came to Asu'a with the rest of their folk, but disappeared into the unmapped north, the icy lands beyond Rimmersgard and its mountains. They chose to separate themselves from the doings of Osten Ard, although that seems to be changing.'

For a moment Simon saw a flicker of deep unease cross the witch woman's sour, practical face.

*And these Norns are helping Elias chase me?* he thought, feeling panic rise again. *Why am I sunk in this nightmare?*

Then, as if his fright had opened a door in his mind, he remembered something. Unpleasant shapes climbed up from the hidden places in his heart, and he struggled to catch his breath.

'Those . . . those pale people. The Norns. I've seen them before!'

'What!?' Geloë and the troll spoke at the same time, leaning forward. Simon, startled by their intensity, backed away.

'When?' Geloë snapped.

'It happened . . . I *think* it happened: it may have been a dream . . . on the night I ran away from the Hayholt. I was in the lich-yard, and I thought I heard something calling my name – a woman's voice. I was so frightened that I ran away, out of the lich-yard and toward Thisterborg.' There was a stirring on the pallet: Malachias nervously shifting position. Simon ignored him and continued.

'There was a fire on top of Thisterborg, up among the Anger Stones. Do you know them?'

'I do.' Geloë's response was matter of fact, but Simon sensed some weight behind the words he did not understand.

'Well, I was cold and frightened, so I climbed up. I'm sorry, but I was so sure that this was a dream. Perhaps it is.'

'Perhaps. Go on.'

'There were men on the top. They were soldiers, I could tell because they wore armor.' Simon felt a thin sweat break on his palms, and rubbed them together. 'One of them was King Elias. I was frightened even more, then, so I hid. Then . . . then there was a horrible creaking noise, and a black wagon came up the far side of the hill.' It was coming back, all coming back . . . or, at least, it *seemed* like all . . . but there were still empty shadows. 'Those pale-skinned people – the Norns, that's what they were – were with it, several of them, dressed in black robes.'

There was a long pause while Simon struggled to remember. Rain drummed on the cottage roof.

'And?' the valada asked at last, gently.

'Elysia Mother-of-God!' Simon swore, and tears started in his eyes. 'I can't remember! They gave him something, something from the wagon. Other things happened, too, but it feels like it's all under a blanket in my head. I can touch it, but I can't tell what it is! They gave him something! I thought it was a dream!' He buried his face in his hands, trying to squeeze the painful thoughts from his whirling head.

Binabik awkwardly patted Simon's knee. 'This is perhaps answering our other question. I, too, pondered over why the Norns should be readying for battle. I wondered if they would be fighting against Elias the High King, as some age-old grievance against mankind. Now, it has the appearance to me that they are *helping* him. Some kind of bargain has been struck. Possibly it was that which Simon saw. But how? How could Elias ever make such compact with the secretive Norns?'

'Pryrates.' As soon as Simon said it, he was sure it was true. 'Morgenes said that Pryrates opened doors, and that terrible things came through. Pryrates was on that hill, too.'

Valada Geloë nodded her head. 'It makes a kind of sense. A question that must be answered, but one that I am sure is beyond our powers, is – what was the bargaining-tally? What could these two, Pryrates and the king, have to offer to the Norns for their aid?'

They shared a long silence.

'What did the book say?' Simon asked abruptly. 'On the dream-road. Did you see the book, too?'

Binabik thumped the heel of his hand against his chest. 'It was there. The runes I saw were of Rimmersgard: *"Du Svardenvyrd."* In your speech it means: "The Spell of the Swords." '

'Or Weird of the Swords,' Geloë added. 'It is a famous book in the circles of the wise, but it has been long lost. I have never seen it. It is said to have been written by Nisses, a priest who was a counselor to King Hjeldin the Mad.'

'The one Hjeldin's tower is named after?' Simon asked her.

'Yes. That is where Hjeldin and Nisses both died.'

Simon considered. 'I saw three swords, too.'

Binabik looked to Geloë. 'Only shapes was I seeing,' the troll said slowly. 'I thought they might have the look of swords.'

The witch woman had not been sure, either. Simon described the silhouettes, but they meant nothing to her or to Binabik.

'So,' the little man said at last, 'we have learned what from the dream-road – that the Norns are giving aid to Elias? This we guessed. That a strange book is playing some part . . . perhaps? This is a new thing. We are given a dream-glimpse of Stormspike, and the halls of the mountain's queen. We may have learned things that we do not understand yet – still, I am thinking, one thing has changed not at all: we must take ourselves to Naglimund. Valada, your house will be protection for a while, but if Josua lives he has need to know of these things.'

Binabik was interrupted from an unexpected quarter. 'Simon,' Malachias said, 'you said someone called you in the lich-yard. It was *my* voice you heard. I was the one calling you.'

Simon could only gape.

Geloë smiled. 'At last, one of our mysteries begins to speak! Go on, child. Tell them what you must.'

Malachias blushed furiously. 'I . . . my name is not Malachias. It is . . . Marya.'

'But Marya is a girl's name,' Simon began, then broke off at the sight of Geloë's widening grin. 'A *girl*. . . ?' he said lamely. He stared at the strange boy's face, and suddenly saw it for what it was. 'A girl,' he grunted, feeling impossibly stupid.

The witch woman chuckled. 'It was obvious, I must say – or it should have been. She had the advantage of traveling with a troll and a boy, and the cloak of confusing, dangerous events, but I told her the deception could not last.'

'Especially not all the way to Naglimund, and that is where I must go.' Marya rubbed her eyes wearily. 'I have an important message to bear to Prince Josua from his niece, Miriamele. Please do not ask me what it is, for I may not tell you.'

'What of your sister?' Binabik asked. 'She will not be able to travel for a long time.' He, too, squinted at the surprising Marya, as if trying to discover how he had been fooled. It did seem obvious, now.

'She is not my sister,' Marya said sadly. 'Leleth was the princess' handmaiden. We were very close. She was frightened to stay in the castle without me, and was desperate to come along.' She looked down at the sleeping child. 'I should never have brought her. I tried to

490

pull her up into the tree before the dogs caught us. If I had only been stronger . . .'

'It is not clear,' Geloë broke in, 'whether the little girl will *ever* be able to travel. She has not moved far from the brink of death. I am sorry to say it, but it is the truth. You must leave her with me.'

Marya started to protest, but Geloë would not listen. Simon was disturbed to see what he thought was a glimmer of relief in the girl's dark eyes. It angered him to think she would leave the wounded child behind, no matter how important the message.

'So,' Binabik said finally, 'where is it we are now? We still must reach Naglimund, and we are blocked by leagues of forest and the steep slopes of Wealdhelm. Not mentioning those who will be in our pursuit.'

Geloë thought carefully. 'It seems clear to me,' she said, 'that you must get through the forest to *Da'ai Chikiza*. That is an old Sithi place, long-deserted, of course. There you can find the Stile, which is an old road through the hills from a time when the Sithi regularly traveled between there and Asu'a – the Hayholt. It is unused now, except by animals, but it will be the easiest, safest place to cross. I can give you a map in the morning. Yes, Da'ai Chikiza . . .' A deep light kindled in her yellow eyes, and she nodded her head slowly, as if lost in thought. A moment later she blinked, and became her brisk self once more. 'Now you should sleep. We should all sleep. The day's doings have left me limp as a willow branch.'

Simon didn't think so. He thought the witch woman looked strong as an oak tree – but he supposed even an oak could suffer in a storm.

Later, as he lay curled in his cloak, the warm bulk of Qantaqa's somewhat intrusive presence against his legs, he tried to push away thoughts of the terrible mountain. Such things were too vast, too murky. Instead, he wondered what Marya must think of him. A boy, Geloë

491

had called him, a boy who did not know what a girl looked like. But that was not fair – when had there been time to think about it?

Why had she been spying in the Hayholt? For the princess, perhaps? And if it had been Marya who called to him in the lich-yard, why? How had she known his name, why had she bothered to learn it? He didn't remember ever seeing her at the castle – or at least not as a girl.

When he at last floated off into sleep, like a tiny boat pushed out onto a black ocean, he felt as though he pursued a receding light, a patch of brightness just out of reach. Outside the windows, rain covered the dark mirror of Geloë's lake.

# 27

# The Gossamer Towers

He tried to ignore the hand on his shoulder, but could not. Opening his eyes, he found the room still quite dark, two angular siftings of stars the only indication of where the windows stood.

'Let me sleep,' he moaned. 'It's too early!'

'Get up, boy!' came the harsh whisper. It was Geloë, her robe loosely drawn about her. 'There is no time to waste.'

Blinking his dry and painful eyes, Simon looked past the kneeling woman to see Binabik quietly repacking his bag. 'What's going on?' he asked, but the troll seemed too busy to talk.

'I have been outside,' Geloë said. 'The lake has been discovered – I assume by the men who were hunting you.'

Simon sat up quickly and reached for his boots. It all seemed so unreal in the near-darkness; nevertheless, he could feel his heart beating swiftly. 'Usires!' he cursed quietly. 'What shall we do? Will they attack us?'

'I do not know,' Geloë answered as she left him to go and wake Malachias – no, *Marya*, Simon reminded himself. 'There are two camps, one at the lake's far end by the inlet stream, one not far from here. Either they know whose house this is and are trying to decide what to do, or they do not yet know the cottage is here at all. They may have arrived after we put the candles out.'

493

A sudden question occurred to him. 'How do you know they're out at the far end?' He peered through the windows. The lake was again shrouded in fog, and there was no sign of campfires. 'It's so dark,' he finished, and turned back to Geloë. She was certainly not dressed to be out prowling in the woods. Her feet were bare!

But even as he looked at her, at the hastily donned robe and the wet beads of mist clinging to her face and hair, he remembered the great wings of the owl who had flown before them to this lake. He could still feel the strong talons that had carried him away when the hateful thing on the Road of Dreams had been crushing out his life.

'I don't suppose it's important, is it?' he finished at last. 'It's only important that we know they're out there.' Despite the faint moonlight, he saw the witch woman grin.

'Right you are, Simon-boy,' she said softly, then went to help Binabik fill two more bags, one each for Simon and Marya.

'Listen,' Geloë said as Simon, now dressed, came over. 'It is obvious you must get out now, before dawn,' she squinted out at the stars for a moment, 'which will not be long in coming. The question is, how?'

'All we can hope,' Binabik grunted, 'is to slip away and try and pass them in the forest, moving with great quietness. We with certainty cannot *fly*.' He grinned, somewhat sourly. Marya, bundling into a cloak the valada had given her, stared at the troll's smile in puzzlement.

'No,' said Geloë seriously, 'but I also doubt you could slip by those terrible hounds. You may not fly, but you can *float* away. I have a boat tied beneath the house. It is not big, but it will hold you all – Qantaqa too, if she does not frolic around.' She affectionately ruffled the ears of the wolf, who reclined by her squatting master.

'And of what good is that?' Binabik asked. 'Shall we paddle out to the center of the lake, then in the morning dare them to swim and get us?' He finished the last bag and pushed one toward Simon, one toward the girl.

494

'There is an inlet stream,' Geloë said. 'It is small and not very fast-flowing, not even as strong as the one you followed on your way here. With four paddles you can easily make your way out of the lake and up it some ways.' Her faint frown was more contemplative than worried. 'Unfortunately, it also passes by one of the two camps. Well, that is not to be helped. You must simply paddle quietly. Perhaps it will even help in your escape. Such a thickheaded man as your Baron Heahferth – believe me, I have had my dealings with him and his like! – would not credit that his quarry might slide by so near.'

'Heahferth is not giving me worry,' Binabik replied. 'It is that one who is truly leading the hunt – the Black Rimmersman, Ingen Jegger.'

'He probably doesn't even sleep,' added Simon. He didn't like the memory of that one at all.

Geloë made a wry face. 'Never fear, then. Or at least, do not let fear overwhelm you. Some useful distraction or other may occur . . . one never knows.' She stood up. 'Come, boy,' she said to Simon, 'you are good-sized. Help me untie the boat and move it silently to the front door bridge.'

'Can you see it?' Geloë hissed, pointing at a dark shape bobbing on the ebony lake near the far corner of the elevated house. Simon, already knee-deep in the water, nodded his head. 'Go quietly, then,' she said – somewhat unnecessarily, Simon thought.

As he waded around the side, head-high to the cottage's stilted floorboards. Simon decided that he had *not* been mistaken last afternoon, when he had felt that somehow things around the hut had changed. That tree there, roots halfway into the water: he had seen it the first day they had arrived, but then – he was sure, by Usires! – it had been on the cottage's *other* side, near the doorplank. How could a tree move?

He found the boat's tie rope with his fingers and slid them up until he encountered the place where it was tied to a sort of hoop hanging down from the bottom of the cottage. As he bent down at a back-aching angle to try and work the knot loose, he wrinkled his nose against the strange reek. Was it the lake, or the underside of the house itself that smelled so? Beside the odor of damp wood and mold, there was also a kind of odd, animal scent – warm and musky, but not unpleasant.

Even as he squinted into the darkness the shadows lightened a bit; he could even see the knot! His pleasure at that, and the rapid untying that followed, was dashed by the cold realization that dawn would be coming soon: the fading darkness was his friend. After pulling the tie line loose, he began wading back, towing the boat quietly behind him. He could just discern the dim shape of Geloë standing huddled beside the long plank that sloped from the hut's entrance; he headed toward her as quickly as he could . . . until he tripped.

With a splash and a muffled cry, he half-fell down onto one knee, then drew himself upright. What had caught at him? It felt like a log. He tried to step over the obstruction, but merely succeeded in putting his bare foot down directly on top of it, and had to stifle the urge to cry out again. Although it lay unmoving and solid, still it had the scaly feel of one of the pikefish from the Hayholt's moat, or one of the stuffed cockindrills Morgenes had kept perched on his shelves. As the ripples quieted, and he heard Geloë's quiet but wary voice asking if he had hurt himself, he looked down.

Although the water was very nearly opaque in the darkness, Simon was sure he could see the outlines of some strange type of log, or rather a vast *branch* of some kind, for he could see that the thing he had tripped over, lying close beneath the surface of the water, joined two other scaly branches. Together they seemed connected to the base of one of the two pillars on which the cottage stood suspended over the lake.

And as he stepped carefully over it, sliding silently through the water toward the shadow that was Geloë, he suddenly realized that what the tree roots – or branches, or whatever they were – what they truly looked like was . . . some kind of monstrous *foot*. A claw, actually, the claw of a bird. What a funny idea! A house did not have bird's feet, anymore than a house got up and . . . walked.

Simon was very quiet as Geloë tied the boat up to the base of the plank.

Everything and everybody was packed into the tiny boat: Binabik perched in the pointed prow, Marya in the middle, Simon seated in the stern with a restless Qantaqa between his knees. The wolf was obviously very uncomfortable; she had whined and resisted when Binabik ordered her into the little craft. He had finally needed to smack her lightly on the snout. The discomfort on the little man's face showed clearly even in the predawn darkness.

The moon had swung far into the blue-black vault of the lightening western sky. Geloë, after handing them the paddles, straightened up.

'Once you have gotten safely out of the lake and a bit upstream, I think you should probably carry the boat overland through the forest to the Aelfwent. It is not a very heavy craft, and you don't need to carry it far. The river is flowing the proper direction, and should get you to Da'ai Chikiza.'

Binabik reached out with his paddle and pushed the boat away from the plank. Geloë stood ankle-deep at the lake's edge as they spun gently out from the shore.

'Remember,' she whispered, 'edge those paddles into the water as you reach the inlet stream. Silence! That is your protection.'

Simon raised his palm. 'Farewell, Valada Geloë.'

'Farewell, young pilgrim.' Her voice was already growing faint, with less than three cubits between them. 'Good luck to you all. Fear not! I will take good care of the little girl.' They slid quietly away, until the witch woman was only a shadow beside the house's near stilt.

The prow of the little boat cut through the water like a barber's blade through silk. At Binabik's gesture they lowered their heads, and the troll silently guided the craft toward the center of a misty lake. As Simon huddled into the thick fur of Qantaqa's back, feeling the pulse of her nervous breath, he watched tiny rings form on the lake's surface beside the boat; at first he thought it might be fish, up early to break their fast on mayflies and mosquitos. Then he felt a tiny drop of moisture splash on the back of his neck, and another. It was raining again.

As they neared the middle, cutting through swarms of hyacinths that lay scattered on the water before them as though cast in the path of a returning hero, the sky began to brighten. Dawn did not announce its arrival: it would be hours before the sun cut through the clouds and became visible in the sky. Rather, it was as if a layer of darkness had been stripped away from the heavens, the first of many veils. The line of trees that had been a blot of obscurity on the horizon became a thatch of distinguishable treetops profiled against the slate-gray sky. The water was black glass around them, but now some details of the shoreline could be seen, the faint, pale tree roots like the twisted legs of beggars, the dim silver shine of a granite outcropping – all standing around the secret lake like a court gallery waiting for the players to arrive, all slowly metamorphosing from gray night shapes to the vivid objects of day.

Qantaqa hunched, surprised, as Marya suddenly leaned forward to peer over the gunwale of the boat. She started to say something, checked herself, and instead pointed a finger out across the bow and slightly to the right.

Simon squinted, then saw it: an anomalous shape in the orderless but somehow symmetrical forest fringe, a square, blocky shape that was a different color from the dark branches around it – a striped blue tent.

Now they could see several more, a crowd of three or four just behind the first. Simon scowled, then smiled disdainfully. How typical of the Baron Heahferth – from what he had heard in his days at the castle, anyway – to carry such luxuries out into the wild forest.

Just beyond the scatter of small tents the lakeshore dipped back for several ells, then reappeared again, leaving a dark space in the middle as though a bite had been taken from the shoreline. Tree branches hung low over the water there; it was impossible to see if it was truly the river inlet, but Simon felt sure that it was.

*Right where Geloë said!* he thought. *Sharp, sharp eyes she's got – but then, that's not much of a surprise, is it?*

He pointed to the dark break in the lake's rim, and Binabik nodded: he had seen it, too.

As they neared the silent camp. Binabik had to paddle a bit harder to keep them scudding along at a good pace; Simon guessed that they must be starting to feel the push of the feeder stream. He delicately lifted his paddle to lower it over the side. Binabik, catching the movement from the corner of his eye, turned and shook his head, silently mouthing *'not yet'*; Simon stopped the small paddle just above the rain-puckered water.

As they slid past the tents, not thirty ells from the shore, Simon saw a dark shape moving among the walls of azure cloth. His throat tightened. It was a sentry: he could see the dull sheen of metal beneath the cloak. He might even be facing in their direction, but it was difficult to tell, for he had the hood of his cloak up around his head.

Within instants the others had also seen the man. Binabik slowly lifted his paddle from the water and they all leaned forward, hoping to show as little profile as possible. Even if the soldier chanced to look out onto the lake, perhaps his eye would pass over them, or see only a log bobbing on the water – but that was really too much to hope for, Simon felt sure. He could not imagine the man failing to spot them if he turned, close as they were.

Even as the progress of the little craft slowed, the dark gap in the shoreline came up before them. It *was* the inlet stream: Simon could see the water rippling faintly where it passed over the rounded back of a stone some few yards up the channel. It had also nearly stopped their forward motion; as a matter of fact, the nose of the boat was beginning to come around, rebuffed by the mild current. They would have to put paddles in the water soon, or be pushed into the bank just below the blue tents.

Then, finished with whatever had caught his attention at the far side of the camp, the sentry turned around to gaze out across the lake.

Within an instant, even before the mounting fear could truly take hold of them, a dark shape dropped from the trees over the camp and skimmed swiftly toward the sentry. It sailed through the branches like a huge gray leaf and fetched up against his neck, but *this* leaf had talons; when he felt them at his throat the armored man gave a shout of horror and dropped his spear, beating at whatever had clutched him. The gray shape fluttered up, wings churning, and hung over his head just beyond his reach. He shouted again, clutching his neck, and fumbled in the dirt for his spear.

'Now!' Binabik hissed. 'Paddle!' He and Marya and Simon drove the wooden blades into the water, pulling desperately. For the first few strokes they seemed somehow snagged, water splashing purposelessly as the boat rocked. Then they began to ease forward, and within moments were pushing against the stronger current of the stream, sliding in beneath the overarching branches.

Simon looked back to see the sentry, head bare, leaping up and down trying to swat the hovering creature. A few of the other men sat up from their bedrolls, beginning to laugh as they watched their comrade, who had dropped his spear and was now throwing rocks at this daft, dangerous bird. The owl dodged the missiles with ease; as Simon lowered the curtain of leafy branches down behind the boat it gave a flirt of its wide white tail and circled up into the shadowed trees.

As they strained forward against the difficult current – surprisingly difficult, since on the surface it did not appear to be moving at all – Simon gave a quiet chortle of triumph.

For a long time they paddled hard against the river's flow. Even had they not felt the need for silence they would have been hard-pressed to make any conversation, the paddling was such strenuous work. At last, close to an hour later, they found a small backwater hedged in by a secretive screen of reeds where they could stop and rest.

The sun was now well up, a glowing blur behind a pearly, sky-wide canopy of clouds. A film of mist still clung to the forest and river, so that their surroundings seemed the landscape of a dream. Somewhere up ahead the stream was passing through or over some obstacle; the quiet purr of moving water was augmented by the chimelike tones of the watercourse leaping and splashing back upon itself.

Simon, panting, watched the girl Marya as she leaned on the gunwale, her cheek resting on her forearm. It was hard to understand how he had ever mistaken her for a boy. What he had seen as foxlike, as a sharpness of feature unusual in a boy, he now saw as delicacy. She was flushed with exertion; Simon stared at her ruddy cheek, and his eye moved down the white length of her extended neck, to the gentle but well-defined protrusion of her collarbone where the boy's shirt she wore gaped open at the throat.

*She's not well-padded . . . not like Hepzibah*, he mused. *Huh! I'd like to see Hepzibah pass as a boy! Still, she's pretty in a kind of thin way. Her hair's so very black.*

Marya's eyes fluttered closed. She continued to breathe deeply. Simon absently stroked Qantaqa's wide head.

'Well made, is she not?' Binabik asked cheerfully. Simon gaped at him, startled.

'What?'

Binabik frowned. 'I am sorry. Perhaps you are calling them "him" in Erkynland? "It," possibly? Still, you must agree that Geloë has done a job of great craft.'

'Binabik,' Simon said, his blush beginning to fade, 'I don't have any idea what you are talking about.'

The little man pounded the gunwale softly with the flat of his hand. 'What a nice work Geloë has accomplished with bark and wood. And so light! We shall not have much trouble, I am thinking, to carry this overland to the Aelfwent.'

'The boat . . .' Simon said, nodding like a village idiot. 'The boat. Yes, it *is* well made.'

Marya sat up. 'Are we going to try and cross to the other river now?' she asked. As she turned again to look out across the thin strip of forest visible through the reeds, Simon noticed the dark circles under her eyes, her strained look. In a way, he was still upset with her for being relieved when Geloë volunteered to keep the child, but he was glad to see that this servant girl seemed concerned, that she wasn't just the kind of girl who laughed and teased all the time.

*Well of course she's not,* he thought a moment later. *As a matter of fact, I don't think I've seen her smile yet. Not that things haven't been frightening – but you don't see* **me** *always frowning and moping.*

'That might perhaps be a good idea,' Binabik said, responding to Marya's question. 'I believe that the noise which is sounding ahead is a gathering of rocks in the stream. If that is being the case, we would anyway have little choice but to carry the boat around. Perhaps Simon would go find out.'

'How many years old are you?' Simon asked Marya. Binabik, surprised, turned around and stared. Marya quirked her lips and looked at Simon for a long moment.

'I am . . .' she began, then paused. 'I will have sixteen years in Octander.'

'Fifteen, then,' said Simon, a little smugly.

'And you?' the girl challenged.

502

Simon bristled. 'Fifteen!'

Binabik coughed. 'Well and good that shipmates should have acquaintance of each other, but . . . perhaps later. Simon, could you go to see if those are indeed rocks ahead?'

He was about to agree, then suddenly did not want to. Was he an errand boy? A child, to run and find out things for the grown-ups? Who had made the decision to go and rescue this stupid girl from a tree, anyway?

'As long as we need to cross to the whatever-it's-called, why bother?' he said. 'Let's just do it.'

The troll stared, then at length nodded his head. 'Very well. I think it will do my friend Qantaqa good to be stretching her legs, besides.' He turned to Marya. 'Wolves are not sailors, you know.'

Now for a few moments Marya stared at Binabik as if he were odder than Simon. Then she burst into ringing laughter.

'That's very true!' she said, and laughed again.

The canoe was indeed feathery light, but they still had difficulty carrying it through the clinging branches and creepers. To keep it at a height where both Binabik and the girl could help bear the load they had to hold the upside-down boat in such a way that the sharp angle of the stern kept thumping against Simon's breastbone. He couldn't see his feet as he walked, either, with the result that time and again he was tripped up in the under-growth. Rain showered down through the overhanging net of boughs and leaves; with his hands occupied, Simon could not even wipe away the drops that ran into his eyes. He was not in the best of all possible moods.

'How far *is* it, Binabik?' he asked at last. 'My chest is being battered to pieces by this by-Usires damnable boat.'

'Not far, I am hoping,' the troll called, his voice echoing strangely from beneath the stretched-bark shell. 'Geloë said that the inlet stream and the Aelfwent run side

503

by side for a long distance, being only a quarter of a league or so apart. Soon we should reach it.'

'Soon it had better be,' Simon said grimly. In front of him Marya made a noise that he was sure was a sound of disgust – disgust with him, probably. He scowled horribly, red hair stringy and wet on his forehead.

At last they heard another sound above the soft drumming of raindrops on leaves, a breathy rush that made Simon think of a room full of murmuring people. Qantaqa leaped ahead, clattering through the underbrush.

'Hah!' Binabik grunted, laying his end of the boat down. 'You see? We have found it! *T'si Suhyasei!*'

'I thought it was named Aelfwent.' Marya rubbed the place where the boat had rested on her shoulder. 'Or is that what trolls always say when they find a river?'

Binabik smiled. 'No. That is a Sithi name. It is a Sithi river, in a way, since they used to be boating upon it when Da'ai Chikiza was their city. You should be knowing that. Aelfwent *means* "Sithi river" in the old tongue of Erkynland.'

'Then what does . . . what you said mean?' Marya asked.

'T'si Suhyasei?' Binabik thought. 'Hard it is to say, exactly. It means something like: "her blood is cool." '

'Her?' Simon asked, digging mud from his boots with a stick. 'What's "her" this time?'

'The forest,' Binabik replied. 'Come now. You can be washing that mud off in the water.'

They carried the boat down the bank, pushing it through a thicket of cattails only with a great deal of stem snapping, until the river was before them – a wide, healthy expanse of water, far bigger than the inlet stream, and with what looked like a far stronger current. They had to lower the boat down into the gully carved by the river's passage; Simon, the tallest, wound up standing knee–deep in the shallows to receive the boat – his boots were indeed washed clean. He held the bobbing craft as

504

Marya and the troll first levered a doubtful Qantaqa over the edge – without much help from the wolf herself – then followed after. Simon climbed in last, taking his place in the stern.

'Your positioning, Simon,' Binabik told him gravely, 'requires great responsibility. We shall find little need to paddle with a current of such vigor, but you must steer, and you must call out when there are rocks ahead so we can all help push away from them.'

'I can do it,' he said quickly. Binabik nodded and let go of the long branch he had been clutching; they eased off from the bank and out onto the surging Aelfwent.

It was a little difficult at first, Simon found. Some of the rocks that they needed to avoid were not even visible above the water's glassy surface; rather, they lay just below, only recognizable by the shiny humps made by the water above them. The first one that Simon did *not* see made a horrible noise scraping along the taut hull, giving them all a moment's scare, but the little boat bounded away from the submerged stone like a sheep fleeing the shears. Soon Simon had the feel of it; in spots the craft seemed almost to skim the top of the water, weightless as a leaf on the river's undulating back.

As they hit a stretch of smoother water, the clamor of the rocks falling away behind them, Simon felt his heart swell within his chest. The playful hands of the river tugged his trailing paddle. A memory of climbing on the Hayholt's broad battlements came to him – breathless with his own power, with the sight of the ordered fields lying so far below. He remembered, too, crouching in the bell chamber of Green Angel Tower, looking down on the huddling houses of Erchester, staring out over the broad world with the wind in his face. Now, in the stern of the little boat, he was again both of the world and above it, far above it, sailing like the spring wind gusting through the treetops. He lifted the paddle in the air before him . . . it was now a sword.

'*Usires was a sailor,*' he abruptly sang, the words

coming back to him in a rush. It was a tune someone had sung to him when he was very young.

> *'Usires was a sailor*
> *He went upon the ocean*
> *He took the Word of God*
> *And he went sailing to Nabban-o!'*

Binabik and Marya turned to look at him; Simon grinned.

> *'Tiyagaris was a soldier*
> *He went upon the ocean*
> *He took the Word of Justice*
> *And went sailing to Nabban-o!*
>
> *King John he was a ruler*
> *He went upon the ocean*
> *He took the word of Aedon*
> *And went sailing to Nabban-o! . . .'*

He trailed off.

'Why do you stop?' Binabik asked. Marya still stared, a speculative look in her eye.

'That's all I know,' Simon said, lowering his paddle back into the boat's rippling wake. 'I don't even know where it's from. I think one of the chambermaids used to sing it when I was small.'

Binabik smiled. 'A good song for river travel, I am thinking, although some of the details have not much historical correctness. Are you sure you can remember no more?'

'That's it.' His failure to recall troubled him little. Just a short hour on the river had redeemed his mood entirely. He had been on a fisherman's boat in the bay, and had enjoyed it . . . but that was nothing to this, to the forest rushing by, and the feeling of the delicate boat beneath him, as sensitive and responsive as a colt.

506

'I have no sailing songs to sing,' the troll said, pleased by Simon's change of mood. 'In high Qanuc the rivers are ice, and used only for the sliding games of trollings. I could be singing perhaps of mighty Chukku, and his adventures . . .'

'I know a river song,' said Marya, running a slender white hand through her thatch of black hair. 'The streets of Meremund are full of sailor's songs.'

'Meremund?' Simon asked. 'How did a castle girl ever get to Meremund?'

Marya curled her lip at him. 'And where do you think the princess and all her court lived before we came to the Hayholt – the wilds of Nascadu?' She snorted. 'Meremund, of course. It is the most beautiful city in the world, where the ocean and the great river Gleniwent meet. *You* wouldn't know, you haven't been there.' She grinned wickedly. 'Castle boy.'

'Then sing!' Binabik said, waving his hand before him. 'The river waits to hear. The forest, too!'

'I hope I remember,' she said, sneaking a glance at Simon, who haughtily returned it – her remark had barely touched the buoyancy of his mood. 'It's a river rider song,' she continued, then cleared her throat and began – tentatively at first, then more confidently – to sing in a sweet, throaty voice.

> '. . . *Now those who sail the Big Pond*
> *Will tell you of its mystery*
> *They'll brag of all those battles*
> *And all that bloody history*
>
> *But talk to any river-dog*
> *Who sails upon the Gleniwent*
> *He'll say God made the oceans*
> *But the River's what he really meant*
>
> *Oh, the Ocean is a question*
> *But the River is an answer*
> *With her rollicking and frolicking*

*As fine as any dancer*
*So let Hell take the shirkers*
*For this old boat won't carry 'em*
*And if we lose some crew or two*
*We'll drink to 'em at Meremund . . .*

*Now some men go away to sea*
*And they're never seen again*
*But every night we river-dogs*
*Are found down at the inn*

*And some may say we drink a bit*
*And punch it up a mite*
*But if the river is your lady*
*That's just how you rest at night*

*Oh, the Ocean is a question*
*But the River is an answer*
*When her rollicking and frolicking*
*As fine as any dancer*
*So let Hell take the shirkers*
*For this old boat won't carry 'em*
*And if we lose some crew or two*
*We'll drink to 'em at Meremund . . .*

*In Meremund! In Meremund!*
*We'll drink to 'em in Meremund*
*If we don't spy 'em floating by*
*It'll save the penny to bury 'em. . . !'*

By the time Marya had gotten to the chorus the second time around, Simon and Binabik knew the words well enough to join in. Qantaqa flattened her ears as they hooted and shouted down the swift-racing Aelfwent.

'Oh the Ocean is a question, but the River is an answer . . .' Simon was singing at the top of his lungs when the nose of the boat dipped down into a trough and bounced up: they were among the rocks again. By the time they had negotiated the roiling waters and were out into the clear, they were all too breathless for singing. Simon, however, was still grinning, and as the gray clouds above the forest roof opened, showering down more rain, he tilted his chin up and caught the drops on his tongue.

'Raining, now,' Binabik said, eyebrows arched beneath the hair plastered to his forehead. 'I am thinking we shall get wet.'

The brief instant of silence was pierced by the troll's high-pitched, gusting laugh.

When the light filtering down through the canopy of trees began to dim, they steered the boat to the side and made camp. After building a fire, using his sack of yellow dust to kindle the damp wood, Binabik produced a parcel of fresh vegetables and fruits from one of the packs Geloë had provided. Qantaqa, left to her own devices, went slinking off into the tall brush, returning some time later with her fur soaking wet and a few streaks of blood adorning her muzzle. Simon looked at Marya, who was meditatively sucking on a peach pit, to see what her reaction would be to this evidence of the brutal side of the wolf's nature, but if the girl noticed she showed no signs of unease.

*She must have worked in the princess' kitchens*, he guessed. *Still, if I had one of Morgenes' stuffed lizards to slip in her cloak,* **then** *she'd jump, I'll wager.*

Thinking about her working in castle kitchens set him to wondering just what it was she *had* done in the princess' service – and now that he thought of it, what had she been doing spying on *him*? But when he tried to ask her questions about the princess, she only shook her head, saying that she could not say anything about her mistress or her services until the message had been delivered at Naglimund.

'I am hoping you will forgive my asking,' Binabik said as he packed away the few supper things and took his walking stick apart, producing at last his flute, 'but what is your plan if Josua is not *at* Naglimund, for receiving your message?'

Marya looked disturbed by this, but still would not say anything more. Simon was tempted to ask Binabik about *their* plans, about Da'ai Chikiza and the Stile, but the troll was already tootling absently on his flute. Night pulled a blanket of darkness over all the great Aldheorte but their tiny fire. Simon and Marya sat listening as the troll set his music to swooping and echoing in the rainy treetops.

They were on the river soon after sunup the next day. The rhythms of the moving water now seemed as familiar as a child's rhyme: the long idle stretches in which it seemed that their boat was a rock upon which they sat while the vast sea of trees marched by on either side, then the dangerous excitement of the fast-running rapids that shook the frail craft as though it were a hooked and wriggling fish. The rain let up in mid-morning, and in its place the sun sprinkled down through the overhanging branches, dotting the river and forest floor with puddles of light.

The welcome respite from the weather – unusually wintry for late Maia, Simon couldn't help noticing, remembering the icy mountain of their shared dream – kept their spirits high. As they floated along through the tunnel of leaning trees, broken here and there by majestic sheets of sunlight that streamed down through gaps in the tangled branches to turn the river briefly into a mirror of polished, golden glass, they entertained each other with talk. Simon, reluctantly at first, told of the people he had known at the castle – Rachel, Tobas the dogkeeper, who daubed his nose black with lamp grease to more easily pass as family among his charges, Peter Gilded-Bowl, giant Ruben and the rest. Binabik spoke more of his journeying, of his youthful travels to the brackish Wran-country and the dismal, exotic wastelands east of his Mintahoq home. Even Marya, despite her initial reticence and the large area of unapproachable topics, made Simon and the troll smile with her imitations of river-sailor and ocean-mariner arguments, and her

510

observations about some of the dubious nobility that surrounded the Princess Miriamele at Meremund and the Hayholt.

Only once did the conversation of the second day's boating turn to the darker subjects that shadowed all the companions' thoughts.

'Binabik,' Simon asked, as they took their midday meal in a sunlit patch of forest-meadow, 'do you really think we've left those men behind? Might there be others looking for us, too?'

The troll flicked an apple pip from his chin. 'I do not know *anything* with sureness, friend Simon – as I have already been saying. Sure I am that we slipped by, that there was no immediate pursuit, but since I cannot be knowing why exactly they seek us, I cannot know whether they can find us. Do they know we are bound for Naglimund? That is not a difficult thing to be supposing. *But*, three things there are in our favor.'

'What things?' Marya asked, a slight frown on her face.

'First, it is easier to hide than find in a forest.' He held up a stubby finger. 'Second, we are taking a back route to Naglimund that is not well-known for hundreds of years.' Another finger. 'Last, to find out our route, those men will have to hear it from Geloë,' his third finger straightened, 'and that is a thing that will not, I think, happen.'

Simon had been secretly worrying about just this. 'Won't they hurt her? Those were men with swords and spears, Binabik. Owls won't scare them off forever if they think we're with her.'

A grave nod. The troll tented his short fingers. 'I am not being unconcerned, Simon. Daughter of the Mountains, I am not! But you know little of Geloë. To think of her only as a village wise woman is to be making a mistake, a mistake Heahferth's men may regret if they do not treat her with respect. A long time Valada Geloë has walked Osten Ard: she has been many years in the forest, and many, many years before that among the

511

Rimmersgarders. Even preceding that, she was coming up from the south into Nabban, and her travels before no one knows. She is one who can be trusted for taking care of herself – far more than I, or even, as was proved with such sadness, that good man Morgenes.' He reached for another apple, the last in the bag. 'But that is enough of such worrying. The river is waiting, and our hearts must be light, so we can faster travel.'

Later in the afternoon, as the shadows of the trees began to blend together into one large blotch of shade stretched across the river, Simon learned more of the mysteries of the Aelfwent.

He was digging through his pack, searching for a bit of rag to wrap around his hands, to protect them from the blisters raised by the coarse paddle. He found something that felt like what he was searching for and pulled it out. It was the White Arrow, still bound in the tattered hem of his shirt. It was surprising to suddenly have it in his hand again, to feel its delicacy laying in his palm like a feather that might be swept away in the first errant breeze. He carefully unwrapped the shielding cloth.

'Look here,' he said to Marya, reaching past Qantaqa to show it nestled on its blanket of rag. 'It's a Sithi White Arrow. I saved the life of a Sitha-man and he gave it to me.' He reconsidered briefly. 'Shot it at me, actually.'

It was a beautiful thing; in the dimming light it was almost luminous, like the shimmering breast of a swan. Marya looked at it for a moment, then touched it with a raised finger.

'It's pretty,' she said, but in her tone there was none of the admiration Simon had hoped to hear.

'Of *course* it's pretty! It's sacred. It means a debt owed. Ask Binabik, he'll tell you.'

'Simon is correct,' the troll called back from the prow. 'That was happening just before we met.'

Marya continued to regard the arrow calmly, as though her mind flew elsewhere. 'It's a lovely thing,' she

512

said, only slightly more conviction in her voice than the time before. 'You're very lucky, Simon.'

He didn't know why, but that made him furious. Didn't she realize what he had been through? Lich-yards, trapped Sithi, the hounds, the enmity of a High King!? Who was *she*, to answer like one of the chambermaids absentmindedly soothing him when he had skinned a knee?

'Of course,' he said, holding the arrow up before him so it caught a beam of near-horizontal sunlight, the riverbank a moving tapestry behind it, 'of course, for all the luck it's brought me so far – attacked, bitten, hungry, chased – I might as well have never got it.' He stared at it crossly, running his eyes over the carvings that might have been the story of his life since he had left the Hayholt, complicated but meaningless.

'I really might as well throw it away,' he said casually. He never *would*, of course, but it was strangely satisfying to pretend that he might. 'I mean to say, what good has it brought me. . . ?'

Binabik's warning cry came in midsentence, but by the time Simon could sort things out it was too late. The boat struck the hidden rock almost directly; the craft lurched, stern breaching the water with a sucking splash. The arrow flew from Simon's hand to go spinning through the air and into the water churning around the rocks. As the boat's rear smacked down, Simon turned to look for it; a moment later they skidded off another submerged stone and he was falling, the boat tipping, falling. . . .

The water was shockingly cold. For an instant it was as though he had fallen through some hole in the world into absolute night. Then he was gasping, breaking the surface, whirling crazily in the turbulent water. He struck a rock, spun away and went under again, terrifying water pushing the air from his nose and mouth. Struggling he got his head to the top again and tensed as the swirling current battered him against one hard object after another. He felt wind on his face for a moment and sucked in, coughing; he felt some of the praise-Usires air making its way into his burning lungs. Then, suddenly, the rocks were past and he was floating free, kicking to keep his head above the plane of the river. To his surprise, the boat was *behind* him now, just sliding around the last of the hump-backed stones. Binabik and Marya were paddling hard, eyes round with fear, but Simon saw the distance gradually growing wider. He was slipping downstream, and as he pivoted his head wildly to either side he saw the riverbanks were shockingly far away. He gasped in another great clout of air.

'Simon!' Binabik yelled. 'Swim back to us! We cannot row fast enough!'

Floundering, he tried to turn about and struggle back to them, but the river pulled him with a thousand invisible fingers. He splashed, trying to form his hands into the paddle shapes Rachel – Morgenes? – had once shown him as they held him suspended in the shallows of the Kynslagh, but the effort seemed laughable against the all-pervading power of the current. He was tiring fast; he could not find his legs anymore, felt nothing but a cold emptiness when he tried to make them kick. The water splashed up into his eyes, prisming the reaching tree branches as he slipped back under the surface.

Something smacked down beside his hand, and he beat his arms against the cold water to climb back up one last time. It was Marya's paddle. With her longer reach she had pushed up to Binabik's place in the prow and stretched out, extending the flat piece of wood to within inches of his grasp. Qantaqa was standing beside her, barking, straining forward almost in mimicry of the girl; the canoe, with so much weight forward, was leaning dangerously.

Simon sent a thought back to where his legs had been, told them to kick if they could hear him, and threw out his hand. He barely felt the paddle as he curled his numb fingers about it, but it was there, just where he needed it to be.

After they had hauled him over the side – a nearly impossible task in itself, since he weighed more than any of them except the wolf – and after he had coughed out or thrown up great quantities of river water, he lay panting and shivering, curled in a ball at the bottom of the boat while the girl and the troll searched for a spot to make landing.

He recovered enough strength to crawl out of the boat by himself on shaking legs. As he fell on his knees, spreading grateful palms on the soft forest floor, Binabik reached down and plucked something loose from the sodden, ragged mess that was Simon's shirt.

'See what was caught up in your clothes,' Binabik said, an odd look on his face. It was the White Arrow. 'Let us make a fire for you, poor Simon. Perhaps you have had a lesson – a cruel lesson, but a serious one – about speaking ill of Sithi gifts while sailing on a Sithi river.'

Denied even the strength to be embarrassed as Binabik helped him shed his clothes and wrapped him in his cloak, Simon fell asleep in front of the blessed fire. His dreams were unsurprisingly dark, full of things that clutched and smothered.

Clouds hovered low the following morning. Simon felt very sick. After chewing and swallowing a couple of strips of dried meat – against the protestations of his queasy stomach – he clambered gingerly into the boat, letting Marya take the stern this time while he huddled in the middle, Qantaqa's warm bulk pressed against him. He slept on and off throughout the long day on the river. The sliding green blur that was the forest made him dizzy, and his head felt hot and much too large, like a potato swelling on the coals. Both Binabik and Marya checked the progress of his fever solicitously. When he woke from the sludgy doze he had fallen into while his two companions ate lunch, and found them bending over him, Marya's cool palm on his forehead, his confused thought was: *What a strange mother and father I have!*

515

They halted for the night just as twilight began creeping through the trees. Simon, swaddled in his cloak like an infant, sat close to the fire, unwrapping his arms only long enough to drink some soup the troll had prepared, a broth of dried beef, turnips and onions.

'We must be getting up with the first footsteps of the sun tomorrow,' Binabik said, proffering the stem end of a turnip to the wolf, who sniffed it with benign indifference. 'Close we are to Da'ai Chikiza, but it would be senseless to come upon it at night when it could not be properly seen. In any way, we will have a long climbing up the Stile from there, and may as well undertake it when the day is warm.'

Simon watched blearily as the troll pulled Morgenes' manuscript from one of the packs and unwrapped it, squatting close to the flickering campfire and tilting the pages to read; he looked like a little monk at prayer over his Book of the Aedon. The wind rustled through the trees overhead, knocking loose water drops that had clung to the leaves, remnants of the afternoon's shower. Mixed in with the dull rush of the waters below was the insistent piping of the tiny river frogs.

It took Simon a while to realize that the soft pressure against his shoulder was not just another strange message from his sick, discomforted body. He laboriously turned his chin past the collar of his heavy wool cloak, freeing a hand to shoo Qantaqa off, only to see Marya's dark head resting on his upper arm, mouth slightly open, breath easing in and out with the rhythms of sleep.

Binabik looked over. 'It was a hard day of working, today,' he smiled. 'Much paddling. If it is not paining you, let her stay there a bit.' He turned back to the manuscript.

Marya stirred against him and murmured something. Simon tugged the cloak that Geloë had loaned her up higher; as it touched her cheek she half-muttered something, reached up a hand and patted clumsily at Simon's chest, then squirmed a little nearer.

516

The sound of her even breathing so close to his ear threaded its way in among the noises of river and night forest. Simon shivered, and felt his eyes becoming heavy, so heavy . . . but his heart was beating swiftly, and it was the sound of his restless blood that led him down a path toward warm darkness.

In the gray, diffuse light of a rainy dawn, with eyes still sticky with sleep and bodies queerly unresponsive from their too-early start, they saw the first bridge.

Simon was in the stern again. Despite the disorientation of boarding the boat and joining the river in near-darkness, he felt better than he had the day before: still light-headed, but much more fit. As they rounded a bend in the river, which leaped along happily, careless of the hour, he saw a strange shape arched across the water ahead. Wiping his eyes free for a moment of the misty drizzle that seemed not so much to fall as to hang in the air, he squinted.

'Binabik,' he asked, leaning forward, 'is that a . . .'

'A bridge it is, yes,' the troll replied cheerily. 'The Gate of Cranes, I think it must be.'

The river bore them ever closer, and they shipped water with their paddles to slow down. The bridge stretched up from the choking undergrowth of the river bank to extend in a slender arc into the trees on the other side. Carved in pale, translucent green stone, it seemed delicate as a span of frozen sea foam. Once covered with intricate carvings, now much of its surface was obscured by moss and twining ivy; the spots that showed through had been worn down, the whorls and curves and hard angles softened, rounded by wind and rain. Perched at its apex, directly over their heads as the little boat slid underneath, a cream-green, translucent stone bird spread its water-worn wings.

They passed through the faint shadow in moments, and were out the other side. The forest suddenly seemed

517

to breathe antiquity, as though they had slid through an open door into the past.

'Long ago have the river roads been swallowed up by Oldheart,' Binabik said quietly as they all turned to watch the bridge dwindling behind them. 'Perhaps even the other works of the Sithi will be fading someday.'

'How could people cross over a river on such a thing?' Marya wondered. 'It looked so . . . so fragile.'

'More fragile than it was once, that is certain,' Binabik said with a wistful backward glance. 'But the Sithi never built . . . never *build* . . . for beauty alone. Their works have strength. Does not the tallest tower in Osten Ard, the work of their hands, still stand in your Hayholt?'

Marya nodded, thinking. Simon trailed his fingers in the cold water.

They passed eleven more bridges, or 'gates' as Binabik called them, since they had for a thousand years or more marked the river entrance to Da'ai Chikiza. Each gate was named for an animal, the troll explained, and corresponded to a phase of the moon. One by one, they drifted beneath Foxes, Roosters, Hares and Doves, each one slightly different in shape, made of pearly moonstone or bright lapis, but all unmistakably the work of the same sublime and reverent hands.

By the time the sun had climbed behind the clouds to its midmorning station they were just slipping beneath the Gate of Nightingales. On the far side of this span, on whose proud carvings flecks of gold still glimmered, the river began to turn, bearing west one more time toward the unseen eastern flank of the Wealdhelm Hills. There were no surface-roiling rocks here; the current moved swiftly and evenly. Simon was in the midst of asking Marya a question when Binabik raised his hand.

As they rounded a bend it was before them: a forest of impossibly graceful towers, set like a jeweled puzzle within the larger forest of trees. The Sithi city, flanking the river on either side, seemed to grow out of the very soil. It seemed the forest's own dream realized in subtle stone, a hundred shades of green and white and pale summer-sky blue. It was an immense thicket of needle-thin stone, of gossamer walkways like bridges of spider-web, of filagreed tower tops and minarets reaching up into the high treetops to catch sun on their faces like icy flowers. The world's past lay open before them, breath-taking and heartrending. It was the most beautiful thing Simon had ever seen.

But as they floated into the city, the river winding around the slender columns, it became apparent that the forest was reclaiming Da'ai Chikiza. The tiled towers, intricate with cracks, were netted in ivy and the twining branches of trees. In many places, where once there had been walls and doors of wood or some other perishable substance, the stone outlines now stood precariously unsupported, like the bleached skeletons of incredible sea creatures. Everywhere the vegetation was thrusting in, clinging to the delicate walls, smothering the whisper-thin spires in uncaring leaves.

In a way, Simon decided, it only made it more beautiful, as though the forest, restless and unfulfilled, had grown a city from out of itself.

Binabik's quiet voice broke the silence, solemn as the moment; the echoes quickly vanished in the choking greenery.

' "Tree of the Singing Wind," they named it: *Da'ai Chikiza*. Once, can you imagine, it was full of music and life. All the windows burned with lamps, and there were bright boats at sail upon the river.' The troll tilted his head back to stare as they passed beneath a last stone bridge, narrow as a feather quill, clothed in images of graceful antlered deer. 'Tree of the Singing Wind,' he repeated, distant as a man lost in memory.

Simon wordlessly steered their little craft over to a bank of stone steps that ended in a platform, nearly flush with the surface of the wide river. They climbed out, tying the boat to a root that had pushed through the cracked white stone. When they had mounted up they stopped, staring silently at the vine-draped walls and mossy corridors. The very air of the ruined city was charged with quiet resonance, like a tuned but unplucked string. Even Qantaqa stood seemingly abashed, tail held low as she sniffed the air. Then her ears straightened, and she whined.

The hiss was almost imperceptible. A line of shadow leaped past Simon's face and struck one of the attenuated walkways with a sharp crack. Sparkling chips of green stone exploded in all directions. Simon whirled to look back.

Standing not a hundred ells away, separated from the companions only by the rolling expanse of river, stood a black-garbed figure holding a bow as long as he was tall. A dozen or so others garbed in blue and black surcoats were scrambling up a pathway to stand beside him. One of them carried a torch.

The black figure lifted a hand to his mouth, showing for an instant a flash of pale beard.

'You have nowhere to go!' Ingen Jegger's voice came faint above the sound of the river. 'Surrender in the King's name!'

'The boat!' Binabik cried, but even as they moved to the steps black-clad Ingen reached out some slender thing toward the torchbearer; fire blossomed at one end. A moment later he had nocked it on his bowstring. As the companions reached the bottom step, a bolt of fire leaped across the river, exploding into the side of the boat. The quivering arrow ignited the bark almost instantly, and the troll had time only to pull one of the packs from the craft before the flames forced him back. Momentarily hidden behind the leaping fire, Simon and Marya darted up the stairs, Binabik close behind. At the top Qantaqa was running from side to side, uttering hoarse barks of dismay.

'Run now!' Binabik snapped. On the far side of the river two more bowmen stepped up to Ingen's side. As

Simon strained toward the cover of the nearest tower he heard the awful hum of another arrow, and saw it skid across the tiles twenty cubits before him. Two more clattered against the tower wall that seemed so achingly far ahead. He heard a cry of pain, and Marya's terrified call.

'Simon!'

He whirled to see Binabik tumble to the ground, a tiny bundle at the girl's feet. Somewhere, a wolf was howling.

# 28

# Drums of Ice

The morning sun of the twenty-fourth day of Maia-month beamed down on Hernysadharc, turning the golden disc atop the highest of the Taig's roofs into a circlet of brilliant flame. The sky was blue as an enamel plate, as though Brynioch of the Skies had chased the clouds away with his heavenly hazel stick, leaving them to lurk sullenly around the upper peaks of the looming Grianspog.

The sudden return of spring should have gladdened Maegwin's heart. All over Hernystir the untimely rains and cruel frosts had drawn a shroud over both the land and her father Lluth's people. Flowers had frozen in the ground, unborn. Apples had dropped small and sour from the gnarled branches in the orchards. The sheep and cows, put out to graze in sodden fields, came back with rolling, frightened eyes, unnerved by hailstones and gusting winds.

A blackbird, insolently waiting until the last moment, hopped up from Maegwin's path into the denuded branches of a cherry tree where he trilled disputatiously. Maegwin paid him no heed, but hitched up her long dress and hurried toward her father's hall.

She ignored the voice calling her name at first, unwilling to be hindered in her errand. Finally, reluctantly, she turned to see her half brother Gwythinn running toward her. She stopped and waited for him, arms folded.

Gwythinn's white tunic was disordered, and his golden neck torque had ridden halfway around to the back, as though he were a child instead of a young man of warrior age. He caught up and stood panting; she gave a snort of dismay and set to straightening out his garments. The prince smirked, but waited patiently while she pulled the torque around to lie against his collarbone. His long brown mane of hair had largely pulled free of the red cloth holding it in a careless horse tail. As she reached around to tie it, their faces were eye-to-eye, although Gwythinn was by no means a short man. Maegwin scowled.

'Bagba's Herd, Gwythinn, look at you! You must do better. You will be king someday!'

'And what has being king to do with how my hair is worn? Besides, I was handsome enough when I started out, but I had to run like the very wind to catch you, you with those long legs.'

Maegwin flushed as she turned away. Her height was something about which, try as she might, she could not be matter-of-fact.

'Well, you've caught me up now. Are you going to the hall?'

'I certainly am.' A sterner expression ran across Gwythinn's face like quicksilver, and he tugged at his long mustache. 'I have things I must say to our father.'

'As do I,' Maegwin nodded, walking now. Their strides and heights so evenly matched, their sorrel-coloured hair so alike it might have been spun from one wheel, any outsider would have guessed they were twins, instead of Maegwin five years older and from a different mother.

'Our best brood sow, Aeghonwye, died evening last. Another one, Gwythinn! What is happening? Is it another plague, like at Abaingeat?'

'If it is a plague,' her brother said grimly, fingering the

leather-wrapped hilt of his sword, 'I know who brought it here. That man is a sickness on legs.' He slapped the pommel and spat. 'I only pray that he speaks out of turn today. Brynioch! Would I love to cross blades with that one!'

Maegwin narrowed her eyes. 'Don't be a fool,' she said crossly, 'Guthwulf has killed a hundred men. And, strange as it may seem, he is a guest at the Taig.'

'A guest who insults my father!' Gwythinn snarled, pulling his elbow from Maegwin's gentle, prisoning grasp. 'A guest who brings threats from a High King drowning in his own poor kingship – a king who struts and bullies and spends golden coins like they were pebbles, then turns to Hernystir and demands we help him!' Gwythinn's voice was rising, and his sister darted a glance around, worried who might hear. There was no one in sight but the pale shapes of the door guards a hundred paces away. 'Where was King Elias when we lost the road to Naarved and Elvritshalla? When bandits and the gods know what else decended on the Frost-march Road?' Face flushed again, the prince looked up to find Maegwin no longer at his side. He turned to see her standing, arms folded, ten steps behind.

'Have you finished, Gwythinn?' she asked. He nodded, but his mouth was tight. 'Good, then. The difference between our father and yourself, fellow, is more than only thirty-some years. In those years he has learned when to speak, and when to keep his thoughts inside. That is why, thanks to him, someday you stand to be King Gwythinn, and not just the Duke of Hernystir-Duchy.'

Gwythinn stared for a long moment. 'I know,' he said at last, 'you would have me be like Eolair, and bow and scrape to the dogs of Erkynland. I know you think Eolair is the sun and moon – regarding not what he thinks of you, king's daughter though you be – but I am not such a man. We are Hernystiri! We crawl for no one!'

Maegwin glared, stung by the jab over her feelings for

the Count of Nad Mullach – about whom Gwythinn was exactly right: the attention he showed her was only that due to a king's gawky, unmarried daughter. But the tears she dreaded did not come; instead, as she looked at Gwythinn, his handsome face twisted by frustration, by pride, and not least by genuine love of his people and land, she saw again the little brother she had once carried on her shoulder – and whom she herself had, from time to time, teased into tears.

'Why are we fighting, Gwythinn?' she asked wearily. 'What has brought this shadow down on our house?'

Her brother lowered his gaze to his boot tops, embarrassed, then extended his hand. 'Friends and allies,' he said. 'Come, let us go in and see Father before the Earl of Utanyeat comes slinking in to bid fond farewells.'

The windows of the Taig's great hall were thrown open; the sunlight streaming through was full of sparkling dust from the rushes spread across the floor. The thick wall timbers, hewed from the oak trees of the Circoille, were fitted so carefully that not a gleam of light showed between them. Up among the roofbeams hung a thousand painted carvings of the gods of the Hernystiri, of heroes and monsters, all twisting slowly in the rafters as reflected light shone warmly on their polished wooden features.

At the hall's far end, sun splashing in on either side, King Lluth ubh-Llythinn sat in his huge oaken chair, beneath the carved stag's head that strained upward from the chair's back, antlers of real horn fixed to its wooden skull. The king was eating a bowl of porridge and honey with a bone spoon while Inahwen, his young wife, sat on a lower chair at his side, putting a tracery of delicate stitching onto the hem of one of Lluth's robes.

As the sentries banged their spear points twice upon their shields to signal Gwythinn's arrival – lesser nobility such as Count Eolair received only a single beat, while the king himself received three, and Maegwin not a one –

Lluth looked up and smiled, placing his bowl down on the arm of his chair and wiping his gray mustache on his sleeve. Inahwen saw the gesture and gave Maegwin a despairing woman-to-woman look that Lluth's daughter resented more than a little. Maegwin had never really gotten used to Gwythinn's mother Fiathna taking the place of her own (Maegwin's mother Penemhwye had died when Maegwin was four), but at least Fiathna had been Lluth's age, not a mere girl like Inahwen! Still, this young, golden-haired woman was good-hearted, although perhaps a little slow of wit. It was not really Inahwen's fault she was a third wife.

'Gwythinn!' Lluth half-rose, brushing crumbs from the lap of his belted yellow robe. 'Are we not lucky to have the sun today?' The king swept a hand window-ward, as pleased as a child who has learned a trick. 'It is a certain thing that we need a little, eh? And perhaps it will help to put our guests from Erkynland,' he made a wry face, his mobile, clever features shifting into a look of bemusement, eyebrows arching above the thick, crooked nose broken in his boyhood, 'to put them in a more agreeable mood. Do you think?'

'No, I do not think that, father,' Gwythinn said, approaching as the king settled back into his antler-crested seat. 'And I hope the answer you give them today, if I may presume, will send them away in an even fouler one.' He pulled up a stool and sat at the king's feet just below the raised platform, sending a harper scuttling. 'One of Guthwulf's soldiers picked a fight with old Craobhan last night. I had a hard time preventing Craobhan from feathering the bastard's back with an arrow.'

Lluth looked troubled for a moment, then the look was gone, hidden behind the smiling mask that Maegwin knew so well.

*Ah, father,* she thought *even **you** are finding it a bit hard to keep the music playing while these creatures bay all around the Taig.* She walked quietly forward and sat on the platform by Gwythinn's stool.

'Well,' the king grinned ruefully, 'sure it is that King Elias could have chosen his diplomats with a bit more care. But today in an hour they are gone, and peace descends again on Hernysadharc.' Lluth snapped his fingers and a serving boy sprang forward to take his dish of porridge away. Inahwen watched critically as it went by.

'There,' she said reproachfully. 'You didn't finish again. What am I to do with your father?' she added, this time directing her gaze to Maegwin, smiling fondly as though Maegwin, too, was a soldier in the constant battle to make Lluth finish his meals.

Maegwin, still at a loss as to how deal with a mother a year younger than herself, hastily broke the silence. 'Aeghonwye died, Father. Our best, and the tenth sow this month. And some of the others have gotten very thin.'

The king frowned. 'This cursed weather. If Elias could but keep this spring sun overhead, I'd give him any tax he asked.' He reached down to pat Maegwin's arm, but was not quite able to reach. 'All we can do is pile more rushes in the barns to keep out the chill. Failing that, we are in the godly hands of Brynioch and Mircha.'

There was another metallic clash of spear on shield, and the door-speaker appeared, hands nervously clasped.

'Your Highness,' he called, 'the Earl of Utanyeat requests an audience.'

Lluth smiled. 'Our guests have decided to say farewell before they take to their horses. Of course! Please, bring Earl Guthwulf in immediately.'

But their guest, followed by several of his armored but unsworded men, was already moving past the ancient servant.

Guthwulf dropped slowly to his knee five paces before the platform. 'Your majesty . . . ah, and the prince, as well. I am fortunate.' There was no hint of mockery in his voice, but his green eyes held an unsubtle fire. 'And Princess Maegwin,' – a smile – 'the Rose of Hernysadharc.'

Maegwin struggled to maintain her composure. 'Sir, there was only one Rose of Hernysadharc,' she said, 'and since she was the mother of your King Elias, I am surprised it should slip your mind.'

Guthwulf nodded gravely. 'Of course, lady, I sought only to pay a compliment, but I must take exception to your calling Elias *my* king. Is he not yours, too, under the High Ward?'

Gwythinn shifted on his stool, turning to see what his father's reaction would be; his scabbard scraped on the wooden platform.

'Of course, of course,' Lluth waved his hand slowly, as if beneath deep water. 'We have been through all this, and I see no need to belabor it. I recognize the debt of my house to King John. We have always honored it, in peace or war.'

'Yes.' The Earl of Utanyeat stood, dusting the knees of his breeches. 'But what about your house's debt to King Elias? He has shown great tolerance . . .'

Inahwen stood up, and the robe she had been sewing slid to the floor. 'You must excuse me,' she said breathlessly, plucking the garment up, 'there are things in the household I should attend to.' The king waved his permission and she walked quickly but carefully between the waiting men and slid out the half-opened door of the hall, as lithely as a doe.

Lluth breathed a quiet sigh; Maegwin looked at him, seeing the always-surprising lines of age that wreathed her father's face.

*He is tired, and she, Inahwen, is frightened,* Maegwin thought. *I wonder what I am? Angry? I'm not sure – exhausted, really.*

As the king stared at Elias' messenger, the room seemed to darken. For a moment Maegwin feared that clouds had covered the sun, that the winter was returning; then she realized it was only her own apprehension, her sudden feeling that something more than her father's peace of mind hung in the balance here.

'Guthwulf,' the king began, and his voice sounded bowed as though beneath a great weight, 'do not think to provoke me today . . . but neither think that you can cow me. The king has shown no tolerance for the troubles of the Hernystiri at all. We have weathered a bitter drought, and now the rains for which we thanked all the gods a thousand times have themselves become a curse. What penalty that Elias can threaten me with can exceed that of seeing my people frightened, our cattle starving? I can pay no greater tithe.'

The Earl of Utanyeat stood silently for a moment, and the blankness of his expression slowly hardened into something that to Maegwin looked unsettlingly like jubilation.

'No greater penalty?' the Earl said, savoring each word as though it felt good on his tongue. 'No greater tithe?' He spat a wad of citril juice on the ground before the king's chair. Several of Lluth's men-at-arms actually cried out in horror; the harper who had been quietly playing in the corner dropped his instrument with a discordant crash.

'*Dog!*' Gwythinn leaped up, his stool clattering away. In a flashing moment his sword was out and at Guthwulf's throat. The earl only stared, his chin tipped ever so slightly back.

'Gwythinn!' Lluth barked, 'Sheathe, damn you, sheathe!'

Guthwulf's lip curled. 'Let him. Go ahead, pup, kill the High King's Hand unarmed!' There was a clanking by the door as some of his men, their astonishment thawing, started to move forward. Guthwulf's hand shot up. 'No! Even if this whelp should slip my weasand from ear to ear, no one shall strike back! You walk out and ride to Erkynland. King Elias will be . . . most interested.' His men, confused, stood in place like armored scarecrows.

'Let him go, Gwythinn,' Lluth said, cold anger in his voice. The prince, face flushed, glared at the Erkynlander for a long moment, then dropped his blade back to his side. Guthwulf passed a finger over the tiny cut on his throat and gazed coolly at his own blood. Maegwin realized she had been holding her breath; at the sight of the crimson smear on the Earl's fingertip, she let it whistle out again.

'You will live to tell Elias yourself, Utanyeat.' Only a slight tremor disturbed the evenness of the king's tone. 'I hope you will tell him as well the mortal insult you have paid to the House of Hern, an insult that would have gained your death had you not been Elias' emissary and King's Hand. Go.'

Guthwulf turned and walked to where his men stood, wild-eyed. When he reached them he pivoted on one heel, facing Llúth across the expanse of the great hall.

'Remember that you could think of no greater tithe you could pay,' he said, 'if someday you hear fire in the beams of the Taig, and your children crying.' He strode heavily through the door.

Maegwin, her hands shaking, bent and picked up a piece of the shattered harp, and wound its curling string around her hand. She raised her head to look at her father and brother; what she saw there made her turn back again to the shard of wood in her palm, and the string pulled tight against her white skin.

Breathing a soft Wrannaman curse, Tiamak stared disconsolately at the empty cage of reeds. It was his third trap, and there had not been a crab yet. The fishhead that had baited it was, of course, gone without trace. Glaring down into the muddy water, he had a sudden nervous premonition that the crabs were somehow a step ahead of him – were perhaps even now waiting for him to drop the cage down lardered with another pop-eyed head. He could picture a whole tribe of them scuttling over with expressions of glee to poke the bait out through the bars

530

with a stick or some other such tool recently granted to crab-kind by some beneficent crustacean deity.

Did the crabs worship him as a soft-shelled providing angel, he wondered, or did they look up at him with the cynical indifference of a gang of ne'er-do-wells taking the measure of a drunkard before relieving him of his purse?

He felt sure it was the latter. He rebaited the carefully woven cage and, with a soft sigh, let it splash down into the water, uncoiling its rope behind as it sank.

The sun was just slipping below the horizon, washing the long sky above the marsh in shades of orange and persimmon-red. As Tiamak poled his flatboat through the Wran's waterways – distinguishable in places from the land only by the lesser height of the vegetation – he had a sinking feeling that today's ill luck was only the beginning of a long rising tide. He had broken his best bowl that morning, the one that he had spent two days writing Roahog the Potter's ancestor-list to pay for; in the afternoon he had shattered a pen nib and spattered a great gobbet of berry-juice ink across his manuscript, ruining an almost completed page. And now, unless the crabs had decided to hold some kind of festival in the cramped confines of his last trap, there was going to be precious little to eat tonight. He was growing so very tired of root soup and rice biscuits.

As he silently approached the last float, a latticework ball of reeds, he offered an unspoken prayer to He Who Always Steps on Sand that even now the little bottom-walkers were pushing and shoving their way into the cage below. Because of his unusual education, which included a year living on Perdruin – unheard of for a Wrannaman – Tiamak did not really believe in He Who Steps on Sand anymore, but he still held a fondness for him, such as might be felt for a senile grandfather who often tumbled down from the house, but once brought nuts and carved toys. Besides, it never hurt to pray, even if one did not believe in the object of prayer. It helped to compose the mind, and, at the very least, it impressed others.

The trap came up slowly, and for a moment Tiamak's heart sped a little in his thin brown chest, as if seeking to drown out the expectant noises of his stomach. But the sensation of resistance was short-lived, probably some clinging root which had held and then slipped away, and the cage suddenly popped up and bobbed on the water's cloudy surface. *Something* was moving inside; he lifted the cage up, interposing it between himself and the sunset-glaring sky, squinting. Two tiny, stalked eyes goggled back at him, eyes that wobbled atop a crab that would disappear in his palm if he folded his fingers over it.

Tiamak snorted. He could imagine what had happened here: the older, rowdier crab-brothers goading the littlest into assaying the trap; the youngling, caught inside, weeping while his crude brothers laughed and waved their claws. Then the giant shadow of Tiamak, the cage suddenly tugged upward, the crab-brothers staring abashedly at each other, wondering how they would explain Baby's absence to Mother.

Still, Tiamak thought, considering the hollowish feeling in his middle, if this was all he had to show for today . . . it was small, but it would go nicely in the soup.

He squinted into the cage again, then upended it, shaking the prisoner out onto his palm. Why delude himself? This was a run-on-the-sandbar day, and that was that.

The crablet made a plopping noise as he dropped it back into the water. He did not even bother to resink the trap.

As he climbed the long ladder from his moored boat to the little house perched in the banyan tree, Tiamak vowed to be content with soup and a biscuit. Gluttony was an obstacle, he reminded himself, an impediment between the soul and the realms of truth. As he reeled the ladder up onto the porch he thought of She Who Birthed

Mankind, who had not even had a nice bowl of root soup, but had subsisted entirely on rocks and dirt and swamp water until they combined in her stomach and she whelped a litter of clay men, the first humans.

There, that made root soup a real bargain, didn't it? Besides, he had much work to do anyway – repair or rewrite the blotched manuscript page, for one thing. Among his tribesmen he was thought of as merely strange, but somewhere out in the world there would be people who would read his revision of *Sovran Remedys of the Wranna Healers* and realize that there were minds of true learning in the marshes. But ay! a crab would have gone down smartly – that and a jug of fern beer.

As Tiamak washed his hands in the water bowl he had put out before leaving, crouching because there was no room to sit between his obsessively scraped and polished writing board and his water jug, he heard a scratching sound on the roof. He listened carefully as he wiped his hands dry on his waistcloth. It came again: a dry rustle, like his broken pen being rubbed across the thatching.

It took him only a moment to slide out the window and climb hand over hand onto the sloping roof. Grasping one of the banyan's long, curving limbs he made his way up to where a little bark-roofed box sat atop the roof peak, an infant house carried on its mother's back. He ducked his head into the box's open end.

It was there, right enough: a gray sparrow, pecking briskly at the seeds that were scattered across the floor. Tiamak reached in a gentle hand to enfold it; then, as carefully as he could, he climbed down the roof and slid in through the window.

He put the sparrow in the crab cage he kept hanging from the roofbeam for just such occasions, and quickly made a fire. When the flames began to lick up from the stone hearth, he removed the bird from the cage, his eyes smarting as the smoke began to coil toward the hole in the ceiling.

The sparrow had lost a feather or two from its tail, and

held one wing out a bit from its side, as though it had come through some scrapes on its way down from Erkynland. He knew it had come from Erkynland because it was the only sparrow he had ever raised. His other birds were marsh doves, but Morgenes insisted on sparrows for some reason – funny old man, he was.

After he had set a pot of water on the flames, Tiamak did what he could for the awkward silver wing, then put down more seeds and a hollow curl of bark full of water. He was tempted to wait until he had eaten to read the message, to hold off the pleasure of faraway news as long as possible, but on a day like this one had been, such patience was too much to expect of himself. He mashed some rice flour up in the mortar, added some pepper and water, then spread the mixture out and rolled it into a cake which he set on the fire stone to bake.

The slip of parchment that had been wrapped around the sparrow's leg was ragged at the edges, and the printed characters were smeared, as though the bird had gotten more than a little wet, but he was used to such things and soon sorted it out. The notation signifying the date when it had been written surprised him: the gray sparrow had taken nearly a month to reach the Wran. The message surprised him even more, but it was not the kind of surprise he had been hoping for.

It was with a feeling of cold weight in his stomach superceding any hunger that he went to the window, looking out past the tangled banyan branches to the fast-blooming stars. He stared into the northern sky, and for a moment could almost believe he felt a cold wind knifing in, driving a wedge of chill through the warm air of the Wran. He was a long time at the window before he noticed the smell of his supper burning.

❧

Count Eolair sat back in the deep-cushioned chair and looked up at the high ceiling. It was covered in religious paintings, painstaking renditions of Usires healing the washerwoman, Sutrin martyred in the arena of the Imperator Crexis, and other such subjects. The colors seemed to be fading somewhat, and many of the pictures were obscured by dust, as though draped in a fine veil. Still, it was an impressive sight, for all that this was one of the smaller antechambers of the Sancellan Aedonitis.

*A millionweight of sandstone, marble, and gold,* Eolair thought, *and all for a monument to something no one has ever seen.*

Unbidden, a wave of homesickness washed over him, as had often happened in this last week. What he would not give to be back in his humble hall in Nad Mullach, surrounded by nieces and nephews and the small monuments of his own people and gods, or at the Taig in Hernysadharc, where a bit of his secret heart always lingered, instead of surrounded here by the land-devouring stone of Nabban! But the scent of war was on the wind, and he could not lock himself away when his king had asked his help. Still, he was weary of traveling. The grass of Hernystir would feel fine beneath his horse's hooves again.

'Count Eolair! Forgive me, please, for keeping you waiting.' Father Dinivan, the lector's young secretary, stood in the far doorway wiping his hands on his black robe. 'Today has been a full one already, and we have not reached the forenoon. Still,' he laughed, 'that is a terribly poor excuse. Please, come into my chambers!'

Eolair followed him out of the antechamber, his boots silent on the old, thick carpets.

'There,' said Dinivan, grinning and warming his hands before the fire, 'is that better? It is a scandal, but we cannot keep the Lord's greatest house warm. The ceilings are too high. And it has been such a cold spring!'

The count smiled. 'Truth to tell, I had not much noticed it. In Hernystir we sleep with our windows open, except in direst winter. We are a people who live out-of-doors.'

Dinivan wagged his eyebrows. 'And we Nabbanai are soft southerners, eh?'

'I did not say that!' Eolair laughed. 'One thing you southerners are, you are masters of clever speech.'

Dinivan sat down in a hard-backed chair. 'Ah, but his Sacredness the lector – who is an Erkynlandish man originally, as you well know – the lector can talk circles around any of us. He is a wise and subtle man.'

'That I know. And it is about him I would speak, Father.'

'Call me Dinivan, please. Ah, it is ever the fate of a great man's secretary – to be sought out for one's proximity rather than one's personality.' He made a mock-downcast face.

Eolair again found himself liking this priest very much. 'Such indeed is your doom, Dinivan. Now hear, please. I suppose you know why my master has sent me here?'

'I would have to be a clod indeed not to know. These are times that set tongues wagging like the tails of excited dogs. Your master reaches out to Leobardis, that they can make some sort of common cause.'

'Indeed.' Eolair stepped away from the fire to draw up a chair near Dinivan's. 'We are delicately balanced: my Lluth, your Lector Ranessin, Elias the High King, Duke Leobardis . . .'

'And Prince Josua, if he lives,' Dinivan said, and his face was worried. 'Yes, a delicate balance. And you know that the lector can do nothing to upset that balance.'

Eolair nodded slowly. 'I know.'

'So why have you come to me?' Dinivan asked kindly.

'I am not quite sure. Only this I would tell you: it seems there is some struggle brewing, as often happens, but I myself fear it is deeper. You might think me a madman, but I forebode that an age is ending, and I fear what the coming one may bring.'

The lector's secretary stared. For a moment his plain

536

face seemed far older, as though he reflected on sorrows long carried.

'I will say only that I share your fears, Count Eolair,' he said at last. 'But I cannot speak for the lector, except to say as I did before: he is a wise and subtle man.' He stroked the Tree at his breast. 'For your hearts-ease, though, I can say this: Duke Leobardis has not yet made up his mind where he will lend his support. Although the High King alternately flatters and threatens him, still Leobardis resists.'

'Well, this is good news,' said Eolair, and smiled warily. 'When I saw the duke this morning he was very distant, as though he feared to be seen listening to me too closely.'

'He has many things to weigh, as does my own master,' Dinivan replied. 'But know this, too – and it is a deep secret. Just this morning I took Baron Devasalles in to see Lector Ranessin. The baron is about to set forth on an embassy that will mean much to both Leobardis and my master, and will have much to do with which way Nabban throws her might in any conflict. I can tell you no more than that, but I hope it is something.'

'It is more than a little,' Eolair said. 'I thank you for your trust, Dinivan.'

Somewhere in the Sancellan Aedonitis a bell rang, deep and low.

'The Clavean Bell calls out the noon hour,' Father Dinivan said. 'Come, let us find us something to eat and a jug of beer, and talk about more pleasant things.' A smile chased across his features, making him young again. 'Did you know I traveled once to Hernystir? Your country is beautiful, Eolair.'

'Although somewhat lacking in stone buildings,' the count replied, patting the wall of Dinivan's chamber.

'And that is one of its beauties,' the priest laughed, leading him out the door.

The old man's beard was white, and long enough that he tucked it into his belt when he walked – which, until this morning, he had been doing for several days. His hair was no darker than his beard. Even his hooded jacket and leggings were made from the thick pelt of a white wolf. The creature's skin had been carefully flayed; the forelegs crossed on his chest, and its jawless head, nailed to a cap of iron, sat upon his own brow. Had it not been for the bits of red crystal in the wolf's empty sockets, and the old man's fierce blue eyes beneath, he would have been nothing but another patch of white in the snow-covered forest that lay between Drorshull Lake and the hills.

The moaning of the wind in the treetops increased, and a spatter of snow dropped from the branches of the tall pine tree onto the man crouching below. He shook himself impatiently, like an animal, and a fine mist rose around him, momentarily breaking the weak sunlight into a fog of tiny rainbows. The wind continued its keening song, and the old man in white reached to his side, grasping something that at first appeared to be only another lump of white – a snow-covered stone or tree stump. He held it up, brushing the powdery whiteness from its top and sides, then lifted away the cloth just far enough to peer inside.

He whispered into the opening and waited, then knitted his brows for an instant as if annoyed or troubled. Setting the object down, he stood up and unbuckled the belt of bleached reindeer hide from around his waist. After first pulling the hood back from his lean, weather-hardened face, he stripped off the wolfskin coat. The sleeveless shirt he wore beneath was the same color as the jacket, the skin of his sinewy arms not much darker, but starting on his right wrist just above the fur gauntlet the head of a snake was drawn in bright inks, scribed in blue and black and blood-red directly on the skin. The body of the snake curved round and round the old man's right arm in a spiral, disappearing into the shoulder of his shirt to reappear writhing sinuously about his left arm and terminate in a curlicued tail at the wrist. This fierce splash of color leaped out against the dull winter forest and the man's white garb and skin; from a short distance it appeared that some flying serpent, halved in midair, was suffering its death agonies two cubits above the frozen earth.

The old man paid no attention to the gooseflesh on his arms until he had finished draping his jacket over the bundle, tucking the loose folds in beneath it. Then he pulled a leather bag from a pouch in his undershirt, squeezed from it a quantity of yellow grease, and briskly rubbed it over his exposed skin, causing the serpent to gleam as though newly-arrived from some humid southern jungle. The task over, he crouched back again on his heels to wait. He was hungry, but he had finished the last of his traveling rations the night before. That was of no importance, anyway, because soon the ones he waited for would come, and then there would be food.

Chin tilted down, cobalt eyes smoldering beneath his icy brows, Jarnauga watched the southern approaches. He was an old, old man, and the rigors of time and weather had made him hard and spare. In a way he looked forward to the hour that was coming soon, when Death called for him and took him to her dark, quiet hall. Silence and solitude held no terror; they had been the warp and weft of his long life. He wanted only to finish the task that had been set before him, to hand on a torch that others might use in the darkness ahead; then he would let life and body go as easily as he shrugged the snow from his bare shoulders.

Thinking of the solemn halls that waited at the final turn of his road, he remembered his beloved Tungoldyr, left behind him a fortnight ago. As he had stood upon his doorstep that last day, the little town where he had spent most of his four and a half score of years had stretched before him, as empty as the legendary Huelheim that awaited him when his work was done. All of Tungoldyr's other inhabitants had fled months before;

only Jarnauga remained in the village called Moon Door, perched among the high Himilfell Mountains, but still in the shadow of distant Sturmrspeik – the Stormspike. The winter had hardened into a cold that even the Rimmersmen of Tungoldyr had never known before, and the nighttime songs of the winds had changed into something that had the sound of howling and weeping in it, until men went mad and were found laughing in the morning, their families dead around them.

Only Jarnauga had remained in his small house as the ice mists became thick as wool in the mountain passes and the narrow streets of the town, Tungoldyr's sloping roofs seeming to float like the ships of ghost warriors sailing the clouds. No one but Jarnauga had been around to see the flickering lights of Stormspike burn brighter and brighter, to hear the sounds of vast, harsh music that wound in and out through the din of thunder, playing across the mountains and valleys of this northernmost province of Rimmersgard.

But now even he – his time come around at last, as made known to him by certain signs and messages – had left Tungoldyr to the creeping darkness and cold. Jarnauga knew that no matter what happened, he would never again see the sun on the wooden houses, or listen to the singing of the mountain rills as they splashed past his front door, down to the swelling Gratuvask. Neither would he stand on his porch in the clear, dark spring nights and see the lights in the sky – the shimmering northern lights that had been there since his boyhood, not the guttering, sickly flares now playing about the dark face of Stormspike. Such things were gone, now. His road ahead was plain, but there was little joy in it.

But not everything was clear, even now. There was still the nagging dream to be dealt with, the dream of the black book and the three swords. It had dogged his sleep for a fortnight, but its meaning was still hidden from him.

His thoughts were interrupted by a blotch of

movement on the southern approach, far away along the rim of the trees dotting the Wealdhelm's western skirts. He squinted briefly, then slowly nodded his head and rose to his feet.

As he was pulling his coat back on, the wind changed direction; a moment later a dim mutter of thunder rolled down from the north. It came again, a low growl like a beast struggling awake from sleep. On its heels, but from the opposite direction, the sound of hooves grew from a murmur to a noise that rivaled the thunder.

As Jarnauga picked up his cage of birds and walked out to meet the riders, the sounds grew together – thunder tolling in the north, the muffled din of approaching horsemen to the south – until they filled the white forest with their cold rumble, like music made on drums of ice.

# 29

# Hunters and Hunted

The hollow roar of the river filled his ears. For a heartbeat it seemed to Simon that the water was the only moving thing – that the archers on the far side, Marya, he himself, all had been frozen into immobility by the impact of the arrow that quivered in Binabik's back. Then another shaft spat past the white-faced girl, splintering noisily against a broken cornice of shining stone, and all was frantic movement once more.

Only half-aware of the insectlike scuttling of the archers across the water, Simon covered the distance back to the girl and troll in three steps. He bent to look, a strange, isolated part of his mind noticing how the boy's leggings Marya wore had tattered holes at the knee, and an arrow snicked through his shirt beneath his arm. At first he thought it had missed him completely; a moment later he felt a flare of pain sizzle along his rib cage.

More darts skimmed past, hitting low on the tiles before them and skipping like stones on a lake. Simon quickly kneeled and scooped the silent troll into his arms, feeling the horrible, stiff arrow quiver between his fingers. He turned, putting his back between the little man and the archers – Binabik was so pale! He was dead, he must be! – then stood. The pain in his ribs burned him again, and he staggered, Marya catching at his elbow.

'Löken's Blood!' screamed the black-garbed Ingen, his

542

far-off voice a faint murmur in Simon's ear. 'You're killing them, you idiots! I said to *keep them there*! Where is Baron Heahferth?!'

Qantaqa had run down to join them; Marya tried to wave the wolf away as she and Simon lumbered up the stairs into Da'ai Chikiza. One last feathered shaft cracked into the step behind them, then the air was still again.

'Heahferth is here, Rimmersman!' a voice shouted amid the clamor of armored men. Simon looked back from the top step. His heart sank.

A dozen men in battle array were rushing past Ingen and his bowmen, heading straight for the Gate of Stags, the bridge Simon and his companions had passed beneath just before coming ashore. The baron himself rode behind them on his red horse, a long spear held above his head. They couldn't have outrun even the foot soldiers for long – the baron's horse would catch them in three breaths.

'Simon! Run!' Marya jerked his arm, pulling him forward at a stumble. 'We must hide in the city!' But Simon knew that was hopeless, too. By the time they reached the first concealment the soldiers would be upon them.

'Heahferth!' Ingen Jegger's voice cried out behind them, a flat, small sound above the river's drone. 'You can't! Don't be a fool, Erkynlander, your horse. . . !'

The rest was lost in water sounds; if Heahferth heard he did not seem to care. In a moment the clangor of his soldiers' feet upon the bridge was matched by the pounding of hoofbeats on stone.

Even as the din of pursuit mounted, Simon caught the toe of his boot on an uprooted tile and pitched forward.

*A spear in the back* . . . he thought to himself in midfall, and: *How did all this happen*? Then he was tumbling painfully onto his shoulder, rolling to protect the cradled body of the troll.

He lay on his back staring up at the patches of sky gleaming through the dark dome of trees, Binabik's not unsubstantial weight perched on his chest. Marya was pulling at his shirt, trying to get him upright. He wanted to tell her it was not important now, no longer worth the bother, but as he sat up on one elbow, propping the troll's body with his other arm, he saw a strange thing happening below.

In the middle of the long, arching bridge, Baron Heahferth and his men had stopped moving – no, that was not quite correct, they were *swaying* in place – the men-at-arms clinging to the bridge's low walls, the baron perched atop his horse, his features not quite distinguishable from this distance, but his pose that of a man who is startled out of sleep. A moment later, for no reason Simon could discern, the horse reared and plunged forward; the men followed, running faster than before. Immediately after – a flicker behind the movement – Simon heard a great crack, as though a giant hand had snapped off a tree trunk for a toothpick. The bridge seemed to come unstuck in the middle.

Before the shocked, fascinated eyes of Simon and Marya, the slender Gate of Stags plunged downward, middle first, stones crumbling loose in great angular shards to crash foaming into the water below. For a few pulsebeats it seemed that Heahferth and his soldiers would reach the far side; then, rippling like a shook-out blanket, the arc of stone folded in on itself, sending a writhing mass of arms, legs, pale faces, and a thrashing horse toppling down amidst the ragged blocks of milky chalcedony, to disappear in gouts of green water and white froth. A few moments later the head of the baron's horse appeared several ells downstream, neck straining upward, then it slid back into the swirling river.

Simon slowly tilted his head around the the base of the bridge. The two archers were on their knees, staring into the torrent; the black-hooded figure of Ingen stood behind them, staring across at the companions. It felt like his pale eyes were only inches away. . . .

'Get *up!*' Marya shouted, pulling at Simon's hair. He

544

freed his gaze from Ingen Jegger's with an almost palpable snap of separation, like a cord fraying through. He climbed to his feet, balancing his small burden, and they turned and fled into the echoes and tall shadows of Da'ai Chikiza.

Simon's arms were aching after a hundred steps, and it felt as though a knife was sliding in and out of his side; he fought to stay even with the girl as they followed the bounding wolf through the ruins of the Sithi city. It was like running through a cave of trees and icicles, a forest of vertical shimmer and dark, mossy corruption. Shattered tile was everywhere, and massive tangles of spiderwebs strung across beautiful, crumbling arches. Simon felt as though he had been swallowed by some incredible ogre with innards of quartz and jade and mother-of-pearl. The river sounds became muted behind them; the rasp of their own hard breathing vied with the scrape of their running feet.

At last, it seemed they were reaching the outskirts of the city: the tall trees, hemlock and cedar and towering pine, were closer together, and the tiled flooring that had been everywhere underfoot now dwindled to pathways coiling at the feet of the forest giants. Simon stopped running. His eyesight was blackening at the edges. He stood in place and felt the earth reel about him. Marya took his hand and led him a few limping steps to an ivy-choked mound of stone that Simon, his sight slowly returning, recognized as a well. He set Binabik's body down gently on the pack that Marya had been carrying, propping the little man's side against the rough cloth, then leaned on the well's rim to suck air into his needy lungs. His side continued to throb.

Marya squatted next to Binabik, pushing away Qantaqa's nose as the wolf prodded at her silent master. Qantaqa took a step back, making a whimpering sound of incomprehension, then lay down with her muzzle on her paws. Simon felt hot tears spring to his eyes.

'He's not dead.'

Simon stared at Marya, then at Binabik's colorless face. 'What?' he asked. 'What do you mean?'

'He's not dead,' she repeated without looking up. Simon kneeled beside her. She was right: the troll's chest was moving almost imperceptibly. A frothy bubble of blood on his lower lip pulsed in time.

'Usires Aedon.' Simon wiped his hand across his dripping forehead. 'We have to take the arrow out.'

Marya looked at him sharply. 'Are you mad? If we do, the life will run out of him! He'll have no chance at all!'

'No.' Simon shook his head. 'The doctor told me, I'm sure he did, but I don't know if I can get it out, anyway. Help me to take off his jacket.'

When they had pried cautiously at the jacket for a moment, they realized there was no possible way to remove it without pulling on the arrow. Simon cursed. He needed something to cut the jacket away, something sharp. He pulled the salvaged pack over by a strap and began to rummage through it. Even in his sorrow and pain he was gratified to discover the White Arrow, still wrapped in its shroud of rags. He pulled it out and began loosening the knot that held the strips of cloth.

'What are you doing?' Marya demanded. 'Haven't we had enough arrows?'

'I need something sharp to cut with,' he grunted. 'It's a pity we've lost part of Binabik's staff . . . it's the part that's got a knife in it.'

'Is *that* what you're doing?' Marya reached into her shirt and pulled out a small knife in a leather sheath, hung on a thong around her neck. 'Geloë told me I should have it,' she explained, unsheathing it and passing it over. 'It's not much good against archers.'

'And bowmen aren't much good at keeping bridges from falling, praise God.' Simon began to saw away at the oiled hide.

'Do you think that's all that happened?' Marya said after a while.

'What do you mean?' Simon panted. It was hard work,

but he had cut upward from the bottom of the jacket and past the arrow, revealing a sticky mass of congealed blood. He pulled the knife blade up toward the collar.

'That the bridge just . . . fell.' Marya looked up at the light filtering down through the twining greenery. 'Maybe the Sithi were angry about what was happening in their city.'

'*Pfah.*' Simon clenched his teeth and split the last piece of hide. 'The Sithi who are alive don't live here anymore, and if the Sithi don't die, like the doctor told me, then there aren't any spirits to make bridges fall.' He spread the wings of the split jacket and winced. The troll's back was covered in drying blood. 'You heard the Rimmersman shouting at Heahferth: he didn't want him to take his horse on the bridge. Now let me think, damn you!'

Marya raised her hand as though to strike him; Simon looked up, and their eyes locked. For the first time he saw that the girl, too, had been crying. 'I gave you my knife!' she said.

Simon shook his head, confused. 'It's just that . . . that devil Ingen may have already found another place to cross. He's got two archers, at least, and who knows what's become of the hounds . . . and . . . and this little man is my friend.' He turned back to the bloodied troll.

Marya was silent for a moment. 'I know,' she said at last.

The arrow had entered at an angle, striking a good hand's length from the center of the spine. By carefully tilting the small body, Simon was able to slide his hand underneath. His fingers quickly found the sharp iron arrowhead protruding from just below Binabik's arm, near the front of his ribs.

'Blazes! It's gone right through him!' Simon thought frantically. 'A moment . . . a moment . . .'

'Break the point off,' Marya suggested, her voice now calm. 'Then you can pull it through more easily – if you're sure you should.'

'Of course!' Simon was elated, and a bit dizzy. 'Of course.'

It took him no little time to cut through the arrow beneath its head; the little knife had been considerably dulled. When he finished, Marya helped him tilt Binabik into the position where the arrow was most flexible. Then, with a silent prayer to the Aedon under his tongue, he eased the arrow out through the wound made by its entry as fresh blood welled around it. He stared at the hateful object for a moment, then threw it away. Qantaqa raised her massive head to watch its flight, gave a rumbling moan, and slumped back down.

They wrapped Binabik in the rags from the White Arrow, along with strips cut from his ruined jacket, then Simon picked up the still faintly-breathing troll and cradled him.

'Geloë said climb the Stile. I don't know where that is, but we'd best continue on to the hills,' he said. Marya nodded.

The glimpses of sun through the treetops told them it was near noontime as they left the overgrown well. They passed quickly through the fringes of the decaying city, and within an hour found the land beginning to slope upward beneath their weary feet. The troll was again becoming a difficult burden. Simon was too proud to say anything, but he was sweating profusely, and his back and arms had begun to ache fully as much as his wounded side. Marya suggested that he cut leg holes in the pack so that it could be used to carry Binabik. After some consideration, Simon discarded the idea. For one thing, it would mean too much jouncing for the helpless, unconscious troll; also, they would have to leave some of the pack's contents behind, and most of that was food.

When the gently rising land began to change into steep, brushy slopes of sedge and thistle, Simon at last waved Marya to a stop. He set the little man down and stood for a moment, hands on hips, sides puffing in and out as he got back his breath.

'We . . . we must . . . I must . . . rest . . .' he huffed. Marya looked up at his flushed face with sympathy.

'You can't carry him all the way to the top of the hills, Simon,' she said gently. 'It looks to get steeper ahead. You'll need your hands to climb with.'

'He's . . . my friend,' Simon said stubbornly. 'I can . . . do it.'

'No, you can't.' Marya shook her head. 'If we can't use the pack to carry him, then we must . . .' Her shoulders slumped, and she slid down to sit on a rock. 'I don't know *what* we must, but we must,' she finished.

Simon sagged down beside her. Qantaqa had disappeared up the slope, bounding nimbly along where it would take the boy and girl long minutes to follow.

Suddenly, an idea came to Simon. 'Qantaqa!' he called, rising to his feet and spilling the pack out on the grassy ground before him. 'Qantaqa! Come here!'

Working feverishly, the unspoken thought of Ingen Jegger a hovering shadow, Simon and Marya wrapped Binabik up neck to toe in the girl's cloak, then balanced the troll stomach down on Qantaqa's back, tying him in place with the last shredded strips of clothing from out of the pack. Simon remembered the position from his involuntary ride to Duke Isgrimnur's camp, but he knew that if the thick cloak was between Binabik's ribs and the wolf's back, the little man would at least be able to breathe. Simon knew it was not a good situation for a wounded, probably dying, troll, but what else could be done? Marya was right; he would need his hands going up the hill.

Once Qantaqa's initial skittishness wore off, she stood passively as the boy and girl worked, turning occasionally to try and sniff Binabik's face where it bobbed at her side. When they finished and started up the slope, the wolf picked her way carefully, as if aware of the importance to her silent burden of a smooth ride.

Now they made better time, scrambling over stones and ancient logs molting their bark in peeling strips. The bright, cloud-blurred ball of sun that peered down through the branches had rolled far toward its western mooring. Scrabbling along, the wolf's gray and white tail floating before his sweat-smarting eyes like a plume of smoke, Simon wondered where the darkness would find them – and what might find them in that darkness.

The going had become very steep, and both Simon and Marya were beribboned with scratchmarks from the clutching undergrowth, when they at last stumbled across a clear, horizontal crease in the side of the hill. They sat down gratefully in the dusty track. Qantaqa looked as though she would not mind exploring farther up the narrow, grass-clotted trail, but instead she slumped down beside them, tongue lolling. Simon untied the troll from the makeshift harness. The little man's condition seemed unchanged, his breathing still terribly shallow. Simon dribbled water into his mouth from the waterskin, then passed it to Marya. When she had finished, Simon cupped his hands, which she filled, and held them out for Qantaqa to drink. Afterward he took several long swallows from the bag himself.

'Do you think this is the Stile?' Marya asked as she ran her hands through her damp black hair. Simon smiled weakly. Wasn't that like a girl, to be arranging her hair in the midst of the forest! She was very flushed, and he saw that it brought out the freckles across the bridge of her nose.

'It looks more like a deer path or some such,' he said at last, turning his attention to where the track wandered away along the flank of the hill. 'I think the Stile is a Sithi thing, Geloë said. But I think we might follow this for a while.'

*She's not really thin, so much,* he thought. *It's more what they call delicate.* He remembered how she reached up and snapped off the overhanging branches, and her coarse river chanteys. No, maybe 'delicate' wasn't quite it, either.

'Let's be off, then,' Marya broke into his ruminations. 'I'm hungry, but I'd rather not be out in the open here when the sun goes down.' She stood up and began collecting the cloth strips to remount Binabik on his steed, who was using *her* last moments of unencumbered freedom to scratch behind one ear.

'I like you, Marya,' Simon blurted out, and then wanted to turn away, to run, to do *something*; instead he bravely stayed where he was, and a moment later the girl looked up at him, smiling – and *she* was the one who looked embarrassed!

'I'm glad,' was all she said, and then moved away up the deer track a few steps to let Simon, hands suddenly clumsy, bind Binabik into place. Suddenly, as he finished tying the last loop beneath the shaggy belly of the hugely patient wolf, he looked at the troll's bloodless face, as slack and still as death – and was angry with himself.

*What a mooncalf!* he thought savagely. *One of your closest friends is dying, you're lost in the middle of nowhere, being chased by armed men and maybe worse – and here you stand moping over a skinny servant girl! Idiot!*

He did not say anything to Marya as he caught up with her, but the expression on his face must have told her something. She gave him a pensive look and they fell into stride with no further conversation.

The sun had dipped down behind the ridged backs of the hills when the deer path began to widen. Within a quarter of a league it became a broad, flat path that might have once been used for wagon travel, although it had long since given over sovereignty to the creeping wilderness. Other, smaller tracks wound alongside, distinguishable mainly as flaws in the smooth cover of brush and trees. They came to a place where these lesser pathways joined with theirs, and within a hundred ells found themselves walking again on ancient stone tiles. Soon after, they reached the Stile.

The wide, cobbled roadway cut across the track they had been following, switching back and forth up the hill in a steep traverse. Tall grasses pushed up between the cracked gray and white tiling, and in places large trees had grown right through the road surface, shouldering the stones up and outward as the trees gained size, so that each was now surrounded by a small slagheap of uprooted stones.

'And this will take us to Naglimund,' Simon said, half to himself. They were the first words either had spoken for a long time.

Marya was about to reply when something on the hilltop caught her eye. She stared, but whatever had made the flash of light was gone.

'Simon, I think I saw something bright up there.' She pointed to the crest of the hill, a good league above them.

'What was it?' he asked, but she only shrugged. 'Armor, perhaps, if the sun would reflect this late in the day,' he answered himself, 'or the walls of Naglimund, or, or who knows. . . ?' He looked up, narrowing his eyes.

'We can't leave the road,' he said finally. 'Not until we get farther, not while there's light. I would never forgive myself if we didn't get Binabik to Naglimund, especially if he . . . if . . .'

'I know, Simon, but I don't think we can make it all the way over the top tonight.' Marya kicked a stone, sending it rolling into the tall grass beside the paving tiles. She winced. 'I have more blisters on one foot than I've had in my whole life before this. And it can't be good for Binabik to bounce on the wolf's back all night,' she met his eyes, '*if* he's even going to live. You've done everything anybody could do, Simon. It's not your fault.'

'I know!' Simon replied angrily. 'Let's walk. We can talk about it while we're moving.'

They trudged on. It did not take long for the wisdom of Marya's words to become uncomfortably obvious. Simon, too, was so scratched and blistered and scuffed that he wanted to lie down and weep – a different Simon, the Simon that had lived his castle-boy life in the labyrinthine Hayholt, *would* have lain down – he would have sat on a stone and demanded dinner and sleep. He was somewhat different now: he still hurt, but there were other things that were more important. Still, there was no good to be done by crippling them all.

At last even Qantaqa began to favor one of her legs. Simon was finally ready to give in when Marya spotted another light on the spine of the hill. This one was no sun reflection: blue twilight was settling over the slopes.

'Torches!' Simon groaned. 'Usires! Why now, when we're almost there?!'

'That's probably why. That Ingen monster must have headed for the top of the Stile to wait for us. We must get away from the road!'

Hearts stone-heavy, they quickly made their way off the Stile's paving and down into a gulley that ran along the width of the hill. They scurried on, stumbling frequently in the fading light, until they found a little clearing no wider than Simon was tall, protected by a stockade of young hemlocks. As he looked up one last time before ducking into the cover of the high brush, Simon thought he saw the gleaming eyes of several more torches winking on the hilltop.

'May those bastards burn in Hell!' he snarled breathlessly, crouching to untie Binabik's limp form from Qantaqa's back. 'Aedon! Usires Aedon! How I wish I had a sword, or a bow!'

'Should you take Binabik off?' Marya whispered. 'What if we have to run again?'

'Then I'll carry him. Besides, if it comes to running, we might as well give up now. I don't think I could run fifty steps, could you?'

Marya ruefully shook her head.

They took turns swigging at the waterskin while Simon massaged Binabik's wrists and ankles, trying to get some blood back into the troll's chill extremities. The little man was breathing better now, but Simon did not feel confident that would last long: a thin film of bloody saliva bulged in and out of his mouth with each breath, and when Simon skinned back the little man's eyelids, as he had once seen Doctor Morgenes do with a fainting chambermaid, the whites of the troll's eyes seemed quite gray.

As Marya fished about in the pack for something to eat, Simon tried to lift one of Qantaqa's paws to see why she was limping. The wolf stopped panting long enough to bare her teeth and snarl at him in a very convincing manner. When he tried to pursue the investigation, she snapped at his hand, jaws clashing hard not an inch from his probing fingers. Simon had almost forgotten she *was* a wolf, and had grown used to handling her as though she were one of Tobas' hounds. He was suddenly grateful she had chastened him so mildly. He left her alone to tongue-wash her ragged pads.

The light dwindled, pinpoint stars blooming in the thickening darkness overhead. Simon was chewing a piece of hard biscuit Marya had found for him, and wishing he had an apple, or anything with juice to it, when a thin, clamoring noise began to untangle itself from the song of the evening's first crickets. Simon and Marya looked at each other, then, for the confirmation that they did not really need, to Qantaqa. The wolf's ears were swung forward, her eyes alert.

There was no need to name the creatures that made that faraway baying noise. Both of them were far too familiar with the sounds of hunting hounds at full cry.

'What should. . . ?' Marya started to ask, but Simon shook his head. He banged his fist in frustration against the trunk of a tree, and absently watched blood rise on the back of his pale knuckles. In a few minutes they would be in full darkness.

'There's nothing we can do,' he hissed. 'If we run, we will only make more of a track for them to follow.' He wanted to lash out again, to break something. Stupid, stupid, stupid, this whole bloody adventure – and to what end?

As he sat fuming, Marya pushed in close against his side, lifting his arm and draping it around her shoulder.

'I'm cold,' was all she said. He wearily leaned his head against hers, tears of frustration and fear welling in his eyes as he listened to the noises from the hillside above. Now he thought he could hear men's voices shouting back and forth above the din of the hounds. What he would give for a sword! Unskilled as he was, he could at least cause them some pain before they took him.

Gently, he lifted Marya's head from his shoulder and bent forward. As he had remembered, Binabik's skin bag was nestled at the bottom of the pack. He pulled it out and ran his fingers through it, searching by touch alone in the obscurity of the clearing.

'What are you doing?' Marya whispered.

Simon found what he was seeking and closed his hand on it. Some of the noises were now coming from the hillside north of them, too, almost at their level of the slope. The trap was closing.

'Hold Qantaqa.' He got up and crawled a short distance, scouring the brush until he found a good-sized broken branch, a thick one longer than his arm. He brought it back and upended Binabik's bag of powder on it, then laid it down carefully. 'I'm making a torch,' he said, pulling out the troll's flints.

'Won't that just lead them to us?' the girl asked, a note of detached curiosity in her voice.

'I won't light it until I have to,' he replied, 'but at least we'll have something . . . something to fight with.'

Her face was in shadow, but he could sense her eyes on him. She knew exactly how much good such a gesture would do them. He hoped – and the hope was very strong – that she would understand why it was a necessary gesture.

The ferocious uproar of the dogs was horribly close now. Simon could hear the sounds of the bushes being beaten down, and the loud cries of the hunters. The sound of branches snapping grew louder, just above them on the hillside and approaching rapidly – too loud a noise for dogs, Simon thought, heart fluttering as he smacked flint against stone. It must be men on horseback. The powder sparked but did not catch. The underbrush was crackling as though a wagon was tumbling through it end over end.

*Catch, damn you, catch!*

Something smashed through the thicket just above their hiding place. Marya's hand clutched his arm hard enough to cause pain.

'Simon!' she cried, and then the powder sputtered and flared; a wavering orange flower blossomed at the tip of the branch. Simon leaped up, swinging it out at the end of his arm, the flames rippling. Something crashed out of the trees. Qantaqa pulled free of Marya's grasp, howling.

*Nightmare!* That was all Simon could think as he lifted the torch; the light reached out, illuminating the thing that stood, startled upright before him.

It was a giant.

In the horrifying, static instant that followed, Simon's mind struggled to absorb what his eyes saw – the thing that towered above him, swaying in the torch glare. At first he thought it some kind of bear, for it was covered all over in pale, shaggy fur. But no, its legs were too long, its arms and black-skinned hands too human. The top of its hairy head was three cubits above Simon's as it leaned forward at the waist, eyes squinting in its leathery, manlike face.

The baying was everywhere, like the music of a ghastly choir of demons. The beast lashed out a long, taloned arm, tearing the flesh of Simon's shoulder, rocking him backward so that he stumbled and almost dropped the torch. The darting light of its flames, briefly illuminated Marya, eyes wide with horror as she clutched Binabik's limp form, trying to drag him back out of the way. The giant opened its mouth and *thundered* – that was the only possible word for the echoing rumble that came out – and lunged at Simon again. He leaped away, catching his foot on something and toppling over, but before the thing could move toward him, its chest-rattling growl turned into a howl of pain. It fell forward, half-slumping to the ground.

Qantaqa had caught it behind a shaggy knee, a gray shadow dashing back to leap again at the giant's legs. The beast snarled and swiped at the wolf, missing her once. The second time its broad hand caught her; she tumbled over and over into the brush.

The giant turned back to Simon, but even as he hopelessly raised the torch before him, and saw its pulsing light reflected in the giant's glossy black eyes, a boiling mass of shapes came through the undergrowth, howling like the wind in a thousand high turrets. They seethed around the giant like an angry ocean – dogs everywhere, leaping and biting at the huge creature as it raged in its thunderstorm voice. It windmilled its arms and broken bodies flew away; one knocked Simon to the ground, his torch skittering, but five more leaped in to fill the place of each one dislodged.

Even as Simon crawled to the torch, his mind a jumble of insane, feverish pictures, light suddenly bloomed everywhere. The vast shape of the beast reeled around the clearing, roaring, and then men came, and there were horses rearing and people shouting. A dark shape leaped over Simon, knocking his torch away once more. The horse slid to a halt just beyond, the rider standing atop his mount with a long spear flicking in and out of the torchlight. A moment later the spear was a great black nail standing out from the breast of the besieged giant, who gave a last shuddering roar and slipped down beneath the convulsing blanket of hounds.

The horseman dismounted. Men with torches ran past him to pull the dogs off; the light revealed the horseman's profile, and Simon climbed to one knee.

'Josua!' he said, then pitched forward. His last sight was the prince's spare face limned in the yellow light of torch flames, eyes widening in surprise.

Time came and went in fitful moments of waking and darkness. He was on a horse before a silent man who smelled of leather and sweat. The man's arm was a stiff band around Simon's middle as they swayed up the Stile.

The horse's hooves clopped on stone, and he found he was watching the swinging tail of the horse before him. There were torches everywhere.

He was looking for Marya, for Binabik, for everyone else . . . where were they all?

Some kind of tunnel was all around now, stone walls echoing with the rippling sound of heartbeats. No, *hoofbeats*. The tunnel seemed to go on forever.

A great wooden door set in the stone loomed before them. It swung open slowly, torchlight flooding out like water through a burst dam, and the shapes of many men were in the spreading light of the entrance.

And now they came down a long slope in the open air, the horses single file, a glimmering snake of torches winding down the path ahead as far as he could see. All around them was a field of bare earth, planted with nothing but naked bars of iron.

Below them, the walls were lined with more torches, the sentries staring up at the procession descending from the hills. The stone walls were before them, now level, now slowly rising up past their heads as they followed the trail downward. The night sky was dark as the inside of a barrel, but salted with stars. Head bobbing, Simon found himself sliding back down into sleep – or the dark sky, it was hard to tell which.

*Naglimund*, he thought, as the light of the torches splashed on his face, and the men shouted and sang on the walls above. Then he was falling away from the light, and darkness covered him like a drift of ebony dust.

# PART THREE

---

# SIMON
# SNOWLOCK

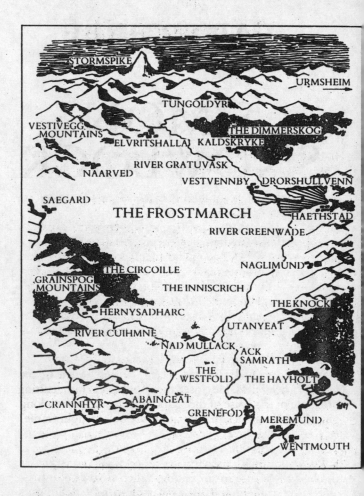

# 30

# A Thousand Nails

Somebody was breaking down the door with axes –
hacking, chopping, splintering away the shielding
timber.

'Doctor!' Simon shouted, sitting up, 'it's the soldiers!
The soldiers have come!'

But he was not in Morgenes' chambers. He was
wrapped in sweat-drenched sheets, on a small bed in a
small, neat room. The sound of blades splitting wood
continued; a moment later the door swung inward, and
the din rose in volume. An unfamiliar face peered around
the edge, pale and long of chin, topped with a sparse crest
of hair that gleamed as coppery red as Simon's own in the
framing sunlight. His one visible eye was blue. The other
was covered by a black patch.

'Ah!' the stranger said, 'you're awake, then. Good.' He
was an Erkynlander by his accent, with a touch of the
northern heaviness. He closed the door behind him, cutting
off some of the noise of the work outside. He wore a long
gray priestly cassock that hung limply on his slight frame.

'I'm Father Strangyeard.' He settled into a high-
backed chair beside Simon; other than the bed and a low
table covered with parchment and odds and ends, it was
the only furniture in the room. When he was comfortable, the stranger leaned forward and patted Simon's
hand.

'How are you feeling? Better, I hope?'

'Yes . . . yes, I suppose so,' Simon looked around. 'Where am I?'

'Naglimund, but you knew that, of course.' Father Strangyeard smiled. 'More specifically, you are in my room . . . my bed, too.' He lifted a hand. 'I hope you found it comfortable. It is not very well-appointed – but, goodness, how foolish of me! You have been sleeping in the forest haven't you?' The priest gave another quick, hesitant smile. 'It *must* be better than the forest, hmmm?'

Simon swung his feet to the cold floor, relieved to find that he was wearing breeches, a little unsettled to see that they weren't his own. 'Where are my friends?' A dark thought came up like a cloud. 'Binabik . . . is he dead?'

Strangyeard pursed his lips, as though Simon had uttered a mild blasphemy. 'Dead? Praise Usires, no – although he is not well, not well at all.'

'May I see him?' Simon slid down to the flags to look for his boots. 'Where is he? And how is Marya?'

'Marya?' the priest's expression was puzzled as he watched Simon crawl about the floor. 'Ah. Your other companion is fine. You will eventually see her as well, I do not doubt.'

The boots were under the writing table. As Simon pulled them on Father Strangyeard reached around and lifted a clean white blouse from the back of the chair.

'Here,' he said. 'My, you *are* in a hurry. Would you like to see your friend first, or have something to eat?'

Simon was already tying the front of the shirt closed. 'Binabik and Marya, then eat food,' he grunted, concentrating. 'And Qantaqa, too.'

'Hard as times have been of late,' the father said in a tone of reproof, 'we never eat wolves at Naglimund. I assume you are counting her as a friend.'

Looking up, Simon saw that the one-eyed man was making a joke.

'Yes,' Simon said, feeling suddenly shy. 'A friend.'

'Then let us go,' the priest said, standing. 'I was told to

make sure you were well provided for, so the sooner I get food into you, the better I will have fulfilled my commission.' He opened the door, admitting another flood of sunshine and noise.

Simon blinked in the strong light, looking up at the high walls of the keep and the vast purple and brown expanse of the Wealdhelm looming above, dwarfing the gray-clad sentries. A congregation of angular stone buildings bulked large at the keep's center, arranged without any of the Hayholt's eccentric beauty, its contrast of styles and eras. The dark smoke-streaked cubes of sandstone, the small lightless windows and heavy doors, looked as if they had been constructed for one purpose only: to keep something out.

Just a stone's throw away, in the midst of the swarming commons yard, a crew of shirtless men were splitting a stack of logs, adding to a pile of timbers already as high as their heads.

'So *that's* what that chopping was,' Simon said, watching the axes flash and fall. 'What are they doing?'

Father Strangyeard turned to follow his glance. 'Ah. Ah. Building a pyre, they are. Going to burn the *Hunë* – the giant.'

'The giant?' It came back in a rush: the snarling, leathery face, the arms of impossible length lashing out at him. 'It isn't dead?'

'Oh, quite dead, yes.' Strangyeard began walking toward the main buildings. Simon fell in behind, sneaking a last look back at the growing stack of spars. 'You see, Simon, some of Josua's men wanted to make a show of it, you understand, cut its head off, mount it on the gate, that sort of thing. The prince said no. He said that it was an evil thing, but it was no animal. They wear clothes of a sort, did you know? Carry clubs, as well, cudgels really. Well, Josua said he'd mount no enemy's head for sport. Said burn it.' Strangyeard tugged at his ear. 'So, they're going to burn it.'

565

'Tonight?' Simon had to stretch to keep up with the priest's long strides.

'Just as soon as the pyre is finished. Prince Josua doesn't want any more made of it than has to be. I'm sure he'd just as lief bury it in the hills, but the people want to see it dead.' Father Strangyeard quickly sketched the sign of the Tree on his breast. 'It's the third one come down from the north this month, you see. One of the others killed the bishop's brother. It's all been most unnatural.'

Binabik was in a small room off the chapel, which stood in the center courtyard of the main keep buildings. He looked very pale, and smaller than Simon expected, as though some of the substance had drained from him, but his smile was cheerful.

'Friend Simon,' he said, sitting up carefully. His small brown torso was swathed in bandages to the collarbone. Simon resisted the urge to pick the little man up and hug him, not wanting to open the healing wounds. Instead he sat on the edge of the pallet and clasped one of Binabik's warm hands.

'I thought you were lost,' Simon said, tongue thick in his mouth.

'As I did, when the arrow struck at me,' the troll said with a rueful shake of the head. 'But apparently nothing of a serious nature was pierced. I have been given good care, and but for a soreness of movement I am nearly new.' He turned to the priest. 'I walked upon the yard today.'

'Good, very good.' Father Strangyeard smiled absently, fiddling with the string that held his eye patch in place. 'Well, I must be going. I'm sure there are many things you companions wish to discuss.' He sidled for the door. 'Simon, please use my room as long as you like. I am sharing Brother Eglaf's room for the nonce. He makes terrible noises when he sleeps, but he is a good man to take me in.'

Simon thanked him. After a last wish for Binabik's continued return to strength, he went out.

'He is a man of very good mind, Simon,' Binabik said as they listened to the priest's footsteps fade down the corridor. 'Master of the castle archives, he is. We have already had fine conversing.'

'He's a little strange, isn't he? Sort of . . . distracted?'

Binabik laughed, then winced and coughed. Simon leaned forward, apprehensive, but the troll waved him back. 'A moment only,' he said. When he had his breath back, he continued. 'Some types of men, Simon, whose minds are very full of thoughts, they are forgetting to speak and act like normal men.'

Simon nodded, looking around at the room. It was much like Strangyeard's: spare, small, with whitewashed walls. Instead of the piles of books and parchment, the writing table bore only a copy of the Book of the Aedon, a red ribbon like a slender tongue keeping the place where the last reader had stopped.

'Do you know where Marya is?' he asked.

'No.' Binabik looked extremely serious. Simon wondered why. 'I expect she gave her message to Josua. Perhaps he sent her back to wherever the princess is, for relaying of a return answer.'

'No!' Simon did not like that idea at all. 'How could all that have happened so fast?'

'So fast?' Binabik smiled. 'This is the morning of the second day we have been in Naglimund.'

Simon was astonished. 'How can that be?! I just woke up!'

Binabik shook his head, sliding back down into the sheets as he did so. 'Not so. You slept through most of yesterday, waking only to take some water, then sleeping again. I would suppose it was the last part of the trip weakening you, on top of your fever from when we rode the river.'

'Usires!' He felt as though his body had betrayed him. 'And Marya's been sent away?'

Binabik raised a placating hand from beneath the sheets. 'I have no such knowledge. That was guess, only.

567

Just as likely she is here somewhere – perhaps staying with some of the womenfolk, or in the quarter of servants. She is, for all said, a servant.'

Simon glowered. Binabik gently took back the hand the boy had tugged free in his agitation. 'Be of patience, Simon-friend,' the troll said. 'You have done a hero's work to be reaching so far. Who knows what may happen next?'

'You are right . . . I suppose . . .' He took a deep breath.

'And you have saved my life,' Binabik pointed out.

'Is that important?' Simon distractedly patted the small hand and stood up. 'You have saved mine as well, several times. Friends are friends.'

Binabik smiled, but his eyes showed weariness. 'Friends are friends,' he agreed. 'Speaking of those things, I must sleep again now. There will be important doings in the days ahead. Will you look on Qantaqa, and how she is being kept? Strangyeard was supposed to be fetching her to me, but I am afraid it has slipped from his busy head like down from a' – he plumped his – 'a pillow.'

'Certainly,' Simon said, pulling open the door. 'Do you know where she is?'

'Strangyeard said . . . the stables . . .' Binabik responded, yawning. Simon let himself out.

As he emerged into the central courtyard, stopping to watch the people passing by, courtiers and servants and clerics, none of them paying him the slightest attention, he was struck by a twofold revelation.

First of all, he had no idea where the stables might be. Second, he was very, very hungry. Father Strangyeard had said something about being sworn to see him provided for, but the priest had wandered off. He *was* a daft old bird!

Suddenly he saw a familiar face across the courtyard. He had already taken several steps before he remembered the name that went with it.

'Sangfugol!' he called, and the harper stopped, looking around to find who had called him. He saw Simon running toward him and shaded his eyes, continuing to look puzzled even as the youth slid to a stop before him.

'Yes?' he said. He was dressed in a rich doublet of lavender, and his dark hair hung gracefully from beneath a matching feathered cap. Even in his clean clothes, Simon felt shabby standing before the politely-smiling musician. 'Do you have some message for me?'

'I'm Simon. You probably don't remember . . . you spoke to me at the funeral feast at the Hayholt.'

Sangfugol stared at him a moment longer, frowning slightly, then his face lightened. 'Simon! Aha, of course! The well-spoken bottle boy. I am truly sorry, I didn't recognize you at all. You have grown a great deal.'

'I have?'

The harper grinned. 'I should say! You certainly didn't have this fuzz on your face when I saw you last.' He reached out and cupped Simon's chin. 'Or at least I don't remember any.'

'Fuzz?' Wonderingly, Simon reached his hand up and felt his cheek. It *did* seem furry . . . but soft, like the hair on the back of his arms.

Sangfugol quirked his lips and laughed. 'How could you not know? When I first got my mannish beard, I was at my mother's glass every day to see how it was coming in.' He raised a hand to his clean-shaven jaw. 'Now I am cutting it off with curses every morning, to keep my face soft for the ladies.'

Simon felt himself blushing. He must seem such a rustic! 'I have been away from looking glasses for a while.'

'Hmmm.' Sangfugol looked him up and down. 'Taller too, if my memory serves. What brings you to Naglimund? Not that I can't guess. There are many here who have fled the Hayholt, my master Prince Josua not least of them.'

'I know,' Simon said. He felt the need to say

569

something that would bring him back to some kind of parity with the well-dressed young man. 'I helped him escape.'

The harper raised an eyebrow. 'True? Well, this sounds an interesting tale, indeed! Have you eaten yet? Or would you like to find some wine? I know the hour is early, but truth to tell, I have not yet been to bed . . . to sleep.'

'Food would be splendid,' Simon said, 'but first I must do something. Can you show me where the stables are?'

Sangfugol smiled. 'What now, young hero? Will you ride down to Erchester to bring Pryrates' head to us in a sack?' Simon blushed again but this time with no little pleasure. 'Come,' the harper said, 'stables, then food.'

The bent, sour-faced man pitchforking hay seemed suspicious when Simon asked after Qantaqa's whereabouts.

'Here, what do you want with him?' the man asked, then shook his head. 'Fair vicious he is. Not right to put him in here. I shouldn't have to, but that's what the prince said. Almost took my hand off, that beast did.'

'Well, then,' Simon said, 'you should be glad to be rid of her. Take me to her.'

'That's a devil-beast, I tell you,' the man said. They followed his limping progress all the way through the dark stables and out the back door to a muddy yard nestled in the shadow of the wall.

'Bring the cows here for slaughter, sometimes,' the man said, pointing to a square pit. 'Don't know why the prince brought this one back alive for poor old Lucuman to mind. Should have put a spear right in the evil bastard, like that giant.'

Simon gave the bent man a look of disgust, then strode forward to the edge of the pit. A rope staked to the ground at the edge trailed down into the hole. It was knotted around the neck of the wolf, who lay on her side at the pit's muddy bottom.

Simon was shocked. 'What have you done to her!?' he shouted, turning on the stablekeeper. Sangfugol, treading the soggy yard more carefully, came up behind.

The old man's suspicion turned to peevishness. 'Didn't do nothing,' he said resentfully, 'Proper devil he is – howled and howled like a fiend. Tried to bite me, too.'

'So would I,' Simon snapped. 'As a matter of fact, I still might. Bring her out of there.'

'How, then?' the man asked, disquieted. 'Just pull on the rope? He's too big by half.'

'*She*, you idiot.' Simon was full of rage to see the wolf – his companion of uncounted miles – lying in a dark, runny hole. He leaned over.

'Qantaqa,' he called. 'Ho, Qantaqa!' She flicked her ears, as though to dislodge a fly, but did not open her eyes. Simon looked around the yard until he saw what he needed: the chopping block, a scarred log stump as big as a man's chest. He wrestled it to the pit while the stableman and the harper looked on in puzzlement.

'Watch now,' he called down to the wolf, then rolled the stump over the edge; it thumped into the soft earth only a cubit from the wolf's hind legs. She lifted her head briefly to look, then lay back.

Simon again peered over the edge of the pit, trying to coax Qantaqa up, but she paid him no heed.

'Be careful, for pity's sake,' Sangfugol said.

'He's lucky that beast's a-resting now,' the other man said, sagely chewing on his thumbnail. 'Should of heard him afore, howling and all.'

Simon swung his feet over the rim of the hole and slid down, landing in the squelching, slippery mud below.

'What are you doing?!' Sangfugol cried. 'Are you mad?'

Simon crouched beside the wolf, and slowly reached his hand forward. She growled at him, but he held his fingers out. Her muddy nose snuffled briefly, then she carefully extended her long tongue and licked the back of his hand. Simon applied himself to scratching her ears,

571

then felt her for cuts or broken bones. None were apparent. He turned and sat the chopping log upright, digging it into the mud beside the pit wall, then went back to Qantaqa. He put his arms around the width of her trunk and coerced her into standing upright.

'He's mad, isn't he?' the sour-faced man half-whispered to Sangfugol.

'Close your mouth,' Simon growled, looking at his clean boots and clothing already smeared with mud. 'Grab the rope and pull when I say pull. Sangfugol, cut his head off if he dallies.'

'Here, now,' the man said reproachfully, but clutched the rope. The harper took up a position behind him to help. Simon urged Qantaqa toward the stump, at last persuading her to put her forelegs up on it. Simon lowered his shoulder to her wide, fur-fringed hindquarters.

'Ready? Haul away!' he cried. The rope went taut. Qantaqa fought it at first, pulling away from the straining men, dropping her considerable weight back on Simon, whose feet were slipping in the ooze. Just as he thought he could feel himself sliding under, to be crushed to death in a mud pit beneath a large wolf, Qantaqa relented and went with the tug of the rope. Simon did slide, then, but had the satisfaction of seeing the wolf scramble kicking over the side of the pit. There was a whoop of surprise and consternation from the stable-keeper and Sangfugol as her yellow-eyed head breached the rim.

Simon used the block himself to climb out. The stable man was cowering in terror before the wolf, who regarded him balefully. Sangfugol, looking more than a little alarmed himself, was cautiously sliding away from her on his rump, for the moment uncaring of the damage to his fine garments.

Simon laughed and helped the harper to his feet. 'Come with me,' he said. 'We will deliver Qantaqa to her friend and master, who you should meet anyway – then perhaps that food we talked of?'

Sangfugol slowly nodded his head. 'Now that I have seen Simon, Companion of Wolves, some of the other things are easier to credit. Let us go, by all means.'

Qantaqa nudged the prostrate stablekeeper one last time, eliciting a whimper of fright. Simon untied her rope from the stake and they set out across the stable, leaving four pairs of muddy footprints behind them.

While Binabik and Qantaqa had their reunion, moderated by Simon in order to protect the still-weak troll from his mount's dangerous exuberance, Sangfugol slipped off to the kitchens. He returned a short while later with a jar of beer, a goodly quantity of mutton, cheese and bread wrapped in a cloth; he was also – Simon was surprised to see – still wearing the same mud-spattered clothes.

'The south battlement, where we're going, is quite dusty,' the harper explained. 'I'm damned if I'm going to ruin another doublet.'

As they headed for the keep's main gate, and the steep staircase up to the battlements, Simon commented on the great number of people who milled about the commons yard, and the tents and lean-tos that dotted the open spaces.

'Come for refuge, many of them,' Sangfugol said. 'Most are off the Frostmarch and out of the Greenwade river valley. Some also from Utanyeat who've found Earl Guthwulf's hand a little too heavy, but mostly they're folk who've been driven from their land by weather or bandits. Or other things – like the Hunën.' He gestured to the completed pyre as they passed. The woodsmen had gone away; the stack of lumber stood mute and significant as a ruined church.

Atop the battlements they settled down on rough-hewn stone. The sun had scaled high into the sky, beating down past the few remaining clouds. Simon wished he had a hat.

'Either you or someone else has brought good weather

573

with them.' Sangfugol opened his doublet to the warmth. 'It has been the strangest Maia weather of my memory – snow flurries on the Frostmarch, cold rains down into Utanyeat . . . hail! We had hail a fortnight ago, icestones big as bird's eggs.' He began to unwrap the food as Simon took in the view. Perched as they were atop the high walls of the inner keep, Naglimund was spread at their feet like a blanket.

The castle hunched in a steep-sided hollow in the Wealdhelm Hills like something held in an upturned palm. Below the western battlements, across from where they sat, lay the castle's broad outer wall; beyond that the crooked streets of Naglimund town sloped down to the outwall of the city. Outside the wall lay a nearly limitless expanse of rocky grazing land and low hills.

On the far side, between the eastern battlements and the stark violet wall of the Wealdhelm, was a long, twisting trail down from the crest of the hills. Dotting the slopes on either side of the pathway were a thousand points of blackly gleaming sunlight.

'What are those?' Simon pointed. Sangfugol squinted his eyes, chewing.

'The nails, you mean?'

'What nails? Those long spikes on the hillside are what I'm asking about.'

The harper nodded. 'The nails. What do you think Naglimund means, anyway? You Hayholt-folk have forgotten your Erkynlandish. "Nail-fort" – that's what it means. Duke Aeswides put them there when he built Naglimund.'

'When was that? And what are they for?' Staring, Simon let the wind take his bread crumbs and swirl them out over the outer bailey.

'Sometime before the Rimmersmen came south, that's all I know,' Sangfugol answered. 'But he got the steel from Rimmersgard, all those bars. The Dvernings made them,' he added significantly, but the name meant nothing to Simon.

'Why, though? It's like an iron garden.'

'To keep the Sithi out,' Sangfugol declared. 'Aeswides was terrified of them, because this was really their land. One of their great cities, I forget the name, was on the far side of the hills here.'

'Da'ai Chikiza,' Simon said quietly, staring at the thicket of tarnished metal.

'That's right,' the harper agreed. 'And the Sithi can't stand iron, it's said. Makes them quite ill, even kills them. So Aeswides surrounded his castle wih those steel "nails" – used to be they were all around the front of the keep as well, but with the Sithi gone they just got in the way: made it hard to bring wagons in on market day, things of that sort. So when King John gave this place to Josua – to keep him and his brother apart as much as possible, I suspect – my master took them all down except the ones there on the slopes. I think they amuse him. He likes old things very much, the prince my master.'

As they shared the jug of beer, Simon related to the harp player a pared-down version of what had happened to him since they had last met, leaving out some of the more inexplicable things since he had no answer to the questions the harper would surely raise. Sangfugol was impressed, but he was most strongly affected by the tale of Josua's rescue and Morgenes' martyrdom.

'Ah, that villain Elias,' he said at last, and Simon was surprised by the look of real anger that clouded the harper's face like a storm. 'King John should have strangled that monster at birth, or barring that, at least made him general of the armies and let him harry the Thrithings-men – anything but putting him on the Dragonbone Chair to be a plague to us all!'

'But he is there,' Simon said, chewing. 'Do you think he will attack us here in Naglimund?'

'Only God and the Devil know,' Sangfugol grinned sourly, 'and the Devil's hedging his bets. He may not know yet that Josua is here, although *that* certainly won't

575

last long. This keep is a strong, strong place. We have long-dead Aeswides to thank for that, anyway. All the same, strong or no, I can't imagine Elias standing by for long while Josua builds power here in the north.'

'But I thought Prince Josua didn't want to be king,' Simon said.

'And he doesn't. But Elias is not the type to understand that. Ambitious men never believe others aren't the same. He's also got Pryrates whispering words of snaky advice in his ear.'

'But haven't Josua and the king been enemies for years? Since long before Pryrates came?'

Sangfugol nodded. 'There has been no shortage of trouble between them. They loved each other once, were closer than most brothers – or so I'm told by Josua's older retainers. But they fell out, and then Hylissa died.'

'Hylissa?' Simon asked.

'Elias' Nabbanai wife. Josua was bringing her to Elias, who was still a prince, at war then for his father in the Thrithings. Their party was waylaid by Thrithings raiders. Josua lost his hand trying to defend Hylissa, but to no avail – the raiders were too many.'

Simon let out a long breath. 'So *that's* how it happened!'

'It was the death of any love between them . . . or so people say.'

After thinking for a while on Sangfugol's words, Simon stood and stretched; the sore spot on his ribs gave him a warning twinge. 'So what will Prince Josua do now?' he asked.

The harper scratched at his arm and stared down at the commons yard. 'I can't even guess,' Sangfugol said. 'Prince Josua is cautious, and slow to action; anyway, they don't usually call me in to discuss strategy.' He smiled. 'There is talk that important emissaries are arriving, and that sometime within a sennight Josua will call a formal Raed.'

'A what?'

'Raed. It's an old Erkynlandish term for council, more or less. People in these parts tend to cling to the older ways. Out in the country, away from the castle, most of them still use the old speech. A Hayholt man like yourself would probably need a local interpreter.'

Simon would not be distracted by talk of rustic foibles. 'A council, you said – a . . . a Raed? Would that be a council of . . . war?'

'These days,' the musician replied, and his face was again somber, 'any council at Naglimund will be a council of war.'

They walked along the battlements.

'I'm surprised,' Sangfugol said, 'that with all the services you have rendered to my master he has not yet called you for an audience.'

'I've only just got out of bed this morning,' Simon said. 'Besides, he may not even have known it was me . . . in a dark clearing, with a dying giant and all.'

'I suppose you're right,' the harper said, clinging to his hat, which was doing its best to take to the gusting winds.

*Still*, Simon thought, *if Marya took him the message from the princess, I should hope she would mention her companions. I never would have thought she was the kind of girl to just forget us.*

He had to be fair, though: what girl suddenly saved from the damp and dangerous wilderness would *not* prefer to spend her time with the gentlefolk of the castle instead of a stringy scullion?

'You haven't by any chance seen the girl Marya who came with us?' he asked.

Sangfugol shook his head. 'People are coming in at the gates every day. And not just the ones fleeing the outlying farms and villages, either. The outriders for Prince Gwythinn of Hernystir came in last night, horses in a lather. The prince's party should be here this evening. Lord Ethelferth of Tinsett has been here for a week with two hundred men. Baron Ordmaer brought a hundred Utersall men just after. Other lords are coming in with their musters from all around. The hunt is afoot, Simon – though the Aedon only knows who's hunting who.'

They had reached the northeastern turret. Sangfugol tipped a salute to the young soldier who was walking sentry. Beyond his gray-cloaked shoulder rose the bulk of the Wealdhelm, the massive hills seeming close enough to reach out and touch.

'Busy as he is,' the harper said suddenly, 'it doesn't seem right that he shouldn't have seen you yet. Do you mind if I put in a word for you? I'm to attend him at dinner tonight.'

'I would certainly like to see him, yes. I was . . . very frightened for his safety. And *my* master gave a great deal so that Josua could return here, to his home.'

Simon was surprised to notice a faint touch of bitterness in his own voice. He hadn't meant it to sound that way, but still, he *had* gone through it here, and it *had* been him and no other who had found Josua, trussed and hanging like a pheasant over a cotsman's doorway.

The tone of the remark had not escaped Sangfugol, either; the look he turned on Simon was compounded of sympathy and amusement.

'I understand. I would advise, however, that you do not put it to my prince in quite that manner. He is a proud, difficult man, Simon, but I am sure he hasn't forgotten you. Things have been, as you know, rather difficult of late in these parts, almost as harrowing as your own journey.'

Simon lifted his chin and stared out at the hills, at the strange shimmer of the wind-ruffled trees. 'I know,' he said. 'If he can see me, it will be an honor. If he cannot . . . well, that is what will be.'

The harper grinned lazily, playful eyes drooping at the corners. 'A proud and fair speech. Come now, let me show you the Nails of Naglimund.'

*

It was truly an astonishing sight in broad daylight. The field of shining poles, starting within a few ells of the ditch below the eastern wall of the castle, slanted up the slope and away for perhaps a quarter of a league, right up to the feet of the hills. They were arranged in symmetrical rows, as though a legion of spearmen had been buried there, leaving only their weapons protruding above the dark soil to show how conscientiously they stood their guard. The road that meandered down from a gaping cavern in the hill's western face wound back and forth between the rows as sinuously as the track of a serpent, stopping at last before the Naglimund's heavy eastern gate.

'And whatever-was-his-name did all this because he was frightened of the Sithi?' Simon asked, bewildered by the strange, silvery-dark crop that stretched before him. 'Why not just put them at the top of the wall?'

'Duke Aeswides was his name. He was Nabban's governor here, and he was breaking precedent to place his castle on Sithi lands. As to why not on the walls, well, I suppose he feared they could find some way to get over a single wall – or *beneath*, perhaps. This way they would need to go through them. You have not seen the half, Simon – these things used to sprout on every side!' Sangfugol swung his arm in an encompassing gesture.

'What did the Sithi do?' Simon asked. 'Did they try and attack?'

Sangfugol frowned. 'Not as I've ever heard. You should really ask old Father Strangyeard about that. He is the archivist and historian of the place.'

Simon smiled. 'I've met him.'

'Interesting old scuffer, isn't he? He told me once that when Aeswides built this place, the Sithi called it . . . called it . . . damn! I should know these old stories, being a balladeer. Anyway, the name they had for it meant something like "Trap that Catches the Hunter" . . . as if Aeswides had just walled himself in or some such: that he had made his own trap.'

'And did he? What happened to him?'

Sangfugol shook his head, and nearly lost his hat again. 'Damn me if I know. Probably got old and died here. I don't think the Sithi paid much attention to him.'

It took them an hour to complete the circuit. They had long ago emptied the jar of beer Sangfugol had brought to wash down their meal, but the harper had prudently brought a skin of wine as well, thus saving them from a dry hike. They were laughing; the older man was teaching Simon a bawdy song about a Nabbanai noble-woman when they reached the main gate and the winding stairs back down to the ground. As they emerged from the gatehouse they found themselves in a milling crowd of workmen and soldiers; most of the latter were off duty, to judge by the disarray of their dress. Everyone was shouting and shoving; Simon quickly found himself crushed between a fat man and a bearded guardsman.

'What's happening?' he called to Sangfugol, who had been pulled a short distance away by the movement of the crowd.

'I'm not sure,' the other called back. 'Perhaps Gwythinn of Hernysadharc has arrived.'

The fat man turned his red face up to Simon. 'Naow, it ain't,' he said cheerfully. His breath stank of beer and onions. 'It's that giant, the one what the prince has killed.' He pointed toward the pyre, which still stood naked at the edge of the commons.

'But I don't see the giant,' Simon said.

'They're just a-fetching him,' the man said. 'I just came with the others, to make sure of seeing. My sister's son was one of the beaters what helped catch the devil-beast!' he added proudly.

Now another wave of sound passed through the crowd: somebody up front could see something, and the word was hurrying back to those who could not. Necks were craned, and children were lifted to the shoulders of patient, dirty-faced mothers.

580

Simon looked around. Sangfugol had disappeared. He stood up on tiptoe, and found that only a few in the throng were as tall as he. Beyond the pyre he saw the bright silks of a tent or awning, and before it the flashing colors of some of the castle's courtiers, sitting on stools and talking, waving their sleeves as they gestured, like a branch full of brilliant birds. He scanned the faces for a glimpse of Marya – perhaps she had already found a noble lady to attach herself to: surely it was not safe for her to go back to the princess at the Hayholt, or wherever she was. None of the faces was hers, however, and before he could look for her elsewhere in the assemblage a line of armored men appeared in one of the archways of the inner wall.

Now the crowd was murmuring in earnest, for the first half-dozen soldiers were followed by a team of horses pulling a high wooden cart. Simon felt a moment of hollowness in his stomach but dismissed it: was he to go all queasy every time a wagon creaked by?

As the wheels ground to a halt, and the soldiers gathered around to unload the pale thing humped high on the bed of the cart, Simon caught a glimpse of crow-black hair and white skin over where the nobles stood, beyond the stacked timbers; when he looked closer, hoping it was Marya, the laughing courtiers had closed in again and there was nothing to see.

It took eight straining guardsmen to lift the pole on which the giant's body hung like a deer from the king's hunting preserve, and even so they still had to slide it from the wagon to the ground before they could get their shoulders comfortably under the bar. The creature had been trussed at knees and elbows; huge hands wagged in the air as its back bumped along the ground. The crowd, which had pushed forward eagerly, now began to fall back with exclamations of fear and disgust.

The thing looked more manlike now, Simon thought, than when it had loomed upright before him in the forest of the Stile. With the skin of its dark face gone slack in death, the menacing snarl erased, it wore the puzzled expression of a man given unfathomable news. As Strangyeard had said, it wore a garment of rough cloth around its waist. A belt of some reddish stones hung dragging in the dust of the commons.

The fat man beside Simon, who had been exhorting the soldiers to march faster, turned a merry eye his way.

'Do you know what he was a-wearing 'round his neck?' he shouted. Simon, hemmed in on both sides, shrugged. 'Skulls!' the man said, as pleased as if he had given them to the dead giant himself. 'Wearing 'em as a necklace, he was. Giving 'em an Aedonite burial, the prince is – even though it's anyone's guess whose they be.' He turned back to the spectacle again.

Several other soldiers had climbed to the top of the pyre, and were helping the bearers move the massive creature into place. When they had wrestled it into place, lying on its back at the summit, they slipped the pole out from between its crossed arms and legs and scrambled down in a group. As the last man leaped down to the ground, the great body slipped forward a little way, and the sudden movement made a woman scream. Several children began to cry. A gray-cloaked officer shouted an order; one of the soldiers leaned forward and thrust a torch deep into the bundles of straw that had been laid around the edges. The flames, strangely colorless in the late afternoon sun, began to bend around the straw, reaching upward toward more substantial food. Wisps of smoke twined around the form of the giant, and some current of air bent his shaggy fur like dry summer grass.

*There!* He had seen her again, beyond the pyre! Trying to push forward, he received a sharp elbow to the ribs from someone fighting to retain their choice viewpoint. He stopped, frustrated, and stared at the spot where he thought he had spotted her.

Then he saw, and he realized it was not Marya. *This* black-haired woman, wrapped in a somber, exquisitely-sewn green cloak, was perhaps twenty years older. She was certainly beautiful, though, with ivory skin and wide, uptilted eyes.

As Simon stared, she in turn watched the burning giant, whose hair was beginning to curl and blacken as the fire climbed the mound of pine logs. The smoke rose like a curtain, obscuring her from Simon's view; he wondered who she was, and why – as the Naglimunders all around shouted and waved their fists at the pillar of smoke – she looked into the blaze with such sad, angry eyes.

# 31
# The Councils
# of the Prince

Although he had been quite hungry while walking the castle walls with Sangfugol, when Father Strangyeard came by to take him to the kitchens – belatedly fulfilling his earlier promise – Simon found that his appetite had fled. The stench of the afternoon's burning was still in his nostrils; he could almost feel the clinging smoke as he walked behind the castle archivist.

As they walked back across the misty commons, after Simon had picked ineffectually at a plate of bread and sausages thumped down before him by a stern kitchen woman, Strangyeard did his best to make conversation.

'Perhaps you're just . . . just tired, lad. Yes, that's what it will be. Appetite should be back in no time. Young people always have an appetite.'

'I'm sure you're right, Father,' Simon said. He *was* tired, and it was easier sometimes to agree with people than to explain. Besides, he was not entirely sure himself what was making him feel so limp, so washed-out.

They walked on a while through the twilit inner ward. 'Oh,' the priest said at last, 'I was meaning to ask you . . . I hope you don't think it's grasping of me . . .'

'Yes?'

'Well, Binbines . . . Binabik, that is, he told me . . . told me of a certain manuscript. A manuscript penned by Doctor Morgenes of Erchester? Such a great man, such a tragic loss to the community of learning . . .' Strangyeard shook his head sorrowfully, then seemed to forget what he had been asking, for he walked several more steps in gloomy contemplation. Simon at last felt compelled to break the silence.

'Doctor Morgenes' book?' he prompted.

'Oh! Oh, yes . . . well, what I wished to ask was – and I'm sure it is too great a favor – Binbines said it was saved, the manuscript, that it came with you in your pack.'

Simon hid a smile. The man took forever! 'I don't know where the pack is.'

'Oh, it's under my bed – your bed, that is, for now. As long as you want, actually. I saw the prince's man put it there. I haven't touched it, I assure you!' he hastened to add.

'Do you want to read it?' Simon was touched by the old man's earnestness. 'By all means. I am too tired to look at it. Besides, I am sure the doctor would prefer it to be examined by a man of learning – which is certainly not me.'

'Truly?' Strangyeard seemed dazzled, fidgeting nervously with his eye patch. He looked as though he might pull it off and throw it into the air with a whoop of glee. 'Oh,' the priest breathed, composing himself, 'that would be splendid.'

Simon felt uncomfortable: the archivist had, after all, moved out of his own room so that Simon, a stranger, could use it. It was embarrassing that he should be so grateful.

*Ah*, he decided, *but it's not me he's grateful to, I don't think, so much as it is the chance to read Morgenes' work on King John. This is a man who loves books the way Rachel loves soap and water.*

They had almost reached the low block of rooms along the southern wall when a shape appeared – a man, unrecognizable in the fog and fast-diminishing light. He made a faint clinking noise as he stepped in front of them.

'I'm searching for the priest Strangyeard,' the man

said, his voice more than a little slurred. He seemed to waver, and the clinking noise came again.

'He is I,' Strangyeard said, a little more highly-pitched than usual, 'umm . . . that is, I am he. What is your business?'

'I seek a certain young man,' the other said, and took a few steps closer. 'Is this him?'

Simon tensed his muscles, but could not help noticing that the approaching figure was not very big. Also, there was something about his walk . . .

'Yes.' Simon and Strangyeard spoke together, then the priest fell silent, plucking distractedly at his headstrap as Simon continued. 'I'm the one. What do you want?'

'The prince wants to speak with you,' the small figure said, closing to within a few feet, peering up at Simon. He jingled faintly.

'Towser!' Simon said happily. 'Towser! What are you doing here!?' He reached out and clamped his hands on the old man's shoulders.

'Who are you, then?' the jester said, startled. 'Do I know you?'

'I don't know – I'm Simon! Doctor Morgenes' apprentice! From the Hayholt!'

'Hmmm,' the jester said doubtfully. Up close he smelled of wine. 'I suppose so . . . it's dim to me, lad, dim. Towser is getting old, like old King Tethtain: "*head snow-capped and weathered like distant Minari-mount,*" ' he squinted, 'and I'm not so sharp with faces as once I was. Are you the one I'm to take to Prince Josua?'

'I suppose.' Simon's mood had lifted. 'Sangfugol must have spoken to him.' He turned to Father Strangyeard. 'I must go with him. I haven't moved that pack – didn't even know it was there.'

The archivist mumbled an acknowledgment and scuttled off in quest of his prize. Simon took the elbow of the old jester as they turned back across the commons yard.

'Whoosh!' said Towser, shivering; the bells on his

586

jacket tinkled again. 'Sun was high today, but the wind is bitter tonight. Bad weather for old bones – can't think why Josua sent me.' He staggered a bit, leaning for a moment on Simon's arm. 'That's not true, really,' he continued. 'He likes to give me things to do. He's not much for my jesting and tricks, you see, but I don't think he likes to see me idle.'

They walked on for a while without speaking.

'How did you get to Naglimund?' Simon asked at last.

'Last wagon caravan up the Wealdhelm Road. Elias has closed it now, the dog. Rough traveling it was, too – had to fight off bandits north of Flett. Everything's falling apart, boy. Everything's going sour.'

The guards at the front of the residence hall scrutinized them carefully in the flickering torchlight, then knocked for the door to be unbolted. Simon and the jester padded down the cold, flagstoned corridor until they reached another heavy-beamed door and another pair of guards.

'Here you are, boy,' Towser said. 'I'm off to bed, had a late night last night. It's good to see a familiar face. Come by soon and have a noggin with me, tell me what you've been up to – yes?' He turned and shuffled off down the hallway, the patchwork of his motley glimmering faintly until he was swallowed by shadows.

Simon stepped up between the impassive guards and rapped on the door.

'Who goes there?' a boy's voice asked.

'Simon of Hayholt, to see the prince.'

The door swung silently in to reveal a solemn-faced child of about ten years dressed in the costume of a page. When he stepped out of the way, Simon moved past him into a curtained antechamber.

'Come through,' a muffled voice called. After some searching he found the entrance, hidden by a curtain.

It was an austere room, scarcely better furnished than Father Strangyeard's. Prince Josua, in gown and night-cap, sat at a table holding a scroll open with his elbow. He did not look up as Simon entered, but waved toward another chair.

'Please, sit down,' he said, arresting Simon halfway into a deep bow. 'I will be a moment, only.'

As Simon sat in the hard, unpadded chair, he saw a movement at the back of the room. A hand pulled the curtain there aside, revealing a sliver of lamplight beyond. A face appeared, dark-eyed, framed in thick black hair – the woman he had seen in the courtyard, watching the burning. She was looking intently at the prince, but when she looked up her stare met Simon's and held it, angry eyes like a cornered cat. The curtain dropped back into place.

Worried, for a moment he considered saying something to Josua. A spy? An assassin? Then he realized why this woman was in the prince's bedchamber, and he felt very foolish.

Josua looked up to the blushing Simon, allowing the scroll to curl on the table before him. 'Now, forgive me.' He rose, and pulled his chair nearer. 'I have been thoughtless. I hope you will understand that I meant no slight to one who helped me escape my imprisonment.'

'No . . . no need to apologize, your Highness,' Simon stammered.

Josua spread the fingers of his left hand, a pained expression on his face. Simon remembered what Sangfugol had said, and wondered what it must be like to lose a hand.

'Please. "Josua" in this room – Prince Josua if you must. When I studied with the Usirean brothers in Nabban they called me "acolyte," or "boy." I do not think I have come so far since then.'

'Yes, sir.'

Josua's eyes flicked away, back to his writing table; in the moment of silence Simon looked him over carefully. In truth, he did not look a great deal more princely than when Simon had seen him in his shackles in Morgenes' chambers. He looked tired, worn by care as surely as a

588

rock is worn by weather. In his nightclothes, high pale brow furrowed in thought, he looked more like a companion archivist to Father Strangyeard than a prince of Erkynland or a son of Prester John.

Josua got up and walked back to his scroll.

'The writings of old Dendinis,' he tapped it against his leather-capped right wrist, 'Aeswides' military architect. Do you know, Naglimund has never been broken by siege? When Fingil of Rimmersgard rolled down from the north, he had to detach two thousand men to keep this castle bottled up, to protect his flank.' He tapped again. 'Dendinis built well.'

There was a pause. At length Simon awkwardly filled it. 'It is a mighty keep, Prince Josua.'

The prince tossed the scroll back onto the table, pursing his lips like a miser counting out his taxes. 'Yes . . . but even a mighty keep can be starved out. Our supply lines are almost impossibly long, and where can we expect to find help?' Josua looked at Simon as if he expected some answer, but the youth could only goggle, without a thought of what to say. 'Perhaps Isgrimnur will bring back cheering news . . .' the prince continued, 'and perhaps not. Word is spreading up from the south that my brother is assembling a great force of troops.' Josua stared at the floor, then looked up suddenly, eyes bright and intent. 'Again, forgive me. I find I am awash in dark thoughts lately, and my words run ahead of my good sense. It is one thing to read of great battles, you know, it is another to try and plan them. Do you know how many things there are to think of? Mustering the local troops, bringing the people and their stock into the castle, shoring up the walls . . . and all these things useless if no one will fight at Elias' back. If we stand alone, we will stand a long time . . . but we will fall at last.'

Simon was disconcerted. It was flattering to have Josua speak so openly with him, but there was also something frightening about a prince so full of foreboding, a prince

589

who was willing to speak to a boy as though to his war council. 'Well,' Simon said at last, 'well . . . surely everything will turn out as God wills it.' He hated himself for such stupidity even as the words were out of his mouth.

Josua only laughed, a sour chuckle. 'Ah, caught up by a mere lad, like Usires on the famous thornbush. You are right, Simon. While we breathe there's hope, and I have you to thank for that.'

'Only in part, Prince Josua.' Did that sound ungrateful, he wondered?

The wintry look returned to the prince's stern face. 'I heard about the doctor. A cruel blow to us all, but even crueler to you, I'm sure. We will miss his wisdom – his goodness, too, but his wisdom more. I hope that others can take up some of the slack.' Josua pulled up the chair again and leaned forward. 'There will be a council, and I think it must be soon. Gwythinn, Lluth of Hernystir's son, will be here tonight. There are already others who have been waiting several days. Many plans hinge on what we decide here, many lives.' Josua nodded his head slowly, musing.

'Is . . . is Duke Isgrimnur alive, Prince?' Simon asked. 'I . . . I spent a night with his men on the journey here, but . . . but I left them.'

'He and his men were here days ago, stopping before continuing toward Elvritshalla. That is why I cannot wait – they might be weeks.' He looked away again.

'Can you wield a sword, Simon?' he asked suddenly. 'Have you been trained?'

'Not really, sir.'

'Then go to the captain of the guards and have him find someone to work with you. We will need every arm, I think, especially strong young ones.'

'Of course, Prince Josua,' Simon said. The prince stood up and walked to his table, turning his back as though the audience was over. Simon sat frozen in his chair, wanting to ask another question, not sure of the propriety. At last he stood up, too, and backed slowly toward the curtained doorway. Josua continued to stare at Dendinis' scroll. Simon was a step from going out when he stopped, squared his shoulders, and asked the question he had been balancing.

'Prince Josua, sire,' he began, and the tall man looked back over his shoulder.

'Yes?'

'Did . . . did the girl Marya . . . the girl who brought you the message from your niece Miriamele . . .' He took a breath. 'Do you know where she is?'

Josua raised an eyebrow. 'Even in our darkest days, we cannot keep our minds from them, can we?' The prince shook his head. 'I'm afraid I cannot help you there, young man. Good night.'

Simon bobbed his head and backed out through the curtain.

As he walked back from his unsettling audience with the prince, Simon wondered what would become of them all. It had seemed such a victory to reach Naglimund. For weeks he had thought of no other goal, followed no other star. Torn away from his home, it had been something to pursue to keep the larger questions at bay. Now what had seemed a paradise of safety compared to the wild journey was suddenly yet another trap. Josua had as much as said it: if they were not overrun, they would be starved.

As soon as he reached Strangyeard's tiny room he crawled into bed, but he heard the sentries call out the hour twice more before he fell asleep.


A groggy Simon answered the rap at the door, opening it to discover a gray morning, a large wolf, and a troll.

'I am startled to be finding you abed!' Binabik grinned wickedly. 'A few days out of the wilderness only and civilization has sunk its claws of laziness into you!'

'I am not,' Simon frowned, 'in bed. Not any longer. But why aren't *you*?'

'In bed?' Binabik asked, stumping slowly into the room and nudging the door closed with his hip. 'I am better – or better enough. Things there are to do.' He squinted around the room as Simon sank back onto the edge of the pallet and contemplated his own unshod feet. 'Do you know where is the pack we saved?' the troll asked at last.

'*Urrh*,' Simon grunted, then waved his hand at the floor. 'It was under the bed, but I think Father Strangyeard took it to get Morgenes' book.'

'Likely it is still there,' Binabik said, lowering himself gingerly to his hands and knees. 'The priest seems to me a man forgetful of people, but who is putting things back in their place when he is finished with them.' He scrabbled under the bed. 'Aha! Here I have found it!'

'Isn't that bad, with your wound?' Simon asked, feeling guilty he had not offered to do it himself. Binabik backed out and stood up, very carefully, Simon noticed.

'Trolls have fast healing,' he said, and smiled broadly, but Simon was still worried.

'I don't think you should be up and around yet,' he said as Binabik rifled through the pack. 'That's no way to get better.'

'A fine trollmother you would make,' Binabik said without looking up. 'Will you be chewing my meat for me, too? *Qinkipa!* Where are those bones!?'

Simon got down on his knees to try and find his boots, but it was difficult with the wolf padding up and down in the narrow chamber.

'Can't Qantaqa wait outside?' he asked as her broad flank bumped him again.

'Both of your friends will be happy to leave if we are bringing you inconvenience, Simon,' the troll said primly. '*Aia!* Here they have been hiding!'

Outdone, the boy stared at the troll. Binabik was brave, clever, kind, had been wounded at Simon's side – and even without these things was anyway too little to hit. Simon made a noise of disgust and frustration and crawled over.

592

'What do you need those bones for?' He peered over Binabik's shoulder. 'Is my arrow still there?'

'The arrow, yes,' his friend replied. 'The bones? Because these are days of decision, and I would be a fool to avoid any wise advising.'

'The prince summoned me last night.'

'I know.' Binabik shook the bones out of their sack and weighed them in his hand. 'I was speaking with him this morning. The Hernystiri have arrived. There will be council tonight.'

'He told you that?' Simon was more than a little disappointed to find that he had not been Josua's only confidante, but a little relieved as well to find the responsibility shared. 'Are you going to go there?'

'As the only man of my people ever to enter the walls of Naglimund? As the apprentice of Ookequk, Singing Man of the Mintahoq trolls? Of course I will go. So also will you.'

'Me?!' He felt caught off balance. 'Why me? What in the name of the good God would I do at a . . . a military council? I'm no soldier. I'm not even a grown man!'

'Certain it is you are not hurrying to be one.' Binabik made a mocking face. 'But even you cannot fight maturity away forever. Besides, your years have no meaning in this. You have seen and heard things that may be important, and Prince Josua would want you there.'

'*Would* want? Did he ask for me?'

The troll blew the hanging hair off his forehead impatiently. 'Not with exactness . . . but he asked *me*, and I will take you. Josua does not know all you have seen.'

'God's Blood, Binabik!'

'Please do not be swearing Aedonite oaths at me. Just because you are having a beard . . . almost . . . does not make you a man to be cursing. Now please let me have some silence to throw the bones, then I have more news to tell.'

Simon sat back, worried and upset. What if they asked

593

him questions? Was he going to be called to speak in front of barons and dukes and generals and all? He, a runaway scullion?

Binabik was crooning softly to himself, gently shaking the bones like a trooper dicing in a tavern. They clicked and then tumbled free onto the slate floor. He examined their position, then scooped them up and tossed them twice more. He pursed his lips and stared intently at the last roll for some time.

'*Clouds in the Pass . . .*' he said at last, musing, '*Wingless Bird . . . Black Crevice.*' He rubbed his lips with the back of his sleeve, then thumped the heel of his hand once on his chest. 'What am I to be making from such a tale?'

'Does it mean something?' Simon asked. 'What are the words you just said?'

'They are the names for certain fallings – certain patterns. Three times we throw, and each throw means different.'

'I don't . . . I . . . can you explain?' Simon said, then almost fell forward as Qantaqa bulled past him to put her head on Binabik's squat thigh.

'Here,' the troll said, 'first: *Clouds in the Pass*. Meaning where we stand now it is hard to see far, but beyond is something very different than what is behind.'

'I could have told you that.'

'Silence, trolling. Do you wish to remain foolish forever? Now, the one that is second was *Wingless Bird*. The second is something of advantage, but here it seems our helplessness might be itself useful, or so I am reading the bones today. Last, what thing it is we should be aware of . . .'

'Or fear?'

'Or fear,' Binabik agreed calmly. '*Black Crevice* – that is a strange one, one I never have gotten for myself. It *could* mean treachery.'

Simon took a breath, remembering. 'Like "false messenger"?'

594

'True. But it is having other meanings, unusual meanings. My master taught me that it could also be things coming from other places, breaking through from *other sides* . . . thus, perhaps something about the mysteries we have found . . . the Norns, your dreams . . . do you see?'

'A little.' He stood up and stretched, then began looking for his shirt. 'What about the other news?'

It took the troll, who was meditatively stroking Qantaqa's back, a moment to look up.

'Ah,' he said at last, and reached into his jacket. 'I have something for your reading.' He pulled out a flattened roll of parchment and handed it up. Simon felt his bare skin tingle.

It was written in crisp but delicate script, a smattering of words in the midst of the unrolled sheet.

*For Simon*
*Here are thanks for your bravery on our journey. May the Good Lord always give you luck, friend.*

It was signed with the single letter '*M.*'

'From her,' he said slowly. He didn't know if he was disappointed or delighted. 'It is from Marya, isn't it? Is this all she sent? Did you see her?'

Binabik nodded his head. He looked sad. 'I saw her, but it was only of a moment. She said also that we would perhaps see her more, but there were things that must be done first.'

'What things? She makes me angry . . . no, I don't mean that. Is she here at Naglimund?'

'She gave me the message, did she not?' Binabik got unsteadily to his feet, but for the moment Simon was too consumed to pay much attention. She had written! She had not forgotten! But she certainly had not written much, and she hadn't come to see him, to talk, to do anything. . . .

*Usires save me, is this being in love?* he suddenly wondered. It was nothing like the ballads he had heard sung

– this was more irritating than uplifting. He had thought he was in love with Hepzibah. He had certainly thought about *her* a great deal, but it had mostly been about the way she looked, she walked. With Marya, he certainly remembered how she looked, but just as much he wondered what she thought.

*What she thinks!* He was disgusted with himself. *I don't even know where she comes from, let alone anything about how she thinks! I don't know the simplest thing about her . . . and if she likes me, it's certainly not something she bothered to write in this letter.*

And that was only the truth, he knew.

*But she said I was brave. She called me friend.*

He looked up from the parchment to see Binabik staring at him. The troll's expression was morose, but Simon was not sure why.

'Binabik,' he began, but then could think of no question whose answer would clear his muddy thoughts. 'Well,' he said at last, 'do you know where the captain of the guard is? I have to get a sword.'

The air was damp, and heavy gray skies hung over them as they walked to the outer ward. A pressing crowd of people streamed through the city gate, some bearing vegetables and flax and other things to sell, many pulling rickety carts that seemed to be heaped with the pitiful entirety of their worldly possessions. Simon's companions, the diminutive troll and the huge, yellow-eyed wolf, made no small impression on these newcomers: some pointed and cried out anxious questions in rustic dialect, others shrank back, making the protective sign of the Tree on their rough-suited breasts. On all faces there were signs of fear – fear of the different, fear of the bad days that had come to Erkynland. Simon felt torn between wishing he could help them and wishing he did not have to see their homely, fretful faces.

Binabik left him at the guardhouse, part of the gate building of the outer ward, then went on to visit with

Father Strangyeard in the castle library. Simon quickly found himself before the captain of the guard, a drawn, harried-looking young man who was several days unshaven. He was bareheaded, his conical helm filled full of tally stones with which he was counting the muster of the outland militias trickling into the castle. He had been told to expect Simon, who was duly flattered the prince had remembered him, and handed the youth over to the ministrations of a bearlike North Erkynlandish guardsman named Haestan.

'Ha'n't got y'r growth yet, have ye?' Haestan growled, tugging his curly brown beard as he eyed Simon's lanky frame. 'A bowman, then, tha's the story. Get ye a sword we will, but t'won't be big enough t'do much. Bow's the thing.'

Together they walked around the outer wall to the armory, a long narrow room behind the ringing smithy. As the arms warden led them down rows of battered armor and tarnished swords, Simon was saddened to see the dregs of the castle armaments, slim protection against the shining legions that Elias would no doubt put into the field.

'No' much left,' Haestan observed. 'Warn't half enough in first place. Hope th'outland levies bring somewhat beside pitchfork and plowshare.'

The limping warden at last found a scabbarded sword that the guardsman deemed to be of proper slenderness for Simon's size. It was crusty with dried oil, and the warden was hard put to mask his frown of distaste. 'Polish it,' he said, ''twill be a fine piece.'

Further search turned up a longbow that lacked only a string, but was otherwise in good enough shape, and a leather quiver.

'Thrithings work,' Haestan said, pointing out the round-eyed deer and rabbits etched on the dark hide. 'Make fine quivers, Thrithings-men do.' Simon had a feeling the guardsman felt a little guilty over the unprepossessing sword.

Back at the guardhouse his new tutor wheedled a bowstring and half a dozen arrows from the quartermaster, then showed Simon how to clean and care for his new weapons.

'Sharp it *away*, lad, sharp it away,' the burly guardsman said, making the blade skitter across the whetstone, 'lest otherways ye'll be a girl afore ye're a man.' Somehow, against logic, he found a gleam of true steel beneath the tarnish and grit.

Simon had hoped to start immediately with sword wielding, or at least some target shooting, but instead Haestan produced a pair of cloth-padded wooden poles and took Simon out the city gate to the hillside above the town. Simon quickly learned how little like real soldier-sparring his play with Jeremias Chandler's-boy had been.

'Spear work'd be more use,' Haestan said as Simon sat on the turf, wheezing over a buffet to the stomach. 'As 'tis, though, we've none t'spare. That's why arrows be y'r game, boy. Still, s'nice t'know some swording for close work. That's when ye'll thank old Haestan a hundredfold.'

'Why . . . not . . . bow. . . ?' Simon panted.

'T'morrow, boy, for bow'n'arrows . . . or day after.' Haestan laughed and extended a broad paw. 'Get on y'r feet. Jolliness' just started for th'day.'

Weary, sore, threshed like wheat until he thought he could feel the chaff trickling from his ears, Simon ate beans and bread at the guards' afternoon meal while Haestan continued the verbal part of his education, most of which Simon missed due to a low and continuous ringing in his ears. He was dismissed at last with a warning to be out sharp early the next morning. He stumbled back to Strangyeard's empty room and fell asleep without even pulling off his boots.

Rain spattered in through the open window, and thunder murmured in the distance. Simon woke to find Binabik waiting for him as he had that morning, as though the long, bruising afternoon had not occurred. That illusion was quickly dispelled when he sat upright: every single muscle was stiff. He felt as though he were a hundred years old.

It took more than a little work for Binabik to convince him to get off the bed. 'Simon, this is no evening of sport for your attending or declining. These are things on which our lives will hang balanced.'

He had returned to his back. 'I believe you . . . but if I get up, I'll die.'

'Enough.' The little man got hold of a wrist, braced his heels against the floor, wincing as he slowly tugged Simon back into a sitting position. There was a deep groan and a thump as one of Simon's booted feet hit the floor, then a long interval of silence before the second joined it.

Long minutes later he was limping out the door at Binabik's side, into the gathering winds and chill rain.

'Will we have to sit through supper as well?' Simon asked. For once in his life he actually felt too sore to eat.

'That I do not think. Josua is a strange one in that way; he is not for eating and drinking much with his court. He has a desire for solitariness. So, I am thinking, all have eaten before. That is indeed how I am reconciling Qantaqa to staying in the room.' He smiled and patted Simon's shoulder. Simon winced. 'All that we will feast on this night will be worrying and arguing. Bad for digestion of troll, man, *or* wolf.'

While the storm blustered loudly outside, the great hall of Naglimund was dry, warmed by three huge open hearths, lit by the flames of countless candles. The slanting beams of the roof disappeared in darkness high above, and the walls were thick with somber religious tapestries.

Scores of tables had been pushed together into the shape of a vast horseshoe; Josua's tall, narrow wooden chair stood at the apex of the arc, inscribed with the Swan of Naglimund. Already half a hundred men had installed themselves at different points along the rim of the shoe, talking avidly among themselves – tall men, dressed in the furred robes and gawdy trinkets of petty nobility for the most part, but some wearing the rough gear of soldiers. Several looked up as the pair walked past, viewing them with appraising eyes before turning back to their discussions.

Binabik elbowed Simon's hip. 'They are thinking perhaps that we are the hired tumblers.' He laughed, but Simon did not think he looked truly amused.

'Who are all these people?' Simon whispered as they sat down at the far end of one of the horseshoe's arms. A page set wine before them and added hot water before shrinking back into the long shadows of the wall.

'Lords of Erkynland loyal to Naglimund and Josua – or at least undecided as yet in their loyalties. The stout one in red and white is Ordmaer, baron of Utersall. He speaks with Grimstede, Ethelferth, and some other lords.' The troll hefted his bronze goblet and drank. 'Hmmm. Our prince is not being profligate with his wine, or perhaps it is that he wishes appreciation for the fine local water.' Binabik's mischievous smile reappeared; Simon slid back in his chair, fearing a similar reappearance of the small, sharp elbow, but the small man only looked past him up the table.

Simon took a long swallow of his wine. It *was* watery; he wondered whether it was the seneschal or the prince himself who was tight with a fithing piece. Still, it was better than nothing, and might serve to ease his aching limbs. When he finished, the page scurried forward and filled it again.

More men trickled in, some animatedly conferring, others coolly surveying those who had already arrived. A very, very old man in sumptuous religious robes entered on the arm of a husky young priest and began to set up various shiny articles near the head of the table; the look on his face was one of definite bad temper. The younger man helped him into a chair and then leaned down and whispered something into his ear. The elder made a reply of seemingly dubious civility; the priest, with a long-suffering glance at the roofbeams, strode from the room.

'Is that the lector?' Simon asked in hushed tones.

Binabik shook his head. 'It seems very doubtful to me that the head of your whole Aedonite church would be here in the den of an outlaw prince. Likely that is Anodis, the bishop of Naglimund.'

As Binabik spoke, a last clutch of men came in, and the troll broke off to watch. Some, with hair in slender braids down their backs, wore the belted white tunics of the Hernystiri. Their apparent leader, an intense, muscular young man with long dark mustaches, was talking to a southerner of some kind, an exceedingly well-dressed fellow who appeared only slightly older. This one, hair carefully curled, robed in delicate shades of heather and blue, was so neatly turned out that Simon felt sure even Sangfugol would be impressed. Some of the old soldiers around the table were openly grinning at the foppishness of his rig.

'And these?' Simon asked. 'The ones in white, with the gold 'round their necks – Hernystirmen, yes?'

'Correct. Prince Gwythinn that is, and his embassy. The other, my guessing is, would be Baron Devasalles of Nabban. He has reputation as a sharp wit, if a bit full of fondness for costume. A brave fighter, too, I was told.'

'How do you know all this, Binabik?' Simon asked, turning his attention from the newcomers back to his friend. 'Do you listen at keyholes?'

The troll drew himself up haughtily. 'I do not live always on mountaintops, you know. Also, I have found Strangyeard and other resources here, while you have been at keeping your bed warm.'

'What!?' Simon's voice came out louder than he had intended it to; he realized he was at least a little drunk. The man seated beside him turned with a curious glance; Simon leaned forward to continue his defense in a quieter tone.

'I have been . . .' he began, then chairs began creaking all over the hall as their occupants suddenly stood. Simon looked up to see the slender figure of Prince Josua, dressed in his customary gray, enter at the hall's far end. His expression was calm but unsmiling. The only indication of his rank was the silver circlet on his brow.

Josua nodded to the assembly and then seated himself; the others quickly followed suit. As the pages came forward to pour wine, the old bishop at Josua's left hand – Hernystir's Gwythinn sat at his right – rose.

'Please, now,' the bishop sounded sour, as a man who does a favor he knows will have no good result, 'bow down your heads as we ask the blessing of Usires Aedon on this table and its deliberation.' So saying, he lifted a beautiful Tree of wrought gold and blue stones and held it before him.

'He who was of our world, but is not wholly of our flesh, hear us now.

'He who was a man, but whose Father was no man, but rather the breathing God, give us comfort.

'Watch over this table, and those who take seat here, and put Your hand on the shoulder of him who is lost and searching.'

The old man took a breath and glared around the table. Simon, straining to watch with his chin sunk on his breast, thought he looked as though he would like to take his jeweled Tree and brain the lot of them.

'Also,' the bishop finished in a rush, 'forgive those assembled for any damnable, prideful foolishness that might be spoken here. We are Your children.'

The old man teetered and dropped into his chair; there was a murmur of low conversation around the table.

'Would you guess, Simon, that the bishop is not happy to be here?' Binabik whispered.

Josua rose. 'Thank you, Bishop Anodis for your . . . heartfelt prayers. And thanks to all who come to this hall.' He looked about the high, firelit chamber, left hand on the table, the other hidden in the folds of his cloak.

'These are grave times,' he intoned, moving his glance from one face to the other. Simon felt the warmth of the room well up in his, and wondered if the prince would say anything about his rescue. He blinked, opening his eyes in time to see Josua's gaze slide quickly over him and return to the center of the room. 'Grave and troubling times. The High King in the Hayholt – and yes, he is my brother, of course, but for our purposes here he is the king – seems to have turned his back on our hardships. Taxes have been raised to the point of cruel punishment, even as the land has suffered beneath fierce drought in Erkynland and Hernystir and terrible storms in the north. At the same time that the Hayholt reaches out to take more than it ever did under King John's reign, Elias has pulled back the troops that once kept the roads open and safe, and which helped to garrison the emptier lands of the Frostmarch and the Wealdhelm.'

'Too true!' shouted Baron Ordmaer, and clanged a flagon on the table. 'God bless you but that's true, Prince Josua!' He turned and waggled his fist for the benefit of the others. There was a chorus of agreement, but there were also others, Bishop Anodis among them, who shook their heads to hear such rash words so early on.

'And thus,' Josua said loudly, quieting the assembly, 'thus we are faced with a problem. What are we to do? That is why I have called you here and, I presume, why you have come. To decide what we may do. To keep those chains,' he lifted his left arm and showed the manacle still clasped there, 'off of our necks, that the king would put on us.'

There was a handful of appreciative cries. The buzz of whispered speech rose as well. Josua was waving his enshackled arm for silence when there came a flash of red in the doorway. A woman swept into the room, long silk dress like a torch flame. It was she whom Simon had seen in Josua's chambers, dark-eyed, imperious. Within moments she had reached the prince's chair, the eyes of the men following her with undisguised interest. Josua seemed uncomfortable: as she bent down to whisper something in his ear, he kept his gaze fixed on his wine cup.

'Who is that woman?' Simon hissed, and was not the only one asking, to judge by the rush of whispers.

'Her name is Vorzheva. Daughter of a clan lord of the Thrithings, she is, as well as being the prince's . . . what? Woman, I suppose. They say she is of great beauty.'

'She is.' Simon continued to stare for a moment, then turned back to the troll. ' "They say"! What do you mean, "they say"? She's right there, isn't she?'

'Ah, but I am having trouble judging.' He smiled. 'It is that I do not like the look of tall women.'

The Lady Vorzheva had apparently finished giving her message. She listened to Josua's reply, then a moment later glided swiftly from the hall, leaving only a final scarlet shimmer in the dark of the doorway.

The prince looked up, and behind his placid face Simon thought he detected something that looked like . . . embarrassment?

'Now,' Josua began, 'we were. . . ? Yes, Baron Devasalles?'

The dandy from Nabban stood up. 'You were saying, your Highness, that we should be considering Elias only as king. But that is obviously not true.'

'What do you mean?' asked the lord of Naglimund, above a disapproving rumble from his liegemen.

'Your pardon, prince, but what I mean is this: if he were only king we would not be here, or at least Duke Leobardis would not have sent me. You are the only other son of Prester John. Why else would we travel so far? Otherwise, those who had complaints with the Hayholt would travel to the Sancellan Mahistrevis, or to the Taig in Hernysadharc. But you *are* his brother, yes? The king's brother?'

A chilly smile flickered across Josua's mouth. 'Yes, Baron, I am. And I understand your meaning.'

'Thank you, Highness.' Devasalles made a small bow.

'Now the question remains. What do *you* want, Prince Josua? Revenge? The throne? Or merely an accommodation with a grasping king, one that will leave you unmolested here at the Naglimund?'

Now there *was* a full-blown growl from the Erkynlanders present, and a few rose, brows beetling and mustaches quivering. But before any of them could seize the moment, young Gwythinn of Hernystir leaped to his feet, leaning across the table toward Baron Devasalles like a horse straining at the bit.

'The gentleman from Nabban wants a word, eh? Well, then, here's mine. Fight! Elias has insulted my father's blood and throne, and has sent the King's Hand to our Taig with threats and harsh words, like a man punishing children. We do not need to weigh the this and that of it – we are ready to fight!'

Several people cheered the Hernystirman's bold words, but Simon, looking fuzzily about the room as he finished the last drops of another cup of wine, saw even more looking worried, talking quietly with their table-mates. Beside him Binabik was frowning, mirroring the expression that shadowed the face of the prince.

'Hear me!' Josua cried. 'Nabban, in the person of Leobardis' emissary, has asked hard but fair questions, and I will answer them.' He turned his cold stare to Devasalles. 'I have no wish to be king, Baron. My brother knew that, yet still he captured me, killed a score of my men, and held me in his dungeons.' He brandished the arm shackle again. 'For that, yes, I *do* wish revenge – but if Elias was ruling well and fairly, I would sacrifice the revenge for the good of Osten Ard, and especially my Erkynland. As to accommodation . . . I do not know if that is possible. Elias has grown dangerous and difficult; some say that he crosses over into madness at times.'

'*Who* says?' Devasalles asked. 'Lords who chafe under his admittedly heavy hand? We speak of a possible war that will tear our nations like rotted cloth. It would be a shame if it started over rumors.'

Josua leaned back and summoned a page, whispering a message to him. The boy virtually flew out of the hall.

A muscular, bearded man in white furs and silver chains stood. 'If the baron remembers me not, I will remind him,' he said, plainly uncomfortable. 'Ethelferth, Lord of Tinsett am I, and I wish to say only this; if my prince says the king has lost his wits, well, that word is good enough for me.' He furrowed his brow and sat.

Josua stood up, slender, gray-clad body uncoiling like a rope. 'Thanks to you, Lord Ethelferth, for your good words. *But,*' he cast his eyes around the assembly, which quieted to watch him, 'no one need take my word for anything, or the words of other of my liegemen. Instead I bring to you one whose firsthand knowledge of Elias's ways you will, I am sure, find easy to trust.' He waved his left hand toward the near door of the hall, the one through which the page had disappeared. The boy had reentered; behind him in the doorway were two figures. One was the Lady Vorzheva. The other, dressed in sky blue, stepped past Vorzheva into the pool of light around the wall sconce.

'My lords,' Josua said, 'the Princess Miriamele – daughter of the High King.'

And Simon, gaping, stared at the short, cropped strands of golden hair that showed beneath the veil and crown, shed of their dark disguise . . . and staring at the oh-so-familiar face, felt a great tumbling inside him. He almost stood, as the others were doing, but his knees went watery and dropped him back into his chair. How? Why? *This* was her secret – her rotten treacherous secret!

'Marya,' he murmured, and as she sat in the chair Gwythinn surrendered to her, acknowledging his gesture with a precise, gracious nod of her head, and as everyone else sat down again, talking aloud in their wonder, Simon finally lurched to his feet.

'You,' he said to Binabik, grabbing the little man's shoulder, 'did . . . did you know?!'

The troll seemed about to say something, then

grimaced instead and shrugged. Simon looked up across the sea of heads to find Marya . . . Miriamele . . . staring at him with wide, sad eyes.

'Damn!' he hissed, then turned and hurried from the room, his eyes pooling with shameful tears.

# 32
# Northern Tidings

'Well, lad,' Towser said, pushing another flagon across the tabletop, 'you couldn't be righter – trouble they are. Always will be.'

Simon squinted at the old jester, who suddenly seemed the repository of all knowledge. 'They write letters to a fellow,' he said, and took a generous swallow, 'lying letters.' He set the cup back down on the wood and watched the wine wash from side to side, threatening to overtop the rim.

Towser leaned back against the wall of his boxlike room. He was in his linen undershirt, and had not shaved for a day or two. 'They do write those letters,' he said, nodding his white-bristled chin gravely. 'Sometimes they lie about you to the other ladies.'

Simon frowned, thinking about it. She had probably done just that, telling the other highborn noble folk about the stupid scullion who had ridden with her on a boat down the Aelfwent. It was probably a merry tale all through the Naglimund.

He took another swig and felt the sour taste come back up, filling his mouth with bile. He set the cup down.

Towser was struggling to his feet. 'Look, look,' the old man said, going to a wooden chest and rummaging about inside. 'Damnation, I know it's here somewhere.'

'I should have realized!' Simon berated himself. 'She

wrote me a note. How could a serving girl have . . . have known how to *spell* better than me?!'

'*Here's* that God-be-cursed lute string!' Towser continued to rummage.

'But Towser, she wrote me a note – said God bless me! Called me "friend." '

'What? Well, that's fine, lad, fine. That's the kind of girl you want, not some stuck up fancy-lady who'll look down on you, like that other. Ah! Here!'

'Hah?' Simon had lost the thread. He was virtually positive he had only been talking of one girl – the arch-traitoress, the identity-shifting Marya . . . *Miriamele* . . . well, it didn't matter very much, did it?'

*But she fell asleep on my shoulder.* Fuzzily, drunkenly, he remembered warm breath on his cheek, and felt a corresponding ache of loss.

'Look at this, lad.' Towser was standing over him, swaying, holding out something white. Simon stared, puzzled.

'What is it?'

'A scarf. For cold weather. Do you see these?' The old man pointed a bent forefinger at a series of characters woven onto the white in dark blue thread. The shape of the runes reminded Simon of something that touched off a throb of cold inside him even through the fog of wine.

'What are they?' he asked, his voice a little clearer than before.

'Rimmersgard runes,' the old jester said, smiling absently. 'They read "Cruinh" – my true name. A girl wove those, wove the scarf. For me. When I was with my dear King John at Elvritshalla.' Unexpectedly, he began to cry, feeling his way back to the table to slump down in the hard chair. Within a few moments the sobbing was over, and water stood in his red-rimmed eyes like puddles after a sunshower. Simon said nothing.

'I should have married that one,' Towser said at last. 'But she would not leave her land – wouldn't come back to the Hayholt. Frightened of foreign ways, she was,

609

frightened to leave her family. She died years ago, poor girl.' He sniffled loudly. 'And how could I have ever left my good John?'

'What do you mean?' Simon asked. He couldn't remember where he'd seen the Rimmersgard runes lately, or at least he did not want to put out the effort to recall. Easier just to sit here in the candlelight and let the old man talk. 'When were th . . . when were you in Rimmersgard?' he prompted.

'Oh, lad, years and years and years.' Towser wiped his eyes without embarrassment and blew his nose into a capacious kerchief. 'It was after the Battle of Naarved. In the year after it was over, that was when I met the girl who made this.'

'What was the Battle of Naarved?' Simon reached out to pour himself more wine, then thought better of it. What, he wondered, was going on in the great hall at this moment?

'Naarved?' Towser goggled. 'You don't know Naarved? Where John beat old King Jormgrun, and became High King over the north?'

'I suppose I do know some of it,' Simon said uncomfortably. What a lot there was to know in the world! 'It was a famous battle?'

'Of course!' Towser's eyes were bright. 'John laid siege to Naarved all through the winter. Jormgrun and his men never thought that southerners, Erkynlanders, could survive the cruel Rimmersgard snows. They were sure that John would have to call off the siege and retreat south. But John did it! Not only did they break Naarved, but in the final storming John went over the wall of the inner keep himself and got the porticullis open – held off ten men until he could cut the guy rope. Then he broke Jormgrun's shield and cut him down before his own heathen altar!'

'Really? And you were there?' Simon *had* heard this story, more or less, but it was exciting to hear it from a firsthand witness.

'As good as. I was in John's camp; he took me everywhere with him, my good old king.'

'How did Isgrimnur get to be duke?'

'Ah.' Towser's hand, which had been wringing the white scarf, went in search of the wine jug and found it. 'It was his father Isbeorn who was the first duke, you see. He was the first of the pagan Rimmersgard nobles to become enlightened – to receive the grace of Usires Aedon. His house was made by John the first house of Rimmersgard. So Isbeorn's son Isgrimnur is duke now, and a more pious Aedonite you'd have a hard time finding.'

'What happened to King Jorg-whatever-was-his-name's sons? Didn't any of them want to become Aedonites?'

'Oh,' Towser waved his hand dismissively, 'I think they all died in the fighting.'

'Hmmm.' Simon sat back, pushing the confusing business of religion and paganism out of his mind to try and visualize the great battle. 'Did King John have Bright-Nail then?' he asked.

'Yes . . . yes, he did.' Towser said. 'God's Tree, he was a beautiful man to watch in battle. Bright-Nail, it shone so brightly and moved so quickly – just a blur of steel it was – that sometimes John looked like he was surrounded by beautiful, holy silver light.' The old jester sighed.

'So who was the girl?' Simon asked.

Towser stared. 'What girl?'

'The one who made the scarf for you.'

'Oh!' Towser frowned, wrinkling. 'Sigmar.' He thought for several long moments. 'Well, you see, we did not leave for almost a year. It's hard work administering a conquered country, you know, hard work. Harder than fighting the damned war, it sometimes seemed to me. She was a girl who cleaned the hall where the king stayed – where I stayed, too. She had hair the color of gold – no, lighter, it was almost white. I lured

611

her in to me, just like taming a wild colt: a kind word here, a bit of extra food for her family there. Ah, she was a pretty one!'

'Did you want to marry her then?'

'I think I did. It's been many a long year, boy. I wanted to take her with me, that's sure as sure. But she wouldn't go.'

Neither spoke for a while. The storm winds moaned outside the thick castle walls, like hounds forgotten by their master. Candle wax dripped and sizzled.

'If you could go back,' Simon said at last, 'if you could be there again . . .' he struggled with the difficult idea, 'would you . . . would you let her get away a second time?'

There was no reply at first. Just when Simon was about to reach up and give a gentle shake, the old man stirred and cleared his throat.

'I don't know,' Towser said slowly. 'It seems as though God made happen what He meant to happen, but we must have choices, eh, boy? Without choices there's no good. I don't know – I don't think I want to unwrap the past that much. Better the way it is, choices right or wrong.'

'But choices are so much easier afterward,' Simon said, clambering to his feet. Towser stared fixedly into the wavering candleflame. 'I mean, at the moment you have to decide on things, you never know enough. It's only later that you see everything.'

He suddenly felt more tired than drunken, caught and tugged at by a wave of fatigue. He gave thanks for the wine, then said good night to the old jester and walked out into the deserted courtyard and the slanting rain.

Simon stood and knocked mud off his boots, watching Haestan stump away across the damp, wind-lashed hillside. The cookfires of the town below bled their smokes upward into the steely sky. Unwrapping the cloth padding from his sword, he watched the white blades of sunlight that thrust down through the clouds on the northwestern horizon, shafts that might signify either the presence of a brighter, better place beyond the storm, or only the impersonal play of light, caring nothing for the world or its problems. Simon stared upward, rolling the batting in his hands, but his mood remained unchanged. He felt lonely. Standing amid the swaying grasses he might as well have been a stone or the stump of a tree.

Binabik had come by that morning, the sound of his rap at the door eventually cutting through Simon's wine-weighted sleep. He had ignored the rapping and the troll's faint words until both stopped, and he could roll back over and doze a little longer. He had no wish to see the little man quite yet, and had been grateful for the impersonal door between them.

Haestan had laughed callously at the greenish tinge Simon wore to the guard barracks, and after promising to take him out sometime soon for some *real* drinking, proceeded to sweat the vapors out of him. Although at first Simon was convinced that his life was being drained from him at the same time, after an hour or so he thought he could feel his blood once more begin to flow through his veins. Haestan worked him even harder than the day before, with cloth-shrouded sword and padded buckler, but Simon was grateful for the distraction: it was a luxury to submerge himself in the relentless, pounding rhythm of sword on shield, of swipe and dodge and counter-swipe.

Now, with the wind knifing through his sweat-sodden shirt, he picked up his gear and started back up the slope to the main gate.

Trudging across the rain-puddled inner courtyard, dodging the squad of guards in thick wool cloaks on their way out to relieve the sentries, it seemed to him that all the color had been bled out of Naglimund. The unhealthy trees, the gray capes of Josua's guardsmen, the priests' somber vestments, every object in his view could have been hewn from stone; even the hurrying pages were only statues that had been given some sort of transitory life, but would eventually grind down into immobility again.

As Simon toyed with, even enjoyed, these gloomy sentiments, his attention was attracted by a gleam of color that suddenly appeared across a long open courtyard, colors whose brightness leaped out like a trumpet call on a quiet evening.

The extravagant silks belonged to three young women who had swung out from an archway to skitter headlong, laughing, across the open court. One wore red and gold, another a yellow like a field of mown hay; the third had a long, shiny dress of dove-gray and blue. It took him only a fraction of an instant to recognize the last as Miriamele.

He was already walking toward the retreating threesome before he knew what he was up to; a moment later he began to trot as they disappeared under the long, columned walkway, the sound of their talk floating back to him like a provocative scent to a chained mastiff. Within thirty long paces he had caught up.

'Miriamele!' he said, and it came out of his mouth very loudly, making him stop short in surprise and embarrassment. 'Princess?' he lamely tacked on as she turned. Recognition was pushed off her face by another emotion that followed quickly behind, one that looked to him terrifyingly like pity.

'Simon?' she questioned, but there was no corresponding doubt in her eyes. They stood, three or four ells between them, facing each other as though across a canyon. For a moment they only stared, each waiting for the other's voice to cross the distance with the proper reply. At last Miriamele said something short and quiet to her two companions, whose faces Simon took no notice of, except to register what he was sure was disapproval in their expressions; the pair backed away, then turned and walked a short distance ahead.

'I . . . I feel strange not calling you Marya . . . Princess.' Simon looked down at the mud splattered on his boottops, his grass-stained pants, and instead of the shame he would have expected felt a kind of strange, fierce pride. Perhaps he *was* a bumpkin; at least he was an honest bumpkin.

The princess looked him over quickly, saving his face for last. 'I'm sorry, Simon. I didn't lie to you because I wanted to, but because I had to.' She unknotted her fingers to make a brief gesture of helplessness. 'I'm sorry.'

'No . . . no need to be sorry. It just . . . just . . .' he searched for words, keeping his own hands resolutely clamped around his scabbard, 'it just makes things strange, I suppose.'

Now he was looking *her* over. He decided that the beautiful dress – which, he noticed, was striped in green, perhaps in stubborn loyalty to her father – both added to the Marya he remembered, and took something away as well. She looked good, he had to admit: her fine, sharp features were now set, like a valuable stone, in a substance that showed them off properly. At the same time there was something missing, something funny and earthy and careless in the Marya who had shared his river journey and the terrifying night on the Stile. There was not much to remind him of it in her subdued face, but a hint still lurked in the close-shorn strands of hair that showed at the neck of her cowl.

'Did you have your hair dyed black?' he asked at last.

She smiled shyly. 'Yes. I decided a long time before I ran away from the Hayholt what I needed to do. I cut my hair off – it was *very* long,' she added proudly, 'then I had a woman in Erchester make it into a wig. Leleth brought it to me. I hid my cut hair beneath it, which was dyed black so I could watch the men around my father unrecognized, hear things I wouldn't otherwise hear . . . find out what was going on.'

Simon, despite his discomfort, was full of admiration

615

for the girl's cunning. 'But why were you spying on *me*? I wasn't important.'

The princess continued to twine and untwine her fingers. 'I really wasn't spying on you, not the first time. I was listening to an argument my father had with my uncle in the chapel. The other times . . . well, I did follow you. I had seen you in the castle, on your own, no one telling you what to do, where to be, who to smile at and talk to . . . I was envious.'

'No one telling me what to do!' Simon grinned in spite of himself. 'You never met Rachel the Dragon then, girl!' He caught himself. 'Princess, I mean.'

Miriamele, who had been smiling, too, again looked uncomfortable. Simon felt a surge of the anger that had burned in him all night. Who was *she* to be uncomfortable around him? Wasn't he the one who had plucked her out of a tree? Didn't she rest her head on his shoulder?

*Yes, but that's a large part of the problem, isn't it?* he thought.

'I have to go.' He hoisted the scabbard as though to show her some detail of its tooling. 'I've been swording it all day. I'm sure your lady friends are waiting for you.' He started to turn, then stopped and bent his knee to her. Her expression became, if anything, more discomforted, more sad than before.

'Princess,' he said, and walked away. He did not look back to see if she watched him go. He held his head up, and his back was very straight.

Binabik, wearing what looked like his good clothes, a white deerskin jacket and a necklace of bird skulls, met him on his way back to the room. Simon greeted him coolly; he was secretly surprised to find that where there had been a vast store of anger only hours before, there now existed only a strange emptiness of spirit.

The troll waited as he scraped more mud from his boots at the doorstep, then followed him into the room while he changed into the other shirt Strangyeard had kindly left for him.

'I am sure you are now angry, Simon,' Binabik began. 'I am wanting you to understand that I did not know about the princess until Josua told me it the night before the last.'

The priest's shirt was long, even on Simon's lank frame; he tucked it into his breeches. 'Why didn't you tell me?' he asked, pleased with the light-headed, casual way he felt. There was no reason he should let the little man's bad faith trouble him; he had been on his own before.

'It was because a promise was made.' Binabik looked very unhappy. 'I was agreeing before I knew to what. But it was only one day you did not know and I did – would there have been much difference made? *She* should have been telling you and me her own self, that is my thinking.'

There was truth to what the little man said, but Simon did not like to hear Miriamele criticized, even though he himself blamed her for vaster but more subtle crimes.

'It isn't important now,' was all he said.

Binabik pulled a poorly-formed smile. 'I am hoping that is so. For now, the important thing is certainly the Raed. Your story should be told, and I am thinking tonight will be the night. With your departure you did not miss much, mostly Baron Devasalles looking for assurances from Prince Josua, should the Nabbanai be committing themselves to his side. But tonight . . .'

'I don't want to go.' He rolled up the sleeves, which hung halfway down over his hands. 'I'm going to see Towser, or maybe Sangfugol.' He fussed with a cuff. 'Is the princess going to be there?'

The troll looked concerned. 'Who can say? But *you* are needed, Simon. The Duke and his Rimmersgarders are here. They have arrived less than an hour gone, cursing and dirty and with their horses blowing froth. There will be discussion of important things tonight.'

Simon stared at the floor. It would be simpler just to

find the harper and drink; it did seem to take one's mind off these kind of problems. Doubtless there would be some of his new guardsmen acquaintances who might be good company, too. They could all go down to Naglimund-town, which he hadn't really seen yet. It would be so much easier than sitting in that great room, that *heavy* room, with the weight of decisions and danger upon them all. Let others do the discussing, the worrying – he was only a scullion, and had been out of his depth for too long. Wasn't that best? Wasn't it?

'I'll go,' he said finally, 'but only if I can decide whether I want to talk or not.'

'Agreed!' said Binabik, and offered a smile, but Simon was not in the mood to dole one out in return. He pulled on his cloak, clean now, but bearing the unmended scars of the road and the forest, and let Binabik lead him away toward the great hall.

'This is it!' shouted Duke Isgrimnur of Elvritshalla. 'What more proof does anyone need! He will have *all* our lands soon enough!'

Isgrimnur, like his men, had not even taken time yet to shed his traveling clothes. Water drizzled from his sodden cloak, pooling on the stone floor. 'To think that I once dandled such an unnatural monster on my lap!' He clutched his chest apoplectically, looking to his men for support. All but the expressionless, slit-eyed Einskaldir nodded their heads in black commiseration.

'Duke!' Josua called out, raising his hand, 'Isgrimnur, please, sit down. You have been shouting since the moment you crashed through the door, and I still do not understand what . . .'

'What your brother the king has done!?' Isgrimnur purpled, and looked as though he might grab the prince and throw him over a broad knee. 'He has stolen my land! He has given it to traitors, and they have imprisoned my son! What more would you have him do to be proved a demon?'

The assembled lords and generals, who had leaped to their feet when the Rimmersmen came tumbling and shouting into the room, began to drop back into the hard wooden chairs, muttering angrily, steel sliding back into a dozen scabbards with a tuneful hiss.

'Must I ask your man to talk for you, good Isgrimnur?' Josua asked. 'Or will you be able to tell us what has happened?'

The old duke glared up the table at the prince for a moment, then slowly lifted his hand and drew it across his face, as though to wipe away the sweat. For a dangerous moment, Simon felt sure that Isgrimnur would cry: the duke's red face crumpled into a mask of helpless despair, his eyes those of a stunned animal. He took a step backward and lowered himself into his seat. 'He has given my land to Skali Sharp-nose,' he said at last, and as the bluster left Isgrimnur's voice the hollowness rang clear. 'I have nothing else, and nowhere to go but here.' He shook his head.

Ethelferth of Tinsett stood up, his broad face full of sympathy. 'Tell us what happened, Duke Isgrimnur,' he said. 'Here we all share one grief for another, but we also share a long history of comradeship. We will be each other's sword and shield.'

The duke looked over to him gratefully. 'Thank you, Lord Ethelferth. You are a good comrade, and a good northern man.' He turned back to the others. 'Forgive me. This is disgraceful, the way I'm going on. It's also no damnable way to give news. Let me tell you of some things you should know about.' Isgrimnur picked up a stray wine flagon and drained it. Several of the other men, anticipating a long story, called for their cups to be refilled.

'Much that has happened you will know, I'm sure, since Josua and many others here were aware already: I told Elias I would not stay at his bidding in the Hayholt any longer, not while blizzards killed my people and buried our towns, and while my young son must rule the Rimmersmen in my stead. The king had resisted me and resisted me for months, but finally said yes. I took my men and started north.

'The first thing was that we were ambushed at Saint Hoderund's; before we walked into the trap, the ambushers killed the keepers of that holy place.' Isgrimnur reached up and patted the wooden tree swinging against his chest. 'We fought them and they fled, escaping when we were slowed by a freakish rainstorm.'

'I had not heard this,' Devasalles of Nabban said, fixing Isgrimnur with a contemplative look. 'Who ambushed you at the abbey?'

'I do not know,' the Rimmersman replied, disgusted. 'Not a single prisoner could we take, although we sent a fair lot of them down the cold road to Hell. Some of them looked like Rimmersgarders. At the time I was sure they were mercenaries – now I am not so quick to think I know. One of my relatives fell to them.

'Secondly, while camped not far north of the Knock, we were set upon by filthy Bukken, a great hive of them, and on open ground, no less. A whole armed camp they attacked! We fought them off, too, but not without great losses . . . Hani, Thrinin, Utë of Saegard . . .'

'Bukken?' It was hard to tell if Devasalles' arched eyebrow was a sign of surprise or contempt. 'Are you telling me that your men were attacked by the little people of legend, Duke Isgrimnur?'

'A legend in the south, maybe,' Einskaldir sneered from his seat, 'a legend in the soft courts of Nabban; in the north we known them as real, and keep our axes sharp.'

Baron Devasalles bristled, but before he would launch an angry reply, Simon felt a movement at his side, and a voice rang out.

'Misunderstanding and ignorance both north and

south are having in plenty,' Binabik said, standing on his chair with one hand on Simon's shoulder. 'The Bukken, the diggers, are not extending their holes much past the northern borders of Erkynland, but what is good fortune for those farther south should not be mistaken for universal truth.'

Devasalles openly gaped in amazement, and he was not the only one. 'And is this one of the Bukken themselves, come as emissary to Erkynland? Now I have seen everything under the sun, and die happy!'

'If I am the strangest thing you see before a year is out . . .' Binabik began, when he was interrupted by Einskaldir, leaping out of his seat to stand beside the startled Isgrimnur.

'It is worse than a Bukka!' he snarled. 'It is a *troll* – a hell-wight!' He tried to push past the duke's restraining arm. 'What is this stealer-of-babies doing here?'

'More good than you, you hulking and bearded idiot!' Binabik snapped back; the assembly collapsed into general shouting and confusion. Simon grabbed the troll's waist, as the little man had leaned so far forward he threatened to tumble onto the wine-stained table. At last Josua's voice could be heard above the clamor, calling angrily for order.

'Aedon's Blood, I will not have this! Are you men or children?! Isgrimnur, Binabik of Yiqanuc is here by my invitation. If your man does not respect the rules of my hall, he may try the hospitality of a tower cell! I wish an apology!' The prince tilted forward like a stooping hawk, and Simon, clutching Binabik's jacket, was struck by the resemblance to the dead High King. Here was Josua as he should be!

Isgrimnur bowed his head. 'I apologize for my liegeman, Josua. He is hotheaded, and not broken to courteous company.' The Rimmersman turned a fierce look on Einskaldir who sat down again, muttering silently in his beard, eyes cast to the floor. 'Our people and the trolls are age-old enemies,' the duke explained.

'The trolls of Yiqanuc are no one's enemy,' Binabik replied, more than a little haughtily. 'It is the Rimmersmen who are so frightened by our great size and strength that they attack wherever they see us – even in the hall of Prince Josua.'

'Enough.' Josua waved his hand in disgust. 'This is no place for the unstoppering of old bottles. Binabik, you will have your say. Isgrimnur, you have a story yet to finish.'

Devasalles cleared his throat. 'One thing only let *me* say, Prince.' He turned to Isgrimnur. 'Faced with the little man from . . . Yiqanuc? . . . I find your story of Bukken easier to credit. Forgive my doubting words, good Duke.'

Isgrimnur's frown softened at the edges. 'Say nothing of it, Baron,' he grumbled. 'I have forgotten it, as I'm sure you've forgotten Einskaldir's foolish speech.'

The duke paused for a moment to marshall his scattered thoughts.

'Well, as I was saying, that was the strangeness of it all. Even in the Frostmarch and the northern wastes the Bukken are scarce – and we are thankful to God it is so. For them to attack an armed force of our size is simply unheard of. The Bukken are small,' his gaze lit briefly on Binabik, and slid off onto Simon. Arrested, the duke frowned again, staring. 'Small . . . they are small . . . but fierce, and dangerous when they attack in numbers.' Shaking his head, as if to banish Simon's disturbing familiarity, Isgrimnur turned his attention back to the others gathered around the long, looping table.

'After escaping the hole dwellers, and making our way here to Naglimund, we quickly resupplied and headed north again. I was anxious to see my home again, and my son and wife.

'The upper Wealdhelm Road and the Frostmarch Road are not good places these days. Those of you whose lands are north of here know what I mean without any more talk needed. We were happy to see the lights of Vestvennby below us the night of the sixth day out.

'The next morning we were met before the gate by Storfot, Thane of Vestvennby – what you would call a baron, I suppose – and a half-hundred of his housecarls. But had he come to welcome his duke?

'Embarrassed – and well he should be, the treacherous dog – he tells me that Elias has called *me* the traitor, and given my lands over to Skali Sharp-nose. Storfot says that Skali wants me to surrender myself, and he, Storfot, will take me to Elvritshalla where my son Isorn is already being held . . . and that Skali will be fair and merciful. Fair! Skali of Kaldskryke, who slew his own brother in a drunken brawl! Would grant me mercy under my own roof!

'If my men hadn't held me back . . . if they hadn't . . .' Duke Isgrimnur had to stop for a moment, twisting his beard in fretful anger. 'Well,' he resumed, 'you may guess I was all for disemboweling Storfot on the instant. Better to die with a sword in my guts, I thought, than to bow to a pig like Skali. But, as Einskaldir pointed out, best of all will be to take back my hall and make Skali eat steel.'

Isgrimnur shared a brief, sour grin with his carl, then turned back to the assembly and slapped his empty scabbard. 'So, that I *promise*. If I have to crawl on my old, fat belly all the way to Elvritshalla, I swear by Dror's Hamm . . . by Usires Aedon, I mean – your pardon, Bishop Anodis – I will be there to put my good sword Kvalnir a yard into his guts.'

Gwythinn, prince of Hernystir, who had been unusually silent, now pounded a fist on the table. His cheeks were flushed, but not, Simon thought, just by wine, although the young Westerner had been drinking that in plenty. 'Good!' the prince said. 'But see, Isgrimnur, see: it is not this Skali who is your greatest enemy – no, it is the king himself!'

A rumble went around the table, but this time it seemed mostly one of approval. The idea of having one's lands taken away and handed to a blood rival struck a deep and threatening spot in almost everyone.

'The Hernystirman speaks rightly!' shouted fat Ordmaer, heaving his bulk up from his seat. 'It is obvious that Elias only kept you at the Hayholt so long in order for Skali to work his treachery. Elias is the enemy behind it all.'

'As he has worked through his only-too-willing tools, Guthwulf and Fengbald and the others, to trample on the rights of most of you here!' Gwythinn had the bit in his teeth now, and he was pulling hard. 'It is Elias who is reaching out to crush us all, until there is no resistance to the reign of misfortune, until the rest of us are taxed into poverty, or ground beneath the heels of Elias' knights. The High King is the enemy, and we must act!'

Gwythinn turned to Josua, overlooking the proceedings like a gray statue. 'It is for you, Prince, to show us the lead. Your brother doubtless has plans for us all, as he has shown so clearly with you and Isgrimnur! Is he not our true, and most dangerous enemy?!'

'*No!* He is not!'

The startling voice cracked like a drover's whip through Naglimund's great hall. Simon, with every other soul in the room, whirled to see who had spoken. It was not the prince, who stood as baffled as everyone else.

For a moment it seemed that the old man had materialized out of the insubstantial air, so suddenly did he step forward from the shadows into the glow of the wall sconce. He was tall, and almost impossibly spare; the torchlight cast deep shadows in the hollows of his cheeks, and beneath the bony ridge of his brow. He wore a cloak of wolfskin, and his long white beard was tucked into his belt; to Simon he looked like some wild spirit of the winter forest.

'Who are you, old man?' Josua called. Two of his guards stepped forward to stand at either side of the prince's chair. 'And how do you come to be in our councils?'

'He is one of Elias' spies!' hissed one of the northern lords, and others echoed him.

624

Isgrimnur stood. 'He is here because *I* brought him, Josua,' the duke growled. 'He was waiting for us on our road to Vestvennby – knew where we were bound, and knew before we did that we would return here. He said that one way or another he was coming to speak to you.'

'And that it would only be better for everyone if I arrived as soon as was possible,' the old man finished, fixing his luminous blue eyes on the prince. 'I have things of importance to tell you – to tell you all.' He turned his disturbing gaze along the length of the table, and the whispering ceased in its wake. 'You may listen or not, that is your choice . . . that is *always* the choice in matters like these.'

'These are children's riddles, man,' mocked Devasalles. 'Whoever are you, and what do you know of the things we debate? In Nabban,' he smiled up at Josua, 'we would send this old fool to the Vilderivan Brothers, whose purview is the care of lunatics.'

'We are not speaking of southern matters here, Baron,' the old man said, with a smile cold as a row of icicles, 'though soon the south, too, will feel chill fingers at its throat.'

'Enough!' Josua cried. 'Speak now, or I shall have you put in chains as a spy indeed. Who are you, and what is your business with us?!'

The old man nodded stiffly. 'Your pardon. I am long out of practice with the ways of courts. Jarnauga is my name, late of Tungoldyr.'

'*Jarnauga!*' Binabik said, climbing back onto his chair to peer at the new arrival. 'Amazing! Jarnuaga! Ho, I am Binabik! I was for long apprenticing with Ookequk!'

The old man pinned the troll with his bright, steely eyes. 'Yes. We shall talk, and soon. But first I have business in this hall, with these men.' He stood straight, facing the prince's chair.

'King Elias is the enemy, I heard the young Hernystir-man say, and I heard others echo him. You are all of you like mice, who speak in hushed tones of the terrible cat,

625

and dream in the walls of doing away with him someday. Not a one of you realizes that it is not the cat who is the problem, but the master who brought him in to kill mice.'

Josua leaned forward, displaying reluctant interest. 'Are you saying that Elias himself is someone's pawn? Who? That devil Pryrates, I suppose?'

'Pryrates *presumes* to deviltry,' the old man sneered, 'but he is a child. I speak of one to whom the lives of kings are flitting moments . . . one who will take away far more than your lands.'

The men began to talk among themselves. 'Has this mad monk broken in upon us to lecture us on the works of the *Devil?*' one of the barons cried. 'It is no secret to us that the Arch-fiend uses men for his purposes.'

'I do not speak of your Aedonite master-demon,' Jarnauga said, then turned his gaze back to the prince's tall chair. 'I speak of the *true* master-demon of Osten Ard, who is as real as this stone,' he squatted and slapped a palm on the floor, 'and as much a part of our land.'

'Blasphemy!' someone shouted. 'Throw him out!'

'No, let him speak!'

'Speak up, old man!'

Jarnauga raised his hands. 'I am not some mad, half-frozen holy man come to save your imperiled souls.' He pinched his mouth in a bleak smile. 'I come to you as one of the League of the Scroll, one who has lived his life beside – and spent that life watching – the deadly mountain called Stormspike. We of the League of the Scroll, as the troll can confirm for you, have for long kept vigil while others slept. Now I come to fulfill a vow made long-ago . . . and to tell you things you will wish you had never heard.'

A nervous silence fell over the hall as the old man walked across the room and pushed open the door that led to the courtyard. The howl of the wind, that had been only a dim moan, was loud in everyone's ears.

'Yuven-month!' Jarnauga said. 'It is only weeks till

626

Midsummer! Listen: can a king, even the High King, do *this?!*' A swirl of rain blew past him like smoke. 'There are fur-clad Hunën, giants, a-hunting men in the Wealdhelm. Bukken crawl from the cold earth to attack armed soldiers on the Frostmarch, and the forge fires of Stormspike in the north burn all night long. I myself have watched the glow against the sky, and heard the icy hammers falling! How do you think Elias has caused all this? Do you not see that there is a black, fell winter coming down on you out of all season, beyond all your power of understanding?'

Isgrimnur stood again, round face pale, eyes squinting. 'What then, man, what? Are you saying, Udun One-Eye help me, that we are fighting . . . the White Foxes out of old legends?' Behind him was a chorus of whispered questions and shocked mumblings.

Jarnauga stared at the duke, and his seamed face softened with an expression that might have been pity, or sorrow. 'Ah, Duke Isgrimnur, bad as the White Foxes – who some know as the Norns – bad as they would be, it would be a boon to us if it were the whole case. But I tell you that Utuk'ku, the queen of the Norns herself, mistress of the dreadful mountain Sturmrspeik, is no more the guiding hand than is Elias.'

'Hold, man, just hold your tongue a moment.' Devasalles leaped up angrily, robes billowing. 'Prince Josua, forgive me, but it is bad enough this madman walks in and disrupts the council, stealing away the floor with no explanation of who or what he is, but now, as emissary for Duke Leobardis, I must waste my time listening to northern bogey tales? This is insufferable!'

As the hubbub of argument rose again, Simon felt a strange, exciting chill. To think that he and Binabik had been in the center of it all, in the middle of a tale that would boggle anything Shem Horsegroom could devise! But as he thought of the story he might tell beside the fire one day, he remembered the muzzles of the Norn hounds, and the pale faces in the dark mountain of his dreams, and again, not for the first time or the last, wished desperately that he was back in the Hayholt kitchen, that nothing had changed, that nothing would ever change. . . .

Old Bishop Anodis, who had been watching the new arrival with the keen, fierce gaze of a gull confronting a newcomer to his favorite scavenging ground, arose.

'I must say, and I feel no shame in admitting it, that I have thought very little of this . . . this *Raed*. Elias has perhaps made mistakes, but His Holiness the Lector Ranessin has offered to mediate, to try and find a way to bring peace between Aedonites, including, of course, their honorable pagan allies,' he nodded perfunctorily in the direction of Gwythinn and his men, 'but all I have heard is talk of war, and the spilling of Aedonite blood in revenge for petty insults.'

'Petty insults?!' Isgrimnur fumed. 'You call the theft of my duchy a petty insult, Bishop? Let you come home to find your church a . . . a damned Hyrka stable, or a nest of trolls, and see if *you* find it a "petty insult"!'

'Nest of trolls?!' said Binabik, rising.

'And this only proves my point,' Anodis snapped, wielding the Tree in his knotted hands as though it were a knife to hold off bandits. 'See, you shout at a churchman when he seeks to correct your foolish ways.' He drew himself up. 'And *now*,' he waved the Tree at Jarnauga, 'now this . . . this . . . bearded hermit comes to tell tales of witches and demons, and drive a wedge larger still between the only sons of the High King! Who does that benefit, eh? *Who does this Jarnauga serve, eh?*' Red and shaking, the bishop collapsed into his chair, taking the flagon of water his acolyte brought and drinking thirstily.

Simon reached up and pulled on Binabik's arm until his friend sat down.

'I am still wanting an explanation for "nest of trolls," ' he growled under his breath, but at Simon's frown he pursed his lips and was silent.

628

Prince Josua sat staring for some time at Jarnauga, who bore the prince's eye as calmly as a cat.

'I have heard of the League of the Scroll,' Josua said at last. 'It was not my understanding that its adherents tried to influence the ways of rulers and states.'

'I have *not* heard of this so-called League,' Devasalles said, 'and I think it is time this strange old man told us who sends him, and what it is that endangers us – if it is not the High King as many here seem to think it is.'

'For once I agree with the Nabbanman,' Gwythinn of Hernystir called out. 'Let Jarnauga tell us all, that we may decide whether to believe him or drive him from the hall.'

In the highest chair Prince Josua nodded. The old Rimmersman looked around at the expectant features, than raised his hands in a strange gesture, touching fingers to thumbs as though to hold a slender thread before his eyes.

'Good,' he said. 'Good. Thus we are on the first steps of the road, the only road that might possibly lead us out of the mountain's black shadow.' He spread his arms, as though drawing the invisible thread out to great length, then opened his hands wide.

'The story of the League is only a small story,' he began, 'but it fits inside a larger story.' Again he walked to the door, which a page had closed to keep the warmth in the high-raftered hall. Jarnauga touched the heavy frame. 'We can close this door, but that does not make the snow and hail go away. In the same manner, you can call *me* mad – that will not make he who menaces you go away, either. He has waited five centuries to take back what he feels is his, and his hand is colder and stronger than any of you can understand. His is the larger story, inside which the tale of the League is nestled like an old arrowhead stuck in a great tree, over which the bark has grown thick until the arrow itself is hidden.

'The winter that is upon us now, the winter that has dethroned summer from its rightful place, is his. It is the symbol of his power as he reaches out and begins to shape things to his will.'

Jarnauga stared fiercely, and for a stretching moment there was no sound but the wind's lonely singing beyond the walls.

'Who?' Josua asked at last. 'What is the name of this thing, old man?'

'I thought you might know, Prince,' Jarnauga replied. 'You are a man who has learned many things.

'Your enemy . . . our enemy . . . died five hundred years ago; the place where his first life ended lies beneath the foundations of the castle where your life began. He is *Ineluki* . . . the Storm King.'

# 33
# From the Ashes of Asu'a

'Stories within stories,' Jarnauga intoned, shucking off his wolfskin cloak. The firelight revealed the twining snakes that banded the skin of his long arms, occasioning fresh whispers. 'I cannot tell you the story of the League of the Scroll without you first understanding the fall of Asu'a. The end of King Eahlstan Fiskerne, he who constructed the League as a wall against darkness, cannot be separated from the end of Ineluki, whose darkness is now upon us. Thus, the stories are woven together, one strand upon the other. If you pull a single thread away it is just that – a single thread. I defy any man to read a tapestry from a solitary strand.'

As he spoke Jarnauga ran slender fingers through his knotted beard, smoothing it and arranging its great length as though it were a kind of tapestry itself, and might lend some sense to his story.

'Long before men came to Osten Ard,' he said, 'the Sithi were here. There is no man or woman who knows when *they* came, but they did, traveling out of the east, out of the rising sun, until they settled at last in this land.

'In Erkynland, on the site where the Hayholt now stands, they made their greatest work of hands, the castle Asu'a. They delved deep into the earth, laying its foundations into the very bones of Osten Ard, then built walls of ivory and pearl and opal stretching up higher

631

than the trees, and towers that stood against the sky like the masts of ships, towers from which all of Osten Ard could be seen, and from which the sharp-eyed Sithi could watch the great ocean bounding the western shore.

'For countless years they lived alone in Osten Ard, building their fragile cities on the mountain slopes and in the deeps of the forest, delicate hill-cities like icy flowers, and forest settlements like earthbound boats with many sails. But Asu'a was the greatest, and the long-lived kings of the Sithi ruled there.

'When men first came, it was as simple herders and fishermen, wandering over some long-vanished land bridge in the northern wastes, fleeing some fearful thing behind them in the west, perhaps, or merely looking for new grazing lands. The Sithi paid them no more mind than they did the deer or the wild cattle, even when the swift generations multiplied, and Man began to build himself stone cities, and forge bronze tools and weapons. As long as they did not take what was the Sithi's, and stayed on the lands the Erl-king had allowed them, there was peace between the peoples.

'Even the empire of Nabban in the south, glorious in its arts and its arms, that put all mortal men of Osten Ard beneath its long shadow, caused no concern to the Sithi, or their king, Iyu'unigato.'

Here Jarnauga looked about for something to drink, and as a page filled a flagon for him the listeners exchanged looks and puzzled murmurs.

'Doctor Morgenes told me about this,' Simon whispered to Binabik. The troll smiled and nodded, but appeared distracted by thoughts of his own.

'There is no need, I'm sure,' Jarnauga resumed, his voice raised to recapture the attention of the muttering throng, 'to speak about the changes that came with the first Rimmersmen. There will be old wounds enough that shall be opened without dwelling on what happened when they found their way across the water, out of the west.

'But what *must* be spoken of is the march of King Fingil down out of the north, and the fall of Asu'a. Five long centuries have covered much of the story with the debris of time and ignorance, but when Eahlstan the Fisher King chartered our League two hundred years ago, it was to find and preserve such knowledge. Thus, there are things I will now tell you that most of you have never heard.

'At the Battle of the Knock, and Ach Samrath Plain, and in the Utanwash – at one place and another Fingil and his armies triumphed, and drew the noose tight around Asu'a. The Sithi lost their last human allies at the Summerfield, Ach Samrath, and with the Hernystiri routed there were none among the Sithi who could stand against northern iron.'

'Routed by treachery!' said Prince Gwythinn, red-faced and trembling. 'Naught but treachery could drive Sinnach from the field – the corruption of the Thri-thingsmen, stabbing the Hernystiri in the back in hopes of some crumbs from Fingil's bloody table!'

'Gwythinn!' Josua barked. 'You have heard Jarnauga: these are old wounds. There is not even a Thrithingsman present. Would you leap across the table and strike Duke Isgrimnur, since he is a Rimmersman?'

'Let him try,' growled Einskaldir.

Gwythinn shook his head, abashed. 'You are right, Josua. Jarnauga, my apologies.' The old man nodded, and Lluth's son turned to Isgrimnur. 'And of course, good Duke, we are here the thickest of allies.'

'No offense was taken, young sir,' Isgrimnur smiled, but beside him Einskaldir caught Gwythinn's eyes and the two stared hard at each other.

'So it was,' Jarnauga continued, as if there had been no interruption, 'that in Asu'a, even though its walls were bound with old and powerful magics, home and heart of the Sithi race though it was, still there was a sense that things were at their ending, that the upstart mortals would throw down the house of their elders, and that the Sithi would pass from Osten Ard forever.

633

'Iyu'unigato the king dressed himself all in mourning white, and with his queen Amerasu spent the long days of Fingil's siege – which quickly became months, then years, for even cold steel could not throw down the work of the Sithi overnight – listening to melancholy music, and the poetry of the Sithi's brighter days in Osten Ard. From the outside, in the camps of the besieging northerners, Asu'a still seemed a place of great power, wrapped tight in glamour and sorceries . . . but inside the gleaming husk the heart was rotting away.

'There was one among the Sithi, though, who wished it otherwise, and was not content to spend his last days keening over lost peace and ravaged innocence. He was Iyu'unigato's son, and his name was . . . Ineluki.'

Without saying a word, but not without a good deal of noise, Bishop Anodis was gathering his things together. He waved his hand for his young acolyte, who helped him to his feet.

'Your pardon, Jarnauga,' Josua said. 'Bishop Anodis, why are you leaving us? As you can hear, there are dreadful things moving against us. We look for your wisdom and the strength of Mother Church to guide us.'

Anodis looked up crossly. 'And I should sit here, in the midst of a war council I never approved of, and listen to this . . . this wild man speaking the names of heathen demons? Look at you all – hanging on his words as though they were every one from the Book of the Aedon.'

'Those of whom I speak were born long before your holy book, Bishop,' said Jarnauga mildly, but there was a fierce, combative tilt to his head.

'It is fantasy,' Anodis grunted. 'You think me a sour old man, but I tell you that such children's tales shall lead you into perdition. The greater sadness, though, is that you may drag all our land down with you.'

He sketched the sign of the Tree before him like a shield, then tottered out on the arm of the young priest.

'Fantasy or no, demons or Sithi,' Josua said, rising

634

from his chair to survey the assembly, 'this is my hall, and I have asked this man to tell us what he knows. There will be no further interruptions.' He cast his eye about the shadowed room, then sat down, satisfied.

'Well you should attend now,' Jarnauga said, 'for this is the meat of what I bring you. I speak of *Ineluki*, son of Iyu'unigato the Erl-king.

'Ineluki, whose name means "here is bright speech" in the Sithi tongue, was the younger of the king's two sons. Together with his older brother Hakatri he had fought the worm Hidohebhi the Black, mother of the red worm Shurakai that Prester John slew, and mother as well of Igjarjuk, the white dragon of the north.'

'Your pardon, Jarnauga?' One of Gwythinn's companions stood. 'This is strange to us, but perhaps not all unfamiliar. We Hernystiri know stories of a black dragon, the mother of all worms, but in them she was called Drochnathair.'

Jarnauga nodded, as a master at a pupil. 'That was her name among the first men in the west, long before Hern built the Taig at Hernysadharc. Thus do bits and pieces of older truth survive in the stories children hear in their beds, or soldiers and hunters share around a campfire. But Hidohebhi was her Sithi name, and she was more powerful than either of her children. In the killing of her, which itself became a long and famous story, Ineluki's brother Hakatri was horribly wounded, burned by the worm's terrible fires. There was no cure for his injuries or their unending pain in all of Osten Ard, but neither did he die. At last the king had him put in a boat with his most trusted servant, and they passed away over the ocean toward the West, where the Sithi hoped there was a land beyond the setting sun, a place without pain, where Hakatri might be whole again.

'Thus Ineluki, despite the great deed of slaying Hidohebhi, became his father's heir under the shadow of Hakatri's fall. Blaming himself, perhaps, he spent long years in the pursuit of knowledge that likely should have

635

been barred to man and Sithi alike. At first he may have thought that he could make his brother well, bring him back from the uncharted west . . . but as with all such quests, soon the search became its own reason and reward, and Ineluki, he whose beauty had once been the silent music of the palace of Asu'a, became more and more a stranger to his people, a searcher in dark places.

'So it was that when the men of the north rose up, pillaging and slaying, to encircle Asu'a at last in a ring of poisonous iron, Ineluki was the one who set his mind to defeating the trap.

'In the deep caverns below Asu'a, lit by cunning mirrors, grew the witchwood gardens, the place where the Sithi tended the trees whose strange wood they used as the southern men used bronze, and as the northerners used iron. The witchwood trees, whose roots, some say, reached down into the very center of the earth, were tended by gardeners as sacred as priests. Every day they spoke the old spells and performed the unchanging rituals that made the witchwood thrive, as the king and his court in the palace above sank more and more into despair and forgetfulness.

'But Ineluki had not forgotten the gardens, nor had he forgotten the dark books he had read, and the shadowy paths he had walked in search of wisdom. In his chambers, where none of the others came anymore, he began a task that he thought would be the saving of Asu'a and the Sithi.

'Somehow, causing himself great pain, he procured black iron, which he gave to the witchwood trees as a monk waters his vines. Many of the trees, no less sensitive than the Sithi themselves, sickened and died, but one survived.

'Ineluki wove this tree 'round with spells, with words older perhaps than the Sithi, and charms that reached down farther even than the witchwood's roots. The tree grew strong again, and this time poisonous iron ran through it like blood. The caretakers of the sacred garden, seeing their charges blighted, fled. They told Iyu'unigato the king, and he was concerned, but seeing as he did the end of all things, would not stop his son. What use was witchwood now, with bright-eyed men all around, and deadly iron in their hands?'

'The growing of the tree sickened Ineluki, even as it did the gardens themselves, but his will was stronger than any illness. He persevered, until at last it was time to reap the sought-for harvest. He took his dreadful planting, the witchwood all shot through with baleful iron, and went up into the forges of Asu'a.

'Haggard, sick to madness, yet full of grim resolve, he watched the master smiths of Asu'a flee before him and did not care. By himself he heated the forge fires hotter than they had ever been; alone he chanted the Words of Making, all the while wielding the Hammer That Shapes, which none but the High Smith had ever held before.

'Alone in the red-lit depths of the forge he made a sword, a terrible gray sword whose very substance seemed to breathe dismay. Such hideous, unholy magics did Ineluki call up during its forging that the very air of Asu'a seemed to crackle with heat, and the walls swayed as though struck by giant fists.

'He took the new-forged sword, then, into his father's great hall, thinking to show his people the thing that would save them. Instead, so terrible was his aspect, and so distressing was the gray sword, shining with an almost unbearable light, that the Sithi ran in horror from the hall, leaving only Ineluki and his father Iyu'unigato.'

In the deepening hush that surrounded Jarnauga's words, a quiet so profound that even the fire seemed to have stopped sputtering, as though it, too, held its breath, Simon felt the hairs on his neck and arms stand upright, and a strange dizziness creep through him.

*A . . . sword! A gray sword! I can see it so clearly! What does it mean? Why does the thought stick in my head?* He

637

scratched hard at his scalp with both hands, as though in his pain he might shake the answer loose.

'When the Erl-king at last saw what his son had made, he must have felt his heart turn to ice in his chest, for the blade Ineluki held was no mere weapon, but a blasphemy against the earth that had yielded both iron and witch-wood. It was a hole in the tapestry of creation, and life leaked away through it.

' "Such a thing should not be," he told his son. "Better that we should go into the forgetful void, better that the mortals gnaw on our bones – better even that we had never lived at all than such a thing should ever be made, let alone used."

'But Ineluki was maddened with the power of the thing, and horribly tangled in the spells that created it. "It is the one weapon that will save us!" he told his father. "Otherwise these creatures, these insects, will swarm over the face of the land, destroying as they go, obliterating beauty they cannot even see or comprehend. It is worth any price to prevent that!"

' "No," said Iyu'unigato, "No. Some prices are too great. Look at you! Even now it has worn your mind and heart away. I am your king, as well as your sire, and I command you to destroy it, before it devours you utterly." '

'But to hear his father demand such a thing, the unmaking of what he had nearly died a-forging – and only done, as he thought, to save his people from final darkness – drove Ineluki past all caring. In that moment he lifted the sword and struck his father down, killing the king of the Sithi.

'Never before had such a thing been done, and when Ineluki saw Iyu'unigato lying before him he wept and wept, not only for his father, but also for himself, and his people. At last he lifted the gray sword up before his eyes. "From sorrow have you come," he said, "and sorrow you have brought with you. Sorrow shall be your name." Thus he named the blade *Jingizu*, which is the word in Sithi-tongue.'

*Sorrow . . . a sword named Sorrow . . .* Simon heard it in his mind as an echo, bouncing back and forth through his thoughts until it seemed it would drown out Jarnauga's words, the storm outside, everything. Why did it sound so terribly familiar? *Sorrow . . . Jingizu . . . Sorrow . . .*

'But the story does not end there,' the northerner said, his voice gaining strength even as its spell flung a pall of unease over the listening company. 'Ineluki, more maddened than ever by what he had done, nevertheless took up his father's crown of white birchwood and proclaimed himself king. So stunned were his family and folk by the murder that they had no stomach to resist it. Some actually welcomed the change in secret, five in particular who, like Ineluki, had been angered by the idea of passive surrender to the surrounding mortals.

'Ineluki, with Sorrow in his hand, was a force unbridled. With his five servants – whom the terrified and superstitious northerners named the Red Hand for their number and fire-colored cloaks – Ineluki took the battle outside the walls of Asu'a, for the first time in almost three years of siege. Only the sheer numbers, the iron-wielding thousands of Fingil's horde, prevented the night-terror that Ineluki had become from breaking the siege. As it was, if the other Sithi had rallied behind them it could be that Sithi kings would still walk the battlements of the Hayholt.

'But Ineluki's people had no will left to fight. Frightened by their new king, horrified by his murder of Iyu'unigato, they instead took advantage of the mayhem caused by Ineluki and his Red Hand to flee Asu'a, led by Amerasu the queen and Shima'onari, son of Ineluki's dragon-doomed brother Hakatri. They escaped into the dark but protective ways of Aldheorte forest, hiding from the blood-mad mortals and their own king.

'Thus it was that Ineluki found himself left with little more than his five warriors in the glittering skeleton of Asu'a. Even his powerful magics had proved too little at the end to withstand the sheer numbers of Fingil's army. The northern shamans spoke their weirds, and the last protective magics fell away from the age-old walls. With pitch and straw and torches the Rimmersmen set the delicate buildings to burning. As the smoke and licking flames rose, the northerners routed out the last of the Sithi – those who had been too weak or timid to flee, or who had felt too much loyalty to their immemorial home. In those fires Fingil's Rimmersmen did terrible deeds; the remaining Sithi had little strength left to resist. Their world had come to an end. The cruel murders, the heartless tortures and ravishings of unresisting victims, the laughing destruction of a thousand exquisite and irreplaceable things – with all these Fingil Redhand's army put his crimson stamp on our history, and left a stain that can never be removed. Doubtless those who had fled to the forest heard the screams and shuddered, and wept to their ancestors for justice.

'In this last, most fatal hour Ineluki took his Red Hand and climbed to the summit of the tallest tower. He had decided, it seems clear, that what the Sithi could no longer inhabit would never be the home of men.

'That day he spoke words more terrible than any he had spoken before, more baleful by far than even those which had helped bind the substance of Sorrow. As his voice boomed out above the conflagration, Rimmersmen fell screaming in the courtyard, faces blackening and with blood running from their eyes and ears. The chanting rose to an intolerable pitch, and then became a vast scream of agony. A huge flash of light turned the sky white, followed a moment later by a darkness so complete that even Fingil, in his tent a mile away, thought he had been struck blind.

'But, in some way, Ineluki had failed. Asu'a still stood, and still burned, although now much of Fingil's army lay wailing and dying on the ground at the tower's base. In the tower top itself, strangely untouched by smoke or flame, the wind sifted six piles of gray ash, scattering them slowly across the floor.'

*Sorrow* . . . Simon's head was whirling, and he had difficulty drawing breath. The torchlight seemed to be flickering wildly. *The hillside. I heard the wagon wheels . . . they brought Sorrow! I remember it was like the Devil in a box . . . the heart of all sorrow.*

'So Ineluki died. One of Fingil's lieutenants, as he breathed his last breath minutes later, swore that he had seen a great form billowing out of the tower, crimson as coals in a fire, writhing like smoke, grasping at the sky like a huge red hand . . .'

'*Nooooo!*' Simon shouted, leaping up. A hand reached up to restrain him, then another, but he shook them off as though they were cobwebs. 'They brought the gray sword, the horrible sword! And then I saw *him!* I saw Ineluki! He was . . . he was. . . !'

The room was wobbling back and forth, and staring faces – Isgrimnur, Binabik, the old man Jarnauga – loomed up before him like fish leaping in a pond. He wanted to say more, to tell them all about the hillside and the white demons, but a black curtain was being pulled before his eyes, and something was roaring in his ears. . . .

Simon ran in dark places, and his only companions were words in the emptiness.

*Mooncalf! Come to us! There is a place here prepared for you!*

*A boy! A mortal child! What did it see, what did it see?*

*Freeze his eyes and carry him down into shade. Cover him with clinging, stinging frost.*

A shape loomed before him, an antler-headed shadow massive as a hill. It wore a crown of pale stones, and its eyes were red fires. Red was its hand, too, and when it clutched and lifted him the fingers burned like fiery brands. White faces flickered up all around, wavering in the darkness like candle flames.

*The wheel is turning, mortal, turning, turning . . . Who are you to stop it?*

*A fly he is, a little fly . . .*

The crimson fingers squeezed, and the fiery eyes glowed with dark and infinite humor. Simon screamed and screamed, but was answered only by pitiless laughter.

He awoke from a strange swirl of chanting voices and clutching hands to find his dream mirrored in the circle of faces that bent over him, pale in the torchlight as a fairy ring of mushrooms. Beyond the blurry faces the walls seemed lined with points of glinting light, mounting up into the darkness above.

'He's waking up,' a voice said, and suddenly the glimmering points came clear as rows of pots hanging on racks. He was lying on the floor of a pantry.

'Doesn't look good,' said a deep voice nervously. 'I'd best get him some more water.'

'I'm sure he'll be fine if you want to go back inside,' the first voice replied, and Simon felt himself squinting and goggling until the face that went with it was no longer a blur. It was Marya – no, it was Miriamele, kneeling beside him; he couldn't help noticing how the hem of her dress lay crumpled beneath her on the dirty stone floor.

'No, no,' the other said: Duke Isgrimnur, pulling nervously at his beard.

'What . . . happened?' Had he fallen and struck his head? He reached up to feel gingerly around, but the soreness was general, and there was no lump.

'Keeled over, you did, boy,' Isgrimnur grunted. 'Shouting about . . . about things you saw. I carried you out here, fair busted a gut doing it, too.'

'And then stood there staring at you lying on the floor,'

said Miriamele, her voice stern. 'It's a good thing I was coming in.' She looked up at the Rimmersman. 'You fight in battles, don't you? What do you do when somebody's wounded – stare at them?'

'That's different,' the Duke said defensively. 'Bandage 'em if they're bleeding. Carry 'em back on their shields if they're dead.'

'Well, that's clever,' Miriamele snapped, but Simon saw a secret smile tug at her lips. 'And if they're not bleeding or dead, I suppose you just step over them? Never mind.' Isgrimnur closed his mouth and tugged at his beard.

The princess continued to wipe Simon's forehead with her dampened handkerchief. He couldn't imagine what good it was doing, but for the moment he was content to just lie back and be tended to. He knew that soon enough he would have to explain himself to somebody.

'I . . . I knew I recognized you, boy.' Isgrimnur said at last. 'You were the lad at Saint Hoderund's, am I right? And that troll . . . I *thought* I saw . . .'

The pantry door opened wider. 'Ah! Simon! I hope you are feeling more of yourself now.'

'Binabik,' Simon said, straining to sit up. Miriamele gently but firmly leaned on his chest, forcing him back down. 'I *did* see it, I did! That was what I couldn't remember! The hillside, and the fire, and . . . and . . .'

'I know, friend Simon, I was understanding many things when you stood up – not all things, however. There is still much unexplained in this riddle.'

'They must think I'm a madman,' Simon groaned, pushing the princess' hand away, but nevertheless enjoying the moment of contact. What *was* she thinking? Now she was looking at him like a grown girl looked at a troublesome younger brother. Damn girls and women both!

'No, Simon,' Binabik said, crouching down beside Miriamele to look him over carefully. 'I have been telling many stories, our adventuring together not least among them. Jarnauga has confirmed much that my master was hinting at. He also received one of Morgenes' last messages. No, you are not thought mad, although I think still many are doubting the real danger. Baron Devasalles especially, I am thinking.'

'Ummm,' Isgrimnur scuffed a boot on the floor. 'If the lad's hale, I think I'd better go back in. Simon, was it? Yes, well . . . you and I, we'll talk more.' The duke maneuvered his considerable bulk out of the narrow pantry and clumped off down the hall.

'And I will be going in, too,' Miriamele said, briskly chasing the worst of the dust from her dress. 'There are things that should not be decided before I have been heard, whatever my uncle thinks.'

Simon wanted to thank her, but could think of nothing to say while lying on his back that would not make him feel more ridiculous than he presently did. By the time he decided to throw over his pride, the princess had gone in a swirl of silks.

'And if you are recovered to sufficiency, Simon,' Binabik said, extending a small, blunt hand, 'then there are things we must hear in the council hall, for I am thinking Naglimund has never seen a Raed quite the like of this one.'

'First of all, young one,' Jarnauga said, 'while I believe all that you have told us, you must know that it was *not* Ineluki you saw on that hillside.' The fires had burned down to dreaming coals, but not a soul had left the hall. 'If you had seen the Storm King, in the form he must now wear, it would have left you a blasted, mindless shell lying beside the Anger Stones. No, what you saw – beside the pale Norns and Elias and his liegemen – was one of the Red Hand. Even so, it seems miraculous to me that you came away from such a night-vision whole in heart and mind.'

'But . . . but . . .' As he began to remember what the old man had been saying just before the wall of forgetfulness had crumbled, spilling the memories of that horrible night – Stoning Night, the doctor had called it – Simon was again puzzled and confused. 'But I thought you said Ineluki and his . . . Red Hand . . . were dead?'

'Dead, yes; their earthly forms burnt away utterly in the last scorching moments. But *something* survived: there was someone or something that was able to recreate the sword Sorrow. Somehow – and it did not need *your* experience to tell me, for this is indeed why the League of the Book was made – Ineluki and his Red Hand survived: as living dreams or thoughts, perhaps, shades held together only by hate, and by the terrible runes of Ineluki's last casting. But somehow the darkness that was Ineluki's mind at the very ending did not die.

'King Ealhstan Fiskerne came three centuries later to the Hayholt, the castle that stood upon the bones of Asu'a. Ealhstan was wise, and a seeker after knowledge, and he found things in the ruins beneath the Hayholt that made him aware that Ineluki had not been completely unmade. He formed the League of which I am a member – and we are dwindling fast now, with the loss of Morgenes and Ooqequk – so that old knowledge would not be lost. Not only knowledge of the Sithi's dark lord, but other things, too, for those were evil times in the north of Osten Ard. Over the years it was discovered, or rather guessed at, that somehow Ineluki, or his spirit or shade or living will, had become manifest again among the only ones who might welcome him.'

'The Norns!' Binabik said, as if suddenly a bank of fog had been swept away before him.

'The Norns,' Jarnauga agreed. 'I doubt that at first even the White Foxes knew what he had become, but soon his influence in Sturmrspeik was doubtless too great for anyone to say him nay. His Red Hand, too, has come back with him, although in no form seen before on this earth.'

'And we had thought that the Löken worshiped by the

645

Black Rimmersmen was only our own fire god, from heathen days,' said Isgrimnur, wondering. 'If I had known how far they had strayed from the path of light . . .' He brushed his fingers against the Tree that hung upon his neck. 'Usires!' he breathed softly.

Prince Josua, who had been listening silently for a long while, leaned forward. 'But why, if it is indeed this demon out of the past who is our truest enemy, does he not show himself? Why does he play at cat's-paw with my brother Elias?'

'Now we are coming to the place where my long years of study atop Tungoldyr cannot be helpful,' Jarnauga shrugged. 'I watched, and I listened, and I watched, for that was what I was there to do – but what goes on in the mind of such as the Storm King is more than I can guess at.'

Ethelferth of Tinsett stood and cleared his throat. Josua nodded for him to speak.

'If all this is true . . . and my head is a-swimming with it all, I tell you . . . then maybe . . . *I* can guess at the last.' He looked around, as though expecting to be shouted down for his presumptuousness, but seeing in the faces around him only worry and confusion, he cleared his throat again and went on. 'The Rimmersman,' he tilted his head toward old Jarnauga, 'said that it was our own Ealhstan Fiskerne who was first a-noticing that this Storm King had come back. That was three hundred years after Fingil took the Hayholt – or whatever was its name then. It's been nigh two hundred year since. It sounds to me as though this . . . demon, I suppose, has taken a long time to get strong again.

'Now,' he continued, 'we all know, we men that've held land in the midst of greedy neighbors,' he snuck a sly look at Ordmaer, but the fat baron had gone quite pale some time before, and seemed insensible to innuendo, 'that the best way to keep yourself safe, and purchase yourself time to grow strong, is to have your neighbors fight each other. Seems to me that's what's going on here. This Rimmersgard demon gives Elias a present, then gets him a-fighting with his barons and dukes and such.' Ethelferth looked around, hitched his tunic and sat down.

'It's not a "Rimmersgard demon," ' Einskaldir growled. 'We're shriven Aedonite men.'

Josua ignored the northerner's comment. 'There is truth to what you say, Lord Ethelferth, but I think those who know Elias will agree that he also has designs of his own.'

'He didn't need any Sithi demon to steal my land,' Isgrimnur said bitterly.

'Nevertheless,' Josua continued, 'I find Jarnauga, and Binabik of Yiqanuc . . . and young Simon, who was Doctor Morgenes' apprentice . . . all too uncomfortably trustworthy. I wish I could say I did not believe these tales, I am not sure yet *what* I believe, but neither can I discount them.' He turned to Jarnauga again, who was prodding at the nearest fire with an iron poker. 'If these dire warnings you bring are true, then tell me one thing: what does Ineluki want?'

The old man stared into the fire, then poked it again vigorously. 'As I said, Prince Josua, my task was to be the League's eyes. Both Morgenes' and young Binabik's master knew more than I of what might lurk in the mind of the Master of Stormspike.' He raised a hand as if to ward off more questions. 'If I had to guess, it would be to say this: think of the hatred that kept Ineluki alive in the void, that brought him back from the fires of his own death . . .'

'What Ineluki wants then,' Josua's voice fell heavily in the dark, breathing hall, 'is revenge?'

Jarnauga only stared into the embers.

'There is much to think on,' the master of Naglimund said, 'and no decisions to be lightly made.' He stood up, tall and pale, slender face a mask before his hidden thoughts. 'We shall return here tomorrow sunset.' He went out, with a gray-cloaked guard on either side.

In the hall men turned to look at each other, then rose, clustering in small silent groups. Simon saw Miriamele, who had never had her chance to speak, go out between Einskaldir and the limping Duke Isgrimnur.

'Come, Simon,' Binabik said, tugging at his sleeve. 'I think I will be letting Qantaqa run, now the rains have gentled some. Of such things we must take advantage. At this point I have still not been robbed of my liking for thinking as I walk with wind in my face . . . and there is much that I should be thinking.'

'Binabik,' Simon said at last, the shocking, wearying day sitting heavily upon him. 'Do you remember the dream I had . . . we all had . . . in Geloë's house? Stormspike . . . and that book?'

'Yes,' said the little man gravely. 'That is one of the things I am worrying with. The words, the words you saw, they catch at me. I am fearing there is a dreadfully important riddle in them.'

'Du . . . Du Swar . . .' Simon struggled with his muddled memories. 'Du . . .'

'*Du Svardenvyrd*, it was,' Binabik sighed. 'The Weird of the Swords.'

The hot air beat painfully on Pryrates' hairless and unprotected face, but he would allow no discomfort to show on his features. As he strode across the foundry floor, robes flapping, he was gratified to see the workmen, themselves masked and heavily cloaked, stare and flinch at his passing. Buoyant in the pulsing forge light, he chuckled as he briefly fancied himself an arch-demon striding the tiles of Hell, petty underdevils scattering before him.

A moment later the mood fell away, and he scowled. Something had happened to that little wretch of a wizard's boy – Pryrates knew it. He had felt it as clearly as if someone had jabbed him with some sharp thing. There was some strange, tenuous bond still between them from Stoning Night; it bit at him, and gnawed at his concentration. That night's business had been too important, too dangerous to bear any kind of interference. Now the boy was thinking of that night again, probably telling all he knew to Lluth, or Josua, or someone. Something serious needed to be done about that nasty, prying boy.

He stopped before the great crucible and drew himself up, arms folded upon his chest. He stood that way for no little while, already angry, growing angrier at the wait. At last one of the foundrymen hurried up and clumsily bent a thick-breeched knee before him.

'How can we serve you, Master Pryrates?' the man said, voice muffled by the damp cloth wrapped across his lower face.

The priest stared silently long enough to change the man's partially-revealed expression from discomfort to real fear.

'Where is your overseer?' he hissed.

'There, Father.' The man pointed to one of the dark openings in the foundry-cavern wall. 'One of the crank wheels be gone on the winch . . . your Eminence.'

Which was gratuitous, since he was still officially no more than a priest, but the sound of it was not inharmonious.

'Well. . . ?' Pryrates asked. The man did not respond, and Pryrates kicked him hard on his leather-clad shin. '*Get* him, then!' he shrilled.

With a head-wagging bow the man limped off, moving like a toddling child in the padded clothes. Pryrates was aware of the beads of sweat forming on his brow, and of the furnace-spewed air that seemed to bake his lungs from the inside, but nevertheless a brief grin stretched his spare features. He had felt worse things: God . . . or Whoever . . . knew he had faced worse.

At last the overseer came, huge and deliberate. His height, when he finally shambled to a halt and stood looming over Pryrates, was almost enough in itself to be regarded as an insult.

'I suppose you know why I've come?' the priest said, black eyes glittering, mouth taut with displeasure.

'About the engines,' the other replied, voice quiet but childishly petulant.

'Yes about the siege engines!' Pryrates snapped. 'Take off that damned mask, Inch, so I can see you when I speak to you.'

The overseer reached up a bristle-haired paw and peeled back the cloth. His ruined face, rippled with burn scars around the empty right eye socket, reinforced the priest's sensation that he stood in one of the ante-rooms of the Great Inferno.

'The engines are not finished,' Inch said stubbornly. 'Lost three men when the big one collapsed Drorsday-last. Slow going.'

'I know they're not finished. Get more men. Aedon knows there are enough slagging about the Hayholt. We'll put some of the nobles to work, let them get a few blisters on their fine hands. But the king wants them finished. Now. He's going into the field in ten days. *Ten days*, damn you!'

Inch's one eyebrow slowly rose, like a drawbridge. 'Naglimund. He's going to Naglimund, isn't he?' There was a hungry light in his eye.

'That's not for such as you to worry about, you scarred ape,' Pryrates said contemptuously. 'Just have them finished! You know why you were given this loftier place – but we can take it back. . . .'

Pryrates could feel Inch's stare on him as he walked away, could feel the man's stonelike presence in the smoky, flickering light. He wondered again whether it had been wise to let the brute live, and if not, whether he should rectify the error.

The priest had reached one of the broad stairheads, with hallways leading left and right, and the next flight of steps ahead, when a dark figure abruptly slid from the shadows.

'Pryrates?'

The priest, whose nerves were such that he might not have cried out if struck with an axe, nevertheless felt his heart quicken.

'Your majesty,' he said evenly.

Elias, in unintended mockery of the foundrymen below, wore his black cloak-hood pulled close around his face. He went that way always these days, at least when he left his chambers — just as he always wore the scabbarded sword. The gaining of that blade had brought the king power such as few mortals had ever had, but it had not come without a price. The red priest was wise enough to know that the reckoning of such bargains was a very subtle science.

'I . . . I cannot sleep, Pryrates.'

'Understandable, my king. There are many burdens on your shoulders.'

'You help me . . . with many. Have you been seeing to the siege engines?'

Pryrates nodded, then realized the hooded Elias might not see it in the dark stairwell. 'Yes, sire. I would like to roast Inch, that pig of an overseer, over one of his own fires. But we will have them, sire, somehow.'

The king was silent for a long while, stroking the hilt of the sword. 'Naglimund must be crushed,' Elias said at last. 'Josua defies me.'

'He is no longer your brother, sire, he is only your enemy,' Pryrates said.

'No, no . . .' Elias said slowly, thinking deeply. 'He *is* my brother. That is why he cannot be allowed to defy me. That seems obvious to me. Is it not obvious, Pryrates?'

'Of course, your Majesty.'

The king pulled his cloak tighter around him, as though to keep out a cold wind, but the air that billowed up from below was thick with the heat of the forges,

651

'Have you found my daughter yet, Pryrates?' Elias asked suddenly, looking up. The priest could faintly see the eye-gleam and shadow of the king's face in the cavern of his hood.

'As I told you, sire, if she is not gone to Nabban, to her mother's family there – and our spies do not think so – then she is at Naglimund with Josua.'

'Miriamele.' The exhaled name drifted down the stone stairwell. 'I must have her back. I must!' The king extended an open hand, slowly closing it into a fist before him. 'She is the one piece of good flesh I shall save from the broken shell of my brother's house. The rest I shall tread into dust.'

'You have the strength now, my king,' Pryrates said. 'And you have powerful friends.'

'Yes.' The High King nodded slowly. 'Yes, that is true. And what of the huntsman Ingen Jegger? He has not found my daughter, but neither has he returned. Where is he?'

'He still hunts the wizard's boy, Majesty. It has become something of a . . . grudge.' Pryrates waved his hand, as though trying to banish the uncomfortable memory of the Black Rimmersman.

'A great deal of effort, it seems to me, has been spent trying to find this boy who you say knows a few of our secrets.' The king frowned and spoke harshly. 'I wish as much trouble had been expended on my own flesh and blood. I am not pleased.' For a moment his shadowed eyes glinted angrily. He turned to go, then stopped.

'Pryrates?' The king's voice had changed again.

'Yes, sire?'

'Do you think I shall sleep better . . . when Naglimund is thrown down, and I have my daughter back?'

'I am sure, my king.'

'Good. I shall enjoy it even more, knowing that.'

Elias slipped away, up the shadowed corridor. Pryrates did not move, but listened as the king's retreating footsteps blended with the hammers of Erkynland, whose clangor sounded monotonously in the deeps below.

# 34
# Forgotten Swords

Vorzheva was angry. The brush trembled in her hand, and the red line trailed onto her chin.

'See what I have done!' she said, irritation thickening her heavy Thrithings accent. 'You are cruel to rush me.' She blotted her mouth with a kerchief and began again.

'By the Aedon, woman, there are more important matters afoot than your lip-painting.' Josua stood up and resumed his pacing.

'Do not speak so to me, sir! And do not walk like that behind me . . .' she waved her hand, searching for words, '. . . to and fro, to and fro. If you must throw me out into the corridor like a camp follower, at least I will first make myself ready.'

The prince picked up a fire iron, then stooped to poke at the coals. 'You are not being "thrown into the corridor," my lady.'

'If I *am* your lady,' Vorzheva scowled, 'then why may I not stay? You are ashamed of me.'

'Because we will speak of things that are not your concern. If you have not noticed, we are preparing for war. I'm sorry if that inconveniences you.' He grunted and stood, laying the poker carefully back against the hearth. 'Go speak with the other ladies. Be glad you do not have to carry my burdens.

Vorzheva spun to face him. 'The other ladies hate me!'

she said, eyes narrowed, a lock of black hair dangling loose across her cheek. 'I hear them whispering about Prince Josua's slut from the grasslands. And *I* hate *them* – the northern cows! In my father's march-land they would be whipped for such . . . such . . .' she struggled with the still unfamiliar tongue, '. . . such disrespect!' She took a breath to still her trembling.

'Why are you so cold to me, sir?' she asked at last. 'And why did you bring me here, to this cold country?'

The prince looked up, and for a moment his stern face softened. 'I sometimes wonder.' He slowly shook his head. 'Please, if you despise the company of the other court ladies, then go and have the harper sing for you. Please. I will not have an argument tonight.'

'Nor any night,' Vorzheva snapped. 'You do not seem to want *me* at all – but old things, yes, yes, those you are interested in! You and your old books!'

Josua's patience was wearing thin. 'The events we will speak of tonight are old, yes, but their importance is to our current struggle. Damnation, woman, I am a prince of the realm, and cannot evade my responsibilities!'

'You do better at that than you think, Prince Josua,' she replied frostily, throwing her cape about her shoulders.

When she reached the doorway, she turned. 'I hate the way you think only of the past – old books, old battles, old history . . .' her lip curled, 'old loves.'

The door swung closed behind her.

'Thanks to you, Prince, for admitting us to your chambers,' Binabik said. His round face was troubled. 'I would not have been making such a request had I not thought this important.'

'Of course, Binabik,' the prince said. 'I, too, prefer to talk in more quiet surroundings.'

The troll and old Jarnauga had pulled up hard wooden

stools to sit beside Josua at his table. Father Strangyeard, who had accompanied them, was walking quietly around the room looking at the tapestries. In all his years at Naglimund it was the first time he had been in the prince's private chambers.

'I am still reeling from the things I heard last night,' Josua said, then gestured at the sheets of parchment Binabik had strewn before him. 'Now you say there is even more I must know?' The prince gave a small, rueful smile. 'God must be chastising me, taking my nightmare of having to command a castle at siege and then complicating it with all this.'

Jarnauga leaned forward. 'As long as you remember, Prince Josua, that it is no nightmare we speak of, but a dark reality. We cannot any of us afford the luxury of thinking this a fantasy.'

'Father Strangyeard and I have been at days of searching in the castle archives,' Binabik said, 'since first I came, trying to find the meaning of the Weird of the Swords.'

'The dream, you mean, that you told me of?' Josua asked, idly thumbing through the pages of writing on the table. 'The one that you and the boy had in the witch woman's house?'

'And not them alone,' Jarnauga declared, his eyes sharp as chips of blue ice. 'The nights before I left Tungoldyr I, too, dreamt of a great book. *Du Svardenvyrd* was written upon it in letters of fire.'

'I have heard of the priest Nisses' book, of course,' the prince said, nodding, 'when I was a young student with the Usirean brothers. It was infamous, but it no longer exists. Surely you are not going to tell me you have found a copy here in our castle library?'

'Not for the lack of our searching,' Binabik replied. 'If it had been anywhere but perhaps the Sancellan Aedonitis, here it would be. Strangyeard has been assembling a library of great wonder.'

'Very kind,' the archivist said, facing the wall as

656

though studying a tapesty so that his unseemly blush of pleasure would not imperil his reputation as a level-headed historian.

'In fact, for all of Strangyeard's and my hunting, it was Jarnauga who has been partway solving our problem,' Binabik continued.

The old man leaned forward and tapped a skinny finger on the parchment. 'It was a stroke of good fortune which I hope bodes well for us all. Morgenes had sent once to ask me questions about Nisses – who was, of course, a Rimmersman like myself – to help fill in some empty spots in his written life of your father, King John. I was of little help, I'm afraid. I told him what I knew. But I remembered his asking.'

'And,' Binabik said, excited, 'another stroke of lucki-ness: the one thing young Simon saved from the destruction of Morgenes' chambers was . . . this book!' He grabbed a sheaf in his stubby brown hand and waved it. ' "The Life and Reign of King John Presbyter, by Morgenes Ercestres" – Doctor Morgenes of Erchester. In another way still, the doctor is with us here!'

'We owe him more than we can say,' Jarnauga pronounced solemnly. 'He saw the dark days coming, and made many preparations – some we *still* do not know of.'

'But the most important to this current moment,' the troll burst in, 'is this: his life of Prester John. Look!' He thrust the papers into Josua's hand. The prince leafed through them, then looked up, smiling faintly.

'Reading Nisses' tangled and archaic language puts me in mind of my student days, prowling the archives of the Sancellan Aedonitis.' He shook his head regretfully. 'This is fascinating, of course, and I pray that I have the time some day to read Morgenes' full work, but I still do not understand.' He held up the page he had been reading. 'Here is a description of the forging of the blade Sorrow, but I see no information that Jarnauga has not already given to us. What help will this be?'

Binabik, with Josua's permission, took back the manuscript. 'We must be looking closer, Prince Josua,' he said. 'Morgenes quotes from Nisses – and the fact that he actually read at least some of *Du Svardenvyrd* only confirms for me Morgenes' resourcefulness – he quotes Nisses as speaking of two *other* "Great Swords." Two more besides Sorrow. Here, let me read what Morgenes tells are Nisses' own words.'

Binabik cleared his throat and began.

*'The first Great Sword came, in its form original, from out of the Sky one thousand years agone.*

*'Usires Aedon. Whom we of Mother Church call the Son and Avatar of God, had hung for nine days and nights, nailed by His Hands and Feet to the Execution Tree in the square before the Temple of Yuvenis in Nabban. This Yuvenis was the heathen god of Justice, and the Nabbanai imperator was wont to hang such dyverse criminals at his courts convicted from the mighty branches of Yuvenis' Tree. So hung Usires of the Lake, guilty of sacrilege and rebellion for proclaiming the Single God. Heels above Head like a carcase of Beef.*

*'There came, that Ninth night, a great Roaring and a streak of fire, and a hurtling Bolt from the Heavens flew down from the sky and smote the Temple into a thousand shards, killing all the heathen judges and priests within. When the reek and fumes were dispersed, the Body of Usires Aedon was gone, and a great shout went up that God had restored Him to Heaven and punished His enemies, although others said that Usires' patient disciples had cut down His body and escayped in the Confusion. These naysayers were quickly made silent, and the Word of a miracle spread throughout all the quarters of the City. Thus began the downfall of the pagan gods of Nabban.*

*'In the smoaking rubble of the Temple there now lay a great and steaming Stone. It was proclaimed by the Aedonites that here was the heathen altar, melted by the vengeful Fires of the One God.*

*'I, Nisses, believe instead that this was a flaming Star of the heavens fallen to Earth, as happens on Occasion.*

*'Now, from this molten wrack was taken a great piece, and the Imperator's swordwrights found it Workable, and the sky-metal was hammered into a great Blade. In mind of the scourging branches which had flaid Usires' Back, the star-sword — as I suppose it to be — was named THORN, and a mighty power there was in it . . .'*

'Thus,' Binabik said, 'the sword Thorn, being passed down through the line of Nabbanai rulers, came at last to . . .'

'To Sir Camaris, my father's most beloved friend.' Josua finished. 'The stories of Camaris' sword Thorn are many, but I had not known before today where it came from . . . if Nisses is to be believed. This passage has somewhat the smack of heresy.'

'Those of his assertions which can be measured against truth measure well, your Highness,' Jarnauga said, stroking his beard.

'Still,' said Josua, 'what does it mean? Camaris' sword was lost when he drowned.'

'Allow me to share more of Nisses' writing,' Binabik replied. 'Here, where he is speaking of the third part of our puzzle.'

*'The second of the Great Swords came from the Sea, traveling across the salt ocean from the West to Osten Ard.*

*'For some years the Sea-Raiders had come seasonally to this land from the far, cold Country they called Ijsgard, only to return across the waves when their pillaging was done.*

*'Then it was, some Tragedy or dire Happening in their native place caused the men of Ijsgard to abandon that land and bring their families in boats to Osten Ard, to settle in Rimmersgard in the North, the land of my Own far more recent birth.*

*'When they had landed, their King Elvrit gave thanks*

659

to Udun and their other Heathenish gods, and commanded that the iron keel of his Dragon-boat should be made into a sword to protect his People in their new land.

'Thus it went that the keel was given to the Dvernings, a Secretive and crafty race, and they separated out the Pure and Significant metal by means unknown, and smithied a long and shining blade.

'But in the haggling over the payment King Elvrit and the master of the Dvernings fell out, and the king did slay the smith and took the sword unpaid-for, which was the cause of much later Woe.

'In thought of their coming to this New country, Elvrit named the sword MINNEYAR, which means "Year of Memory." '

The troll finished, and walked to the table to drink from the water-ewer there.

'So, Binabik of Yiqanuc, two powerful swords,' Josua said. 'Perhaps this dreadful year has softened my mind, but I cannot think what significance they have to us.'

'Three swords,' Jarnauga offered, 'counting Ineluki's *Jingizu* – what we call Sorrow. *Three* great swords.'

'You must read this last part of Nisses' book that Morgenes cited, Prince Josua,' Strangyeard said, joining them at last. He picked up the parchment that Binabik had laid on the table. 'Here, please. This bit of rhyme from the end of the madman's writings.'

> '*When frost doth grow on Claves' bell* . . .'

Josua read aloud,

> '*And Shadows walk upon the road*
> *When water blackens in the Well*
> *Three Swords must come again.*
>
> '*When Bukken from the Earth do creep*
> *And Hunën from the heights descend*
> *When Nightmare throttles peaceful Sleep*

660

*Three Swords must come again.*

*'To turn the stride of treading Fate*
*To clear the fogging Mists of Time*
*If Early shall resist Too Late*
*Three Swords must come again . . .'*

'I think . . . I think I understand,' the prince said, with mounting interest. 'This almost appears to be a prophecy of our own day – as if Nisses somehow knew that Ineluki would someday return.'

'Yes,' Jarnauga said, combing his beard with his fingers as he looked over Josua's shoulder, 'and apparently, if things are to be made right, "Three swords must come again." '

'Our understanding, Prince,' Binabik said, 'is that if somehow the Storm King can be defeated, it is by our finding the three swords.'

'The three swords of which Nisses speaks?' Josua asked.

'So it would seem.'

'But, if what the boy Simon saw is correct, Sorrow is already in the hands of my brother.' The prince frowned, his pale brow creased with the lines of thought. 'If it were a simple thing to go and take it from him in the Hayholt, we would not be cowering here in Naglimund.'

'We shall worry about Sorrow last, Prince,' Jarnauga said. 'We must move now to secure the other two. I am named for my eyes and my trained sight, but even *I* cannot see the future. Perhaps a way will come for us to take Sorrow from Elias, or perhaps he will make some mistake. No, it is Thorn and Minneyar we must now find.'

Josua leaned back in his chair, crossing one ankle over the other and pressing his fingers on his lidded eyes. 'This is like a children's story!' he exclaimed. 'How are mere men to survive such times? Chill winter in Yuven-month . . . the risen Storm King who is a dead Sithi prince . . .

661

and now a desperate search for long-forgotten swords – madness! Folly!' He opened his eyes and sat up. 'But what can we do? I believe it all . . . so I must be mad, too.'

The prince stood up and began to pace. The others watched him, grateful that despite the slenderness of their hope they had at least convinced Josua of the grim, strange truth.

'Father Strangyeard,' he said at last, 'would you go and find Duke Isgrimnur? I sent my pages and all others away so we would have privacy.'

'Certainly,' the archivist said, and hurried from the room, robes flapping on his lanky frame.

'No matter what happens,' Josua said, 'I will have much to explain at tonight's Raed. I would have Isgrimnur beside me. The barons know him as a practical man, where I am still somewhat suspect for my years in Nabban and my odd ways.' The prince smiled wearily. 'If these mad things are true, then our task is more complex than even it was. If the Duke of Elvritshalla will stand beside me, then I think the barons will too – although I do not think I will share this latest bit of information, even if it does represent a thin shard of hope. I mistrust the ability of some of the lords to keep such amazing things a secret.'

The prince sighed. 'It was bad enough to have Elias alone for an enemy.' He stood, staring at the blazing hearth. His eyes glinted, as if full of some reflecting moisture. 'My poor brother.'

Binabik looked up, startled by the prince's tone.

'My poor brother,' Josua said again. 'He must be riding the nightmare now in earnest – the Storm King! The White Foxes! I cannot think he knew what he was doing.'

'*Somebody* had knowledge of what they did, Prince,' the troll declared. 'Stormspike's master and his minions do not, I am thinking, go dancing house to house like peddlers, a-selling of their wares.'

'Oh, I doubt not that Pryrates reached out to them somehow,' Josua said. 'I know him and his unholy thirst for forbidden knowledge from the old days, in the seminary of the Usirean brothers.' He shook his head sorrowfully. 'But Elias, although brave as a bear, was always mistrustful of secrets in old books, and scornful of scholarship. He also feared talk of spirits or the demonic. He became worse after . . . after his wife died. I wonder what he thought worth the terror he must reap for this bargain. I wonder if he now regrets it – what terrible allies! Poor, foolish Elias . . .'

It was raining again, and when Strangyeard came back with the duke, they were both soaked from their trip across the long courtyard. Isgrimnur stood in the doorway of Josua's chambers stamping like a nervous horse.

'I was just seeing to my wife,' he explained. 'She and the other women left ahead of Skali's arrival, and went to Thane Tonnrud, her uncle. She has brought half a dozen of my men and a score of women and children. She's got the frostbite in her fingers, poor Gutrun.'

'I am sorry to call you away from her, Isgrimnur, especially if she is injured,' the prince apologized, rising and clasping the old duke's hand.

'Ah, there's not much I can do. She has our girls to help her.' He frowned, but there was pride in his voice. 'She's a strong woman. She made strong sons for me.'

'And we shall bring help to Isorn, your eldest, never fear.' Josua led Isgrimnur to the table and handed him Morgenes' manuscript. 'It may be, though, that we shall be fighting more than one battle.'

When the duke had read of the Weird of the Swords, and asked some few questions, he read the pages again.

'This bit of rhyme, then?' he asked at last. 'You think that's the key to the whole thing?'

'If you mean the sort of key that *locks* a door,' Jarnauga said, 'yes, we hope so. For that is what we must do, it

663

seems: find the swords of Nisses' prophecy, swords that will keep the Storm King at bay.'

'But your boy claimed Elias has the Sithi one – and in fact I saw him wearing an unfamiliar sword when he told me I could leave for Elvritshalla. A great, strange-looking thing it was.'

'This we know, Duke,' Binabik chimed. 'It is the other two we must first find.'

Isgrimnur squinted suspiciously at the troll. 'And what do you want from me, little man?'

'Only your help, in any way you can render it,' Josua said, reaching out to pat the Rimmersman's shoulder. 'And Binabik of Yiqanuc is here for the same reasons.'

'Have you heard aught of the fate of *Minneyar*, Elvrit's sword?' Jarnauga asked. 'I confess I should know, since it is the purpose of our League to gather such wisdom, but Minneyar has gone out of the tales we know.'

'I know this from my grandmother, who was a storyteller,' Isgrimnur said, chewing his mustache as he remembered. 'It went through Elvrit's line to Fingil Redhand, and from Fingil to his son Hjeldin, and then when Hjeldin fell from the tower – with Nisses dead on the floor behind him – Hjeldin's lieutenant Ikferdig took it, along with Fingil's crown of the Rimmersmen, and the mastery of the Hayholt.'

'Ikferdig died in the Hayholt,' Strangyeard said shyly, warming his hands at the hearth. ' "The Burned King," he is called in my books.'

'Dead by the dragon-fire of red Shurakai,' Jarnauga said. 'Roasted in his throne room like a coney.'

'So . . .' Binabik said thoughtfully, while gentle Strangyeard shivered at Jarnauga's words, 'Minneyar is either within the walls of the Hayholt somewhere . . . or it has been unmade by the red dragon's fiery breathing.'

Josua stood up and walked to the fireplace, where he stood staring into the wavering flames. Strangyeard inched away so as not to crowd his prince.

'Two confounding and unhappy alternatives,' Josua

said, and grimaced, turning to Father Strangyeard. 'You have brought me no good news today, you wise men.' At this, the archivist looked morose. 'First you tell me our only hope is to find this trio of legendary blades, and now you say that two of them are in the stronghold of my enemy brother – if they exist at all.' The prince sighed in dismay. 'What of the third? Does Pryrates use it to cut his beef at table?'

'*Thorn*,' Binabik said, climbing up to perch on the table's edge. 'The sword of the great knight who was Camaris.'

'Made from the star-stone which destroyed the temple of Yuvenis in old Nabban,' Jarnauga said. 'But surely it went into the sea with great Camaris, when he was swept overboard in the Bay of Firannos.'

'You see!' spat Josua. 'Two held by my brother, and the third in the even tighter grip of the jealous ocean. We are cursed before we begin.'

'It no doubt would have also seemed an impossible chance that Morgenes' work would have survived the destruction of him and his chambers,' Jarnauga said, and his voice was stern, 'and then would come safely through danger and despair to us here, so we could read Nisses' prophecy. But it did survive. And it did reach us. There is *always* hope.'

'Excuse me, Prince, but there seems only one thing to do,' Binabik said, nodding sagely atop the table. 'It is back to the archives and searching again, until we find the answer to the riddle of Thorn and the other blades. And we must be finding it soon.'

'Soon indeed,' said Jarnauga, 'for we are wasting diamond-precious time.'

'By all means,' said Josua, pulling his chair over by the hearth and slumping down into it, 'by all means make haste, but I deeply fear that our time has already run out.'

'Damn and damn and damn,' Simon said, hurling yet one more rock from the battlement into the teeth of the wind. Naglimund seemed to stand in a great expanse of soapy gray nothingness, a mountain sprouting from a sea of swirling rain. 'Damn,' he added, as he bent to search for another on the wet stone wall.

Sangfugol looked over, his fine cap a limp, sodden mass on his head. 'Simon,' he said crossly, 'you cannot have it both ways. First you curse them all for dragging you along behind them like a peddler's sack, then you blaspheme and hurl stones because you are not invited to the afternoon's deliberations.'

'I know,' Simon said, sending another projectile down from the castle walls. 'I don't know what I want. I don't know anything.'

The harper scowled. 'What I would like to know is: what are we doing up here? Are there not better places to feel miserable and left out? It is cold as a well digger's privy parts on these battlements.' He allowed his teeth to chatter for a moment, hoping to inspire pity. 'Why are we up here?'

'Because it clears a man's head, a little wind and rain,' Towser called, making his way back along the battlement toward his two companions. 'There is no better cure for a night of drinking.' The little old man winked at Simon, who guessed that Towser would have gone down long ago, but for the enjoyable sight of Sangfugol shivering in his beautiful gray velvet robe.

'Well,' the harper growled, miserable as a soaked cat, 'you drink like a man in his youth, Towser – or in his second childhood – thus, I suppose it is no surprise to see you prance on the walls for fun, just like a rascally boy.'

'Ah, Sangfugol,' Towser said with a wrinkly smile, watching another of Simon's missiles send up a gout of water from the rain-pocked pond that eddied where the commons yard had been, 'you are too . . . Ho!' Towser pointed. 'Is that not Duke Isgrimnur? I had heard he was returned. *Ho, Duke!*' The jester shouted and waved at the stout figure. Isgrimnur, squinting against the slanting raindrops, looked up. 'Duke Isgrimnur! It's Towser!'

'Is that who it is?' the Duke cried. 'Damn me, it is, you old whoreson!'

'Come up, come up!' Towser said. 'Come and tell me what is the news!'

'I shouldn't be amazed,' Sangfugol said sardonically as the duke ankled across the submerged commons toward the curling staircase in the wall. 'The only person beside an old madman who would come up of his free will *would* be a Rimmersman. It's probably even too warm for him, since it's not actually sleeting or snowing.'

Isgrimnur had a tired smile and a nod for Simon and the harper, then turned and clasped the jester's veined hand and gave him a comradely smack on the shoulder. He was so much taller and bulkier than Towser that he looked like a mother bear cuffing her cub.

While the duke and the jester exchanged tidings, Simon threw stones and listened, and Sangfugol stood with a look of patient, hopeless suffering. Soon, un-surprisingly, the Rimmersman's talk came around from mutual friends and homely things to darker topics. As Isgrimnur spoke of the gathering threat of war, and the shadow in the north, Simon felt the cold that the chill winds had – strangely – helped dispel for a while come shouldering back. When the duke began to speak in hushed tones of the Ruler of the North, then sheared off, saying some things were too fear-fraught to speak of openly, the cold seemed to slide further into Simon's being. He stared out into the murky distance, at the dark fist of storm that hovered beyond the rain on the northern horizon, and felt himself slipping back into his journey on the dream-road . . .

. . . *The naked thrust of the stone mountain, its halo of indigo and yellow flames. The silver-masked queen in her icy throne, and the chanting voices in the rocky fastness* . . . Black thoughts pressed down on him, crushing him like the

667

rim of a broad wheel. It would be easy, he was sure, to go forward into the darkness, into the warmth beyond the storm's chill . . .

. . . *It's so close . . . so close . . .*

'Simon!' a voice said in his ear. A hand grasped his elbow. He looked down, startled, to see the edge of the battlement inches from his foot, and the wind-lashed water of the courtyard directly below.

'What are you doing?' Sangfugol asked, giving his arm a shake. 'If you went over this little wall, you would have more than broken bones.'

'I was . . .' Simon said, feeling a dark mist still clouding his thoughts, a mist that was slow to clear, 'I . . .'

'Thorn?' Towser said loudly, responding to something Isgrimnur had said. Simon turned to see the little jester tugging at the Rimmersman's cloak like an importunate child. '*Thorn*, did you say? Well, then, why did you not come to me immediately? Why not come to old Towser? I know all there is to know, if anybody does!'

The old man turned to Simon and the harper. 'Why, who was with our John longer than anyone? Who? I was, of course. Joked and tumbled and played for him sixty years. And the great Camaris, too. I saw him come to the court.' He turned back around to face the duke, and there was a light in his eyes that Simon had not seen before. 'I am the man you want,' Towser said proudly. 'Quick! Take me to Prince Josua.'

The bandy-legged old jester almost seemed to dance, so light were his steps as he led the somewhat dumbfounded Rimmersman toward the stairs.

'Thank God and His angels,' said Sangfugol, watching them go. 'I suggest we go immediately to pour something inside us – a wetness within to make up for the wetness without.'

He led Simon, who was still shaking his head, down from the rainy battlements into the echoing, torch-lit stairwell, out of the northern winds for a little while and into the warmth.

'We understand your place in these events, good Towser,' Josua said impatiently. The prince, perhaps to ward off the all-pervasive chill, had wrapped a woolen scarf tightly around his throat. The tip of his slender nose was pink.

'I'm just setting the place, so to speak, Your Highness,' Towser said complacently. 'If I might have a cup of wine to help ease the talk, I will get to the main course directly.'

'Isgrimnur,' Josua groaned, 'would you be good enough to find our venerable jester something to drink, or I fear we shall be here until Aedontide waiting for the rest of the story.'

The duke of Elvritshalla went to the cedar cabinet beside Josua's table and found a ewer of red Perdruin wine. 'Here,' he said, handing a filled flagon to Towser, who sipped and smiled.

*It's not the wine he's wanting*, the Rimmersman thought, *it's the attention. These are grim enough days for the young and useful, let alone for an old trickster whose master is two years dead.*

He stared at the jester's seamed face, and for a moment thought he saw the child's countenance trapped beneath, as behind a thin curtain.

*God grant me a quick, honorable death*, Isgrimnur prayed, *and never let me be one of those old fools who sits by the campfire telling the young men that things will never be as good as they once were. Still*, he thought as he moved back to his chair, listening to the lupine howling of the winds outside, *still, it may be true this time. Maybe we **have** seen the better days. Maybe there is nothing left now but a losing battle against creeping darkness.*

'You see,' Towser was saying, 'Camaris' sword Thorn

*didn't* go with him into the ocean. He had given it over for safekeeping to his squire, Colmund of Rodstanby.'

'*Gave* away his sword?' Josua said, puzzled. 'That accords with none of the stories I have ever heard of Camaris-sá-Vinitta.'

'Ah, but you did not know him that last year . . . and how could you, since you had only just come into the world?' Towser took another swig and stared meditatively up at the ceiling. 'Sir Camaris grew strange and fell after your mother Queen Ebekah died. He was her special protector, you know, and he worshipped the very tiles she trod upon – as if she were Elysia the Mother of God herself. I always thought he blamed himself for her death, as though he could somehow have cured her ill-health by force of arms, or by the purity of his heart . . . poor idiot.'

Seeing Josua's impatience, Isgrimnur leaned forward. 'So he gave the star-sword Thorn to his squire?'

'Yes, yes,' said the old man testily, not liking to be rushed. 'When Camaris was lost in the sea off Harcha-island, Colmund took it for his own. He went back and reclaimed his family's lands at Rodstanby in the Frost-march, and became the baron of a good-sized province. Thorn was a famous weapon through all the world, and when his enemies saw it – for it was unmistakable, all shiny black but for the silver hilt, a beautiful, perilous thing – they would none of them face him. He seldom even had to draw it from its scabbard.'

'So it is then at Rodstanby?' Binabik said excitedly from the corner. 'That is near within two days' ride from where we are now sitting!'

'No, no, no,' growled Towser, waving his flagon for Isgrimnur to fill again. 'If you would only wait, troll, I will tell you all.'

Before Binabik or the prince or anyone else could respond, Jarnauga stood up from his crouch by the fire and leaned toward the little jester. 'Towser,' he said, and his voice was as hard and cold as ice in the roof thatches,

670

'we cannot wait on your pace. There is a grave darkness spreading from the north, a cold and fatal shadow. We *must* have the sword, do you understand?' He brought his sharp face even closer to Towser's, and the little man's tufted eyebrows shot upward in alarm. 'We must find Thorn, for soon the Storm King himself will be knocking at our door. *Do you understand?*'

Towser gaped as Jarnauga dropped back into his long-limbed squat beside the hearth.

*Well*, Isgrimnur mused, *if we wanted the latest news shouted all over Naglimund, now we'll have it done. Still, it does look as though he's put a bit of a burr under Towser's saddle.*

It took a few moments for the jester to be able to tear his startled, fascinated eyes from the glare-eyed northerner. When he turned, he no longer looked to be enjoying his status quite as much.

'Colmund,' he began, 'Sir Colmund heard traveler's tales of the dragon Igjarjuk's legendary hoard, in the heights of the mountain Urmsheim. It was a treasure said to be richer than any other in the wide world.'

'Only a flatlander would be thinking of searching out a mountain dragon – and for gold!' Binabik said disgustedly. 'My people have long lived near Urmsheim, and we are living long because we are not going there.'

'But you see,' old Towser said, 'the dragon has been only a story for generations. No one has seen it, no one has heard of it . . . except for snow-maddened wanderers. And Colmund had the sword Thorn, a magic sword to lead him on a quest for the magic dragon's hoard!'

'But what idiocy!' Josua said. 'Did he not have everything he wanted? A powerful barony? The sword of a hero? Why should he go rabbiting off after such a madman's vision?'

'Damn me, Josua,' Isgrimnur swore, 'why do men do *any* of the things they do? Why did they hang Our Lord Usires topsides-down from the Tree? Why should Elias imprison his brother and make bargains with demons when he is already High King of all Osten Ard?'

'There are indeed things in men and women that make them reach for what is beyond their grasp,' Jarnauga said from his hearth corner. 'Sometimes the things they seek lie beyond the bounds of understanding.'

Binabik jumped lightly to the floor. 'Too much talk is this of things we can never know,' he said. 'Our question still is: where is the sword? *Where is Thorn?*'

'Lost in the north, I'm sure,' Towser said. 'I have never heard that Sir Colmund came back from his quest. One traveler's tale was that he had made himself a king of the Hunën, and lives there still in a fortress of ice.'

'It sounds as though his story has been muddied and mixed with old memories of Ineluki,' Jarnauga said thoughtfully.

'He made it as far as the monastery of Saint Skendi at Vestvennby,' Father Strangyeard piped up unexpectedly from the back of the room. He had gone out quickly and come back without anyone's noticing; he wore a faint flush of pleasure high on his thin cheeks. 'Towser's words sparked a memory. I thought I had some of the monastic books of Skendi's order, salvaged from its burning during the Frostmarch wars. Here is the household ledger for the Founding-year 1131. See, it lists the outfitting of Colmund's party.' He passed it proudly to Josua, who held it up to the firelight.

'Dried meat and fruits,' Josua read, straining to make out the faded words. 'Wool cloaks, two horses . . .' He looked up. 'It says here a party of "a dozen and one" – thirteen.' He passed the book on to Binabik, who took it back to pore over with Jarnauga by the fire.

'Then they must have run into bad luck,' Towser said, refilling his flagon. 'The stories I heard said he set out from Rodstanby with over two dozen of his hand-picked best.'

Isgrimnur was staring after the troll. *He's certainly clever enough*, the Rimmersman thought, *although I don't* trust him or his kind much. And what's his hold on that boy? I'm not sure I like that either, although I think the stories they both tell are largely true.

'What good is all this to us now?' he said aloud. 'If the sword is lost, it is lost, and we must simply make the best of our defenses here.'

'Duke Isgrimnur,' Binabik said, 'you are not understanding, perhaps: there is no choice for us. If indeed the Storm King is our greater enemy – as I think we are all agreeing, now – then the only thing for hope, it seems, is that we acquire the three swords. Two are for now denied from us. That leaves Thorn, and we must find it – if finding is possible.'

'Don't instruct me, little man,' Isgrimnur growled, but Josua waved his hand wearily to forestall their argument.

'Quiet now,' the prince said. 'Please, let me think. My brain is fevered with so many madnesses heaped one atop the other. I need some moments of quiet.'

Strangyeard, Jarnauga, and Binabik pored over the monastery ledger and Morgenes' manuscript, talking in whispers; Towser finished his wine, Isgrimnur sipping moodily beside him. Josua sat staring into the fire. The prince's weary features looked like parchment pulled over bone; the Duke of Elvritshalla could hardly bear to look at him.

*His father looked no worse in his last dying days*, Isgrimnur brooded. *Has he the strength to lead us through a siege, as it looks to come to soon? Has he even the strength himself to survive? He has ever been a thinker, a worrier . . . although, in fairness, he is no slouch with sword and shield.* Without thinking he got up and stumped over to the the prince's side, laying an ursine paw on Josua's shoulder.

The prince looked up. 'Can you spare me a good man, old friend? Do you have one who knows the northeast country?'

Isgrimnur looked thoughtful. 'I have two or three. Frekke, though, is too old for a journey such as I imagine

673

you are thinking of. Einskaldir would not leave my side unless I pushed him out of the gate of Naglimund at spear-point. Besides, I have a mind we will need his fierceness here, when the fighting grows hot and bloody. He is a badger: fierce-blooded, and best when he is backed into a hole.' The duke mused. 'Of the rest, I would give you Sludig. He is young and fit, but he is also clever. Yes, Sludig will be the man for you.'

'Good.' Josua nodded his head slowly. 'I have some three or four I will send, but a small party is better than a large.'

'For what, exactly?' Isgrimnur looked around the room, at its sparse solidity, and wondered again whether they were chasing phantoms, whether the wintry weather had somehow chilled their better judgement.

'To search for Camaris' sword, Uncle Bear-skin,' the prince said with a ghost of a smile. 'It is doubtless madness, and we have nothing better to go on than old stories and a few faded words in old books, but it is not a chance we can afford to ignore. It is storm-fraught winter in the summer month of Yuven. None of our doubts can change that.' He looked around the room, mouth pursed in thought.

'Binabik of Yiqanuc,' he called at last, and the troll hurried over. 'Will you lead a party on the trail of Thorn? You know the northern mountains better than anyone here except perhaps Jarnauga, who I hope will go, too.'

'I would be full of honor, Prince,' Binabik said, and dropped to one knee. Even Isgrimnur was forced to grin.

'I am honored, too, Prince Josua,' Jarnauga said, rising, 'but I think it is not to be. Here at Naglimund I will best serve. My legs are old, but my eyes are still keen. I will help Strangyeard in the archives, for there are many questions still to answer, many riddles behind the story of the Storm King, and the whereabouts of Fingil's sword Minneyar. And there may yet be other ways I can serve, as well.'

'Your Highness,' Binabik asked, 'if there is a place

unfilled, may I have your permission to take young Simon? Morgenes was asking as his last wish that the boy be watched over by my master. With Ookequk's death I am master now, and would not be shirking this watching-over.'

Josua looked skeptical. 'And you would look after him by taking him on a mad expedition into the unmapped north?'

Binabik raised an eyebrow. 'Unmapped by big people, perhaps. It is the commons yard of my Qanuc-folk. Also, is it more safe to leave him shut up in a castle set for warring with the High King?'

The prince brought his long hand up to his face, as though his head pained him. 'You are right, I suppose. If these slender threads of hope come to naught, there will be no safe places for those who have sided with the Lord of Naglimund. If the boy wishes to go, you may take him.' He brought his hand down and clasped Binabik's shoulder. 'Very well, little man – little but brave. Go back to your books, and I shall send you three good Erkynlanders and Isgrimnur's man Sludig in the morning.'

'My thanks, Prince Josua,' Binabik nodded. 'But I think it is at night tomorrow we should be leaving. We will be a small party, and our best hope is in not attracting evil attention.'

'So be it,' said Josua, rising and lifting his hand as though in benediction. 'Who knows if this is some fool's errand or the rescue of us all? You should be going out amid trumpets and applause. Instead necessity must override honor, and stealth must be the watchword. Know that our thoughts are with you.'

Isgrimnur hesitated, then leaned forward and clasped Binabik's small hand. 'Damned strange this is,' he said, 'but God be with you. If Sludig should get contentious, be forgiving. He is high-spirited, but his heart is good and his loyalty strong.'

'Thank you, Duke,' the troll said seriously. 'May your god be blessing us indeed. We go into unknown places.'

675

'As do all mortals,' Josua added. 'Sooner or later.'

'What! You told the prince and everyone I would go *where?*' Simon balled his fists in anger. 'What right did you have to do that?!'

'Simon-friend,' Binabik calmly responded. 'You are under no order to go. I was only asking Josua's permission for your being on this search, and it was granted. The choosing is for you.'

'S'bloody Tree! What else can I do now? If I say no, everyone will think I'm a coward!'

'Simon.' The little man put on a look of patience. 'First, please do not be using your new-learned soldier curses on me. We Qanuc are a courteous folk. For second, it is not good worrying so on other's opinions. Anyway, staying at Naglimund will certainly not be for cowards.'

Simon hissed a great frosty cloud of breath and hugged himself. He stared up at the murky sky, at the dull blur of sun secreted behind the clouds.

*Why are people always making decisions for me without asking first? Am I a child?*

He stood for some moments, red-faced from more than the chill, until Binabik reached out a small, gentle hand.

'My friend, I am sorrowful this was not the honor I was hoping it to be – an honor of dreadful, dreadful danger, of course, but an honor. I have explained of what importance we think this quest, of how the fate of Naglimund and all the north may hang on its accomplishing. And, of course, that all may be perishing without fame or song in the white northern waste.' He patted Simon's knuckles solemnly, then reached into the pocket of his fur-lined jacket. 'Here,' he said, and put something hard and cold into Simon's fingers.

Momentarily distracted, he opened his hand to look. It

was a ring, a plain, thin circlet of some golden metal. On it was inscribed a simple design: a long oval with a tipped triangle at one end.

'The fish sign of the League of the Scroll,' Binabik said. 'Morgenes tied this thing to the sparrow's leg, along with the note of which I was speaking before. The end of the note told this was for you.'

Simon held it up, trying to catch a gleam of the dull sunlight. 'I never saw Morgenes wear it,' he said, a little surprised that it startled up no memories. 'Do all the League members have one? Besides, how could I be worthy to wear it? I can hardly read. My spelling isn't very good, either.'

Binabik smiled. 'My master did not have such a ring, or at least I never was seeing it. As for the other: Morgenes was wanting you to have it, and that is permission enough, I have sureness.'

'Binabik,' Simon said, squinting, 'it has writing on the inside.' He held it up for the troll to inspect. 'I can't read it.'

The troll narrowed his eyes. 'It is writing in some Sithi tongue,' he said, turning the ring to peruse its inner rim, 'hard to read for being very small, and in a style I do not know.' He studied it a moment longer.

' "Dragon," that character means,' Binabik read at last. 'And this one means, I believe, "death" – *"Death and the Dragon"? – "Death of the Dragon"?'* He looked up at Simon, grinned and shrugged. 'What it might be meaning, I have no idea. My knowledge is not deep enough. Some conceit of your doctor's, is my guessing – or perhaps a family motto. Perhaps Jarnauga could read it with more ease.'

It slid easily onto the third finger of Simon's right hand, as though it had been made for him. Morgenes had been so small! How could he have worn this?

'Do you think it's a *magic* ring?' he asked suddenly, narrowing his eyes as though he might detect spells swarming around the golden circle like minuscule bees.

'If so,' Binabik said, mock-somberly, 'Morgenes included no grammarye for explaining its using.' He shook his head. 'I think it not a likelihood. A keepsake, from a man who was caring for you.'

'Why are you giving it to me now?' Simon asked, feeling a certain sorrowful tightness behind his eyes that he was determined to resist.

'Because I must be leaving tomorrow night to go north. If you decide for remaining here, we might not have opportunity to meet again.'

'Binabik!' The tightening increased. He felt like a small child pushed back and forth between bullying elders.

'The truth it is, only.' The troll's round face was entirely serious now. He raised his hand to forestall more protests and questions. 'Now you must be deciding, my good friend. I go into the snow and ice country, on an errand that may be foolishness, and which may claim the lives of the fools who are following it. Those who remain are facing the anger of a king's army. An evil choosing, I fear.' Binabik nodded his head gravely. 'But, Simon, whichever it is for you, going north or staying to fight for Naglimund – and princess – we will be the best of comrades still, yes?'

He stood on tiptoe to clap Simon on the upper arm, then turned and walked away across the courtyard toward the archives.

Simon found her standing alone, tossing pebbles into the castle well. She wore a heavy traveling cloak and hood against the cold.

'Hello, Princess,' he said. She looked up and smiled, sadly. For some reason she seemed much older today, like a grown woman.

'Welcome, Simon.' Her breath made a halo of mist about her head.

He began to bend his knee in a bow, but she was no longer looking. Another stone rattled down the well. He considered sitting down, which seemed the natural thing to do, but the only place to sit was on the edge of the well, which would either put him uncomfortably close to the princess or leave him facing in the wrong direction. He decided to remain on his feet. 'And how have you been?' he said at last. She sighed.

'My uncle treats me as though I am made of eggshells and cobwebs – like I would shatter if I lifted anything, or if anyone bumped into me.'

'I'm sure . . . I'm sure that he is only worried for your safety, after the dangerous journey you had to get here.'

'The dangerous journey *we* had, but nobody's following *you* around to make sure you don't skin your knee. They're even teaching you how to fight with a sword!'

'Miri . . . Princess!' Simon was more than a little shocked. 'You don't want to fight with swords, do you?!'

She looked up at him, and their eyes met. For an instant her stare burned like the noonday sun with some inexplicable longing; a moment later she wearily dropped her gaze again.

'No,' she said, 'I suppose not. But, oh, I do wish to do *something*!'

Surprised, he heard the real pain in her voice, and in that moment remembered her as she had been on the flight up the Stile, uncomplaining and strong, as good a companion as could be wished.

'What . . . what do you want to do?'

She looked up again, pleased by the serious tone of his question. 'Well,' she began, 'it's no secret that Josua is having trouble convincing Devasalles that his master Duke Leobardis should support the prince against my father. Josua could send me to Nabban!'

'Send *you* . . . to Nabban?'

'Of course, you idiot.' She frowned. 'On my mother's side I am of the Ingadarine House, a very noble family of Nabban. My aunt is married to Leobardis! Who better to go and convince the duke!?' She clapped her gloved hands for emphasis.

'Oh . . .' Simon was unsure of what to say. 'Perhaps Josua thinks that it would be . . . would be . . . I don't know.' He considered. 'I mean to say, should the High King's daughter be the one to . . . to arrange alliances against him?'

'And who knows the High King's ways better?' Now she was angry.

'Do you . . .' He hesitated, but his curiosity won out. 'How do you feel toward your father?'

'Do I hate him?' Her tone was bitter. 'I hate what he has become. I hate what the men around him have put him up to. If he would suddenly find goodness in his heart, and see the error of his ways . . . well, then I would love him again.'

A whole procession of stones went down the well as Simon stood uncomfortably by.

'I'm sorry, Simon,' she said at last. 'I have become very bad at talking with people. My old nurse would be shocked at how much I have forgotten, running around in the forest. How are you, and what have you been doing?'

'Binabik has asked me to go with him on a mission for Josua,' he said, bringing the subject up more abruptly than he had meant to. 'To the *north*,' he added significantly.

Instead of showing the expressions of worry and fear he had expected, the princess' face seemed to light up from within; although she smiled at him, she did not truly seem to see him. 'Oh, Simon,' she said, 'how brave. How fine. Can you . . . when do you leave?'

'Tomorrow night,' he said, dimly aware that somehow, by some mysterious process, *asked to go* had become *going*. 'But I haven't decided yet,' he said feebly. 'I thought I might be more needed here, at Naglimund – to wield a spear on the walls.' He tacked on the last just in case there was any possibility she thought he might be staying behind to work in the kitchens, or something like.

'Oh, but Simon,' Miriamele said, reaching up suddenly to take his cold hand in her leather-gloved fingers. 'If my uncle needs you to do it, you must! We have so little hope left, from all I have heard.'

She reached up to her neck and quickly unfastened the sky-blue scarf she wore, a slender gauzy strip; she handed it to him. 'Take this and bear it for me,' she said. Simon felt the blood come roaring up into his cheeks, and struggled to keep his lips from stretching into a shocked, mooncalfish grin.

'Thank you . . . Princess,' he said at last.

'If you wear it,' she said, standing up, 'it will be almost as though I were there myself.' She did a funny little dance step, and laughed.

Simon was trying without success to understand what exactly had happened, and how it had happened so fast. 'It will be, princess,' he said. 'Like you were there.'

Something in the way he said it tripped up her sudden mood: her expression turned sober, even sad. She smiled again, a slower, more rueful smile, then quickly stepped forward, startling Simon so that he almost raised a hand to ward her off. She brushed his cheek with her cool lips.

'I know you will be brave, Simon. Come back safely. I shall pray for you.'

Immediately she was gone, running across the courtyard like a little girl, her dark cape a smoky swirl as she disappeared into the twilit archway. Simon stood holding her scarf. He thought of it, and her smile when she kissed his cheek, and he felt something smolder into flame inside of him. It seemed, in some way he did not fully understand, that a single torch had been lit against the vast gray chill looming in the north. It was only a single point of brightness in a dreadful storm . . . but even a lone fire could bring a traveler home safe.

He rolled the soft cloth into a ball and slipped it into his shirt.

'I am glad you have come so quickly,' Lady Vorzheva said. The brilliance of her yellow dress seemed reflected in her dark eyes.

'My lady honors me,' the monk replied, his eyes straying about the room.

Vorzheva laughed harshly. 'You are the only one who thinks it honorable to visit me. But no matter. You understand what it is you must do?'

'I am sure that I have it correctly. It is a matter difficult in execution, but easily grasped in concept.' He bowed his head.

'Good. Then wait no longer, for the more wait, the less chance of success. Also more chance for tongues to wag.' She whirled away to the back chamber in a rush of silks.

'Uh . . . my lady?' The man blew on his fingers. The prince's chambers were cold, the fire unlit. 'There is the matter of . . . payment?'

'I thought you did this as honor for me, sir?' Vorzheva called from the back room.

'Welladay, madam, I am but a poor man. What you ask will take resources.' He blew on his fingers again, then thrust his hands deep into his robe.

She came back bearing a purse of shiny cloth. 'That I know. Here. It is in gold, as I promised – half now, half when I receive proof that your task is completed.' She handed him the purse, then drew back. 'You stink of wine! Is that the sort of man you are, trusted with this grave task?'

'It is the sacramental wine, my lady. Sometimes on my difficult road it is the only thing to drink. You must understand.' He favored her with a diffident smile, then made the sign of the Tree over the gold before stowing it in the pocket of his robe. 'We do what we must to serve God's will.'

Vorzheva nodded slowly. 'That I can understand. Do not fail me, sir. You serve a great purpose, and not just for me.'

'I understand, Lady.' He bowed, then turned and left. Vorzheva stood and stared at the parchments strewn on the prince's table and let out a deep breath. The thing was done.

Twilight of the day after he spoke to the princess found Simon in the chambers of Prince Josua, preparing to say farewell. In a sort of daze, as though he had just awakened, he stood listening as the prince had his final words with Binabik. The boy and the troll had spent the whole of the dark day preparing their kit, obtaining a new fur-lined cloak and helmet for Simon, along with a light mail shirt to wear beneath his outer clothing. The coat of thin ringlets, Haestan had pointed out, would not save him from a direct sword blow or an arrow to the heart, but would stand him in good stead in the case of some less than deadly assault.

Simon found the weight of it reassuring, but Haestan warned him that at the end of a long day's journey he might not feel so cheerful about it.

'Y'r soldier carries many burdens, boy,' the big man told him, 'an' sometimes keepin' alive's th'hardest one.'

Haestan himself had been one of the three Erkynlanders to step forward when the captains had called for men. Like his two companions, Ethelbearn, a scarred, bushy-mustached veteran nearly as big as Haestan, and Grimmric, a slender, hawkish man with bad teeth and watchful eyes, he had spent so long preparing for siege that any sort of action was welcome, even something as dangerous and mysterious as this quest looked to be. When Haestan found out Simon was going too, he was even more adamant in his desire to join them.

'T'send such a boy's madness,' he growled, ''special when he's not finished learning t'swing sword or shoot arrow. I'd best go an' keep at teachin' 'im.'

Duke Isgrimnur's man Sludig was also there, a young Rimmersman attired like the Erkynlanders in furs and conical helmet. In place of the longsword the others carried, blond-bearded Sludig had two notch-bladed hand axes thrust in his belt. He grinned cheerfully at Simon, anticipating his question.

'Sometimes one gets stuck in a skull or rib cage,' the Rimmersgarder said. He spoke the Westerling tongue nimbly, with almost as little accent as the duke. 'It is nice to have another to use until you get the first one out.'

Nodding, Simon tried to smile back.

'Well met again, Simon.' Sludig extended a callused hand.

'Again?'

'We met once before, at Hoderund's abbey,' Sludig laughed. 'But you spent the journey arse-end-up across Einskaldir's saddle. I hope that is not the only way you know how to ride.'

Simon blushed, clasped the northerner's hand, then turned away.

'We have turned up little to help you on your way,' Jarnauga was regretfully telling Binabik. 'The Skendian monks left scant word about Colmund's expedition besides the transactions of its outfitting. They probably thought him a madman.'

'Most likely they had it correctly,' the troll observed. He was burnishing the bone-handled knife he had carved to replace the missing piece of his staff.

'We did find one thing,' said Strangyeard. The priest's hair stood up in wild tufts, and his eye patch sat a little off-center, as though he had come straight from spending an entire night poring over his books . . . which he had. 'The abbey's book-keeper wrote: "The Baron does not know how long his journeying to the Rhymer's Tree shall last . . ." '

'It is unfamiliar,' Jarnauga said, 'in fact, it is probably something the monk misheard, or got third hand . . . but it *is* a name. Perhaps it will make more sense when you reach the mountain Urmsheim.'

'Perhaps,' said Josua thoughtfully, 'it is a town along the way, a village at the mountain's foot?'

'Perhaps,' Binabik answered doubtfully, 'but from what I am knowing of those places, there is nothing lying between the ruins of the Skendi monastery and the mountains – nothing there is but ice, trees, and rocks, of course. Plenty of those things there are.'

As final farewells were spoken, Simon heard Sangfugol's voice drift out from the room in back, where he was singing for the Lady Vorzheva.

> '. . . And shall I go a-wandering
> Out in the winter's chill?
> Or shall I come now home again?
> Whate'er thou sayest, I will . . .'

Simon picked up his quiver and looked for the third or fourth time to make sure the White Arrow was still there. Bewildered, as though caught in some slow and clinging dream, he realized that he was setting off on a journey once more – and again he was not quite sure why. His time at Naglimund had been so brief. Now it was over, at least for a long while. As he touched the blue scarf tied loosely at his throat he realized he might not see any of the others in this room again, anybody at Naglimund . . . Sangfugol, old Towser, or Miriamele. He thought he felt his heart trip for a moment, the beat stuttering like a drunkard, and was reaching for something to lean on when he felt a strong hand clasp his elbow.

'There you be, lad.' It was Haestan. 'Bad enow that ye've no learnin' with the sword an' bow, now we're goin' t'put you t'horseback.'

'Horseback?' Simon said. 'I'll like that.'

'No y'wont,' Haestan smirked. 'Not for month or two.'

Josua said a few words to each one of them, and then

there were warm, solemn handclasps all around. A short while later they were in the dark, cold courtyard where Qantaqa and seven, stamping, steaming horses awaited them, five for riding and a pair for carrying heavy gear. If there was a moon, it was hidden like a sleeping cat in the blanket of clouds.

'Good it is that we have *this* darkness,' Binabik said, swinging up into the new saddle on Qantaqa's gray back. The men, seeing the troll's steed for the first time, exchanged wondering looks as Binabik clicked his tongue and the wolf sprang out before them. A group of soldiers quietly raised the oiled porticullis, and they were out under the broad sky, the field of shadowy nails spread around them as they made for the close-looming hills.

'Good-bye, everyone,' Simon said quietly. They started up the sloping path.

High above on the Stile, at the crest of the hill overlooking Naglimund, a black shape was watching.

Even with his keen eyes, Ingen Jegger could make out little more in the moonless murk than that someone had left the castle by the eastern gate. That, however, was more than enough to raise his interest.

He stood, rubbing his hands, and considered calling one of his men to go down with him and get a better look. Instead he lifted his fist to his mouth and hooted like a snow owl. Seconds later a huge shape appeared from the scrub growth and leaped onto the Stile beside him. It was a hound, bigger even than the one killed by the troll's tame wolf, shining white in the moonlight, its eyes twin pearl slots in a long, grinning face. It growled, a deep, cavernous rumble, and swiveled its head from side to side, nostrils wrinkling.

'Yes, Niku'a, yes,' Ingen hissed quietly. 'It is time to hunt once more.'

A moment later the Stile was empty. The leaves rattled ever so gently beside the ancient tiles, but no wind was blowing.

# 35

# The Raven and the Cauldron

Maegwin winced as the clanging began again, the doleful clatter that signified so much – and none of it good. One of the other girls, a small, fair-skinned beauty that Maegwin had assessed at first glance as a quitter, let go of the bar they were all pushing to cover her ears. The heavy piece of fencing meant to hold the gate closed nearly tumbled free, but Maegwin and the two other girls clung on grimly.

'Bagba's Herd, Cifgha,' she snarled at the one who had let loose, 'are you mad?! If this had fallen, someone might have been crushed, or at least broken a foot!'

'I'm sorry, I am, my lady,' the girl said, cheeks flushed, 'it's just that loud noise . . . it frightens me!' She stepped back to take her place again, and they all pushed, trying to get the massive oak bar over the top and into the notch that would hold the paddock closed. Inside the restraining fence a close-packed congregation of red cattle grunted, as unsettled as the young women by the continual din.

With a scrape and thump the log fell down into place, and they all turned, panting, to slump with their backs against the gate.

'Merciful are the gods,' Maegwin groaned, 'my spine is breaking!'

'It's not right,' Cifgha opined, staring ruefully at the bleeding scratches on her palms. 'It's men's work!'

687

The metallic clamor stopped, and for a moment the very silence seemed to sing. Lluth's daughter sighed and took in a deep breath of frosty air.

'No, little Cifgha,' she said, 'what the men are doing now is men's work, and whatever is left to do is women's work – unless you want to carry a sword and spear.'

'Cifgha?' one of the other girls said, laughing. 'She won't even kill a spider.'

'I always call Tuilleth to do it,' Cifgha said, proud of her fastidiousness, 'and he always comes to me.'

Maegwin made a sour face. 'Well, we had better get used to dealing with our own spiders. There will not be many menfolk around in the days to come, and those who remain will have much else to do.'

'It's different for you, Princess,' Cifgha said. 'You're big and strong.'

Maegwin stared hard at her but did not answer.

'You don't think the fighting will go on all summer, do you?' asked another girl, as if speaking of a particularly dreary chore. Maegwin turned to look at them all, at their sweat-dampened faces and their eyes already roaming, looking for something more interesting to talk about. For a moment she wanted to shout, to frighten them into realizing that this was not a tournament, not a game of some sort, but deadly serious.

*But why rub their faces in the mud now?* she thought, relenting. *Soon enough we will all of us get more than we need of it.*

'I don't know if it will last that long, Gwelan,' she said, and shook her head. 'I hope not. I truly hope not.'

As she made her way down from the paddocks toward the great hall, the two men again started to beat the huge bronze cauldron that hung upside down in its frame of oaken poles before the Taig's front doors. As she trotted past, the noise of the men furiously ringing the cauldron with iron-tipped cudgels was so loud that she had to cover her ears with her hands. She wondered again how her father and his advisors could think, let alone plan life-and-death strategy with this awful ruckus just outside the hall. Still, if Rhynn's Cauldron was not rung, it would take days to warn each of the outlying towns one by one, especially those that clung to the slopes of the Grianspog. This way those villages and manor halls within earshot of the cauldron would send riders to those beyond. The lord of the Taig had rung the cauldron in times of danger since long before the days when Hern the Hunter and Oinduth his mighty spear had made of their land a great kingdom. Children who had never heard it sounded still recognized it instantly, so many stories of Rhynn's Cauldron were told.

The Taig's high windows today were shuttered against the chill wind and mists. Maegwin found her father and his counselors in earnest discussion before the fireplace.

'My daughter,' Lluth said, standing. He expended visible effort to produce a smile for her.

'I took some women and got the last of the cattle into the big paddock,' Maegwin reported. 'I don't think it's right to squeeze them all so tightly. The cows are miserable.'

Lluth waved a dismissive hand. 'Better we lose some few now than have to try and round them up if we must fall back to the hills in a hurry.'

At the far end of the hall the door opened, and the sentries banged their swords against their shields once, as though to echo the piercing noise of the Summons of the Cauldron. 'I do thank you, Maegwin,' the king said, turning from her to greet the new arrival.

'Eolair!' he called out as the count strode forward, still dressed in travel-stained clothes. 'You are swift in returning from the healers. Good. How are your men?'

The Count of Nad Mullach approached, dropped briefly to one knee, then stood again at Lluth's impatient gesture. 'Five are able-bodied; the two wounded do not look well. The other four I shall call Skali to account for

689

personally.' He saw Lluth's daughter at last and smiled his broad smile, but his brow remained knitted in a weary, troubled study. 'My Lady Maegwin,' he said, and bowed again, kissing her long-fingered hand, which, she was embarrassed to notice, was smudged with dirt from the paddock fence.

'I heard you were back, Count,' she said. 'I only wish it were in happier circumstances.'

'It's a terrible shame about your brave Mullachi, Eolair,' the king said, returning to sit with old Craobhan and his other trusted men. 'But thanks be to Brynioch and Murhagh One-arm that you stumbled on to that scout party. If not, Skali and his bastard northerners would have been on us unawares. After the skirmish with your men gets back to him, he'll make a much more cautious approach, I'm sure – he may even change his mind altogether.'

'I wish that were true, my king,' Eolair said, shaking his head sadly. Maegwin's heart softened to see how bravely he bore his weariness; she silently cursed her childish emotions. 'But,' he continued, 'I fear it is not. For Skali to make such a treacherous attack so far from his home he must feel sure the odds are leaning his way.'

'Why, though, why?' Lluth protested. 'We have been at peace with the Rimmersmen for years!'

'I think, sire, that has little to do with it.' Eolair was respectful but unafraid to correct his king. 'If old Isgrimnur still ruled in Elvritshalla, you would be right to wonder, but Skali is Elias' creature entirely, I think. Rumor in Nabban said Elias will go into the field against Josua any day. He knows we have refused Guthwulf's ultimatum, and he fears to have the Hernystiri unencumbered at his back when he moves against Naglimund.'

'But Gwythinn is still there!' said Maegwin, frightened.

'And with half a hundred of our best men, worse luck,' old Craobhan growled from beside the fireplace.

Eolair turned to give Maegwin a kind look, the condescending sort, she felt sure. 'Your brother is doubtless safer behind the thick stone walls of Josua's castle then he would be here in Hernysadharc. Also, if he hears of our plight and can ride out, his fifty men will be at *Skali's* back, to our advantage.'

King Lluth rubbed his eyes as though to wring out the dismay and worry of the last day. 'I do not know, Eolair, I do not know. I have a bad feeling about this all. It takes no soothsayer to see an ill-omened year, which this has been from its first instant.'

'I'm still here, father,' Maegwin said, and went forward to kneel beside him. 'I will stay with you.' The king patted her hand.

Eolair smiled and nodded at the girl's words to her father, but his mind was obviously on his two dying men, and on the vast force of Rimmersmen moving down the Frostmarch into the Inniscrich, a great wave of sharp, sentient iron.

'Those who stay will perhaps not thank us,' he said beneath his breath.

Outside the brazen voice of the cauldron sang out across Hernysadharc, shouting ceaselessly to the hills beyond: *Beware . . . Beware . . . Beware . . .*

Baron Devasalles and his small Nabbanai contingent had somehow contrived to make their row of chambers in Naglimund's drafty east wing into a little bit of their southern home. Although the freakish weather was too cold to allow the wide-open windows and doors so prevalent in balmy Nabban, they had covered the stone walls with bright green and sky-blue tapestries and filled every available surface with candles and guttering oil lamps so that the shuttered rooms bloomed with light.

*It's brighter in here at noon than it is outside,* Isgrimnur decided. *But it's like old Jarnauga said – they won't be able to*

*make everything else go away so easy as they have the wintry
dark, not by half.*

The duke's nostrils twitched like those of a frightened
horse. Devasalles had set out pots of scented oils
everywhere, some afloat with lighted wicks like white
worms, filling the chamber with the thick smells of
island spices.

*I wonder if it's the smell of everyone's fear he doesn't like, or
that of good honest iron?* Isgrimnur grunted in distaste and
slid his chair over by the hallway door.

Devasalles had been surprised to find the duke and
Prince Josua at his door, unannounced and unexpected,
but had quickly invited them in, throwing aside some of
the multicolored robes that draped the hard chairs so his
guests could seat themselves.

'I'm sorry to disturb you, Baron,' Josua said, leaning
forward to rest his elbows on his knees, 'but I wished to
speak to you alone before we conclude the Raed tonight.'

'Of course, my prince, of course.' Devasalles nodded
encouragingly. Isgrimnur, disdainfully observing the
man's shining hair and the glinting baubles he wore at
neck and wrist, wondered how he could be the deadly
swordsman his reputation declared him.

*Looks like he might catch a hilt on his own necklaces and
hang himself.*

Josua hurried explained the events of the last two days,
which were the real reason the Raed had not continued.
Devasalles, who, like the rest of the assembled lords, had
doubted but accepted the prince's claim of illness, raised
his eyebrow but said nothing.

'I could not talk openly; I still cannot,' Josua amplified.
'In the mad crush, the muster of local forces, the comings
and goings, it would be only too easy for someone of bad
faith or one of Elias' spies to take the news of our fears
and plans to the High King.'

'But our fears are known to all,' Devasalles said, 'and
we have made no plans – yet.'

'By the time I am ready to speak of these things to all

the lords, I will have made the gates secure – but you see, Baron, you do not yet know all the story.'

With that the prince proceeded to tell Devasalles all the latest discoveries, of the three swords and the prophetic poem in the mad priest's book, and how these things matched with the dreams of many.

'But if you will tell all your liegemen this soon enough, why tell me now?' Devasalles asked. By the doorway Isgrimnur snorted: he, too, had wondered this same thing.

'Because I *need* your lord Leobardis, and I need him now!' Josua said. 'I need Nabban!' He stood and began a circuit of the room, facing the walls as though he studied their hangings, but his gaze was focused on a point somewhere leagues beyond the stone and woven cloth.

'I have needed your duke's pledge from the beginning, but I need him more now than ever I did. Elias has given Rimmersgard, for all practical purposes, to Skali and his Kaldskryke Raven-clan. Thus he has put a knife against King Lluth's back; the Hernystiri will be able to send me many fewer men, forced as they will be to keep a quantity back to defend their lands. Already Gwythinn, who a week ago was chafing to be at Elias, is anxious to return and help his father defend Hernysadharc and its outlands.'

Josua whirled to stare Devasalles in the eyes. The prince's face was a mask of cold pride, but his hand twisted at his shirt-front, something neither Isgrimnur or the baron failed to notice. 'If Duke Leobardis ever hopes to be more than a lackey to Elias, he *must* throw in his lot with me now.'

'But why do you tell this to me?' Devasalles asked. He looked honestly puzzled. 'I know all of this last, and the other things – the swords and the book and all – make no difference.'

'Damn it, man, they do!' Josua snapped back, his voice rising almost to a shout. 'Without Leobardis, and with Hernystir under the northern threat, my brother will have us as snug as if we were nailed in a barrel, and also he is dealing with demons – and who can know what dread advantage that means?! We have made some small, feeble attempt to counter those forces, but what good will come of it – even if it succeeds, against all likelihood – if all the freeholds have been already thrown down?! Neither your duke nor anyone else will ever answer King Elias with anything but "yes, master," from now on!'

The baron shook his head again, and his necklaces chinked gently. 'I am confused, my lord. Can it be that you do not know? I sent a message to the Sancellan Mahistrevis in Nabban by my fastest rider the night before yesterday, telling Leobardis I believed you would fight, and that he should move to put his men into the field in your support.'

'What?' Isgrimnur leaped up, his astonishment echoing the prince's. They both stood swaying over Devasalles, their expressions those of men ambushed by night.

'Why have you not told me?' Josua demanded.

'But my prince, I *did* tell you,' Devasalles sputtered, 'or at least, since I was advised you might not be disturbed, I sent a message to your chambers with my seal on it. Surely you read it?'

'Blessed Usires and his Mother!' Josua smacked his open left hand against his thigh. 'I have only myself to blame, for it sits even now on my bedside table. Deornoth brought it to me, but I was waiting for a quieter moment. I suppose I forgot. Still it is no harm done, and your news is excellent.'

'You say Leobardis will ride?' Isgrimnur asked suspiciously. 'How are you so sure? You seemed to have more than a few doubts yourself.'

'Duke Isgrimnur,' Devasalles' tone was frosty, 'surely you realize I was only fulfilling my duty. In truth, Duke Leobardis has long been in sympathy with Prince Josua. Likewise, he has feared Elias is becoming overbold. The troops have been on alert for weeks.'

'Then why send you?' Josua asked. 'What did he think to discover that he did not have already from me, through my messengers?'

'He sought nothing new,' Devasalles said, 'although there has been far more learned here than I think any of us bargained for. No, he sent my embassy more to make a show for certain others in Nabban.'

'There is resistance among his liegemen?' Josua asked, eyes bright.

'Of course, but that is not unusual . . . nor is it the source of my mission. It was to undermine resistance from a closer source.' Here, although the smallish chamber was obviously empty but for the three of them, Devasalles darted a look on all sides.

'It is his wife and son who resist most strongly his making common cause with you,' Devasalles said at last.

'You mean the eldest, Benigaris?'

'Yes, else he or one of Leobardis' younger sons should have been here in my stead.' The baron shrugged. 'Benigaris sees much he likes in Elias' rule, and the Duchess Nessalanta . . .' The Nabbanai emissary shrugged again.

'She, too, favors the High King's chances,' Josua smiled bitterly. 'Nessalanta is a clever woman. Too bad that now she will be forced, willy-nilly, to support her husband's choice of allies. She might well be correct in her misgivings.'

'Josua!' Isgrimnur was shocked.

'I only jest, old friend,' the prince said, but his expression belied him. 'So the duke will go into the field then, good Devasalles?'

'As soon as possible, Prince Josua. With the cream of Nabban's knights in his train.'

'And a strong dollop of pikemen and archers as well, I hope. Well, Aedon's grace on us all, Baron.'

He and Isgrimnur said their farewells and went out into the dark corridor, the bright colors of the baron's chamber left behind them like a dream abandoned at the lip of awakening.

'One person I know will be very glad of this news, Isgrimnur.'

The duke raised a questioning eyebrow.

'My niece. Miriamele was very upset when she thought Leobardis might not come over. Nessalanta is her aunt, after all. She'll be glad of this news, indeed.'

'Let us go tell her,' Isgrimnur proposed, taking Josua's elbow and guiding him out toward the courtyard. 'She may be with the other court ladies. I'm tired of looking at whiskery soldiers. I may be an old man, but I still like to look on a lady or two from time to time.'

'So be it.' Josua smiled, the first unforced example Isgrimnur had seen in several days. 'Then we'll go by and visit your wife, and you may tell her about your undiminished love of the ladies.'

'Prince Josua,' the old duke said carefully, 'you'll never be too damn old or exalted that I can't knuckle your ears, just you see if I can't.'

'Not today, Uncle,' Josua smirked. 'I'll need 'em to appreciate just what Gutrun has to say to you.'

The wind soughing in off the water carried the smell of cypress. Tiamak, wiping beads of sweat from his brow, gave silent thanks to He Who Always Steps on Sand for the unexpected breeze. Coming back from checking his trap line he had felt the storm-charged air descend on the Wran: hot, angry air that came and would not go away, like a march crocodile circling a leaking skiff.

Again Tiamak wiped his forehead dry, and reached for the bowl of yellowroot tea steeping on the firestone. As he sipped, not without some pain to his cracked lips, he worried over what he should do.

It was Morgenes' strange message that disturbed him. For days its ominous words had rattled in his head like pebbles in a dry gourd as he poled his boat through the byways of the Wran, or made his way to market in Kwanitupul, the trading village that crouched along the outlet stream from lake Eadne. He made the three-day flatboat trip to Kwanitupul once every new moon, putting his unusual schooling to good advantage at the marketing stalls, helping the smaller Wrannamen merchants to bargain with the Nabbanai and Perdruinese traders who worked the Wran's coastal villages. The taxing journey to Kwanitupul was a necessity, if only to earn a few coins and perhaps a bag of rice. The rice he used to supplement that occasional crab too stupid or too cocksure to avoid his traps. There were not many crabs so obliging, however, which was the reason Tiamak's usual table fare was fish and roots.

As he crouched in his tiny, banyan-perched cabin, anxiously turning over Morgenes' message for the hundredth time, he thought back to the bustling, hilly streets of Ansis Pelippé, Perdruin's capital, where he and the old doctor had first met.

As much as the clamor and spectacle of the vast trading port, a hundred, no, *many* hundreds of times the size of Kwanitupul – a fact that his fellow Wrannamen would never believe, provincial, sandscuffing louts that they were – it was the smells Tiamak remembered most strongly, the million shifting scents: the dank salt smell of the wharves, spiced with the tang of the fishing boats; the cook fires in the streets where bearded island men offered skewers of bubbling, charred mutton; the musk of sweating, champing horses whose proud riders, merchants and soldiers cantered boldly down the middle of the cobbled streets, letting the pedestrians scatter where they might; and of course, the swirling odors of saffron and quickweed, of cinnamon and mantinges, that eddied through the Spice District like fleeting, exotic solicitations.

Just the memories made him so hungry he almost wanted to weep, but Tiamak steeled himself. There was work to be done, and he could not be distracted by such fleshly obsessions. Morgenes needed him, somehow, and Tiamak had to be ready.

In fact, it had been food that had brought him to Morgenes' attention, all those years ago in Perdruin. The doctor, on some kind of apothecarical search through the trading districts of Ansis Pellipé, had bumped into and almost knocked over the Wrannaman youth, so intently was young Tiamak eyeing an array of marchpane on a baker's table. The doctor was amused and intrigued by the marsh lad so far from home, whose apologies to the older man were so full of carefully-learned Nabbanai idiom. When Morgenes learned that the boy was in Perdruin's capitol to study with the Usirean Brothers, and was the first of his village to leave the swampy Wran, he bought him a large square of marchpane and a cup of milk. From that moment on Morgenes was as a god to the astounded Tiamak.

The smudged sheet of parchment before him, even though itself a copy of the original message that had fallen to pieces from handling, was nevertheless becoming hard to read. He had stared at it so many times, however, that it no longer mattered. He had even placed it back into its original ciphers and retranslated it, just to make sure he had not missed some subtle but important detail.

*'The time of the Conqueror Star is surely upon us . . .'* the doctor had written, in the course of warning Tiamak this would likely be his last letter for a long while. Tiamak's help would be needed, Morgenes assured him, *'. . . if certain dreadful things which – it is said – are hinted at in the infamous lost book of the priest Nisses . . .'* were to be avoided.

The first time he had gone to Kwanitupul after receiving Morgenes' sparrow-borne message, Tiamak asked Middastri, a Perdruinese merchant with whom he sometimes drank a bowl of beer, what dreadful things were happening in Erchester, the city where Morgenes lived in Erkynland. Middastri said he had heard of strife between the High King Elias and Lluth of Hernystir, and of course everyone had been talking about the falling out between Elias and his brother Prince Josua for months, but beyond that the merchant could think of nothing special. Tiamak, who from Morgenes' message had feared danger of a vaster and more immediate sort, had felt a little better. Still, the import of the doctor's message tugged at him.

'The infamous lost book . . .' How had Morgenes known the secret? Tiamak had not told anyone; he had wanted to surprise the doctor with it on a visit he had planned to make next spring, his first time ever north of Perdruin. Now it appeared Morgenes already knew something of his prize – but why didn't he say so? Why should he instead hint and riddle and suggest, like a crab carefully poking the fish head out of one of Tiamak's traps?

The Wrannaman set down his bowl of tea and moved across the low-ceilinged room, hardly rising from his bent-kneed crouch. The hot, sour wind began to blow a little more strongly, rocking the house on its tall stilts, lifting the thatch with a serpentine hiss. He searched in his wooden chest for the leaf-wrapped thing, carefully hidden below the stack of parchment that was his own rewriting of *Sovran Remedys of the Wranna Healers*, what Tiamak secretly liked to think of as his 'great work.' Finding it at last he brought it out and unwrapped it, not for the first time in the last fortnight.

As it lay beside his transcription of Morgenes' message, he was taken by the contrast. Morgenes' words were painstakingly copied in black root-ink on cheap parchment, beaten so thin a candle flame held a handsbreadth away might puff it into flame. The other, the prize, was scribed on a sheet of tight-stretched skin or hide. The reddish brown words trailed crazily across the page, as though the writer had been a-horseback, or sitting at table during an earth tremor.

This last was the jewel of Tiamak's collection – indeed, if he was right about what it was, would be the crowning gem of *anyone's* collection. He had found it in a great pile of other used parchments a trader in Kwanitupul was selling for scribing practice. The trader had not known who the chest of papers had belonged to, only that he had gotten it as part of a blind lot of household goods in Nabban. Fearing that his good fortune might evaporate, Tiamak had stifled the urge to question further and bought it on the spot – along with a sheaf of other parchments – for one shiny Nabbanai quinis-piece.

He stared at it again – although he had read this more times even than Morgenes' message, if such was possible – and especially at the top of the parchment, not so much torn as gnawed, whose disfigurement ended with the letters '. . . ARDENVYRD.'

Was not Nisses' famous, vanished volume – some even called it imaginary – named *Du Svardenvyrd*? How had Morgenes known? Tiamak had not yet told anyone of his lucky find.

Beneath the title the northern runes, smeared in some places, flaking away into rust-colored powder in others, were nevertheless quite readable, written in the archaic Nabbanai of five centuries gone.

> '. . . *Bringe from Nuanni's Rocke Garden*
> *The Man who tho' Blinded canne See*
> *Discover the Blayde that delivers The Rose*
> *At the foote of the Rimmer's greate Tree*
> *Find the Call whose lowde Claime*
> *Speakes the Call-bearer's name*
> *In a Shippe on the Shallowest Sea –*
> *– When Blayde, Call, and Man*
> *Come to Prince's right Hande*
> *Then the Prisoned shall once more go Free* . . .'

Below the strange poem a single name was printed in large, awkward runes '*NISSES.*'

Although Tiamak stared and stared, inspiration still remained anguishingly distant. At last, sighing, he rolled the ancient scroll back in its jacket of preservative leaves and tucked it into his burrwood chest.

What, then, did Morgenes want him to do? Bring this thing to the doctor himself at the Hayholt? Or should he instead send it to another wise one, like the witch woman Geloë, fat Ookequk up in Yiqanuc, or the fellow in Nabban? Perhaps the wisest plan was merely to wait for Doctor Morgenes' further word, instead of hurrying off foolishly without full understanding. After all, from what Middastri had told him, whatever Morgenes feared must still be a long way off; there was certainly time to wait until he knew what it was that the doctor wanted.

*Time and patience*, he counseled himself, *time and patience . . .*

Outside his window the cypress branches groaned, suffering beneath the wind's rough handling.

The chamber door flew open. Sangfugol and the lady Vorzheva leaped up guiltily, as if they had been caught in some impropriety, although the length of the chamber separated them. As they looked up, wide-eyed, the minstrel's lute, which had been propped against his chair, tilted and fell over at his feet. He hurriedly caught it up and held it against his breast as though it were an injured child.

'Damn you, Vorzheva, what have you done!?' Josua demanded. Duke Isgrimnur stood behind him in the doorway wearing a worried look.

'Be calm, Josua,' he urged, tugging at the prince's gray jerkin.

'When I have the truth from this . . . this woman,' Josua spat. 'Until then, stay out of this, old friend.'

Color was returning fast to Vorzheva's cheeks.

701

'What is your meaning?' she said. 'You knock in doors like a bull, and shout questions. What is your meaning?'

'Do not seek to gull me. I have just come from speaking to the gate-captain; I am sure he wishes I had never found him, so angry I was. He told me that Miriamele went out yesterday forenoon with my permission – which was no permission, but instead my seal attached to a false document!'

'And why do you shout at me?' the lady asked haughtily. Sangfugol began to sidle toward the chamber door, still clutching his wounded instrument.

'That you know full well,' Josua growled, the flush finally beginning to fade from his pale features, 'and stay where you are, harper, for I am not done with you. You have been much in my lady's confidence of late.'

'At your command, Prince Josua,' Sangfugol said haltingly, 'to ease her loneliness. But of the Princess Miriamele I swear I know nothing!'

Josua moved forward into the chamber, swinging the heavy door shut behind him without a look back. Isgrimnur, nimble despite his years and girth, skipped out of its way.

'Good Vorzheva, do not treat me as though I were one of the wagon boys you grew up with. All I have heard from you is how the poor princess is sad, the poor princess is missing her family. Now Miriamele is gone out the gate with some villain, and some other confederate has used my seal ring to give her safe passage! I am no fool!'

The dark-haired woman returned his stare for a moment, then her lip began to tremble. Angry tears started in her eyes as she sat back down, long skirts rustling.

'Very well, Prince Josua,' she said, 'cut my head off if you like. I have helped the poor girl to go away to her family in Nabban. If you were not so heartless, you would have sent her yourself, with armed men to escort. Instead, all she has for company is a kind monk.' She pulled a kerchief from the bosom of her dress and dabbed her eyes. 'Still, she is happier that way, than to be cooped up here like a bird in a cage.'

'Tears of Elysia!' Josua swore, throwing his hand in the air. 'You foolish woman! Miriamele wanted only to play at being an emissary – she thought to find glory by bringing her Nabbanai relatives into this struggle on my side.'

'Perhaps it is not fair to say "glory," Josua,' Isgrimnur cautioned. 'I think the princess honestly means to help.'

'And what is wrong with that?!' asked Vorzheva defiantly. 'You need the help of Nabban, do you not? Or are you too proud?'

'God help me, the Nabbanai are with us already! Do you understand? I have just seen Baron Devasalles an hour gone. But now the High King's daughter is out needlessly wandering the land somewhere, with all of her father's troops about to go into the field, and his spies swarming everywhere like maggot-flies.'

Josua waved his arms in frustration, then slumped into his chair, long legs stretched before him.

'It is too much for me, Isgrimnur,' he said wearily. 'And you wonder why I do not declare myself a rival for Elias' throne? I cannot even keep a young girl safely under my roof.'

Isgrimnur smiled dolefully. 'Her father didn't have much luck in keeping her either, as I recall.'

'Still.' The prince brought his hand up to knead his brow. 'Usires, my very head throbs with it all.'

'Now, Josua,' the duke said, casting a look at the others to warn them to keep silence, 'all is not lost. We must simply put a troop of good men out to beat the bushes for Miriamele and this monk, this . . . Cedric or whatever . . .'

'Cadrach,' said Josua tonelessly.

'Yes, then, Cadrach. Well, a young girl and a holy friar cannot move that quickly afoot. We shall simply put some men to horse and get after them.'

'Unless the Lady Vorzheva here has hidden horses for them as well,' Josua said sourly. He sat up. 'You haven't, have you?!'

Vorzheva could not meet his gaze.

'Merciful Aedon!' Josua swore. 'That is the final trick! I shall send you back to your barbarian father in a sack, you wildcat!'

'Prince Josua?' It was the harper. When he got no response he cleared his throat and tried again. 'My prince?'

'What?' Josua said irritably. 'Yes, you may go. I will have words with you later. Go.'

'No sir . . . that is, did you say the monk's name was . . . Cadrach?'

'Yes, so the gate-captain said. He spoke with the man a bit. Why, do you know him, or know his haunts?'

'Well, no, Prince Josua, but I think the boy Simon met him. He told me much of his adventures, and the name sounds quite familiar. Oh, sir, if it is him, the princess may be in some danger.'

'What do you mean?' Josua leaned forward.

'The Cadrach Simon told me of was a rogue and a cutpurse, sir. That one also went in the guise of a monk, but he was no Aedonite man, that's sure.'

'It cannot be!' Vorzheva said. The kohl around her eyes had run onto her cheeks. 'I have met this man, and he quoted me from the Book of Aedon. He is a good, kind man, Brother Cadrach.'

'Even a demon can quote the Book,' Isgrimnur said, shaking his head sorrowfully.

The prince had sprung to his feet, and was moving to the door.

'We must put men out at once, Isgrimnur,' he said, then stopped and turned back, taking Vorzheva by the arm. 'Come, lady,' he said brusquely. 'You will not undo your damage, but you may at least come along and tell us all you know, where you have hid the horses and all such.' He pulled her to her feet.

'But I cannot go out!' she said, shocked. 'Look, I have been weeping! My face, it is terrible.'

'For the hurt you have done to me, and maybe to my foolish niece as well, it is a small enough penalty. Come!'

He hurried her before him out of the chamber, Isgrimnur following. Their arguing voices echoed down the stone corridor.

Sangfugol, left behind, looked sorrowfully down at his lute. There was a long crack twisting the length of its curved, ashwood back, and one of the strings hung loose in a useless curl.

'Scant music but sour will be made tonight,' he said.

It was still an hour before dawn when Lluth came to her bedside. She had not been able to sleep all night, stretched tight inside with worry for him, but as he bent over to touch her arm she pretended sleep, wanting to spare him the only thing left from which she *could* spare him: the knowledge of her own great fear.

'Maegwin,' he said softly. Her eyes shut fast, she fought the urge to reach up and hug him tight. Full-armored but for his helmet, as she knew from the sound of his walk and the scent of polishing oil, he might have trouble straightening up again if she pulled him down so close. Even the parting she could stand, bitter though it was. The thought of him showing his weariness and his age this night of all nights, she could not.

'Is that you, Father?' she said at last.

'It is.'

'And are you going now?'

'I must. The sun will be up soon, and we hope to reach the edge of the Combwood by midmorning.'

She sat up. The fire had burned out, and even with her eyes open she could not see much. Faintly, through the walls, she could hear the sound of her stepmother

Inahwen sobbing. Maegwin felt a twinge of anger at such a display made of grief.

'Brynioch's Shield over you, father,' she said, reaching out a blind hand to find his battered face. 'I wish I was a son, to fight at your side.'

She felt his lips curl beneath her fingers. 'Ah, Maegwin, you were ever a fierce one. Have you not duty enough here? It will not be easy being mistress of the Taig while I am gone.'

'You forget your wife.'

Lluth smiled again in the dark. 'I do not. You are strong, Maegwin, stronger than she. You must lend her some of your strength.'

'She usually gets what she wants.'

The king's voice was gentle, but he caught her wrist in a firm hand. 'Don't, daughter. Along with Gwythinn, you are the three I love most in all the world. Help her.'

Maegwin hated to cry. She pulled her hand from her father's grasp and rubbed her eyes fiercely. 'I will,' she said. 'Forgive me.'

'No forgiveness necessary,' he answered, then took her hand once more and squeezed. 'Farewell, daughter, until I come back again. There are cruel ravens in our field, and we have work to do chasing them out again.'

She was up and out of bed then, and threw her arms around him. A moment later the door opened and closed, and she heard his steps going slowly up the hall, the clink of spurs like sad music.

Later, when she cried, it was with the blankets over her head so that no one would hear.

# 36
# Fresh Wounds and Old Scars

The horses were more than a little afraid of Qantaqa, so Binabik rode the great gray wolf well ahead of Simon and the others, carrying a hooded lamp to show the way in the blanketing darkness. As the tiny caravan made its way along the skirt of the hills the shuddering light bobbed before them like a corpse-candle.

The moon cowered within its nest of clouds, and their progress was slow and cautious. Between the gentle, jogging rhythm of the horse beneath him, and the feel of its warm, broad back, Simon nearly fell asleep several times, only to be startled awake by thin, scrabbling fingers at his face: the branches of close-hovering trees. There was little talk. From time to time one of the men whispered a word of encouragement to his mount, or Binabik called back softly to warn of some upcoming obstacle; but for those sounds, and the muffled percussion of hoofbeats, they might have been a gray pilgrimage of lost souls.

When the moonlight finally began to seep through a rent in the cloud ceiling, not long before dawn, they stopped to make camp. Vaporous breath caught the moon's glow, making it seem they exhaled silver-blue clouds as they tied up their mounts and the two packhorses. They lit no fire. Ethelbearn took first watch;

the others, wrapped in their heavy cloaks, curled up on the damp ground to snatch what sleep they could.

Simon awoke to a morning sky like thin gruel, and nose and ears that seemed to have magically turned to ice in the night. As he crouched by the small fire chewing the bread and hard cheese Binabik had doled out, Sludig sat down beside him. The young Rimmersman's cheeks were polished red by the brisk wind.

'This is like our early spring weather, back in my home,' he grinned, skewering a heel of bread on the long blade of his knife and holding it over the flame. 'It makes a man of you quick, you will see.'

'I hope there are other ways of becoming a man besides freezing to death,' Simon grunted, rubbing his hands together.

'You can kill a bear with a spear,' Sludig said. 'We do that, also.'

Simon could not tell whether he was joking.

Binabik, who had just sent Qantaqa off to hunt, came over and sat down cross-legged. 'Well, the two of you, are you ready to be at hard riding today?' he said. Simon did not respond, since his mouth was full of bread; when a moment later Sludig had not answered either, Simon looked up. The Rimmersman was staring straight into the fire, his mouth in a set, straight line. The silence was uncomfortable.

Simon swallowed. 'I suppose so, Binabik,' he said quickly. 'Do we have far to go?'

Binabik smiled blithely, as though the Rimmersman's silence were perfectly natural. 'We will be going as far as we shall wish. Today it seems good to ride long, since the skies are clear. Sooner than we are wishing we may be found by rain and snow.'

'Do we know where we're headed?'

'In part, friend Simon.' Binabik took a length of twig from the outskirts of the firepit and began to scratch lines in the moist earth. 'Here is standing Naglimund,' he said, drawing a rough circle. He then made a line of scallop shapes starting at the circle's right flank and extending up for some distance. 'That, the Wealdhelm. This cross is being us here.' He made a mark not far past the circle. Then in quick succession he drew a large oval near the far end of the mountains, a few smaller circles scattered around its rim, and what seemed to be another line of hills out beyond.

'So, then,' he said, hunkering down close over his furrowed patch of ground. 'Soon it is we shall be approaching this lake,' he indicated the large elliptical shape, 'which is called Drorshull.'

Sludig, who seemingly against his will had leaned over to look, straightened up. 'Drorshullvenn – the Lake of Dror's Hammer.' He frowned and tilted forward once more, making a dot with his finger along the lake's western rim. 'There is Vestvennby – the thaneland of that traitor, Storfot. I would like very much to pass through there by night.' He wiped the breadcrumbs from the blade of his dagger and held it up to catch the weak firelight.

'We will not, however, be going to there,' Binabik said sternly, 'and for you revenge must wait. We are passing to the other side, past Hullnir to Haethstad, nearby where is the Abbey of Saint Skendi, then most likely up across the plain of the north, toward the mountains. No stopping before for cutting of throats.' He pushed his stick up beyond the lake toward the row of rounded shapes.'

'That is because you trolls do not understand honor,' Sludig said bitterly, staring at Binabik from beneath his thick blond eyebrows.

'Sludig,' Simon said pleadingly, but Binabik did not respond to the man's baiting.

'We are having a task to perform,' the troll responded calmly. 'Isgrimnur, your duke, wishes it, and his will is not served with faithfulness by creeping off at nighttimes to slit the throat of Storfot. That is not a troll's lack of honor, Sludig.'

The Rimmersman looked hard at him for a moment, then shook his head. 'You are right.' There was, to Simon's surprise, no sullenness remaining in his voice. 'I am angry, and my words were poorly chosen.' He got up and walked away toward where Grimmric and Haestan stood reburdening the horses; as he went he flexed his supple, muscular shoulders as though to loosen knots. Simon and the troll stared after him for a moment.

'He apologized,' Simon said.

'All Rimmersmen are not being that cold one Einskaldir,' his friend replied. 'But, also, all trolls are not either being Binabik.'

It was a very long day's ride, up along the flank of the hills under the cover of the trees. When they finally stopped for their evening meal, Simon knew for certain the truth of Haestan's earlier warnings: although his horse walked slowly, and their march had been over mild terrain, his legs and crotch felt as though he had spent the day attached to some dreadful torture device. Haestan, not without a grin, kindly explained to him that after a night's stiffening the worst would be yet to come; he then offered him as much of the wineskin as he cared to drink. When Simon eventually curled up that evening between the humped and mossy roots of a nearly leafless oak tree he was feeling a little better, although the wine made him think he heard voices singing strange songs on the wind.

When he woke up in the morning it was to discover that not only was everything Haestan had claimed true tenfold, but snow was swirling down as well, covering Wealdhelm Hills and travelers alike in a cold, clinging white coverlet. Even shivering in the weak Yuven daylight he could still hear the wind-voices. What they were saying was clear: they mocked calendars, and fleered at travelers who thought they could walk with impunity into winter's new kingdom.

The Princess Miriamele stared with horror at the scene spread before her. What had been since the beginning of the morning's ride a riot of colors and black smoke on the horizon now lay clear as she and Cadrach stood on the hillside overlooking the Inniscrich. It was a tapestry of death, woven in flesh and metal and shredded earth.

'Merciful Elysia,' she gasped, reining in her shying horse, 'what has happened here!? Is this my father's work?'

The small round man squinted, mouth working for a moment in what the princess took for silent prayer. 'Most of the dead are Hernystiri, my lady,' he said at last, 'and I'm guessing the others are Rimmersmen, from the look of them.' He frowned on the scene below as a group of startled ravens all leaped up at once like a clutch of flies, circled, then settled again. 'It appears the battle, or the retreating part of it, has moved away west.'

Miriamele found her eyes filling with frightened tears, and reached up a fist to scour them away. 'The survivors must be falling back to Hernysadharc, to the Taig. Why has this happened? Has *everyone* gone mad?'

'Everyone was mad already, my lady,' Cadrach said with a strange, sorrowful smile. 'It is merely that the times have brought it out in them.'

They had ridden swiftly for the first day and a half, pushing the Lady Vorzheva's horses to their gasping limit until they reached and crossed the Greenwade River at its upper fork, some twenty-five leagues southwest of Naglimund. They then slowed their pace, giving the horses a chance to rest in case they should again need to ride in haste.

Miriamele rode well in the manly style, which was appropriate to the garments she wore, the breeches and jerkin in which she had disguised herself in her escape from the Hayholt. Her shorn hair was again black-dyed, although little of it showed beneath the traveling hood worn as much against the cold as against discovery;

Brother Cadrach riding beside her in his travel-stained gray habit was no more likely than she to attract notice. In any case, there were few other travelers on the river road in such discouraging weather, and in the midst of such perilous times. The princess had begun to feel quite confident that their escape was safely effected.

Since the middle of the day before they had ridden along the dike road above the wide, swollen river with the braying of distant trumpets in their ears, shrill brazen voices that outstripped even the moan of the rain-laden wind. At first it was frightening, raising the specter of some vengeful troop of her uncle's or her father's at their heels, but soon it became apparent that she and Cadrach were approaching the source of the clamor, rather than the reverse. Then, this morning, they had seen the first signature of battle: lonely trails of black smoke inking the now-calm sky.

'Isn't there anything we can do?' Miriamele asked, dismounted and standing beside her gently blowing horse. But for the birds the scene below them was as motionless as if carved in gray and red stone.

'And what might we do, my lady?' Cadrach asked, still a-saddle. He took a swig from his wineskin.

'I don't know. You're a priest! Mustn't you say a *mansa* for their souls?'

'For whose souls, princess? Those of my pagan countrymen, or those of the good Aedonites from Rimmersgard who have come down to pay this call on them?' His bitter words seemed to hang like smoke.

Miriamele turned to stare at the little man, whose eyes now seemed quite unlike those of the jocular companion of the last few days. When he told stories or sang his Hernystiri riding and drinking songs, he fairly glittered with cheer. Now he looked like a man savoring the doubtful victory of a dire prophecy fulfilled.

'All Hernystiri are not pagans!' she said, angry with his strange mood. 'You yourself are an Aedonite monk!'

'Should I go down, then, and ask who is pagan and who is not?' He waved a plump hand at the unmoving spectacle of carnage. 'No, my lady, the only work still to be done here will be done by scavengers.' He prodded his horse with his heels and rode ahead a short distance.

Miriamele stood and stared, pressing her cheek against the horse's neck. 'Surely no religious man could stand by and see such a scene unmoved,' she called after him, 'even that red monster Pryrates!' Cadrach hunched at the mention of the king's counselor as if struck in the back, then rode a few more paces before stopping to sit for a while in silence.

'Come, lady,' he said at last over his shoulder. 'We must get down from this hillside, where we are in such plain view. Not all scavengers are feathered, and some go on two legs.'

Dry-eyed now, the princess shrugged wordlessly and clambered back into the saddle, following the monk down the forested slope that ran beside the bloodied Inniscrich.

As he slept that night in their camp on the hillside above the flat, white, treeless expanse of Drorshull lake, Simon dreamed again of the wheel.

Once more he found himself snagged helplessly, tossed about like a child's doll of rags, lifted aloft on the wheel's vast rim. Cold winds buffeted him, and shards of ice scored his face as he was drawn up into freezing blackness.

At the summit of the ponderous revolution, wind-ripped and bleeding, he saw a gleam in the darkness, a luminous vertical stripe that reached from the impenetrable blackness above to the equally murky depths below. It was a white tree, whose broad trunk and thin branches glowed as though stuffed with stars. He tried to pull himself free from the wheel's grip, to leap out toward the beckoning whiteness, but it seemed he was held fast. With one great, final effort he tore loose and jumped.

He plunged downward through a universe of glowing leaves, as though he flew among the lamps of stars; he cried out for blessed Usires to save him, for God's help, but no hands caught at him as he plummeted through the cold firmament. . . .

Hullnir, at the slowly-freezing lake's eastern rim, was a town empty of even ghosts. Half-buried beneath the drifting snows, its houses unroofed by wind and hail, it lay like the carcass of a starved elk beneath dark, indifferent skies.

'Have Skali and his ravens so soon wrung the life from all the northland?' Sludig asked, his eyes wide.

'As like they all fled th'late frost,' Grimmric said, pulling his cloak tight beneath his narrow chin. 'Too cold here, too far away from th'few roads open.'

'It is probable Haethstad will be the same,' Binabik said, urging Qantaqa back up the slope. 'Good it is that we had no plan to find supplies on our way.'

Here at the lake's far end the hills began to fade, and a great arm of the northern Aldheorte reached out to cloak their last, low slopes. It was different than the southern part of the forest Simon had seen, and not only because of the snow that now carpeted the forest floor, stealing away the very sound of their passage. Here the trees were straight and tall, dark green pines and spruce that stood like pillars beneath their white mantles, separating wide, shadowy corridors. The riders moved as through pale catacombs, snow sifting down from above like the ash of ages.

'There is someone there, Brother Cadrach!' Miriamele hissed. She pointed. 'There! Can't you see the gleam – it's metal!'

714

Cadrach lowered the wineskin and stared. His mouth was stained purplish red at the corners. He scowled and squinted, as if to satisfy a whim of hers. A moment later the frown deepened.

'By the Good God, you are right, Princess,' he whispered, drawing back on his reins. 'There is something there, sure enough.' He handed the traces to her and slipped down onto the thick green grass, then, with a gestured admonition to silence, he crept forward; using a broad tree trunk to shield his almost equally stout form, he moved to within a hundred paces of the glimmering object, craning his neck around to peer at it like a child playing hide-and-seek. After a moment he turned back and beckoned. Miriamele rode forward, bringing Cadrach's horse beside her own.

It was a man who lay half-propped against the sprawling base of an oak tree, clad in armor that still shone in a few spots, despite the fearful battering it had taken. Lying in the grass at his side was the hilt of a shattered sword, and a broken pole and green pennant which bore the blazoned White Stag of Hernystir.

'Elysia Mother of God!' Miriamele said as she hurried forward. 'Is he still alive?'

Cadrach quickly tied the horses up to one of the oak's arching roots and then moved to her side. 'It doesn't look likely.'

'But he is!' the princess said, 'Listen . . . he is breathing!'

The monk kneeled down to look at the man whose breath indeed sounded haltingly within the chamber of his half-open helmet. Cadrach tilted up the mask beneath the winged crest to expose a mustached face almost hidden by runnels of dried blood.

'Hound of Heaven,' Cadrach sighed, 'it is Arthpreas – the Count of Cuimhne.'

'You know him?' Miriamele said, searching in her saddlebag for the waterskin. She found it, and moistened a piece of cloth.

715

'Know of him, really,' Cadrach said, and gestured at the two birds stitched on the knight's tattered surcoat. 'He's the liege-lord of Cuimhne, near Nad Mullach, he is. His sign is the twin meadowlarks.'

Miriamele dabbed at Arthpreas' face while the monk gingerly explored the bloodied rents in his armor. The knight's eyes fluttered.

'He's awakening!' the princess said, breathing in sharply. 'Cadrach, I think he will live!'

'Not long, Lady,' the small man said quietly. 'There is a wound here in his belly as wide as my hand. Let me give him the last words, and he can die in peace.'

The count groaned and a little blood ran over the rim of his lip. Miriamele tenderly wiped it from his chin. His eyes trembled open.

'*E gundhain sluith, ma connalbehn . . .*' the knight muttered in Hernystiri. He coughed weakly, and more blood bubbled onto his lips. 'There's a good . . . lad. Did they . . . take the Stag?'

'What does he mean?' Miriamele whispered. Cadrach pointed to the torn banner on the grass beneath the count's arm.

'You rescued it, Count Arthpreas,' she said, holding her face close to his. 'It's safe. What happened?'

'Skali's Raven-warriors . . . they were everywhere.' A long cough, and the knight's eyes opened wider. 'Ah, my brave boys . . . dead, all dead . . . hacked up like, like . . .' Arthpreas gave a painful, dry sob. His eyes stared up at the sky, moving slowly as if tracing the movements of clouds.

'And where is the king?' he said at last. 'Where is our brave old king? The *goirach* northerners were all around him, Brynioch rot them, *Brynioch na ferth ub . . . ub strocinh . . .*'

'The king?' Miriamele whispered. 'He must mean Lluth.'

The count's eyes suddenly lit on Cadrach, and for a moment were kindled as though by an inner spark.

716

'Padreic?' he said, and lifted a shaking, bloodied hand to lay it on the monk's wrist. Cadrach flinched and made as though to draw away, but his eyes seemed caught, lit by a strange gleam. 'Is it you, Padreic *feir*? Have you . . . come back. . . ?'

The knight stiffened then, and gave vent to a long, racking cough which brought the red flow up like an underground spring. A moment later his eyes rolled up beneath his dark lashes.

'Dead,' Cadrach said after a moment, a harsh note in his voice. 'Usires save him, and God comfort his soul.' He made the sign of the tree over Arthpreas' unmoving breast and stood up.

'He called you Padreic,' Miriamele said, staring abstractedly at the cloth she held, now entirely crimson.

'He mistook me,' the monk said. 'A dying man looking for an old friend. Come. We have no shovels for digging a grave. Let us at least find stones to cover him. He was . . . I am told he was a good man.'

As Cadrach walked away across the clearing, Miriamele carefully pulled the armored gauntlet from Arthpreas' hand, then wrapped it in the torn green banner.

'Please come and help me, my lady,' Cadrach called. 'We cannot afford to be spending much time here.'

'I will come,' she said, slipping the bundle into her saddlebag. 'This much time we can afford.'

Simon and his companions made their way slowly around the long circumference of the lake, along a peninsula of tall trees and drifting snow. On their left lay the frozen mirror of Drorshull; the white shoulders of the upper Wealdhelm loomed on the right. The song of the wind was loud enough to drown all conversation softer than a full shout. As Simon rode, watching Haestan's wide, dark back jounce along before him, it seemed they were all solitary islands in a cold sea: in constant sight of each other, but separated by untrafficked expanses. He found his thoughts turning inward, lulled by the monotonous pacing of his horse.

Strangely, in his mind's inlooking eye, the Naglimund they had just left seemed as insubstantial as a distant memory of childhood. Even the faces of Miriamele and Josua were hard to recapture, as though he tried to summon the features of strangers whose importance had not been discovered until long after they were gone. Instead, he found vivid memories of the Hayholt . . . of long summer evenings in the commons yard, itchy with mown grass and insects, or of breezy spring afternoons climbing on the walls, when the heady scent of the rose hedges in the courtyard pulled at him like warm hands. Remembering the slightly damp odor of the walls around his tiny cot, pushed into a corner in the servant's quarters, he felt himself a king in exile, as though he had lost a palace to some foreign usurper – as, in a way, he had.

The others seemed just as enfolded in their own thoughts; but for Grimmric's whistling – a thin trill of music that only occasionally rose above the wind, but seemed nevertheless constant – the trip around Drorshull Lake was made in silence.

Several times, when he could make her out through the fluttering snowflakes, he thought he saw Qantaqa stop and tilt her head as though to listen. When they finally made camp that night, with the main body of the lake now lying behind them to the southwest, he asked Binabik about it.

'Does she hear something, Binabik? Is there something ahead of us?'

The troll shook his head, extending his now unmittened hands closer to the small fire. 'Perhaps, but things that are before us, even in such weather, Qantaqa smells them – it is into the wind that we are walking. More likely it is she hears a sound from behind or to either side.'

Simon thought about that for a moment. Certainly nothing had followed them from barren Hullnir, devoid even of birds.

'Someone is behind us?' he said.

'I am doubting. Who? And for what reason?'

Nevertheless, Sludig, bringing up the rear of the column, had also noticed the wolf's seeming uneasiness. Although he was still not entirely comfortable with Binabik, and certainly was not ready to trust Qantaqa – he rolled his sleeping cloak at the far side of camp when he slept – he did not doubt the gray wolf's keen senses. As the others sat eating hard bread and dried venison, he had taken out his whetstone to sharpen his hand axes.

'Here between the Dimmerskog – the forest north of us – and Drorshullven,' Sludig said frowning, 'it has always been wild country, even when Isgrimnur or his father ruled in Elvritshalla and winter knew its place. These days, who knows what walks the white waste, or the Trollfells beyond?' He scraped rhythmically.

'Trolls, for one thing,' said Binabik sardonically, 'but I can be assuring you there is scant fear of troll-folk descending upon us in the night for killing and plunder.'

Sludig grinned sourly and continued sharpening his axe.

'Th'Rimmersman speaks sense,' Haestan said, giving Binabik a displeased look. 'An' tis not trolls I'm fearin' myself.'

'Are we near to your country, Binabik?' Simon asked. 'To Yiqanuc?'

'We will be approaching with more closeness when we reach the mountains, but the place of my birth is in actuality, I think, east of where it is we are heading.'

'You think?'

'Do not be forgetting, we are still not sure with exactness where we go. "The Rhymer's Tree" – a tree of rhymes? I know the mountain called Urmsheim, where it is *supposed* this Colmund went, is standing somewhere to the north, between Rimmersgard and Yiqanuc, but a

719

big mountain it is.' The troll shrugged. 'Is the tree on it? Before it? Or somewhere else all together? I cannot know at this time.'

Simon and the others stared glumly into the fire. It was one thing to undertake a perilous mission for your sovereign, it was another thing to search blindly in the white wilderness.

The flames hissed as they bit at the damp wood. Qantaqa rose from where she stretched on the naked snow and cocked her head. She walked purposefully to the edge of the clearing they had chosen, in a grove of pines on the low hillside. After a suspenseful interval she walked back and lay down again. No one said a word, but a moment of tension had passed, leaving their hearts a little lighter once more.

When they had all finished eating, more logs were fed onto the blaze, which popped and steamed in cheerful spite of the flurrying snow. As Binabik and Haestan talked quietly, and Simon used Ethelbearn's whetstone on his own sword, a thin melody rose up. Simon turned to see Grimmric whistling, lips pursed, eyes fixed on the wavering flames. When he looked up and saw Simon staring at him, the wiry Erkynlander gave him a snaggle-toothed smile.

'Put me t'mind of somethin',' he said. 'N'old winter song, it was.'

'What then?' Ethelbearn asked. 'Sing it, man. No harm in quiet song.'

'Yes, go ahead,' Simon seconded.

Grimmric looked over to Haestan and the troll, as if fearing an objection from that quarter, but they were still enmeshed in their discussion. 'Well, then,' he said. 'Suppose there's no harm in't.' He cleared his throat and looked down, as if embarrassed by the sudden attention. 'S'just a song my old father'd sing when we'd go out of a Decander afternoon t'cut wood.' He cleared his throat. 'A winter song,' he added, then cleared his throat again and sang, in a scratchy but not untuneful voice.

*'Ice is a-growin' in th' thatch*
*And snow is upon th' sill.*
*Someone's a-knockin' at th' door*
*Out in th' winter's chill.*

*Sing you hey-a-ho, an' who can it be?*

*Fire is a-burnin' in th' grate*
*Shadows is on th' wall.*
*Pretty Arda, she answers up*
*Inside her latchlocked hall.*

*Sing you hey-a-ho, an' who can it be?*

*Comes then a voice from winter-dark,*
*"Open up your door.*
*Let me in for to share your fire*
*An' to warm my hands before."*

*Sing you hey-a-ho, an' who can it be?*

*Arda, chaste an' chary maid*
*She answers. "Tell me, sir-o,*
*Who can you be, who walks abroad*
*When nought outside should stir-o?"*

*Sing you hey-a-ho, an' who can it be?*

*"A holy man," th' voice replies,*
*"Who has not food nor shelter."*
*Th' words all spoke so piteous*
*If she were ice, 'twould melt her.*

*Sing you hey-a-ho, an' who can it be?*

*"Then I will let you in, good Father,*
*Old bones will soon be warmer.*
*A maid can trust a man o' God*
*That he will never harm her".*

*Sing you hey-a-ho, an' who can it be?*

*Open th' door an' who stand there?*
*A man who's nothin' holy.*

721

*Old One-Eye with his cloak an' staff.*
*An' his wide-brim hat pulled lowly.*

*"I lied, I lied, t'get inside,"*
*Old One-Eye grins and dances,*
*"Th' frost's my home, but I love t'roam*
*An' a maid is worth th' chances" . . .'*


'Holy Usires, are you mad?!' Sludig leaped up, startling everybody. His eyes wide with horror, he made the sign of the Tree broadly before him, as though to fend off a charging beast. 'Are you mad?' he asked again, staring at the dumbfounded Grimmric.

The Erkynlander looked around at his other companions, shrugging helplessly. 'What's wrong with this Rimmersman, troll?' he asked.

Binabik squinted up at Sludig, who was still standing. 'What *is* the wrongness, Sludig? We are none of us understanding.'

The northerner looked around at the uncomprehending faces. 'Are you all without your senses?' he asked. 'Do you not know of who you are singing?'

'Old One-Eye?' Grimmric said, eyebrow cocked in puzzlement. 'S'just a song, northman. Learned it from m'father.'

'That is Udun One-Eye you sing of – Udun Rimmer, the black old god of my people. We worshipped him in Rimmersgard when we were sunk in our heathen ignorance. Do not call up Udun Skyfather when you walk in his country, or he will come – to your grief.'

'Udun the Rimer . . .' Binabik said wonderingly.

'If you don't believe in him any more,' Simon asked, 'why are you afraid to speak of him?'

Sludig stared, his mouth still taut with worry. 'I did not say I did not believe in him . . . Aedon forgive me . . . I said we Rimmersmen no longer worship him.' After a moment he lowered himself back to the ground. 'I am sure you think me foolish. Better *that* than we call

722

down jealous old gods on ourselves. We are in *his* country now.'

'S'just a song,' Grimmric said defensively. 'I wasna callin' down *anythin'*. S'just a bloody song.'

'Binabik, is that why we call it "Udensday"?' Simon began, then broke off when he saw the troll was not listening. Instead, the little man wore a broad, cheerful grin, as though he had just swallowed a draught of some pleasing liquor.

'That is it, certainly!' the little man said, and turned to pale, stern-faced Sludig. 'You have thought of it, my friend.'

'What are you talking about?' the blond-bearded northman asked with some irritation. 'I do not understand you.'

'What we are looking for. The place where Colmund was going: The Rhymer's Tree. Except we were at thinking "rhyme" like poetry, but you have now said it. "Udun Rimmer" – Udun the Rimer. "Rime" meaning "frost." It is a *Rimer's* Tree we are searching for.'

Sludig retained his blank look for a moment, then slowly nodded his head. 'Blessed Elysia, troll – the *Uduntree*. Why did I not think of it? The Uduntree!'

'You know the place Binabik is talking about?' Simon was slowly catching on.

'Of course. It is an old, old legend of ours – a tree entirely of ice. The old tales say that Udun made it grow so he could climb to the sky and make himself king over all the gods.'

'But what good is legend t'us?' Simon heard Haestan ask, but even as the words came to his ears he felt a strange, heavy chill folding around him like a blanket of sleet. The icy, white tree . . . he saw it again: the white trunk stretching up into the darkness, the impenetrable white tower, a great, looming pale stripe against the blackness . . . it stood squarely in the track of his life, and somehow he knew there was no path around it . . . no way around the slender, white finger – beckoning, warning, waiting.

723

*The white tree.*

'Because the legend tells where it is, too,' a voice said, echoing as if down a long corridor. 'Even if there is no such thing, we know that Sir Colmund must have gone where the legend points – the northern face of Urmsheim.'

'Sludig is correct,' someone said . . . Binabik said. 'We are needing only to go where Colmund was going with Thorn – nothing else is having importance.' The troll's voice seemed very far away.

'I think I . . . I have to go to sleep,' Simon said, his tongue thick. He got up and stumbled away from the fire, practically unnoticed by the others, who were talking animatedly of riding distances and mountain travel. He curled up in his thick cloak and felt the snowy world revolve dizzyingly around him. He shut his eyes and, though he still felt every pitch and yaw, at the same time he began sliding heavily, helplessly down into dream-thick sleep.

All the next day they continued along the forested bight of snow between the lake and the settling hills, hoping to make Haethstad at the lake's northeastern tip by late afternoon. If its inhabitants had not fled the harsh winter and headed west, the companions decided, Sludig could go down by himself and restock some of their stores. Even if it lay deserted, they could perhaps take shelter in an abandoned hall for the night and dry out their things before the long trip across the waste. Thus, it was with some anticipation they traveled, making good time along the lakeshore.

Haethstad, a village of some two dozen longhouses, stood on a promontory of land scarcely wider than the town itself; seen from the hillside above, the village seemed to sprout from the frozen lake.

The cheering effect of their first glimpse lasted only about halfway down the sloping road into the vale. It became increasingly obvious that although the buildings stood, they were no more than burned-out shells.

724

'Damn my eyes,' Sludig said angrily, 'this is not just a village abandoned, troll. They were driven out.'

'If they were lucky enow t'get out at all,' Haestan muttered.

'I think I must be agreeing with you, Sludig,' Binabik said. 'Still we must go and look there, to see how recent this burning is.'

As they rode down to the bottom of the glen, Simon stared at the scorched remains of Haethstad, and could not help remembering the calcined skeleton of Saint Hoderund's abbey.

*The priest at the Hayholt always used to say fire purifies,* he thought. *If that's true, then why does fire, does burning, frighten everyone? Well, by the Aedon, I suppose no one wants to be purified **that** thoroughly.*

'Oh, no,' Haestan said, Simon almost ran into him as the big guardsman reined up. 'Oh, the good God,' he added.

Simon peered around him to see a line of dark shapes filing out of the trees near the village, moving slowly into the snowy road not a hundred ells before them – men on horseback. Simon counted them as they made their way out into the open . . . seven, eight, nine. They were all armored. The leader wore a black iron helm shaped like a hound's head, showing the profile of the snarling muzzle as he turned to give orders. The nine started forward.

'That one – the dog-headed one.' Sludig pulled his axes out and pointed at the approaching men. 'He is the one who led the ambush on us at Hoderund's. He is the one I owe for young Hove, and the monks at the abbey!'

'Never'll we take 'em,' Haestan said calmly. 'They'll carve us up – nine men t'six, and two of us a troll and boy.'

Binabik said nothing, but calmly unscrewed his walking stick, which had been thrust beneath the cinch strap of Qantaqa's saddle. As he reassembled it, a matter of instants only, he said: 'We must run.'

Sludig was already spurring his horse forward, but

Haestan and Ethelbearn reached him within a couple of paces and caught at his elbows. The Rimmersman, who had not even donned his helmet, tried to shake them off; he had a distant look in his blue eyes.

'God damn't, man,' Haestan said, 'come on! At least we've got chance in 'mong th' trees!'

The leader of the approaching riders shouted something, and the others kicked their horses into a trot. White mist flurried up from their horses' hooves as though they ran on sea foam.

'Turn 'im!' Haestan shouted to Ethelbearn, grabbing the reins of Sludig's horse as he himself wheeled about; Ethelbearn gave a smart smack with his sword hilt to the flank of the Rimmersman's mount and they spun away from the oncoming riders, who were howling along at full gallop now behind them, waving axes and swords. Simon was trembling so that he feared he might fall from his saddle.

'Binabik, where?' he shouted, his voice cracking.

'The trees,' Binabik called back, as Qantaqa jumped forward. 'Death it would be to climb back up the road. Ride, Simon, and stay to me nearly!'

Now the horses of his companions were rearing and kicking on all sides as they headed off the wide path, away from the blackened ruins of Haethstad. Simon managed to slide his bow from where it hung over his shoulder, then leaned his head down over his horse's neck and dug in the spurs. With a bone-jarring surge they were suddenly leaping over the snow and into the ever-thickening forest.

Simon saw Binabik's small back, and the bobbing gray of Qantaqa's hindquarters as the trees loomed up dizzyingly on all sides. Shouts echoed from behind, and he looked back to see his other four companions in a close knot, with the dark mass of their pursuers beyond, fanning out through the forest. He heard a sound like the tearing of parchment, and for a brief moment saw an arrow quivering in a tree trunk just before him.

The muffled drumfire of hoofbeats was everywhere, filling his ears even as he clung for his life to the pitching saddle. A whistling black thread was suddenly drawn out and snapped before his face, and then another: the pursuers were outflanking them, loosing their arrows almost broadside. Simon heard himself scream something at the plunging shapes flashing along beyond the near trees, and several more of the hissing darts snapped past. Clinging to his pommel, he reached the hand that held the bow back to draw an arrow from his jouncing quiver, but when he brought it forward he saw it flash pale against his horse's shoulder. It was the White Arrow – what should he do?

In a split instant that seemed much longer he pushed it back over his shoulder into the quiver, pulling out another. A mocking voice somewhere in his head laughed to see him picking and choosing arrows at such a moment. He almost lost bow and arrow both as his horse lurched around a snow-spattered tree that seemed to leap up in their path. A moment later he heard a shout of pain and the terrified, terrifying scream of a falling horse. He darted a look over his shoulder to see only three of his companions behind him, and – farther behind every moment – a thrashing tangle of arms and kicking horselegs and roiling snow. The pursuers went over and around the downed rider, undeterred.

*Who was it?* was his brief, flickering thought.

'Up the hill, the hill!' Binabik shouted hoarsely from somewhere to Simon's right. He saw the flag of Qantaqa's tail as the wolf leaped up an incline into heavier trees, a thick clot of pines that stood like uncaring sentinels as the shouting chaos slashed past them. Simon yanked hard on his right-hand rein, having no idea if the horse would pay him any heed at all; a moment later they canted to the side and bolted up the slope behind the bounding wolf. The other three companions rushed past him, pulling up their steaming horses within the sparse shelter of a crown of staff-straight trunks.

Sludig still wore no helmet, and the thin one was surely Grimmric, but the other man, bulky and helmeted, had gone a short way up the slope; before Simon could turn to see who it was he heard a hoarse shout of triumph. The riders were upon them.

After a frozen moment he nocked his arrow and lifted the bow, but the whooping attackers were moving in and out among the trees so quickly that his shot flew harmlessly over the head of the nearest man and disappeared. Simon let fly a second arrow, and thought he saw it strike the leg of one of the armored riders. Somebody shouted in pain. Sludig, with an answering howl, spurred his white horse forward, pulling his helm down over his head. Two of the attackers peeled off from the pack and angled toward him. Simon saw him duck the sword swipe of the first and, turning, crash his axe-blade into the man's ribs as he swept past, bright blood rilling from the gash in the man's armor. As he turned from the first man the second nearly caught him; Sludig had time only to deflect the man's swing with his other axe, but still took a clanging blow to the helmet. Simon saw the Rimmersman wobble and almost fall as the attacker wheeled around.

Before they came together again Simon heard an ear-piercing screech and pivoted to see another horse and rider stagger toward him, a troll-less Qantaqa teeth-clinging to the man's unarmored leg, scrabbling with her claws at the shrilling horse's side. Simon pulled his sword from the scabbard, but as the rider struck helplessly at the wolf his reeling steed plunged into Simon's own mount. Simon's blade spiraled away, then he, too, was briefly without weight or tether. A long instant later the air was thumped from him as though by a giant's fist. He skidded to a face-down halt a short way from where his horse struggled with the other in a panicked, whinnying knot. Through a biting mask of snow, Simon saw Qantaqa pull herself out from beneath the two horses and sprint away. The man, caught shrieking beneath, could not escape.

728

Climbing painfully to his feet, spitting icy grit, Simon snatched at his bow and quiver lying nearby. He heard the sounds of combat move away up the hill and turned to follow on foot.

Somebody laughed.

Not twenty paces below him, seated astride a motionless gray horse, was the man in the black armor who wore the head of a ravening hound. A stark, pyramidal shape was blazoned in white on his black jerkin.

'There you are, boy,' Dog-face said, deep voice tolling inside his helmet. 'I have been looking for you.'

Simon turned and dug up the snowy hill, stumbling, sinking into the knee-high drifts. The man in black laughed happily and followed.

Picking himself up yet again, tasting his own blood from his torn nose and lip, Simon stopped at last, backed against a leaning spruce. He grabbed at an arrow and let the quiver drop, then nocked it and pulled back the bowstring. The man in black stopped, still half a dozen ells below, tilting his helmeted head to one side as if imitating the hound he resembled.

'Now kill me, boy, if you can,' he mocked. 'Shoot!' He spurred his horse up the hill toward where Simon stood shivering.

There was a hiss and a sharp, fleshy slap. Suddenly the gray horse was rearing up, up, mane-flinging head thrown back, an arrow shuddering in its breast. The dog-faced rider was thrown down hard into the snow; he lay as if boneless, even as his twitching horse fell to its knees and rolled heavily onto him. Simon stared with fascination. A moment later he was staring with even more surprise at the bow he still held in his outstretched arm. The arrow had not left the string.

'H-Haestan. . . ?' he said, turning to look up the slope. Three figures stood there, in a gap between the trees.

They were none of them Haestan. They were none of them men. They had bright, feline eyes, and their mouths were set in hard lines.

The Sitha who had shot the arrow nocked another and lowered it until its delicately quivering head came to a halt pointed at Simon's eyes.

'*T'si im t'si*', *Sudhoda'ya*,' he said, his small, newly-formed smile as cold as marble. 'Blood . . . as you say . . . for blood.'

# 37
# Jiriki's Hunt

Simon stared helplessly at the black arrowhead, at the trio of thin faces. His jaw trembled.

'*Ske'i! Ske'i!*' a voice cried, 'Stop!'

Two of the Sithi turned to look up the hill to their right, but the one coolly holding the bent bow never wavered.

'*Ske'i, ras-Zida'ya!*' the small figure shouted, and then, leaping forward, fell into a snow-churning roll to stop at last in a flurry of gleaming powder a few paces from Simon.

Binabik got slowly to his knees, coated in snow as though he had been floured by a hurrying baker.

'W-What?' Simon forced his numb lips to shape words, but the troll signaled him to silence with an urgent flutter of his squat fingers.

'Shhh. Slowly be putting down the bow you are holding – slowly!' As the boy followed this direction, Binabik spouted another rush of words in the unfamiliar language, waving his hands imploringly at the unblinking Sithi.

'What . . . where are the others . . .' Simon whispered, but Binabik silenced him again, this time with a small but violent head-shake.

'No time is there, no time . . . for your life we are fighting.' The troll raised his own hands in the air, and

Simon, having dropped the bow, did the same, turning his palms outward. 'You have not, I am hoping, lost the White Arrow?'

'I . . . I don't know.'

'Daughter of the Mountains, I must hope not. Slowly drop your quiver. There.' He sputtered out a little bit more of what Simon took to be Sithi-tongue, then kicked at the quiver so that the arrows scattered across the broken snow like dark jackstraws . . . all but one. Only its triangular tip, pearl-blue like a liquid drop of sky, stood out against the surrounding whiteness.

'Oh, praise to the High Places,' Binabik sighed. '*Staj'a Ame ine!*' he called to the Sithi, who watched like cats whose avian quarry has chosen to turn and sing instead of fly away. 'The White Arrow! You cannot be in ignorance of this! *Im sheyis tsi-keo'su d'a Yana o Lingit!*'

'This is . . . rare,' the Sitha with the bow said, lowering it slightly. His accent was odd, but his command of the Western Speech very good. He blinked. 'To be taught the Rules of Song by a troll.' His cold smile returned briefly. 'You may spare us your exhortations . . . and your crude translations. Pick up your arrow and bring it here to me.' He hissed a few words to the other two as Binabik bent to the quiver. They looked back once more at Simon and the troll, then dashed up the hill with startling speed, seeming to barely dimple the snow as they went, so quick and light were their steps. The one remaining behind kept his arrow trained in Simon's general direction as Binabik went trudging forward.

'Hand it toward me,' the Sitha directed. 'Feathers first, troll. Now, step back toward your companion.'

He eased up on the bow to examine the slender white object, allowing the arrow to slide forward until the string was almost slack and he could hold the nocked arrow and bowstave in one hand. Simon was aware for the first time of the shallow rasp of his own rapid breathing. He lowered his shaking hands a bit as Binabik crunched to halt nearby.

'It was given to this young man for a service he was rendering,' Binabik said defiantly. The Sitha looked up at him and cocked a slanting eyebrow.

He seemed, at Simon's first glance, much like the first one of his kindred Simon had seen – the same high-boned cheeks and strange, birdlike movements. He was dressed in pants and jacket of shimmery white cloth, dotted at shoulders, sleeves and waist with slender dark green scales. His hair, almost black, but also with a strange greenish tinge, he wore in two complicated braids, one falling before each ear. Boots, belt, and quiver were of soft milk-hued leather. Simon realized that it was only the Sitha's position upslope, and silhouetted against the drab sky, that allowed him to be clearly seen: if the Fair One were to stand against the snow, in a copse of trees, he would be as invisible as the wind.

'*Isi-isi'ye!*' the Sitha muttered feelingly, and turned to hold the arrow to the shrouded sun. Lowering it, he stared wonderingly at Simon for a moment, then narrowed his eyes.

'Where did you · find this, *Sudhoda'ya*?' he asked harshly. 'How did one such as you come by such a thing?'

'It was given to me!' Simon said, color coming back into his cheeks and strength to his voice. He knew what he knew. 'I saved one of your people. He shot it at a tree, then ran away.'

The Sitha again looked him over carefully, and seemed about to say something more. Instead, he turned his attention up the hillside. A bird whistled a long, complex call, or so Simon thought at first, until he saw the small movements of the white-clad Sitha's lips. He waited, still as a statue, until there came an answering trill.

'Go now, before me,' he said, swinging around to gesture with his bow at the troll and boy. They walked with difficulty up the steep slope, their captor moving lightly behind them, slowly turning the White Arrow over and over in his slender fingers.

Within the space of a few hundred heartbeats they

733

reached the rounded top of the knoll and started down the other side. There, four Sithi crouched around a tree-rimmed, snow-blanketed gully, the two Simon had already seen, recognizable only by the bluish tint to their braided hair, and another pair whose tresses were smoky gray – although, like the others, their golden faces were unwrinkled. At the gully's bottom, beneath the menacing quadrangle of Sithi arrows, sat Haestan, Grimmric, and Sludig. They were each one bloodied, and wore the hopelessly defiant expressions of cornered animals.

'Bones of Saint Ealhstan!' Haestan swore when he saw the new arrivals. 'Ah, God, boy, 'was hopin' y'got away.' He shook his head. 'Still, better than bein' a dead'un, I suppose.'

'Do you see, troll?' Sludig said bitterly, his bearded face smeared with red. 'Do you see what we have called on ourselves? Demons! We should never have mocked . . . that dark one.'

The Sitha who held the Arrow, seemingly the leader, said a few words in his language to the others, and gestured for Simon's companions to climb from the pit.

'Demons they are not,' Binabik said as he and Simon braced their legs to help the others scramble up, a difficult task on the shifting snow. 'They are Sithi, and they will do us no harm. It is, after all is said, their own White Arrow that is compelling them.'

The Sithi's leader gave the troll a sour look but said nothing. Grimmric came gasping up onto level ground. 'Sith . . . Sithi?' he said, struggling for breath. A cut just below his scalp had painted his forehead with a solid swath of crimson. 'Now we've gone walkin' into old, old stories, an' that's sure. Sithi-folk! May Usires th' Aedon protect us all.' He made the sign of the Tree and wearily turned to help the staggering Sludig.

'What happened?' Simon asked. 'How did you . . . what happened to . . . ?'

'The ones who pursued us are dead,' Sludig said, sagging back against a tree trunk. His byrnie was slashed

734

in several places, and his helmet, which dangled from his hand, was scraped and dented like an old pot. 'We did for some ourselves. The rest,' he flapped a limp hand at the Sithi guards, 'fell with bodies full of arrows.'

'They'd shot us too, sure, if the troll hadna spoken in their tongue,' Haestan said. He smiled faintly at Binabik. 'We didna think bad of ye when y'ran. Prayin' for ye, we were.'

'I went for finding Simon. He is my charge,' Binabik said simply.

'But . . .' Simon looked around, hoping against hope, but saw no other prisoner. 'Then . . . then that was Ethelbearn who fell. Before we reached the first hill.'

Haestan nodded slowly. ''Twas.'

'Damn their souls!' Grimmric swore. 'Th'were Rimmersmen, those murd'rin' bastards!'

'Skali's,' Sludig said, eyes hard. The Sithi began making gestures for them to get up. 'Two of them wore the Kaldskryke raven,' he continued, rising. 'Oh, how I am praying to catch him with nothing between us but our axes.'

'You are waiting with a host of many others,' Binabik said.

'Wait!' Simon said, feeling terribly hollow: this was not right. He turned to the leader of the Sithi company. 'You have been looking at my arrow. You know my story is true. You cannot take us anywhere, or do anything, until we see what has happened to our companion.'

The Sitha looked at him appraisingly. 'I do *not* know your story is true, manchild, but we will find out soon enough. Sooner than you might wish. As to the other . . .' He took a moment to survey Simon's ragged party. 'Very well. We shall allow you to see to your other man.' He spoke to his comrades, and they followed the men down the hill. The quiet company passed the arrow-plumped corpses of two of their attackers, eyes wide and mouths agape. Snow was already sifting back over their still forms, covering the scarlet stains.

They found Ethelbearn a hundred ells from the lake road. The broken shaft of an ashwood arrow stood out from the side of his neck below his beard, and his splayed, twisted posture told that his horse had rolled over him in its death throes.

'He wasna long a-dyin',' Haestan said, tears standing in his eyes. 'Aedon be praised, 'twas quick.'

They dug a hole for him as best they could, hacking at the hard ground with swords and axes; the Sithi stood by, unconcerned as geese. The companions wrapped Ethelbearn in his thick cloak and lowered him into the shallow grave. When he was covered over, Simon pushed the dead man's sword into the earth as a marker.

'Take his helmet,' Haestan said to Sludig, and Grimmric nodded.

'He'd not want it t'go unused,' the other Erkynlander agreed.

Sludig hung his own ruined helm on the pommel of Ethelbearn's sword before taking the one held out to him. 'We will avenge you, man,' the Rimmersgarder said. 'Blood for blood.'

Silence settled over them. Snow filtered down through the trees as they stood regarding the patch of naked ground. Soon it would all be white again.

'Come,' the Sitha chief said at last. 'We have waited for you long enough. There is someone who will want to see this arrow.'

Simon was last to move. *I scarcely had time to know you, Ethelbearn*, he thought. *But you had a good loud laugh. I will remember that*.

They turned and headed back into the cold hills.

The spider hung motionless, like a dull brown gem in an intricate necklace. The web was complete, now, the last strands laid delicately in place; it stretched from one side of the ceiling corner to the other, quivering gently in the rising air as though strummed by invisible hands.

For a moment Isgrimnur lost the thread of talk, important talk though it was. His eyes had drifted from the worried faces huddled near the fireplace in the great hall, roving up to the darkened corner, and to the tiny builder at rest.

*There's sense*, he told himself. *You build something and then you stay there. That's the way it's meant to be. Not this running here, running there, never see your blood-family or your home roofs for a year at a time.*

He thought of his wife: sharp-eyed, red-cheeked Gutrun. She had not offered him a solitary word of rebuke, but he knew it angered her that he had been gone so long from Elvritshalla, that he had left their oldest son, the pride of her heart, to rule a great duchy . . . and to fail. Not that Isorn or anyone else in Rimmersgard could have stopped Skali and his followers, not with the High King behind him. Still, it had been young Isorn who had been master while his father was gone, and it was Isorn who would be remembered as the one who had seen the Kaldskryke clan, traditional enemies of the Elvritshallamen, strut into the Longhouse as masters.

*And I was looking forward to coming home this time*, the old duke thought sadly. *It would have been nice to tend to my horses and cows, and settle a few local disputes, and watch my children raise their own children. Instead, all the land is being torn up again like leaky thatch. God save me, I had enough of fighting when I was younger . . . for all my talk.*

Fighting was, after all, mostly for young men, whose grip on life was light and careless. And to give the old men something to talk about, to remember when they sat warm in their halls with winter moaning outside.

*A damned old dog like me is just about ready to lie down and sleep by the fire.*

He plucked at his beard, and watched the spider scramble toward the darkened roof corner, where an unwary fly had made an unexpected stop.

*We thought John had forged a peace that would last a thousand years. Instead, it has not survived his death by two summers. You build and you build some more, laying strand over strand like that little fellow up there, only to have a wind come along and blow everything to pieces.*

'. . . and so I have near-crippled two horses to bring these tidings as fast as I could, Lord,' the young man finished as Isgrimnur turned his ear back to the urgent discussion.

'You have done magnificently, Deornoth,' Josua said, 'Please rise.'

His face still damp from his ride, the lank-haired soldier stood, wrapping himself more tightly in the thick blanket the prince had given him. He looked much as he had that other time, when, garbed in the costume of the holy monk for the Saint Tunath's Day festivities, he had brought the prince news of his father's death.

The prince laid his hand upon Deornoth's shoulder. 'I am glad to have you back. I feared for your safety, and cursed myself for having to send you on such a dangerous errand.' He turned to the others. 'So. You have heard Deornoth's report. Elias has at last gone into the field. He is bound for Naglimund with . . . Deornoth? You said. . . ?'

'Some thousand knights and more, and near ten thousand foot,' the soldier said unhappily. 'That averages the different reports in a way that seems most reliable.'

'I'm sure,' Josua waved his hand. 'And we have perhaps a fortnight at most until he is at our walls.'

'I should think so, sire,' Deornoth nodded.

'And what of *my* master?' Devasalles asked.

'Well, Baron,' the soldier began, then clenched his teeth until a fit of shivering had passed, 'Nad Mullach was in a mad uproar – understandably, of course, with what is happening to the west . . .' he broke off to look over to Prince Gwythinn, who sat a short way off from the rest, staring miserably at the ceiling.

738

'Go on,' said Josua calmly, 'we will hear it all.'

Deornoth turned his gaze away from the Hernystir-man. 'So, as I said, good information was hard to come by. However, according to several of the rivermen up from Abaingeat on the coast, your Duke Leobardis has set sail from Nabban, and is even now on the high seas, probably to make landfall near Crannhyr.'

'With how many men?' Isgrimnur rumbled.

Deornoth shrugged. 'Different people say different things. Three hundred horse, perhaps, two thousand or so foot.'

'That sounds correct, Prince Josua,' Devasalles said, lips pursed contemplatively. 'Many of the liege-lords doubtless would not go along, frightened as they are of crossing the High King, and the Perdruinese will stay neutral, as they usually do. Count Streáwe knows he will do better helping both sides, and saving his ships to haul goods.'

'So we may hope for Leobardis' strong help, although I might have wished it stronger still.' Josua looked around the circle of men.

'Even if these Nabbanai should beat Elias to the gate,' Baron Ordmaer said, fear poorly hidden on his plump features, 'still Elias will have three times our numbers.'

'But we have the walls, sir,' Josua replied, his narrow face stern. 'We are in a strong, strong place.' He turned back to Deornoth, and his expression softened. 'Give us the last of your news, my faithful friend, and then you must sleep. I fear for your health, and I will need you strong in the days ahead.'

Deornoth mustered a faint smile. 'Yes, sire. The tidings that are left are not happy ones either, I fear. The Hernystiri have been driven from the field at Inniscrich.' He started to glance at the place where Gwythinn sat, but instead dropped his eyes. 'They say King Lluth has been wounded, and his armies have fallen back into the Grianspog Mountains, the better to harry Skali and his men.'

Josua looked gravely over to the Hernystiri prince. 'So. It is at least better than you feared, Gwythinn. Your father yet lives, and continues the fight.'

The young man turned. His eyes were red. 'Yes! They continue the fight, while I sit here inside stone walls, drinking ale and eating bread and cheese like a fat townsman. My father may be dying! How can I stay here?'

'And do you think you can beat Skali with your half-hundred men, lad?' Isgrimnur asked, not unkindly. 'Or would you seek a quick, glorious death, rather than wait to see what is the best policy?'

'I am not so foolish as that,' Gwythinn replied coldly. 'And, Bagba's Herd, Isgrimnur, who are you to be saying such to me? What of that "foot of steel" you are saving for Skali's guts?!'

'Different,' Isgrimnur muttered, embarrassed. 'I did not speak of storming Elvritshalla with my dozen knights.'

'And all I mean to do is steal around the flank of Skali's ravens, and go to my people in the mountains.'

Unable to meet Prince Gwythinn's bright, demanding stare, Isgrimnur let his eyes slide back up to the roof corner, where the brown spider was industriously wrapping something in clinging silk.

'Gwythinn,' Josua said soothingly, 'I ask only that you wait until we can speak more. One or two days will make little difference.'

The young Hernystirman stood up, his chair scraping against the stone flags. '*Wait!* That is all that you *do* is wait, Josua! Wait for the local muster, wait for Leobardis and his army, wait for . . . wait for Elias to climb the walls and put Naglimund to the torch! I am tired of waiting!' He raised an unsteady hand to forestall Josua's protests. 'Do not forget, Josua, I am a prince, too! I came to you out of the friendship of our fathers. And now *my* father is wounded, and harried by northern devils. If he dies unsuccored, and I am become king, will you order me then? Will you still think to hold me back? *Brynioch!* I cannot understand such craven reluctance!'

Before he reached the door he turned. 'I will tell my men to prepare for our departure tomorrow at sunset. If you think of some reason why I should not go, one that has escaped me, you know where I may be found!'

As the prince flung the door shut behind him, Josua rose to his feet.

'I think there are many here who . . .' he paused and shook his head wearily, 'who feel the need of some food and drink – you not least, Deornoth. But I ask you to remain a short moment while these others go ahead, so I may ask you of some private matters.' He waved Devasalles and the rest off to the dining hall, and watched them shuffle out, talking quietly among themselves. 'Isgrimnur,' he called, and the duke stopped in the doorway to look back inquiringly. 'You stay also, please.'

When Isgrimnur had settled himself in a chair again, Josua looked expectantly to Deornoth.

'And have you other news for me?' the prince asked. The soldier frowned.

'If I had aught else of good tiding, my prince, I would have told you first, before the others arrived. I could find no trace of your niece or the monk who accompanies her, but for one peasant farmer near the Greenwade fork who saw a pair of their description fording the river there some days ago, heading south.'

'Which is no more than what we knew they would do, as the Lady Vorzheva told us. But by now they are well into the Inniscrich, and the Blessed Usires alone knows what may happen, or where they will go next. Our only luck is that I am sure my brother Elias will march his army up the skirt of the hills, since in this wet season the Wealdhelm Road is the only safe place for the heavy wagons.' He stared at the wavering flames of the fire. 'Well, then,' he said at last, 'my thanks, Deornoth. If all my liegemen were such as you then I could laugh at the King's threat.'

'The men are a good lot, sire,' the young knight said
loyally.

'Go on, now.' The prince extended his hand to pat
Deornoth's knee. 'Get some food, and then some sleep.
You will not be needed for duty until tomorrow.'

'Yes, sire.' The young Erkynlander threw off his
blanket and stood, his back straight as a gatepost as he
walked from the room. After he was gone, Josua and
Isgrimnur sat in silence.

'Miriamele gone God knows where, and Leobardis
racing Elias to our gates.' The prince shook his head and
kneaded his temples with his hand. 'Lluth wounded, the
Hernystiri in retreat, and Elias' tool Skali master from the
Vestivegg to the Grianspog. And atop all else, demons
out of legend walking the mortal earth.' He showed the
duke a grim smile. 'The net grows tighter, Uncle.'

Isgrimnur tangled his fingers in his beard. 'The web is
swaying in the wind, Josua. A strong wind.'

He left the remark unexplained, and silence crept back
into the high hall.

The man in the hound mask cursed weakly and spat
another gobbet of blood onto the snow. Any lesser man,
he knew, would now be dead, lying in the snow with his
legs crushed and his ribs collapsed, but the thought was
only faintly gratifying. All the years of ritual training and
hardening toil that had saved his life when the dying
horse rolled over him would be for naught unless he
could reach somewhere sheltered and dry. Another hour
or two of exposure would finish the work his dying steed
had begun.

The damnable Sithi – and *their* unexpected involve-
ment was nothing short of astonishing – had led their
human captives within a few feet of where he had lain
hidden, buried under a half-foot of snow. He had
summoned all his reserves of strength and courage to stay

preternaturally still while the Fair Folk had scanned the area. They must have concluded he had crawled away somewhere to die – which, of course, he had hoped they would – and a few moments later they had continued on their way.

Now he huddled shivering where he had dug out from beneath the obscuring white blanket, summoning his strength for the next move. His only hope was to somehow get back to Haethstad, where a pair of his own men should now be waiting. He damned himself a hundred times for ever trusting those louts of Skali's – drunken pillagers and woman-beaters that they were, unfit to polish his boots. If only he had not been forced to send his own off on another mission.

He shook his head in an attempt to clear it of the swirling, jiggling specks of light that floated against the gradually darkening sky, then pursed his cracked lips. The hoot of a snow owl issued incongruously from the snarling hound muzzle. While he waited he tried once more, impossibly, to stand – even to crawl. It was no use: something was gravely wrong with both legs. Ignoring the scalding pain from his cracked ribs, he used his hands to drag himself a little farther toward the trees, then had to stop, laid flat out and panting.

A moment later he felt hot wind, and lifted his head. The black muzzle of his helmet was doubled, as though in some queer mirror, by a grinning white snout only inches away.

'Niku'a,' he gasped, in a language quite unlike his native Black Rimmerspakk. 'Come here, Udun damn you! Come!'

The great hound took another step closer, until he loomed over his injured master.

'Now . . . hold,' the man said, reaching up strong hands to clasp the white leather collar. 'And pull!'

A moment later he groaned in agony as the dog did pull, but he hung on, teeth clenched and eyes bulging behind the unchanging canine features of the helmet. The

743

hammering, tearing pain almost pushed him over into insensibility as the hound drew him bumping across the snow, but he did not relax his grip until he reached the cover of the trees. Only then did he at last let go, let everything go. He slid down into darkness, and brief surcease to pain.

When he awoke the gray of the sky had gone several shades darker, and the wind had swept a powdery layer of snow across him like a blanket. The great hound Niku'a still waited, unconcerned and unshivering despite his short fur, as though lounging before a blazing hearth. The man on the ground was not surprised: he well knew the icy black kennels of Sturmrspeik, and knew how these beasts were raised. Looking at Niku'a's red mouth and curving teeth, and the tiny white eyes like drops of some milky poison, he was again grateful that it was he who followed the hounds, and not the other way around.

He pulled off the helmet – not without effort, since the fall had changed its shape – and pitched it into the snow at his side. With his knife he cut his black cloak into long strips; soon after he began laboriously sawing down some of the slenderest young trees. It was horrible work on his agonized ribs, but he did his best to ignore the flashing pain and go on. He had two excellent reasons to survive: his duty to tell his masters of the unexpected attack by the Sithi, and his own heightened desire for revenge on this ragtag lot who had thwarted him too many times.

The moon's blue-white eye was peering curiously through the treetops when he at last finished cutting. He used the strips of his cloak to bind a number of the shorter staves tightly to each leg as splints; then, sitting with his legs stiffly before him like a child playing noughts and crosses in the dirt, he bound short crosspieces to the tops of the two long staves remaining. Clutching them carefully he grabbed again at Niku'a's collar, letting the long, corpse-white dog drag him up onto his feet where he swayed precariously until he could get the new-made crutches under his arms.

He took a few steps, swiveling awkwardly on his unbending legs. It would do well enough, he decided, wincing at the sickening pain – not that he had any choice.

He looked at the snarling-mouthed helmet lying in the snow, thinking of the effort it would take to reach it, and the now-useless weight of the thing. Then he leaned down, gasping, and picked it up anyway. It had been given him in the sacred caverns of Sturmrspeik, by Herself, when She named him Her sacred hunter – he, a mortal! He could no more leave it lying in the snow than he could leave his own beating heart. He remembered that impossible, heady moment, the blue lights flickering in the Chamber of the Breathing Harp, when he had knelt before the throne, before the serene shimmer of Her silver mask.

His excruciating pain lulled for a moment by the wine of memory, Niku'a silently padding at his heels, Ingen Jegger moved haltingly down the long, tree-covered hill, and began to think carefully about revenge.

Simon and his companions, now lessened by one, did not have much stomach for talk, nor did their captors encourage any. They trudged silently and slowly through the snow-carpeted foothills as gray afternoon edged into evening.

Somehow the Sithi seemed to know exactly where they wanted to go, although to Simon the pine-spotted slopes were featureless, one spot indistinguishable from another. The leader's amber eyes were always moving in his masklike face, but he never seemed to be searching for anything; rather he gave the impression that he read the subtle language of the terrain as knowledgeably as Father Strangyeard surveyed his bookshelves.

The only time the Sitha leader displayed any reaction was early in their march, when Qantaqa came trotting down an incline and fell in at Binabik's side, nose twitching as she sniffed his hand, tail nervously tucked. The Sitha raised a half-curious eyebrow, then looked around to catch the glances of his fellows, whose narrow eyes had narrowed further. He made no sign that Simon could distinguish, but the wolf was allowed to pace along unhindered.

Daylight was fading when the strange walking-party turned north at last, and within a short time they were slowly circling the base of a steep slope whose snowy flanks were studded with jutting, naked stone. Simon, shock and numbness worn off enough to make him all too aware of his achingly cold feet, gave silent thanks as the chief of their captors waved them to a halt.

'Here,' he said, gesturing to a large outcropping that thrust up high above their heads. 'At the bottom.' He pointed again, this time to a wide, waist-high fissure in the face of the stone. Before any of them could say a word, two of the Sithi guards slipped nimbly past them and slid themselves headfirst into the opening. In a moment they had vanished.

'You,' he said to Simon. 'Go after.'

There were angry mutters from Haestan and the other two soldiers, but Simon, despite his unusual situation, felt strangely confident. Kneeling, he poked his head through the opening.

It was a slender, shining tunnel, an ice-lined tube that twisted steeply up and away from him, seemingly hollowed from the very stone of the mountain. He decided that the Sitha who had gone before him must have climbed up beyond the next bend. There was no sign of them, and no one could hide in this glass-smooth, narrow passage, barely wide enough to allow him to raise his arms.

He ducked back out into the chill open air.

'How can I go through it? It's almost straight up, and it's covered in ice. I'll just slide back down.'

746

'Look above your head,' the chief Sitha replied. 'You will understand.'

Simon reentered the tunnel, pushing in a little farther so that his shoulders and upper body were inside too, and he could turn on his back to look up. The ice of the tunnel ceiling, if one could call something half an arm's length away a ceiling, was scored with a regular series of horizontal cuts that extended the visible length of the passage. Each was a few inches deep, and wide enough to hold both hands comfortably side by side. He realized after some thought that he was intended to pull himself up with his hands and feet, bracing his back against the floor of the tunnel.

Viewing the prospect with some dismay, since he had no idea how long the tunnel might be, or what else might conceivably be sharing it with him, he considered backing out of the narrow passageway once more. After a moment he changed his mind. The Sithi had shinnied up before him as quickly as squirrels, and for some reason he felt the urge to show them that, if not as nimble as they, he was still bold enough to follow without coaxing.

The climb was difficult, but not impossibly so. The tunnel turned often enough that he could make frequent stops to rest, bracing his feet against the bends in the passage. As he slowly grabbed, pulled and braced, time after muscle-cramping time, the advantage of such an entrance tunnel – if this was, as it seemed, an entrance – became obvious: it was difficult going to clamber up, and would be near-impossible for any animal but a two-legged one; anyone who needed to get out could slide down it as swiftly as a snake.

He was just considering stopping for another rest when he heard voices speaking the liquid Sithi language just beyond his head. A moment later strong hands reached down, grasping him by the harness-straps of his chain mail and pulling him upward. He popped out of the tunnel with a gasp of surprise and tumbled onto a warm stone floor puddled with snowmelt. The two Sithi who had dragged him out crouched by the passage mouth, faces obscure in the near-darkness. The only light in the room – which was not really a room so much as a rock cavern carefully swept clean of debris – came from a door-sized crevice in the opposite wall. Through this gap spilled a yellow gleam, painting a bright swath on the cavern floor. As Simon pulled himself to his knees he felt a slender, restraining hand laid on his shoulder. The dark-haired Sitha beside him pointed up at the low ceiling, then made a waving motion and gestured at the tunnel mouth.

'Wait,' he said calmly, his speech not as fluent as his leader's. 'We must wait.'

Haestan was next up, grumbling and cursing. The two Sithi had to worry his bulky form out of the opening like a cork from a wine jug. Binabik appeared on his heels – the nimble troll had easily caught up with the Erkynlander – followed within a short while by Sludig and Grimmric. The three remaining Sithi clambered lithely up behind them.

No sooner had the last of the Fair Ones issued from the tunnel then the party went forward again, passing through the rock doorway and into a short passage beyond where they could at last stand upright. Lamps of some kind of milky golden crystal or glass had been set into niches in the wall, and their flickering light was enough to mask the glow of the door at the far end until they were almost upon it. One of the Sithi stepped to this gap in the stone, which unlike the last was shrouded with a hanging of dark cloth, and called out. An instant later two more of their kindred pushed past the cloth. Each of them held a short sword made of what looked to be some dark metal. They stood silently alert, betraying no surprise or curiosity, as the leader of the captors spoke.

'We will bind your hands.' As he said this the other Sithi produced coiled lengths of shiny black cord from beneath their clothing.

Sludig stepped back a pace, bumping into one of the

guards, who made a quiet hissing noise but offered no violence.

'No,' the Rimmersman said, his voice dangerously tight, 'I will not let them. No man will bind me against my will.'

'Nor me,' Haestan said.

'Don't be foolish,' Simon said, and stepped forward, offering his own crossed wrists. 'We will probably get out of this with our skins, but not if you start a fight.'

'Simon is speaking rightly,' Binabik said, 'I, too, will let them tie me. You are not having sense if you do otherwise. Simon's White Arrow is genuine. It is being the reason they did not kill us, and why they brought us here.'

'But how can we . . .' Sludig began.

'Also,' Binabik cut him off, 'what would you plan for doing? Even if these folk here you fought and overcame, and the others who most likely wait beyond, what then? Should you slide downward through the tunnel you would no doubt be crashing onto Qantaqa, who waits at the bottom. I think such a startling thing would give you little chance to tell her you were no enemy.'

Sludig looked down at the troll for a moment, plainly thinking of the possibilities attendant on being mistaken by a frightened Qantaqa. At last he called up a weak smile.

'Again you win, troll.' He put his hands forward.

The black cords were cool and scaly like snakeskin, but flexible as oiled leather thongs. Simon found that a couple of loops held his hands as immobile as if they had been caught in an ogre's fist. When the Sithi had finished with the others, the group was led forward once more, through the cloth-covered door and into a dazzling wash of light.

It seemed, when Simon tried to remember it later, as though they had stepped through the clouds and into a brilliant, shining land – some nearer neighbor to the sun. After the bleak snows and the featureless tunnels, the difference was like the wild carousal of the Ninth Day festival after the eight gray days that preceded.

Light, and its handmaiden color, was everywhere. The room was a rock chamber less than twice a man's height but very wide. Tree roots twined graspingly down the walls. In one corner, thirty paces away, a glinting stream of water ran down a grooved stone to arch, splashing, into a pond cupped in a natural basin of stone. The delicate chime of its fall wound in and out of the strange, subtle music that filled the air.

Lamps like the ones that lined the stone hallway were everywhere, casting, according to their making, beams of yellow, ivory, pale chalky blue or rose, painting the stone grotto with a hundred different hues where they ran against each other. In the center of the floor, not far from the edge of the rippling pool, a fire was animatedly ablaze, the smoke vanishing into a crevice above.

'Elysia, Mother of the Holy Aedon,' Sludig said, awed.

'Never know there was a rabbit hole here,' Grimmric shook his head, 'an' they got a palace.'

Perhaps a dozen Sithi, all male as far as Simon could tell on brief inspection, were ranged about the chamber. Several of them sat calmly before another pair scated on a high stone. One held a long flutelike instrument and the other was singing; the music was so strange to Simon that it took him a few moments before he could separate voice from flute, and the continuing melody of the waterfall from either. Still, the exquisite, quavering song they played tugged achingly at his heart even as it lifted the short hairs on the back of his neck. Despite the unfamiliarity there was something in it that made him want to sink down on the spot, never to move again while such gentle music lasted.

Those not gathered around the musicians were talking quietly, or merely lying on their backs staring upward, as if they could gaze out through the solid stone of the hillside and into the night sky beyond. Most turned briefly to survey the captives at the chamber's entrance, but in the manner, Simon felt, that a man listening to a good story might lift his head to watch a cat walk past.

He and his companions, who had been quite unprepared for this, stood gaping. The leader of their guards crossed the room toward the far wall where two more figures sat facing each other over a table that was a tall, flattened knob of shiny white stone. Both stared intently at something on the tabletop, lit by another of the strange lamps set in a niche in the rock face close by. The warder stopped and stood quietly a short distance away, as though waiting to be recognized.

The Sitha who sat with his back to the companions was dressed in a beautiful high-collared jacket of leaf-green, with pants and high boots of the same shade. His long, braided hair was of a red even more fiery than Simon's, and his hands, as he moved something across the tabletop, glittered with rings. Across from him, watching the movements of his hand intently, sat one wrapped in a loose white robe rucked up around his braceleted forearms, his hair a pale shade of heather or blue. A crow's feather, shiny black, hung down before one ear. Even as Simon watched, the white-gowned Sitha flashed his teeth and spoke to his companion, then reached out to slide some object forward. Simon's stare grew more intense; he blinked.

It was the very Sitha-man he had rescued from the cotsman's trap. He was positive.

'That's him!' he whispered excitedly to Binabik. 'The one whose arrow it is!'

Even as he spoke, their warder approached the table, and the one Simon recognized looked up. The warder quickly said something, but the white-robed one only flicked a glance over toward the prisoners and waved a dismissive hand, returning his attention to what Simon had at last decided was either some kind of map or gaming board. His red-haired companion never turned, and a moment later their captor came back.

'You must wait until Lord Jiriki has finished.' He brought his expressionless gaze to bear on Simon. 'Since the arrow is yours, you may go unbound. The others may not.'

Simon, only a stone's throw from the one who had made the debt-pledge but still being ignored, was tempted to push forward and confront the white-robed Sitha – Jereekee, if that was his name. Binabik, who felt his tension, bumped him in warning.

'If the others must remain tied, then so will I,' Simon said at last. For the first time he thought he saw something unexpected slide across his captor's face: a look of discomfort.

'It *is* a White Arrow,' the guard leader said. 'You should not be prisoned unless it is proven you have come by it through foul means, but I cannot free your companions.'

'Then I will stay tied,' Simon said firmly.

The other stared at him for a moment, then shuttered his eyes in a slow, reptilian blink, reopening them to smile unhappily.

'So it must be,' he said. 'I do not like binding a bearer of the *Staj'a Ame*, but I see little choice. On my heart it will be, right or wrong.' Then, strangely, he bobbed his head in an almost respectful manner, fixing his luminous eyes on Simon's. 'My mother named me An'nai,' he said.

Caught off balance, Simon let a long moment pass until he felt Binabik's boot grinding on his toe. 'Oh!' he said, 'I am . . . my mother named me Simon . . . Seoman, actually.' Then, seeing the Sitha nod, satisfied, he hurriedly added: 'and these are my companions – Binabik of Yiqanuc, Haestan and Grimmric of Erkynland, and Sludig of Rimmersgard.'

Perhaps, Simon thought, since the Sitha had seemed to place such importance on the sharing of his name, this forced introduction would help protect his companions.

An'nai bobbed his head again and glided off, once more taking up a position near the stone table. His fellow

752

guards, after lending surprisingly gentle help to the bound companions so that they could sit down, dispersed around the cavern.

Simon and the others talked quietly for a long while, hushed by the strange twining music more than their situation.

'Still,' said Sludig at last, after complaining bitterly about the treatment they had received, 'at least we are alive. Few who encounter demons are so lucky.'

'Y'r a top, Simon-lad!' Haestan laughed. 'A spinnin' top! Got the Fair Folk bowin' and scrapin'. Let's be sure t'ask for bag o' gold 'fore we go on our way.'

'Bowing and scraping!' Simon smirked in unhappy self-mockery. 'Am I free? Am I unbound? Am I eating supper?'

'True.' Haestan shook his head sadly. 'A bit'd go down nice. And a jar or so.'

'I am thinking we will receive nothing until Jiriki sees us,' Binabik said, 'but if he is indeed the person that Simon rescued, we may yet be eating well.'

'Do you think he's important?' Simon asked. 'An'nai called him "Lord Jiriki." '

'If there is not more than one living of that name . . .' Binabik began, but was interrupted by An'nai's return. He was accompanied by the selfsame Jiriki, who clutched in his hand the White Arrow.

'Please,' Jiriki called two of the other Sithi over, 'untie them now.' He turned and said something rapid in his flowing tongue. The musical words somehow had the sound of a reproach. An'nai accepted Jiriki's admonishment expressionlessly, if such it was, only lowering his eyes.

Simon, carefully watching, was certain that minus the effects of hanging in a trap, and the bruises and gashes of the cotsman's attack, this was the same Sitha.

Jiriki waved a hand and An'nai walked away. Because of his confident movements, and the deference that those around him showed, Simon had at first taken him to be older, or at least of an age with the other Sithi. Now, despite the strange timelessness of their golden faces, Simon suddenly felt that the Lord Jiriki was, by Sithi standards anyway, still young.

As the newly freed prisoners rubbed feeling back into their wrists, Jiriki held up the arrow. 'Forgive the wait. An'nai misjudged, because he knows how seriously I take the playing of *shent*.' His eyes moved from the companions to the arrow and back again. 'I never thought to meet you again, Seoman,' he said with a birdlike chin tilt, and a smile that never quite reached his eyes. 'But a debt is a debt . . . and the *Staj'a Ame* is even more. You have changed since our first meeting. Then you looked more like one of the forest animals than like your human kindred. You seemed lost, in many ways.' His gaze burned brightly.

'You've changed, too,' Simon said.

A shadow of pain crossed Jiriki's angular face. 'Three nights and two days I spent hanging in that mortal's trap. Soon I would have died, even if the woodsman had not come – from shame, that is.' His expression changed, as if he had shut his hurt beneath a lid. 'Come,' he said, 'we must give you food. It is unfortunate, but we cannot feed you as well as I would like. We bring little with us to our,' he gestured around the chamber while searching for the proper word, 'hunting lodge.' Although he was far more fluent with the Westerling speech than Simon would ever have dreamed at their first meeting, still there was something halting yet precise in his manner that indicated how alien that tongue was to him.

'You are here to . . . hunt?' Simon asked as they were led forward to sit before the fire. 'What is it you hunt? The hills seem so barren now.'

'Ah, but the game we seek is more plentiful than ever,' Jiriki said, walking past them and toward a row of objects draped with a shimmering cloth, set along one wall of the cavern.

The green–clad, red–haired one stood up from the

754

gaming table, where Jiriki's place had been taken by An'nai, and spoke in tones both questioning and perhaps angry, all in the Sithi-speech.

'Only showing our visitors the fruits of our hunt, Uncle Khendraja'aro,' Jiriki said cheerfully, but again Simon felt something missing from the Sitha's smile.

Jiriki crouched gracefully beside the row of covered objects, alighting like a sea bird. With a flourish he pulled the shroud away, revealing a row of half a dozen large, white-haired heads, dead features frozen in expressions of snarling hatred.

'Chukku's Stones!' Binabik swore as the others gasped.

It took Simon a shocked instant to recognize the leathery-skinned faces for what they were.

'Giants!' he said at last. 'Hunën!'

'Yes,' Prince Jiriki said, then turned. There was a flash of danger in his voice. 'And you, trespassing mortals . . . what do *you* hunt in my father's hills?'

# 38
# Songs of the Eldest

Deornoth woke in chill darkness, sweating. The wind hissed and wailed outside, clawing at the shuttered windows like a flight of the lonely dead. His heart leaped as he saw the dark shape looming over him, silhouetted by the embers in the fireplace.

'Captain!' It was one of the men, voice a panicked whisper. 'There's someone comin' down on th' gate! Armed men!'

'God's Tree!' he cursed, struggling into his boots. Shrugging his mailshirt over his head, he snatched up his scabbard and helmet and followed the soldier out.

Four more men were huddled on the top platform of the gatehouse, hunkered down behind the rampart. The wind pushed him staggering, and he quickly dropped into a crouch.

'There, Captain!' It was the one who had awakened him. 'Comin' up th' road through th' town.' He leaned past Deornoth to point.

The moonlight, shining through the streaming clouds, silvered the shabby thatching of Naglimund-town's huddled roofs. There was indeed movement on the road, a small company of horsemen, perhaps a dozen in number.

The men on the gatehouse watched the riders' slow approach. One of the soldiers groaned quietly.

Deornoth, too, felt the ache of waiting. It was better when the horns were shrilling, and the field was full of shouting.

*It is this waiting that has unmanned us all*, Deornoth thought. *Once we have been blooded again, our Naglimunders will do proudly.*

'There must be more, a-hidin'!' one of the soldiers breathed. 'What should we do?' Even with the crying of the wind, his voice seemed loud. How could the approaching riders not hear?

'Nothing,' Deornoth said firmly. 'Wait.'

The waiting seemed to last days. As the horsemen drew nearer, the moon picked out shining spearpoints and the gleam of helmets. The silent riders reined in before the massive gate, and sat as if listening.

One of the gatemen stood, drawing his bow and sighting on the breast of the leading rider. Even as Deornoth leaped toward him, seeing the straining lines on the guardsman's face, his desperate eye, there came a loud pounding from below. Deornoth caught the bow arm and forced it up; the arrow spat forth and out into the windy darkness over the town.

'*By the good God, open your door!*' a man shouted, and once more a spear-butt was thumped against the timbers. It was a Rimmersman's voice, with an edge almost, Deornoth thought, of madness. 'Are you all asleep?! Let us in! I am Isorn, Isgrimnur's son, escaped from the hand of our enemies!'

'Look! See how the clouds break! Don't you think that is a hopeful sign, Velligis?'

As he spoke, Duke Leobardis swung his pointing hand in a broad arc to the cabin's open window, nearly smacking his mailed arm against the head of his sweating squire in the process. The squire ducked, swallowing a silent oath as he juggled the duke's greaves, and turned to cuff a young page who had not gotten out of his way fast enough. The page, who had been trying to make himself as unobtrusive as possible in the ship's crowded cabin, renewed his desperate efforts to shrink out of sight entirely.

'Perhaps we are, in some way, the thin end of the wedge that will put an end to this madness.' Leobardis clanked to the window, his squire scrambling along the floor behind him, struggling to hold a half-fastened greave in place. The gravid sky did indeed show long, rippled streaks of blue, as if Crannhyr's dark and bulky cliffs, looming over the bay where Leobardis' flagship *Emettin's Jewel* rolled at close anchor, caught and tore at the lowering clouds.

Velligis, a great round man in golden escritorial robes, stumped to the window to stand at the duke's side.

'How, my lord, can throwing oil on the fire help to extinguish it? It is, if you will pardon my forwardness, folly to think so.'

The hammering of the muster-drum echoed across the water. Leobardis brushed lank white hair out of his eyes. 'I know how the lector feels,' he said, 'and I know he directs you, beloved Escritor, to try and persuade me out of this. His Sacredness' love of peace . . . well, it is admirable, but it will not come about by talking.'

Velligis opened a small brass casket and shook out a sugar-sweet, which he delicately placed on his tongue. 'This is perilously close to sacrilege, Duke Leobardis. Is prayer "talking"? Is the intercession of His Sacredness the Lector Ranessin somehow of less validity than the force of your armies? If that is so, then our faith in the word of Usires, and of his first acolyte Sutrines, is a mockery.' The escritor sighed heavily, and sucked.

The duke's cheeks pinkened; he waved the squire away, bending creakily to fasten the last buckle himself, then waved for his surcoat of rich blue with the Benidrivine kingfisher gold-blazoned on the chest.

'God bless me, Velligis,' he said testily, 'but I haven't

758

the mind for arguing with you today. I have been pushed too far by the High King Elias, and now I must do what is needed.'

'But you do not go into battle by yourself,' the large man said, speaking with some heat for the first time. 'You lead hundreds, nay, thousands of men – of souls – and their well-being is in your care. The seeds of catastrophe are fluttering in the wind, and Mother Church has a responsibility to see they do not find fertile soil.'

Leobardis shook his head sadly as the small page shyly lifted his golden helmet, and its crest of blue-dyed horsehair.

'Fertile soil is everywhere these days, Velligis, and catastrophe is already growing – if you'll forgive my theft of your poetic words. The thing is, we must try and nip it while it is budding. Come.' He patted the escritor's fleshy arm. 'It is time to go down to the landing-boat. Walk with me.'

'Certainly, my good Duke, certainly.' Velligis turned slightly to the side to ease through the narrow doorway. 'You will forgive me if I do not accompany you ashore just yet. I have been somewhat unsteady on my legs of late. I am getting old, I fear.'

'Ah, but your rhetoric has not lost its vigor,' Leobardis replied as they moved slowly across the deck. A small figure wrapped in a dark robe crossed his path, pausing to nod briefly, hands folded on its breast. The escritor frowned, but Duke Leobardis returned the nod with a smile.

'Nin Reisu has been with *Emettin's Jewel* a long time,' he said, 'and she is the finest of seawatchers. I forgive her the formalities – Niskies are strange folk anyway, Velligis, as you would know if you were a sailing man. Come, my boat is this way.'

The harbor wind made of Leobardis' cloak a sail, billowing blue against the uncertain sky.

*

759

Leobardis saw his youngest son Varellan waiting at landfall, looking too small to fill out his gleaming armor. His thin face peered anxiously from the hollow of his helmet while he surveyed the gathering Nabbanai forces, as if his father might hold him responsible for any slipshod formations among the milling, swearing soldiers. Several of them pushed past him as unconcernedly as if he were the drummer boy, cursing cheerfully at a pair of horses who, frightened by the confusion, had leaped off the gangplank into the shallow water, taking their handler with them. Varellan backed away from the splashing, whinnying chaos, his forehead wrinkled in a frown that did not go away even when he saw the duke step from the grounded boat and wade the last few paces to the rocky shore of Hernystir's south coast.

'My lord,' he said, and hesitated; Leobardis guessed he was wondering whether to climb down from his horse and bend a knee. The duke had to restrain a scowl. He blamed Nessalanta for the boy's timidity, since she had hung on to him as a drunkard to his jug, unwilling to admit that the last of her children was grown. Of course, he perhaps owned some responsibility himself. He should never have poked fun at the boy's half-formed interest in the priesthood. Still, that had been years ago, and there was no turning the boy's path now; he would be a soldier if it killed him.

'So, Varellan,' he said, and looked around. 'Well then, my son, it looks as though all is in good order.'

Although the evidence of his eyes told him his father was either mad or overkind, the young man flashed a grateful smile. 'We shall be unshipped in two hours, I would say. Will we march tonight?'

'After a week at sea? The men would kill us both and find a new ducal family. Although I suppose they would have to dispatch Benigaris, too, if they wanted to finish the line. Speaking of your brother, why is he not here?'

He spoke lightly, but he found the absence of his eldest

child irritating. After weeks of bitter argument over whether Nabban should cling to neutrality, and a stormy reaction to the duke's decision to support Josua, Benigaris had turned his coat and announced his desire to ride with his father and the armies. Benigaris could not give up an opportunity to lead the Legions of the Kingfisher in battle, the duke felt sure, even if it meant giving up a chance to rest his hocks for a short while on the throne of the Sancellan Mahistrevis.

He realized he was woolgathering. 'No, no, Varellan, we must give the men a night in Crannhyr, although merrymaking may prove scarce with Lluth's war gone so poorly to the north. Where did you say Benigaris was?'

Varellan colored. 'I didn't, my lord. I'm sorry. He rode up to the town with his friend Count Aspitis Preves.'

Leobardis ignored his son's discomfort. 'By the Tree, I would not have thought it too much to expect my son and heir to meet me. Well, so, let us go and see how things are with our other commanders.' He snapped his fingers and the squire brought the duke's horse up, harness bells jingling.

They found Mylin-sá-Ingadaris underneath his house's white and red albatross banner. The old man, who had been Leobardis' cordial enemy for years, hailed the duke over. He and Varellan sat watching as Mylin oversaw the final unloading of his two carracks, then joined the old earl in his striped tent for a flagon of sweet Ingadarine wine.

After talking marching squares and fewtering – and putting up with Varellan's half-successful attempts to join in – Leobardis thanked Earl Mylin for his hospitality and went out, youngest son trailing behind. Taking the reins back from their squires, they continued on through the bustling encampment, paying brief courtesy visits to the camps of some of the other nobles.

The pair had just turned about to ride back up the

strand when the duke caught sight of a familiar figure on a big-chested roan charger, sauntering down the road from town with another rider at his side.

Benigaris' silver armor, his most cherished possession, was so thick with engravings and costly tracings of ilenite inlay that light declined to reflect from it properly, making it appear almost gray. Corseted by his breastplate, which corrected the overabundancy of his figure, Benigaris looked every inch a brave and doughty knight. Young Aspitis beside him also wore armor of beautiful workmanship: the family osprey crest had been inlaid on his breastplate in mother of pearl. He wore no surcoat that might cover it up, but went, like Benigaris, plated all over like a gleaming crab.

Benigaris said something to his companion; Aspitis Preves laughed, then rode away. Benigaris came down the road, crunching across the gravelly beach toward his father and younger brother.

'That was Count Aspitis, was it not?' Leobardis asked, trying to keep the bitterness he felt in the back of his throat from his voice. 'Is the Prevan House now become our enemy, that he cannot come and salute his duke?'

Benigaris leaned over in his saddle and patted his horse's neck. Leobardis could not see if he looked up through his thick, dark brows. 'I told Aspitis that you and I would speak privately, Father. He would have come, but I sent him away. He went out of respect for you.' He turned to Varellan, who looked aswim in his bright armor, and gave the boy a brief nod.

Feeling slightly overbalanced, the duke changed the subject. 'What took you to town, my son?'

'News, sire. I thought Aspitis, since he has been here before, might help me to gather useful tidings.'

'You were gone a long time.' Leobardis could not summon the strength to be angry. 'What did you find, Benigaris – anything?'

'Nothing we had not already heard from the Abaingeat boats. Lluth is wounded and has fallen back to the

762

mountains. Skali controls Hernysadharc, but has not the armies to extend himself any farther, not until the Hernystirmen in the Grianspog have been subdued. So the coast is yet free, and all the ground this side of the Ach Samrath – Nad Mullach, Cuimhne, all the river lands up to Inniscrich.'

Leobardis rubbed his head, squinting at the glaring streak the sun made on the surface of the ocean. 'Perhaps we could best serve Prince Josua if we were to break this nearer siege. If we were to bring our two thousand men against Skali Sharp-nose's back, Lluth's armies would be freed up – what's left of them – and Elias' back would be naked as he lays siege to the Naglimund.'

He weighed the plan and liked it. It seemed to him something his brother Camaris might have done: swift, forceful, a stroke like a snapping whip. Camaris had always approached warfare like the pure weapon he was, as straightforward and unhesitating as a shining hammer.

Benigaris was shaking his head, something like real alarm on his face. 'Oh, no, sire! No! Why, if we were to do that, all Skali would have to do is melt into the Circoille, or climb up into the same Grianspog mountains. Then *we* would be pegged down like a stretched hide, waiting for the Rimmersmen to come out. Meanwhile Elias would reduce Naglimund and be free to turn on us. We would be cracked like a hazelnut between the High King and the Raven.' He shook his head emphatically, as if the idea frightened him.

Leobardis turned away from the dazzling sun. 'I suppose you make good sense, Benigaris . . . although I seem to remember you arguing differently not long ago.'

'That was until you made your decision to put the army in the field, my lord.' Benigaris lifted his helmet and rolled it in his hands for a moment before hanging it back on his pommel. 'Now that we are committed, I am a Nascadu lion.'

Leobardis took a deep breath. The tang of war was in the air, and it was a scent that filled him with unease and regret. Still, the sundering of Osten Ard after the long years of John's peace – the High King's Ward – seemed to have brought his headstrong son back to his side. It was something for which to be grateful, however insignificant in the tide of greater events. The Duke of Nabban offered a silent prayer of thanks to his confusing but ultimately beneficent God.

'Praise Usires Aedon for bringing you back to us!' Isgrimnur said, and felt tears coming again. He leaned over the bed and gave Isorn's shoulder a rough, joyful shake, earning a sharp glance from Gutrun, who had not left her grown son's side since he had come in the night before.

Isorn, no stranger to his mother's stern ways, grinned weakly up at Isgrimnur. He had the duke's blue eyes and broad features, but much of the sheen of youth seemed to have vanished since his father had seen him last: he was drawn, shadowed. Something seemed to have been drained from him, for all his stock-shouldered bulk.

*It's just hardship and worry that's been at him*, the duke decided. *He's a strong boy. Look at him, how he puts up with his mother's fussing. He'll be a fine man – no. He is a fine man. When he's duke after me . . . after we send Skali shouting down to Hell . . .*

'Isorn!' A new voice sent the errant thought fluttering away. 'It is a miracle to have you back among us.' Prince Josua leaned forward and clasped Isorn's hand with his own left hand. Gutrun nodded approvingly. She did not rise to curtsy to the prince, motherhood apparently overriding manners on this occasion. Josua did not seem to mind.

'The devil it's a miracle,' Isgrimnur said gruffly, and frowned to keep his swelling heart from causing him any embarrassment. 'He got 'em out through wits and courage, and that's God's truth.'

'Isgrimnur . . .' Gutrun warned him. Josua laughed.

'Of course. Let me say then, Isorn, that your courage and wit were miraculous.'

Isorn sat higher in the bed, readjusting the bandaged leg that lay pillowed atop the coverlet like the relic of a saint. 'That's far too kind, Your Highness. Had not some of Skali's Kaldskryke-men been without the stomach for torture of their fellows, we would be there still – as ice-stiffened corpses.'

'Isorn!' his mother said, annoyed. 'Do not speak of such things. It flies in the face of God's mercy.'

'But it's true, Mother. Skali's own Ravens gave us the knives that permitted our escape.' He turned to Josua. 'There are dark things afoot in Elvritshalla – over all of Rimmersgard, Prince Josua! You must believe me! Skali is not alone. The town was full of Black Rimmersmen out of the lands around Stormspike. It was them that Sharp-nose left to guard us. It was those God-cursed monsters who tortured our men – for nothing! We had nothing to hide from them! They did it for pleasure, if such a thing can be imagined. Nights we went to sleep hearing the cries of our fellows, wondering who they would take next.'

He moaned softly and lifted his hand from Gutrun's restraining grasp to rub at his temples, as if to scour the memory. 'Even Skali's own men found it sickening. I think they are beginning to wonder what their thane has gotten them into.'

'We believe you,' Josua said gently; the look he lifted to standing Isgrimnur was etched with worry.

'But there were others, too – ones who came by night, hooded in black. Even our guards did not see *their* faces!' Although Isorn's voice remained quiet, his eyes were round in the remembering. 'They did not even *move* like men – the Aedon be my witness! They were out of the cold wastes beyond the mountains. We could feel the chill of them as they passed our prison! We were more frightened of being near to them than of all the Black

Rimmersmen's hot irons.' Isorn shook his head and lay back on the pillow. 'I am sorry, Father . . . Prince Josua. I am very tired.'

'He is a strong man, Isgrimnur,' the prince said as they walked up the puddled corridor. The roof here was leaking, as so many were in Naglimund after a winter of hard weather, and a spring and summer of the same.

'I only wish I had not left him alone to face that whoreson Skali. Be-damned!' Skidding on the wet stone, Isgrimnur cursed his age and clumsiness.

'He did all that could be done, Uncle. You should be proud of him.'

'I am.'

They walked on for a while before Josua spoke. 'I must confess, having Isorn here makes it easier for me to ask of you . . . what I must ask.'

Isgrimnur tugged at his beard. 'And what is that?'

'A boon. One that I would not beg if . . .' He hesitated. 'No. Let us go to my chamber. This is a thing that should be discussed in solitude.' He hooked his right arm through the duke's elbow, the leather-capped stump on his wrist a mute reproach in advance of any rejection.

Isgrimnur tugged at his beard again until it hurt. He had a feeling he would not like what he was about to hear. 'By the Tree, let's get a jug of wine to take with us, Josua. I sorely need it.'

'*For the love of Usires!* By the crimson mallet of Dror! The bones of Saint Eahlstan and Saint Skendi! Are you *mad*?! Why should I leave Naglimund?' Isgrimnur trembled in surprise and anger.

'I would not ask it if there was any other way, Isgrimnur.' The prince spoke patiently, but even through the mist of his rage the duke could see the anguish Josua felt. 'I have lain awake two nights without sleep, trying to think of another way. I cannot. Somebody must find the Princess Miriamele.'

Isgrimnur took a long swallow of wine, feeling some dribble down his beard, but not caring. 'Why?' he said at last, and set the jar down with a table-rattling thump. 'And why *me*, God damn it all? Why me?'

The prince was all strained patience. 'She must be found because she is vitally important . . . as well as my only niece. What if I die, Isgrimnur? What if we hold off Elias, break the siege, but I stop an arrow, or tumble from the castle wall? Who will the people rally behind – not just the barons and the warlords, but the common people, those who came flocking into my walls for protection? It will be hard enough to fight Elias with me at your head – strange and fickle as I am thought – but what if I die?'

Isgrimnur stared at the floor. 'There is Lluth. And Leobardis.'

Josua shook his head harshly. 'King Lluth is wounded, maybe dying. Leobardis is the Duke of Nabban – at war with Erkynland within the memory of some. The Sancellan itself is a reminder of a time when Nabban ruled all. Even you, Uncle, good and much-respected man as you are, could not hold a force together that would stand against Elias. He is a son of Prester John! He was raised to the Dragonbone Chair by John himself. For all his wicked deeds, it will take someone from the family to unseat him . . . and you know it!'

Isgrimnur's long silence was his answer.

'But why me?' he said at last.

'Because Miriamele would not come back for anyone else I could send. Deornoth? He is as brave and as loyal as a hunting hawk, but he would have to carry the princess back to Naglimund in a sack. Beside myself, you are the only one who could ever bring her unresisting, and she must come willingly, for it would be disaster if you were found out. Soon enough Elias may discover she is gone, and then he will set the south afire to find her.'

Josua walked to his desk and absently ruffled a stack of parchments. 'Think carefully, Isgrimnur. Forget for a moment that it is yourself we speak of. Who else has traveled as far, and has as many friends in strange places? Who else, if you will forgive me, has seen the wrong end of so many dark alleys in Ansis Pelippé and Nabban?'

Isgrimnur grinned sourly, in spite of himself. 'But still it makes no sense, Josua. How can I leave my men, with Elias coming against us? And how could I hope to perform such a secret thing, well known as I am?'

'For the first, that is why it seems to me a sign from God that Isorn has come. Einskaldir, we both would agree, has not the restraint to command. Isorn does. Anyway, Uncle, he deserves the chance to make good. Elvritshalla's fall has battered his young pride.'

'It's battered pride that makes a boy a man,' the duke growled. 'Go on.'

'As to the second, well, you *are* well-known, but you have been seldom south of Erkynland in twenty years. In any case, we shall disguise you.'

'Disguise?' Isgrimnur pawed distractedly at the braids of his beard as Josua walked to his chamber door and called out. The duke had a strange, heavy feeling around his heart. He had been dreading the fight, not so much for himself as for his people, his wife . . . now his son was here, too, giving him another stone of worry to carry. But to leave, even riding into danger as great as he left behind . . . it seemed unsupportably like cowardice, like treason.

*But I was sworn to Josua's father – my dear old John – how can I not do what his son asks? And his arguments make all too much be-damned sense.*

'Here,' the prince said, stepping away from the door to allow someone in. It was Father Strangyeard, his pink, eye-patched face creased in a shy smile, tall frame stooped over his burden: a bundle of dark cloth.

'I hope it fits,' he said. 'They seldom do; I don't know why, just another gentle reminder, another of the Master's little burdens.' He trailed off, then seemed to find the thread again. 'Eglaf was most kind to lend it. He is about your size, I think, although not quite so tall.'

'Eglaf?' Isgrimnur said, mystified. 'Who is Eglaf? Josua, what is this nonsense?'

'Brother Eglaf, of course,' Strangyeard explained.

'Your disguise, Isgrimnur,' Josua amplified. The castle archivist shook out the bundle, revealing a woolen set of black priestly vestments. 'You are a devout man, Uncle,' the prince said. 'I am sure you will be able to carry it off.' The duke could have sworn Josua was resisting a smile.

'What? Priest's robes?' Isgrimnur was beginning to see the outlines of the thing, and he was not pleased.

'How better to pass unnoticed in Nabban, where Mother Church is queen, and priests of every stripe nearly outnumber the rest of the citizens?' Josua *was* smiling.

Isgrimnur was furious. 'Josua, I feared for your wits before, but now I know you have lost them completely! This is the maddest scheme I have ever seen! And on top of everything else, who ever heard of an Aedonite priest with a beard?!' He snorted scornfully.

The prince – with a warning glance to Father Strangyeard, who put the robes down on a chair and backed toward the door – walked to his table and lifted a cloth, revealing . . . a basin of hot water, and a gleaming, fresh-stropped razor.

Isgrimnur's eruptive bellow rattled the very crockery in the castle kitchen below.

'Speak, mortal men. Do you come to our hills as spies?'

A chilly silence followed Prince Jiriki's words. From the corner of his eye Simon watched Haestan reach backward, feeling along the wall for something to use as a weapon; Sludig and Grimmric glared at the Sithi who surrounded them, certain that any moment they would be set upon.

'No, Prince Jiriki,' Binabik said hastily. 'Surely you are seeing we had no expectations of finding your people

769

here. We are from Naglimund, Prince Josua's sending, on an errand of terrible import. We are seeking . . .'

The troll hesitated, as though afraid to say too much. Finally, with a shrug, he continued.

'We go to the dragon-mountain for searching Camaris-sá-Vinitta's sword Thorn.'

Jiriki narrowed his eyes, and behind him the green-clad one he had called his uncle let out a thin whistle of breath.

'What would you do with such a thing?' Khendraja'aro demanded.

Binabik would not answer this, but stared unhappily at the cavern floor. The very air seemed to thicken as the moments passed.

'It's to save us from Ineluki the Storm King!' Simon blurted out. None of the Sithi moved a muscle except to blink. No one said a word.

'Speak more,' Jiriki said at last.

'If we must,' Binabik said. 'It is part of a story near as long as your *Ua'kiza Tumet'ai nei-R'i'anis* – the Song of the Fall of Tumet'ai. We will try for telling you what we can.'

The troll hurriedly explained the main facts. It seemed to Simon that he deliberately omitted many things; once or twice in the telling Binabik looked up and caught his eye, seemingly warning him to silence.

Binabik told the silent Sithi of Naglimund's preparations and the crimes of the High King; he explained the words of Jarnauga, and the book of Nisses, reciting the rhyme that led them on toward Urmsheim.

The finish of the story left the troll facing Jiriki's bland stare, the uncle's more skeptical expression, and a silence so complete that the ringing echo of the waterfall seemed to swell until it filled the whole world with noise. What a place of madness and dreams this was, and what a mad story they were suddenly living in! Simon felt his heart racing, but not from fear alone.

'This is hard to credit, son of my sister,' Khendraja'aro

770

said at last, spreading his beringed hands in an unfamiliar gesture.

'It is, Uncle. But I think this is not the time to speak of it.'

'But the *other one* the boy spoke of . . .' Khendraja'aro began, his yellow eyes troubled, his voice full of building anger. 'The black one below *Nakkiga* . . .'

'Not now.' There was an edge to the Sithi prince's voice. He turned to the five outsiders. 'Apologies are called for. It is not good that we should discuss such things while you still have not eaten. You are our guests.' Simon felt a wave of relief at these words and swayed a little, his knees suddenly weak.

Noticing this, Jiriki waved them toward the fire. 'Sit down. We must be forgiven for our suspicion. Understand, although I owe you blood debt, Seoman – you *are* my *Hikka Sta'ja* – your race has done ours little kindness.'

'I must be disagreeing with you in a part, Prince Jiriki,' Binabik replied, seating himself on a flat rock near the fire. 'Of all Sithi, your family should be knowing that we Qanuc have never brought you any harm.'

Jiriki looked down on the little man, and his taut features relaxed into an expression almost of fondness. 'You have caught me in ungraciousness, Binbiniqega-benik. After only the Western men, whom we knew best, we once loved the Qanuc well.'

Binabik lifted his head, a look of astonishment on his round face. 'How are you knowing my full name? I have not given mention of it, and my companions have not been either.'

Jiriki laughed, a hissing sound, but strangely cheering, with not a hint of insincerity. In that moment Simon felt a fierce, sudden liking for him.

'Ah, troll,' the prince said, 'someone as traveled as you are should not be surprised that your name is known. How many Qanuc beside your master and yourself are ever seen south of the mountains?'

'You were knowing my master? He is dead now.'

Binabik pulled off his gloves and flexed his fingers. Simon and the others were finding seats of their own.

'He knew us,' Jiriki said. 'Did he not teach you to speak our language? You said the troll spoke to you, An'nai?'

'He did, my prince. Mostly correctly.'

Binabik flushed, pleased but embarrassed. 'Ookequk was teaching me some, but he never told me where he had been learning it. I had the thought perhaps *his* master had given it to *him*.'

'Sit now, sit,' said Jiriki, gesturing for Haestan, Sludig and Grimmric to follow Simon and Binabik's example. They came like dogs who fear a beating and found themselves places near the fire. Several of the other Sithi approached bearing salvers of intricately carved and polished wood, high-laden with all manner of things: butter and dark brown bread, a wheel of pungent, salty cheese, small red and yellow fruits that Simon had never seen before. There were also several bowls of quite recognizable berries, and even a pile of slow-dripping honeycombs. When Simon reached and took two of the sticky combs, Jiriki laughed again, a quiet sibilance like a jay in a distant tree.

'Everywhere is winter,' he said, 'but in the sheltered fastnesses of Jao-é-Tinukai'i, the bees do not know it. Take all you like.'

Captors-turned-hosts now served the companions an unfamiliar but potent wine, filling their wooden goblets from stone ewers. Simon wondered if some prayer might be said before starting, but the Sithi had already begun to eat. Haestan, Sludig, and Grimmric were looking around miserably, wanting to begin but still full of fear and distrust. They watched intently as Binabik broke bread and took a mouthful of buttered crust. Some moments later, when he was not only still alive but eating merrily, the men felt safe to attack the Sithi fare, which they did with the vigor of reprieved prisoners.

Dabbing honey from his chin, Simon paused to watch the Sithi. The Fair Folk ate slowly, sometimes staring at a berry between their fingers for long instants before lifting it to their mouths. There was little speech, but when one of them made some remark in their liquid tongue, or gave voice to a brief trill of song, all the others listened. Most often there was no response, but if one of them had some answer they all listened to that, too. There was much quiet laughter, but no shouting and no arguing, and Simon never heard anyone interrupt while another was speaking.

An'nai had moved over to sit near Simon and Binabik. One of the Sithi made a solemn statement that drew a laugh from the others. Simon asked An'nai to explain the joke.

The white-jacketed Sitha looked slightly uncomfortable. 'Ki'ushapo said that your friends eat as though they fear their food might run away.' He gestured to Haestan, who was pushing food into his mouth with both hands.

Simon was not sure what An'nai meant – surely they had seen hungry people before? – but he smiled anyway.

As the meal wore on, and a seemingly inexhaustible river of wine replenished the wooden goblets, the Rimmersman and the two Erkynlandish guardsmen began to enjoy themselves. At one point Sludig stood, tumbler sloshing in his hand, and proposed a hearty toast to his new Sithi friends. Jiriki smiled and nodded, but Khendraja'aro stiffened; when Sludig swung into an old northern drinking song, the prince's uncle slipped quietly off to the corner of the broad cavern to stare into the rippling, lamplit pond.

The other Sithi at table laughed as Sludig sang the choruses in his braying voice, and swayed to his tipsy rhythm, whispering occasionally among themselves. Sludig and Haestan and Grimmric seemed quite happy now, and even Binabik was grinning as he sucked on a pear rind – but Simon, remembering the enthralling music he had heard the Sithi play, felt a glow of shame for his companion, as though the Rimmersman were a festival bear dancing for crumbs in Main Row.

After watching for some while he got up, wiping his hands on his shirtfront. Binabik rose, too, and after asking Jiriki's permission went down the covered passageway to have a look after Qantaqa. The three soldiers were all laughing uproariously among themselves, telling, Simon had no doubt, drunken soldier jokes. He walked to one of the wall niches to examine the strange lamps. Abruptly he was reminded of the glowing crystal Morgenes had given him – could it have been Sithi-work? – and felt a cold, lonely tug at his heart. He lifted one of the lamps and saw a faint shadow of the bones in his hand, as though the flesh was only muddied water. Stare as he might, he could not fathom how the flame had been introduced to the inside of the translucent crystal.

Sensing someone watching, he turned. Jiriki was staring, cat-eyes agleam on the far side of the fire circle. Simon started, surprised; the prince nodded.

Haestan, the wine gone to his shaggy head, had challenged one of the Sithi – the one An'nai had named Ki'ushapo – to wrist-wrestle. Ki'ushapo, yellow-braided, dressed in black and gray, was receiving drunken advice from Grimmric. It was clear why the skinny guardsman thought his aid well-directed: the Sitha was a head shorter than Haestan, and looked to be barely more than half his weight. As the Sitha, with a bemused expression, leaned forward across the smooth stone to clasp Haestan's broad hand, Jiriki stood up and edged past them, making his graceful way across the chamber toward Simon.

It was still difficult, Simon thought, to reconcile this confident, clever being with the maddened creature he had found in the cotsman's wire. Still, when Jiriki turned his head a certain way, or flexed his long-jointed fingers, it was possible to see again the wildness that had frightened and fascinated. And whenever the firelight caught the prince's gold-flecked amber eyes, they shone ancient as jewels from the black soil of the forest.

'Come, Seoman,' the Sitha said, 'I will show you something.' He slid his hand under the youth's elbow and steered him toward the pool where Khendraja'aro sat trailing his fingers in the water. As they passed the fire, Simon saw that the wrist-wrestling contest was at full heat. The opponents were locked in struggle, neither with an advantage yet, but Haestan's bearded face was clenched in a lock-toothed grin of strain. The slender Sitha, by contrast, showed little effect from the standoff, except his gray-clad arm quivering with the tension of their striving. Simon did not think this boded well for Haestan's chances. Sludig, watching the small frustrate the large, sat open-mouthed.

Jiriki fluted something to his uncle as they approached, but Khendraja'aro did not respond: his ageless face seemed closed, shut like a door. Simon followed the prince past him along the cavern wall. A moment later, before his astonished eyes, Jiriki disappeared.

He had only stepped into another tunnel, one that hooked around behind the stone sluice of the little waterfall. Simon went in after him; the tunnel curled upward in rough stone steps, lit by a row of lamps.

'Follow me, please,' Jiriki said, and began to climb.

It seemed they mounted far up into the hill, spiraling around and around for some time. At last they passed the last lamp, and traveled a careful way in near-darkness, until finally Simon became aware of the gleam of stars before him. A moment later the passageway widened into a small cave, one end of which was open to the night sky.

He followed Jiriki to the cavern's edge, which was a waist-high lip of stone. The rock face of the hill dropped away below: ten bare cubits down to the tops of the tall evergreens, fifty more to the snow-matted ground. The night was clear, the stars shining fiercely against the blackness, and the forest was all around, like a vast secret.

After they had stood some while, Jiriki said: 'I owe you a life, manchild. Do not fear I will forget.'

Simon said nothing, afraid to speak in case he should break the spell that allowed him to stand in the very midst of the forest night, a spy in God's dark garden. An owl called.

There passed another interval of silence, then the Sitha lightly touched Simon's arm and pointed out above the silent ocean of trees.

'There. To the north, beneath Lu'yasa's Staff . . .' He indicated a line of three stars in the lowest part of the velvety sky. 'Can you see the outline of the mountains?'

Simon stared. He thought there might be a faint luminescence on the murky horizon, the barest hint of some great white shape so far away as to seem out of reach of the same moonlight that glowed on trees and snow beneath them. 'I think so,' he said quietly.

'That is where you go. The peak men call Urmsheim is in that range, although you would need a clearer night to see it well.' He sighed. 'Your friend Binabik tonight spoke of lost Tumet'ai. Once it could be seen from here, away there in the east,' he pointed into the darkness, 'from this very perch, but that was in my great-grandfather's day. In daylight the *Seni Anzi'in* . . . The Tower of the Walking Dawn . . . would catch the rising sun in its roofs of crystal and gold. They say it was like a beautiful torch burning on the morning horizon . . .'

He broke off, turning his eyes finally to Simon, the rest of his face obscured by nightshadow.

'Tumet'ai is long buried,' he said, and shrugged. 'Nothing lasts, not even the Sithi . . . not even time itself.'

'How . . . how old are you?'

Jiriki smiled, teeth glinting in the moonlight. 'Older than you, Seoman. Let us go down now. You have seen and survived many things today, and no doubt you need sleep.'

When they got back to the firelit cavern, the three guardsmen were wrapped in their cloaks, snoring lustily. Binabik had returned, and sat listening as several Sithi sang a slow, mournful song that droned like a beehive and ran like a river, and seemed to fill the cave like the thick scent of some rare, dying flower.

Curled in his own cloak, watching the firelight flicker on the stones above him, Simon was lulled to sleep by the strange music of Jiriki's tribe.

# 39
# High King's Hand

Simon awakened to find the cavern light changed. The fire still burned, thin yellow flames among the white ashes, but the lamps had been extinguished. Daylight filtered down through crevices in the ceiling that had been invisible the night before, transforming the stone chamber into a pillared hall of light and shadow.

His three soldier companions still slept, tangled in their cloaks snoring, sprawled like battle casualties. The cavern was otherwise empty but for Binabik, who sat cross-legged before the fire tootling absently on his walking-stick flute.

Simon sat up groggily. 'Where are the Sithi?'

Binabik did not turn, but piped a few more notes. 'Greetings, good friend,' he said at last. 'Was your sleep satisfying?'

'I suppose,' Simon grunted, rolling back over to stare at the dust flecks shimmering near the cavern's roof. 'Where did the Sithi go?'

'Out for hunting, as it were. Come and raise yourself. I need your assistance.'

Simon groaned, but dragged himself up into a sitting position.

'Hunting for giants?' he asked a short while later through a mouthful of fruit. Haestan's snores were becoming so loud that Binabik had put his flute down in disgust.

'Hunting whatever is threatening to their borders, I suppose.' The troll stared at something before him on the stone cavern floor. '*Kikkasut*! This is making no good sense. I am not liking it one least bit.'

'What doesn't make sense?' Simon lazily surveyed the rock chamber 'Is this a Sithi house?'

Binabik looked over, frowning. 'I suppose it is good you have regained your ability for the asking of many questions at once. No, this is not a Sithi house, as such. It is, I am thinking, what Jiriki called it: a hunting lodge, a place for their hunters to stay while roaming afield. As for your other question, it is these bones that are nonsensical – or rather, *too much* sense they make.'

The knucklebones lay in a heap before Binabik's knees. Simon looked them over. 'What does that mean?'

'I will tell you. Perhaps it would be good your using this time to wash the dirt and blood and juice of berries from your face.' The troll flashed a sour yellow grin, pointing to the pool in the corner. 'There is suitable for washing.'

He waited until Simon had ducked his head once in the bitingly cold water.

'Aaah!' the youth said, shivering. 'Cold!'

'You may be seeing,' Binabik resumed, unperturbed by Simon's complaints, 'that I have been at throwing my bones this morning. What they are saying is this: *The Shadowed Path*, *Unwrapped Dart*, and *Black Crevice*. Much confusion and worry this is causing me.'

'Why?' Simon splashed more water on his face and rubbed it off with his jerkin sleeve, which was itself none too clean.

'Because I was casting the bones before we left Naglimund,' Binabik said crossly, 'and the same figures I was getting! Exactly!'

'But why should that be bad?' Something bright lying at the pool's edge caught his eye. He picked it up carefully, and discovered it was a round looking glass set in a splendidly carved wooden frame. The rim of the dark glass was etched with unfamiliar characters.

'Bad it often is when things are always the same,' Binabik answered, 'but with the bones it is more than that. The bones to me are guides to wisdom, yes?'

'Mmm-hmmh.' Simon polished the mirror on his shirtfront.

'Well, what if you were opening your Book of the Aedon to discover that all its pages suddenly were having only one verse – the same verse, over then over?'

'Do you mean a Book I had already seen? That hadn't been like that before? I suppose it would be magic.'

'Well, then,' Binabik said, mollified, 'there you are seeing my problem. There are hundreds of ways the bones can find themselves. To be the same cast six times in running – I can only think it bad. Much as I have studied, still I am not liking the word "magic" – but some force there is gripping the bones, as a powerful wind is pushing all flags the same way . . . Simon? Are you listening?'

Staring fixedly at the mirror, Simon was astonished to find an unfamiliar face looking back. The stranger had an elongated, large-boned face, blue-shadowed eyes, and a growth of red–gold whiskers on chin, cheeks and upper lip. Simon was further amazed to realize that – of course! – he was only seeing himself, thinned and weathered by his travels, the first growth of man's beard darkening his jaws. What kind of face was this, he suddenly wondered? He still had not a man's features, worn and stern, but he fancied that he had sloughed off some of his mooncalfishness. Nonetheless, he found something disappointing in the long-chinned, shock-haired youth who stared back at him.

*Is this what I looked like to Miriamele? Like a farmer's son – a ploughboy?*

And even as he thought of the princess, it seemed that he saw a flash of her features in the glass, almost growing out of his own. For a dizzy instant they were meshed together, like two cloudy souls in one body; an instant later it was Miriamele alone whose face he saw – or

Malachias, rather, for her hair was short and black, and she wore boy's clothes. A colorless sky lay beyond her, spotted with dark thunderheads. There was another, too, who stood just behind, a round-faced man in a gray hood. Simon had seen him before, he was sure so sure – who *was* he?

'Simon!' Binabik's voice splashed him like the cold pool-water, just as the elusive name flitted within reach. Startled, he juggled the mirror for a moment. When he clutched it tight again, no face was there but his own.

'Are you turning sick?' the troll asked, worried by the slack, puzzled expression Simon turned toward him.

'No . . . I don't think so . . .'

'Then if you are washed, come to help me. We shall go to speaking of the auguries later, when your attention is not so delicate.' Binabik stood, dropping the knuckle-bones back into their leather sack.

Binabik went first down the ice chute, warning Simon to keep his toes pointed and his hands close to his head. The headlong seconds rushing down the tunnel were like a dream of falling from a high place, and when he thumped down into the soft snow beneath the tunnel mouth, bright, chill daylight in his eyes, he was content to sit for a moment and enjoy the feel of his heart's rapid beating.

A moment later he was bowled over by a surprising clout on the back, followed by the smothering descent of a mountain of muscle and fur.

'Qantaqa!' he heard Binabik shout, laughing. 'If it is your friends who are receiving such treatment, I am glad I am no enemy!'

Simon pushed the wolf away, gasping, only to face a renewed, rough-tongued assault on his face. At last, with Binabik's aid, he rolled free. Qantaqa sprang to her feet whining excitedly, circled the youth and troll once, then sprang away into the snowy wood.

'Now,' Binabik said, brushing snow from his black

781

hair, 'we must be finding where the Sithi have been putting up our horses.'

'Not far, Qanuc-man.'

Simon jumped. He turned to see a line of Sithi file silently out of the trees, Jiriki's green-jacketed uncle at its head. 'And why do you seek them?'

Binabik smiled. 'Certainly not for escaping you, good Khendraja'aro. Your hospitality is too lavish for us to hurry away from it. No, there are certain things only I wish to make sure we still have, things I was obtaining with some trouble at Naglimund that we will need on the roads ahead.'

Khendraja'aro looked down on the troll expressionlessly for a moment, then signaled to two of the other Sithi. 'Sijandi, Ki'ushapo – show them.'

The yellow-haired pair walked a few steps along the hillside, away from the tunnel-mouth, then stopped, waiting for Simon and the troll to follow. When Simon looked back he saw Khendraja'aro still watching, an unreadable expression in his bright, narrowed eyes.

They found the horses put up a few furlongs away, in a small cavern hidden by a pair of snow-laden pine trees. The cave was snug and dry; all six horses were contentedly chewing away at a pile of sweet-smelling hay.

'Where did all this come from?' Simon asked, surprised.

'We often bring our own horses,' Ki'ushapo replied, speaking the Western tongue carefully. 'Does it surprise you to find we have a stable for them?'

As Binabik rooted around in one of the saddlebags, Simon explored the cavern, noting the light spilling through a crevice high in the wall, and a stone trough filled with clean water. Propped against the far side was a pile of helmets, axes and swords. Simon recognized one of the blades as his own, from the armory of Naglimund.

'These are ours, Binabik!' he said. 'How did they get here?'

Ki'ushapo spoke slowly, as though to a child. 'We put

them here after we took them from you and your companions. Here they are safe and dry.'

Simon looked at the Sitha suspiciously. 'But I thought that you couldn't touch iron – that it was poison to you!' He stopped short, fearful that he had ventured onto forbidden ground, but Ki'ushapo only exchanged a glance with his silent companion before replying.

'So, you have heard tales of the Days of Black Iron,' he said. 'Yes, it was once thus, but those of us who survived those days have learned much. We know now what waters to drink, and from which certain springs, so that we can handle mortal iron for a little time without harm. Why did you think we allowed you to keep your coat of mail? But, of course, we have no liking for it, and do not use it . . . or even touch it when there is no need.' He looked over to Binabik, who was still rummaging intently in the traveling bags. 'We shall leave you to finish your search,' the Sitha said. 'You will find nothing missing – at least nothing you had when you came into our hands.'

Binabik looked up. 'Of course,' he said. 'I am only in worry over things that may have been lost during the fighting of yesterday.'

'Of course,' Ki'ushapo replied. He and the quiet Sijandi went out beneath the branches of the entrance.

'Ah!' Binabik said at last, holding up a sack that clinked like a purse full of gold Imperators. 'A worry eased, this is.' He dropped it back in the saddle bag.

'What is it?' Simon asked, irritated to be asking another question.

Binabik grinned wickedly. 'More Qanuc tricks, ones that will be found very useful soon. Come, we should be returning. If the others wake up, stiff with drink and alone, they may have fright and be doing something foolish.'

Qantaqa found them on their short journey back, her mouth and nose daubed with the blood of some luckless animal. She bounded several times around them, then stopped, hackles lifting as she sniffed at the air. She lowered her head and sniffed again, then went loping ahead.

Jiriki and An'nai had joined Khendraja'aro. The prince had shed his white robe for a jacket of tan and blue. He held a tall bow, unstrung, and wore a quiver full of brown-fletched arrows.

Qantaqa circled the Sithi, growling and sniffing, but her tail waved in the air behind her as though she greeted old acquaintances. She lunged forward toward the blithe Fair Folk, then dodged back, rumbling deep in her throat and shaking her head as though snapping the neck of a rabbit. When Binabik and Simon joined the circle, she came forward long enough to touch Binabik's hand with her black nose, then danced away again and resumed her nervous circling.

'Did you find all your possessions in good order?' Jiriki asked.

Binabik nodded. 'Yes, with certainty. Thanks to you for seeing to our horses.'

Jiriki negligently waved his slender hand. 'And what now to do?' he asked.

'I am thinking we should be on our road soon,' the troll responded, shading his eyes to look at the gray-blue sky.

'Surely not this day,' Jiriki said. 'Rest this afternoon, and eat with us again. We still have much to speak of, and you can leave tomorrow by dawn light.'

'You . . . and your uncle . . . show much kindness to us, Prince Jiriki. And honor.' Binabik bowed.

'We are not a kind race, Binbiniqegabenik, not as we once were, but we *are* a courteous one. Come.'

After a splendid lunch of bread, sweet milk, and a wonderfully odd, tangy soup made from nuts and snowflowers, the long afternoon was spent by Sithi and men alike in quiet talk and singing and long naps.

Simon slept shallowly, and dreamed of Miriamele standing atop the ocean as though it were a floor of uneven green marble, beckoning him to come to her. In his dream he saw furious black clouds on the horizon, and called out, trying to give warning. The princess did not hear over the gathering wind, only smiled and beckoned. He knew he could not stand on the waves, and dove in to swim toward her, but he felt the cold waters, pulling him down, tugging him under. . . .

When he fought free of the dream at last, it was to awaken in dying afternoon. The pillars of light had dimmed, and leaned as though drunken. Some of the Sitha were setting the crystal lamps in their wall niches, but even watching the process gave Simon no better understanding of what lit them: after being put in place they simply, slowly, began to glow with gentle, suffusive light.

Simon joined his companions at the stone circle around the fire. They were alone: the Sithi, although hospitable and even friendly, nevertheless seemed to prefer their own company, sitting in small knots around the cavern.

'Boy,' Haestan said, reaching up to clap his shoulder, 'we feared ye'd sleep all th' day.'

'I would sleep too, if I ate as much bread as he,' Sludig said, cleaning his nails with a sliver of wood.

'All here were agreeing on an early leave-taking tomorrow,' Binabik said, and Grimmric and Haestan nodded. 'There is no certainty this mildness of weather will continue long, and it is far we must still go.'

'Mild weather?' said Simon, frowning at the stiffness in his legs as he sat down. 'It's snowing like mad.'

Binabik chuckled deep in his throat. 'Ho, friend Simon, talk to a snow-dweller if you are wanting to know cold weather. This is like our Qanuc spring, when we play naked in the snows of Mintahoq. When we are reaching the mountains, then, I am sorry to say, you will be feeling *real* coldness.'

*He doesn't look very sorry at all*, Simon thought. 'So when do we start out?'

'First light in the east,' Sludig said. 'The sooner,' he

785

added significantly, looking around the cavern at their unusual hosts, 'the better.'

Binabik eyed him, then turned back to Simon. 'So we shall be at putting things in order tonight.'

Jiriki had appeared as though from thin air to join them at the fireside. 'Ah,' he said, 'I wish to speak to you about just these matters.'

'Surely there is no problem had with our leaving?' Binabik asked, his cheerful expression not entirely masking a certain anxiousness. Haestan and Grimmric looked worried, Sludig ever-so-faintly resentful.

'I think not,' the Sitha replied. 'But there are certain things I wish to send with you.' He reached a long-fingered hand into his robe with a fluid gesture, producing Simon's White Arrow.

'This is yours, Seoman,' he said.

'What? But it . . . it belongs to you, Prince Jiriki.'

The Sitha lifted his head for a moment, as though listening to some distant call, then lowered his gaze once more. 'No, Seoman, it is not mine until I earn it back – a life for a life.' He held it up between his two hands, like a length of string, so that the slanting light from above burnished the minute and complicated designs along its length.

'I know you cannot read these writings,' Jiriki said slowly, 'but I will tell you that they are Words of Making, scribed on the arrow by Vindaomeyo the Fletcher himself – deep, deep in the past, before we of the First People were torn apart into the Three Tribes. It is as much a part of my family as if it were made with my own bone and sinew – and as much a part of me. I did not give it lightly – few mortals have *ever* held a *Sta'ja Ame* – and I certainly could not take it back until I had paid the debt it signifies.' So saying, he handed it to Simon, whose fingers trembled as they touched the arrow's smooth barrel.

'I . . . I didn't understand . . .' he stammered, feeling as if *he* were the one suddenly under obligation. He shrugged, unable to say more.

'So,' Jiriki said, turning to Binabik and the others. 'My destiny, as you mortals might have it, seems strangely bound with this manchild. You will not then find it too surprising when I tell you what else I would send along with you on your unusual and probably fruitless errand.'

After a moment, Binabik asked 'And what is that being, Prince?'

Jiriki smiled, a feline, self-satisfied smile. 'Myself,' he answered. 'I will go with you.'

The young pikeman stood long seconds, unsure of whether to interrupt the prince's thoughts. Josua was staring out into the middle distance, knuckles white as he clutched the parapet of Naglimund's western wall.

At last the prince seemed to notice the foreign presence. He turned, revealing a face so unnaturally pale that the soldier took a half step back.

'Y'r Highness. . . ?' he asked, finding it hard to look into Josua's eyes. The prince's stare, the soldier thought, was like that of the wounded fox he'd once seen the hounds take, and tear before it was dead.

'Send me Deornoth,' the prince said, and forced himself to smile, which the young soldier thought the most horrible thing of all. 'And send me the old man Jarnauga – the Rimmersman. Do you know him?'

'I think so, Y'r Highness. With th'one-eyed father in book-room.'

'Good man.' Josua's face tilted toward the sky, watching the mass of inky clouds as though they were a book of prophecy. The pikeman hesitated, unsure of whether he was dismissed, then turned to sidle off.

'You, man,' the prince said, stopping him in midstep.

'Y'r Highness?'

'What is your name?' He might have been asking the sky.

'Ostrael, Highness . . . Ostrael Firsfram's son, Lord . . . out Runchester.'

The prince looked over briefly, then his gaze flicked back to the darkening horizon as though irresistibly drawn. 'When were you last home in Runchester, my good man?'

'Elysiamansa 'fore last, Prince Josua, but I send 'em half my gettin's, Lord.'

The prince pulled his high collar closer, and nodded his head as though at great wisdom. 'Very well, then . . . Ostrael Firsfram's son. Go and send Deornoth and Jarnauga. Go now.'

Long before this day the young pikeman had been told that the prince was half-mad. As he clomped down the gatehouse stairs in his heavy boots, he thought of Josua's face, remembering with a shiver the bright, ecstatic eyes of painted martyrs in his family's Book of the Aedon – and not only the singing martyrs, but also the weary sadness of Usires Himself, led in chains to the Execution Tree.

'And the scouts are certain, Highness?' Deornoth asked carefully. He did not want to give offense, but he sensed a wildness in the prince today that he did not understand.

'God's Tree, Deornoth, of course they are certain! You know them both – dependable men. The High King is at the Greenwade Ford, less than ten leagues away. He'll be before the walls by tomorrow morning. With considerable strength.'

'So Leobardis is too slow.' Deornoth squinted his eyes, looking not south where Elias' armies crept inexorably nearer, but west, where somewhere beyond the late-morning mist the Legions of the Kingfisher were laboring across the Inniscrich and the southern Frostmarch.

'Barring a miracle,' the prince said. 'Go to, Deornoth. Tell Sir Eadgram to hold all in readiness. I want every spear sharp, every bow tight-strung, and not a drop of wine in the gatehouse . . . or in the gatekeepers. Understood?'

'Of course, Highness,' Deornoth nodded. He felt a quickening of his breath, a slightly sickening thrill of anticipation in his stomach. By the Merciful God, they would give the High King a taste of Naglimund honor – he knew they would!

Someone cleared his throat warningly. It was Jarnauga, scaling the stairs up to the broad walkway as effortlessly as a man half his age. He wore one of Strangyeard's loose black robes, and had tucked the end of his long beard under the belt.

'I answer your summons, Prince Josua,' he said, stiffly courteous.

'Thank you, Jarnauga,' Josua replied. 'Go on, Deornoth. I will talk with you at supper.'

'Yes, Highness.' Deornoth bowed, helmet in hand, then was gone down the stairway two steps at a time.

Josua waited some moments after he was gone to speak.

'Look there, old man, look,' he said at last, sweeping his arm out over the clutter of Naglimund-town and the meadows and farmland beyond, the greens and yellows dark-painted by the glowering sky. 'The rats are coming to gnaw at our walls. We will not see this untroubled view for a long time, if ever.'

'Elias' approach is the talk of the castle, Josua.'

'As it should be.' The prince, as if he had drunk his fill of the sights before him, turned his back to the parapet and fixed the bright-eyed old man with his own intent stare. 'Did you see Isgrimnur off?'

'Yes. He was not pleased to be leaving in secret, and before dawn.'

'Well, what else could be done? After we put about the story of his mission to Perdruin, it would have been difficult if anyone had seen him go in priest's robes – and as beardless as when he was a boy in Elvritshalla.' The prince forced a grim, clench-jawed smile. 'God knows,

Jarnauga, though I made sport of his disguising himself, it is a knife in my guts to have pulled that good man from his family and sent him out to try and recover my own failing.'

'You are master here, Josua; sometimes being master means less of some kinds of freedom than that given to the meanest serf.'

The prince tucked his right arm into his cloak. 'Did he take Kvalnir?'

Jarnauga grinned. 'Sheathed beneath his outer robe. May your God save the one who tries to rob that fat old monk.'

The prince's tired smile widened for a moment. 'Even God Himself won't be able to help them, in the mood Isgrimnur's in.' The smile did not outlast the moment. 'Now, Jarnauga, walk with me here on the battlements. I need your good eyes and wise words.'

'I can indeed look farther than most, Josua – so my father taught me, and my mother. That is why I am named "Iron-eyes" in our Rimmerspakk: I was taught to see through veils of deception as black iron cuts spells. But as to the other, I can promise no wisdom worthy of the name at this late hour.'

The prince made a dismissive gesture. 'You have helped us already, I suspect, to see much we would not have. Tell me of this League of the Scroll. Did they send you to Tungoldyr to spy on Stormspike?'

The old man fell in at Josua's side, his sleeves fluttering like black pennants. 'No, Prince, that is not the League's way. My father, too, was a Scrollbearer.' He lifted a golden chain out of the neck of his vestments, showing Josua a carved quill and scroll that hung upon it. 'He raised me to take up his place, and I would have done no less to please him. The League does not compel; it asks only that one does what one can do.'

Josua walked silently, thinking. 'If only a land could be so ruled,' he said at last. 'If only men would do what they should.' He turned his thoughtful, gray-eyed stare to the old Rimmersman. 'But things are not always so easy – the wrong and right not always so apparent. Surely this League of yours must have its high priest, or its prince? Was that Morgenes?'

Jarnauga quirked his lips. 'There are indeed times when it would benefit us to have a leader, a strong hand. Our woeful unpreparedness for these events shows that.' Jarnauga shook his head. 'And we would have granted such leadership to Doctor Morgenes in an instant if he had asked – he was a man of incredible wisdom, Josua; I hope that you appreciated him when you knew him. But he would not have it. He wanted only to search, and to read, and to ask questions. Still, thank whatever powers that we had him as long as we did. His foresight is, at this moment, our only shield.'

Josua stopped, leaning with his elbows on the parapet. 'So this League of yours has never had a leader?'

'Not since King Eahlstan Fiskerne – your Saint Eahlstan – brought it together . . .' He paused, remembering. 'There almost was one, and within my time. He was a young Hernystirman, another of Morgenes' discoveries. He had nearly Morgenes' skill, although less caution, so that he studied things Morgenes would not. He had ambitions, and argued that we should make ourselves more of a force for good. He might have one day been the leader you speak of, Josua: a man of great wisdom and strength. . . .'

When the old man did not continue, Josua looked over to see Jarnauga's eyes fixed on the western horizon. 'What happened?' the prince asked. 'Is he dead?'

'No,' Jarnauga answered slowly, eyes still drawn out across the rolling plain, 'no, I do not think so. He . . . changed. Something frightened him, or hurt him, or . . . or something. He left us long ago.'

'So you *do* have failures,' Josua said, starting to walk again. The old man did not follow.

'Oh, certainly,' he said, lifting his hand as if to shade

his brow, staring out into the dim distance. 'Pryrates was one of ours once, too.'

Before the prince could reply to this he was interrupted.

'Josua!' someone cried from the courtyard. The lines around the prince's mouth tightened.

'Lady Vorzheva,' he said, turning to look down to where she stood indignantly in a dress of gleaming red, hair aswirl in the wind like black smoke. Towser skulked uncomfortably at her side. 'What would you of me?' the prince demanded. 'You should be in the keep. As a matter of fact, I *order* you to the keep.'

'I have been there,' she called crossly. Lifting the hem of her dress she ankled toward the stairway, talking as she went. 'And I will soon go back, do you not worry. But first, I must one time more see the sun – or would you rather keep me in a black cell?'

Despite his exasperation, Josua was hard-pressed to keep his face entirely stern. 'Heaven knows that there are windows in the keep, Lady.' He lowered his frown to Towser. 'Can you not at least keep her off the walls, Towser? Soon we are at siege.'

The little man shrugged and limped up the stairs after Vorzheva.

'Show me the armies of your terrible brother,' she said, a little breathless as she reached the prince's side.

'If his armies were here, *you* would not be,' Josua said irritably. 'There is nothing to see, yet. Now please go down.'

'Josua?' Jarnauga was still squinting into the cloudy west. 'I think there *is* perhaps something to see.'

'What?!' In an instant, the prince was beside the old Rimmersman, his body pitched awkwardly against the parapet as he strained to find what the man saw. 'Is it Elias? So soon? I see nothing!' He slapped his palm on the stone in frustration.

'I doubt it is the High King, coming from so westerly a direction,' Jarnauga said. 'Do not be surprised you do not see them. As I told you, I was trained to look where others could not. Nevertheless, they are there: many horses and men – too far away still to guess how many – coming toward us. There.' He pointed.

'Praise Usires!' Josua said, excited. 'You must be right! It can only be Leobardis!' He straightened up, suddenly full of life, even as his face clouded with worry. 'This is delicate,' he said, half to himself. 'The Nabbanai must not come too close, else they will be useless to us, caught between Elias and the walls of Naglimund. Then we shall have to bring them in, where they will be just more mouths to feed.' He strode for the stairs. 'If they stay too far, we will not be able to protect them when Elias turns on them. We must send riders!' He went down the stairs at a bound, shouting for Deornoth and Eadgram, the Lord Constable of Naglimund.

'Oh, Towser,' Vorzheva said, her cheeks flushed with the wind and the pace of events, 'we shall be saved after all! Everything will be better.'

'Just as well with me, my lady,' the jester responded. 'I've been through this all before with my master John, you know . . . and I'm not anxious to do it again.'

Soldiers were cursing and shouting now in the castle courtyard below. Josua stood on the rim of the well, his slender sword in his hand, calling instructions. The sound of metal on metal, as spear butts clanged on shields, and helmets and swords were hurriedly taken from the corners where they had been laid, rose past the walls like an invocation.

Count Aspitis Preves exchanged a few terse words with Benigaris, then pulled his horse up beside the duke's, matching him stride for stride through the high, dewy grass. The dawn sun was a shining smudge above the gray horizon.

'Young Aspitis!' Leobardis said heartily. 'What news?'

If he and his son were to be on better terms, he must try to show kindness to Benigaris' intimates – even to Aspitis, whom he considered one of the Prevan House's less impressive products.

'The scouts have just rejoined us, my lord Duke.' the Count, a handsome, slender youth, was quite pale. 'We are less than five leagues from the walls of Naglimund, my lord.'

'Good! With luck we shall be there in early afternoon!'

'But Elias is ahead of us.' Aspitis looked over to the duke's son, who shook his head and cursed beneath his breath.

'He has already laid the siege in strength?' Leobardis asked, surprised. 'How? Has he learned to make his armies fly?'

'Well, no, lord, it is not Elias,' Aspitis hurried to amend himself, 'it is a large force riding beneath the flag of the Boar and Spears – Earl Guthwulf to Utanyeat's banner. They have a half a league or so on us, and will keep us from the gates.'

The duke shook his head, relieved. 'How many does Guthwulf have?'

'Perhaps a hundred horse, my lord, but the High King cannot be too far behind.'

'Well, little should we care,' Leobardis said, reining up at the edge of one of the many small streams that crisscrossed the meadowlands east of Greenwade. 'Let the High King's Hand and his troop languish there. We are more use to Josua at a short distance, where we can harry the besiegers, and keep the lines of supply open.' With a splash he rode down into the ford. Benigaris and the count spurred after him.

'But father,' Benigaris said, catching up, 'think now! Our scouts say Guthwulf has moved ahead of the king's army, and with only a hundred knights.' Aspitis Preves nodded confirmation, and Benigaris drew his dark brows together in a frown of earnestness. 'We have thrice that, and if we send fast riders ahead we can muster

Josua's forces, too. We could smash Guthwulf against Naglimund's walls as between hammer and anvil.' He grinned, and clapped his father's armored shoulder. 'Think how *that* would sit with King Elias – make him think twice, wouldn't it?'

Leobardis rode silently for a long minute. He looked back at the rippling banners of his legions stretching back several furlongs across the meadows. The sun had, for a moment, found a thinner spot in the overcast, bringing color to the wind-bowed grass. It reminded him of the Lakelands east of his palace.

'Call the trumpeter,' he said, and Aspitis turned and shouted an order.

'Héa! I'll send riders ahead to Naglimund, father,' Benigaris said, smiling almost with relief. The duke could see how much his son longed for glory, but it would be Nabban's glory, too.

'Pick your fastest riders, my son,' he called as Benigaris rode back through the lines. 'For we shall move more swiftly than anyone dreams we can!' He raised his voice to a great shout, turning heads all through the field. 'The legions shall ride! For Nabban and Mother Church! Let our enemies beware!'

Benigaris returned shortly to pronounce the messengers dispatched. Duke Leobardis let the trumpets ring out, then sound again, and the great army set out at speed. Their hoofbeats sounded, rolling like rapid drumbeats in the meadow-dells as they passed out of the Inniscrich. The sun rose in the muddy morning sky, and the banners streamed blue and gold. The Kingfisher flew to Naglimund.

Josua was still pulling on his unadorned, bright-polished helm as he went through the gate at the head of two-score mounted knights. The harper Sangfugol ran alongside, holding something up to him; the prince reined in and slowed his horse to a walk.

'What, man?' he asked impatiently, scanning the misty horizon.

The harper struggled for breath. 'It is . . . your father's banner, Prince Josua,' he said, passing it up. 'Brought . . . out of the Hayholt. You carry no standard but Naglimund's gray Swan – what better one for yourself could you wish?'

The prince stared at the red and white pennant, half-unfolded in his lap. The firedrake's eye glared sternly, as if some interloper threatened the sacred Tree about which it had enwrapped itself. Deornoth and Isorn, with a few of the other knights nearby, smiled expectantly.

'No,' said Josua, handing it back. His look was cold. 'I am not my father. And I am no king.'

He turned, wrapping the reins around his right arm, and lifted his hand.

'Forward!' he shouted. 'We go to meet friends and allies!'

He and his troop rode down through the sloping streets of the town. A few flowers, thrown by well-wishers from atop the castle walls, fluttered into the churned, muddy roadway behind them.

'What do you see there, Rimmersman?' Towser demanded, frowning. 'Why are you mumbling so?'

Josua's small force was now only a colorful blur, fast disappearing in the distance.

'There is a troop of mounted men coming along the rim of the hills to the south,' Jarnauga said. 'It looks from here not a large army, but they are still distant.' He closed his eyes for a moment as if trying to remember something, then reopened them, staring into the distance.

Towser reflexively made the sign of the Tree; the old Rimmersman's eyes were so bright and shone so fiercely, like lamps of sapphire!

'A boar's head on crossed spears,' Jarnauga hissed, 'whose is it?'

'Guthwulf,' Towser said, confused. The Rimmersman might have been watching phantoms, for all the horizon revealed to the old jester. 'Earl of Utanyeat – the King's Hand.' Farther down the wall the Lady Vorzheva stared wistfully after the prince's vanishing horsemen.

'He comes from the south, then, ahead of Elias' full army. It looks as though Leobardis has seen him: the Nabbanai have turned toward the southern hills, as though to engage him.'

'How many . . . how many men?' Towser asked, feeling ever more muddled. 'How can you see such a thing, now? I see nothing, and my sight's the one thing that hasn't . . .'

'A hundred knights, perhaps fewer,' Jarnauga interrupted. 'That's what is troubling: *why are they so few*. . . ?'

'Merciful God! What is the duke up to?' Josua swore, rising in his stirrups to gain better vantage. 'He has turned east and is galloping full tilt toward the southern hills! Has he lost his wits?!'

'My lord, look!' Deornoth shouted across to him. 'Look there, on the skirts of Bullback Hill!'

'By the love of the Aedon, it's the king's army! What is Leobardis doing? Does he think to attack Elias unsupported?' Josua slapped his horse's neck and spurred forward.

'It looks a small force only, Prince Josua,' called Deornoth. 'An advance party, perhaps.'

'Why didn't he send riders?' the prince asked plaintively. 'Look, they will try and push them toward Naglimund, to trap them against the wall. Why in God's name did Leobardis not send riders to me?!' He sighed and turned to Isorn, who had pushed his father's bear-helm back from his brow to better scan the horizon. 'Now we will have our mettle tested after all, friend.'

The inevitability of fighting seemed to have drawn serenity over Josua like a mantle. His eyes were calm, and he wore an odd half-smile. Isorn grinned over at Deornoth, who was loosening his shield from his saddle pommel, then looked back to the prince.

'Let them test it, Lord,' said the duke's son.

'Ride on!' the prince shouted. 'The despoiler of Utanyeat is before us! Ride!' So crying, he spurred his piebald charger into a gallop, making the sod spurt beneath the horse's hooves.

'For Naglimund!' Deornoth shouted, lifting his sword high. 'For Naglimund and our prince!'

'Guthwulf is standing fast!' Jarnauga said. 'He holds on the hillside, even as the Nabbanai come against him. Josua has turned to meet them.'

'They are fighting?' Vorzheva asked, frightened. 'What is happening to the prince?'

'He has not reached the battle – there!' Jarnauga was striding down the wall toward the southwestern turret. 'Guthwulf's knights take the first charge of the Nabbanai! It is all confusion!' He squinted and knuckled his eyes.

'What?! What?!' Towser put a finger in his mouth, staring and gnawing. 'Do not go silent on me, Rimmersman!'

'It is hard to make out what happens from this far,' said Jarnauga, unnecessarily, for neither of his two companions, nor anyone else on the castle walls could see anything but a faint smear of movement in the shadow of misty Bullback Hill. 'The prince bears down on the fighting, and Leobardis' and Guthwulf's knights are scattered along the hillslopes. Now . . . now . . .' He trailed off, concentrating.

'Ah!' said Towser in disgust, slapping his skinny thigh. 'By Saint Muirfath and the Archangel, this is worse than anything I can think of. I might as well read this in . . . in a book! Damn you, man – *speak!*'

Deornoth found it all unfolding before him as in a dream – the murky shimmer of armor, the shouting and the muffled crash of blade on shield. As the prince's troop bore down on the combatants, he saw the faces of the Nabbanai knights come slowly up, and the Erkylanders' too, an eddy of surprise rippling out through the battle at their approach. For a timeless instant he felt himself a fleck of shining foam, prisoned at the crest of a hanging wave. A moment later, with a shocking roar and clash of arms, the battle was all around them, as Josua's knights came full against the flank of Guthwulf's Boar and Spears.

Abruptly there was someone before him, a blank, helmeted face above the rolling eyes and red mouth of a war-charger. Deornoth felt a blow to his shoulder that rocked him in his saddle; the knight's lance struck his shield and slid away. He saw the man's dark surcoat before him for an instant, and swung his sword with both hands, feeling a shivering impact as it caromed past the shield and struck the knight's chest, toppling him from his steed down into the mud and bloodied grass.

For a moment he was clear; he looked around, trying to find Josua's banner, and felt a distant throb in his shoulder. The prince and Isorn, Isgrimnur's son, were fighting back to back in the midst of a swirling surge of Guthwulf's knights. Josua's swift hand darted out, and Naidel pierced the visor of one of the black-crested horsemen. The man's hands flew to his metal-clad face, covered in an instant with red, then he was yanked down out of sight as his reinless horse reared.

Deornoth saw Leobardis, the duke of Nabban, sitting

799

his horse at the farthest southeastern edge of the battle beneath his billowing kingfisher flag. Two knights held their balking horses close by, and Deornoth guessed the large one in the chasework armor to be his son, Benigaris. Damn the man! Duke Leobardis was old, but what was Benigaris doing on the fringe of things?! This was war!

A shape loomed before him, and Deornoth spurred left to dodge a downrushing battleaxe. The rider blew past, unturning, but was followed by another. For a while all was swept from his head but the dance of stroke on stroke as he traded blows with the Utanyeater; the clangor of the field seemed to subside to a dull rush, like the sound of falling water. At last he found an opening in the man's guard and crashed a swordstroke against his helm, crumpling it in at the visor-hinge. The knight toppled sideways and off, his foot caught in the stirrup so that he hung like a butchered hog in a pantry. His maddened horse dragged him away.

Earl Guthwulf, black-mantled and black-helmeted, was now only a stone's throw away, dealing blows left and right with his great broadsword, holding off two blue-coated Nabbanai horsemen as if they were boys. Deornoth leaned down in his saddle to spur toward him – what glory, to trade blows with the Monster of Utanyeat! – when a toppling horse beside him spun his own mount around.

Pausing, still as muddled as if he dreamed, he found he had been driven down the hill toward the outer edge of the battle. The blue and gold banner of Leobardis was before him; the duke, white hair streaming from beneath his helm, stood high in the stirrups shouting exhortations at his men, then pulled his visor down over his bright eyes, preparing to spur forward into the fray.

The dream turned to nightmare as Deornoth watched. The one whom he took for Benigaris, moving so slowly that Deornoth almost felt he could reach out a hand and stop him, pulled back his long blade and carefully, deliberately, pushed it into the back of the duke's neck under the helm. In the milling crowd, with the battle crashing all around them, it seemed that no one but Deornoth saw this terrible act. Leobardis arched his back as the blade was withdrawn, scarlet-streaked, and brought trembling, gauntleted hands up to his throat, holding them there for a moment as if trying to speak through some all-swaying grief. A moment later the duke sagged forward in his saddle, leaning into his horse's white neck and smearing the mane with his unprisoned blood before rolling off his saddle to the ground.

Benigaris looked down for a moment, as if contemplating a bird tumbled from its nest, then tugged his horn to his lips. For a moment, with shouting chaos on every side, Deornoth thought he saw a gleam in the black slot of Benigaris' helmet, as if the duke's son caught his eye across the heads of all the fighting men between them.

The horn sounded, long and harsh, and many heads turned.

'*Tambana Leobardis eis!*' Benigaris bellowed, his voice a dreadful thing, ragged and sorrowful. 'The Duke is down! My father is killed! Fall back!'

He sounded the horn again, and even as Deornoth stared in unbelieving horror there came another horn call from the hillside above them. A line of armored horsemen sprang out of the shadowed concealment of the trees.

'Lights of the North!' Jarnauga groaned, sending Towser into another paroxysm of frustration.

'Tell us! How goes the battle!?'

'I fear it is lost,' the Rimmersman said, his voice a hollow echo. 'Someone has fallen.'

'Oh!' Vorzheva gasped, tears standing in her eyes. 'Josua! It is not Josua?!'

801

'I cannot tell. I think it may be Leobardis. But now another force of men comes down the hillside, out of the trees. Red-coated, on their banner . . . an eagle?'

'Falshire,' Towser groaned, and pulling off his belled hat flung it clattering onto the stone. 'Mother of God, it is Earl Fengbald! Oh, Usires Aedon, save our prince! The whoreson bastards!'

'They ride down on Josua like a hammer,' Jarnauga said. 'And the Nabbanai are confused, I think. They . . . they . . .'

'Fall back!' Benigaris shouted, and Aspitis Preves at his side plucked the banner from the stunned arms of Leobardis' squire, riding the young man down beneath his horse's hooves.

'They are too many!' Aspitis cried. 'Retreat! The duke is dead!'

Deornoth pulled his horse around and plunged back through the melee toward Josua.

'A trap!' he shouted. Fengbald's knights were thundering down the hillside, lances agleam. 'It is a trap, Josua!'

He cut his way through two of Guthwulf's Boars who would have blocked his path, taking hard blows on his shield and helm, running the second man straight through the throat and almost losing his sword as it stuck in the spine. He saw a rill of blood run past his visor, and did not know if it was some other's or his own.

The prince was calling back his knights, Isorn's horn blaring above the screaming and clashing of arms.

'Benigaris has killed the duke!' Deornoth cried. Josua looked up, startled, as the blood-stained figure bore down on him. 'Benigaris has stabbed him in the back! We are trapped!'

For a brief instant the prince hesitated, lifting his hand as though to raise his visor and look around. Fengbald

802

and his Eagles had pitched toward the Naglimunders' flank, trying to cut them off from their retreat.

A moment later the prince raised his rein-wrapped shield arm. 'Your horn, Isorn!' he shouted. 'We must cut our way out! Back! Back to Naglimund! We are betrayed!'

With a blast of the horn and a great cry of anger, the prince's knights surged forward, directly into Fengbald's wide-strung crimson line. Deornoth goaded his horse forward, trying to reach the front, and watched as Josua's whirling blade snaked through the guard of the first Eagle, striking serpentlike beneath the man's arm, in and out. A moment later Deornoth found a host of red-surcoats before him. He swung his blade, and cursed; although he did not know it, beneath his helm his cheeks were wet with tears.

Fengbald's men, startled by the ferocity of their attackers, wheeled slowly about, and in that instant the Naglimunders broke through. Behind them the Nabbanai legions were in full retreat, flying brokenly back toward the Inniscrich. Guthwulf did not pursue them, but rather sent his troops to join Fengbald in pursuit of Josua's fleeing knights.

Deornoth hugged his charger's neck. He could hear its breath rasping as they galloped full out, back across the meadows and fallow farmland. The sound of pursuit gradually fell away as the walls of Naglimund rose ahead.

The gate was raised, a black, open mouth. Staring at it, his head throbbing like a beaten drum. Deornoth suddenly wanted very much to be swallowed – to go sliding down into deep, lightless oblivion, and never come out again.

# 40

# The Green Tent

'No, Prince Josua. We cannot allow you to do such a foolish thing.' Isorn sat down heavily, favoring his leg.

'Cannot?' The prince lifted his gaze from the floor to the Rimmersman. 'Are you my keepers? Am I a child-regent or an idiot, that I should be told what to do?'

'My prince,' Deornoth said, resting a hand on Isorn's knee to urge him to silence, 'you are master here, of course. Do we not follow you? Have we not all sworn our allegiance?' Heads around the room nodded somberly. 'But you ask much of us, you must know that. After such treachery as has been done to us, do you really think you can trust the king at all?'

'I know him as none of you do,' Josua, as if burned by some inner fire, leaped up from his chair and paced to his table. 'He wants me dead, certainly, but not this way. Not so dishonorably. If he swears safe conduct – and if we avoid obvious stupidity – then I will return unharmed. He still wants to act the High King, and the High King does not slay his brother unarmed beneath a flag of truce.'

'Then why did he throw you in th'cell you told of?' asked Ethelferth of Tinsett, scowling. 'Are you thinkin' that's proof of honor?'

'No,' Josua replied, 'but I don't think that was Elias' idea. I see no other hand but Pryrates' there – at least until

after the deed was done. Elias has become a monster –
God help me, for he was my brother once in more than
blood – but he still has a queer sense of honor, I think.'

Deornoth hissed air. 'Such as he showed to Leobardis?'

'The honor of a wolf, who slays the weak and flees the
strong,' Isorn sneered.

'I think not.' Josua's patient grimace was stretched
tighter. 'Benigaris' patricide has the feeling of a grudge,
to me. I suspect that Elias . . .'

'Prince Josua, with your pardon . . .' Jarnauga interrupted, raising eyebrows around the room. 'Do you not
think you are stretching to find excuses for your brother?
These are useful concerns that your liegemen have. Just
because Elias asks for parley does not mean you are
bound to go to him. No one will question your honor if
you do not.'

'*Aedon save me*, man, I care not a *whit* for what anyone
thinks of my honor!' the prince snapped. 'I know my
brother, and I know him in ways none of you can
understand – and don't tell me he has changed, Jarnauga,'
he glared, forestalling the old man's words, 'for no one
knows that better than I do. But nevertheless I will go,
and I need not explain any more. I wish you all to leave
me, now. I have other matters to think on.'

Turning from the table, he waved them from the
room.

'Has he gone mad, Deornoth?' Isorn asked, his wide face
heavy with apprehension. 'How can he walk into the
king's bloody hands this way?'

'Stubbornness, Isorn – oh, who am I to say? Perhaps he
*does* know what he speaks of.' Deornoth shook his head.
'Is that damned thing still there?'

'The tent? Yes. Just out of bowshot from the walls –
also well out of range of Elias' encampment, as well.'

Deornoth walked slowly, allowing the young Rimmersman to set the pace his wounded leg demanded.
'God save us, Isorn, I have never seen him like this, and I

have served him since I was old enough to draw sword. It is as if he seeks to prove Gwythinn wrong, who called him "reluctant." ' Deornoth sighed. 'Welladay, if there is no stopping him, we must then do our best to protect him. The king's herald said two guards, no more?'

'And for the king the same.'

Deornoth nodded, thinking. 'If this arm of mine,' he indicated the white linen sling, 'is movable by the day past tomorrow, then no force on earth will keep me from being one of those guards.'

'And I shall be the other,' Isorn said.

'I think better you should be inside the walls with a score or so mounted men. Let us speak to the Lord Constable Eadgram. If there is an ambush – if even a sparrow is seen to fly from the king's camp toward that tent – you can be there in a few heartbeats.'

Isorn nodded. 'I suppose. Perhaps we can talk to the wise man Jarnauga, ask him to give Josua some charm to protect him.'

'What he needs, and it hurts me to say it, is a spell to protect him against his own rashness.' Deornoth stepped over a large puddle. 'Anyway, no charm is proof against a dagger in the back.'

Lluth's lips were in constant, silent movement, as though offering an endless series of explanations. His mumbling had slipped over into soundlessness the day before; Maegwin cursed herself for not having taken note of his last words, but she had been sure he would find voice again, as he had many times before since his wounding. This time, she could sense, he would not.

The king's eyes were closed, but his wax-pale face worked ceaselessly through changing expressions of fear and sorrow. Touching his burning forehead, feeling the muscles flexing weakly in the unfulfilled rhythms of speech, she again felt as though she *must* cry, as though the tears welling inside her, unshed, would eventually force their way out through her very skin. But she had not wept since the night her father had led the army out into the Inniscrich – not even when they had brought him back in a litter, maddened by pain, the yards of cloth bandaging his stomach soggy with dark blood. If she had not cried then, she never would again. Tears were for children and idiots.

A hand touched her shoulder. 'Maegwin. Princess.' It was Eolair, his clever face folded in grief as neatly as a summer robe stored for the winter. 'I must speak to you outside.'

'Go away, Count,' she said, looking back to the rough bed of logs and straw. 'My father is dying.'

'I share your grief, Lady.' His touch was heavier, like an animal nosing blindly in the dark. 'Believe me, I do. But the living must live, the gods know, and your people have need of you this moment.' As if he felt his words too cold, too proud, he gave her arm a brief squeeze and let go. 'Please. Lluth ubh-Llythinn would not want it any other way.'

Maegwin bit back a bitter rejoinder. He was right, of course. She stood, her knees aching from the stone cavern floor, and followed him past her silent stepmother Inahwen, who sat at the foot of the bed staring at the guttering torches on the wall.

*Look at us*, Maegwin thought, wonderingly. *It took the Hernystiri a thousand, thousand years to crawl out of the caves into the sunlight.* She ducked her head to pass beneath the low spot of the cavern ceiling, squinting her eyes against the gritty torchsmoke. *And yet, it has taken less than a month to drive us back in again. We are becoming animals. The gods have turned their backs on us.*

She lifted her head up again as she emerged into daylight behind Eolair. The clutter of the daytime camp was all around her; carefully-watched children playing on the muddy ground, court women – many in the tatters of their best clothing – on their knees preparing squirrel and hare for the stew pot and grinding grain on flat stones. The trees growing close all around on the rock-studded slope of the mountain bent grudgingly to the wind.

The men were nearly all gone; those not dead on the Inniscrich or having their wounds tended in the honeycomb of caves were out hunting, or guarding the lower slopes against any move by Skali's army to finally crush Hernystir's battered resistance.

*All we have left are memories*, she thought, looking down at her own stained and ragged skirt, *and the hiding holes of the Grianspog. We are treed like a fox. When Elias the master comes to take the prey from his hound Skali, we are finished.*

'What is it you want, Count Eolair?' she asked.

'It is not what I am wanting, Maegwin,' he said, shaking his head. 'It's Skali. Some of the sentries came back to say he's been down at the bottom of the Moir Brach all morning, shouting for your father.'

'Let the pig shout,' Maegwin scowled. 'Why doesn't one of the *men* put an arrow into his dirty hide?'

'He's not near in bowshot, princess. And he has half a hundred men with him. No, I think we should go down and listen to him – from cover, of course, out of sight.'

'Of course,' she said scornfully. 'Why should we care what Sharpnose has to say? Come to demand surrender again, I don't doubt.'

'Possibly.' Count Eolair lowered his eyes, thinking, and Maegwin felt a rush of sorrow for him, that he should have to bear up under her ill will. 'But I think there is something else here, Lady. He has been there an hour and more, the men say.'

'Very well,' she said, wanting to get away from Lluth's dark bed, and hating herself for the wish. 'Let me put on my shoes and I will come with you.'

It took the better part of an hour to climb down the forested mountain side. The ground was wet and the air was chilly; Maegwin's breath rushed out in little clouds as she picked her way down the gullies after Eolair. The gray cold had driven the birds out of the Circoille, or numbed them into silence. No sound accompanied their passing but the shivering murmur of wind-raked branches.

Watching the Count of Nad Mullach making his nimble way through the undergrowth, so like a child with his slender back and shiny tail of hair, with his movements so quick and unthinking, Maegwin was again filled with a dull, hopeless love for him. It seemed such a ridiculous way for her to feel – tall, gawky child of a dying man – that it turned into a kind of anger. When Eolair turned back to help her over a jutting stone, she frowned as if he had offered her insult instead of his hand.

The men huddled in the copse of trees overlooking the long ridge called Moir Brach looked up in startlement at the approach of Eolair and Maegwin, but quickly lowered their bows again and beckoned the pair forward. Peering through the bracken down the finger of stone for which the ridge was named, she saw a milling crowd of antlike shapes at the bottom, some three furlongs away.

'He just stopped speaking a moment ago,' one of the sentries whispered – a young boy, eyes wide with nervousness. 'He'll start again, Princess, you'll see.'

As if in planned confirmation, one of the figures strode out from the throng of men in helmets and capes who surrounded a wagon and team of horses. The figure raised his hands to his mouth and stood facing slightly to the north of the watchers' hiding-place.

'. . . the last time . . .' his voice drifted up, muffled by distance. 'I offer you . . . hostages . . . return for . . .'

Maegwin strained to make out the words. *Information?*

'. . . about the wizard's boy, and . . . princess.'

Eolair snapped a glance over to Maegwin, who sat stock-still. What did they want with her?

'If you do not tell . . . where . . . princess is . . . we will . . . these hostages.'

The man who spoke – and Maegwin was sure in her heart it was Skali himself, just from the wide-legged stance, and the sour, mocking tone that even distance could not wholly obscure – waved an arm, and a struggling figure in a rag of light blue was taken from the wagon and brought to where he stood. Maegwin stared, feeling an ugly pressure on her heart. She was sure that light blue dress belonged to Cifgha . . . little Cifgha, pretty and stupid.

'. . . If you do *not* tell us . . . you know . . . the princess Miriamele, things . . . poorly for these . . .' Skali gestured and the kicking, thinly crying girl – who might not *really* be Cifgha, Maegwin tried to tell herself – was thrown back onto the wagon, amidst other pale captives, lying in a row on the wagon bed like fingers.

So, it was the princess Miriamele they sought, she marveled – the High King's daughter! Had she run away? Been stolen?

'Can't we do *anything*?' she whispered to Eolair. 'And who is "the wizard's boy"?'

The count shook his head roughly, frustration in every line of his face. 'What could we do, princess? Skali'd like nothing more than to have us come down. He has ten times the men we have!'

Long minutes passed in silence as Maegwin watched, fury tugging at her emotions like a demanding child. She was thinking of what else to say to Eolair and these others – how she'd tell them that if none of the *men* wanted to go with her, she'd go down to the Taig herself and rescue Skali's captives . . . or, more likely, die bravely in the attempt – when the thickset figure below, helmet off now, showing the tiny yellow smudge that was his hair and beard, walked back out to the base of the Moir Brach.

'Very well!' he roared. '. . . And Lokën curse . . . stiff backs! We . . . and take these with . . .' The little figure pointed at the wagon. 'But . . . leave you a *gift!*' Something was untied from one of the horses, a dark bundle, and dumped at Skali Sharp-nose's feet. 'Just in case . . . waiting for help! . . . Little use against . . . Kaldskryke!'

A moment later he mounted his horse, and with the harsh rasp of a horn he and his Rimmersmen clattered off up the valley toward Hernysadharc, the wagon bumping along behind them.

They waited an hour before making their way cautiously down the bank, moving as watchfully as a doe crossing a clearing. Reaching the bottom of the Moir Brach, they scuttled to the black-wrapped bundle Skali had left behind.

When it was opened the men cried out in horror and wept, great racking sobs of helpless grief . . . but Maegwin did not shed a tear, even when she saw what Skali and his butchers had done to her brother Gwythinn before he died. When Eolair put an arm around her shoulders to help her away from the blood-soaked blanket she shook him off angrily, then turned and slapped hard at his cheek. He did not protect himself, but only stared at her. The tears that filled his eyes, she knew, were not from the blow – and in that moment it made her hate him all the more.

But her own eyes remained dry.

Flakes of snow filled the air – confusing vision, weighting garments, chilling fingers and ears to a painful tingle – but Jiriki and his three Sithi companions seemed not to mind it much. As Simon and the others plodded along on their horses, the Sithi walked jauntily ahead, often stopping to wait for the riders to catch up, patient as well-fed cats, an indecipherable serenity behind their luminous eyes. Walking all day from sunrise to twilight, Jiriki and his fellows nevertheless seemed as lightfooted around the camp that night as they had at dawn.

811

Simon hesitantly approached An'nai while the others hunted deadwood for the evening's fire.

'May I ask you some questions?' he asked.

The Sitha lifted his imperturbable stare. 'Ask.'

'Why was Prince Jiriki's uncle angry that he decided to come with us? And why did he bring you three along?'

An'nai brought a spidery hand up to his mouth as though to cover a smile, although no smile had been present. A moment later he lowered it again, revealing the same impassive expression.

'What passes between the prince and S'hue Khendraja'aro is not mine to hold, so I cannot share it, either.' He nodded once, gravely. 'As to the other, perhaps he can best answer it himself . . . yes, Jiriki?'

Simon looked up, startled, to find the prince standing behind him, thin lips taut in a smile.

'Why did I bring these?' Jiriki asked, making a sweeping gesture from An'nai to the other two Sithi, returning from a search around the thickly-forested perimeter of the camping-place. 'Ki'ushapo and Sijandi I brought because someone must look after the horses.'

'Look after the horses?'

Jiriki raised an eyebrow, then snapped his fingers. 'Troll,' he called over his shoulder, 'if this manchild is your student, then you are a poor teacher indeed! Yes, Seoman, the horses – or did you expect to see them climb the mountains beside you?'

Simon was flummoxed. 'But . . . climb? The horses? I didn't think about . . . I mean to say, couldn't we just leave them. Let them go?' It did not seem fair; he had never felt much more than a dangling tassel on his journey – except, of course, for the White Arrow – and now the Sitha was holding him accountable for the horses!

'Let them go?' Jiriki's voice was harsh, almost angry, but his face was bland. 'Leave them to perish, you mean? Once they have been ridden far beyond where they would themselves go, we would free them to struggle back across the snowy wastes or die?'

Simon was about to protest, to point out that it wasn't *his* responsibility, but decided it was not worth arguing.

'No,' he said instead. 'No, we should not leave them alone to die.'

'Beside,' Sludig said, walking by with an armload of wood, 'how then would we get back across the wastes ourselves?'

'Exactly,' said Jiriki, his smile stretching; he was pleased. 'So I bring Ki'ushapo and Sijandi. They will tend the horses and prepare things for my . . . for our return.' He brought the tips of his two index figures together, as if to indicate some kind of completion. 'Now, An'nai,' he continued, 'is a more complex matter. His reason for being here is more like mine.' He looked down at the other Sitha.

'Honor,' An'nai said, eyes downcast, staring at his own interlaced fingers. 'I bound the *Hikka Sta'ja* – the Arrow-Bearer. I did not show proper respect for a . . . sacred guest. Thus, I come to atone.'

'A small debt,' Jiriki said softly, 'when compared with my great one, but An'nai will do what he must.'

Simon wondered if An'nai had decided on his own, or if Jiriki had somehow forced him to join them. It was hard to know anything about these Sithi, how they thought, what they wanted. They were so damnably different, so slow and so subtle!

'Come now,' Binabik announced. A tiny streamer of flame wavered before him, and he fanned it with his hands. 'Now we are starting a fire, and I am sure you will all be interested in a little food and wine, for the warming of inner spaces.'

In the next few days' riding they left the northern Aldehorte behind, coming down off the last decrement of the Wealdhelm hills onto the flat, snow-swept waste.

There was always cold, now, every long night, every dreary white day – bitter, biting cold. The snow flew continuously into Simon's face, stinging his eyes, burning and cracking his lips. His face reddened painfully, as if he had gone too long in the sun, and he could hardly hold the reins of his horse for shivering. It was like being thrown out of doors forever, a punishment that had gone on too long. Still, there was nothing he could do to remedy the situation but offer silent prayers to Usires each day for the strength to last until camp was made.

*At least*, he reflected sadly, his ears stinging even beneath the hooded cloak, *at least Binabik is having a good time*.

The troll was, indeed, in his very element – riding ahead, urging his companions on, laughing from time to time for sheer pleasure as he and Qantaqa leaped along the mounting drifts. Long evenings around the fire, while the other mortal companions shivered and oiled their sleet-saturated gloves and boots, Binabik detailed the different types of snow, and the various signals portending avalanches, all to prepare them for the mountains that loomed implacably on the horizon before them, stern and judgmental as gods in their crowns of white snow.

Every day the great range before them seemed larger without ever seeming a foot closer, no matter how far they rode. After a week in the warmthless, featureless wastes, Simon began to long for the ill-rumored Dimmerskog forest, or even the wind-lashed heights of the mountains themselves – anything but this endless, bone-chilling plain of snow.

They passed the ruins of Saint Skendi's abbey on the sixth day. It was nearly covered in snowdrifts: only the spire of the chapel protruded more than a short distance above the surface, an iron Tree encircled by the coils of some serpentine beast crowning its rotting roof. Rising up through the frost-laden mist before them, it might have been a ship near-sunken in a sea of purest white.

'Whatever secrets it may be holding – whatever it

knows of Colmund or the sword Thorn – it is holding them too tightly for us,' Binabik said as their horses trudged past the drowning abbey. Sludig made a Tree on his forehead and heart, his eyes troubled, but the Sithi circled slowly, staring as though they had never seen anything quite so interesting.

As the travelers huddled around the campfire that night, Sludig demanded to know why Jiriki and his comrades had spent so much time examining the lost monastery.

'Because,' the prince said, 'we found it pleasing.'

'What does that mean?' Sludig asked in irritated puzzlement, looking to Haestan and Grimmric as if they might know what the Sitha meant.

'It is better not to speak of these things, perhaps,' said An'nai, making a flattening gesture with his spread fingers. 'We are companions at this fire.'

Jiriki looked solemnly into the fire for a moment, then his face split in an odd, mischievous grin. Simon marveled; sometimes it was hard to think of Jiriki as being any older than himself, so young and reckless did his behavior occasionally seem. But Simon also remembered the cavern overlooking the forest. Youth and great age mixed confusedly together; that was what Jiriki was like.

'We stare at things that interest us,' Jiriki said, 'just as mortals do. It is only the reasons that are different, and ours you would probably not understand.' His wide smile seemed completely friendly, but now Simon detected a discordant note, something out of place.

'The question, northman,' Jiriki continued, 'is why should our staring offend you so?'

For a moment silence descended over the fire circle as Sludig stared hard at the Sithi prince. The flames popped and sputtered on the damp wood, and the wind hooted, making the horses shift nervously.

Sludig lowered his eyes. 'You may look at what you please, of course,' he said, smiling sadly; his blond beard was flecked with melting snow. 'It is only that it reminded me of Saegard – of the Skipphavven. It was as if you mocked something dear to me.'

'Skipphavven?' Haestan rumbled, sunk in his furs. 'Never heard of't. Is't a church?'

'Boats . . .' Grimmric said, screwing up his narrow face in remembrance. 'There's boats there.'

Sludig nodded, face serious. 'You would say Ship-haven. It is where the longships of Rimmersgard lie.'

'But Rimmersmen dunna' sail!' Haestan was sur-prised. 'In all Osten Ard, no other race be so landbound!'

'Ah, but we did.' Sludig's face glowed with reflected firelight. 'Before we came across the sea – when we lived in Ijsgard, in the lost West – our fathers burned men and buried ships. At least, that is what our tales say.'

'Burned men. . . ?' Simon wondered.

'The dead,' Sludig explained. 'Our fathers built death-ships of new ashwood and put the dead to flame on the water, sending their souls up with the smoke. But our great longships, those that carried us on the world's oceans and rivers – the ships that were our lives as surely as a cotsman's acre or a shepherd's flock – those we buried in the ground when they were too old to be seaworthy, so that their souls would go into the trees, and make them grow straight and tall to become new ships.'

'But that was across th'ocean y'said – long ago,' Grimmric pointed out. 'Saegard is here is't not? In Osten Ard?'

The Sithi around the fire were silent and unmoving, watching intently as Sludig answered.

'It is. That is where the keel of Elvrit's boat first touched land, and where he said; "We have come across the black ocean to a new home." '

Sludig looked around the circle. 'They buried the great longships there. "Never will we go back across that dragon-haunted sea," Elvrit said. All along the valley floor of Saegard at the mountains' feet lie the mounds of the last ships. On the headland at the water's edge, beneath the biggest howe, they buried Elvrit's ship Sotfengsel, leaving only its tall mast thrusting up from the earth like a tree with no branches – it was that I saw in my mind when I saw the abbey.'

He shook his head, eyes bright with memories. 'Mistletoe grows on Sotfengsel's mast. Every year, on the day of Elvrit's death, the white berries of the mistletoe are gathered by young maidens of Saegard, and taken to the church . . .'

Sludig trailed off. The fire hissed.

'What you do not tell,' Jiriki said after a while, 'is how your Rimmersgard people came to this land only to drive others from it.'

Simon breathed in sharply. He had sensed something like this beneath the prince's placid surface.

Sludig replied with surprising mildness, perhaps still thinking of the pious maidens of Saegard. 'I cannot undo what my ancestors have done.'

'There is truth to that,' Jiriki said, 'but neither will we *Zida'ya* – we Sithi – make the same mistake our kin made before us.' He turned his fierce stare on Binabik, who met it solemnly. 'Some things should be made clear between us all, Binbiniqegabenik. I spoke only truth when I gave my reasons for accompanying you: some interest that I have in where you go, and a frail, unusual bond between the manchild and myself. Do not for a moment believe that I share your fears or struggles. As far as I am concerned, you and your High King may grind each other to dust.'

'With respectfulness, Prince Jiriki,' Binabik said, 'you are not examining the full truth. If it was only the struggling of mortal kings and princes that concerned us, we would all of us be defending Naglimund. You know that we five, at least, are having other goals.'

'Then know *this*,' Jiriki said stiffly. 'Though the years that have passed since we were sundered from the *Hikeda'ya* – those you call the Norns – are as numerous as snowflakes, still we are one blood. How could we take

817

the side of upstart men against our kin? Why should we, when once we walked together beneath the sun, coming out of the ultimate East? What allegiance could we possibly owe to mortals, who have destroyed us as eagerly as they destroy all else . . . even themselves?

None of the humans but Binabik could meet his cold gaze. Jiriki lifted a long finger before him. 'And the one you whisperingly call the Storm King . . . he whose name was *Ineluki* . . .' He smiled bitterly as the companions stirred and shivered. 'Ah, even his name is fearsome! He was the best of us once – beautiful to see, wise far beyond the understanding of mortals, bright-burning as a flame! – if he is now a thing of dark horror, cold and hateful, whose is the fault? If now, bodiless and vengeful, he schemes to brush mankind from the face of his land like dust from a page – *why should we not rejoice*? It was not Ineluki who drove us into exile, so that we must hide among Aldheorte's dark trees like deer, wary always of discovery. We strode Osten Ard in the sunlight before men came, and the works of our hands were beautiful beneath the stars. What have mortals ever brought to us but suffering?!'

No one could make reply, but in the stillness after Jiriki's words a plaintive, quiet sound arose. It hovered in the darkness, full of unknown words, a melody of spectral beauty.

When he had finishing singing, An'nai looked to his silent prince and his Sithi companions, then to those who faced them across the dancing flames.

'It is a song of ours that mortals once sang,' he murmured. 'The western men loved it of old, and gave it words in their tongue. I will . . . I will try to give it words in yours.'

He looked up into the sky as he thought. The wind was slowing, and as the snow flurries died the stars shone through, cold and remote.

'Moss grows on the stones of Sení Ojhisá.'

An'nai sang at last, the clicks and liquid vowels of Sithi speech muted.

> 'The shadows are lingering, still as if listening
> The trees have embraced Da'ai Chikiza's bright towers
> The shadows all whispering, dark on the leaves.
>
> Long grass is waving above Enki-e-Sha'osaye
> The shadows are growing, upon the sward lengthening
> The grave of Nenais'u wears a mantle of flowers
> The shadowed brook silent, and no one there grieves.
>
> Where are they gone?
> Now the woods are all silence.
> Where are they gone?
> The song vanished away.
> Why will they come no more
> Dancing at twilight?
> Their lamps the stars' messengers
> At ending of day . . .

As An'nai's voice rose, caressing the mournful words, Simon felt a longing such as he had never felt – a homesickness for a home he had never known, a sense of loss over something that had never belonged to him. No one spoke as An'nai sang. No one could have.

> 'Sea beats above the dark streets of Jhiná-T'seneí
> The shadows are hiding, in deep grottoes slumbering
> Blue ice freezes Tumet'ai, entombs its sweet bowers
> The shadows have stained all the pattern Time weaves.
>
> Where are they gone?
> Now the woods are all silence.
> Where are they gone?
> The song vanished away.
> Why will they come no more

> *Dancing at twilight?*
> *Their lamps the stars' messengers*
> *At ending of day . . .'*

The song ended. The fire was a solitary bright spot in a wasteland of shadows.

The green tent stood by itself in the damp emptiness of the plain before the walls of Naglimund. Its sides heaved and rippled in the wind, as though it alone, of all the other things that might move unseen in that vastly open place, was breathingly alive.

Gritting his teeth against a superstitious shiver, although the dank, knifelike wind was reason enough to let them go a-chattering, Deornoth looked over to Josua, riding slightly ahead.

*Look at him,* he thought. *It's as though he saw his brother already – just as if his eyes could seee right through the green silk and the black dragon crest, right into Elias' heart.*

Gazing back to the third and last member of their party, Deornoth felt his heavy heart sink further. The young soldier whom Josua had insisted on bringing – Ostrael, his name was – looked ready to faint from pure fright. His blunt, square features, their sun-reddening faded now by the sunless weeks of spring, were screwed tight in barely-suppressed terror.

*Th'Aedon save us if he's got to be any use. Why on earth did Josua pick him?*

As they slowly approached, the tent flap parted. Deornoth tensed, ready to grab for his bow. He had an instant to curse himself for allowing his prince to do such a foolish, foolish thing as this, but the green-cloaked soldier who emerged only looked up at them incuriously, then stepped to the side of the door, holding the flap open.

Deornoth signed respectfully for Josua to wait and

spurred his horse into a quick circuit of the green tent. It was large, a dozen paces or more on each side, and the guy ropes thrummed with the wind-buffeted weight of it, but the flattened grass all around was empty of ambushers.

'Very well, Ostrael,' he said, returning, 'you will stand here, next to this man,' he indicated the other soldier, 'with at least one of your shoulders visible in the doorway at all times, yes?'

Taking the young pikeman's sickly smile for an affirmative, Deornoth turned to the king's guard. The man's bearded face was familiar; doubtless he had seen him at the Hayholt. 'If you, too, would stand near the doorway, it would be better for all concerned.'

The guard showed him a curled lip, but edged a step nearer the entrance.

Josua had already dismounted and moved to the door, but Deornoth stepped quickly through ahead of him with one hand resting lightly on his sword hilt.

'There is scarcely need for such caution, Deornoth,' a soft but penetrating voice said, 'that is your name, is it not? After all, we are all gentlemen here.'

Deornoth blinked as Josua stepped in behind him. It was bitingly cold inside, and dark. The walls glowed faintly, letting in only a green fraction of the light outside, as though the tent's occupants floated inside a huge but imperfectly-cut emerald.

A pale face loomed before him, the black eyes pinpoint holes into nothingness. Pryrates' scarlet robe was rusty brown in the green murk, the color of dried blood. 'And Josua!' he said, horrible levity in his voice. 'We meet again. Who would ever have thought so many things would have happened since our last conversation. . . ?'

'Shut your mouth, priest – or whatever you are,' the prince snapped back. There was such cold strength in his voice that even Pryrates blinked in surprise, like a startled lizard. 'Where is my brother?'

'I am here, Josua,' a voice said, a deep, cracked whisper that seemed to echo the wind.

A figure sat in a high-backed chair in the corner of the tent, a low table resting nearby, another chair before it – the only furniture in the huge shadowy tent. Josua moved closer. Deornoth pulled his cloak tighter, and followed, more from an urge not to be left with Pryrates than any hurry to see the king.

The prince took the chair facing his brother. Elias, sat, strangely stiff, his eyes bright as gems in his hawkish face, his black hair and pale brow bound by the iron crown of the Hayholt. Propped between his legs was a sword, scabbarded in black leather. The High King's powerful hands rested on the pommel, above the strange double hilt. Although he stared for a moment, Deornoth's eyes did not want to rest on the sword; it gave him a queasy, unwell feeling, like glancing down from some great height. Instead he looked back up to the king, but this was scarcely better: in the freezing cold of the tent, the air so chill that a mist of breath hung before Deornoth's own eyes, Elias wore only a sleeveless jerkin, his white arms bare to his heavy bracelets, the sinews pulsing beneath the skin as though they had a life of their own.

'So, brother,' the king said, baring his teeth in a smile, 'you are looking well.'

'As you are not,' Josua said flatly, but Deornoth could see the worried pinch of his eyes. Something was terribly wrong here; anyone could sense it. 'You called for the parley, Elias. What do you want?'

The king narrowed his eyes, masking them in green shadow, and waited a long while before he replied. 'My daughter. I want my daughter. There is another, too . . . a boy – but he is less important. No, it is Miriamele I chiefly want. If you hand her over to me, I will give my word of safe conduct to all children and womenfolk in Naglimund. Otherwise, all who hide behind its walls and thwart me . . . will die.'

He said this last with such casual lack of malice that Deornoth was startled by the hungry look that flitted nakedly across his face.

'I do not have her, Elias,' Josua replied slowly.

'Where is she?'

'I do not know.'

'*Liar!*' The king's voice was so full of anger that Deornoth almost drew his sword, expecting Elias to leap from his chair. Instead, the king remained nearly motionless, only gesturing for Pryrates to refill his goblet from a ewer full of some black fluid.

'Do not think me a bad host for not offering you any,' Elias said after he had taken a long swallow; he smiled grimly. 'I fear this liquor would not agree with you.' He handed the cup to Pryrates, who took it gingerly between his fingertips and lowered it to the table. 'Now,' Elias resumed, his tone almost reasonable, 'can we not spare ourselves this useless byplay? I want my daughter, and I will have her.' His tone turned grotesquely plaintive. 'Does not a father have a right to the daughter he loved and raised?'

Josua took a deep breath. 'What rights you have are between you and her. I do not have her, and I would not give her unwilling to you if I did.' He continued hastily, before the king could respond. 'Come, Elias, please – you were my brother once, in all things. Our father loved us both, you more than me, but he loved this land more. Can you not see what you are doing? Not just with this struggle – Aedon knows this land has seen war a–plenty. But there is something else here. Pryrates knows what I speak of. He it was that guided your first steps down the path, I do not doubt!'

Deornoth saw Pryrates turn, spewing a surprised cloud of breath at the prince's words.

'Please, Elias,' Josua said, his stern face full of woe. 'Turn back only from the course you have chosen, send that cursed sword back to those unholy ones who would poison you *and* Osten Ard . . . and I will lay my life in your hands. I will open Naglimund's gates to you as a maiden unshuts her window for a lover! I will turn every stone in heaven and earth to find Miriamele! Throw away the sword, Elias! Throw it away! Not by accident was it named Sorrow!'

The king stared at Josua as if stunned. Pryrates, muttering, rushed forward, but Deornoth leaped and caught him. The priest squirmed beneath his restraining arm like a snake, and his touch was horrible, but Deornoth held fast.

'Do not move!' he hissed in Pryrates' ear. 'Though you blast me with a spell, still I will cut the life from you before I die!' He prodded the side of the scarlet robe with his drawn dagger, just far enough to touch cloaked flesh. 'You have no place in this – neither do I! This is between brothers.'

Pryrates became quiet. Josua was leaning forward, staring at the High King. Elias looked on, as though he had trouble seeing what was before him.

'She is beautiful, my Miriamele,' he half-whispered. 'In her I sometimes see her mother Hylissa – poor, dead girl!' The king's face, frozen a moment before in malice, collapsed into confusion. 'How could Josua have let it happen? How could he? She was so young. . . .'

Groping, his white hand reached out. Josua held his own out too late. Instead of catching it, the king's long, cold fingers alighted on the leatherbound stump of the prince's right wrist. His eyes flared into life, and his face stiffened into a mask of rage.

'Go to your hiding-hole, traitor!' he snarled as Josua snatched his arm away. 'Liar! *Liar!* I will shake it down around your ears!'

Such hatred beat out from the king that Deornoth staggered back, letting Pryrates wriggle free.

'*I will ruin you so completely,*' Elias thundered, squirming in his chair as Josua walked to the tent door, '*that God All-powerful will search a thousand years and never find even your **soul***!'

*The young soldier Ostrael was so terrified by the faces of Deornoth and the prince that he wept silently all the wind-wracked way back to Naglimund's brooding walls.*

# 41

# Cold Fire and
# Grudging Stone

The dream gradually receded, melting like mist, a terrifying dream in which he was surrounded by choking green sea. There was no up or down, only sourceless light all around, and a host of slicing shadows, sharks, each one with the lifeless black eyes of Pryrates.

As the sea slid away, Deornoth broke surface, flailing up out of sleep into bleary half-wakefulness. The walls of the guard barracks were spotted with cold moonlight, and the steady breathing of the other men was like the wind pushing through dry leaves.

Even as his heart fluttered swiftly in his breast he felt sleep reaching out again to reclaim his exhausted soul, soothing him with feathery fingers, whispering voicelessly in his ear. He began to slide back, the tidal pull of dream gentler than before. This time it carried him toward a brighter place, a place of morning damp and gentle noontime sun: his father's freeholding in Hewenshire, where he had grown up working in the fields beside his sisters and older brother. A part of him had not left the barracks – it was before dawn, he knew, the ninth day of Yuven – but another part had fallen back into the past. Again he smelled the musk of turned earth, and heard the patient creaking of the plow traces and the measured chirp of cart wheels as the ox pulled the wagon down the road toward market.

The creaking became louder, even as the pungent, muddy smell of the furrows began to fade. The plow was coming closer; the wain sounded to be just behind. Were the ox-drivers asleep? Had someone let the oxen wander trampling into the fields? He felt a childish horror.

*My Da'll be right mad – was't me? Was I s'posed to watch 'em?* He knew how his father would look, the puckered, rage-mottled face that would hear no excuse, the face, young Deornoth had always thought, of God sending a sinner down to Hell. *Mother Elysia. Da's goin' t' get th' strop to me, sure. . . .*

He sat upright on his pallet, breathing hard. His heart was stumbling as badly as after the shark-dream, but it began to slow as he looked around the barracks.

*How long have you been dead, Father?* he wondered, wiping the swiftly-cooling sweat from his forehead with his wrist. *Why do you haunt me still? Have not the years and prayers. . . ?*

Deornoth suddenly felt a cold finger of fear trace his spine. He was awake now, was he not? Then why hadn't the remorseless creaking noise disappeared with his half-dream?

He was on his feet in a moment, shouting, dead father's ghost blown out like a candle.

'Up, men, up! To arms! The siege is begun!'

Struggling into his mailcoat he went down the line of cots, kicking wakefulness into the groggy and wine-addled, calling instructions to those whom his first cry had brought suddenly to life. There were shouts of alarm from the gatehouse above, and the ragged bleat of a trumpet.

His helmet sat askew on his head, and his shield thumped his side as he trotted out the door struggling with his sword belt. Poking his head into the other barracks room he saw the denizens already up and swiftly arming themselves.

'Ho, Naglimunders!' he called, waving a fist while he held the belt closed with the other. 'Now the test, God love us, now the test!'

826

He smiled at the ragged shout that answered him and headed for the stairs, straightening his helmet.

The top of the Greater Gatehouse, in the western curtain wall, looked strangely misshapen by the light of the half-moon overhead: the hoardings had been finished only days before, wooden walls and roof that would protect the defenders from arrows. Already the top of the gatehouse was swarming with partially-dressed guards, flitting forms weirdly banded by the moonbeams that bled past the hoarding-walls.

Torches bloomed along the wall as archers and pike-men took their positions. Another trumpet squalled, like a rooster who had despaired of dawn's arrival, summoning more soldiers out to the courtyard below.

The shrill protest of wooden wheels grew louder. Deornoth stared out across the denuded, down-sloping plain before the town wall, looking for the source of the noise – knowing what it would be, but still unprepared for the actual sight.

'God's Bloody Tree!' he swore, and heard the man beside him repeat the oath.

Moving toward them as slowly as hobbled giants, taking form out of the predawn shadows, were six great siege towers, their wooden summits fully as high as Naglimund's mighty curtain wall. Hung all over in dark hides, they slouched forward like tree-tall, square-headed bears; the grunts and cries of the hidden men who pushed them, and the screech of the wheels, big as houses, seemed the voices of monsters unseen since the Eldest Days.

Deornoth felt a not-unpleasant rush of fear. The King had come at last, and now his army was at their door. By the Good God, people would sing of this someday, whatever happened.

'Save your arrows, fools!' he shouted, as a few of the defenders launched wild shots into the darkness, the missiles falling far short of their still-distant targets. 'Wait, wait, wait! Soon enough they will be closer than you'll like!'

Elias's army, in response to the flowering of fire on Naglimund's walls, let their drums thunder out through the darkness, a great rolling rumble that gradually resolved into a plodding two-part tread, as of titan footsteps. The defenders blew horns from every tower – a faint and tinny sound against the crash of the drums, but one that nonetheless betokened life and resistance.

Deornoth felt a touch at his shoulder and looked up to see two armored shapes beside him: bear-helmed Isorn, and glowering Einskaldir in a cap of steel unadorned but for a metal beak that hooked down over the nose. The dark-bearded Rimmersman's eyes burned like the torchlight as he laid a firm hand on his master Isgrimnur's son, moving Isorn carefully but forcibly out of the way so he could stride to the parapet. Staring out into the dimness, Einskaldir growled doglike under his breath.

'There,' he snarled, pointing to the bases of the siege towers, 'at the big bears' feet. The stone-chuckers and the ram.' He indicated other large engines moving in the wake of the towers. Several were catapults, long, strong arms cocked back like the heads of startled snakes. Others seemed merely hide-covered boxes, their workings hidden by their armor, designed to come safely like hard-shelled crabs through the arrows and stones to the wall, where they would perform whatever tasks they had been assigned.

'Where is the prince?' Deornoth asked, unable to tear his eyes from the crawling engines.

'Coming,' Isorn replied, standing on his toes to try to look over Einskaldir. 'He has been with Jarnauga and the archive-master since you returned from the parley. I hope they are preparing some wondrous device to give us strength, or to sap the king's. S'truth, Deornoth, look at them all.' He pointed at the dark, swarming shapes of the king's army, numerous as ants behind the slow-rolling towers. 'They are so damnably many.'

'Aedon's wounds,' Einskaldir snarled, and turned a

red eye back on Isorn. 'Let them come. We will eat them and spit them out.'

'There,' said Deornoth, and hoped he had made a smile come to his face, as he intended. 'With God, the prince, and Einskaldir, what have we to fear?'

The king's army came onto the flatlands in the trail of siege engines, swarming over the mist-soaked meadows like flies on a green appleskin. Tents seemed to push up everywhere from the moist earth like angular mushrooms.

Dawn came quietly as the besiegers moved into place. The hidden sun peeled away only a single layer of night's darkness, leaving the world suspended in directionless gray light.

The great siege towers, which had stood in place for a long hour, like dozing sentries, suddenly moved forward again. Soldiers dodged in and out among the mighty wheels, heaving on the guy ropes as the massive engines rolled laboriously uphill. At last they came within range; the archers on the walls let fly, shouting with terrified joy when the arrows went hissing out, as though they let go the tight tethers on their hearts with the bowstrings. After the first wobbly barrage they began to find the range; many of the king's men dropped dead in their tracks, or lay wounded as the remorseless wheels of their own engines ground them screaming into the turf. But for every one who fell, arrow-pierced, another of the helmeted and blue-jacketed engineers leaped forward to take up his guy rope. The siege towers rumbled on toward the walls, undeterred.

Now the king's archers on the ground were close enough to return fire. Arrows flickered back and forth between the walls and the earth below like maddened bees. As the engines rattled and creaked toward the curtain wall the sun broke through for a short moment; already the battlements were red-sprinkled in places, as if with a gentle rain.

'Deornoth!' The soldier's white face, dirt-streaked, shone within his helmet like a full moon. 'Grimstede bids you come, and soon! They have brought ladders against the wall below Dendinis' Tower!'

'S'Tree!' Deornoth clenched his teeth in frustration and turned to look for Isorn. The Rimmersman had taken a bow from a wounded guardsman and was helping to keep clear the last few ells of ground between the nearest siege tower and the wall, skewering any soldier fool enough to come out from the stalled tower's protective skirts and try and take up the loose guy ropes fluttering in the wind.

'Isorn!' Deornoth shouted, 'while we keep the towers at bay, they bring ladders to the southwest wall!'

'Go then!' Isgrimnur's son did not look up from his arrow tip. 'I will join you when I may!'

'But where is Einskaldir?!' From the corner of his eye he saw the messenger jigging up and down in fearful impatience.

'God knows!'

Cursing again under his breath, Deornoth lowered his head and ran clumsily along behind Sir Grimstede's messenger. He gathered half a dozen guardsmen as he went, tired men who had slumped down for a moment in the lee of the battlement to catch their breath. Summoned, they shook their heads regretfully, but donned their helms and followed; Deornoth was well-trusted; many called him the Prince's Right Hand.

*But Josua had poor luck with his first right hand*, Deornoth thought sourly as he hunched along the walkway, sweating despite the cold gray air. *I hope he keeps this one longer. And where is the prince, anyway? Of all times he should be seen . . .*

Rounding the great bulk of Dendinis' Tower, he was shocked to see Sir Grimstede's men falling back, and the swarming red-and-blue colors of Baron Godwig's Cellodshiremen pouring over the battlement onto the curtain wall.

'For Josua!' he shouted, leaping forward. The men behind him echoed his cry. They came against the besiegers with a tinny crash of sword on sword, and for a moment pushed the Shiremen back. One toppled from the walls, shrieking, windmilling his arms as though the chill wind might bear him up. Grimstede's men took heart and pushed forward. While the enemy was engaged again, Deornoth pulled a pike from the stiff grasp of a sprawled corpse, suffering a hard blow to his body from a stray spear butt, and pushed the first of the tall ladders away from the wall. A moment later two of his guardsmen had joined him, and together they levered the ladder out; it went shivering into open space as the besiegers on it clung and cursed, their mouths gaping like black empty holes. For a moment it stood free, halfway between earth and heaven and perpendicular to both; then the ladder overbalanced backward toward the ground below, shedding soldiers like fruit from a shaken branch.

Soon all but a pair of red-and-blue lay in their blood on the walkway. The defenders pushed the remaining three ladders away, and Grimstede had his men roll up one of the large stones they had not had time to move at the assault's beginning. They tipped it over the low spot on the wall so that it went crashing down on the toppled ladders, splintering them like kindling and killing one of the laddermen who sat where he had tumbled, staring idiotically as the great stone rolled down upon him.

One of the defending guardsmen – a bearded young fellow who had diced with Deornoth once – lay dead, his neck broken by the edge of a shield. Four of Sir Grimstede's men had also fallen, crumpled like wind-toppled scarecrows among seven men of Cellodshire who had also not survived the failed assault.

Deornoth was feeling the blow on his stomach, and stood panting as gap-toothed Grimstede limped over to stand beside him, a ragged, bloody hole in the calf of his boot.

''Tis seven here, an' half-dozen more toombled off th' ladder,' the knight said, staring down with satisfaction on the writhing bodies and wreckage below. 'All down th' wall it's th' same. Losin' far more than we, King Elias, is, far more.'

Deornoth felt ill, and his wounded shoulder throbbed as though a nail had been driven into it.

'The king *has* . . . far more than we do,' he replied. '. . . He can . . . toss them away like apple peelings.' Now he knew he would be sick, and moved toward the edge of the wall.

'Apple peelings . . .' He said again, and leaned over the parapet, too pained to feel shame.

'Read it again, please,' Jarnauga said quietly, staring at his knitted fingers.

Father Strangyeard looked up, his weary mouth open to form a question. Instead, a bone-jarring thump from outside brought a look of panic to the one-eyed priest's face, and he quickly traced a Tree on the breast of his black robe.

'Stones!' he said, his voice shrill. 'They are . . . they are throwing stones over the wall! Shouldn't we . . . isn't there. . . ?'

'The men fighting atop the walls are in danger too,' the old Rimmersgarder said, his face stern. 'We are here because we best serve here. Our comrades search for one sword in the white north, against lethal odds. Another is in the hands of our enemy already, even as he besieges our walls. What little hope there is of discovering what happened to Fingil's blade Minneyar lies with us.' His expression softened as he regarded the worried Strangyeard. 'The few stones that reach the inner keep must come over the high wall behind this room. We are at little risk. Now please, read that passage again. There is something in it I cannot quite touch, but that seems important.'

The tall priest stared down at the page for some moments, and as the room fell into silence a wave of cries and exhortations, muffled by distance, stole through the window like a mist. Strangyeard's mouth twitched.

'Read,' suggested Jarnauga.

The priest cleared his throat.

' " . . . And so John went down into the tunnels beneath the Hayholt – steaming vents and sweating passageways alive with the breath of Shurakai. Unarmed but for a spear and shield, his very boot-leather smoking as he neared the firedrake's den, he was, there is little doubt, as frightened as he ever would be in his long life . . . " '

Strangyeard broke off. 'What use is this, Jarnauga?' Something thudded into the soil a short distance away with a sound like the fall of a giant's hammer. Strangyeard stoically ignored it. 'Do . . . do you want me to go on? Through all King John's battle with the dragon?'

'No.' Jarnauga waved a gnarled hand. 'Go to the ending passage.' The priest carefully turned a few leaves.

' " . . . Thus it was that he came out again, into the light, beyond any hope of return. Those few who had remained at the cave mouth – this itself an indication of great bravery, for who could know what might happen at the door of an angered dragon's tunnel? – swore great oaths of joy and astonishment; joy, when they saw John of Warinsten come up alive from the worm's den, and astonishment at the massive claw, crimson-scaled and hook-taloned, that he bore upon his bloody shoulder. As they went shouting down the road before him, leading his horse triumphantly through the gates of Erchester, the people came gaping to their windows and into the streets. Some say that those who had loudest prophesied John's horrible death, and the dire consequences to themselves of the young knight's actions, were now most audible in

> *their acclaim of his great deed. As word spread, the rows*
> *were quickly lined with clamoring citizens who threw*
> *flowers before John as he rode, Bright-Nail lifted before*
> *him like a torch-flame, through the city that was now his*
> *own . . ." '*

Sighing, Strangeyard gently put the manuscript pages back into the cedar box he had found to house them. 'A lovely and frightening story, I would say, Jarnauga, and Morgenes, hmmmm, yes, he puts things wonderfully – but what use to us? – no disrespect, you understand.'

Jarnauga squinted at his own prominent knuckles, and frowned. 'I do not know. Something, there is *something* there. Doctor Morgenes, whether he wished to or no, put something there. Sky and clouds and stones! I can almost touch it! I feel blind!'

Another wash of noise came through the window: loud, worried shouts and the weighty chink of armor as a troop of guards jogged past in the commons outside.

'I do not think we have long to ponder, Jarnauga,' Strangeyard said finally.

'Nor do I,' said the old man, and rubbed his eyes.

All through the afternoon the tide of King Elias' army dashed itself against Naglimund's stony cliffs. The weak sunlight struck glinting shards of reflection from polished metal as wave after wave of mailed and helmeted soldiers swarmed up the ladders, only to be repelled by the castle's defenders. Here and there the king's forces found a momentary breach in the ring of stern men and grudging stone, but they were always pushed back. Fat Ordmaer, baron of Uttersall, held one such gap alone for long minutes, battling hand to hand with the scaling-soldiers mounting the ladders from below, slaying four of them and keeping the rest at bay until help arrived, although he got his own deathwound in the fighting.

It was Prince Josua himself who brought up a troop of guards, securing the length of wall and destroying the ladder. Josua's sword Naidel was a ray of sunlight flickering through leaves, snicking swiftly in and out, making dead men from living while his attackers swung clumsy broadswords or inadequate daggers.

The prince cried when Ordmaer's body was found. There had been no love lost between the baron and himself, but Ordmaer's death had been a heroic one, and in the pulse of battle his fall suddenly seemed to Josua representative of all the others – all the pikemen and archers and foot-soldiers on both sides, dying in their own blood beneath cold, cloudy skies. The prince ordered that the baron's great, limp bulk be carried down to the castle chapel. His guardsmen, cursing silently, complied.

As the reddening sun crawled toward the western horizon, King Elias' army seemed to sag, to let up; their attempts to push the siege engines against the curtain wall in the hissing face of arrow-fire grew half-hearted, and the scalers began to abandon their ladders at the first resistance from the heights above. It was hard for Erkynlander to kill Erkynlander, even at the High King's command. It was harder still when those brother Erkynlanders fought like denned badgers.

As sunset came on a mournful horn blast floated across the field from the lines of tents, and Elias' forces began to fall back, dragging the wounded and also many of the dead, leaving the hide-covered siege towers and miner's frames where they stood awaiting the next morning's assault. As the horn sounded again the drums beat loudly, as though to remind the defenders that the king's great army, like the green ocean, could send waves forever. Eventually, the drums seemed to say, even the stubbornest stone would crumble.

The siege towers, standing like solitary obelisks before the walls, were another obvious reminder of Elias' intent to return. The damp hides hung upon them permitted no mere flaming arrow to do damage, but Eadgram the Lord Constable had been pondering all day. After seeking some advice from Jarnauga and Strangyeard, he had at last devised a plan.

Silently, even as the last of the king's men limped down the slope toward their encampment, Eadgram bade his men load oil-filled winesacks onto the throwing arms of Naglimund's two small slingstones. When the arms were released, the oilsacks whistled across the open distance beyond the wall to splatter over the towers' leather mantling. This done, it was a simple matter to send a few fiery pitch-tipped arrows streaking through the blue twilight; within moments the four huge towers had become billowing torches.

There was nothing the king's men could do to quell the blaze. The defenders on the walls clapped their hands together and stamped and shouted, weary but heartened, as orange light danced on the battlements.

When King Elias rode out from the camp, wrapped in his great black cloak like a man of shadows, Naglimund's defenders jeered. When he lifted his strange gray sword, and shouted like a madman for rain to fall and quench the fiery towers, they laughed uneasily. It was only after a while, as the king rode back and forth, crow-black cape flapping in the cold wind, that they began to understand from the horrible anger in Elias' echoing voice that he truly *expected* rain to come at his summoning, and that he was outraged it had not. The laughter faded into a fearful silence. Naglimund's defenders, one by one, left off their celebrating and climbed down from the walls to tend their wounds. The siege, after all, had barely begun. There was no respite in view, and no rest this side of Heaven.

'I've been having strange dreams again, Binabik.'

Simon had ridden his horse up alongside Qantaqa, some yards ahead of the rest of the company. It was clear but terribly cold, this their sixth day riding across the White Waste.

'Dreams of what sort?'

Simon readjusted the mask the troll had made him, a strip of hide with a slit cut in it, to mask the fierce glare of the snow. 'Of Green Angel Tower . . . or some tower. Last night I dreamed that it was running with blood.'

Binabik squinted behind his own mask, then pointed to a faint band of gray running along the horizon at the base of the mountains. 'That, I am sure, is the edge of the Dimmerskog – or the *Qilakitsoq*, as my folk properly name it: the Shadow-wood. We should be upon it with another day or so.'

Staring at the dreary strip, Simon felt his frustrations boiling up.

'I don't care about the damnable forest,' he snapped, 'and I'm sick to death of ice and snow, ice and snow! We shall freeze and die in this awful wilderness! What about the dreams I'm having?!!'

The troll bobbed along for a moment as Qantaqa made her way over a series of small drifts. Through the song of the wind Haestan could be heard shouting something to someone.

'I am already full of sorrow.' Binabik spoke measuredly, as if matching his speech to the cadence of their progress. 'Awake I lay two nights in Naglimund, worrying what harm I would do in bringing you along for this journey. I have no knowledge of what your dreams mean, and the only way for finding it would be to walk the Road of Dreams.'

'As we did at Geloë's house?'

'But I am having no faith in my unaided powers for that – not here, not now. It is possible your dreams could give us aid, but still I do not find it wise to walk the dream-road now. Here we are all, then, and this is what

837

our fate will be. I can only say I have been doing what seemed best.'

Simon thought about this and grunted.

*Here we all are. Binabik is right; here we all are, too far in to turn back.*

'Is Inelu . . .' he made the sign of the Tree with fingers trembling from more than chill, '. . . is the Storm King . . . the Devil?' he asked at last.

Binabik frowned deeply.

'The Devil? The Enemy of your God? Why are you asking that? You have heard Jarnauga's words – you know what Ineluki is.'

'I suppose.' He shivered. 'It's just that . . . I see him in my dreams. I think it's him, anyway. Red eyes, that's all I see, really, and everything else black . . . like burned-up logs with the hot places still showing through.' He felt ill just remembering.

The troll shrugged, hands caught up in the wolf's neck ruff. 'He is not your Devil, friend Simon. He *is* evil, though, or at least I am thinking that the things he wants will be evil for the rest of us. That is evil enough.'

'And . . . the dragon?' Simon said hesitantly a moment later. Binabik turned his head sharply, presenting his strange, slitted gaze.

'Dragon?'

'The one who lives on the mountain. The one whose name I can't say.'

Binabik laughed explosively, his breath a cloud. 'Igjarjuk is its name! Daughter of the Mountains, you are having many worries, young friend! Devils! Dragons!' He caught one of his own tears on the finger of his glove and held up. 'Look!' he chuckled. 'As if there was need of making more ice.'

'But there *was* a dragon!' Simon answered hotly. 'Everyone said so!'

'Long ago, Simon. It is an ill-omened place, but that is being as much for its isolation as anything else, is my guessing. Qanuc legends tell a great ice-worm lived there once, and my people do not go there, but now I think it to be more likely a haunt of snow leopards and such creatures. Not that there will not be things of danger. The Hunën, as we are well-knowing, range far afield these days.'

'So then, truly I have little to fear? The most terrible things have been running through my head at night.'

'I was not saying you had little to fear, Simon. We must never be forgetting that we have enemies; some, it would seem, are very powerful indeed.'

Another frigid night in the Waste; another campfire in the dark emptiness of the surrounding snowfields. Simon would have liked nothing better in the entire world than to be curled up in a bed at Naglimund, covered in blankets, even if the bloodiest battle in the history of Osten Ard raged just outside the door. He was sure that if just now someone offered him a warm, dry place to sleep, he would lie or kill or take Usires' name in vain to get it. He was positive, as he sat wrapped in his saddle blanket trying to keep his teeth from chattering, that he could feel his very eyelashes freezing on his lids.

Wolves were yipping and wailing in the unending darkness beyond the faint firelight, carrying on long and mournfully intricate conversations. Two nights before, when the companions had first begun to hear their singing, Qantaqa spent the entire evening pacing nervously around the campfire circle. She had since grown used to the night cries of her fellows, and only responded with an occasional uneasy whimper.

'Why dunna she talk b-b-back at 'em?' Haestan asked worried. A plainsman of the Erkynlandish north, he had no more love for wolves than did Sludig, although he had grown almost fond of Binabik's mount. 'Why dunna she tell 'em t'go p-plague someone else?'

'Like men, not all tribes of Qantaqa's kind are at peace,' Binabik replied, setting no one's mind at ease.

Tonight the great she-wolf was doing her stalwart best

to ignore the howling – pretending sleep, but giving herself away as her pricked ears swiveled toward the louder cries. The wolfsong, Simon decided as he huddled deeper in his blanket, was about the loneliest sound he had ever heard.

*Why am I here?* he wondered. *Why are any of us here? Searching through this horrible snow for some sword no one has even thought about in years. Meanwhile, the Princess and all the rest of them are back at the castle waiting for the king to attack! Stupid! Binabik grew up in the mountains, in the snow – Grimmric and Haestan and Sludig are soldiers – the Aedon alone knows what the Sithi want. So why am I here? It's stupid!*

The howling quieted. A long forefinger touched Simon's hand, making him jump.

'Do you listen to the wolves, Seoman?' Jiriki asked.

'It's hard n–not to.'

'They sing such fierce songs.' The Sitha shook his head. 'They are like your mortal kind. They sing of where they have been, and what they have seen and scented. They tell each other where the elk are running, and who has taken whom to mate, but mostly they are merely crying "*I am! Here I am!*" ' Jiriki smiled, veiling his eyes as he watched the dying fire.

'And th–that's what you think we . . . we m–m–mortals are saying?'

'With words and without them,' the prince responded. 'You must try to see things with our eyes: to the Zida'ya, your folk often seem as children. You see that the long-lived Sithi do not sleep, that we stay awake throughout the long night of history. You men, like children, wish to remain at the fire with your elders, to hear the songs and stories and watch the dancing.' He gestured around, as though the darkness was peopled with invisible revelers.

'But you cannot, Simon,' he continued kindly. 'You may not. It is given to your folk to sleep the final sleep, just as it is given to our kind to walk and sing beneath the stars the night long. Perhaps there is even a richness in your sleeping dreams that we Zida'ya do not understand.'

The stars hanging in the black-crystal sky seemed to slide away, to sink deeper into the vast night. Simon thought of the Sithi, and of a life that did not end, and could not make himself understand what it might be like. Chilled to the bone – even, it seemed, to his soul – he leaned close to the fire, pulling off his damp mittens to warm his hands.

'But the Sithi *can* d-die, c-c-can't they?' he asked cautiously, cursing his frozen stuttering speech.

Jiriki leaned close, his eyes narrowing, and for a frightening moment Simon thought the Sitha was going to strike him for his temerity. Instead, Jiriki took Simon's trembling hand and tilted it.

'Your ring,' he said, staring at the fish-shaped curlicue, 'I had not seen it before. Who gave you this?'

'My . . . my master, I su . . . . suppose he was,' Simon stammered. 'Doctor Morgenes of the Hayholt. He sent it after me, to B-B-Binabik.' The cool, strong clutch of the Sithi prince's hand was unsettling, but he dared not pull away.

'So you are one of your kind who knows the Secret?' Jiriki asked, watching him intently. The depth of his golden eyes, rust-tinged by the fire's reflection, was frightening.

'S-Secret? N-N-No! No, I don't know any secret!'

Jiriki stared at him for a moment, holding him still with his eyes as surely as if he had grasped Simon's head in both hands.

'Then why should he give you the ring?' Jiriki asked, mostly to himself, shaking his head as he released Simon's hand. 'And I myself gave you a White Arrow! The Ancestors have made for us a strange road indeed.' He turned back to stare at the wavering fire, and would not answer Simon's questions.

*Secrets,* Simon thought angrily, *more secrets! Binabik has them. Morgenes had them, the Sithi are full of them! I don't want to know about any other secrets! Why have I been picked up for this punishment? Why is everyone forever forcing their horrible secrets on me?!*

He cried silently for a while, hugging his knees and shivering, wishing for impossible things.

They reached the eastern outskirts of the Dimmerskog on the afternoon of the next day. Although the forest was covered in a thick blanket of white snow, it nevertheless seemed, as Binabik had named it, a place of shadows. The company did not pass beneath its eaves, and might have chosen not to even had their path lain that way, so thick with foreboding was the wood's atmosphere. The trees, despite their size – and some of them were huge indeed – seemed dwarfish and twisted, as though they squirmed bitterly beneath their burden of needled branches and snow. The open spaces between the contorted trunks seemed to bend away crazily like tunnels dug by some huge and drunken mole, leading at last to dangerous, secretive depths.

Passing in near silence, his horse's hooves crunching softly in the snow, Simon imagined following the gaping pathways into the bark-pillared, white-roofed halls of Dimmerskog, coming at last to – who could guess? Perhaps to the dark, malicious heart of the forest, a place where the trees breathed together and passed endless rumors with the scaly rub of branch on branch, or the malicious exhalation of wind through twigs and frozen leaves.

They camped that night in the open again, even though the Dimmerskog crouched only a short distance away like a sleeping animal. None of them wanted to spend a night beneath the forest's branches – especially Sludig, who had been raised on stories of the ghastly things that stalked the wood's pale corridors. The Sithi did not seem to care, but Jiriki spent part of the evening oiling his dark witchwood sword. Again the company huddled around a naked fire, and the east wind razored past them all the long evening, sending great powdery spouts of snow whirling all around, and sporting among the Dimmerskog's upper reaches. When they lay down that night to sleep it was to the sound of the forest creaking, and the wind-ridden branches sawing one against the other.

Two more days of slow riding brought them around the forest and across the last stretch of open, icy land to the foothills of the mountains. The landscape was bleak, and the daylight glared off the snowcrust until Simon's head throbbed from squinting, but the weather seemed a little warmer. The snow still fell, but the harrying wind did not drive past cloak and coat as it did out of the mountains' broad lee.

'Look!' Sludig cried, pointing away up the sloping apron of the foothills.

At first Simon saw nothing but the ubiquitous snow-capped rocks and trees. Then, as his eye slid along the line of low hills to the east, he saw movement. Two strangely-shaped figures – or was it four, oddly com-mingled? – were silhouetted on the ridgetop a furlong away.

'Wolves?' he asked nervously.

Binabik rode Qantaqa out from the party until they stood clear, then cupped his gloved hands in his mouth. '*Yah aqonik mij-ayah nu tutusiq, henimaatuq?*' he called. His words echoed briefly and then died amid the shrouded hills. 'In truth there should be no shouting,' he whispered to a puzzled Simon. 'Higher up it might be the causing of snowslides.'

'But who are you. . . ?'

'Sshhh.' Binabik waved his hand. A moment later the two shapes moved down the ridge a short way toward the companions. Now Simon could see that the pair were small men, each astride a shaggy, twist-horned ram. Trolls!

One of them called out. Binabik, after listening intently, turned with a smile to his comrades.

'They wish for knowing where we go, and if that is not being a flesh-eating Rimmersman in our midst, and is he a prisoner?'

'The devil take them!' Sludig growled. Binabik's smile widened, and he turned back to the ridge.

'*Binbiniqegabenik ea sikka!*' he shouted. '*Uc sikkan mohinaq da Yijarjuk!*'

The two round fur-hooded heads regarded them blankly for a moment, like sunbaffled owls. A moment later one rapped his chest with his hand, and the other waved his mittened arm in a wide circle as they turned their mounts and rode off up the ridge in a cloud of powdery snow.

'What was all that?' Sludig asked, nettled.

Binabik's grin seemed strained. 'I told them we were to go to Urmsheim,' he explained. 'One gave the sign to ward off evil, the other was using a charm against madmen.'

After making their way up into the hills, the company made camp in a rocky dale gouged into the hem of Urmsheim's mantle.

'Here it is we should leave the horses, and those things we need not be carrying,' Binabik said as he surveyed the sheltered site.

Jiriki strode to the mouth of the dale and leaned backward, staring up toward Urmsheim's craggy, snowcapped head, pink-tinged on its westerly face by the setting sun. The wind billowed his cloak and blew his hair up around his face like wisps of lavender clouds.

'It has been long since I have seen this place,' he said.

'Have you climbed this mountain before?' Simon asked, struggling with his horse's cinch buckle.

'I have never seen the peak's far side,' the Sitha answered. 'This will be something new for me – to see the easternmost realm of the *Hikeda'ya*.'

844

'The Norns?'

'Everything north of the mountains was ceded to them long ago, at the time of the Parting.' Jiriki strode back up the gulley. 'Ki'ushapo, you and Sijandi must prepare a shelter for the horses. See, there is some scrub growing here, under the leaning rocks, that may be a boon if you run short of hay.' He lapsed over into the Sithi tongue, and An'nai and the other two began to set up a campsite more permanent than any the company had enjoyed since leaving the hunting lodge.

'Here, Simon, see what I have brought!' Binabik called.

The youth made his way past the three soldiers, who were splitting the small trees they had felled into firewood. The troll was squatting on the ground pulling oilskin-wrapped bundles from his saddlebag.

'The blacksmith at Naglimund thought me as mad as I am small,' Binabik smiled as Simon approached, 'but he made for me the things I was wanting.'

Unlaced, the pouches disgorged all kinds of strange objects – spike-covered metal plates with straps and buckles, odd hammers with pointy heads, and harnesses that looked as though they might be made to fit very small horses.

'What are all these things?'

'For the wooing and winning of mountains,' Binabik smirked. 'Even the Qanuc, with all our nimblefootedness, do not go climbing to the highest reaches unprepared. See, these are for wearing on boots,' he indicated the spiked plates, 'and these are ice-axes – very useful they are. Sludig will have seen them, no doubt.'

'And the harnesses?'

'So we may be roping ourselves together. Thus, if the sleet is blowing, or we are on dragon-snow or too-thin ice, when one falls the others can then be bearing up his weight. If there had been the time, I would have made preparation of a harness for Qantaqa, too. She will be

upset at staying behind, and we will have a sad parting.'
The troll hummed a quiet tune as he oiled and polished.

Simon stared silently at Binabik's tools. Somehow he had thought climbing the mountain would be something like climbing the stairs of Green Angel Tower – steeply uphill, but essentially no more than a difficult hike. This talk of people falling, and thin ice . . .

'Ho, Simon-lad!' It was Grimmric. 'Come make y'rself useful. Pick up some of th' chippings. We'll have one last good blaze 'fore we go t'killing ourselves up-mountain.'

The white tower again loomed in his dreams that night. He clung desperately to its blood-slickened sides as wolves howled below him, and a dark, red-eyed shape rang the baleful bells above.

The innkeeper looked up, mouth open to speak, then stopped. He blinked and swallowed, like a frog.

The stranger was a monk, robed and hooded in black, his garb spattered in places with the mud of the road. What was arresting was his size: he was fairly tall but broad as an ale barrel, wide enough that the tavern room – not the brightest to begin with – had perceptibly darkened when he pushed through the doorway.

'I . . . I'm sorry, Father.' The innkeeper smiled ingratiatingly. Here was a man of the Aedonite God who looked as though he could squeeze the sin right out of you if he chose. 'What were you asking?'

'I said I've been to every inn on every street in the wharf district, and I've had no luck. My back aches. Give me a mug of your best.' He stumped over to a table and lowered his bulk onto a creaking bench. 'This damnable Abaingeat has more inns than it has roads.' His accent, the innkeeper noted, was a Rimmersman's. That explained the raw, pink look of his face: the innkeeper had heard it said that the men of Rimmersgard had such thick beards they had to shave thrice daily – those few who didn't just let them grow.

'We are a harbor town, Father,' he said, setting a healthy flagon down before the scowling, rumpled monk. 'And with the things that are going on these days – ' he shrugged and made a face, 'well, there are plenty of strangers wanting rooms.'

The monk wiped foam from his upper lip and frowned. 'I know. A damnable shame. Poor Lluth . . .'

The innkeeper looked around nervously, but the Erkynlandish guardsmen in the corner were paying no attention. 'You said you have had no luck, Father,' he said, changing the subject. 'Might I be asking what you're seeking?'

'A monk,' the big man growled, 'a *brother* monk, that is – and a young boy. I have scoured the wharf from top to bottom.'

The tavernmaster smiled, polishing a metal flagon with his apron. 'And you came here last? Begging your pardon, Father, but I think your God's seen fit to test you.'

The big man grunted, then looked up from his ale. 'What do you mean?'

'They were here, they were – if it's the same two.'

His satisfied smile froze on his face as the monk lurched up from the bench. His reddened face was inches from the innkeeper's own.

'When?'

'T–two, three d–days ago – I'm not sure . . .'

'Are you really not sure,' the monk asked menacingly, 'or do you just want money?' He patted his robe. The innkeeper did not know if it was a purse or a knife this strange man of God was patting for; he had never much trusted Usires' followers anyway, and living in Hernystir's most cosmopolitan town had not improved his opinion of them.

'Oh, no, Father, truly! They . . . they were in a few

days past. Asked after a boat going down-coast to Perdruin. The monk was a short fellow, bald? The lad thin-faced, black hair? They were here.'

'What did you tell 'em?'

'To go see Old Gealsgiath down by the Eirgid Ramh – that's the tavern with the oar painted on the front door, down near land's end!'

He broke off in alarm as the monk's huge hands folded over his shoulders. The innkeeper, a reasonably strong man, felt himself clasped as securely as a child. A moment later he was reeling from a rib-crushing hug, and could only stand wheezing as the monk pressed a gold Imperator into his hand.

'Merciful Usires bless your inn, Hernystirman!' the big man bellowed, turning heads clear out in the street. 'This is the first piece of luck I have had since I began this God-cursed search!' He crashed out through the door-way like a man leaving a burning house.

The innkeeper took a painful breath, and clutched the coin, still warm from the monk's great paw.

'Mad as a mooncalf, these Aedonites,' he told himself. 'Touched.'

She stood at the railing and watched Abaingeat sliding away, drawing back into the fog. The wind ruffled her close-cropped black hair.

'Brother Cadrach!' she called. 'Come here. Is there anything so glorious?' She gestured at the growing strip of green ocean that separated them from the misty shoreline. Gulls wheeled and screeched above the boat's foaming wake.

The monk waved a limp hand from where he crouched beside a clutch of lashed-down barrels. 'You enjoy yourself . . . Malachias. I have never been much of a seafarer. God knows, I do not think this voyage will change that.' He wiped spray– or sweat – from his forehead. Cadrach had not touched a drop of wine since they had set foot on shipboard.

Miriamele looked up to see a pair of Hernystiri sailors watching her curiously from the foredeck. She dipped her head and walked over to seat herself next to the monk.

'Why did you come with me?' she asked after a while. 'That is something I still do not understand.'

The monk did not look up. 'I came because the lady paid me.'

Miriamele pulled her hood forward. 'There is nothing like the ocean to remind you of what is important,' she said quietly, and smiled. Cadrach's returned smile was weak.

'Ah, by the Good Lord, that's true,' he groaned. 'I am reminded that life is sweet, that the sea is treacherous, and that I am a fool.'

Miriamele nodded solemnly, staring up at the bellying sails. 'Those are good things to remember,' she said.

# 42

# Beneath the Uduntree

'There's no hurrying it, Elias,' Guthwulf growled. 'No hurrying. Naglimund's a tough nut . . . tough – you knew it'd be . . .' He could hear himself slurring his words; he had needed to get drunk just to face his old companion. The Earl of Utanyeat no longer felt comfortable around the king, and felt even less so bringing him bad news.

'You have had a fortnight. I have given you everything – troops, siege engines – everything!' The king pulled at the skin of his face, frowning. He was drawn and sickly, and had not yet met Guthwulf's eyes. 'I can wait no longer. Tomorrow is Midsummer's Eve!'

'And why should that matter?' Guthwulf, feeling chilled and sick, turned away and spat out the now-tasteless lump of citril root he had been chewing. The king's tent was as cold and dank as the bottom of a well. 'No one has ever taken one of the great houses in a fortnight except by treachery, even if they were poorly defended – these Naglimunders have fought like cornered animals. Be patient, Highness; patience is all we need. We can starve them out in a matter of months.'

'Months!' Elias' laugh was hollow. 'Months, he says, Pryrates!'

The red priest offered a skeletal smile.

The king's laughter abruptly ceased, and he lowered

his chin until it almost touched the pommel of the long gray sword propped between his knees. There was something about that sword that Guthwulf did not like, although he knew it was foolish to have such thoughts about a mere thing. Still, everywhere that Elias went these days the sword was with him, like some pampered lapdog. 'Today is your last chance, Utanyeat.' The High King's voice was thick and heavy. 'Either the gate is opened, or I must make . . . other arrangements.'

Guthwulf stood, swaying. 'Are you mad, Elias? Are you mad? How can we possibly . . . the miners have scarcely dug halfway . . .' He trailed off dizzily, wondering if he'd gone too far. 'Why should we care whether tomorrow is Midsummer's Eve?' He dropped to a knee again, imploring. 'Talk to me, Elias.'

The Earl had feared an explosive response from his angry king, but he had also, distantly, hoped for some faint return of their old camaraderie. He got neither.

'You cannot understand, Utanyeat,' Elias replied, and his staring red-rimmed eyes were fixed on the tent wall, or empty air. 'I have . . . other obligations. Tomorrow everything will change.'

Simon had thought he had gained an understanding of winter. After the trek across the desolate blankness of the Waste, the endless white days of wind and snow and stinging eyes, he had been sure there were no further lessons winter could teach him. After the first few days on Urmsheim he was amazed by his former innocence.

They traveled along the slender ice paths roped in file, digging in carefully with toe and heel before taking each step. At times the rising wind plucked at them as though they were tree leaves, and they had to shrink back against the Urmsheim's icy side and cling until the wind subsided. The footing, too, was treacherous; Simon, who had thought himself quite a climber as master of the

851

Hayholt's high places, now found himself skidding and clinging on narrow trackways barely two cubits from wall to precipice, a whirling cloud of powdery snow the only thing between the path and the distant earth. Looking down from Green Angel Tower, which had once seemed the world's summit, now seemed as childish and comforting as standing atop a stool in the castle kitchen.

From the mountain path he could soon see the tops of other peaks, and clouds eddying about them. The northeast of Osten Ard lay spread before him, but so distant he turned away from the view. It would not do to stare down from such heights. It made his heart race and the breath catch in his throat. Simon wished with all his heart he had remained behind, but now his only hope to come down again was to keep climbing.

He found himself often in prayer, and hoped that the loftiness of their location would speed his words to Heaven all the faster.

The sickening heights and his own fast-failing confidence were terrifying enough, but Simon was also connected by the cord around his waist to all the rest of the party but the unbound Sithi. Thus, there were not just his own mistakes to worry over: misstep by one of the others could pull them all down, like a weighted fishing line, and send them plunging into the limitless, vertiginous depths. Their progress was painfully slow, but no one, Simon least of all, wanted it otherwise.

Not that all the lessons of the mountain were painful ones. Although the air was so thin and achingly cold that he sometimes felt another breath might turn him to frozen stone, the very iciness of the atmosphere brought with it an odd exaltation, a sensation of openness and insubstantiality, as though a startling wind blew right through him.

The icy mountain face itself was a thing of painful beauty. Simon had never dreamed that ice might have color; the tame variety he knew, that which festooned the roofs of the Hayholt at Aedontide and shrouded the wells in Jonever, was diamond-clear or milky white. By contrast, the icy armor of Urmsheim, warped, twisted, and buckled by wind and the seemingly distant sun, was a dream-forest of colors and strange shapes. Great ice-towers shot through with veins of sea-green and violet leaned out above the heads of the toiling party. Else-where the ice cliffs had cracked and fallen in crystalline chunks, gemlike raw edges etched in stormy blue, crumbling into tesselate confusion like the abandoned blocks of some giant architect.

In one place the black bones of two frozen, long-dead trees stood like abandoned sentinels before the rim of a white-misted crevice. The ice sheet that stretched between them had been melted parchment-thin by the sun; the mummified trees seemed the gateposts of Heaven, the ice between them a shimmering, evanescent fan that shattered the dayshine into a glowing rainbow of ruby and nectarine light, into swirls of gold and lavender and pale rose that – Simon felt sure – would make even the famous windows of the Sancellan Aedonitis seem dull as pondwater and candle-drip.

But even as its brilliant skin beguiled the eyes, the mountain's cold heart schemed against its unwanted guests. Late in the afternoon of the first day, even as Simon and his mortal comrades were trying to grow used to the strange and deliberate pace forced upon them by Binabik's shoe-spikes – the Sithi, who disdained such devices, nevertheless climbed almost as slowly and carefully as the others – darkness overtook the sky as suddenly and thoroughly as ink spilled upon a blotter.

'Lie down!' Binabik yelled, even as Simon and the two Erkynlandish soldiers were staring up curiously at the spot where, moments before, the sun had hung in the heavens. Behind Haestan and Grimmric, Sludig had already flung himself down onto the hard snow. 'Down to the ground!' the troll shouted. Haestan pulled Simon down.

Even as he was wondering if Binabik had seen something dangerous on the trail ahead – and if so what the Sithi were doing, since they had disappeared where the path bent around part of Urmsheim's southeastern flank – Simon heard the pitch of the wind, which had been a low, steady whistle for hours, rise to a shriek. He felt a tug, then a hard pull, and dug his fingers through the powdery snow into the icy pack beneath. A moment later a crash of thunder banged painfully in both his ears. Even as the first drumbeat was echoing down the valley below, another shook him as Qantaqa might a captured rat. He whimpered and clung to the ground as the wind raked him with bony fingers, and the thunder crashed again and again, the mountain they clung to an anvil for some gargantuan and terrible blacksmith.

The storm halted as abruptly as it had descended. Simon crouched in place for long moments after the wind's scream had subsided, his forehead pressed against the freezing ground. When he sat up at last, his ears ringing, the white sun was emerging from the inksplatter of clouds. Beside him Haestan was sitting up like a baffled child, his nose bleeding and his beard full of snow.

'By th'Aedon!' he swore. 'By th' sufferin', bleedin', sorrowful Aedon and God th'Highest.' He wiped his nose with the back of his hand and stared stupidly at the red streak left on his fur glove. 'What. . . ?'

'Lucky we are we stood on a wide part of the path,' Binabik said, climbing to his feet. Although he, too, was covered in clinging snow, he looked almost cheerful. 'Here the storms come fast.'

'Fast . . .' Simon muttered, looking down. He had pierced the ankle of his right boot with the spikes strapped to the left, and the way it stung he was sure he had drawn blood.

A moment later Jiriki's slender form appeared at the bend of the trail.

'Have you lost anyone?' he shouted. When Binabik called back that all were safe, the Sitha gave a mocking salute and vanished again.

'I don't see any snow on *him*,' Sludig remarked sourly.

'Mountain storms are moving quickly,' the troll replied. 'But so are Sithi.'

The seven travelers spent the first night together against the back wall of a shallow ice cave on the mountain's eastern face, with the far edge of the narrow path only five or six cubits away, the black abyss waiting below. As he sat shivering in the penetrating cold, comforted but unwarmed by the quiet singing of Jiriki and An'nai, he remembered something Doctor Morgenes had once told him in the heart of a drowsy afternoon, when Simon had complained about living in the crowded, unprivate servant's quarters.

'*Never make your home in a place*,' the old man had said, too lazy in the spring warmth to do more than a wag a finger. '*Make a home for yourself inside your own head. You'll find what you need to furnish it – memory, friends you can trust, love of learning, and other such things.*' Morgenes had grinned. '*That way it will go with you wherever you journey. You'll never lack for a home – unless you lose your head, of course . . .*'

He was still not quite sure what exactly it was that the doctor had meant; more than anything, he felt sure, he wanted a home to call his own once more. Father Strangyeard's bare room at Naglimund had begun to feel like one in only a week. Still, there was a sort of romance to the idea of living free on the road, making your home wherever you stopped, like a Hyrka horsetrader. But he was ready for other things. It began to seem as though he himself had been on the move for years – how long had it been, anyway?

As he counted carefully back by the changes of the moon, with help from Binabik where he had trouble remembering, he was dumbfounded to realize that it had been . . . less than two months! Astonishing, but true: the troll confirmed his guess, that three weeks of Yuven had passed, and Simon knew for a fact that his journey had begun on ill-fated Stoning Night, the last hours of Avrel. How the world had changed in seven weeks! And – he reflected dully, as he tumbled toward sleep – mostly for the worse.

In late morning the company was climbing a massive slab of ice that had slid down from the mountain's shoulder to lie athwart the path like a vast, discarded package, when Urmsheim struck again. With a horrifying, grating sound a long wedge of the icy slab crackled from blue-gray to white and broke loose, sliding away beneath Grimmric's feet to plunge, crumbling, down the mountainside. The Erkynlander had time only for a brief surprised shout; a moment later he had tumbled out of sight into the gash the wedge had left behind. Before he could think, Simon felt himself jerked ahead by Grimmric's fall. He tumbled forward, flinging out a desperate hand to catch at the ice-wall; the black crevice came ever closer. Helplessly horrified, he saw a thin slice of empty air through the crack in the path, and beyond that the dim form of the crags half a league below. He screamed and felt himself skid forward, his fingers clutching fruitlessly at the slippery path.

Binabik was leading the rope, and his experienced swiftness allowed him to dive forward when he heard the shattering ice; he sprawled face down, clutching the ice with one gloved hand, digging his axe and spikes in as deeply as he could. Haestan's broad hand now caught at Simon's belt, but even the bearded guardsman's bulk could not halt their inexorable slide. Grimmric's hidden weight pulled them down, even as he cried piteously below the crevice-edge and swung from side to side, suspended by the rope above snow-swirling nothingness. At the back of the line Sludig dug in, temporarily halting Simon and Haestan's movement, and shouted anxiously for the Sithi.

An'nai and Prince Jiriki came pelting back along the mountain path, touching as lightly on the powdery surface as snow hares. They quickly dug their own axes deep into the ice and lashed them to the end of Binabik's rope with swift knots. The troll, thus freed, edged around the crevice with the two Sithi, and back to help Sludig.

Simon felt the tug on his belt strengthen, and the crevice slowly began to recede. He was sliding backward. He wasn't going to die! – at least, it seemed, not this moment. As he regained his footing he bent to snatch up one of his fallen mittens, and his head pounded.

With all the party now heaving at the ropes, they at last brought Grimmric – senseless now, his face gray within his hood – back up through the gap in the ice where he could be dragged to safety. It was long minutes after he awoke before Grimmric could recognize his companions, and he was shaking as with a deadly fever. Sludig and Haestan rigged a sling from two fur cloaks to carry him until they could stop and make camp.

When they found a deep cleft that ran back into the mountain until it reached actual stone, the sun was only slightly past the midpoint of the sky, but they had no choice except to make early camp. They lit a small fire, scarcely more than knee-high, with kindling they had scavenged at Urmsheim's feet and carried up into its heights for just such a reason. Shuddering Grimmric lay beside it, teeth a-chatter, waiting for the troll-draught that Binabik, mixing herbs and powders from his pack with snowmelt was laboring to prepare. No one begrudged Grimmric the precious heat.

As the afternoon progressed, and the narrow sliver of sun that arrowed down into the cleft rose up the blue walls and then disappeared, an even deeper and more agonizing chill set in. Simon, his muscles trembling like lute strings, ears aching despite his fur hood, felt himself sliding – as precipitously and helplessly as he had slid toward the naked emptiness of the crevice – toward a waking dream. But instead of the bleak cold he expected, his dream reached out to welcome him with warm and fragrant arms.

*It was summer again – how long had it been? No mind, for the seasons had swung around at last, and the hot, expectant air was full of the sizzle of bees. The spring's flowers now hung swollen and overripe, crisping brown at the edges like Judith's mutton pies baking in the castle ovens. In the fields below the Hayholt's walls the grass was turning yellow, beginning the alchemical transformation that would end in Autumn, when it would be piled in golden, fragrant ricks, dotting the land like tiny cottages.*

*Simon could hear the shepherds singing drowsily, echoing the bees as they led their bleating charges across the meadows. Summer! Soon, he knew, would come the festivals . . . Saint Sutrin's, Hlafmansa – but first his own favorite, Midsummer's Eve . . .*

*Midsummer's Eve, when everything was different and all was disguised, when bemasked friends and costumed enemies mingled unknowing in the breathless darkness . . . when music played all through the sleepless night, and the Hedge Garden was festooned with silver ribbons, and laughing, leaping shapes populated the Moon's Hours . . .*

'Seoman?' A hand was on his shoulder, gently shaking. 'Seoman, you are weeping. Wake up.'

'The dancers . . . the masks . . .'

'Wake up!' The hand shook him again, more vigorously. He opened his eyes to see Jiriki's narrow face, all forehead and cheekbones in the dim, angled light.

'You seemed to be having a frightening dream,' the Sitha said as he sank into a crouch at Simon's side.

'But . . . but it wasn't really.' He shivered. 'It was s-summer . . . it was Midsummer's Eve . . .'

'Ah.' Jiriki raised an eyebrow, then shrugged sinuously. 'I think, perhaps you have been wandering in realms where you should not go.'

'What could be bad about summer?'

The prince of the Sithi shrugged again, then produced from inside his cloak – with a gesture like a favorite uncle producing a toy to distract a sniffling child – a shiny object in a delicately-carved wooden frame.

'Do you know what this is?' Jiriki asked.

'A . . . a mirror . . .' Simon was unaware of what the Sitha was asking. Did he know Simon had handled it in the cave?

Jiriki smiled. 'Yes. A very special mirror, one that has a very long history. Do you know what can be done with such a thing? Besides shaving the face as men do?' he reached over and tapped a cool finger on Simon's furry cheek. 'Can you guess?'

'S-s-see things that are f-far away?' he replied after a moment's hesitation, then waited for the explosion of temper he was sure would come.

The Sitha stared. 'You have heard of the mirrors of the Fair folk?' he said at last, wondering. 'Still they are the subject of tales and songs?'

Now Simon had a chance to slide away from the truth. Instead, he surprised himself.

'No. I looked at it when we were in your hunting lodge.'

Even more surprisingly, this admission only widened Jiriki's eyes. 'You saw other places in it? More than reflection?'

'I saw . . . I saw Princes M-Miriamele – my friend,' he nodded, and patted her blue scarf where it wound about his neck. 'It was like a dream.'

The Sitha scowled down at the mirror, not angrily, but as if it were the surface of a pool beneath which darted an elusive fish he wished to locate.

'You are a strong-willed young man,' Jiriki said slowly, 'stronger than you know – either that or you are

859

touched by other powers, somehow . . .' He looked from Simon back to the mirror, and was silent for a time.

'It is a very old thing, this mirror,' he said at last. 'It is said to be a scale of the Greater Worm.'

'What does that mean?'

'The Greater Worm, the one that many stories say encircles the world. We Sithi, though, see the Worm as circling all worlds at once, those of waking and those of dreaming . . . those that were, and those that will be. His tail is in his mouth, so he has no end or beginning.'

'A worm? Do you mean a d–d–dragon?'

Jiriki nodded once, an abrupt motion like a bird pecking grain. 'It is also told that all dragons are descended from the Greater Worm, and that each is less than the ones that went before. Igjarjuk and Shurakai were less great than their mother Hidohebhi, as she in turn was not as great as her parent Khaerukama'o the Golden. Someday, if all this is true, the dragons will disappear altogether – if they have not already.'

'That w–would be good,' Simon said.

'Would it?' Jiriki smiled again, but his eyes were cold, shiny stones. 'Men grow while the great worms . . . and others . . . diminish. That seems to be the way of things.' He stretched, with the shuddering, slippery grace of a new-wakened cat. 'The way of things,' he repeated. 'Still, I brought out this scale of the Greater Worm to show you something. Would you like to see, manchild?'

Simon nodded.

'This has been a difficult journey for you.' Jiriki flicked a glance over his shoulder to where the others were gathered around Grimmric and the tiny campfire. Only An'nai glanced up, and some unreadable communication flickered between the two Sithi. 'Look,' said Jiriki a moment later.

The looking glass, cupped in his hands like a precious drink of water, seemed almost to ripple. The darkness it held – split by a jagged slash of light gray, the reflection of the sky above their crevice – seemed to slowly sprout points of green light, like strange vegetable stars germinating in the evening sky. 'I will show you a *true* summer,' Jiriki said softly, 'truer than any you have known.'

The flecks of shining green began to flutter and coalesce, sparkling emerald fishes rising to the surface of a shadowy pond. Simon felt himself sinking into the mirror, although he did not move from where he leaned above it. The green became many greens, as many shades and tints as ever were. In a moment they had resolved themselves into a startling confusion of bridges and towers and trees: a city and a forest grown together, sprouting as one in the midst of a grassy plain – not a city a forest had grown over, like Da'ai Chikiza, but a thriving, living amalgam of plant and polished stone, myrtle, jade, and viridian.

'*Enki-e-Shao'saye*,' Jiriki whispered. The grass on the plain bent luxuriantly before the wind; scarlet, white, and sky-blue pennants fluttered like blossoms amid the city's branching spires. 'The last and greatest city of the Summer.'

'Where . . . is . . . it . . . ?' Simon breathed, astonished and bewitched by its beauty.

'Not so much *where*, manchild, as *when*. The world is not only vaster than you know, Seoman, it is also far, far older. Enki-e-Shao'saye is long crumbled now. It lay east of the great forest.'

'Crumbled?'

'It was the last place where Zida'ya and Hikeda'ya lived together, before the Parting. It was a city of great craft and greater beauty; the very wind in the towers made music, and the lamps of night shone bright as stars. Nenais'u danced under moonlight by her forest pool, and the admiring trees leaned down to watch.' He shook his head slowly. 'All gone. Those were the summer-days of my people. We are now far into the Autumn . . .'

'Gone . . . ?' Simon could still not grasp the tragedy. It seemed as though he could reach into the mirror, touch

861

one of the needle-sharp towers with his finger. He felt tears struggling to break free. No home. The Sithi had lost their homes . . . they were lonely and homeless in the world.

Jiriki passed his hand over the glass, and it clouded. 'Gone,' he said. 'But as long as there is memory, Summer remains. And even Winter passes.' He turned and looked long at Simon, and the agonized expression on the youth's face at last brought a small, careful smile to his own.

'Do not mourn so,' he said, and patted Simon's arm. 'Brightness is not completely erased from the world – not yet. And not all beautiful places have fallen to ruin. Still there is Jao é-Tinukai'i, the dwelling of my family and people. Perhaps someday, if we both come down safely from this mountain, you will see it.' He grinned his strange grin, thinking of something. 'Perhaps you will . . .'

The rest of the climb up Urmsheim – three more days on narrow, dangerous pathways scarcely more than ice-ribbons, over sheer, glassy sheets by laboriously hacked hand and footholds; two more nights of evil, teeth-grinding cold – passed by Simon like a fleeting but painful dream. Through the terrible weariness that beset him he held onto Jiriki's gift of summer – for it *was* a gift, he knew – and was comforted. Even as his numb fingers struggled to cling, and his numb feet to stay on the path, he thought that somewhere there would be warmth again, and something like a bed and clean clothes – even a bath would be welcome! All those things were out there somewhere, if he could just keep his head down and get off the mountain alive.

When you stopped to think about it, he reflected, there weren't many things in life one truly *needed*. To want too much was worse than greed: it was stupidity – a waste of precious time and effort.

The company slowly worked their way around the

862

body of the mountain until the sun rose each morning to shine over their right shoulders. The air was growing painfully thin, forcing frequent halts for the catching of breath; even hardy Jiriki and uncomplaining An'nai were moving more slowly, limbs weighted as though by heavy garments. The human companions, except for the troll, positively dragged. Grimmric had revived, thanks to the potency of Binabik's Qanuc elixir, but shivered and coughed as he climbed.

From time to time the wind increased, sending the clouds that hugged Urmsheim's shoulders flying like tattered ghosts. The mountain's silent neighbors would slowly materialize, jagged peaks holding lofty convention far above the surface of Osten Ard, indifferent to the sordid and minuscule landscape at their feet. Binabik, as comfortable breathing the insubstantial air of the Roof of the World as he had been sitting in Naglimund's pantry, pointed out wide, craggy Mintahoq in the east to his gasping companions, as well as several of the other mountains compassing the troll-fells of Yiqanuc.

They came upon it suddenly, while fully half the mountain's height still towered above them. Struggling over a rocky outcropping, the rope pulled taut as a bowstring between them, every breath burning their lungs, they heard one of the Sithi – who had climbed ahead and out of sight – let out a strange, whistling cry. The companions scrambled toward the top with all possible haste; the question of what they were hurrying toward dangled unspoken. Binabik, leading the line, stopped on the hillcrest; he swayed a little to keep his balance.

'Daughter of the Mountains!' the troll gasped, a plume of vapor rising from his mouth. He stood and did not move for long moments. Simon carefully mounted the last few steps.

At first he saw nothing before him but another wide valley of snow, its white wall rising across from them, open on the right to the air and sky and a succession of snowy cliffs that dropped away down the side of Urmsheim. He turned to Binabik to ask what had made him cry out. The question died on his lips.

On the left hand the valley dug deep into the mountain's face, the valley floor sloping up as its high walls gradually angled together. At their apex, stretching up from the ground to the triangle of gray-blue sky, loomed the Uduntree.

'Elysia Mother of God!' Simon said, his voice cracking. 'Mother of God,' he repeated.

At first, confronted by the vast, mad, implausibility of the thing, he thought it *was* a tree – a titanic tree of ice a thousand feet tall, myriad branches sparkling and coruscating in the noonday sun, shadowed at its impossible summit by a halo of mist. It was only as he finally convinced himself it was real – that such a thing could exist in a world that also contained such mundane objects as pigs and fences and mixing-bowls – that he began to understand what it was: a frozen waterfall, the accumulation of years of icy snowmelt captured in a million icicles, a crystalline tracery down the jagged stone-spine that formed the Uduntree's trunk.

Jiriki and An'nai stood transfixed a few ells below the valley floor, staring up at the tree. Simon, following Binabik, began struggling down the slope toward them, feeling the rope around his waist grow tense as Grimmric reached the summit and was himself struck motionless; Simon then waited patiently as the process was repeated two more times for Haestan and Sludig. At last they all made their stumbling, preoccupied way down to the deep snow of the valley floor. The Sithi were quietly singing, and paid no heed to the arrival of their human companions.

For a long while no one spoke. The majesty of the Uduntree almost seemed to suck the breath from their bodies, and for a great span of time the companions just stood and stared, feeling emptied.

'Let us be going forward,' Binabik said at last. Simon started resentfully. The troll's voice seemed a rude intrusion.

''Tis th' d–d–damnedest sight my eyes have ever h– held,' Grimmric stuttered.

'Here old black One-Eye climbed to the stars,' Sludig said quietly. 'God save me from blasphemy, but I can feel his presence still.'

Binabik started out across the open valley floor. The others followed after a few moments, tugged along by the troll's harness rope. The snow was thigh-deep and slow going. After they had moved some thirty difficult steps, Simon finally tore his eyes from the spectacle to look back. An'nai and Jiriki had not joined them; the two Sithi still stood side by side, as if waiting for something.

They moved forward. The valley walls leaned ever closer above their heads as though fascinated by these rare travelers. Simon could see that the base of the ice-tree was a huge, jumbled, hole-dotted rockery sheltered beneath the arching lower branches – not true branches, but rather layer upon spreading layer of melted and refrozen icicles, each one wider than the one above, so that the bottommost branches made a ceiling half as wide as a tourney field over the strew of boulders.

They had come close enough that the great ice-pillar seemed to extend through the very roof of the sky. As he bent his neck painfully for one last glimpse at the near-vanished peak of the tree, a rush of surprise and fear ran over him, blackening his sight for a moment.

*The tower! From my dreams, the tower with branches!* Stunned, he tripped and tumbled into the snow. Haestan reached down a broad hand and lifted him without a word. Simon chanced another look up, and a frightening sensation that was more than mere dizziness sluiced over him.

'Binabik!' he cried. The troll, just passing into the violet darkness of the Uduntree's shadow, turned swiftly.

865

'Quiet, Simon!' he hissed. 'We have no knowing if we may knock sharp ice loose, much to our regret.'

Simon made his way forward through the clinging snow as quickly as he could.

'Binabik, this is the tower I dreamed – a white tower with branches like a tree! This is it!'

The troll surveyed the clutter of huge boulders and shattered rock in the tree's dark underside. 'I thought it was your belief you saw Green Angel Tower, from the Hayholt?'

'I did – that is to say, it was part of both. But since I'd never seen this before, I didn't know that some of *it* was some of *this*! Do you understand?!'

Binabik cocked a bushy black eyebrow. 'When we are next finding time, I will cast the bones. Now we have a mission still unperformed.'

He waited until the others had straggled up before speaking again. 'It is my thought,' he said at last, 'that we should be soon making a camp. Then we can spend the last hours of daylight hunting for some sign of Colmund's company, or the sword Thorn.'

'Are them . . .' Haestan indicated the now-distant Sithi, '. . . goin' t'help?'

Before Binabik could voice an opinion, Grimmric whistled excitedly and pointed up at the jumble of rocks. 'Look, you!' he said, 'I think there's been someone stayin' here before. Look at th' rocks there!'

Simon followed the soldier's finger to a spot farther up the sloping pile of rocks, where several rows of stones had been piled in the mouth of one of the cavelike holes.

'Y'r right!' Haestan exclaimed. 'He's right! Sure as Tunath's Bones lie north t'south, someone made th'selves a camp there.'

'Careful!' Binabik said urgently, but Simon had already shed his harness and was making his way up the scree, setting off tiny avalanches where he stepped incautiously. He reached the cave in short moments, and stood, teetering on a loose stone.

'This wall was made by men, that's certain!' he called back excitedly. The cavern mouth was perhaps three ells wide, and somebody had hurriedly but not unskillfully set rock to rock across the front – to keep in warmth, perhaps? To keep out animals?

'Kindly do not shout, Simon,' Binabik said. 'We will be up directly with you.'

Waiting impatiently, all thoughts of thin air and killing cold in abeyance, Simon watched the company climb after him. Even as Haestan began his clamber up the pile, the two Sithi appeared beneath the eaves of the Uduntree. After taking in the scene for a moment they mounted up to the cave as nimbly as branch-leaping squirrels.

It took a moment for Simon's eyes to adjust to the more profound darkness inside the low cavern. When he could finally see, it took only a moment more for his eyes to widen with shock.

'Binabik! It's . . . they're . . .'

The troll, able to stand upright at his side where Simon crouched, brought the heel of his hand against his breastbone.

'Qinkipa. . . !' he said. 'They have been waiting for our coming.'

The cave was scattered with the brown bones of men. The skeletons, naked but for fittings and jewelry of corroded black and green metal, sat propped against the cavern's walls. A thin layer of ice covered everything, like preserving glass.

'Is it Colmund?' Simon asked.

'Usires save us,' Sludig choked behind him, 'get out, the air must be poison!'

'There is no poison here,' Binabik chided him. 'As to whether it is Sir Colmund's party – the chances seem to me good.'

'It is interesting to wonder how they might have died,' Jiriki's voice was startlingly resonant in the small cavern. 'If they froze, why did they not huddle together for

867

warmth?' He indicated the scattering of the bodies about the chamber. 'If they were killed by some animal – or each other – then why are the bones arranged so carefully, as if each lay down to die in turn?'

'There are mysteries here worth much talking someday,' the troll responded, 'but we have other duties, and light is failing fast.'

'All of you,' Sludig said, his voice strained with some terrible urgency, 'come here! Here!'

He stood over one of the skeletons. Although the bones had collapsed into a madder-colored heap, still it had the look of someone caught in the act of prayer, kneeling with arms outstretched. Between the bones of its two hands, which lay half-submerged in ice like stones in a bowl of milk, was a long bundle wrapped in frosted, rotting oilcloth.

All the air suddenly seemed to leak out of the cavern. A taut, deadening silence fell on the company. The troll and the Rimmersman kneeled, as if in imitation of the ancient bones, and began chipping away at the frozen bundle with their ice-axes. The oilcloth came away in chips, like bark. A long strip splintered away to reveal a profound blackness beneath.

'It's not metal,' said Simon in disappointment.

'Nor is Thorn made of metal,' Binabik grunted, 'or of no metal you have ever been seeing.'

Sludig was able to wiggle the point of his axe in beneath the petrified cloth, and with Haestan's straining help they tore loose another strip. Simon gasped. Binabik was right: this thing emerging like a jet-black butterfly from its prisoning chrysalis was not only a sword, it was a sword like no other he had ever seen: long as a man's arms spread wide, fingertip to fingertip, and black. The purity of its blackness was unmarred by the colors that sparkled on its edge, as though the blade was so supernaturally sharp that it even sliced the dim light of the cavern into rainbows. Had it not been for the silver cord wrapped around the hilt as a handgrip – leaving the uncovered guard and pommel as pitchy as the rest of its length – it would have seemed to bear no relationship to mankind at all. Rather, despite its symmetry, it would have seemed some natural growth, some pure essence of nature's blackness extruded by chance in the form of an exquisite sword.

'*Thorn*,' Binabik whispered, a sort of reverence coloring his satisfaction.

'Thorn,' Jiriki repeated, and Simon could not even try to guess the thoughts behind *his* naming of the thing.

'So this *is* it, then?' Sludig said at last. 'It is a beautiful thing. What could kill them with such a blade in their possession?'

'Who can know what happened to Colmund?' Binabik said. 'But even a sword like Thorn you cannot eat when there is being no food.'

They all continued to stare at the blade. Grimmric, who was closest to the cave mouth, at last straightened out his crouch, hugging himself with thin arms.

'As th'troll says, y'can't eat swords. I'm goin' t'make fire for th'night.' He stepped outside the cavern and stood, stretching. He whistled a little; the tune, weak at first, grew stronger.

'There is scrub brush in the rock crevices that might burn with our kindling,' Sludig called after him.

Haestan leaned forward, then touched the black blade with a cautious finger. 'Cold,' he smiled. 'No surprise that, is't?' He turned to Binabik, oddly diffident. 'May I lift it?'

The troll nodded. 'Carefully.'

Haestan slipped his fingers gently under the cord-wrapped hilt and pulled, but the sword did not move. 'Frozen,' he guessed. He tugged again, harder, with no better result. 'Frozen up hard, 'tis,' he panted, pulling now with all his might. His breath rose in a cloud.

Sludig leaned over to help him. Grimmric, outside the cavern, stopped whistling and said something unintelligible.

As the Rimmersman and the Erkynlander both heaved, the black sword at last began to move, but rather than snapping free of prisoning ice the blade merely slid a little to one side, then stopped.

'It is not frozen,' Sludig gasped. 'It is as heavy as a millstone. We two together can barely move it!'

'How will we get it down the mountain, Binabik?' Simon asked. He wanted to laugh. It was all so silly and strange – to find a magic sword and then not be able to carry it away! He reached his own hand forward and felt the deep, cool weight of the thing – and something else. A warming? Yes, some indefinable life beneath the cold surface, like a sleeping serpent stirring into wakefulness – or was he imagining things?'

Binabik stared at the immobile blade and scratched his shaggy hair, thinking. A moment later Grimmric appeared in the cavern, waving his arms. As they turned to look at him, he slumped to his knees, then toppled over, limp as a sack of meal.

A black arrow, a thorn of a different sort, quivered in his back.

Blue light bathed the silver mask, touching its contours, with pale fire. The face beneath had once been the model for its sculpted, inhuman beauty, but what the mask now covered no living creature could say. The world had made uncountable revolutions since the face of Utuk'ku had disappeared forever behind its gleaming lines.

The blue-brushed mask turned and surveyed the giant, many-shadowed stone hall, eyeing her scurrying servitors as they labored to do all that she had bid them. Their voices were raised in songs of praise and remembrance; their white hair fluttered in the eternal winds of the Chamber of the Harp. She listened with approval as the clatter of witchwood hammers echoed through the endless maze of corridors riddling frozen Nakkiga, the

870

mountain the Norns called *Mask of Tears*. The mortals called her home Stormspike, and Utuk'ku knew that it haunted their dreams . . . as it should. The silver face nodded, satisfied. All was in readiness.

Suspended in the mist that crowned the Great Well, the Harp suddenly moaned, a desolate sound like wind in the high passes. The Norn Queen knew it was not His voice – not He who could make the Breathing Harp sing and howl, not He whose wrathful song sent the entire well-chamber thundering with impossible musics. Some lesser voice was crawling through the Harp, trapped in its infinite complexities like an insect in a sealed maze.

She lifted a silver-and-white-gloved finger mere inches above the black stone of her chair and made a small gesture. The moan became louder, and something quivered into substantiality in the fog above the Well – the gray sword Jingizu, pulsing with painful light. Something held it: a shadowy figure, its hand a formless knot around Jingizu's hilt.

Utuk'ku understood. She did not have to see the supplicant; the sword was there, far more real than any mortal temporarily allowed to possess it.

*Who comes before the Queen of the Hikeda'ya?* she asked, knowing the answer full well.

*Elias, High King of Osten Ard*, the shadowy figure replied. *I have decided to accept the terms of your master.*

The word 'master' nettled her. *Mortal*, she said at last, with queenly languor, *what you wish will be given to you. But you have waited long . . . almost too long.*

*There were . . .* The shadowy thing holding the sword swayed, as if weary. How fleshy, how weak these mortals were! How could they have caused such damage? *I thought*, it continued, *. . . that things would be . . . different. Now I submit.*

*Of course you do. And you shall receive what was promised to you.*

*Thank you, O Queen. And I shall give you what I have promised in return . . .*

*Of course you will.*

She lowered her gloved fingers, and the apparition vanished. Red light bloomed deep in the Well as He came. As He took possession of it, the Harp vibrated to a note of perfect triumph.

'I . . . don't want t'die. . . !' Grimmric wheezed. A froth of blood on his chin and cheek, his crooked teeth standing in his gaping mouth, he looked like a hare caught and savaged by hounds. 'It's . . . it's so bloody cold,' he shivered.

'Who did it?' Simon squeaked, losing control of his voice in shock and panic.

'Whoever,' Haestan muttered, ashen-faced as he bent over his stricken countryman, 'they got us like coney up a plug-hole.'

'We must get out!' Sludig snapped.

'Wrap cloaks around arms,' Binabik said, assembling his blowpipe from the pieces of his walking stick. 'We are having no shields against arrows, but that will be some help.'

Without a word Jiriki stepped over Haestan and the fallen Grimmric, moving toward the mouth of the cave. An'nai, tight-lipped, followed.

'Prince Jiriki. . . ?' Binabik began, but the Sithi paid no heed.

'Come then,' Sludig said, 'we cannot let them go out alone.' He snatched up his blade from the cloak where he had set it.

Even as the others followed the Sithi to the cave mouth, Simon looked down at the black sword Thorn. They had come such a long way to find it – were they to lose it now? What if they escaped, but were cut off from the cavern and could not come back? He put his hand on its hilt and again felt the strange, thrumming sensation. He tugged, and to his amazement it came up in his hand.

The weight of it was tremendous, but using two hands he was able to lift it off the frozen cave floor.

What was happening here? He was dizzied. Two strong men could not lift it, but he could. *Magic?*

Simon cautiously carried the long, achingly heavy blade to where his companions stood. Haestan untied his cloak, but instead of wrapping it around his arm for protection he laid it gently over Grimmric. The wounded man coughed, bringing up more blood. Both Erkynlanders were crying.

Before Simon could say a word about the sword, Jiriki strode from the cave mouth onto the rocky porch, cocky as a juggler.

'Stand forward!' he shouted, and the icy walls of the valley sent the echoes tumbling back. 'Who attacks the company of Prince Jiriki i-Sa'onserei, son of Shima'onari and scion of the House of Year-Dancing? Who would war on the Ziday'a?'

In answer a dozen figures clambered down the sloping valley walls and stood, a hundred ells from the base of Uduntree. All were armed, all wore glare-masks and hooded white cloaks, and each bore on his breast the triangular badge of Stormspike.

'Norns?' Simon gasped, forgetting for an instant the strange object cradled in his arms.

'These are not Hikeda'ya,' said An'nai shortly. 'They are mortals who do Utuk'ku's bidding.'

One of the cloaked men took a limping, stiff-legged pace forward. Simon recognized the sunburned skin and pale beard. 'Go away, Ziday'a,' Ingen Jegger said. His voice was slow and cold. 'The Queen's Huntsman has no quarrel with you. It is those mortals cowering behind who have thwarted me, and who cannot be allowed to leave this place.'

'They are under my protection, mortal man.' Prince Jiriki patted his sword. 'Go back and sit beneath Utuk'ku's table – you will get no scraps here.'

Ingen Jegger nodded. 'So be it.' He waved a negligent

873

hand and one of his huntsmen swiftly drew his bow and fired. Jiriki sprang aside, pulling Sludig along, who had stood just at his back. The arrow shattered on a rock beside the cave mouth.

'Down!' the prince shouted, even as An'nai let fly an arrow in return. The huntsmen scattered, leaving one of their company face down in the snow. Simon and his companions went skittering down the slippery rocks to the base of the ice-tree as arrows hummed past.

Within minutes both sides' meager ration of arrows had been exhausted, but not before Jiriki had feathered another of Ingen's raiders, putting a barb in the running man's eye as neatly as shooting an apple balanced on a stone wall. Nearby, Sludig was stricken in the fleshy part of his thigh, but the arrow had caromed off a stone first and the Rimmersman was able to pluck the head out and limp to shelter.

Simon crouched behind a stone promontory, part of the Uduntree's trunk, cursing himself for leaving his bow and precious arrows in the cave. He watched as An'nai, his own quiver exhausted, cast bow aside and pulled his slender dark sword from its sheath; the face of the Sitha was as implacable as if he had been mending fences. Simon was sure his own must be a mirror of his overwhelming inner fear, of his tripping heart and hollow stomach. He looked down at Thorn, and felt a pulse of life in it. The heaviness had become different somehow, animate, as though it were full of rattling bees; it seemed a bound animal, stirring as it breathed the enticing scents of freedom.

A short way to his left, on the far side of the stone trunk, Haestan and Sludig were slinking forward, using the great curving branches of ice for cover. Safe now from arrows, Ingen was gathering his huntsmen for a charge on the valley floor.

'Simon!' a voice hissed. Startled, he turned around to see Binabik crouching on the stone prominence above his head.

874

'What will we do?' Simon asked, trying to keep his voice level but not succeeding. The troll, however, was staring down at the black length of Thorn, nestled in Simon's arms like a child.

'How. . . ?' Binabik asked, his round face full of surprise.

'I don't know, I only picked it up! I don't know! *What are we going to do?*'

The troll shook his head. 'You are now to stay right here. I am going to help with what I can. I wish that I had a spear.' He sprang down lightly, his heel spattering Simon with a flirt of gravel as he bounded past.

'For Josua Lackhand!' Haestan shouted, and charged out from the eaves of the Uduntree onto the white valley floor, Sludig limping purposefully behind. As soon as they reached the deep snow they slowed as if running in treacle. Ingen's huntsmen slogged toward them, performing the same halting, deadly dance.

Haestan swung up his heavy sword, but before he even reached the attackers the first white-cloaked figure fell, clutching his throat.

'Yiqanuc!' Binabik shouted in triumph, then crouched to reload his blowpipe.

The clang of swords reverberated as the first of Ingen's men reached Haestan and Sludig. The Sithi were there a moment later, moving nimbly over the snow, but still the companions were far outnumbered. A moment later tall Haestan caught the flat of a blade on his hooded skull and went down in a puff of snow. Only An'nai leaping forward to stand over him prevented his being skewered on the spot.

Blades shimmered in the thin sunlight, and cries of pain and rage almost drowned the clash of metal. Simon saw with a sinking heart that Binabik, whose remaining darts had proved useless against the thick cloaks of huntsmen, was pulling his long knife from his belt.

*How can he be so brave? He's too small – they'll kill him before he can get close enough to use it!*

875

'Binabik!' he shouted, and climbed to his feet. He lifted the heavy black sword over his head, feeling its great weight dragging at him even as he stumbled forward.

The ground suddenly pitched beneath his feet. He staggered, spreadlegged, and then felt the very mountain seem to sway. A rumbling screech pierced his ears, like the sound of a heavy stone dragged across a quarry. The combatants stopped, dumbfounded, and stared down at their feet.

With another horrible shriek of tortured ice the ground began to bulge. In the center of the valley floor, only a few cubits from where Ingen Jegger stood gaping in horrible confusion, a great slab of ice pushed upward, cracking and buckling as it came, snow sliding off in great drifts.

Propelled by the sudden shifting of the ground beneath him, Simon tripped and tumbled forward, holding tightly onto Thorn, and came to a stop virtually in the middle of the combatants. No one seemed to notice him: they were all frozen in place as if the very ice of the Uduntree had turned their blood to immobilizing frost, goggling at the impossible thing pushing its way up from beneath the snow.

The ice dragon.

A snakelike head as long as a man thrust out of the new-formed crevice, white-scaled above a toothy mouth, the staring eyes blue and occluded. It waved sinuously from side to side on its long neck, as though curiously observing the minute creatures who had awakened it from years-long slumber. Then, terrifyingly swift, it darted out and caught one of the huntsmen in its jaws, biting him in half and swallowing his legs. His crushed, bloodied torso fell into the snow like a discarded rag.

'*Igjarjuk*! – it is Igjarjuk!' came Binabik's thin shout. The gleaming ivory head snapped up another shrieking, white-cloaked morsel. As the rest scattered, their faces emptied by unthinking horror, splay-clawed white feet

876

gripped the crevice's rim, and the dragon's long body, back covered with strange, pale fur, yellowed as old parchment, humped slowly up from below. A whiplike tail, long as a jousting run, swept two of the huntsmen wailing into the pit.

Simon sat stunned upon the snow, unable to force belief in the monstrous thing that crouched on the rim of the ice-crevice like a cat on a chairback. The long-snouted head dipped to regard him, and the murky, unblinking blue eyes fixed his with calm, ageless malice. His head throbbed, as though he tried to stare through water – those eyes, hollow as glacial crevices! It saw him, it *knew* him in some way – it was as old as the bones of the mountains, as wise and cruel and uncaring as Time itself.

The jaws parted and a sliver of black tongue knifed out, tasting the air. The head bobbed closer.

'*Ske'i*, spawn of Hidohebhi!' a voice shouted. An instant later An'nai had vaulted onto the creature's hindquarters, grasping the thick fur for support. Singing, he lifted his sword and hacked at a scaly leg. Simon got to his feet and stumbled back, even as the dragon brought up its tail and smashed the Sitha away; An'nai flew fifty cubits to land crumpled in the snow at the valley's exposed rim, nothing beyond him but mist. Jiriki ran after with a cry of anger and despair.

'Simon!' the troll shouted, '*Run!* We can do nothing!'

Even as he spoke the mist that had enshrouded Simon's wits began to clear. In a moment he was on his feet, flying after Jiriki. Binabik, who had been perched on the crevice's far rim, flung himself backward as the dragon lashed out, and the great jaws snapped shut on nothing with a sound like an iron gate. The troll fell into a rift in the ice and disappeared.

Jiriki huddled over the body of An'nai, motionless as a statue. Pelting toward him, Simon looked back over his shoulder to see Igjarjuk slithering down from the broken battlement of ice and moving across the little valley, short legs gripping the ice as it wound along the ground, quickly narrowing the distance between itself and its stumbling prey.

Simon tried to shout Jiriki's name, but his throat caught; all that came out was a strangled grunt. The Sitha turned around. His amber eyes were bright. He climbed to his feet beside the body of his comrade, holding his long, rune-carved witchwood sword up before him.

'Come, Old One!' Jiriki cried. 'Come to me and taste *Indreju*, you bastard child of Hidohebhi!'

Simon grimaced as he dug toward the prince. No need to shout – the dragon was coming of its own accord.

'Get behind . . .' Jiriki started to say as Simon reached him, then the Sitha abruptly pitched forward; the snow beneath him had fallen away. Jiriki skidded backward toward the valley's edge and the empty distance beyond. Desperately, he reached out to grab at the snow. He stopped, clinging, his feet dangling over nothingness. An'nai, a bloodied tangle, lay undisturbed a cubit away.

'Jiriki. . . !' Simon stopped. There was a noise like thunder behind. He whirled to see the vast white bulk of Igjarjuk bearing down, head flailing from side to side with the motion of the driving legs. Diving to one side, away from Jiriki and An'nai, he rolled and came up on his feet. The blue saucer-eyes tracked him, and the creature, now only a hundred paces away, swerved to follow.

Simon realized he was still carrying Thorn. He lifted it up; it was suddenly light as a willow-wand, and seemed to sing in his hands, like a wind-sawed rope. He glanced back over his shoulder: a few paces of ground was all, then empty air. One of the distant peaks hovered in the swirling mists across the chasm – white, quiet, serene.

*Usires save me*, he wondered, *why doesn't the dragon make a sound?* His mind seemed to float loose inside his body. One hand stole up to Miriamele's scarf at his throat, and then he grasped the silver-wrapped hilt once more. Igjarjuk's head loomed, the gullet a black pit, the eye a blue lantern. The world seemed constructed of silence.

What should he shout at the last?

He remembered what Jiriki had once said of mortals, even as the frosty musk of the dragon blew down on him, a stench like sour cold earth and wet stones.

'Here I am!' he cried, and brought Thorn whistling toward the baleful eye. '*I am . . . Simon!*'

Something caught at the blade, and a gout of black blood spat at him, burning like fire, like ice, searing his face even as a great white something crashed through and carried him down into darkness.

# 43
# The Harrowing

The robin, orange breast glinting like a fading ember, lighted on one of the elm's low branches. He turned his head slowly from side to side surveying the herb garden, and chirped impatiently, as if displeased to find everything in such poor order.

Josua watched him fly away, dipping over the garden wall, then arching sharply upward to speed past the battlements of the inner keep. Within a moment he was a speck of black against the bright gray dawn.

'The first robin I have seen in a very long time. Perhaps it is a hopeful sign in this dark Yuven.'

The prince turned, surprised, to see Jarnauga standing on the path, eyes fixed on the spot where the bird had disappeared. The old man, apparently unmindful of the cold, wore only breeches and a thin shirt; his white feet were bare.

'Good morningtide, Jarnauga,' Josua said, pulling the neck of his cloak a little tighter, as if the Rimmersman's unsusceptibility increased his own chill. 'What brings you out to the garden so early?'

'This old body needs very little sleep, Prince Josua,' he smiled. 'And I might ask you the same in turn, but I think I know the answer.'

Josua nodded morosely. 'I have not slept well since I first entered my brother's dungeons. While my comfort has improved since then, worry has taken the place of hanging in chains as a denier of rest.'

'There are many kinds of imprisonment,' Jarnauga nodded.

They walked quietly for a while through the maze of walkways. The garden was the lady Vorzheva's onetime pride, set out to her meticulous guidelines – for a girl born in a wagon, the prince's courtiers whispered, she was certainly a stickler for elegance – but had now been allowed to deteriorate due to poor weather, as well as an abundance of more pressing concerns.

'Something is amiss, Jarnauga,' Josua said at last. 'I can sense it. I can almost feel it, as a fisherman feels the weather. What is my brother doing?'

'It seems to me he is doing his best to kill us all,' the old man replied, a tight grin creasing his leathery face. 'Is that what is "amiss"?'

'No,' the prince said seriously. 'No. That is just the problem. We have held him off for a month, with bitter losses – Baron Ordmaer, Sir Grimstede, Wuldorcene of Caldsae, as well as hundreds of stout yeomen – but it has been nearly a fortnight since he has mounted a serious assault. The attacks have been . . . cursory. He is going through the motions of a siege. Why?' He sat down on a low bench, and Jarnauga sat beside him. 'Why?' he repeated.

'A siege is not always won by force of arms. Perhaps he is planning to starve us out.'

'But then why bother to attack at all? We have inflicted terrible losses on them. Why not just wait? It is as though he seeks only to keep us inside, and himself outside. What is Elias doing?'

The old man shrugged. 'As I have told you: I can see much, but the insides of men's hearts are beyond my vision. We have survived so far. Let us be thankful.'

'I am. But I know my brother. He is not the type to sit patiently and wait. There is something in the wind, some plan . . .' He trailed off into silence and sat staring at an overgrown bed of mockfoil. The flowers had never opened, and weeds stood insolently among the twining stems like carrion-eaters mingling with a dying herd.

'He could have been a magnificent king, you know,' Josua said suddenly, as if in answer to some unspoken question. 'There was a time when he was just strong, and not a bully. That is to say, he was sometimes cruel when we were younger, but it was only that innocent sort of cruelty that big boys show to the smaller ones. He even taught me some things – swordplay, wrestling. I never taught him anything. He was not very interested in the things I knew about.'

The prince smiled sadly, and for a moment a child's fragile look seemed to shine through his close-pared features.

'We might even have been friends . . .' The prince knitted his long fingers and blew warm breath into them. 'If only Hylissa had lived.'

'Miriamele's mother?' Jarnauga asked quietly.

'She was very beautiful – southern, you know – black hair, white teeth. She was very shy, but when she smiled it was as though a lamp had been lit. And she loved my brother – as best she could. But he frightened her: so loud, so big. And she was very small . . . slim like a willow, jumped if one only touched her shoulder . . .'

The prince said no more, but sat lost in thought. Watery sunshine broke through the clouds on the horizon, bringing a little color to the drab garden.

'You sound as though you thought much of her,' the old man said gently.

'Oh, I loved her.' Josua's voice was matter-of-fact, his eyes still firmly fixed on the tangled mockfoil. 'I burned for love of her. I prayed to God to take the love away, even though I knew that I would be but a husk, the living core of me scooped out. Not that my prayer did any good. And I think she loved me, too; I was her only friend, she often said. No one else knew her as I did.'

'Did Elias suspect?'

'Of course. He suspected anyone who as much as stood near her at court pageants, and I was with her constantly. But always honorably,' he added hurriedly, then stopped. 'Why should I be so earnest about that, even now? Usires forgive me, I wish we *had* betrayed him!' Josua's teeth were clenched. 'I wish she were my dead lover, instead of only my brother's dead wife.' He stared accusingly at the knob of scarred flesh protruding from his right sleeve. 'Her death lies on my conscience like a great stone – it was my fault! My God, we are a haunted family.'

He broke off at the clatter of footsteps on the path.

'Prince Josua! Prince Josua, where are you?'

'Here,' the prince called distractedly, and a moment later one of his guards stumbled into view around a hedge-wall.

'My prince,' he gasped, bending a knee, 'Sir Deornoth says you must come at once!'

'Are they onto the walls again?' Josua asked, standing and shaking dew from his wool cloak. His voice still sounded distant.

'No, sire,' the guard said, his mustached mouth opening and closing in excitement as though he were a whiskered fish. 'It's your brother – I mean the King, sire. He's pulling back. The siege is ending.'

The prince gave Jarnauga a puzzled, worried glance as they hurried up the path behind the excited guard.

'The High King has given over!' Deornoth shouted as Josua made his way up the steps, cloak billowing in the wind. 'See! He turns tail and runs!'

Deornoth turned and gave Isorn a comradely smack on the shoulder. The duke's son grinned, but Einskaldir beside him glared fiercely at the young Erkynlander, lest he should think to try anything so foolish on him.

'What now, what?' Josua said, pushing up beside Deornoth on the sagging curtain wall. Directly below them lay the shattered ruins of a miner's box, evidence of

883

a futile attempt to drop the curtain wall by tunneling beneath it. The wall had dipped a few feet, but held: Dendinis had built for the ages. The miners, even as they had set fire to the wooden pillars shoring their tunnel, had been felled by the few stones they had themselves shaken loose.

In the distance lay Elias' camp, an anthill of scurrying activity. The remaining siege-engines had been toppled and shattered so that they would benefit no one else; the rows and rows of tents had vanished, as if swept up and carried away by gale winds. Thin sounds – the distant cry of drovers, the crack of whips – floated up as the High King's wagons were loaded.

'He is retreating!' Deornoth said happily. 'We have done it!'

Josua shook his head. 'Why? Why should he? We have whittled away a bare fraction of his troops.'

'Perhaps he realizes now how strong Naglimund is,' Isorn said, squinting.

'Then why not wait us out?' the prince demanded. 'Aedon! What goes on here? I can believe Elias himself might go back to the Hayholt – but why not leave even a token siege in place?'

'To lure us out,' Einskaldir said quietly. 'Onto open ground.' Scowling, he rubbed a rough thumb over the blade of his knife.

'It could be,' the prince said, 'but he should know me better.'

'Josua . . .' Jarnauga was looking out beyond the decamping army, into the morning haze cloaking the northern horizon. 'There are strange clouds away to the north.'

The others stared, but could see nothing but the dim beginnings of the Frostmarch.

'What sort of clouds?' the prince asked at last.

'Storm clouds. Very strange. Like none I have ever seen south of the mountains.'

The prince stood at the window listening to the murmur of the trailing wind, his forehead pressed against the cold stone frame. The spare courtyard below was moon-painted, and the trees swayed.

Vorzheva extended a white arm from beneath the fur coverlet.

'Josua, what is it? It is cold. Shut the window, and come back to your bed.'

He did not turn. 'The wind goes everywhere,' he said quietly. 'There is no keeping it out, and there is no staying it when it wishes to depart.'

'It is too late at night for your riddles, Josua,' she said, yawning and running fingers through her inky hair, so that it spread upon the sheet like black wings.

'It is perhaps too late for many things,' he replied, and went to sit on the bed beside her. His hand gently stroked her long neck, but still he looked out toward the window. 'I am sorry, Vorzheva. I am . . . confusing, I know. I have never been the right man – not for my tutors, not for my brother, or my father . . . and not for you. I sometimes wonder if I was born out of my time.' He lifted his finger to trace her cheek, and her warm breath was on his hand. 'When I see the world as it has been presented to me, I feel only a deep loneliness.'

'Lonely!?' Vorzheva sat up. The fur robe fell away; her smooth ivory skin was banded in moonlight. 'By my clan, Josua, you are a cruel man! Still you punish me for my mistake in trying to help the princess. How can you share my bed and call yourself lonely? Go away, you moping boy, go sleep with one of those cold northern girls, or in some monk's den. Go then!'

She struck at him, and he caught her arm. She was strong despite her slenderness, and she slapped him twice with her other hand before he could roll atop her and pinion her.

'Peace, lady, peace!' he said, and then laughed, although his face stung. Vorzheva scowled and struggled. 'You are right,' he said. 'I have done you insult, and I ask your apology. I sue for peace.' He leaned down and kissed her on the neck, and then again on her anger-reddened cheek.

'Come nearer and I will bite you,' she hissed. Her body trembled against his. 'I was frightened for you when you went to battle, Josua. I thought you would die.'

'I was no less frightened, my lady. There is much in the world to fear.'

'And now you feel you are alone.'

'One can be lonely,' the prince said, offering his lip to be bitten, 'in the highest and best of company.'

Her arm, now free, closed around his neck to pull him closer. The moonlight silvered their intertwined limbs.

Josua dropped his bone spoon back into the soup bowl, and angrily watched the small eddies wash back and forth across the surface. The dining hall hummed with the rush of many voices.

'I cannot eat. I must know!'

Vorzheva, eating in silence, but with her usual good appetite, shot him a disquieted glance down the table.

'Whatever is happening, my prince,' Deornoth said shyly, 'you must have your strength.'

'You will need it to speak to your people, Prince Josua,' Isorn commented around a mouthful of bread. 'They are upset and puzzled. The king is gone. Why no celebration?'

'You know damnably well why not!' Josua snapped, then raised his hand to his temple in pain. 'Surely you can see it is some trap – that Elias would not give up so easily?'

'I suppose,' said Isorn, but did not seem convinced. 'That does not mean the people who have been crowded in the inner keep like cattle – ' he gestured with a large

886

hand at the milling folks pressed around the prince's table on all sides, most sitting on the floor or against the walls of the dining hall, chairs too precious for any but the noblest, – 'that *they* will understand. Take it from one who spent a hellish winter snowbound in Elvritshalla.' Isorn bit off another great hunk of bread.

Josua sighed and turned to Jarnauga. The old man, his serpent tattoos strangely mobile in the lanternlight, was deep in conversation with Father Strangyeard.

'Jarnauga,' the prince said quietly. 'You said you wished to talk to me of a dream you had.'

The old Rimmersgarder excused himself from the priest. 'Yes, Josua,' he answered, leaning close, 'but perhaps we should wait until we might speak privately.' He cocked an ear to the clamor of the dining hall. 'Then again, no one could eavesdrop in here even if he sat under your chair.' He showed a frosty smile.

'I have had dreams again,' he said at last, eyes jewel-bright beneath his brows. 'I have no power to summon them, but they sometimes come unbidden. Something has happened to the company sent to Urmsheim.'

'Something?' Josua's face was shadowed, slack.

'I only dreamed,' Jarnauga said defensively, 'but I felt a great rupture – pain and terror – and I felt the boy Simon calling out . . . calling out in fear and anger . . . and something else . . .'

'Could what has happened to them be the cause of the storm you saw this morning?' the prince asked leadenly, as if hearing bad news long expected.

'I do not think so. Urmsheim is in a range farther east, behind Drorshull lake and across the Wastes.'

'Are they alive?'

'I have no way of knowing. It was a dream, and a short, strange one at that.'

They walked later in silence on the high castle walls. The wind had rolled the clouds away, and the moon turned the deserted town below to bone and parchment.

Staring out in to the black northern sky, Josua exhaled steamily. 'So even the faint hope of Thorn is gone.'

'I did not say so.'

'You had no need. And I suppose you and Strangyeard are no nearer to discovering what has become of Fingil's sword Minneyar?'

'Sadly, no.'

'Then what more needs to be done to assure our downfall. God has played a cruel joke on . . .' Josua broke off as the old man clenched his arm.

'Prince Josua,' he said, gazing squint-eyed at the horizon, 'you convince me never to taunt the gods, even those who are not your own.' He sounded shaken, old for the first time.

'What do you mean?'

'You asked what more could be done to us?' The old man snorted in bitter humor. 'The storm clouds, that black storm in the north? It is moving toward us – and very swiftly, too.'

Young Ostrael of Runchester stood shivering on the curtain wall and reflected on what his father had once said.

*''Tis good t'serve thy prince. Tha'll see a bit o' th' world as soldier, boy.'* Firsfram had told him, folding his leathery farmer's hand over his son's shoulder, even as his mother, red-eyed, silently watched. *'Maybe an' tha'll go t'Southern Islands, or down Nabban-way, an' get thasel' out o' this be-damned Frostmarch wind.'*

His father was gone now. He'd disappeared last winter, dragged off by wolves during that terrible cold Decander . . . wolves or something else, for no trace of him was ever found. And Firsfram's son, the southern life still untasted, stood on a wall in the freezing wind, and felt the cold penetrating his very heart.

Ostrael's mother and sisters huddled below, with

hundreds of the other dispossessed, in makeshift barracks inside Naglimund's heavy stone keep. The walls of the keep provided far better shelter from the wind than did Ostrael's high perch, but even stone walls, no matter how thick, could not keep out the dreadful music of the approaching storm.

His eyes were drawn, fearfully but irresistibly, up to the dark blot roiling on the horizon, spreading as it came like gray ink poured into water. It was a smear, a blank space, as if something had rubbed away the stuff of reality. It was a spot where the very sky seemed to tilt, funneling the clouds downward into a slow-swirling mass like the tail of a whirlpool. From time to time bright prickles of lightning leaped across the top of the storm. And always, always, there was the horrible sound of drumming, distant as a spatter of rain on a thick roof, insistent as the chattering of Ostrael's teeth.

The hot air and fabled sun-dotted hills of Nabban seemed more and more to Firsfram's son like the Book-stories told by priests, a bit of imaginary comfort to drag one along, to hide the terror of inescapable death.

The storm came on, throbbing with drums like a hive of wasps.

Deornoth's lantern guttered in the stiff wind and nearly flickered out; he shielded it with his cloak until the flame grew steady once more. Beside him, Isorn Isgrimnurson stared out into the cold, lightning-scratched darkness.

'God's Tree! It's black as night,' Deornoth groaned. 'Just past noon, yet I can scarcely see at all.'

Isorn's mouth opened, a dark slash in his pale, lantern-lit face, but no sound came out. His jaw worked.

'All will be well,' Doernoth said, frightened himself by the strong young Rimmersman's fear. ''Tis just a storm – some evil, petty trick of Pryrates' . . .' Even as he said it he felt sure it was a lie. The black clouds that masked the sun, dragging night to the very gates of Naglimund, brought with them a dread that pressed on his very being like a weight, like the stone lid of a casket. What magician's summoning was this, what mere wizardry, that could push an icy spear of horror right into his very guts?

The storm trudged toward them, a clot of darkness, spreading far beyond the castle walls on either side, looming above the highest battlements, shot through with the blue-white flicker of lightning. The huddled town and countryside leaped into relief for a moment, then vanished again in the murk. The throbbing of drumbeats echoed against the curtain wall.

As the lightning flashed once more, momentarily counterfeiting the stolen daylight, Deornoth saw something that caused him to turn and grasp Isorn's broad arm so tightly the Rimmersman winced.

'Get the prince,' Deornoth's voice was hollow.

Isorn looked up, his superstitious fear of the storm overcome by the strangeness of Deornoth's manner. The young knight's face had gone slack, empty like a meal bag, even as his fingernails drew an unnoticed rill of blood from Isorn's arm.

'What . . . what is it?'

'Get Prince Josua,' Deornoth repeated. 'Go!'

The Rimmersman, with a backward glance at his friend, made the sign of the Tree, and staggered along the battlement toward the stairs.

Numb, heavy as lead, Deornoth stood and wished that he had been killed at Bullback Hill – even that he had died in disgrace – rather than see what was before him.

When Isorn returned with the prince and Jarnauga, Deornoth was still staring. There was no need to ask what he saw, for the lightning illuminated all.

A great army had come to Naglimund. Within the storm's swirling mist stood a vast forest of bristling spears. A galaxy of bright eyes gleamed in the darkness.

The drums rolled again, like thunder, and the storm settled over castle and town, a great, billowing tent of rain and black clouds and freezing fog.

The eyes gazed up at the walls – thousands of shining eyes, all full of fierce anticipation. White hair streamed in the wind, narrow white faces turned upward in their dark helms, staring at the walls of Naglimund. Speartips glinted blue in another flash of skyfire. The invaders peered silently upward like an army of ghosts, pale as blindfish, ethereal as moonsheen. The drums pulsed. In the mist, other, longer shadows stalked: giant shapes cloaked in armor, carrying great gnarled clubs. The drums pulsed again, then fell silent.

'*Merciful Aedon, give me rest,*' Isorn prayed. '*In Your arms will I sleep, upon Thy bosom . . .*'

'Who are they, Josua?' Deornoth asked quietly, as if merely curious.

'The White Foxes – the Norns,' the prince answered. 'They are Elias' reinforcements.' He lifted his hand wearily, as if to block the spectral legion from his sight. 'They are the Storm King's children.'

'Your Eminence, please!' Father Strangyeard tugged at the old man's arm, gently at first, then with increasing force. The old man clung to the bench like a whelk, a small shape in the darkness of the herb garden.

'We must pray, Strangyeard,' Bishop Anodis repeated stubbornly. 'Get you down on your knees.'

The throbbing, percussive sound of the storm intensified. The archive-master felt a panicky urge to run – somewhere, anywhere.

'This is . . . it is no natural twilight, Bishop. You must come inside, now. Please.'

'I knew I should not have stayed. I *told* Prince Josua not to resist the rightful king,' Anodis added plaintively. 'God is angry with us. We must pray to be shown the rightful path – we must remember His martyrdom on the Tree . . .' He waved his hand convulsively, as though swatting at flies.

'This? This is not God's doing,' Strangyeard replied, a scowl on his usually pleasant face. 'This is the work of your "rightful king" – he and his pet warlock.'

The bishop paid him no heed. 'Blessed Usires,' he babbled, crawling away from the priest toward the shadowy tangle of the mockfoil bed, 'Your humble supplicants repent of their sins. We have thwarted Your will, and in doing so have drawn Your just wrath . . .'

'Bishop Anodis!' cried Strangyeard in nervous exasperation, taking a step to follow him, then halting in surprise. A dense, swirling cold seemed to descend over the garden. A moment later, as the archive-master shuddered in the deepening chill, the sound of drumming stopped.

'Something . . .' A frosty wind flapped Stangyeard's hood in his face.

'O, yea, we have sinned m-m-mightily in our haughtiness, we puny men!' Anodis sang out, rattling through the mockfoil. 'We p-pray . . . we . . . p-p-pray. . . ?' he trailed off, his voice rising curiously.

'Bishop?'

There was a shudder of movement in the depth of the mockfoil. Strangyeard saw the old man's face appear, mouth agape. Something seemed to catch at him; dirt began to gout up all around, further obscuring events in the shadowy vegetation. The bishop screamed, a thin, keening sound.

'Anodis!' Strangyeard shouted, plunging into the mockfoil. 'Bishop!'

The screaming stopped. Strangyeard halted a moment later, standing over the bishop's huddled form. Slowly, as if the old man were revealing the end of some elaborate trick, the bishop rolled to one side.

Part of his face was a wash of red blood. A black head sat on the ground beside him, like a doll thrown aside by a forgetful child. The head, chewing rapidly, turned grinning toward Strangyeard. Its tiny eyes were white as bleached currants, the scraggly whiskers shiny with the bishop's blood. As it reached a long-fingered hand out of the hole to pull the bishop closer, two more heads popped from the ground on either side. The archive-master took a step backward. A scream lodged in his throat like a stone. The ground convulsed again – here, there, on all sides. Thin black hands wriggling like mole-snouts pushed up through the soil.

Strangyeard tumbled backward and fell, dragging himself toward the path, certain that any moment a clammy hand would close on his ankle. His mouth was stretched wide in a rictus of fear, but no sound came. He had lost his sandals in the undergrowth, and he lurched up the path toward the chapel on noiseless bare feet. The world seemed damply blanketed in silence; it choked him, and squeezed at his heart. Even the crash of the chapel door behind him seemed muffled. As he fumbled the bolt home a curtain of featureless gray came down before his eyes, and he fell into it gratefully, like a soft bed.

The flames of countless torches now rose among the Norns like blossoms in a poppy field, throwing the horridly beautiful faces into scarlet half-silhouette, adding grotesquely to the stature of the battle-garbed Hunën lurking behind. Soldiers clambered up onto the castle walls, only to stare down in shocked silence.

Five ghostly figures on horses pale as spider silk rode out into the open space before the curtain wall. The torchlight played on their hooded white cloaks, and the red pyramid of Stormspike glimmered and pulsed on their long rectangular shields. Fear seemed to surround these hooded ones like a cloud, reaching out into the hearts of all who saw them. The watchers on the walls felt a terrible, helpless weakness fall upon them.

The lead horseman lifted his spear; the four behind him did the same. The drums sounded three times.

*'Where is the master of* **Ujin e-d'a Sikhunae** *– The Snare That Traps the Hunter?'* The first horseman's voice was a mocking, echoing moan, like wind blowing down a long canyon. *'Where is the master of the House of a Thousand Nails?'*

The hovering storm breathed for long moments before the reply came.

'I am here.' Josua stepped forward, a slender shadow atop the gatehouse. 'What does such a strange band of travelers want at my door?' His voice was calm, but there was in it a faint quaver.

*'Why . . . we have come to see how the nails have rusted, while we have grown strong.'* The words came slowly, forced out in a hiss of air, as if the horseman was unused to speech. *'We have come, mortal, to have a little of our own back. This time it is man-blood that will spill on the soil of Osten Ard. We have come to pull your house down about your ears.'*

The implacable power and hatred of the hollow voice was such that many of the soldiers cried out and began to scramble down the walls back into the castle below. As Josua stood on the gate, unspeaking, a cry shrilled above the groans and frightened whispers of the Naglimunders.

'Diggers! There are diggers within the walls!'

The prince turned at a movement close by. It was Deornoth, climbing up on unsteady legs to stand at his side.

'The gardens of the keep are full of Bukken,' the young knight said. His eyes were wide as he looked down on the white horsemen.

The prince took a step forward. 'You speak as though of revenge,' he shouted to the pale multitude below. 'But that is a lie! You come at the bidding of the High King Elias – a mortal. You serve a mortal, as a tickbird does a cockindrill. Come then. Do your worst! You will find that not all the nails of Naglimund are rusted, and that there is iron here that can still deal death to the Sithi!'

A ragged cheer went up from those soldiers still atop the walls. The first rider spurred his horse forward a pace.

'*We are the Red Hand!*' His voice was cold as the grave. '*We serve no one but Ineluki, the Lord of Storms. Our reasons are our own – as your death will be your own!*'

He waved his spear above his head, and the drums burst out again. Shrill horns wailed.

'Bring up those wagons!' Josua shouted from the gatehouse roof. 'Block the way! They will try and throw down the gate!'

But instead of bringing up a ram to try and shatter the heavy steel and stout timbers of the gate, the Norns stood silent, watching as the five horsemen rode unhurriedly forward. One of the guards atop the wall loosed an arrow. It was followed by a score of others, but if they struck the riders it was only to pass through them: the pale horsemen faltered not a step.

The drums beat furiously, the pipes and strange trumpets groaned and shrieked. Dismounting, the riders appeared and disappeared in flashes of lightning as they strode the last few steps to the gate.

With dreadful deliberateness, the leader reached up to pull open his hooded cloak. A scarlet light seemed to spill forth. As he tore it away, it was as though he turned inside-out; suddenly he was all formlessness and smoldering red glare. The others did the same. Five beings of shifting, flickering lines grew and stood revealed – larger than before, each tall as two men, faceless, billowing like burning vermilion silk.

A black mouth opened in the leader's eyeless face as he lifted his arms to the gate and placed his burning hands against it.

'*Death!*' he bellowed, and his voice seemed to shake the very fundament of the walls. The iron hinges began to glow a dull orange.

'*Hei ma'akajao-zha!*' The massive spars blackened and smoked. Josua, tugging frantically at the dumbstruck Deornoth's arm, leaped down to the top of the wall.

*'T'si anh pra INELUKI!'*

As the prince's soldiers dove shrieking down the staircases there was a burst of light, a deafening crack louder than drums or thunder, and the mighty gate burst into steaming, sparkling flinders. The shards hissed down in a deadly rain as the wall collapsed on either side, crushing men beneath it even as they tried to flee.

Armored Norns leaped into the smoking gap in the walls. Some lifted long tubes of wood or bone, touching them at the end with flaming brands. Horrible gouts of fire leaped out of the pipes, turning fleeing soldiers into jigging, wailing torches. Great dark shapes pushed through the rubble: the Hunën, swinging long iron-studded clubs in their shaggy hands, howling like maddened bears as they crushed all in their path. Shattered bodies flew before them like ninepins.

Some of the soldiers, courageously resisting the choking fear, turned to fight. A giant went down with two spears in its guts, but a moment later the spearmen were dead, feathered with white-fletched Norn arrows. The pallid Norns were pushing through the fuming breach in the wall like maggots, shouting as they came.

Deornoth pulled a stumbling Josua toward the inner keep. The prince's soot-blackened face was wet with tears and blood.

'Elias has sown the dragon's teeth,' Josua choked as Deornoth pulled him past a gurgling soldier. Deornoth thought he recognized the young pikeman Ostrael, who had stood sentry at the king's parley, buried beneath the squirming black bodies of a score of diggers. 'My brother has planted seeds for the death of all men!' Josua railed. 'He is mad!'

Before Deornoth could reply – and what reply, he briefly wondered, could he possibly make? – two Norn soldiers, eyes fire-gleaming within the slits of their helms, rounded the corner of the inner keep dragging a shrieking girl. Spotting Deornoth, one hissed something, then reached down with his dark, slender sword and dragged the blade across the girl's throat. She dropped twitching to the earth behind them.

Deornoth felt the bile rising in his throat as he threw himself forward, sword upraised. The prince was there even before him, Naidel flickering like the lightning that etched the black sky – afternoon, it was only afternoon! *This is the hour at last, then,* he thought wildly. Steel rang on polished witchwood. *There must be honor,* the thought was desperate. *Even if there is no one to see it . . . God will see . . .*

The white faces, hateful and hating, swam before his sweat-stinging eyes.

No dream of Hell, no woodcut in any of his many books, no warning of any of his Aedonite teachers could prepare Father Strangyeard for the howling inferno Naglimund had become. Lightning sizzled across the sky, thunder roared, and the voices of slayers and victims alike rose to the heavens like the babble of the damned. Despite the wind and driving rains, fires were leaping up everywhere in the darkness, killing many who thought to hide behind stout doors from the madness outside.

Limping along in the shadows of the inner hallways, he saw Norns clambering in through the shattered windows of the chapel, and stood helplessly by while they caught poor Brother Eglaf, who was kneeling in prayer before the altar. Strangyeard could no more stay to watch the horror to come than he could do anything to help his fellow man of God. Slipping outside with his eyes full of blinding tears and his heart heavy as lead in his breast, he headed for the inner keep and the prince's rooms.

Hiding in the black depths of a hedge he saw stout Ethelferth of Tinsett and two of his guardsmen smashed to a red pulp beneath the cudgel of a barking giant.

He watched trembling as Lord Constable Eadgram

bled to death standing upright, swarmed by squeaking diggers.

He saw one of the court ladies ripped limb from limb by another of the shaggy Hunën while another woman crouched on the ground nearby, face blank with madness.

All through the shattered freehold these tragedies were mirrored a thousandfold, a nightmare seemingly without end.

Weeping out a prayer to Usires, certain that God's face was turned away from Naglimund's death throes but praying nevertheless in desperate, passionate reflex, he staggered around to the front of the inner keep. Two scorched, unhelmeted knights stood there in a tangle of corpses, eyes showing hunted-animal white. It was a long moment until he recognized Deornoth and the prince, and another heart-freezing wait before he could convince them to follow him.

It was quieter in the residence's maze of hallways. The Norns had broken in; a few bodies lay crumpled against the walls or splayed out on the stone flags, but most of the people had fled toward the chapel or the dining hall, and the Norns had not stayed to search. That would come later.

Isorn unbarred the door at Josua's shouted command. Isgrimnur's son, with Einskaldir and a handful of Erkynlander and Rimmersman soldiers, stood guard over the Lady Vorzheva and the Duchess Gutrun. A few other courtiers were huddled there as well, Towser and the harper Sangfugol among them.

While the prince pulled himself coldly from Vorzheva's weeping embrace, Strangyeard discovered Jarnauga lying on a pallet in the corner; a blood-soaked bandage was twined haphazardly around his head.

'The roof of the library fell,' the old Rimmersman said, smiling bitterly. 'The flames, I fear, have taken nearly all.'

898

For Father Strangyeard this was, in some way, the worst blow of all. He burst out in fresh weeping, tears even trickling down from beneath his eye patch.

'Worse . . . it could be worse,' he gulped finally. 'You might have gone with them, my friend.'

Jarnauga shook his white head and winced. 'No. Not quite yet. Soon, though. I did save one thing.' He pulled from out of his robe the battered parchment of Morgenes' manuscript, the top page now ribboned with blood. 'Carry it safe. It will be of some use still, I hope.'

Strangyeard took it carefully, tying it with a cord from Josua's table and slipping it into the inner pocket of his cassock. 'Can you stand?' he asked Jarnauga.

The old man nodded carefully, and the priest helped him to his feet.

'Prince Josua,' Strangyeard said, holding Jarnauga's elbow. 'I have thought of something.'

The prince turned from his urgent conferral with Deornoth and the others to stare impatiently at the archive-master.

'What is it?' His eyebrows singed away, Josua's forehead seemed more prominent than ever, a pale lunar bulge beneath his close-cropped hair. 'Do you wish me to build a new library?' The prince sagged wearily against the wall as the clamor built outside. 'I am sorry, Strangyeard. That was a foolish thing to say. What has come to your mind?'

'There is a way out.'

Several of the dirt-streaked, desperate faces turned toward him.

'What?' Josua asked, bending forward to stare intently. 'Shall we march out through the gate? I hear it has been opened for us.'

Strangyeard's sense of urgency gave him the strength to stare the prince down. 'There is a hidden passageway leading out of the guardroom to the Eastern Gate,' he said. 'I should know – you have had me staring at Dendinis' castle plans for months in preparation for the siege.' He thought of the rolls of irreplaceable brown parchment, covered in the fading ink of Dendinis' careful notes, ashes now, charred in the rubble of the library. He fought down more tears. 'If . . . if we c-can get there we may escape up the Stile into the Wealdhelm Hills.'

'And from there what?' Towser asked querulously. 'Starve in the hills? Eaten by wolves in the Oldheart Forest?'

'Would you rather be eaten here and now, by less pleasant things?' Deornoth snapped. His heart had sped at the priest's words; the faint return of hope was almost too painful, but he would bear anything to get his prince to safety.

'We will have to fight our way out,' Isorn said. 'Even now I can hear the Norns filling the residence. We have women and some children.'

Josua stared around the room at nearly a score of weary, frightened faces.

'Better to die outside than to be burned alive here, I suppose,' he said at last. He lifted his hand in a gesture of benediction or resignation. 'Let us go swiftly.'

'One thing, Prince Josua.' Hearing him, the prince came to where the priest was aiding struggling Jarnauga. 'If we can make our way to the Tunnel Gate,' Strangyeard said quietly, 'we have still another problem to solve. It was built for defense, not escape. It can be as easily opened as closed from the inside.'

Josua wiped ash from his brow. 'You are saying that we must find some way to block it behind us?'

'If we are to have any hope of escape.'

The prince sighed. A cut on his lip dripped blood onto his chin. 'Let us reach the gate at all, then we shall do what must be done.'

They burst through the door in a pack, surprising a pair of Norns who waited in the corridor. Einskaldir crashed his axe through the helmet of the nearest, throwing sparks in the darkened hallway. Before the other could do more than raise his short sword, he had been skewered between Isorn and one of the Naglimund guardsmen. Deornoth and the prince quickly herded the courtiers out.

Much of the din of slaughter had died away. Only an occasional scream of pain or rising chant of triumph floated through the empty hallways. Eye-stinging smoke, licking flames, and the mocking songs of the Norns gave the residence the look of some terrible underworld, some labyrinth on the edge of the Great Pit.

In the savaged ruins of the castle gardens they were set on by chittering diggers. One of the soldiers fell dead with a jagged Bukken knife in his back, and as the rest of the company fought off the others, one of Vorzheva's maidservants was dragged squealing down into a gash in the black earth. Deornoth leaped forward to try and save her, impaling a squirming, whistling black body on the end of his sword, but she was gone.

Only her delicate slipper lying in the rain-spattered mud showed she had even existed.

Two of the immense Hunën had discovered the wine cellars, and were fighting drunkenly over the last barrel before the inner keep's guardhouse, clubbing and scratching each other in roaring fury. One giant's arm hung limp at his side, and the other had gotten such a terrible wound to his head that a flap of skin hung free, and his face was a sheet of blood. Still they tore at each other, snarling their incomprehensible language in the wreckage of shattered casks and the crushed bodies of Naglimund's defenders.

Crouched in the mud at the edge of the gardens, Josua and Strangyeard squinted against the driving rain.

'The guardroom door is closed,' Josua said. 'We might be able to get across the open yard, but if it has been bolted from the inside we are doomed. We would never burst it open in time.'

Strangyeard shivered. 'Even if we did, we would not then . . . not then be able to bolt it behind us.'

Josua looked at Deornoth, who said nothing.

'Still,' the prince hissed, 'it is what we came for. We shall run.'

When they had formed up the small company, they set out at a stumbling dash. The two Hunën, one of them with his great teeth fastened in his fellow's throat, were rolling on the ground, locked still in howling battle like gods of the primordial past. Oblivious to the humans passing by, one of them threw out a massive leg in a paroxysm of pain and knocked the harper Sangfugol sprawling. Isorn and old Towser hurriedly turned back and picked him up; as they did so a shrill, excited shout came from across the courtyard.

A dozen Norns, two of them on tall white horses, turned at their fellow's call. Seeing the prince's party they gave a great cry and spurred forward, galloping past the now-senseless giants.

Isorn reached the door and pulled. It sprang open, but even as the terrified company began to push inside the first rider was upon them, a high helm upon his head, a long spear poised in his hand.

Dark-bearded Einskaldir dashed forward with a snarl like a cornered dog, ducking the serpentine strike of the lance, then leaping and throwing himself against the Norn's side. He caught the Norn's flapping cloak in his hand and pushed away, tumbling to the ground and bringing his enemy down after him. The riderless horse skidded on the wet cobbles. Kneeling over the fallen Norn, Einskaldir brought his axe down hard, then crashed it down again. Blind to all around him, he would have been pierced by the spear of the second Norn rider, but Deornoth hefted and threw the lid of a broken barrel, knocking the rider off his horse and into one of the hedges. The howling foot-troops were bearing down fast as Deornoth pulled the foaming Einskaldir off the Norn's hacked corpse.

They drove through the door moments ahead of the attackers, and Isorn and two of the other pursuers rammed it shut. Spears crashed against the heavy wood; a moment later one of the Norns called out in a high-pitched, clicking voice.

'Axes!' Jarnauga said. 'I know that much of the Hikeda'ya tongue. They are going for axes.'

'Strangyeard!' Josua shouted, 'where is the damned passageway?'

'It's . . . it's so dark,' the priest quavered. Indeed, the room was lit only by the inconstant light of orange flames beginning to burn through the roofbeams. Smoke was gathering beneath the low ceiling. 'I . . . I think it is on the south side . . .' he began. Einskaldir and several others sprang to the wall and began pulling down the heavy arrases.

'The door!' Einskaldir barked. 'Locked,' he added a moment later.

The keyhole in the heavy wooden door was empty. Josua stared for a moment, even as a sliver of axe-blade crashed through the door from the courtyard outside. 'Break it down,' he said. 'You others, pile what you can before the other door.'

In the matter of moments Einskaldir and Isorn had hacked the bolt right out of the jamb, while Deornoth lifted an unlit torch to the smoldering ceiling. An instant later the door was knocked off its hinges and they were through, fleeing up the sloping corridor. Another piece splintered out of the door behind them.

They ran for several furlongs, the stronger helping the weaker. One of the courtiers at last fell weeping to the ground, unable to go farther. Isorn went to pick him up, but his mother Gutrun, herself staggeringly tired, waved him off.

'Leave him lie,' she said. 'He can keep up.'

Isorn looked hard at her, then shrugged. As they continued up the slanting stone pathway, they heard the man struggle to his feet, cursing them, and follow.

Even as the doors loomed before them, swart and solid

903

in the light of the solitary torch, extending from the floor of the passageway to the roof, the sound of pursuit came echoing up behind them. Fearing the worst, Josua stretched out his hand to one of the iron rings and pulled. The door swung inward with a soft groan of its hinges.

'Usires be praised,' Isorn said.

'Get the women and others through,' Josua ordered, and a moment later two of the soldiers had led them well up the passageway beyond the mighty doors.

'Now we come to it,' Josua said. 'Either we must find some way to seal this door, or else we must leave enough men behind to slow our pursuers.'

'I will stay,' Einskaldir growled. 'I have tasted faërie-blood tonight. I would not mind more.' He patted his hilt.

'No. It is for me, and me alone.' Jarnauga coughed and sagged on Strangyeard's arm, then straightened. The tall priest turned to look at the old man, and suddenly understood.

'I am dying,' Jarnauga said. 'I was not meant to leave Naglimund. I always knew that. You need only leave me a sword.'

'You have not the strength!' Einskaldir said angrily, as if disappointed.

'I have enough to close *this* door,' the old man said gently. 'See?' He pointed to the great hinges. 'They are wrought very fine. Once the door is shut, a blade broken off in the hinge-crevice will balk the stoutest pursuer. Go.'

The prince turned as if to object; a clicking shout reverberated up the passageway. 'Very well,' he said softly. 'God bless you, old man.'

'No need,' Jarnauga said. He pulled something shiny from around his neck and pressed it into Strangyeard's hand. 'Strange to make a friend at the very last,' Jarnauga said. The priest's eye filled with tears, and he kissed the Rimmersman's cheek.

'My friend,' he whispered, and went through the open door.

The last they saw was Jarnauga's bright gaze catch the torchlights as he put his shoulder to the door. It swung closed, damping the sounds of pursuit. The bolts inside slid solidly into place.

After climbing a long stairway they emerged at last into the windy, rain–lashed evening. The storm had thinned, and as they stood on the naked hillside below the wooded Stile they could see fire flickering in the ruins of Naglimund below, and black, inhuman shapes dancing among the vaulting flames.

Josua stood and stared for a long while, sooty face streaked by the rain. His small party huddled trembling behind him, waiting to take to the path once more.

The prince raised his left fist.

'Elias!' he shouted, and the wind whipped the echoes away. 'You have brought death and worse to our father's kingdom! You have raised an ancient evil, and shattered the High King's Ward! You have unhoused me, and destroyed much that I loved.' He stopped and fought back tears. 'Now you are king *no longer!* I will take the crown from you. *I will take it, I swear!*'

Deornoth took his elbow and led him away from the pathway's edge. Josua's subjects stood waiting for him, cold and frightened, homeless in the wild Wealdhelm. He bowed his head for a moment, in weariness or prayer, and led them into the darkness.

# 44
# Blood and the Spinning World

*The dragon's black blood had spilled over him, burning like a
fire. In the instant of its touch he had felt his own life subdued.
The dreadful essence coursed through him, scalding away his
spirit, and leaving only dragon-life. It was as if he had himself
become – in the failing moment before darkness came – the
Worm's secret heart.*

*Igjarjuk's smolderingly slow and intricate life captured him. He
spread; he changed, and the changing was as painful as both
death and birth.*

*His bones became heavy, solid as stone and curvingly
reptilian. His skin hardened into gemlike scales, and he felt his
pelt sliding on his back like a mailshirt of diamonds.*

*The dragon's heartblood now moved powerfully in his
breast, ponderous as the movement of a dark star in the empty
night, strong and hot as the very forge-fires of the earth. His
claws sank into the world's stony skin, and his age-old heart
pulsed . . . and pulsed . . . and pulsed . . . He grew into the
brittle, ancient cleverness of the dragonfolk, feeling first the birth
of his long-lived race in the earth's infant days, then the weight
of uncountable years pressing upon him, dark millennia rushing
by like roiling waters. He was one of the Eldest of all races, one
of the cooling earth's firstborn, and he lay coiled beneath the
world's surface as the least of worms might lie hidden in the rind
of an apple . . .*

*The old black blood raced through him. Still he grew, and he perceived and named all things of the spinning world. Its skin, the earth's skin, became his own – the crawling surface on which all living things were born, where they struggled and failed, surrendering at last to become a part of him once more. Its bones were his bones, the rocky pillars on which all things stood, and through which he felt every tremor of breathing life.*

*He was Simon. Yet he was the serpent. And he was nevertheless the very earth in its infinitude and detail. And still he grew, and growing, felt his mortal life slipping away . . .*

*In the sudden loneliness of his majesty, fearing that he would lose everything, he reached out to touch those he had known. He could feel their warm lives, sensing them like sparks in a great, windy darkness. So many lives – so important, so small . . .*

*He saw Rachel – bent, old. She sat on a stool in an empty room, holding her gray head in her hands. When had she become so small? A broom lay at her feet, an orderly mound of dust beside it. The castle room was fast darkening.*

*Prince Josua stood on a hillside, looking down. A faint flame-hued light painted his grim face. He could see Josua's doubt and pain; he tried to reach out and give him reassurance, but these lives were only to see, not to touch.*

*A small brown man he did not know poled his flat boat up a stream. Great trees dangled their branches in the water, and clouds of midges hovered. The little man patted protectively at a sheaf of parchment tucked into his belt. A breeze rattled the trailing branches, and the little man smiled gratefully.*

*A large man – Isgrimnur? Where was his beard? – paced on a weather-warped pier and stared out at the darkening sky, at the wind-lashed ocean.*

*A beautiful old man, his long white hair tangled, sat playing with a crowd of half-naked children. His blue eyes were mild, distant, wrinkled in a happy squint.*

*Miriamele, hair close-cropped, looked out from the rail of a ship at the heavy clouds massing on the horizon. The sails snapped and rippled above her head. He wanted to watch her for a longer time, but the vision whirled away like a falling leaf.*

*A tall Hernystiri woman dressed in black kneeled before two cairns of stones in a grove of slender birch trees, high on the side of a wind-swept mountain.*

*King Elias stared into the depth of a wine cup, eyes red-rimmed. Sorrow lay across his knees. The gray sword was a wild thing feigning sleep . . .*

*Morgenes suddenly appeared before him, crowned in flame; and the sight drove an icy spear of pain even into his dragon's heart. The old man was holding a great book, and his lips moved in anguished, silent cries, as though he shouted a warning . . . beware the false messenger . . . beware . . .*

*The faces slipped away, but for one last ghost.*

*A boy, thin and awkward, made his way through dark tunnels beneath the earth, crying and crawling through the labyrinth like a trapped insect. Every detail, every twist and turn unwound tortuously before his eyes.*

*The boy stood on a hillside beneath the moon, staring in horror at white-faced figures and a gray sword, but a dark cloud covered the boy in shadow.*

*The same boy, older now, stood before a great white tower. A golden light flashed on his finger, although the boy stood in deep and darkening shadow. Bells were tolling, and the roof had burst into flames . . .*

*Darkness was engulfing him now, pulling him away toward other, stranger places — but he did not wish to go on to those places. Not until he remembered the name of that child, that gawky boy who labored in ignorance. He would not go on; he would remember . . .*

*The boy's name was . . . the boy's name was . . . Simon! Simon.*

*And then his sight faded . . .*

908

'Seoman,' the voice said, quite loud now; he realized it had been calling him for some time.

He opened his eyes. The colors were so intense he quickly shut them, blinded. Spinning wheels of silver and red danced before the darkness of his closed lids.

'Come, Seoman, come and rejoin your companions. There is need of you here.'

He unlidded halfway, letting himself grow used to the light. There were now no colors at all – everything was white. He groaned, trying to move, and felt a terrible weakness, as though some heavy thing pressed down on him all around; at the same time he felt himself as transparent and fragile as if he were spun from pure glass. Even with closed eyes he thought he could feel light passing through him, filling him with a radiance that brought no warmth.

A shadow crossed his sensitive face, seeming almost to have tangible weight. Something wet and cold touched his lips. He swallowed, felt a bite of pain, coughed, and drank again. It seemed he could taste everywhere the water had ever been – the icy peak, the swollen rain cloud, the stony mountain sluice.

He opened his eyes wider. All was indeed over-whelmingly white, except for the golden face of Jiriki looming nearby. He was in a cave, the walls pale with ash but for the traces of faint lines; furs and wooden carvings and decorated bowls were stacked along the edge of the stone floor. Simon's heavy hands, numb yet strangely acute, clutched at the fur coverlet and probed weakly at the wooden cot on which he lay. How. . . ?

'I . . .' He coughed again.

'You are sore, you are tired. That is expected.' The Sitha frowned, but his luminous eyes did not change expression. 'You have done a very terrible thing, Simon, do you know? You have saved my life twice.'

'Mmmmm.' His head was responding as slowly as his muscles. What exactly had happened? There had been the mountain . . . the cave . . . and the . . .

'The dragon!' Simon said, choking, and tried to sit up. As the fur robe slid down he felt the chill of the room in earnest. Light was leaking past a skin hanging at the room's far end. A wave of dizziness left him limp, and set his head and face to throbbing. He sagged back.

'Gone,' Jiriki said shortly. 'Dead or not I do not know, but gone. When you struck, it tumbled past you and down into the abyss. I could not mark where it fell in the snows and ice of the great deeps. You wielded the sword Thorn like a warrior true, Seoman Snowlock.'

'I . . .' He took a shaky breath and tried again. Talking made his face hurt. 'I don't think . . . it was me. Thorn . . . *used* me. It . . . *wanted* to be saved, I think. That must sound foolish, but . . .'

'No. I think you may be correct. Look.' Jiriki pointed to the cave wall a few feet away. Thorn lay cushioned there on the prince's cloak, black and remote as the bottom of a well. Could such a thing have ever felt alive in his hand? 'It was easy enough to carry here,' Jiriki said, 'perhaps this was a direction it wished to go.'

The Sitha's words set in motion a slow wheel of thought in Simon's mind.

*The sword wanted to come here – but where is here? And how did we get . . . Oh, Mother of God, the dragon. . . !*

'Jiriki!' he gasped, 'the others! Where are the others?'

The prince nodded gently. 'Ah, yes. I had hoped to wait longer, but I see I have no choice.' He closed his wide, bright eyes for a moment.

'An'nai and Grimmric are dead. They have been buried on the mountain Urmsheim.' He sighed, and made a complicated gesture with his hands. 'You do not know what it means to bury a mortal and a Sitha together, Seoman. It has been seldom done, and never in five centuries. An'nai's deeds will live until world's end in the Dance of Years, the annals of our people, and Grimmric's name will now live with his. They will lie forever beneath the Uduntree.' Jiriki closed his eyes and sat for a silent moment. 'The others . . . well, they have all survived.'

Simon felt a clutch at his heart, but pushed away thoughts of the fallen pair for later. He stared at the ash-painted ceiling, and saw that the lines were faint scribings of great serpents and long-tusked beasts, winding all across the roof and walls. The blank eyes of the creatures troubled him: when he looked too long, they seemed to move. He turned back to the Sitha.

'Where's Binabik?' He asked. 'I want to speak to him. I had the strangest dream . . . the strangest dream . . .'

Before Jiriki could speak, Haestan poked his head in through the cave mouth. 'Th'king doesna want t'talk,' he said, then saw Simon. 'Y'r up, lad!' he crowed. 'That's fine!'

'What king?' Simon asked, confused. 'Not Elias, I hope?'

'No, lad,' Haestan shook his head. 'After . . . after what happened up on the mountain, th'trolls found us. You were sleepin' for some days. We're on Mintahoq, now – the troll-mountain.'

'And Binabik is with his family?'

'Not quite.' Haestan looked at Jiriki. The Sitha nodded. 'Binabik – Sludig, too – th'king's holdin' them for prisoners. Under sentence o' death, some say.'

'What!? Prisoners?!' Simon exploded, then sagged back down as a band of pain tightened cruelly around his head. 'Why?'

'Sludig because he is a hated Rimmersman,' Jiriki said. 'Binabik, they say, has committed some terrible crime against the troll-king. We do not know yet what it is, Seoman Snowlock.'

Simon shook his head in amazement. 'This is madness. I've gone mad, or I'm still dreaming.' He turned accusingly to Jiriki. 'And why do you keep calling me that name?'

'Don't . . .' Haestan began, but Jiriki ignored him, producing instead from his jacket the looking glass. Simon sat up and took it, the fine carvings on its frame rough to his sensitive fingers. The wind howled outside he cave, and cold air crept in below the door-cloth.

Was all the world covered with ice, now? Would he never again escape the winter?

In other circumstances he would have been quite taken with the reddish golden whiskers which were coming in thickly all over his face, but his attention was captured by the long scar running up from his jaw, over his cheek and past his left eye. The surrounding skin was livid and new-looking. He touched it and winced, then slid his fingers up to his scalp.

A long swath of his hair had turned as white as the Urmsheim snows.

'You have been marked, Seoman,' Jiriki reached out and touched his cheek with a long finger. 'For better or for worse, you have been marked.'

Simon let the mirror drop, and covered his face with his hands.

# Appendix

## People

### ERKYNLANDERS

Barnabas – Hayholt chapel sexton

Beornoth – one of Jack Mundwode's mythical band

Breyugar – Count of the Westfold, Lord Constable of the Hayholt under Elias

Caleb – Shem Horsegroom's apprentice

Colmund – Camaris squire, later baron of Rodstanby

Deorhelm – soldier at *Dragon and Fisherman*

Deornoth, Sir – Josua's knight, sometimes called 'Prince's Right Hand'

Dreosan, Father – chaplain of Hayholt

Eadgram, Sir – Lord Constable of Naglimund

Eahlferend – Simon's fisherman father, husband of Susanna

Eahlstan Fiskerne – Fisher King, first Erkynlandish master of Hayholt

Eglaf, Brother – Naglimund monk, friend of Strangyeard

Elias – Prince, Prester John's elder son, later High King

Elispeth – midwife at Hayholt

Ethelbearn – soldier, Simon's companion on journey from Naglimund

Ethelferth – Lord of Tinsett

Fengbald – Earl of Falshire

Freawaru – innkeeper, master of *Dragon and Fisherman* in Flett

Godstan – soldier at *Dragon and Fisherman*

Godwig – Baron of Cellodshire

Grimmric – soldier, Simon's companion on journey from Naglimund

Grimstede, Sir – Erkynlandish noble, supporter of Josua

Guthwulf – Earl of Utanyeat, High King's Hand

Haestan – Naglimund guardsman, Simon's companion

Heahferth – Baron of Woodsall

Heanfax – innkeeper's boy

Helfcene, Father – Chancellor of Hayholt

Hepzibah – castle chambermaid

Hruse – Jack Mundwode's wife in song

Inch – Doctor's assistant, later foundry-master

Isaak – page

Jack Mundwode – mythical forest bandit

Jael – castle chambermaid

Jakob – castle chandler

Jeremias – chandler's boy

John – King John Presbyter, High King

Josua – Prince, John's younger son, lord of Naglimund, called 'Lackhand'

Judith – Cook and Kitchen Mistress

Langrian – Hoderundian monk

Leleth – Miriamele's handmaiden

Lofsunu – soldier, Hepzibah's intended

Lucuman – stable-worker at Naglimund

Malachias – castle boy

Marya – Miriamele's servant

Miriamele – Princess, Elias' only child

Morgenes, Doctor – Scrollbearer, King John's castle doctor, Simon's friend

Noah – King John's squire

Ordmaer – Baron of Utersall
Osgal – one of Mundwode's mythical band
Ostrael – pikeman, son of Firsfram of Runchester
Peter Gilded-Bowl – Seneschal of Hayholt
Rachel – Mistress of Chambermaids
Rebah – castle kitchen maid
Ruben the Bear – castle smith
Sangfugol – Josua's harper
Sarrah – castle chambermaid
Scenesefa – Hoderundian monk
Shem Horsegroom – castle groom
Simon (Seoman) – a castle scullion
Sophrona – Linen Mistress
Strangyeard, Father – Archivist of Naglimund
Susanna – Simon's chambermaid mother
Tobas – castle houndmaster
Towser – jester (original name: Cruinh)
Wuldorcene – Baron of Caldsae


## HERNYSTIRI

Arthpreas – Count of Cuimnhe
Bagba – Cattle God
Brynioch of the Skies – Sky God
Cadrach-ec-Crannhyr, Brother – monk of indeterminate
    Order
Cifgha – young lady of Taig
Craobhan – old knight, advisor to King Lluth
Cryunnos – a God
Dochais – Hoderundian monk
Efiathe – original name of Queen Ebekah of Erkynland,
    called 'Rose of Hernysadharc'
Eoin-ec-Cluias – legendary poet
Eolair – Count of Nad Mullach, emissary of King Lluth
Fiathna – Gwythinn's mother, Lluth's second wife
Gealsgiath – ship's captain, called 'Old'

Gormhbata – legendary chieftain

Gwelan – young lady of Taig

Gwythinn – Prince, Lluth's son, Maegwin's half brother

Hern – Founder of Hernystir

Inahwen – Lluth's third wife

Lluth-ubh-Llythinn – King of Hernystir

Maegwin – Princess, Lluth's daughter, Gwythinn's half sister

Mircha – Rain Goddess, wife of Brynioch

Murhagh One-Arm – a God

Penemhwye – Maegwin's mother, Lluth's first wife

Red Hathrayhinn – character in Cadrach story

Rhynn – a God

Sinnach – Prince, Battle of Knock war-leader

Tethtain – King, only Hernystiri master of Hayholt, called 'Holly King'

Tuilleth – young Hernystiri knight


## RIMMERSMEN

Bindesekk – Isgrimnur's spy

Dror – Ancient War God

Einskaldir – Rimmersgard chieftain

Elvrit – First Osten Ard king of Rimmersmen

Fingil – King, first master of Hayholt, 'Bloody King'

Frayja – Ancient Harvest Goddess

Frekke – old soldier

Gutrun – Duchess of Elvritshalla

Hani – young soldier killed by Bukken

Hengfisk – Hoderundian priest

Hjeldin – King, Fingil's son, 'Mad King'

Hoderun, Saint – priest from Battle of Knock

Hove – young soldier, relative of Isgrimnur

Ikferdig – King, Hjeldin's lieutenant, 'Burned King'

Ingen Jegger – Black Rimmersman, master of Norn hounds

Isbeorn – Isgrimnur's father, first Rimmersgard duke under John
Isgrimnur – Duke of Elvritshalla
Isorn – Isgrimnur and Gutrun's son
Ithineg the Harper – character in Cadrach story
Jarnauga – Scrollbearer from Tungoldyr
Jormgrun – King of Rimmersgard, killed by John at Naarved
Löken – Ancient Fire God
Memur – Ancient Wisdom God
Nisse – (Nisses) Hjeldin's priest-helper, writer of *Du Svardenvyrd*
Sigmar – young Rimmerswoman courted by Towser
Skali – Thane of Kaldskryke, called 'Sharp-nose'
Skendi – Saint, founder of abbey
Sludig – young soldier, Simon's companion
Storfot – Thane of Vestvennby
Thrinin – soldier killed by Bukken
Tonnrud – Thane of Skoggey, Duchess Gutrun's uncle
Udun – Ancient Sky God
Utë – of Saegard, soldier killed by Bukken


NABBANAI

Aeswides (probably Nabbanization of Erk. name) – first lord of Naglimund
Anitulles – former Imperator
Antippa, Lady – daughter of Leobardis and Nessalanta
Ardrivis – last Imperator, uncle of Camaris
Aspitis Preves – count of Eadne, master of Prevan House, Benigaris' friend
Benidrivine – Nabbanai noble house, kingfisher crest
Benidrivis – first duke under John, father of Leobardis and Camaris
Benigaris – son of Duke Leobardis and Nessalanta

Camaris-sá-Vinitta – brother of Leobardis, friend of
    Prester John
Clavean – Nabbanai noble house, pelican crest
Claves – former Imperator
Crexis the Goat – former Imperator
Dendinis – architect of Naglimund
Devasalles – Baron, intended of Lady Antippa
Dinivan – Lector Ranessin's secretary
Domitis – Bishop of Saint Sutrin's cathedral in Erchester
Elysia – mother of Usires
Emettin – legendary knight
Enfortis – Imperator at time of Fall of Asu'a
Fluiren, Sir – famous Johannine knight of disgraced
    Sulian House
Gelles – soldier at market
Hylissa – Miriamele's late mother, Elias' wife,
    Nessalanta's sister
Ingadarine – noble family, albatross house-crest
Leobardis – Duke of Nabban, father of Benigaris,
    Varellan, Antippa
Mylin-sá-Ingadaris – Earl, master of Ingadarine House,
    Nessalanta's brother
Nessalanta – Duchess of Nabban, Benigaris' mother,
    Miriamele's aunt
Nin Reisu – Niskie aboard Emettin's Jewel
Nuanni (Nuannis) – ancient sea god of Nabban
Pelippa – noblewoman from Book of Aedon, Saint,
    called 'of the Island'
Plesinnen Myrmenis (Plesinnen of Myrme) –
    philosopher
Prevan – noble family, osprey house-crest
Pryrates, Father – priest, alchemist, wizard, Elias'
    counselor
Quincines – Abbot of Saint Hoderund's
Ranessin, Lector – (born Oswine of Stanshire, an
    Erkynlander) Head of Church
Rhiappa – Saint, called 'Rhiap' in Erkynland

Sulis – Rogue noble, former master of Hayholt, 'Heron King'
Tiyagaris – first Imperator
Turis – soldier at market
Usires Aedon – Aedonite religion's Son of God
Varellan – Duke Leobardis' youngest son
Velligis – Escritor
Vilderivis – Saint
Yuvenis – ancient chief god of Nabban

# SITHI

Amerasu – Erl–queen, mother of Ineluki and Hakatri
An'nai – Jiriki's lieutenant, hunting companion
Finaju – Sithi-woman in Cadrach story
Hakatri – Ineluki's elder brother, gravely wounded by Hidohebhi
Ineluki – Prince, now Storm King
Isiki – Sithi Kikkasut (Bird God)
Iyu'unigato – Erl-king, Ineluki's father
Jiriki, (i-Sa'onserei) – Prince, son of Shima'onari
Kendharaja'aro – Jiriki's uncle
Ki'ushapo – Jiriki's hunting companion
Mezumiiru – Sithi sedda (Moon Goddess)
Nenais'u – Sithi woman from An'nai's song, lived in Enki e-Shaosaye
Shima'onari – King of Sithi, Jiriki's father, son of Hakatri
Sijandi – Jiriki's hunting companion
Utuk'ku – Queen of the Norns, mistress of Nakkiga
Vindaomeyo the Fletcher – ancient Sithi arrow-maker of Tumet'ai

## OTHERS

Binabik (QANUC) – (Binbiniqegabenik) Ookequk's apprentice, Simon's friend

Chukku (QANUC) – legendary troll hero

He Who Always Steps on Sand (WRAN) – god

Kikkasut (QANUC) – king of birds

Lingit (QANUC) – legendary son of Sedda, father of Qanuc and men

Lost Piqipeg – legendary troll hero

Middastri (PERDRUINESE) – trader, friend of Tiamak

Ookequk (QANUC) – Singing Man of Mintahoq tribe, Binabik's master

Qinkipa of the Snows (QANUC) – snow and cold goddess

Raohog (WRAN) – potter

Sedda (QANUC) – moon goddess

She Who Birthed Mankind (WRAN) – goddess

Streáwe (PERDRUINESE) – Count of Ansis Pelippé

Tallistro, Sir (PERDRUINESE) – famous knight of Johannine Table

Tiamak (WRAN) – scholar, correspondent of Morgenes

Tohuq (QANUC) – sky god

Vorzheva (THRITHINGS) – Josua's companion, daughter of a Thrithings-chief

Yana (QANUC) – legendary daughter of Sedda, mother of Sithi

# Places

*Cellodshire* – Erkylandish barony west of Gleniwent

*Da'ai Chikiza* (Sithi: 'Tree of the Singing Winds') – abandoned Sithi city on east side of Wealdhelm, in Aldheorte

*Eirgid Ramh* (Hernystiri) – Abaingeat tavern, haunt of Old Gealsgiath

*Enki-e-Shaosaye* (Sithi) – 'Summer-city' east of Aldheorte, long-ruined

*Ereb Irigú* (Sithi: 'Western Gate') – the Knock; in Rimmerspakk: Du Knokkegard

*Hewenshire* – northern Erkynlandish town east of Naglimund

*Hullnir* – eastern Rimmersgard village on northeast rim of Drorshullven

*Jao é-Tinukai'i* (Sithi: 'Boat on [the] Ocean [of] Trees') – Only thriving Sithi settlement, in Aldheorte

*Jhiná-T'seneí* (Sithi) – city of An'nai's song, now beneath ocean

*Little Nose* – mountain in Yiqanuc where Binabik's parents died

*Moir Brach* (Hernystiri) – long, finger-shaped ridge off Grianspog Mountains

*Nakkiga* (Sithi: Mask of Tears) – Stormspike, Sturmrspeik (Rimmerspakk)

*Qilakitsoq* (Qanuc: Shadow-wood) – Troll name for Dimmerskog

*Runchester* – northern Erkynlandish town on Frostmarch

*Sení Anzi'in* (Sithi: Tower of the Walking Dawn) – Tumet'ai's great tower

*Sení Ojhisá* (Sithi) – cited in An'nai's song

*Skoggey* – central Rimmersgard freehold east of Elvritshalla

*T'si Suhyasei* (Sithi: 'Her Blood is Cool') – river running through Da'ai Chikiza; in Erkynlandish: Aelfwent

*Tan'ja Stairs* – great Asu'a stairs, formerly centerpiece of Asu'a

*Tumet'ai* (Sithi) – northern city buried under ice east of Yiqanuc

*Ujin e-d'a Sikhunae* (Sithi: 'Trap that captures the Hunter') – Sithi name for Naglimund

*Woodsall* – barony between Hayholt and southwestern Aldheorte

# Creatures

*Aeghonwye* – Maegwin's brood sow
*Atarin* – Camaris' horse
*Croich-ma-Feareg* – legendary Hernystiri giant
*Greater Worm* – Sithi-myth, original dragon from which
  all others are descended
*Hidohebhi* – Black Worm, mother of Shurakai and
  Igjarjuk, slain by Ineluki; in Hernystir: Drochnathair
*Igjarjuk* – Ice-worm of Urmsheim
*Khaerukama'o the Golden* – dragon, father of Hidohebhi
*Niku'a* – Ingen Jegger's lead hound
*One-Eye* – Ookequk's ram
*Qantaqa* – Binabik's wolf companion
*Rim* – plow horse
*Shurakai* – Firedrake slain beneath Hayholt, whose bones
  are Dragonbone Chair

# Things

*Boar and Spears* – emblem of Guthwulf of Utanyeat
*Bright-Nail* – sword of Prester John, containing nail from
  the Tree, and finger bone from Saint Eahlstan Fiskerne
*Citril* – sour, aromatic root for chewing
*Ciyan* – a Nabbanai fruit shrub, very rare
*Fire Drake and Tree* – emblem of King John
*Ilenite* – a costly, shimmery metal
*Indreju* – Jiriki's witchwood sword
*Kvalnir* – Isgrimnur's sword
*Lu'yasa's Staff* – line of three stars in the sky's northeast
  quadrant early Yuven
*Mantinges* – a spice
*Mezumiiru's Net* – star cluster; to Qanuc: Sedda's Blanket

922

*Minneyar* – iron sword of King Fingil, inherited through line of Elvrit

*Mockfoil* – a flowering herb

*Naidel* – Josua's sword

*Oinduth* – Hern's black spear

*Quickweed* – a spice

*Pillar and Tree* – emblem of Mother Church

*Rhynn's Cauldron* – Hernystiri battle-summoner

*Shent* – Sithi game of skill

*Sorrow* – sword of iron and witchwood smithied by Ineluki, gift to Elias (Sithi: *Jingizu*)

*Sotfengsel* – Elvrit's ship, buried at Skipphavven

*Thorn* – star-sword of Camaris

*Tree* – the Execution Tree, on which Usires was hanged upside down before temple of Yuvenis in Nabban, now sacred symbol of Aedonite religion

*Knucklebones* – Binabik's auguring tools:
  Wingless Bird
  Fish-Spear
  The Shadowed Path
  Torch at the Cave-Mouth
  Balking Ram
  Clouds in the Pass
  The Black Crevice
  Unwrapped Dart

*Holidays*
  Feyever 2 – Candlemansa
  Marris 25 – Elysiamansa
  Avrel 1 – All Fool's Day
  Avrel 30 – Stoning Night
  Maia 1 – Belthainn Day
  Yuven 23 – Midsummer's Eve
  Tiyagar 15 – Saint Sutrin's Day
  Anitul 1 – Hlafmansa
  Septander 20 – Saint Granis' Day
  Octander 30 – Harrows Eve

Novander 1 – Soul's Day
Decander 21 – Saint Tunath's Day
Decander 24 – Aedonmansa

*Months*
Jonever, Feyever, Marris, Avrel, Maia, Yuven, Tiyagar, Anitul, Septander, Octander, Novander, Decander
*Days of the Week*
Sunday, Moonday, Tiasday, Udunsday, Drorsday, Frayday, Satrinsday

# A Guide to Pronunciation

## ERKYNLANDISH

Erkynlandish names are divided into two types, Old Erkynlandish (O.E.) and Warinstenner. Those names which are based on types from Prester John's native island of Warinsten (mostly the names of castle servants or John's immediate family) have been represented as variants on Biblical names (Elias – Elijah, Ebekah, Rebecca, etc.) Old Erkynlandish names should be pronounced like modern English, except as follows:

*a* – always *ah*, as in 'father'
*ae* – *ay* of 'say'
*c* – k as in 'keen'.
*e* – *ai* as in 'air,' except at the end of names, when it is also sounded, but with an *eh* or *uh* sound, i.e., Hruse – 'Rooz-uh'
*ea* – sounds as *a* in 'mark,' except at beginning of word or name, where it has the same value as *ae*
*g* – always hard *g*, as in 'glad'
*h* – hard *h* of 'help'

924

*i* – short *i* of 'in'
*j* – hard *j* of 'jaw'
*o* – long but soft *o*, as in 'orb'
*u* – *oo* sound of 'wood,' never *yoo* as in 'music'

## HERNYSTIRI

The Hernystiri names and words can be pronounced in largely the same way as the O.E., with a few exceptions:

*th* – always the *th* in 'other,' never as in 'thing'
*ch* – a guttural, as in Scottish 'loch'
*y* – pronounce *yr* like 'beer,' *ye* like 'spy'
*h* – unvoiced except at the beginning of word or after *t* or *c*
*e* – *ay* as in 'ray'
*ll* – same as single *l*: Lluth – Luth

## RIMMERSPAKK

Names and words in Rimmerspakk differ from O.E. pronunciation in the following:

*j* – pronounced *y*: Jarnauga – Yarnauga; Hjeldin – Hyeldin (*H* nearly silent here)
*ei* – long *i* as in 'crime'
*ë* – *ee*, as in 'sweet'
*ö* – *oo*, as in 'coop'
*au* – *ow*, as in 'cow'

## NABBANAI

The Nabbanai language holds basically to the rules of a romance language, i.e., the vowels are pronounced 'ah-eh–ih–oh–ooh,' the consonants are all sounded, etc. There are some exceptions.

*i* – most names take emphasis on second to last syllable: Ben-i-GAR-is. When this syllable has an *i*, it is sounded long (Ardrivis: Ar-DRY-vis) unless it comes before a double consonant (Antippa: An-TIHP-pa)

*e* – at end of name, *es* is sounded long: Gelles – Gel-leez

*y* – is pronounced as a long *i*, as in 'mild'

## QANUC

Troll–language is considerably different than the other human languages. There are three hard 'k' sounds, signified by: *c*, *q*, and *k*. The only difference intelligible to most non-Qanuc is a slight clucking sound on the *q*, but it is not to be encouraged in beginners. For our purposes, all three will sound with the *k* of 'keep'. Also, the Qanuc *u* is pronounced *uh*, as in 'bug'. Other interpretations are up to the reader, but he or she will not go far wrong pronouncing phonetically.

## SITHI

Even more than the language of Yiqanuc, the language of the Zida'ya is virtually unpronounceable by untrained tongues, and so is easiest rendered phonetically, since the chance of any of us being judged by experts is slight (but not nonexistent, as Binabik learned). These rules may be applied, however.

*i* – when the first vowel, pronounced *ih*, as in 'clip.' When later in word, especially at end, pronounced *ee*, as in 'fleet': Jiriki – Jih-REE-kee

*ai* – pronounced like long *i*, as in 'time'

' (aprostrophe) – represents a clicking sound, and should not be voiced by mortal readers.

## EXCEPTIONAL NAMES

*Geloë* – Her origins are unknown, and so is the source of her name. It is pronounced 'Juh-LO-ee' or 'Juh-LOY.' Both are correct.

*Ingen Jegger* – He is a Black Rimmersman, and the 'J' in Jegger is sounded, just as in 'jump.'

*Miriamele* – Although born in the Erkynlandish court, hers is a Nabbanai name that developed a strange pronunciation – perhaps due to some family influence or confusion of her dual heritage – and sounds as 'Mih-ree-uh-MEL.'

*Vorzheva* – A Thrithings-woman, her name is pronounced 'Vor-SHAY-va,' with the *zh* sounding harshly, like the Hungarian *zs*.

# Words and Phrases

## NABBANAI

Aedonis Fiyellis extulanin mei – 'Faithful Aedon save me'
Cansim Felis – 'Song of Joy'
Cenit – 'Dog,' 'Hound'
Cuelos – 'Death'
Duos wulstei – 'God willing'
Escritor – 'Writer': one of group of advisors to Lector
Hue Fauge – 'What's going on'
Lector – 'Speaker': head of Church

Mansa sea Cuelossan – 'Mass for the Dead'
Mulveiz nei cenit drenisend – 'Let sleeping hounds lie'
Oveiz mei – 'Hear me'
Sa Asdridan Condiquilles – 'The Conqueror Star'
Tambana Leobardis eis – 'Leobardis is (has) fallen'
Timior cuelos exaltat mei – 'Fear of death lift me'
Vasir Sombris, feata concordin – 'Shadow-father, accept this bargain'


## HERNYSTIRI

Brynioch na ferth ub strocinh . . . – 'Brynioch has turned away . . .'
E gundhain sluith, ma connalbehn . . . – 'We fought well, my dear one . . .'
Feir – 'Brother' or 'Comrade'
Goirach – 'Mad' or 'Wild'
Sithi – 'Peaceful Ones'


## RIMMERSPAKK

Im todsten-grukker – 'A grave-robber'
Vaer – 'Beware'
Vawer es do ükunde? – 'Who is this child?'


## QANUC

Aia – 'Back' (Hinik Aia – get back)
Bhojujik mo qunquc – (idiom) 'If the bears don't eat you, it's home.'
Binbiniqegabenik ea sikka! Uc Sikkam mo-hinaq da

928

Yijarjuk! – 'I am (Binabik)! We are going to
  Urmsheim!'
Boghanik – 'Bukken'
Chash – 'True' or 'Correct'
Chok – 'Run'
Croohok – 'Rimmersmen'
Hinik – 'Go' or 'Get away'
Ko muhuhok na mik aqa nop. – 'When it falls on your
  head, then you know it's a rock.'
Mikmok hanno so gijiq – (idiom) 'If you want to carry a
  hungry weasel in your pocket, it's your business.'
Nihut – 'Attack'
Ninit – 'Come'
Sosa – 'Come' (imperative)
Ummu – 'Now'
Yah aqonik mij-ayah nu tutusiq, henimaatuq. – 'Ho,
  brothers, stop and speak with me.'


## SITHI

Aí Samu'sithech'a – 'Hail Samu'sitech'a'
Asu'a – 'Looking eastward'
Hei ma'akajao-zha – 'Bring it (the castle) down'
Hikeda'ya – 'Children of Cloud': Norns
Hikka – 'Bearer'
Im sheyis t'si keo'su d'a Yana o Lingit – 'For the shared
  blood of our Ancestors (Yana and Lingit)'
Ine – 'It is'
Isi-isi'ye – 'It is (indeed) that'
Ras – term of respect 'sir' or 'noble sir'
Ruakha – 'Dying'
S'hue – 'Lord'
Skei' – 'Stop'
Staja Ame – 'White Arrow'
Sudhoda'ya – 'Sunset-children': Mortals
T'si anh pra Ineluki! – 'By Ineluki's blood!'

T'si e–isi'ha as–irigú! – 'There is blood on the eastern gate!'

T'si im T'si – 'Blood for blood'

Ua'kiza Tumet'ai nei–R'i'anis – 'Song of the Fall of Tumet'ai'

Zida'ya – 'Children of Dawn': Sithi

# STONE OF FAREWELL

## Memory, Sorrow and Thorn
## Book Two

### *Tad Williams*

In Osten Ard, the evil of the Storm King covers the land,
the country is riven by war, and nature, unbalanced by the
tide of evil, slips into a permanent winter. Simon, once a
kitchen boy, now a hero hiding in the troll stronghold of
Yiqanuc, has prophetic dreams . . . only he and his
companions can save the land, but to do this he must
embark on the second part of his quest . . .
to the Stone of Farewell.

'Reminiscent of Tolkien's *Lord of the Rings* . . . an epic
fantasy you can get lost in for days, not just hours' *LOCUS*